To Kill a King

by Anette Sederquist

RoseDog Books
PITTSBURGH, PENNSYLVANIA 15238

RoseDog Books
585 Alpha Drive
Suite 103
Pittsburgh, PA 15238
Visit our website at *www.rosedogbookstore.com*

ISBN: 978-1-4809-7600-9
eISBN: 978-1-4809-7623-8

Elk's Pass

Cassandra had made her way through Elk's Pass hundreds of times on her way to her Father's Castle; never had the weather been this wicked. The magical coach was rocked by ferocious headwinds, ice, and snow pelted the windows. The northern face and valley below were blanketed with over a foot of snow. This area had been occupied by Monks for thousands of years, they had several talents one of which, was control of the weather. She couldn't help but wonder if the rumors the Hex were crossing the mountains contained some truth.

Even in a magic carriage; they could hardly expect to arrive at the North Castle before dark. Not that she was anxious to see her Father, knowing that this visit was near the end of her freedom. Bringing along Marion, her roommate from the Academy, was not a wise choice either. She was too impressed with the idea of the Grand Emperor, Noble Warlocks, and Lords. She was also outspoken, and on many occasions, made quite a few enemies. She had provoked a few professors too; all in all, she was trouble, but never boring and always fun. Marion was her best friend and the only one she trusted with all the nuances and secrets of the High Sorcerers.

Having Professor McMillan traveling with them was her Mother's idea. It seems her Mother had an evil premonition that Cassandra was just not ready for her new station in the hierarchy, along with some notions of danger and foreboding. Besides, having the most noted and esteemed Professor for additional training would not hurt. Having another ally would only help. That and the fact Mother didn't trust Father any further than she could spell him. Perhaps having an exceptional Warlock to give advice would not hurt her; she would take all the help she was offered.

Soon she would marry a suitable Lord, take on the responsibilities of Sorcerers of the North High Castle, raise the appropriate number of children, and move eventually into the position of High Empress. She had always been the good daughter and the excellent student she was expected to be. She had performed her duties as High Sorcerers flawlessly. Now after years of school, three liaisons and courtships, and three children she would never know or love; she would finally be allowed one season of freedom. The thought that independence would not come into her life again for a few hundred years depressed her. The dark black, luxurious custom magical carriage disheartened her. The stuffy air swallowed her happiness; this storm had her last nerve splayed open. The never answered question lingered in her mind: Why her? She never wanted this, never. This was to be her Sister's lot. Why had the heavens given her this burden?

The Professor's bulk took up most of the carriage. He was over seven feet in height with muscles that were unusual to see on a man of his years. His hair was stunningly silver, which hung to his shoulders in an old style of cut. His black suit with white starched ruffle shirt didn't give him the appearance of a Professor; more like a dignitary. Every bump sent his body flying and his head up to hit the ceiling. Good thing Marion was a Witch Sprite: petite, agile, and beautiful. It helped to have Marion on her side of the carriage, giving Casandra a little more room. Marion's hair and skin changed with her whim; this was a talent of Sprites. This evening she was a sickly shade of greens, not a suitable companion to the brown riding suit she wore. Oh, this carriage ride might be getting the best of her as well. Opening the window for a moment might help everyone. Time to take a fresh breath of air and ease the tension growing from this ruckus of a ride.

Casandra threw open the curtains to crack the window when Marion screamed she saw men riding beside the carriage. Dr. McMillan pulled open the window and stuck out his head. Seeing nothing, he settled back inside and said, "You must have been dreaming, Marion."

Marion quickly snapped, "I know what I saw, and I am sure it was some of those barbarians from Hex come to take us away and siphon off our powers, just as the stories have said. They tear out the heart and brains and eat them, then make a soup of the blood and bones. They bottle the rest of the body parts to use in the spells they weave. It is the only way they can have any magic, you know."

The Professor, cool, calm, and righteous as always, stated, "My dear Marion, you either have a compelling and wonderful imagination, or you are a complete dunderhead without a brain, which no barbarian would even consider consuming. As for these stories; well, I would not give them much credence. Assuredly they are tales contrived by peasants to frighten their children around campfires."

"Oh, really," pronounced Marion, "So you think these peasants would lie and create fiction to amuse each other? Tell me, Professor, what do you know about these peasants that I live among? For that matter, what do you know about Sprites?" At least now Marion's color was turning somewhat normal for her; a pale violet red.

"My Dear Marion," began the Professor, "I will admit to knowing very little about either; however, no one has substantiated that the Hexian's are or have ever been cannibals."

"My Dear Professor, I would appreciate it if you would stop calling me, your Dear! I am not, nor will I ever be your Dear! Also, my friends in the woods find it offensive that people continually use their name to refer to people. I personally find it patronizing!" Marion crossed her arms and glared at him.

"Hum. It is not spelled the same." Marion turned a deeper shade of red as the Professor calmly placed his hands folded in his lap. Eyeing Marion, he said, "I see why you are called Sprites; you certainly are spirited." Placing his hand on his chin, he added, "This might be the perfect opportunity for me to find out more about your Sprite world. Why, I could spend this coming year studying you, perhaps write a paper, no, a book. Ah, it would be the first written I believe. You say you understand these forest friends of yours?"

Marion was ready to explode, turning completely red. "You really do know nothing about us, do you? No one at the Academy knew anything about Sprites!"

"Quite understandable, since you were the very first Sprite to attend," the Professor added.

Marion cried, "What? Was I the first? How is it I did not know this until after I spent eight years of my life there? Now, I find out from an odd Professor aboard the most horrendous carriage ride of my life I was the first! And I must say I am certainly glad I never took your advanced magic course!"

Casandra would have to change this topic of conversation, or the rest of this trip would be a nightmare of raging magical rants between them. Now would be an excellent time to apply some of the knowledge of those eight, long years. She would use diplomacy, yes, yes. Rule number one: first and foremost, find common ground. They both want the world to know more about Sprites.

Casandra held up her hands and began asking Marion a question: "Marion, do you remember the first day of school, when I was assigned to your room?"

Marion laughed and said, "How could I forget? I kicked you out. I told you I had no intention of living with a high and mighty Sorceress. I was just a lowly Witch Sprite and not about to put up with your bigotry. Casandra, how could I compete with you? You were gorgeous, glamorous, smart, happy, perfect; everything I was not." Smiling, she said, "Turned out I was the bigot. Really, I had no idea who you were. You have become the most loving, giving, and tolerant friend a Sprite ever had."

Casandra reached for her hand and held it. "I am the lucky one here. Marion, that first day I knew nothing about Sprites. Like the Professor, I found out quickly they are mighty feisty, strong, brilliant, talented, beautiful, and above all honest. You are right. Life would have been more manageable if anyone there at the school or the students had known anything about Sprites.

Nonetheless, the Professor is right, too. Here is the opportunity to let others know you and your world." Marion started to object, but Casandra continued before Marion's stubborn side came flying out. "You have done nothing but moan and grunt about what you will do with this education that has been given you. You complain that Sprites are not used to help in the hierarchy. They are ignored, found to be cute and entertaining, nothing more. I say show them what you got;

stop complaining and start changing things. This could be an excellent start, and it may help you find your own way forward. You can't keep following me around, you know."

Marion stiffened, pouted, and said, "I am not following you around! I am coming to see what all the fuss is about with these Lord and Ladies of the Imperial Court. Not often does a Sprite get a chance like this." She eyed Casandra. "Wait...there were plenty of times you were happy I was there to help your sorry butt out of some sticky situations."

Casandra put a finger over Marion's mouth and said, "Shhh...he reports to my Mother, remember." They all chuckled, and the Professor swore he would not reveal this tidbit of knowledge.

Marion added, "Speaking of knowledge; I suppose it would be interesting to show the Professor just how much he doesn't know."

Their laughter was halted abruptly as the carriage lunged to the ground. It was as if the air was pulled out from under it. Everyone's breath stopped until the decent slowed, and the carriage righted itself. The Professor magically turned the lights off from inside the carriage. The evening had crept over the mountaintop during their discussion, and the automatic lights had switched on.

Thank the Night his cool head was with them. "Ladies, please do not let whoever has stopped this coach know who we are. As far as they are concerned, we are nothing more than servants heading to the Castle of the North. We must say, we were summoned by the Emperor as extra help for the upcoming holidays, and the expected visit of the High Sorcerers and Lords and Ladies of the continent."

Marion did a quick spell changing everyone's appearance. She couldn't do much in such a short time, but hair, eyes, and clothing colors were second nature to her. The Professor's hair and eyes turned black and his clothes a pale olive green; the color of her stomach. Casandra's straight black hair turned red and curly, her clothes changed from royal blue to light pink; nice contrast with her naturally creamy skin. Marion thought green cat eyes would be a nice touch and so different from her deep aqua blue. There was not much time to do more. Casandra was perfect all the time, a stunning beauty no matter what changes Marion would make. Casandra vanished her crown and torque. They all looked the part of a servant...sort of.

Before they could discuss who they would pretend to be, the door flew open. Everyone was thrown out into the cold on to a thick bed of snow. Standing knee deep in snow, Casandra saw the driver of the coach thrown to the ground. A tall, dark-haired man with a deep scar running diagonally across his right cheek started barking orders. "Stand up you...tell us where you are going. The rest of you stand aside."

Before the stunned driver could answer, the Professor stepped forward. "Is this called for? You're nothing but common thieves; take what you will and be on your way."

A bandit from behind them said, "If we are nothing more than thieves, why do we ask your destination?" They all turned to find not one, but six men of various shapes and sizes, with great fur coats and hats. One man walked to them. His eyes were the color of emeralds and his face strong and regal, certainly not a robber. He was tall and muscular, and very handsome. Casandra thought his hair was black like hers, but it was hard to see with his fur hat. He demanded to the Professor, "Sir, state your name, business, and destination."

"Who are you? Some kind of Military?" asked the Professor.

The man merely smiled and said, "Who I am, who we are, is of no concern to you. Understand that we will know who you are, your names, and destination before you will return to the warmth of your fine carriage. Now, is that clear? Each of you, in turn, will give your name, your destination, and why you are going wherever it is you're going to in this hell of a storm. And we will begin with you Sir, who asks too many questions."

The Professor sighed and told him his name was George McMillan, and they were going to the North Castle for the upcoming holidays. He would provide some magical scientific entertainment.

Casandra thought it was smart that he used his real name in case they check identification. She sure hoped Marion would catch that; what if she did not? Casandra quickly stepped up to the emerald-eyed man, gathered all the charm she could exude and said, "I am Sandra Selvilla. We are all traveling to the North Castle. This is Marion Donnan; we are extra servants for the Holidays."

All the men snickered, and someone said, "I could take a guess at what kind of servant you two would be." Laughing, the green-eyed man turned to Casandra and said, "With your stunning beauty and charm, and the expensive dazzling attire you both wear. You are the whores; only the best for the Emperor." This comment had all of them laughing and holding their sides.

Casandra was feeling slightly insulted. Marion took over the conversation in true Marion fashion. "Gentlemen, while I am sure none of you have ever had the luxury of pairing with high blood whores, we will excuse your ignorance. Just to stand and speak with us would cost you a gold fab; anything more than these few questions will cost much more. I, for one, am freezing and would consider continued questioning for your fur coat and hat. Everything comes at a price, gentleman; especially information. We are not free or cheap."

The handsome man stopped chuckling and answered "Ah, Sprites. They have a tongue on them no matter the continent; brave, too. While I would happily accept your offer; we are about other business tonight. Pleasure is not among that business. You three are not the interrogees we need to find." Turning to Casandra, he winked and said, "Although a kiss from this lovely lady might just be worth the price of my coat."

Marion moaned and said, "Why in the heavens do the handsome ones always pick you?"

At that, Casandra laughed, relaxed, eyed the young man, and said, "That coat does look invitingly warm."

Her smile went right to his heart. How a woman of the evening could pull at his soul's strings and make him want to scream, Yes, he wasn't sure. He stepped directly into her arms. He was immediately pulled back by two of his men. The man with the scar laughingly told him to get a hold of himself. He said, "These women of magic are playing tricks on you, Son."

The man with the scar pushed them into the carriage and told them to leave quickly. The young, green-eyed man poked his head in the door and said, "Ladies, this is your lucky day. You have been released and have gained a golden fab for your time. We are gentlemen, after all. Good evening to you." He looked to Casandra. "May the heavens willingly find you again, and I will get that kiss, and more. This is the truth." With that, he tossed in a gold fab.

The driver and the Professor used all their magic rocketing them away. While Casandra warmed the carriage and returned her crown and torque; Marion restored their appearances and produced woolen coats and blankets. They hardly spoke until entering the village of the Castle when the Professor said, "We will, of course, have to tell of our mishap. However, I think it would be advisable to refrain from mentioning the part about pretending to be Women of the Night."

Marion laughed, "That is very wise, Professor; we will just say we told them we were your magical assistants."

The Professor commented, "Ah, how clever of you, Marion. You young ladies are very resourceful." He laughed and said, "I think I understand the events you referred to earlier in the evening." He looked to both. "Casandra is right. I should not know this information, and I am glad I don't." With that, the carriage stopped in the courtyard of the Castle.

The Other Side of the Mountain

Years of labor had brought Devon to the other side of Elk's mountain. As he stood on the edge of the cliff gazing out over Elk Pass, he wondered how many generations had lived and died inside the caves tunneling a pathway to the northern continent. His entire life had been arranged so he would be standing here, on this cliff, on this day. His training in war tactics, the schooling, the politics, the social gatherings, the parade of women; was all to prepare for the occasion. All this to prove his worth to his country and Father, the King of the Warlocks of the nations of the Hex and Bezier. Devon was a strong Warlock and Wizard combination, but his talent and true powers were the weather.

The Army swarmed around him, staking out the territory for the most secluded area to camp for the next days. Soon the Generals would come through the tunnel and start shouting orders for everyone, including him. He would take these moments to relish the view of the lush green valley below and dream of how easy life must be for the ordinary folk living in snug little cottages covered with thatched roofs. He could clearly see a lovely river running through the valley like someone laid a gleaming ribbon of blue and silver on the land, and dots which must be homes and villages scattered here and there.

On the cliffs across from him, he could just make out what looked to be some sort of shrine, and homes built into the walls of the opposing mountain. He thought that must be the Monastery. The notorious Monks who could control the weather and grant prayers. However, they only granted prayers of the ethical integrity of course; they would be the judge of that. It was also the likely reason God was cupreous with his gifts. If the prayers were not of integrity and humbly given, one could not expect God to grant the prayer. History had marked this as the cradle of civilizations, and they these strange Monks the first to walk on the land of Corinthians. It was said, all the many peoples on every continent had derived from these Monks.

Devon was not sure he believed that. If that were true, why were Monks so different from all the others? Their powers were frail and no match for the Emperor, nor for the many Kings. Wizards, Banisters, Lords, Chancellors, Sorcerers, or Witch Queens; all held more power. Yet, it might explain his strange and rare gift of weather control. He wondered how different his life would be if he had not made that little water sprout for his little Sister to play with; would he would be standing here now, part of these intricate ridiculous plans his Father and the foolish Generals' calculated?

His eyes gravitated to that river. How deep was it? Would it have enough water running through it to create a good storm of snow and ice? Would the storm devastate the land below, the people or the Monks? He would be responsible for that and of course the creation of a new breed with the High Sorcerous. These were his duties, to fight in the war that would inevitably follow would be his choice and his honor. His name would be remembered through the ages as the Prince who spearheaded Hexians to the highest rank among the continents. His people would be recognized and respected at last, and no longer known as the Barbarians. Of course, those Monks might have prayers of higher integrity, and all the plans of the King and Generals may be ended by God. A God most of the world no longer believed in.

"Master Devon." Devon's guardian Ernst grabbed him by the shoulder and pulled him back from the edge of the cliff. "Sir, you may create clouds, but I have yet to see you take a stroll on them. You can see everything simply fine from a few feet back. It would be a shame to lose you now from a fall down the hill; no one would be writing of that in the history books. You would be known only as the Prince who fell to his death while gazing on Monk's Mountain." Ernst was laughing as he walked away.

Devon was laughing too. Ernst had been at his side since the day at the beach when his Father caught him playing with water sprouts. Ernst was with him always; in person as his bodyguard and in his heart. Sometimes he felt as if Ernst was more of a Father to him than the King. Ernst was a strange-looking man and did not look a bit like most. Devon's Sister said Ernst was handsome, in a compelling way. He was powerful; Devon had seen him work his magic, and it was awe-inspiring. Ernst was tall and lanky with thinning hair tied at the back of his neck; perhaps the reason he always wore that worn-out floppy leather hat. His clothes were perpetually black. He wore black shirts, black snakeskin pants, and coat, black boots, black hair, black eyes. He was clean, but the man never looked like he changed clothes. The only obvious thing about him was the scar on his right cheek. Devon had asked many times how he acquired that scar. Every time, Ernst would have a completely different story of how that came to be. His best story was fighting the fire-breathing dragons at the top of the world. Devon would have to say Ernst's past was as black as the clothes he wore. He knew nothing about Ernst's history; at least the part before his service to Devon.

The Generals were coming; noise blared as they came stumbling out of the tunnel. No doubt the first thing out their mouths would be admonishing everyone else for being too loud and bring attention to their location. General Brad was the oldest of the King's Generals, with grey hair, light skin and he still had a good physique. He was by far the most intelligent of his Father's advisors. His eyes twinkled when he was pleased, but his green eyes glimmered red if angered.

General Due Bre exited next; Due Bre's frame was sturdy and well over seven-foot-tall. He wore his blond hair in the traditional straight shortcut, and his green eyes could stare any man down. He was incredibly handsome; Sorcerers and Witches followed him on every campaign.

General Due Bre spoke first, "Nice job at the tunnels, but a little too low for my height." Considering he was seven feet tall, it would have to take another two years to tunnel to his height. General Brad was the first to mention that everyone should bring down the noise level or the location would be discovered before the mission was carried out. General Martin said nothing, he just rolled his eyes and came over to greet Devon.

"Devon, I see you were one of the first through, as it should be, lad. I believe we will name this passageway and cliff for you: Devon's Pass. It has a ring to it don't you think?" He patted Devon on the shoulder wearing a broad smile on his face, chuckling.

Devon could only smile. Of all the Generals, this Warlock was indeed his favorite, and the only one he trusted besides Ernst. Martin had been a part of his training from the time Devon was ten years old; a friend and mentor; sometimes a partner in fun and fraternizing. He was a Warlock of five hundred, but he hardly looked his age and never acted it. He was short for the average Hexian; build like a bull, five ten or so, with thick golden wavy hair. His face was sharp and square which wore a perpetual full smile with the whitest straight teeth. Of course, he held the trademark of power emerald green eyes. Devon would follow this man into battle; he would not question or disobey his orders. The other Generals...well, he had plenty of reason to doubt their loyalty, powers, and abilities.

Martin looked out at the valley and said, "Beautiful view; I can see why the Monks chose this valley. If God is anywhere, surely it is in this valley. I think I might swing over and have a few prayers said in our favor." He smiled and continued, "Prince, it is time for us to finalize our plans and I have some information about your Sorcerous. Let's find our tent and get settled in for the night. The word is we only have days before carriages will be flying, God surely was a help in the caves and tunnels. We did not count on the completion of the tunnel. This is a gift; we need to take advantage of it."

Ernst, Martin, and Devon continued down the mountain's side to find their tents. Devon's mind went directly to fear; here was his moment to shine. Suddenly the weight of the world was on his shoulders; it was time to perform all the magic he had practiced. The camp was struck just inside the tree line with hopes that tree cover would mask the tents. Tonight there would be no fires or songs, only soldiers waiting for orders. They were on the edges of war, but not today…not until the Sorcerers was in their hands and the traitors well-paid.

Ernst stopped halfway through camp and pointed out their tent, it was big enough for two men to sleep in, all that he needed. They made their way to the center of camp to the General's tent. It was huge in comparison to theirs. Inside a full table with dried meats, fruit, bread, and wine, with chairs for two dozen. The other Generals had been seated with wine in their hands, along with their Warlock's attachés: Major Winston, Coronel Greystone, and General Martin's Coronel Fetcher.

General Due Bre handed them each a glass of wine and then held his up for a toast. "To the young Prince who will lead our way to victory." Cheers echoed through the tent.

Devon thought to himself, there was no pressure on him. He drained his glass and took a seat for dinner. Dinner was uneventfully occupied with small talk of the wonderment of the tunnels, the beauty of the mountains, and valley of the Monks. Many tales of the Monk's miracles along with the origin and the story of creation and division filled the dinner.

It was a fanciful story, Devon had heard many times in history classes. The legend recounted the story of people who came from another world, a world that was war-torn and collapsing. They crashed in the Northern slope of Elk Mountain. Those that lived entered God's Valley. The survivors began the slow process of building another civilization. The fertile soils of the valley produced wonderous properties in the foods. The crystals in the ground seem to promote strange side effects in some of the people: magical powers, mystical visions, and physical changes occurred. Some children were born tiny, others large or with changing colors of skin and hair. The ways of conception and births evolved as well. Women no longer had one child at a time causing many young Mothers to die in childbirth.

Yet, over time the populous grew, and the valley became depleted of the vegetation. Meats became infrequent, and laws were ignored. Disagreements broke out among clusters of people. Soon ridicule and fear caused the leading group to banish the dissenting groups from the Valley of Gods. Others left to hunt and find food and shelter in other lands. Only a handful of Monks remained, holding fast to the strange religion they brought with them. Hundreds of years passed with each group segregating from one another. They traveled to finding homes on other continents and in other countries. The land was always shifting and changing as the continents moved from the upper hemisphere to the lower and side to side. Some groups of people could not sustain themselves and had just disappeared. This continued until the magic was found to stop the shifting of continents. It was unknown how that was accomplished; until the Emperor and Empress began holding the energy of Corinthians.

Dinner ended, the table cleared of dishes by soldiers and more wine was poured. Maps filled the center of the table. General Brad began outlining the revised plan, "Gentlemen, our informants have seen the Emperor travel to the South to the countries of Diamante, Tallia, and Tigra. He is aligning them to his will. Also, he has made an overture to Count Rakie, our sly ruthless neighbor, for the intention of marriage to his daughter the High Sorcerers." Everyone mumbled and shifted in the seats. He continued, "I know, if his country falls into their alliance our country cannot withstand armies coming at us from the South, East, and North. At least the Night has blessed us with a western coastline. Count Rakie, the snake, had made as assurances he would stand with us when his Father passed. However, his Father the old King continues to live on, if only by a thread. Now it seems the lure of one day being the Emperor holds much greater interest to the Count. Over the next few days, the coach of the Emperor, Count, and the Sorcerers will pass through Elk's Pass and the Old Valley of Gods. It would be wonderful to snatch all three but to the King's plan. We need to kill the Emperor if we get the chance. He will be traveling with a full guard and regiment; it would be unlikely we could accomplish that without tipping our hand too early. We are to confront the High Sorcerers; spell her and take her blood. However, we are expecting a large show of force around her too. The Count's interrogation is imperative. Without question, he will be stopped at any cost. He will concede to our will, or he will die. Any questions so far?"

"General, how will we force the Count? He is a full Warlock and a master the Sciences of Magic, as well as a skilled soldier." the Major asked.

"Good question for General Brad."

"Ah..." Brad stood. He was the shortest of the Generals in this room full of tall emerald-eyed men. "I have a master's in science too. I have developed a poison and the antidote, of course. I administer one and withhold the other; until our Count consents to hand over his Bride on the way to their honeymoon. Timing is everything to the success of this plan. Devon, your ability to charm this Sorcerous will make short work of this war. The use of your weather power to down the Sorcerous carriage is essential for success. We need a sample of her blood."

Devon only nodded, hoping no one else at this table felt his nerves unravel. This was ridiculous; how could he develop a storm to bring down carriages? Charming the High Sorcerous into his bed was even more implausible.

Thankfully Martin stood and began sharing his information. "To help you, dear boy, we have a new sketch of the Sorcerous and new information." He unfolded a paper with the likeness of a beautiful face. She had grown into a beautiful young woman since the last picture he had of her. Martin continued, "This is in gray pencil, but her coloring is brilliant. She has aqua blue eyes the color of Montego Bay; it is said one can see the waves of the ocean in them. The Princess has straight long black silky hair, ruby red lips and a figure that would make any Warlock see stars. She is around five seven and always wears a jeweled crown and torque of jewels which is a great part of her power source. If you are lucky enough to come across her, remove them at once; they also send a beacon of her presence to the Emperor and his Army."

He returned to his seat. This was additional information, but he had hoped for more. Casandra was no ordinary girl. If this sketch was correct, she was a woman who had Kings fall to her feet. Her power was not in some silly crown and torque. She was a mystic, and history was made with the manifestation of Sorcerers like Casandra De Volt.

A hand on Devon's shoulders brought him out of his thoughts; the General was asking how soon he could begin the weather change. He took in a breath and started sharing his thoughts. "After seeing the pass, I don't think bringing the temperature down will be difficult at all. However, the water source may not be great enough to produce the snow I had hoped for. I need to work out some calculations and get a closer look at the river and its source. I need to practice with the wind to shear snow from the mountain tops without creating avalanches."

Martin laughed, saying, "It would be nice, Devon, if you could spare the camp from avalanches."

Devon paled, but the others laughed. They had a lot more confidence in him than he had in himself. He smiled too but said, "That was his plan."

General Brad stood, "I have ordered everyone into khaki uniforms. We do not want to stand out in the snow with our greens. You all are dismissed; be here before sunrise gentlemen." With that General, Brad left the tent, and the group broke up to retire. Martin asked him to stay behind, he had questions for him. After saying his good nights, Ernst said he would see him at their tent. Martin poured more wine and turned his chair to face him.

"Devon." he began, "I have known you since you were only as tall as my knees. So, do not even try to lie to me. You are worried and unsure of your abilities. I also know you are overthinking. With you, everything must be calculated down to the last detail. This is a fine trait when building cities or controlling the weather. People and emotions cannot be measured, mixed, and nailed together. This plan can work but Son you need to learn how to change and shift with the events as they happen. Today we landed here thinking we had weeks to create snow and ice in this valley; now we know we have only days. Our traitor has turned on us; we need him to have the incentive to work with us. Lucky for us Henry is a selfish bastard without honor, and only concerned with his own hide. Without that; our whole plan would be a complete wash."

Devon knew Martin was right, but his lecture was not helping him feel any better. "You are right Martin, I don't adapt well to change. The weather is one thing, with all the Warlocks here and the power they can generate I know I can bring the snow and storm. The woman…she is another issue altogether. I am no charmer of high blood, let's face it. I have only seduced barmaids, a Wizard or two, and the occasional Warlock's daughter. Never have I been in the presence of a High Sorcerous, and do not tell me a Witch counts, you know it doesn't." Martin laughed, and Devon continued, "That's another thing; you always laugh at my insecurities."

Martin straightened in his chair and dropped his smile, "Son, I only laugh because I see so much of myself in you; trust me I know exactly how you are feeling. You are right to feel intimidated. I know I sure was at my experience with a real High Sorcerous. It is late, and we need to face one thing at a time. The Sorcerous can wait. Let us just concentrate on the snow. You get some sleep, tomorrow will be here soon. Be here early for breakfast, and I will help with the calculations. We will take a few men down to the river to look around. I will send a party out to find the source of the river early. You are the Prince who cut through that mountain. You will create a storm and bring down carriages. Let's just keep it at that for tonight, all right?"

Devon did feel better, but there were so many questions about the Sorcerous. Was Martin with a Sorcerous and never shared that? Martin was right again, one thing at a time. Snow, he would concentrate on snow. He could not help but smile and wish his mentor a goodnight along with his thanks. Martin shoved the sketch into Devon's hands, gave him a quick hug, then they parted for their beds. Devon was sure he would not sleep, not with a picture of Casandra in his hands. Devon entered the tent with Ernst already snoring. He laid on his bedroll wondering what it would be like to love a High Sorcerous; the next thing he knew Ernst was nudging him to wake up.

Devon rolled over only to realize he had slept; more from too much wine than anything else. Now his head was pounding. This was not a good start to the day. A day in which he needed all his powers and wits.

They entered the tent with General Martin smiling and very much prepared. Breakfast was on a side table, maps on the dining table and Martin was sitting calculating where each regiment would be most effective in moving snow from the mountaintop. He looked up as Devon and Ernst entered. "Ah, there you are; reports on the river and water source should be back soon. I sent troopers out before sunrise, I could not sleep well. Want to look over my suggestions on the snow removal? Or, perhaps you need a little something to wake you from that hungover look."

Devon smiled and said, "That would be great. I wasn't watching how much wine I drank, but I did sleep well."

Ernst said, "I can attest to that; he snored and mumbled half the night. Do we have anything here that has caffeine in it?"

"Yes, Ernst help yourself to coffee or the black tea at the side table. That should help you too, Devon. Here are some powers to add to it to relive that headache." Martin handed him two packs of powder which he dumped in the coffee and hoped it would take effect quickly.

The next hour they refigured where, to begin with, the snow. The reports came in. Fortunately, a large lake was just on the east side of Monks Mountain. They decided the Generals would concentrate on creating winds to shear the snow from Elk's Mountain because it was not inhabited by any creatures other than Elk. Devon would lower the temperature in the valley and release water from the damn the Monks had built. Then he would begin billowing snow from the east. As soon as the valley had adequate snow cover to hold the temperature down, they all could set the energies for creating a storm in the upper sky.

Devon stood in a clearing in the middle of the woods and just concentrated on cold; feeling cold, seeing cold and hearing the soft sounds of snow. Everyone worked together; the Warlocks, Wizards, and Witches managed a small wind to push the snow down from Elk's mountain. Devon's powers were too strong to move just a little snow and would take less energy than lowering the temperature. It was early in spring, so the ground was still cold from the winter that just passed. He reached with his mind and pulled up the cold from the field until the temperature dropped. He turned his attention to the water of the lake and sprayed a fine mist up into the air over the damn. Snow and ice covered all the trees by ten in the morning. He was standing in the cold white snow sweating like a hot summer day. Yet, the air around him was cold as ice.

Devon became aware of someone staring at him then his concentration broke for the first time. Generals, Warlocks, and soldiers surrounded him. Martin was laughing like always. "I don't know why you needed our help, you filled this whole valley by yourself."

Devon said, "What are you talking about, General?"

"Devon, we stopped for a break about two hours ago; we ran out of energy after bringing only enough snow to barely cover the ground. You just add twenty inches on the forest floor. We ate for energy and came to watch you. You are fascinating to observe, you filled the entire valley with snow. You really are prodigious,"

General Due Bre said, half-laughing. "Come have something to eat then we'll start the storm."

Devon didn't think he was hungry. Once he began to eat, he was starving, and for the first time, he felt cold. After the early lunch, they all returned to the clearing to start a storm. The sky held just the right Nimbostratus clouds that would produce a rousing storm. The winds began to swirl, and Devon added ice from the lake and snow from the ground. Everything was whirling and speeding when Devon detected an object. No, he felt several carriages; could it be the Count? No, they had informants to let them know when the Count left Belissa Villa. This had to be the Emperor, or perhaps it was the Sorcerers.

"General…carriages to the south. Do you want me to lower them?" Devon shouted.

"I don't see them. Look for a seal on the side of the carriage. If it is the Emperor's seal, take them down, unless there are too many soldiers." Martin yelled.

Devon lifted himself up into the treetops. He could only make out a seal on one carriage, but the uniforms of the Imperial guard were unmistakable. Devon relayed this to Martin. In turn, Martin asked, "How many?" Devon said it looked to be a full company. Martin said, "Come down from there. That is too many for us but keep the storm rocking them just to annoy them."

Devon did just that but stayed just to see how much control he had over the carriage with the seal of the Emperor. He rocked it up, down and then right to the left. Martin mentally screamed at him to get down. Devon released the carriage pushing it right as hard as he could. It flew into the side of Monks Mountain. As he descended, he could hear the screams and commotion of the guards flying to the Emperor's rescue. Devon softly landed on his feet to three Generals staring at him with unlimited anger. Ernst grabbed his arm, and they all went directly to the General's tent.

Martin said, "Explain yourself!"

"Ha…well…I was just sort of testing myself to see what kind of control I had over the Emperor carriage while keeping the storm going, Sir." Devon was not sure if that was weaseling out of the fact he deliberately slammed the carriage aside Monks Mountain or if he should admit to just being curious.

General Due Bre added, "Well, I think you did a fine job; that is, right up until you slammed the carriage against that cliff. That is what you did?"

Devon could not help but look at his feet while saying, "Yes Sir." Before anyone could add anything, a young soldier burst into the tent.

"Sirs pardon me, but the Major told me to report to you immediately about the broken carriage."

General Due Bre said, "Yes, soldier, please inform us."

"Well Sirs, it seems the carriage broke to pieces against the wall of the cliff, but the occupants slid to the floor of the valley unharmed. Major said it was the angle and slope of the hill. He said it was probably a thrilling ride. They were retrieved by their soldiers and have left the valley since the storm has subsided, Sir. Any messages for the Major, Sirs?"

"Yes." General Due Bre face held stern, "Please have him return here as soon as he has finished surveying the area. You are dismissed."

General Due Bre busted into laughter as soon as the young soldier left. "I am sorry, Gentleman. I just cannot get the picture of the Emperor sliding on his ass down a cliff out of my head. Oh, my, I will never forget this day, and I will have many laughs retelling this story in the years to come."

Everyone was laughing. Devon wasn't smiling because he knew he had narrowly managed to slip insubordination charges aside for an exceedingly great story the Generals could tell at parties.

They decided to take shifts helping Devon keep up the storm. Just before sunset, Devon sensed a single carriage. He wasn't making a mistake like last time. Martin had spent an hour screaming at him about not following a direct order. He told General Brad and Major Winston at once. General Brad sent the Major and Ernst up to check it out.

They returned to say it looked like there were some ladies and one gentleman inside, with just a driver on top; no seal or insignia on the coach. It was just a luxurious black coach, as far as they could see. Snickering, General Brad said, "Devon, do you think you could bring it down without smashing it and killing everyone inside?"

"Yes Sir, I think I can." smiled Devon. The afternoon's adventure with the Emperor had given him the confidence he hadn't had the day before. "Do you think it is the Sorcerous?"

The General said, "No, she would at least have a guard with her. Here, I will conjure up some fur coats and hats to cover our uniforms. Ernst take down the driver before he can get a sword or spell us. Men do not give them time to create any magic. Bring out the occupants as soon as they hit the ground and hold them. The Major and I will stand back see how much power there is; keep Devon safe. Devon, just question them and don't give away who we are. We just need their names and destination. Keep it simple and short. We know it isn't the Count; so use this for practice."

Devon stood in the clearing and felt the carriage. The invisible flying horses were frightened of the wind and were struggling, so he whispered them down into the woods with thoughts of warm carrots and rest. Devon held the wind back from the carriage and pointed it straight down. This was fun; he knew he had frightened them. Good, they would talk faster if they were a little scared. He slowed and softened the landing. The soldiers opened the door and pulled out two women and a man. Ernst threw the driver off the top of the carriage into the snow. Only the driver was dressed for the cold. Magic...he could feel the heat from the inside of the carriage and magic emanating from all three occupants. Ernst asked the driver his destination. The man from the coach was insulting them as robbers. He told them to take what they wanted and leave them to travel on. He had an attitude of smugness; and they were not too frightened by the fall, interesting.

Devon stepped up. "If we are nothing more than thieves, why do we ask your destination?" This man is lying, thought Devon as he continued to question him. "Sir state your name, business, and destination."

Who is this man thought Devon? Now he is questioning me. Get control here, Devon.

"Who I am, who we are, is of no concern to you. Understand that we will know who you are and your names and destination before you will return to the warmth of your fine carriage. Now is that clear... each of you, in turn, will give your name, your destination, and why you are going wherever it is you're going to this hell of a storm. And... we will begin with you, Sir, who asks too many questions."

The man said he was a magician to entertain at the North Castle. A Scientific Magician, Devon was not so sure, but he was giving his real name. We would probe him but before he could the most beautiful woman came into his vision with red hair, green eyes...wait, she had cat eyes. She was telling the truth about her name and her friend's name but servants, not these two. Someone from behind him made a comment about them being whores. He looked at this redhead; no, she was no whore. Her whole body stiffened. Devon thought he'd add to that just to watch her squirm. "With your stunning beauty and charm and the expensive dazzling attire, you must be the whores. Only the best for the Emperor." They all laughed. The little Sprite stepped right up to him so close he had to step back; now she is sassy. She wanted money for just talking to her, audacious little Sprite.

So, he said. "Ah, Sprites. They have a tongue on them no matter the continent; brave too. While I would happily accept your offer, but we are about other business tonight. Pleasure is not among that business. You three are not the interrogees we need to find." Turning to the redhead, he winked and said, "Although a kiss from this lovely lady might just be worth the price of my coat." She was speaking, but Devon could only look at her eyes. Her eyes were turning blue than green, they were saying yes come to me, kiss me. Before he knew it, he was pulled away from her, and the three were pushed in the carriage. He jerked away from the Generals and lunged into the carriage. He had to have one more look. Was she the Sorcerer? "Ladies, this is your lucky day. You have been released and gained a golden fab for your time. We are gentlemen, after all. Good evening to you. Heavens willing, I will meet you again, and I will get that kiss. This is the truth." With that, he tossed in a gold fab.

The carriage flew straight up with unbelievable power. Devon turned to General Brad. "What are you doing? That was the High Sorcerous. We just released the one prize we needed."

General Brad laughed. Why did all Generals laugh at him? It was so frustrating. Shaking his head, General Brad turned to Devon, "Prince, I think you may be right. If she wasn't the High Sorcerous Casandra, she was the most powerful whore I have ever run across. That Witch had you in the palm of her hand with just a smile. She is not to overpower you Son, you are to control her. I think we have some work to do. We need to train you to equalize that energy; not get swept away in it."

Devon was embarrassed. All these men knew he had been overpowered. The General put an arm around Devan and started walking back to the general's tent. "My Prince. Don't be downhearted; that smile took my breath away too. Good thing the Major wasn't in full view of her; he and the others pulled you away. I was too transfixed. Ernst pushed them in the carriage knowing full well you would go in after her." Devon smiled; these generals were there for his support. Devon would have to remember that.

At the Generals' tents, the briefing was combined with dinner. They had a hardy hot meal that night and fires were glowing throughout the camp. There was no worry they would be seen; the crucial carriages had flown by. The Count wouldn't leave until daylight it was too late in the day for him to fly. Their spies would inform them the second he left his Villa and send the Counts route to the Generals. If he came through the pass, Devon would have no problem taking him down to the clearing. No storm was needed to hide anything. If he traveled the long way around the mountain, it meant the Emperor had warned him. General Gage would detain him on the flats until they could get there.

Everyone agreed Devon had given too much information. The old man McMillian guessed they were the army and even said so, just by the way Devon asked his questions. Devon's little sarcastic rant to get a last look at the woman practically told them they were from Bezier. Hexian's were known for their ill temper and brashness. Rumors had come back to them long ago saying they were known as barbarians and ate their captors. All at the table agreed, it was ninety-nine to one chance they had encountered the High Sorcerous. None of them could believe the Emperor allowed her to travel alone without guards. This encounter with her had been an exceptional windfall. Now they knew who they were dealing with. She was an immensely powerful being who was not only beautiful but smart, talented, and brave. None of the three gave off one ounce of fear. This was valuable information. An intimation or manipulated would not control this Sorcerous.

General Martin placed a small bottle of blood on the table. “I count this as an immense success, the redhead’s blood. Now we can make a little gift for her.” The Generals all laughed. Devon wondered why.

Everyone looked worn out, they retired early and went to their tents. As Devon stared at the tent ceiling, he could not find sleep. He felt exhausted from keeping the temperature low and wind blowing through the valley. Devon thought he would never go into a deep sleep until this was over. He reached into his pocket to look at his pencil drawing of the High Sorcerous. Was that her really…was she even real? She had changed her hair, and her eyes; this sketch did not look like her. It looked like her shadow. He was sure he would dream of that redhead tonight, maybe every night for many nights to come. He wondered, what present were they making for her?

The Flats of Peroba

The day began before the sunrise with word of the Count's landing in the Peroba Flats. He left his Villa taking the long route to the North Castle. The Emperor must have warned him; the Count was probably in bed with the Emperor. Devon dressed quickly grabbed some bread and cheese, then ran to the Generals tent for orders.

For the first time General Brad, the highest ranking among them, took over the command. "General Due Bre you will oversee breaking camp. Leave it looking like no one was here just in case the Emperor sends Scouts to check on the mishaps they incurred yesterday. Lead our men back through the tunnels and use magic to cover the entrance. Station centuries to keep the tunnels free of someone accidentally finding its opening. We will meet up with you at the Bezier Palace. This should not take long. Martin take your regiment. Also, Devon and Ernst will join us. Devon, you should be quiet and learn from this opportunity, listen and learn Son. Let's get going."

Devon was relieved not just to be included in this venture, but because at last he could relax and release the weather and temperature in the valley. He was suddenly cold and exhausted. He returned to his tent to pack and get that fur coat. They jumped on their mounts and flew out of Elk Pass and east to the Flats of Peroba.

Landing on the flats, they could see the Count's men surrounded in the middle of the encampment. When they entered the General's tent, Gage was seated across from the Count. General Gage was part Wizard, part Elf. He was a tall, slender built man in mid-age with steel gray eyes and white hair at his temples giving his Elf lineage away.

Count Rakie was tall, well built with coffee-colored skin, large chocolate brown eyes, and dark sable hair which waved and curled to just above his shoulders. He turned on a brilliant wide smiled with perfect teeth, and said, "Well, now that we are all here. I guess this interrogation can begin, then I can be on my way." The Prince was always in awe of the Count. He could see why women fell over themselves with that charming smile. "Do I see the young Prince here? I am honored and impressed. I must be more important than I thought. Have no fear Prince I am still loyal to the consortium and your Father."

General Brad stood in front of the Count and offered his hand. Reluctantly the Count rose, shook his hand and reseated himself. "Well Count Rakie, I see you still hold yourself high in regard. You do realize that conceit is one of the reasons your Father the King passed you over as the next heir of your Kingdom?" He paused and watched the Count's face pale. "General Gage I see you have not offered any refreshments. This early morning and the ride have my throat dry."

Gage stood and apologized, "I am sorry gentlemen, how thoughtless of me; please everyone enter." He left the tent returning with two bottles of wine; a Corporal entered with cups and a platter of food. Everyone but the Count helped themselves to food and wine.

Smiling Gage turned to the Count. "You're not hungry Sir?" The Count shook his head no. "Well, you certainly must be thirsty. This is my best wine, right from your land I believe." The Count just glared at him.

General Brad laughed at the Count, "I see you're worried about being poisoned by the food and drink. Don't be, as you see...we are all eating and drinking. Besides you have already been poisoned by simply shaking my hand."

The Count's eyes widened, and his mouth opened. Devon saw Ernst's mouth drop too and checked his own face to find he was gapping like fish. That cunning old General, he must remember not to trust that man.

The Count swallowed and collected himself, "If that is so, then the poison must be on your hands, and you will also die. I don't know what kind of ploy you are pushing on me, but I am not that stupid. Besides everyone and everything we touch would be poisoned; including the food and wine bottle, you contaminated. Is it your plot to assonate everyone in this tent?"

General Brad chuckled, "Now, now give me a little more credit than that Count. I drank the antidote this morning. In fact, when word came that you had left Belissa Villa. You are such a scoundrel. Running to inform the Emperor, are you?" He wiped his hands on a napkin and continued with the Count, "The poison is an alcohol base and is absorbed into the skin immediately, leaving no residue. Marvelous isn't it. Within seconds you had been infected and will die a slow and horrendous death over the next few months. I am very proud of this discovery. I believe I will make millions of Fab with this one. Of course, you dabble in brewing yourself if I remember correctly. I have been playing with potions for over five hundred years. It is a great stress reliever; puttering in a laboratory, don't you think Count?"

The Count was at a loss for words and reached for the wine pouring a large cup. He drank it all down and poured a second. "I see, I am poisoned. I think you want to give me that antidote rather than watch me die. What is it you want from me for the price of my life, General?"

General Gage entered the conversation, "See Brad, I told you he was a reasonable man to deal with. Did I not tell you he wasn't trying to sidetrack our agreement and go off on his own? The Count is not taking a deal from the Emperor and hand clasping with the High Sorcerous to someday elevate himself to the Emperor position. Of course, the Emperor's Son stands in his way, but Henry is clever. The Count would find a way to murder him easily enough. He killed two of his own Brothers, although he messed up badly on the one and lost his station."

The Count stood yelling, "You know nothing, you ass!"

General Brad calmly said, "Sit down Henry. May I call you Henry? I feel we have bonded somehow over this poisoning."

The Count sat red in the face and resigned, "Please General feel free to call me whatever like. Let's just get on with this."

The General began to lay the plan before Henry knowing he would accept the offer. "You will proceed to the North Castle and accept this offer to wed the Emperor's daughter. Try to push the wedding forward without raising suspicions. The sooner this ends, the better. Convince the young woman to consummate your marriage in weeks if possible." Henry started to protest, "We understand the normal length of time is a year. Just do your best Henry. You are to insist the honeymoon and pairing be on your lovely secluded island Azula. Assure the Emperor you have painstakingly planned every detail; include the nesting for reproduction with excellent security. What could be better for the young lady then total privacy and safety? We have already provided this for you at our expense. Trust me it is lovely; she will be very impressed."

"You have been plotting this for a long while, haven't you?" The Count was impressed, Devon thought they had torn him down to nothing. Now they were giving him a sense of importance, feeding his ego. This was a classic military move.

General Gage said, "Yes and we chose you, we know you, Henry. You are one of the few who could pull the wool over the Emperor's eyes. You only need to deceive him and charm the Miss De Volt. Your reputation as a great lover of all sexes has you our number one choice. All you must do is bring your Bride to Azula, and we will handle the rest. You can go off on a wonderful vacation, and enjoy yourself. Then return two weeks later as a Father. Take your wife back to Belissa Villa pregnant. No one will be the wiser."

The Count chuckled, "Won't the Bride be wiser as to who bedded her? Really, gentlemen, this is a half-baked insane plan you have. It seems I am the only one taking any chances in this; with my life and my heirs to the throne."

General Brad sat still and stern, "Count you will be compensated. Your part is a simple one; bring the Bride to Azula, and we will handle everything there. That is all you need to know; that is all you will know. In exchange for this, we will see you are made the Emperor while you are still young enough to enjoy the privileges. She will be sent off to be the Empress very shortly, and you will be rid of her. Then you can have all those lovely young men to play with. You will work with us as Emperor, and we will make you wealthy beyond your dreams. However, you only have two choices today. Will you live or die?"

Without hesitation, the Count said, "I will live; give me the antidote."

General Brad said, "Not so fast, young man. First, go to the Castle. Convince the Emperor and Sorcerous you are her true love. It would be safest for her to only carry one egg, suggest that. Then, bring the written contract to Bezier Castle before the week is out. It will be easy for you to know when to leave, you will begin feeling very tired, sick, and dizzy. Get Casandra to agree to the quick marriage, not the normal years wait. Then you get the antidote… and please try not to look desperate."

General Gage added, "Count do this correctly; we do have eyes in North Castle." The Count did look desperate. "Don't worry Henry they want you. Well, they want an alliance with you and your Father's Kingdom. Besides you are a young, fit, tall, dark, handsome, powerful Warlock; who is as charming as can be when you are motivated. We have given you excellent motivation. You will thank us one day. Now, go, take the long way to the North. You don't want to arouse suspicion, and you want the Emperor to feel you can follow his orders. He told you to take the flats, it seems robbers are in Elk's Pass. Go. Take your men and leave."

The Count stood and looked like he wanted to speak but thought better of it. He nodded his head and walked from the tent. Then he turned with a charming smile and politely spoke. "Gentlemen, I am already one of the richest men in the world, and I have no desire to rule any land. You have a week to find an irresistible offer." He disappeared through the doorway of the tent.

General Gage went to tent flap and watched as the Count mounted his Pegagus and leaped into the sky. He returned to his seat and sighed, "The man is the most arrogant, vile, sneaky Warlock of all time. Why did the King choose him?"

General Brad said, "That is exactly why he was chosen. It is because of his cleverness, and the King hates him too. Well, that is done."

Martin spoke for the first time. "It's a little surreal after years of discussion and planning, and all the missteps and revisions; we are finally here. Today our plan is in motion, I need more wine."

Gage said, "Not too much wine Martin. We are only at the beginning. The hardest part is yet to come. Now we need to work on outsmarting that Sorcerous. She will be much more difficult than that sniveling idiot Henry. Word is she is fearless, intelligent, and powerful."

Martin poured everyone more wine and said, "Precisely why she was chosen, gentlemen. Those are the characteristics we will breed into our populist. As the oracles predicted we have the exact person to do that. Devon, it is time to teach you a thing or two about powerful, intelligent women."

General Brad said, "Yes Devon, you kept quiet just as I had asked. Tell us what you learned today?"

"Sir," Devon paused thinking of what he should share, "I have learned many things. I hardly know where to begin." He was searching for the lessons, what were they; never trust anyone, no, not that.

Martin said, "Come, Son, you are among friends here. Be as honest with them as you would if it were just me sitting here."

Devon released a breath, "Well, never trust General Brad not to poison me to get what he wants." Everyone laughed. "No, never trust anyone, not totally. Two; keep gloves on to shake hands with any opponents. Three; be as informed and prepared as you all have been before undertaking a crazy lunatic plan. Last and I think this is the most important, know your enemy. Plan everything based on facts about him. You must have spent days planning and practicing. You even practiced what you would say to him, and who would say it and how. This was really incredible."

General Brad laughed, "Perfect young man. You are right about almost everything. Except it has taken years to set this up, months practicing the conversation between General Gage and me. We weren't sure it would be us, you know. So, all the generals practiced all the parts. We had no way of knowing who would be acting this out, or whether it would be in Elk's Pass, or here in the flats. Devon, you can trust everyone in this room to carry out this lunatic plan. Think young man, is this really a lunatic plan? It is for the future of our races, the whole planet, not just our consortium. If we don't mix the blood, only the Emperors line will remain. Everyone else will only have one or two traits of magic. Look to the peasants the Nomads to see we are right. They hardly have any magic left. Look to the Count, do we really want him to reproduce?"

Martin said, "Oh my Night, can you imagine a race of brilliant powerful and fearless Sorcerous matched to the sleazy, cunning, traitorous, backstabbing, egotist Warlocks. The thought sends chills through my soul."

Everyone looked at each other solemnly, then burst out laughing. Devon said, "Alright, I understand. After this meeting with the Count and the Sorcerous, believe me, I understand. Call me a lunatic and teach me about powerful, fearless, and intelligent women; who I might add just happens to be gorgeous." So, the drinking and adventures of these men's experience with magical women began to unfold. This might be a long night, but it looked to be one of the most exciting and fun of his life.

The North Castle

The carriage door opened. The Emperor's figure could be seen standing in the doorway to the entrance of the North Castle lights. Casandra knew she was in deep trouble. It was very late, and she had hoped their meeting would not take place until morning. He never, in all her years coming to the Castle stood at the doorway to receive her. This was bad; very, very bad. Oh, was that her Brother standing behind him. No, this was getting worse. Her heart sunk before she stepped out of the carriage.

The Emperor was shouting. "Casandra where have you been! You have vanquished you crown and torque again! I thought we had an understanding worked out the first year of the Academy. You are never to take your torque off! What is going on with you? Why are you traveling without your guard? Where are they? I pay excessively for your protection, and you just leave them in the dust. I thought we had come to an understanding about that too, the second year at the Academy! Who are these people with you? Really, Casandra, you have outdone yourself this time. I can't wait to have you married and settle down. This has got to stop! Do you understand you are a High Sorcerous and this behavior is completely unacceptable?"

The rant continued across the main hallway of the entrance and into the vestibule. Finally, Casandra stopped and screamed, "We were stopped by the Hexian's, caught in the most ferrous storm and delayed! We are tired, hungry, and freezing, so if you don't mind Father, could we continue this conversation by the fire." She pushed the doors open to the smaller parlor where she knew the hearth would have a great fire roaring, then stomped as close as she could without catching on fire. The others followed, and her Father stopped bellowing; she was sure it was from shock. Casandra had never spoken to him with such disrespect. She was already regretting it as she looked at his face, "I am sorry Father, I meant no disrespect. We have had an arduous journey this evening."

The Emperor nodded and said "I see you have. I apologize for ranting at you without giving you time to speak." He turned to Bryan and said, "Son would you please ask the servants to get your Sister and her friends some wine and food. While I begin to sort this out."

"Certainly Father." Bryan gave Casandra a quick hug and kiss on the cheek and said, "See you made it through, good." Then softer so no one could hear. "I told him you were fine, I could feel it." He grinned at her and left to fetch the food.

Casandra said, "Bring hot tea please."

Everyone settled around the fire and introductions began. The Professor initiated the conversation. "Sir let me introduce myself, make our apologies and explanations of the trip here. I take full responsibility for the removal of the Vanguard and logo on the carriage. Casandra's Mother, the Empress, and I felt moving her around with such an interrogee only courts attention. She asked me to accompany these lovely ladies, and be their guardian and chaperone while on holiday. I am Professor McMillan. I teach Advanced Scientific Magic at the Academy; I am a Level 5000. Emperor and ladies, please don't reveal that to anyone; best to keep that under cover. I believe I am the highest Magical Master there is. So, while the encounter this evening was adventurous, to say the least; we were never in real danger. Fortunately for us, I didn't have to use too much of my power. The Hexian's aren't 100 percent sure who they pulled down from the sky."

The Emperor was apparently taken back by the Professor. For that matter, both Casandra and Marion had no idea of his power and wondered what in the world was a Magical Master and a Level 5000.

The Emperor cleared his throat, "Well we must talk further Professor, and I do thank you for bringing these girls home in one piece. Now I remember you, your Beatrice's advisor. Marion, I also remember you Sprite; you're her good friend." Smiling finally the Emperor continued, "I like you, and I am glad you're here. You don't lie and deceive. That is a rare and wonderful trait. Tell me about this adventure you had this evening."

Marion began the story like only Marion could. Bryan came with warm food, wine, and tea. The Emperor and Prince listened carefully; stopping them occasionally asking why they chose to do this or that. They probed about the men that confronted them and asked many questions about the storm and carriage. Her Brother was even questioning things. That was new, he must be taking a more active role in the Kingdom.

Finally, the Emperor stood walked to the fireplace and put his hand on the mantle; which was as tall as his head. He stared into the fire as everyone quieted and waited for him to speak. The Emperor was a handsome, tall, muscular Warlock with beautiful aqua blue eyes and golden red-blond hair. He began softly, "I knew today as we crossed the flats. Crows, crows don't fly in the flats. It is nothing but desert. I was sure they followed us. Someone is using them as spies." He returned to his chair, "I came through Elk Pass just hours before you. My driver notified me of snow on the ground. I pulled back the curtain, sure enough, there was snow. I was thinking, the Monks keep this pass clear. I stilled and felt the magic. Not the low hum of the Monk's magic. No, this was a high vibration of chaotic energies, coming from more than one Maj or Warlock. I looked to Elk Mountain and at the top of a tree line was a young man with black hair whipping in the wind. He might have been the young man you describe Casandra, but we were not close enough to get a good look at his eyes. He was in a uniform. Before I could tell what country, the uniform was from, the carriage began to fly about in the air. We were thrown into the cliff. I was so surprised. It was a few seconds before I fashioned a sleigh shape out of the ruins of the carriage for my driver, the Major, and I to fly down the hill. I knew this was no accident right then, after hearing your tale; I am sure of it. I looked for the man in the tree top, but he was gone. Actually, the ride down the mountainside was rather exhilarating. I must admit I haven't had that much fun in a while, with that much magic whirling around me. I thought it best to come straight to the Castle and try to stop you from going through the Pass. Unfortunately, you couldn't be reached. I have worried since. I contacted your Mother and found out what time you left. She assured me you had more than adequate protection, and that this was not part of her premonition. Then I lost your position when you vanquished your torque. I know, I understand now it was necessary. The next time this happens, I will know that it is a distress signal and get you help. I should have known you would not do that again without just cause. I'm sorry Casandra you have done everything I have asked of you always. I will not doubt you again."

"Thank you, Father, that means more than I can say." Casandra wanted to run to her Father and hug him, but that was not his way. He had never been demonstrative with her; she didn't expect it to start now. It was enough knowing he appreciated her and trusted her. That had taken twenty years to accomplish. Since Sorcerers lived to a thousand years or more, there was plenty of time to work on touching or speaking the words I love you.

The Emperor smiled and sat forward in his chair, "Knowing what happened to me was not an accident; I was certain you would have a story for me, and one I would not like repeated. Before you arrived, I had Elf's clear this room. There are ears and eyes on us in this Castle. It is so large it is almost impossible to keep rooms clean from spies. Information, vital information has gotten out to the consortium. Negotiating with our tactics being known has been difficult. I ask all of you to refrain from talking about anything that might be used against us. If this was the Hex, the more I learn I believe it is, then everything about us they don't know is an advantage. An advantage for us, war is close, I feel it. We must do all we can to prevent that action. This time I am not so sure we would win."

They all sat silently, each with their thoughts until the Emperor said, "It is late, and we have all had an exciting day. Tomorrow will be a difficult one too, so let's get some sleep. There will be a meeting to-morrow at midmorning in the library. Remember your journey and see if you can remember anything else about your abduction. I will have the library cleared in the morning. I want everyone who is here tonight to attend. Do you understand?"

They all answered yes at once and understood this was an order. Everyone left the warmth of the sitting room and followed the maids up to the stairs to their bedrooms. The Professor's bedroom was at the beginning of the hall. Bryan gave her a hug and said he'd see her at breakfast. Kathryn her Sister-in-law and High Sorcerer of the Castle, and their children would be thrilled to see her, but they would already be asleep. He walked away to the east wing. She and Marion would have adjoining rooms on the west side adjacent to her Father's suite. The Castle was magnificent, luxurious, and overwhelming as it always had been. Marion was in awe and excited to inspect every vase, statue, and painting. Casandra entered her room with an inviting fire waiting, and a hot tub of water for a bath sitting in front of the fireplace. Some days it was fabulous to be 'The Empress to be.' The maid helped her undress, and she jumped in the warm water.

Marion came rushing into Casandra's room, "Oh, you have one too. I'm taking a bath. I'll be back to talk after, Bye." and off she flew.

Casandra had never known a creature quite like Marion. She had only two speeds; fast and off. Casandra loved her dearly because Marion never held her thoughts or feelings back from Casandra. Marion was the most endearing person in Casandra's world. Now wouldn't she hate hearing her use that word? Casandra relaxed in the tub scrubbing the dirt of the day away. She wondered about that emerald eye magi. He held the power that was for sure, but she felt like it was strained. Of course, if he held weather magic, and he was trying to probe her, the professor, and Marion while keeping the cold and storm; he had to be powerful. Now that was fascinating. His eyes could hardly hold back his thoughts, and he was just about to fall into her arms where she could see every one of those thoughts and plans. She had been so close to un-covering who he really was, why he was there, and who he was looking for. He was looking for someone; if only those Warlocks hadn't held him back. Of course, they were Warlocks, not ordinary soldiers. She would have to tell that to her Father in the morning meeting. She remembered seeing them grab the man when his coat opened she could see a piece of a uniform; they were Hex! They were not sure who she was until she tried to draw the young officer in. It took all their strength to pull him away. Why didn't she remember until now? Well, a lot was happening all at once. Besides he had riled her by calling her a whore. Never in her life had she been thought of like that. Her Mother was right, a correct decision was never made in anger, which was why she spent hours learning to control emotions. While he gave them too much information, she just might have done the same. She should have used a weaker pull on him. Maybe then they would know about their plan.

"All work and no play Casandra. What is on your mind, you have a somber look about you. Are you brooding about that handsome man you tried to put a spell on?" joked Marion. She sat on the bed with her nightgown on taunting her.

"What do you mean tried; I did put a spell on him. The poor man will never be the same and never be satisfied until he gets his kiss. He won't even know what's wrong with him." Casandra laughed. "You know what I just realized, those men were Warlocks. I was relaxing in my warm tub when I played it back in my mind. I placed a strong spell on that young officer. Those Warlocks needed all their strength to pull him out of my spell before I saw their plot. The young man's coat opened, and I saw a Hex uniform. Think back Marion do you remember anything odd?" Casandra climbed from the tub and dried quickly in front of the fire. She put on her gown and saw the maid had left a hand mirror, brush, and a pot of tea. "Here's tea want some?"

Marion squealed, "Of course, I never turn down tea. Sit, I'll brush your hair out while I think about it." The two girls sat on the bed. Casandra enjoying the hair brushing while Marion was thinking, and both drinking their tea.

Soon Marion said, "Well there was one odd thing, they all wore fur coats, but the one man only dress in black. Did you see that scar? I have seen scars like that made by Witches stealing power. He had black hair and eyes, he reminded me of pictures I have seen of Arlequin Wizards."

"Can't be. A Wizard? They have long been gone from this world. Father says there is only a handful." said Casandra. "This is another thing we need to tell Father. Marion, could I ask...well, did we really look like whores?"

"Ah." sighed Marion, "So, that's what got you into a snit. He got to you. I saw you snap to attention, so did he. That's why he went on about it, I thought you looked good for the short time I had to change everyone. Put the mirror down. I'll do it again, and you can judge for yourself."

Marion worked the magic and then handed Casandra the mirror. Casandra couldn't believe it, she looked so different. Marion had given her cat eyes. "Really, Marion you gave me actual cat eyes. No wonder they thought we were whores, good Night! I was thinking of using red hair when I start my season, but this may be a bit too wild. I want to have fun; not get molested."

Laughing Marion changed her back, "Ha, then you put a glamor on top of it, and a spell. I'm surprised we made it out of there. If it hadn't been for the weird guy with the scar pushing us in the carriage, we might never have made it back here."

"You're right. That is another thing about that guy; he was not affected by the spell." Casandra pondered almost to herself.

Marion suddenly got serious, "He wasn't, nor by the cold yet he wore no coat. Casandra! I am also certain he was the one outside the window when you pulled back the curtains, and I screamed. He knew who we were all along. Who is he and why did he not give us up? We need to tell your Father."

"Yes, we will in the morning, and we should not be speaking about this tonight, in this room," whispered Casandra.

Marion handed the brush back to Casandra. She noticed her arm was bleeding, "Casandra your arm is bleeding." She grabbed her arm and saw a small hole in her arm. "How did you do that? What is that?"

Casandra looked scared, "I have no idea. I didn't even feel anything, maybe when the carriage dropped this happened." Casandra waved her hand, the hole disappeared. Marion sprinkled Sprite dust on it, and the blood vanished.

"Casandra, could I sleep with you tonight; just tonight? Suddenly I am spooked." Marion gave her a pout.

"If you hadn't asked, I would have asked you. Something is not right. My Mother's darn premonition is happening. I hate it when she is right." They huddled together under the blankets, trying not to think about the events of the day and trying to sleep. Casandra had thought she was a woman of the world, a highly skilled Sorcerous. She had not one but three steamy affairs. Casandra was a Mother herself to three children Casandra gifted for those Countries. Yet tonight, she was beginning to think she just may be what others had said behind her back; a girl, spoiled, coddled, overprotected, unaware of the dangers in the real world. Sleep could not come fast enough.

Mornings Light

Casandra had hoped the morning light would paint the fears they had before bed differently; it didn't. The early sunlight against the dark blue curtains and bedsheets seemed cold and harsh. The decorative paintings of flowers looked worn and ominous. Her Father had not changed a thing in her room or her Sisters adjoining room since the night of the fire. It was too painful to ask why. She went to the windows and closed the drapes that had been left open. Looking out on the dawn she saw three black crows circling the village below. Father had said eyes and ears were watching. He had seen crows out on the flats. Suddenly she was no longer sleepy. She quietly dressed leaving Marion to sleep a little longer.

Downstairs the only sounds of the morning were coming from the kitchen. The smell of coffee filled the rooms, that would help clear Casandra's head. She entered the kitchen, and everyone turned. Maggie screamed, "There's my baby!" Before she knew it, she was in a tight bear hug. Maggie released her but kept her in her arms, "My child I was so worried yesterday when you didn't make it here for dinner. I wanted to speak with you last night, but you Father cornered you, and it got to be very late. I had to be up early this morning to make breakfast and get preparations going. You brought along friends. I wasn't counting on so many guests. My you look wonderful. You are more beautiful every time you come for a visit. You're quiet, what's wrong. Oh, forgive me, you had quite a scare falling from the sky yesterday and running into Barbarians. Speak girl. Where is your voice?"

The first time since landing in the courtyard Casandra's world turned normal. This was the women who would be the first to meet her at the doorway. She was a short, powerful Sorcerer with blue-violet and white hair and aqua eyes. She was still beautiful and shapely, but no one knew how old she was. Maggie was her Nanny until she was sent off to school. Casandra and Bryan insisted their Father keep her on at the Castle, so he put her in the kitchen. However, Mags was so bossy she was soon elevated to the headmistress. Now she oversaw all the cooking and maids. Casandra kissed her cheek and said, "Mags I love you, but I really need coffee before I can answer a million questions."

"Oh, it is just being made. Everyone is up with the sun this morning, very unusual. That Professor was already in here looking for coffee as well. I gave him the last cup. I told him I would serve more out on the dining room balcony. It looks to be a spectacular sunrise. I thought everyone would enjoy the view of the meadow, mountains, and lake. He said he needed to inspect the meadow, odd, so he dashed out of here with some of our best china. I hope he can be trusted to return it in one piece."

Casandra was thrilled that her Maggie would never change, "Well, Mags, the Professor can be trusted. Mother sent him with me as my protector. He has already done that very well. I do need a few moments with him before Father wakes. Father isn't down, yet is he?"

"No, so far everything is peaceful." Maggie chuckled and handed her a large mug of coffee, not the good china.

"Mags, I do want to have a long talk with you and fill you in on my last year at school. I also have questions, but I would like it to be a private talk. How is it you already know of the carriage ride?" asked Casandra.

"My child you know these walls have ears," Maggie whispered. "My schedule is so full; your Brother's family, your friends, the gentlemen from Belissa Villa, and those grandchildren don't eat the same food as grownups yet. Your nephews eat a whole different meal each lunch and dinner. There is a special dinner in two days, a party tomorrow, in a few nights there is the big ball and hunting party on Saturday. I only hope people leave by Sunday night. Just thinking about it makes me tired. The only time I will have is this afternoon. How about tea at my cottage, about four? Everything should be organized by then."

Casandra was weary just hearing Mags list off her duties, she laughed, "Well, I will make sure to set that time aside for you. At your cottage, at four then." She rushed out to find the Professor before Mags could add to the conversation.

She wondered why men from Belissa Villa were coming to the Castle and why there were so many special events. The thought struck like a lightning bolt, a match. Father wouldn't make a marriage for her without her input! This was Father, of course, he would! Her heart sunk, she would not even have a week without the weight of her station put on her. She had known from the time she went off to secondary school her marriage would be prearranged. Everything in her life had been strategically decided; schools, liaisons with each country, her marriage, number and sex of her children. The only thing she could choose was her friends and her season of freedom. Often, she had wondered if she had any control over those either; stop Casandra! She was trained to think and not feel. She was no longer a child this would be just another fragment, a small inconvenience in her life. Thank the Night she was not required to live with her husband or love him. She only had to procreate and be married in name. But Belissa Villa in Diamante, they were the lowest cruelest sneakiest snakes of beings. Why would the Emperor want offspring from that? There was much more to this. Regrettably, she was sure she would find out soon enough.

Casandra found the Professor in the garden just below the balcony. She called, "Professor could I speak with you?"

He spun around looking startled, "Miss Casandra you are up with the birds. I am surprised. I thought you and Marion would be sleeping in this morning. I assumed that was the reason your Father planned a late morning meeting with us."

Casandra stopped next to him and gazed at the last of the sunrise. Colors of pink, orange, and gold painted the clouds above them. This morning's sky reminded her of the morning she was taken from the

Castle so many years ago. That was before her life changed; a time when she could feel and not force herself to think instead.

"Casandra? You look to be a million miles away. Come back, Dear." The Professor's voice was soft and caring.

"Not miles Professor… years, to be precise." He sighed as if he understood, she continued, "The sun woke me early, Marion still sleeps… I hope. We both had some revelations before falling to sleep. I had forgotten to make sure the drapes were closed. The sun streamed through my window and woke me; I got up to shut the drapes. I saw crows in the meadow, then I was wide awake." She paused, "Maggie told me you went out to the meadow to investigate something; I surmised you had seen them too. Tell me did you find them?"

"Not really. As soon as I came out of the garden, the crows stopped circling and flew off to the west. Odd, the garden holds plenty of food for crows. I expected it was their destination, but they were more interested in peering in the windows above. As soon as they spied me, they flew like the wind. Perhaps they were the eyes your Father mentioned yesterday." The Professor looked worried.

"Yes perhaps, you know the scullery crew already knows of our mishap in the carriage. I feel like we are targets, and I am not comfortable. Let's refill our cups on the balcony. I have some questions about something you said last evening. Professor, what is a level 5000? I have never heard of this." Casandra turned and walked up the stairs.

They climbed the stairs to the balcony, but the Professor didn't speak until he was seated with a steamy cup. "I suppose I opened a can of worms with that comment. It really is a long story, my Dear."

"No one is around now. I had the feeling I was the only one in the room which was ignorant of the term" said Casandra.

"Very well, it is time you learn. It's time you know who I am." He set his cup down and started teaching. "In my family, I was the eighth son. My Father was Brother to the King of Antico, so I was far removed from ever being part of the hierarchy of society. Of course, I was still on the edges. Hence I was well schooled and exceeded in Science of Magic, Histories, and Diplomacy. I attended the Academy, then the University. However, with so many older Brothers there was little left as far as a career choice. The Army seemed a reasonable choice, but when I took my season, I stumbled onto the Monastery. A group of us decided an adventure of climbing Elk Mountain would be just the thing to distract us from making any decisions about our future. There was a terrible accident. Three of my friends fell to their death. Only one friend and I survived. Kent was not hurt badly he carried me miles to the Monks for help. He returned with my parents several days later. It was decided I could not be moved and would heal faster at the Monastery. What they had not told me was I was never expected to heal. My legs had taken a terrible beating, the bones were crushed, if lived I would become invalid. Fortunately for me, the Monks did not take that attitude. They never told me of my fate. Instead, they prayed continually over me. They trained me to meditate, a strange and wonderful experience. My bones did heal and my heart too. More importantly, my brain finally stopped wondering around. I found peace and understanding; a knowing that had eluded me all my life. To strengthen my muscles, they taught me their system of magical arts. It is an ancient way of fighting brought from the old world. The Monks combine the mystic with a traditional system of exercise and wisdom. Single-mindedness sounds simple; however, it is the most strenuous exercise I have ever known. Every grade or level is tallied, to this day I am at a Level 5000. Is that enough of an answer for you my Dear?"

Casandra thought for a moment, "So, this is a way of fighting or healing?"

"Both, and it is much more. It is connecting our soul and spirit to all. Anything else?" the Professor smiled.

Not even thinking she said, "Yes, can you teach me?"

The professor laughed, "That my Dear, is the exact reason I was sent here by your Mother. I have only taught this skill to a few women. You have been in training already for many years. This is wonderful, it so much easier teaching a willing student."

Casandra's eyes were opened wide she said, "This is the reason you have been my advisor for all these years, and I have been in at least one of your classes every year at the Academy. I also wager the private lessons on 'a single viewpoint' were not to help me concentrate for exams. Tell me, Professor, could all the rumors about you be true as well?"

The Professor almost blushed, "I have no idea what those rumors might be my Dear."

Marion bounced out the dining room door. "There you go throwing around that word 'Dear' again, Professor. Mags said coffee would be out here." She spied the table with china and coffee, "Oh my, good china, I know that is not for me. Is Mags trying to impress someone?" Marion must be in a good mood her coloring was a sunny yellow.

"It wasn't me either." Casandra grinned at the professor. "I got an old mug." Casandra watched the Professor. He deliberately averted his eyes, probing him would not only be rude; it would probably not reveal any more information. She would continue questioning the professor in private. She knew he was mysterious for a reason she would find out why later.

The Emperor walked out on the balcony smiling, "Well it seems we have early risers. Good, we can start our day earlier." He turned and motioned for Major, his assistant, advisor, and longtime friend. "Major get Bryan up, so we can get started with our day."

Major stuck his head out the door and said, "Yes your Majesty. Princess Casandra wonderful to see you, and congratulations on the honors at school. Marion, you are lovely as ever, and Professor McMillian good to see you again." Off he went to get Casandra's Brother.

Marion asked "Your Majesty, could you explain something. Is Major a Major in the army or is he your assistant? I have never understood his name."

The Emperor went to the coffee server and helped himself, "Major is his name, Marion. I am privileged to know why it is his name, but I have been sworn to secrecy about divulging the reason. Let's just say his parents were weird." Everyone laughed. Then the Emperor continued, "It is hard to put names and labels on people, Marion. Major is foremost my very best friend in the world. I keep him close just as Casandra keeps you close. Who would Mags be impressing? The good china is in use. Ah, Professor McMillian, I would watch myself if I were you."

Marion chimed in. "I knew it was not set out for me, his Majesty is right. Watch out." The Professor blushed.

Mags appeared at the door and said. "Who are we watching out for?"

The Emperor turned and said, "Breakfast! It must be around here somewhere. I did find the coffee on the balcony. Are you eavesdropping Mags? Are you the source of the rumors that fly through the Kingdom?"

Mags placed both her hands on her hips and said, "Me? Not likely. I don't have time for such nonsense! What with parties and Balls, extra guests that I am not informed about showing up on my doorstep."

The Emperor stopped short. "So, it's your doorstep now? I thought I was the boss here."

Mags took two steps, stood in from of him and said, "You may be in charge of the Kingdom, but I take care of the Castle. I am announcing breakfast is served. This morning it is served by yourselves. Everything is set out on the buffet; I am hoping the extra servants we hired to show up by noon, or you will be serving yourself lunch too. Dinner, well, I am going to start working on dinner now, if you will excuse me, your Majesty."

"You are impertinent Mags. I should throw you out on your bum!" said the Emperor.

Mags just laughed and said, "You can't. I know too much about you and the Kingdom."

Emperor just frowned. Bryan and Major came out. Bryan made his way to the coffee and said, "Good morning everyone; Father have you been at it with Mags again? You have that look on your face. Oh, who is she trying to impress? We have good china."

That brought the smile back to the Emperor's face.

Breakfast was a whirlwind; Kathryn and children appeared. Kathryn was a beautiful petite Sorcerer, with flaming red hair and deep blue eyes. Her size did not make demure her power; it could be seen in the waves of her aura. She would be the next Empress, and she would be phenomenal. Casandra's three nephews were ecstatic to see her; throwing themselves at her and laughing and jabbering at once. The grown-ups were no better. The family was asking questions about graduation. Kathryn was fascinated with the Professors news of the Academy; he had also been her advisor at school. They must have shared a friendship as they communicated with ease. Marion was in her element, asking questions and changing topics faster than anyone could follow. Casandra couldn't remember a time at the dining room table filled with such joy and noise.

Walter the butler entered and told the Emperor the Elves were there. He stood up and said, "This shouldn't take the Elves long. I would like everyone, except the children, of course, to come into the Library as soon as you are finished with breakfast. Kathryn, you may not play a part in this, but you should know what is about to happen too." Kathryn nodded in agreement, and the mood among them dropped to one of seriousness. Everyone quickly finished, and Kathryn took the children into the kitchen to find the Nanny.

They arrived in the Library to a warm fire in the hearth in the middle of the north wall. Spheres of light were dangled from the ceiling, the oak table customarily filled with books, maps, and globes of the world was empty. Three chairs were placed on each side of the table. Books lined the walls on three sides of the twenty-foot-high Library from the floor to ceiling. The royal blue drapes of the enormous windows that overlooked the stunning views of the mountain range, lake, and meadow were shut. Casandra loved the library. As a child, she spent hours curled up in one of the many winged back chairs enjoying the bright light from the windows, marvelous view, and the books. Her spirit drained, all her life she had issues with the feeling of being closed in. The effect of the lighting in the room was a maudlin one.

Casandra went to the window and opened the drapes. A familiar voice said, "Lady, there are spies with us. Please keep the drapes closed."

Casandra knew that voice well. "Eric, you are still telling me what I can and cannot do?" She turned and smiled at him. When she was a child he was her companion; as a young adult, he had been her keeper. He was in charge of her personal guard at school and the Castle. He had come up the ranks in service to her. She wondered if he would be along on her season. If he were, she would not have much fun. He stood almost seven feet tall with silver-white hair and grey-white eyes with gold rims. All her friends were madly in love with him, as she had been too.

Eric smiled sweetly and said teasingly. "It seems to be my mission in life. You don't seem happy to see me. Am I no longer your friend?"

Casandra said, "You are my Father's Vanguard, first. I know this." She closed the drapes and turned to see him with a look of concerned for her. "I am sorry Eric, I have a terrible feeling this meeting is going to be about me. And...I am not going to like."

He smiled. "Or maybe you will like it. Maybe I will be chosen to go on your holiday. Now that should make your day." He laughed and turned to leave.

Eric announced the room clean of spies, the Elves left the room, and her Father began taking charge. He seated himself at the head of the table and said, "Casandra, please take the seat to my left. Everyone else can sit where they like. Kathryn, I assume Bryan told you of our journeys to the Castle yesterday."

Kathryn said, "Yes your Majesty. Your adventure was exciting, to say the least."

The Emperor said, "Good, then unless anyone here has remembered something that would add any clarification or explain the events of Elks Mountain we will move on and open the discussion to other topics."

Marion was the first to speak, "Your Majesty Casandra and I did have something to add. The man who pushed the driver to the ground looked Arlequin." Everyone at the table had an intake of air, but Marion didn't let that stop her. "He had black hair and eyes and was dressed all in black too with a jagged scar running down his right cheek. It was odd he wasn't wearing a coat; all the others were. It was freezing outside the carriage. The wind was whipping around us, and we all were shivering. Also, when Casandra sent out her spell, he picked all three of us up and pushed us into the coach."

The Emperor stopped her and looked to Casandra, "Spell? You didn't mention a spell last evening."

"I know Father." said Casandra, "I really hadn't thought of it until we had relaxed after our bath. The young man and the five others were trying to probe us, to distinguish our powers or maybe just to see if we were lying. I was curious to find out what they were about, so I cast a spell on the young man. It felt like he was the most vulnerable. I am sure he was controlling the weather and probing us at the same time. I almost had his mind when two of the men pulled the young man away from me. Then we were pushed into the carriage. I realized the young man's coat opened. I saw a Hex uniform. Your Majesty, I believe they were all Warlocks."

The Emperor placed his hands in prayer position and muttered, "Good mother of night."

Marion softly said, "Earlier Sir, before the carriage fell to the ground Casandra was going to open the window to get some fresh air. When she pulled the curtains aside, I saw the Arlequin riding next to us. I didn't put it all together until last night, but today I am sure of it. Sir, that means he had seen us before we had donned our disguises. He had to know who we were, and he didn't give us up to the Warlocks. He was strong enough to push us into the carriage with Casandra still working her spell."

Everyone sat silent for a few minutes just taking all the implications into their heads. The Professor added. "Your Majesty, there was much magic going on in a short amount of time. My focus was to keep the power levels of myself and the young ladies to a minimum. I was worried they would know who we were if our powers were full strength. When Casandra created the spell I was surprised, and immediately tried to check it, stop it. I realized last night while in bed, my power was zapped. Someone had shut me down and threw me into the carriage. This has bothered me all morning, well this and those nosey crows outside my window. If an Arlequin Wizard were in our mist, as Marion suggests, I would have my answer."

"Crows you say." Confirmed the Emperor, "I have known they were more than just crows, as the mice in this Castle are not just mice! Augh, but that is another matter altogether. An Arlequin Wizard; that was an assassination attempt and a kidnapping attempt. Or…maybe they were just practicing."

Prince Bryan spoke, "No, not an attempt. They tried and failed to kill you, Father. Only because you love to ski did your mind jump and save you and the Major, but why did they not take Casandra? This Arlequin knew who you were. Why did he save you?"

"Think my love." said Kathryn, "Would they hold her for ransom or money? They would get that. Evidently, they don't need money, or she would not have been released. For magic, again, it would seem they had their own magic. What other value is she?" Kathryn paused, again everyone was silent, "Alright I'll say it; procreation. The only problem was she is not carrying any eggs. If they had any magic, they'd knew that too."

"I don't think the Hex has evolved that far to even consider the idea you propose Kathryn." Bryan shook his head, and Kathryn sat back in her chair blushing.

The Emperor stood, "Bryan's right, that is outlandish, preposterous, and ridiculous!" He stopped and thought, "But I am afraid it is also possible. This brings to light a whole new host of problems. Also, our next item of discussion. Casandra, I had hoped to speak with you privately about this, but now that this has been brought up, it is time to hand fast. You need to have the royal family that is required of you. Your Brother and I, and the council have been considering a suitable husband for you. There are many out there and the Ball this week will be a wonderful time to announce it. We have narrowed it down to three, but one man stands out to be the best. Perhaps not your first choice, but one that will cement the counties interest."

Casandra held in her emotions, focused and calmly said, "It is the sleazy Count Rakie, isn't it? It is hard for me to fathom why you would want to include the blood of terrorists, traitors, and malefactors into the royal family. I suppose you have your reasons and I would hear them now if you please."

The Emperor rubbed his hand across his face. Clearly, he was discomforted by Casandra. Good, she thought, let him feel unpleasant. It was only fair; she would feel no less under the body of Rakie.

"Casandra, listen to us. We do know this is a strange and an unlikely choice, but we have a plan." Bryan took her hand, "If you would only be open to it. We would not stick you with a lecherous lying man for hundreds of years. There is no possibility we would allow him to come near the throne or be the Emperor. Nor would we ever think to have offspring with the Belissa Villa. This is nothing more than a political maneuver to cement the Continental Council and keep the peace. Our world cannot withstand another war; we have lost too much magic, on both sides. Diamante is the country that stands between our coalition and Bezier. We may have brought Diamante to its knees in the last war, but we have never had control over it."

"I know my history, Brother," Casandra said coolly. "I am acuity knowledgeable of my responsibilities to the realm. I have known all my life my marriage would never include love. Hell, I have never expected to like my husband. Also, let's move past the lesson of politics and on to my children. My children, Brother, children I get to keep, to love and care for. Explain why my children should be half Diamante; horrendously born without one strand of integrity." She said all this without once raising her voice, or with any malice. She looked around the room everyone was just staring or numbly looking at her. Casandra had only felt this commanding at school in the classroom or in other countries, never here at North Castle. She had never felt this in the presence of her Brother, the Prince or her Father. She might as well use this while it lasted, she knew it wouldn't be long before the Emperor snatched it back. "Well, you said you had a plan. Speak!"

Red-faced her Brother said, "Our scientists have developed an impermeable egg. In fact, you can help design each of the children as you like. However, one egg must be fertilized by him; for this to work he must be deceived. He must see that one of his children is somewhat like him, the others will be all yours. He has no place in his Kingdom of Diamentia. The only reason he has estates and money is that he stole it from his dead Brother. He also stole his Brother's wife too, now dead. His Mother insisted he remained royalty and named him Count. He is a winemaker. We understand his Father, the King, is on his deathbed, and the Count is hated by his Brothers. The Queen is removed from service after the death of a King. She will not be in a position to help her Son any longer. He would jump at this chance to be brought up in the world. We will offer him a job as a diplomat. After the mating, he would be traveling, far away from you. We understand he prefers men so he will be just as happy about this arrangement as you. We have already arranged an accident out at sea when he takes his annual visit to the East. Not right away understand; it would only mean one year of tolerance from you."

Casandra sat and listened carefully. She moved her emotion well down, down beyond her feet, far away from her. She had been trained to not react to only think, never feel. She watched her Brother the whole time. Without even probing she knew Bryan was straightforward and honest with her. Now, she turned to her Father who was staring at her in disbelief. Casandra looked over to Kathryn who smiled knowingly. She was the only one in this room that understood her predicament. Casandra and Kathryn had bonded immediately after her Brother 's marriage. She will be the one she could talk to about Count Rakie.

"Well, it seems you gentlemen have worked everything out, barring any unforeseen problems. Which can be handled well enough between all of us in this room." She pushed out her chair and stood. She supposed that was an agreement of sorts. It was the closest contract she would give them. "Of course, this is subject to the approval of both the Count and me. If there is no attraction, well, all this preparation is for nothing. If that is all I would like to ride Sheba, and I promised to visit Mags at four. Marion, would you like to ride with me?" She couldn't believe how disconnected she felt. She was speaking like she had just ordered dinner, not decided on a husband. She wasn't sure how long she could hold this peacefulness and needed to be out of the room, quickly.

"Casandra!" the Emperor screamed, "Sit down. I have a few things to say yet. You are so like your Mother, completely cold. If I live to be a thousand years, I will never understand either of you. I must say I did not expect this much detachment. I am sorry this had to be put on you so soon after your graduation, but things have escalated. The Hex has infiltrated every country. They are working to destroy the financial establishments and business with an elite black market. They are using the Belissa Villa to do this, although we can't prove it. We need to take Diamante, you are the quickest and least painful way of doing it. War will only weaken the Continents and cost Fabs; not to mention the loss of occult blood from all. The sooner we can arrange this marriage the better. So, I am also asking you to defer your season of freedom."

It was good Casandra sat when her Father ordered her, for surely, she would have fallen to the floor. Twenty-five years she had waited to be free for one season without hearing her Mother's or Father's voice in her head. Just once Casandra wanted not to wear the torque and crown or feel the weight of the responsibility. She felt the anger growing so hot inside her, she thought she would ignite. Casandra knew too well what she could do with that flame. She had cremated many things in her life by releasing that flame. A voice in her head said single-minded focus Casandra, see a river running through you, see it now Casandra. She realized it was the Professor's voice, he was speaking silently to her. She followed the advice, drew in a cleansing breath. She looked at her Father and said, "That Father is unacceptable." Calmly she continued, "You and my Brother have cleverly and meticulously devised a devious questionable and clearly unethical plan. You will dupe and kill the Count of Belissa Villa and uproot the Hexian's, all in one blow, me. You can put your evil little heads together and get me my time of freedom. I must say you have upset me, even disappointed me. You very well know what can happen to a High Sorcerer who is extremely upset. Why we can self-consume." She took in another breath while they all sat back in their chairs with their mouths gaping open.

"Then where would your little plans be? Up in smoke, that's where, literally!" Her Father's face was in a rage. Had she been too sarcastic? Too threatening? Well too bad…he had overstepped himself this time. Besides how many times had he been sarcastic to her. She didn't think he had ever cared a smidgeon for her. The worst he could do was kill her, and if this plan of his backfired, that might happen yet. She would take this time to tell him that. "Father you look like you would like to strangle me." She said with a wicked smile on her face, "Well consider this…if this plan you and my Brother devised goes haywire; I am sure the Count will do that for you. If the Hexian's find out your scheme, I will surely be the first dead. The Continental Council may not feel pain, but I will if I die, as I will in giving birth. You need to understand this! Your proposition is a lose/lose situation for me. You can be as angry as you like. You have caused me nothing but anger and pain all my life. Maybe in death, I can be happy and at peace." Casandra didn't wait for an answer from the Emperor. The shock and hurt on his face said all she needed to know. Casandra had wounded him gravely, but he would strike back. She didn't wait for the storm. Casandra stood and walked from the room, using all her strength to place one foot in front of the next. She straightened her back; held her head high and exited with as much dignity as her Mother could. The moment she closed the door, she ran, as fast and as far from the Castle as she could.

The Emperor stood to go after Casandra, but the Major stopped him. "Let her go your Majesty. She needs time to come to terms with this. You have been plotting this for almost a year. This is her first taste of your plan. I will have Eric follow her without being seen. After yesterday we can't have her off on her own; even in the palace grounds." Major started for the door.

The Emperor said, "Thank you, Major. Also, for not reminding me you told me this would happen, and I should not approach her in this manner."

Major turned and smiled and said, "You're welcome Sir, I would never throw that up to you now. I will wait until you decide not to follow my advice the next time."

The Emperor almost fell into his chair muttering, "She hates me."

Marion stood up and said, "Hates you? Your Majesty, I beg your pardon, but Casandra does not hate you. She has completed every one of your commands, only to please you. Yes, right now your daughter is angry with you, but Casandra does love you. I know she had told me many times. She is the one who thinks you hate her."

"How can that be?" the Emperor looked confused.

Marion was reluctant to say, but Prince Bryan stepped in, "Father, she has told me that too. You took all your children with you on the day of the Great War. You left her here at the palace alone."

"That was because she was just a baby. She was only four years old at the time, and I regret that to this day. She was kidnapped. We almost lost her, I always worry about her safety. She is in my heart daily." The Emperor sighed.

Kathryn went to the Emperor and touched his hand. "Your Majesty, may I speak freely?" He nodded yes. "Casandra has been away for a long time, at school. When she did come home for the summer season, you were running the Kingdom and teaching Bryan how to rule. Casandra has been diligent at school, training of sorcery, and all the diplomacy of her station. Even today, she did not refuse to marry the Count but only asked for her season of freedom. This is the first time she has asked anything of you. It must have wounded her deeply for you to refuse her when I have never known you to refuse anything Bryan asked of you."

"I was the one who asked her to give up her season. She was the one who demanded!" the Emperor shouted.

"Well," Kathryn said, "I am sorry, but I think it is unreasonable to ask any young women, much less the Emperor's daughter, to spend only weeks planning her wedding. If you remember Bryan and I had over a year to plan ours. Besides, it is not possible to get all the invitations out that quickly, even if you started today. You need the Count to agree first."

"Kathryn is right Father and think of how it would look. The world would think you care little to nothing about your daughter. It will take weeks to engineer the eggs, and I promised Casandra could be a part of that. Also, have you said anything to Mother about this?"

"Oh, your Mother. No, not really."

Professor McMillian removed a document from his coat pocket. "Yes, your Majesty, remember Casandra's Mother, the Empress. One of the many reasons I was retained by the Empress to take this trip is to deliver this letter to you. Along with representing her in just the circumstances as we find ourselves in today. Would you like to read it in private?"

"What is this? No, I think I would like you to explain this. This meeting has gone on too long already." The Emperor placed his hand on the envelope and pushed it back to the Professor. "Go on."

"As you wish your Majesty." The Professor breathed in deeply and began. "It is time I reveal who I am and the real reason I am here with these young ladies. I will be brief; however, you should have a tad of background on how I came to this business. The one hundred and third Empress appointed me many years ago, to keep an eye on the High Sorcerers at the Academy. I was made a professor and began my stewardship of the highborn sorcerer and those with prodigious high energies, like Kathryn. I was Kathryn's advisor and friend; just as I was Beatrice's advisor and friend and Casandra's. When Beatrice became the Empress, she asked me to be her personal advisor. Just like the Major is to you, and someday I am sure Marion will be to Casandra. While I am here to protect these ladies during the season, I am also here to train them. Casandra in the Monks Arts, and Marion… well, Marion on everything she will need to become Casandra's advisor."

Marion glared at him. "No one asked me about this! I am beginning to understand how Casandra feels."

"Part of your training, my dear." The Professor corrected himself, "I retract the previous endearment and will work on not using them. Marion, we will talk about this later. However, this is a good observation

Marion, of how Casandra feels. Compassion and understanding are a large part of advising. Now, moving on. Both Prince Bryan and Kathryn have made excellent points as to the arrangements of both the nuptials and the logistics of manufacturing the eggs. I would add one point that concerns me. The plans you have for the Count, are as Casandra referred to them, devious, questionable, and I believe she added unethically. While I don't know the Count personally, he is not a stupid Warlock, your Majesty. In fact, he is known to be anything but stupid. He is remarkably intelligent, cunning, clever, and even brilliant at scheming. Are you aware of this many papers and books he has written on a variety of topics? He will see right through your proposal if you try to arrange a quick wedding, as well as be highly insulted. Remember he comes here with his own agenda. Before we tug him into this marriage, we need to know his motives."

The Professor picked up the document, "Now, as for representing the Empress, she has been worried about the contract of marriage you would offer Casandra for years. I believe because her own contract had so many loopholes she has provided some protection for her daughter. This letter is a reminder of your agreement signed the day she left this Castle to become Empress. She is concerned you might have forgotten the details. Specifically, the details surrounding the rights of marriage of the royal children. The Empress was cognizant and privileged to the contract between Prince Bryan and Mistress Kathryn long before their proposed engagement. However, Casandra's visit to you was to just be a rest stop before starting her Season of Freedom. The Empress had a strong inclination that plans for a wedding would be pressed on Casandra. Also, that she is deliberately being excluded from those plans. Hence, the reason I carry this document with me...and I might add, a very worthy reason Casandra's season of freedom will not be postponed. At least not without the expressed permission of the Empress." The Professor noticed the Emperor had a look of astonishment. He added, "I know your Majesty, I am always rather amazed at the Empress ability to comprehend the nuances of the state of affairs, and always be so equipped to handle it with such grace and foresight. It boggles the mind. Women are a wonder don't you think?"

The Emperor just sat looking at the Professor like he had three heads. The Prince stood and said, "Well, your Majesty I would say that settles it. Casandra will have her season; you should really be the one to tell her. She would love hearing it from you. Yes. If you do that, I will gladly go speak to Mother on your behalf, about our plan. I believe we can have her here in time for negotiations and the Ball."

"She surely will." said the Professor. "I spoke with her this morning, and she was already packing."

The Emperor looked resigned said, "That woman is Continents away. Yet, she still controls me. Yes, Professor, the Empress has always boggled my mind." He left to find Casandra. The Emperor wished he could send Bryan to talk to his Sister he would prefer to speak with the Empress. What would he say to Casandra, what could he say?

Count Rakie

The Count was exhausted. He wondered if the poison was already at work. Over the past hours, he wavered between feeling like he was poisoned and knowing the Generals were playing him. Following the suggestion to take the long route to the North Castle was a waste of time, and perhaps his life if he was poisoned. However, it did give him time to reflect. Everyone had always underestimated him; his Brothers, his Father and most of all those outside his Kingdom. They all believed he was nothing more than a ruthless, selfish fool. He was no one's fool. Rakie was his Mother's son, born with inherent genius. His late wife was even more ingenious than him. How he missed her, how he had loved her. Had he known the risk of her having children; he would have never allowed it. She would be able to understand and resolve these issues within minutes. Eliana was not here, so think Henry focus. It was the damn poison that puzzled him. He had not placed it into his equation.

"We are stopping for rest," he shouted to his men. They circled the base of the North Forest and found a space to accommodate them and give the Pegasus grasses and water. If he pushed, they could land at the North Castle in the middle of the night. However, he would not be at his best to negotiate with the Emperor or introduce himself to Casandra. All his plans had changed in an instant. When he completed his task, he hoped he would never be bothered again with any of these fools. He was the wealthiest man on any continent, he needed no one.

His Chancellor Ski and his Major Addison came directly to his tent. Addison announced. "Dinner is being prepared, Henry. I have brought wine. It is early, but should we consider making this our camp for the night. It will be wise to be rested, and it will give us an opportunity for a discussion of our plans."

The Count looked up and said, "My thoughts exactly. There are some new facts I need to address with both of you. First, I need to do something about those damn crows. I need privacy to think and speak with you." Henry left the tent. Crows had been around him for months, and he was sick of being stalked. He wished he could have vanished them, but the Hex would find another way to spy. It was best to keep feeding them only the information Henry wanted them to know. All three walked to Paxton and Sutton's tent, "Gentleman, I am sorry to impose on you, but I must ask you to take on the role of pretense once again. Those crows are stalking, and I have a business. Make your conversations believable. Remember what we have rehearsed. Oh, one more thing, circumstances have been complicated. You all heard the conversation with Gage. It is true, he has poisoned me." Shock hit everyone in the tent, they hadn't believed it true, "Please do talk about this. However, if any of you can devise a way to fool the Hex and gain the Emperor's support; please tell me. Remember spies are everywhere."

The three soldiers stood, the Count waved his hand, they turned into a duplicate of the Count, Chancellor Ski, and Addison. They walked from the tent, and the three soldiers sat around the cook's campfire.

"Henry!" said the Chancellor "I was afraid something ruthless would happen, but not until we were well away. Poison, really that is astonishing. I thought I had misinterpreted the conversation in the Generals tent. You look fine, how are you feeling?" Henry said he felt nothing and wasn't sure he was poisoned. The Chancellor sighed, "So it is true, you are to deliver the young Princess De Volt to the Hex on a silver platter. This is by all accounts malevolent, even for the ruthless coward King of Hex. Henry, this is only a small step back for us. Let's pour the wine and thrash this out."

The Addison poured and said, "Henry, I don't see this as a step back at all, but an opportunity." He laughed and said, "They have unknowing secured cooperation with the Emperor."

The Count said, "Please tell me how my poisoning is an advantage."

Addison said, "Have you forgotten? I know her. Your brilliant idea having me impersonate the young Prince from Carleton has given you a marked edge in this adventure from the start. You hold information about her not even her Mother and Father know. She can hold a secret closer than you know. Remember the Princess is the child of her Mother. She holds to love, compassion, and ethics in her soul. You can use this to appeal to all three."

The Count sat and thought, "Well I can't just blurt it out like a coward. Oh, lady please save my life. Rescue me Please. It must be subtle; I will allow her to discover my illness, by her own cleverness."

The Chancellor said, "You are brilliant Addison. However, I think it prudent not to let all the royalty know. They may decide it to be a convent way to take you out of the running altogether. Addison, you need to check Henry for poison."

"Of course, you are also right Chancellor." The Count swallowed his wine with satisfaction. The energies of his late wife still ran through his brain, thank the Night. Her soul reminded him of the custom of blood bonding. It was only done in Diamentia. It assured no one ever indeed died. Thoughts, memories, and ideas were carried from generations to generation by this method. Henry held untold quantities of knowledge through this method, as well as holding souls for safe keeping. Perhaps he would blood bond with Casandra, share his experience and take some of hers. He would have to trust her first, know if she was intelligent, confident, and worthy of him. The dammed Continents always confused confidence with conceit. Well, most were too arrogant to see the difference.

The Emperor

The Emperor followed the energy of the torque. As he had thought she was riding her Sheba. The stableman saddled his horse, and the Emperor headed toward the lake. He found Casandra walking Sheba through the fields by the lake. She looked calm, serene; she made a pretty picture on the old mare with the backdrop of the swaying wild grasses and ripples on the blue lake. It might be better to let her be.

"No, your Majesty it is time you make peace with your daughter. I understand better than anyone your reluctance to share the events of the Great War." Eric was speaking to him. Was he behind him?

"Eric, become visible. You know I hate it when you walk behind me. I am beginning to believe you only do that to annoy me." The Emperor stopped and waited for Eric to bring his horse next to him.

Eric's horse stopped beside him, and he answered. "I am sorry your Majesty. I was spying on our Sorcerous, not skulking you, remember. The Major asked me to follow her." He said, "Casandra is young, and you have always sheltered her from the war. It has only worked against you. Now she has the misconstrued belief you don't love her. Your omission of the truth is only another way of lying. Unfortunately, she has unknowingly taken the distance you placed around her as animosity; when it has been meant for her protection."

Eric paused wondering if he should go on; he and the King had heated arguments of the girl. The Emperor usually won. This time Eric could feel the deep hurt in both of their souls. He would have to say something, "Sometimes Sir, you forget she is her Mother child. She has all the qualities of the Empress, and your strong emotions run in her blood. Like her Mother, she is highly intuitive. Not to mention she graduated with the highest of honors. I would venture to say her three liaisons have been lesson enough on manipulation. Use truth, your Majesty, she will see through anything else, I would like to take this opportunity to make a point about her Season…"

The Emperor turned in his saddle and stopped him, "Everyone wants to make a point with me today about her Season. The four of them laid out the many facts about my ill-fated decision suggesting she postpone her Season. The most compelling one is the fact the Empress is on her way here to make sure all the rules and observance of royal engagements be followed strictly."

Eric smirked and asked, "The Empress is on her way here now? Of course, I should have known. That is the important detail the Major needed to work out; along with all the other details." A crow flew overhead. They both watched, and Eric said, "All these spies your Majesty… and Elk's Mountain…something is happening. I don't like it. Not at all."

The Emperor sighed. "I fear you are right. Eric, you have been her Mother, Father, friend, and protector. If this does not go well…be there for her; as you always have." The Emperor kick his horse and rode across the meadow.

Casandra was standing near the lake, allowing her horse to eat the wild grass. When she saw her Father, she gathered Sheba's reins to leave. The Emperor shouted, "Casandra don't leave, we need to talk."

She stood still and waited for her Father to come to her. "Father now is not the best time. I will be better later."

"Now is a perfect time, you don't have to talk. I will not force you to make any decisions, just listen." The Emperor dismounted and walked to stand beside her. "You had a good idea, getting some fresh air and a ride. It has helped me to clear my head, see things differently. I have not come to the lake since…well, a long while. Casandra, I need to tell you…I …you should know about many things. I am sorry, I can't seem to find the right words." He stood helpless before her, looking down at her he saw just how remarkably beautiful she was. Her face was strong and noble, she resembled her Grandmother, his Mother. Her black hair shined in the suns light, just as Beatrice's hair did. Her eyes were open wide and matched his perfectly. She had the best of all their features, and the Gods had placed them on her with grace. "If I remember right there are boulders ahead. Let's walk the horse there. You know these boulders hold magic, only the truth can be spoken there."

As they walked, he said, "After you left the others made some excellent points about not having a quick wedding. It would be suspicious, and not rather flattering to the Count. It may just run him away. Kathryn reminded me of her royal wedding. That was a zoo if you asked me." He smiled at her.

Casandra smiled back, "Does that mean I am to have my season?"

He said, "Yes, six or eight weeks you will need a few here to make the necessary arrangements."

Her whole body seemed to relax, "Yes thank you, Father,, that will be perfect." She had questions, but she was not about to push him. This was the only battle she had ever won. She would enjoy the win.

The Emperor was quiet, Casandra asked, "It really is wonderful. You have made me very happy Father. However, that is not all you want to speak to me about, is it?"

They had reached the boulders, he took the reins of the horses and tied them to a tree limb. "No," he said, "Sit down this will take a while. I want you to know I have never lied to you. I have omitted facts. No, I will not make excuses. I deliberately withheld facts and refused to speak to you about many things. I have also ordered others to never to tell you. Now you need to know. The trip through Elk's Mountain has demanded the truth. Casandra I am going to tell you the story of the Great War. Not the one you know from history class, but the one that really happened to your family." She started to say something, but he held up his right hand and said. "Please just listen. You may ask questions after I am finished. These are difficult memories just let me speak."

She nodded and made herself comfortable on her boulder. Her Father looked to the sky as if asking for help then out to the lake like he was pulling his memories from it. "The Empress, my Mother at that time, had visions of the Hexian's, great battles and the royals being slaughtered and kidnapped. She told us of treason in all the Kingdoms. No one believed her. The Hexian's had one small Kingdom at the time; a small army and no navy, and they were on the other side of our world. My Mother was adamant her dreams were true. Soon Oracles in other countries reported the same visions and even your Mother. My Father and the science magi decided to explore the country of Hex. He sent me and others to investigate. We learned they had organized. They were a people with an army, navy, and a strong Kingdom. The Emperor and Council believed they wanted power and land, theirs was largely desert, and their natural resources could not sustain them any longer. Well, you have learned this much from history, haven't you?" Her Father stopped to look at the sky once again.

"The Empress believed they were losing their magic and needed our blood to restore their powers. Before that could be proven, we were attacked from within. She was the first to die. The Emperor sent soldiers and your Mother and me to check on her. Your Mother had a vision she would be assassinated. We arrived to find the Bayonne Temple filled with her blood, still warm. I will not forget, never forget the sights and sounds. Her head was on the altar, her legs and arms cover the floor. All who served her and defended her lay dead or dying. The ones who could speak said traitors within the walls revolted and left with Sorcerers and their children. Those who worked and lived within the walls of the Temple for years were Hexian spies."

He looked to the lake for peace or words, Cassandra couldn't tell which. "They had let the army enter the Temple. I sought revenge. I ran after them killing as many as I could find. I was mad with rage, your Mother found me a day later, strangling men. My sword had been lost, I resorted to squeezing the life out of men with my bare hands. She stood above me and just watched. When I saw her face, I stopped. She had a face of complete detachment. I didn't understand that day, but now I know that detachment is what the Empress needs. This is how our world has survived. The Emperor steers the Kingdom; the Empress see the vision. She is the one in control of the Kingdoms destiny. There have been times I have ignored the Empress, as have the Continental Council. Every time, it has been a very damaging decision."

The Emperor went to his horse and came back with wine and cups. He poured two cups full and handed one to Casandra before continuing. "When I returned to the Temple your Mother had put the Empress back together in a casket. She had cleaned and removed all the bodies and sent the injured to the medics. Your Mother handed me a contract and said sign this. It released our bond of marriage and named her the Empress. The only women I loved, her and my Mother, both gone to me forever. We should have had hundreds of years together before this would happen. Well, the women seem to be able to handle emotions. Men need those emotions to fight and kill. She calmly sent me home with Mother's casket and took on the duties of Empress."

He sat down and looked long at Casandra, he wondered what she thought she was so quiet. "When I returned to the Castle my Father told me of all the other Kingdoms. The death toll would have been higher had it not been for my Mother's warning. The Kings were prepared, but the Temples and holy people were not. Even the Monks were murdered, no one had imagined they would be a target. My Mother's theory had been right, but still, no one believed it. Even now it is still scoffed at. My Father couldn't handle fighting a war, which was left to me. He fell into a depression. I had hoped he come out of it but before he could he too was murdered protecting you. My lovely Casandra, you were not even four years of age, just a baby and your Mother's child. Your Brothers and Sister were older. They needed to witness, to learn because they would rule. You, you were the child given to your Mother, you were hers to train. Mark was twenty years old, and already in the army, Sarah was just seventeen, but she could fight too. Bryan had just turned eleven, I kept Sarah and him away from the war. They were attached to the Generals as Aides. I thought that was a safe place for my children. I decided to have you stay with your Grandfather, I thought you would help him recover. Your Mother and I both felt the Temple was not safe. We were protecting you, we thought we were protecting all our children. It turns out we were wrong, very wrong."

Her Father asked if she wanted more wine, she yes, but her head was spinning without the wine. She had just learned things she had been asking all her life, and she had never gotten answers until today. Her parents did love her, maybe she wasn't second best after all.

The Emperor continued, "I had kept your Brother in the unit between the main force and the Castle. The Generals, Sarah, and Bryan were at the same camp, another one of my bad decisions. I was with the main force. We were attacked before dawn and drawn forward in the forests then out into the flats. By the time I realized it was a hoax, so the Hex could take the main camp and attack the Castle, it was dawn. We turned the army to the camp first only to find it overrun. Sarah was found outside Bryan's tent with a fatal wound to her heart. Bryan was found in the brush outside the camp with only scratches. He later told me Sarah had hidden him there and returned to guard the tent as if he was in it. Mark was speared in his back in his sleep, he at least was spared fear in death. I rushed Bryan to the Castle and found my Father beheaded and you missing."

He drank down his wine and continued, "Mags heard a noise in your chambers and got up to investigate. The window was open. She saw a man carrying you as he ran across the meadow toward the lake. She called the guards, but they were in a fight for the Castle. Mags went out to follow the man. He must have come by boat because they lost his trail at the lake. The sun had risen by then. She told us she could not see a ripple on the water. He must have used magic to cover your trail. Your Mother and I waited for weeks expecting a ransom demand, but nothing came. Four weeks later you were returned by a Monk to the Temple. He said some man dropped you off saying he could no longer take care of you. If not for one of the Monks from the Temple recognizing you, we might never have gotten you back. To this day, that four weeks has been a mystery.

Casandra started to ask about that, but the Emperor held up his cup, "I am almost done Casandra; let me finish. Your Mother was in so much grief and fear after that she was just inconsolable. We commissioned the Science of Magic to develop some device that could keep track of you and your Brother. Four months later they came to us with a crown and torque; a choker that would look like a token of the royal station you and your Bother both held. In reality, they both would track you. They are made of magic and given energy by me. I placed it around your neck, and only Eric or I can remove it. You can vanquish it by covering the energy, but even you cannot remove it until you are married. Yours will remain with you until I withdraw the energy, as I have done with Bryan's. Casandra that energy is love. All the love I hold in my heart goes into tracking you. Your Mother couldn't do this, as Empress she must press her emotions into the earth to function in her duties. I know I have not held you often or told you I love you, but I wish I could have."

Her Father walked to her and said. "Please stand Casandra." He reached out and held her and kissed her on the top of her head and said. "I do love you dearly with all of my heart." When they parted, she heard the torque fall to the ground. She looked down. Her torque was at her feet, it was no longer sparkling gold with stripes of stones but black. She just stood there shocked with tears streaming down her face. She looked up to her Father. Tears were on his cheeks too, love was in his eyes; beautiful aqua eyes that matched hers. The Emperor reached down and placed the torque around her neck, once again it was golden. "Now you may ask me questions."

"Why have you waited so long to tell me this? When did you tell Bryan?'

The Emperor said, "Bryan was eleven years old when the war began he understood. He was there throughout the war. He was the one who found his Sarah dead, they were so close. You went to your Mother's Temple until after the war was over. You were so young; how do you explain death and kidnapping to a four-year-old. We had no idea what happened to you when you went missing. We were careful with what we said to you, we didn't want to bring back any bad memories. We questioned you, but you seemed to remember nothing. Your Mother was glad, she was afraid you saw too much here at the Castle with the fire and the Emperor's death. She said it was a blessing your mind was blank. We never wanted to scare you or make you feel insecure. You came back to the Castle to live, and we hired Eric to care for you. Then you were sent off to school. I had always meant to tell you…I just could never bring myself to it. Time just got away from me; I turn around and here you are all grown up, but I still see my four-year-old baby."

Casandra could feel the weight of the torque lighten; then he turned his head and just that quick the pressure returned. He said, "With all that has happened this week I would like you to keep the torque on, especially with the Count being here. We will work something out for your holiday. Perhaps you could vanquish it for a given amount of time. I will ask the Professor about that. First things first; you must meet the Count. When he leaves, we will work out details of our next moves. Casandra if you find the Count unpleasant or not to your liking, don't feel like you must take him as your husband. I will handle the Council something can be done differently."

If only her Father had come to her and explained things to her all this mess would never have happened. Yet, that would not have been her Father. She had always loved him, now more than ever. Casandra stood and took his hands, "Father I love you. I always have. I didn't mean those things I said in the Library. Forgive me. I was upset about the Count and not having any involvement with my choices. If I can't tolerate him, I will tell you." He smiled, "It seems I have inherited your deep emotions maybe someday I can put them to good use like you have in making the torques work for Bryan and me. I understand. Finally, I truly understand." She paused, "I will keep the torque on, and I believe you should think about making torques for your grandchildren. I may not have all the powers of an Empress, but this week has been more than strange. I feel the evil, I have been having nightmares. These are dreams I haven't had since I was a child about the Castle being on fire and a man carrying me down to the lake."

The Emperor said, "Do you see his face?"

"No," said Casandra "I wish I could. I can only see emptiness, blackness, and a song, or maybe it was a chant." She remembered Mags. "This day is flying by. I promised Mags I would have tea."

They retrieved their horses, and the Emperor said, "Tell Mags I told you the whole story. She has been nagging me for years to tell you. She will be glad. I need to get back to prepare for your Mother."

"MOTHER?" Casandra was stunned, "She is coming here? This was not planned. When? Does Mags know?"

Her Father laughed, "Well, she is coming by magic, but still it takes a while. Hopefully by tomorrow. The Empress will not allow your engagement without her approval. That is another thing I was wrong about. This marriage should look as normal as possible. I assume Major told Mags. However, it wouldn't hurt to mention it when you see her."

The Cottage

The Emperor and Casandra parted, he rode to the Castle. She took the path along the lake to the little cottage nestled at the beginning of the woods, smoke was billowing from the cottage chimney. She left Sheba in the front yard, closed the gate and knocked on the door. Mags called, "If that is you, Casandra, why do you knock. You have always just barged in what makes this day different, and you are late."

She entered the familiar house that felt more home to her than anywhere. It was just a three-room cottage; kitchen, living area, and bedroom. Warmth and cheerfulness exuded from walls which were painted a pale pink. All the material on the chairs, windows, and tablecloth were a pastel print of roses. Real roses of mixed colors were on the kitchen table, no matter the time of year. Here it was warm, cozy, and safe. Casandra apologized, "Father wanted to talk to me it took a long while, I am sorry. He said I should tell you he spoke to me about the night of Grandpa's death. So, you can stop nagging him."

Maggie turned with the kettle and a plate of cookies in her hand and almost dropped them. She stood, not moving, not speaking, Casandra was worried. "Mags are you alright? Say something."

Mags set the pot and cookies on the table and sat down, "Well, I am not often without words but this, well." She just stared into the fire.

“I understand why they didn’t tell me when I was small, but I could have known before now. It explains so much; the over-protectiveness and the reason so many people including you refusing to answer my questions. Many things make sense now, as well as my possible marriage. Do you know Count Rakie is coming for me to decide on? Oh, and Mother is coming too. Did Major tell you?”

Maggie had been staring in space thinking of the night of the fire, then she heard the words marriage and Empress. That brought her back to the present. “The Empress, yes the Major did tell me. When? What about marriage? Not to that Count! They wouldn’t, couldn’t. Belissa’s are scoundrels every last one of them, they can’t be trusted. Well, the Empress will have a thing or two to say about this. Is she bringing servants, or do I need to hire more? These times I can’t trust servants either. Have some tea and tell me everything about school too, and that boy who loves you so.”

The light was fading, and the sunlight was behind the Castle walls before Casandra thought to leave the little cottage. Time passed too quickly with Mags, Casandra told her everything. Even about the boy, the one who loved her, the one she could never see again. Dinner would be ready soon, and Sheba needed to return to the stable, but Casandra wanted to know one thing before she left. “Mags, I need to know about the night of the fire, I remember nothing. Can you tell me what that man looked like who stole me?”

Mags stiffened, “Baby, I only saw his back. He was running down the garden path towards the lake. All I saw was blackness. The sky was still dark, he was dark. I wish I could tell you more. We must hurry, or we’ll be late for dinner.” They both hugged and left the cottage.

Devon

Devon's head was not made for wine; he would be glad to get back home where he could drink ale. The Generals were entertaining; however, Devon didn't believe half the stories they told of their escapades. Evidently, they were making some of these things up. Like changing their appearance or hiding their powers to keep their identity hidden. They bragged about luring Sorcerer into their beds, for one or another devious purpose. Most of the time, merely to test them or take their blood for the science magi. They even had categories for them. Somehow this seemed wrong to Devon. He wanted his people to have land with a Kingdom filled with prosperity, power, and long lives filled with magic. He understood their people were dying out and needed new blood to enter their populace for it to survive. Yet, kidnapping and misrepresentation seemed wrong and wicked.

The morning after the meeting with the Count, camp broke, and they all headed back to Engelton Castle. On their return, they reported to his Father. He was pleased with the result and dismissed everyone but Devon.

The King said, "Son, I know you like to keep company with your friends, but this evening I would like you to join me for dinner. Go and clean up and come to the dining room to have dinner with your family.

Nothing much will be done for a week or so. You will have plenty of time to carouse."

Devon said, "Yes Father." He went to his rooms; he fell into his bed. How he wished he could stay there for a week. He had spent months using his magic cutting through the mountain, then brought the carriages down in Elk's Pass. All Father had to say was, 'Job well-done gentleman.' He thought when he asked him to stay behind he would at least acknowledge his part in the plan. Devon wanted to find time to speak with the King about his foolish ideas. After the stories the Generals told, he no longer wanted to be at the center of this disaster. Devon felt strongly this would end badly.

The thought of dinner with the family, while his three Sisters were all talking at once, did not sound pleasant to him. He surely would have a headache before the main course. He wanted to plead exhaustion, but he was his Mother's child, and that would hurt her deeply. She was sad and fragile. Devon could count the times he saw his Mother smile and never in the presence of his Father. He was beginning to understand why. His headache returned, was it the wine or his thoughts? Maybe dinner would help. He left the bed and went to the bath and dress for dinner.

Devon could hear his Sisters chitchat and giggles from the staircase, and he was in no mood for them. Hopefully, this would be a swift dinner. The dining room was at the far end of the Castle which overlooked the Bezier Bay and the cliffs of Engelton. Huge picture windows offered the view of a two hundred foot drop to Bezier Port. The room was typically used for State Dinners, but when his family was home, they would all occupy the table at the far end with the view of the sunset on the bay. The carpet was the emerald green of their flag with the emblem of the country, a quarter moon, and star on the green field. The wallpaper on the walls held golden stars, and the tables were all covered in white clothes with pink flowers from his Mother's garden. Crystal chandeliers hung around the coved ceilings filled with frescos of the deserts of Hex.

When he entered the room, his Sisters came running at him at once, screaming. "Devon, you are finally home. The messenger came days ago, where were you?" Jessica pulled him into a tight hug.

Joan turned him around and kissed both cheeks, and said "Forget that Devon, did you meet the Sorcerous? What was she like?"

Janet spun him and said, "Never mind all that, what was she wearing? How was her hair done?"

He couldn't help but chuckle, his Sisters were overbearing, but there was no doubt of their love for him. He supposed being raised in this ruin of a Castle, in a small country kept them cloistered and naive. Devon had felt out of place among the Generals, his limited worldly experience had taken away his confidence. He needed to have empathy for his Sisters, they hadn't been privileged to the refinements of society. "Sisters please, let me breathe...I will share everything with you at dinner. I promise, but first I so need an ale." Devon put his arm around Janet and walked her to the table, "Janet." he said. "The Sorcerer changed her appearance for us, and I don't think her fashion was suitable for a lady of high station. You may not want to duplicate it." They all giggled.

His Mother stood at the foot of the table, she was smiling too. Did she find that amusing? He wondered, or was that smile just for him? Devon went to her and hugged her, then kissed her on both cheeks. "Mother you look beautiful tonight."

She drew him into another hug and whispered in his ear, "Come to see me tonight before you sleep we must talk, no matter how late." She stood back and smiled just for him. "You are learning to be charming in your travels, Son. Flattery is as good of a weapon as a sword, remember that. Although I am hoping that complement was true."

Before he could answer his Mother, the King walked in, and her smile went out the door. The room filled with quiet, everyone took their places for dinner. Dinner was long with a barrage of questions from everyone at the table but his Mother. She sat quietly and intently listening to all the details. His Sisters truly wanted plenty of information on everything; from the mining of Elk Mountain to the encounter with the Princess of the North Castle. The most questions were asked about the party of three he brought down in Elks Pass. He understood his Sisters curiosity, but not his Father's. His Mother was clearly distressed at the King's interest. During dessert, Devon ended with the account of the Emperor sliding on his ass down the cliff. Even his Mother laughed at that story.

When the laughter died down the King stood. “Devon, I have some sweet liquor the Count has asked me to try. Come to my study, and we will have a glass together.” The King went to the Queen kissed her cheek and said his Goodnights to the ladies.

Devon stood up and said, “I will see all you tomorrow but don’t count on me for breakfast, I plan to sleep late. I just ate more food in this one meal than I have in one day on the trail.” He followed his Father to the study.

Of all the rooms in the Castle, this one was the most filled. It bordered on chaotic. The table in the center was the only piece of furniture that was not cluttered with maps, papers, and odds and ends of unidentifiable objects. Devon supposed because he used the table for meetings with his Generals he kept it clean. The ceiling was tall, but there was only one small window in this room giving the space a gloomy atmosphere. This Castle had been built into the side of Mount Engel. The north and west side of the Castle and Courtyard plunged hundreds of feet to the floor of the valley and bay. The largest city of the Kingdom sat at the bottom, Engelton. The major battle of the Great War had nearly destroyed the Castle and Engelton. Holes, chips, and burn marks still marred much of the external Castle walls. When the war ended, the King said he would not remove the scars until his peoples were healed, whole, and as prosperous as the Continents of the Consortium. The mountain and city had been known a Whalen, but when the King moved his family and his people into the Castle and Country, he changed the name. In honor of Devon’s Grandfather, he named the Castle Engelton and in recognition of his Grandmother the country was named Bezier. True to the King’s word the only rooms changed were the ones used for the family and the Dining Room. Devon had been ecstatic when he could enter the army and move out of this private museum.

The King handed him a glass filled with thick amber liquid. Devon followed the Kings actions and swallowed a small bit, it was a robust concoction. At first, it burnt his throat, but as it went down, warmth filled his entire body. The hardy dinner, ale, and this drink made him need bed not a long talk with his Father.

“What is this drink, Father? It certainly is potent. I couldn’t be drinking this all night.”

The King chose to sit in one of two old chairs by the hearth Devon took the chair opposite his Father. The King laughed and said, "No, too much of this would make any man sick not drunk. The Count said it was a drink to sip at the end of the evening, to settle the stomach, and set anyone to sleep. He set a little magic on it and had thought of calling it that. I like it, I will buy more. It gives me a warm and comfortable feeling." He took another sip and sighed, "Devon, our plan is unfolding right on schedule, thanks to you. I am so proud of you. I couldn't praise you in front of the Generals. They have worked for almost one hundred years to get us to this day. I would not affront any of my men. You can understand how elated they feel knowing all their work is coming to fruition. The Sorcerous blood will bring our people health, and magic. Son, we are creating our own magical dynasty. You will be at the top of that hierarchy. General Martin had a concern you were not ready for a tryst with the Sorcerer. How do you feel about this? Are you having any second thoughts?"

Devon almost choked on his drink, his Father was having a talk about sex. Oh, no this was extreme. He was comfortable talking with his peers, definitely not the Generals, and indeed never the King.

Thank the gods the King continued, "I see I am making you uncomfortable, you think I am talking about sex, don't you? Well, I am not. I am talking about power Son. Taking a Sorcerer is not at all like having sex or loving a woman. She is not a real woman. Casandra is a High Sorcerer, which is a completely different entity. The sooner you get that into your mind, the better, and the less pain your heart will feel. Trust me, I know this for a fact."

Devon's heart stopped dead, "Father, my Mother, is a High Sorcerer!"

"Ah, yes, she is, but not one of such power as the De Volts. Son, they have been breeding high powered children for thousands of years. We, on the other hand, have been at this only a few hundred years. Do you realize your Grandfather was the first full-blooded Warlock to pair with a High Sorcerer in Hex, I am just the second? It took years of us filtrating into the Academy to even understand the intricate method used to build the magical power they enjoy. Who knew it was hidden in the silly, senseless, and archaic social hierarchy. We can never stand up to them unless we are on an equal footing. Using this Sorceress's eggs and body will guarantee our bloodline produces powerful Warlocks and Witches rapidly. However, the real beauty of our plan is they will never know it even happened. There will be no war and no bloodshed."

"Father I understand all of this." said Devon, "I also am keenly aware that I must create the illusion of being Henry Rakie. The issue is the Count is many times more powerful than I am, she will know. If the woman I stopped in the pass is the High Sorcerous, she will devour me."

"That is not an issue at all if you listen and learn." said the King. "Your Grandfather and I both learned how to charm a Sorcerer, even siphon off their powers and use it for ourselves. In turn, we have taught other Warlocks. The Science Magi's have created accounts that are hidden in our University. You will begin tomorrow for private tutelage with professor Moondale, use your time wisely. Once the Count comes for his antidote and we do a small blood bond with him, you're off to the southern shores. There is nothing like practice. The shores will be filled with sorcerous of all ages and powers for your practice."

Devon was in shock, and he was fully awake. He did not need a picture of his Grandfather siphoning off his Grandmothers power or his Father with his Mother.

The King sighed. "You don't believe your Father. The reason we have reinstated magic into our army and people is that of your Father and Grandfather knowledge. Not because we fought a war, but because we have used our powers and our brains. Your Grandfather charmed a mediocre Sorcerer from a middle-class royal family. He was the one that infiltrated the Academy. I won your Mother to my side, and I bedded the Empress herself while we were at the Academy. I coerced both into revealing their method of propagation. Had I not done that; you would not be here now. This is not a request. As your King, I order you to proceed."

Devon stood and placed his glass on the table. He was angry with his Father that he had ordered Devon as his King, and he had taken advantage of his Mother. This was hardly what he had been told of his parent's love story. He knew better than argue with the man, and he would no longer question why his Mother never smiled, "Yes Sir. What time do I report to the school of science?"

The door to the study opened, and his Mother poked her head in. "You two have been in here long enough. I would like to spend a little time with my Son too. You and the girls have monopolized him all evening. I suspect he will be off with his friends and back in service before we have a chance to talk."

The King went to the door and opened it taking Devon's Mother in his arms. He tenderly brushed a hand through her hair and said, "I am sorry my love, you are right. I have been monopolizing him. It is late, we should all get some sleep. I promise tomorrow after he finished at the School of Science, I will see to it you and he have some time alone." Then he bent down placed a tender kiss on her lips, and slowly ended at her neck, kissing her long and hard.

His Mother looked up into his Father's eyes lovingly, "Thank you, King. It is late, I will be in a much better disposition to listen to all your adventures tomorrow Devon, but why are you studying at the science school?"

The King stood behind the Queen and began rubbing her shoulders, "My Dear, Devon has just expressed an interest in medicine. Can you believe it, a Son who is in medicine? It will be handy in the field, too, if there is war. I told him to go look, dip his toe in see if it is for him. Aren't you proud, he is your child, you created him." The King waved a hand over the Queen's head and winked at Devon.

"Yes, I am. Devon, you are special, and I love you." His Mother swayed and said, "Suddenly I am so tired I can hardly stand."

"Let's get you to bed darling." The King lead the way to the Queen's chambers then opened the door. "Go on in Elizabeth. I am going to walk Devon to his room."

The thirty feet to his room seemed to stretch on forever. Devon didn't know if he should be impressed or appalled at the power his Father held over his Mother. He couldn't think of a thing to say to his Father. Devon opened the door to his room and said, "Goodnight Father."

The King placed his hand on the door and said, "Seeing is believing Devon. Think about that display. Make sure to visit with your Mother tomorrow afternoon. Afterward, join me in the study for an ale before dinner." The soft, pleasant face his Father wore for his Mother was gone, the stern King's face stood before him.

"Yes Father, in the afternoon then." Devon watched him walk back to his Mother's room and enter. They kept separate sleeping chambers.

Tonight, it looked like they would sleep together, one more thing he did not want to think about. The sight of his Mother's transformation in the study haunted his sleep and the face of the redheaded lady of Elks Pass.

Crows Flying

Casandra was up early again, after breakfast she and Marion decided to tour the Castle. They dressed in their tunics, pants, and boots. The Emperor commented, "Casandra do you only wear pants? That is the only apparel I have seen you in since you arrived. Your Mother should arrive any time, and the Count sometime later today. That outfit will not impress a man."

"Well, the Empress nor the Count are here yet, and we want to go outside where the sun is shining. The Count is old and will probably not want to go do anything." Casandra tugged on Marion's arm and pulled her out into the hall.

The Prince came out into the hall and whispered to the Emperor. "She is in for a surprise, you haven't given her a description of him?"

The Emperor smiled, "I have been a little busy, and she didn't ask either. She seems content. I'll wager she's going up on the roof again."

Casandra ran up the stairs with Marion following behind her, "Marion have I ever shown you the falconry?"

"No. What is falconry? I mean I know what a falcon is but not a Falconry." said Marion.

Casandra put an arm around Marion, "Come with me, my friend." She took Marion upstairs, up a bell tower and up two sets of ladders to the top of the ramparts of the Castle. Cages holding the birds were built to look like small homes with roofs, windows, and doors. Marion thought they were adorable. She walked up to one and stooped to look in the little window.

Casandra shouted, "Don't Marion, there might be a hawk or falcon in there!"

Marion jumped back just before a beak came out looking for breakfast. They both laughed when a stern voice said, "Who's bothering my falcons?" They turned to see Gregory, the keeper. He recognized Casandra, "Well, it's about time I get a visit from you. Last time you were here, you didn't even come see me. My heart was broken."

Casandra ran to him and gave him a hug. He was always a tall skinny man. Now that he was older he was putting a little weight on around the middle, "Gregory I am so sorry our visit last year was so short. I have brought my friend Marion to see the Falcons. Marion, meet Gregory, he was the only one who would teach me anything at the Castle when I was young."

Gregory removed his hat and offered his hand to Marion. "Good to meet you, Miss. It was more like the Emperor couldn't keep this one off the roof. She was always up here climbing around. He ordered me to teach her about the birds, so I was stuck with her."

Casandra gave him another hug. "You loved having me; you even told me you did. Mags said you cried when I went off to school. Marion, I had my own bird when I was young. Gregory taught me to train him. He was one of Father's best hunters. Are you hunting today?"

"No, Miss Casandra. I will hunt tomorrow for the big dinner you're having. Today it's only the crows we are after." Gregory stopped. "Just a minute, ladies." He looked over the ladder, satisfied he came back. "Making sure the mice weren't around. The Emperor was up here this morning early. He said I should chase the crows and catch the mice and feed them to the birds. Strange things are around this Castle these days. We must watch what we say. He seems worried."

Marion said, "He has a lot to be worried about. We all think the crows are spies, and the mice are too. I haven't seen a cat. A few cats would chase the mice."

Gregory laughed, "The man's allergic, he gets the worst case of sneezing you ever saw. We had to banish those years previously. Mags won't let a dog or cat in the Castle. Says they bring in too much dirt. Mice are the ones that make the dirt. I told her that many times."

All three heads turned southward at the sound of crows coming in from the flats. Georgy put on his gloves, opened a cage door and put a hood on one of the Falcons. The bird was black and blue. A blue that ran from royal to light gray-blue. "Care to release Rufus Miss?"

"Not me! He was the one who tried to peck my eye." Marion stepped back.

"I would love to!" Casandra put on a glove reached in and harnessed the bird. He immediately jumped on her gloved hand. She took him out of the cage went to the wall and unharnessed him. She lowered her left arm, removed the hood then pushed her arm forward and up. Rufus spread his wings, glided, then flapped strong and steady. Soon he caught the wind, and Rufus soared.

Casandra giggled, "That sight always makes my heart light, look at him go. He's after it, hunting."

Marion asked, "How does he know what he's after?"

Gregory said, "Those birds are in his territory, he will chase them miles away or eat them. He's a wild one. Rufus will chase anything, and he may see a rabbit or dove and before I know I'll be eating it for dinner."

Casandra pointed, "What's that in the sky Gregory? It doesn't look like a bird exactly."

"I believe that's a group of Pegasus. Those must be the guests your Father wanted me to watch for. I had better go ring the bell. Watch for Rufus Miss."

The Count, her heart came back down. She looked to the sky, but Rufus was nowhere in sight. "Marion come and stand behind the pillar with me. Let's see what this Count looks like."

"Hiding from him Casandra? That is not like you." chipped Marion.

"Oh, please stop. I just don't want the Count seeing me like this. Besides, don't tell me you're not curious." Snipped Casandra.

"I want to see the flying horse, not many of those around to see. I heard pegasus are costly, millions of fabs." Marion followed and knelt down by the Castle rampart.

"Who are we spying on girls?" Gregory was standing above them with a big smile on his face.

Marion nonchalantly said, "Casandra's future husband, Shhh."

"Well, you stay there then. I'll watch for Rufus." He took the glove from Casandra and walked to the edge waiting for his bird.

Casandra had spent many hours on this roof, watching and waiting for the Emperor, her Mother or spying just like now at the dignitaries coming and going. This would be her first sight of Count Rakie. Would she know the moment he landed if she could mate with him? No... she had been wrong so many times about men, why would this time be any different. She would not trust her first impression. The others had been boys her age and easy to see through. Rakie was older and over one hundred years old. He was almost as old as her Father; this time would be much different. The party circled the courtyard, she and Marion ducked. She hoped he didn't see her dressed in her pants. Her Father was there to greet them; good they would know which one he was. A white-haired old man got off his horse first. She hoped that wasn't him. He bowed to her Father and began speaking. Marion said, "I can't hear, is that old man Rakie?" Casandra put her hand over Marion's mouth. When Casandra turned back, her Father was shaking hands with a young man dressed fashionably in a tan jacket, dark pants, and boots. He stood taller than her Father, with broad shoulders and he seemed very fit. His hair was a chocolate brown, from a distance he looked handsome. Maybe she lucked out and at least would have a nice-looking husband. At just that moment Rufus appeared flying directly to Gregory, squawking loudly with a rabbit hanging from his claws. All the men in the Courtyard looked up. The Count turned his face up and removed his hat, his eyes were the same color as his hair, his skin was a copper color, and he had a very handsome face. He looked straight at her nodded and gave her a bright smile with perfectly straight teeth. Casandra had never seen eyes like that, she froze. Marion pulled her down with a squeak. Oh, damn she knew they all heard because they were all laughing. The Sorcerers and Sprite laid out flat on the roof.

Gregory was laughing too. He yelled down to the courtyard, "Seems we will be having some rabbit for dinner, your Majesty. I've also caught a couple of those mice too."

"Good, the Count was just mentioning a hawk chased off some crows over the forest. Nice work Gregory. Was that Rufus you sent out?" Father yelled back.

"Yes sir, he's one grand bird," Gregory yelled back.

"Yes, he is. I didn't know he could catch mice. Maybe we should let him fly free in the Castle." Her Father yelled up to the ramparts.

"Mags wouldn't like that, Sir. She doesn't like animals in the Castle unless they are for dinner." The men below were laughing again. "Besides these mice were outside mice climbing up the ramparts, you know Sir. The ones that are always causing trouble." He yelled back.

That's it, Cassandra hauled off and swatted Gregory's leg. "Whoa, think one of them still has some life in it." He stomped like he was squashing it. Roars of laughter came from below, and Casandra was mortified. What an introduction to her new husband.

The Emperor led the Count into the foyer and made the introductions. "Prince Bryan, would you show Chancellor Ski and Major Addison their rooms and settle their men in the barracks? Have Mags take them food and wine. Come back to the library when you're finished. Count Rakie, please follow me."

They walked to the library. "Count Rakie, can I offer you, wine, food? Please take a seat."

The Count walked to the windows and stared, "If it isn't too much trouble a coffee would be wonderful. The trip here was…hump, I will say long. Please sit Emperor. If you don't mind, I would like to stand for a bit and admire this view. I see you still enjoy many relaxing hours looking out this window, the view is spectacular."

"Yes, I do. Unfortunately, it can also be a great distraction as well. Somedays it keeps me from my work. Please, by all means, walk about if you like. I know how it is to be in the saddle for days. You have some beautiful Pegasus, they are not an animal seen on this side of the ocean. How in the world did you get them here? I thought they were deathly afraid of water? I have only managed to have a few myself." The Emperor sat in his chair behind his desk.

"It wasn't easy, trust me, or cheap. Pegasus must be put in a deep sleep with spells and potions. That isn't the hard part; getting them on the ship is the hard part. They are heavy to carry." The Count chuckled, "Was that your daughter on the ramparts?"

"Yes. Well, one girl was. I told Casandra earlier to get ready for your arrival. She was an avid falconer when she was young. She had to see the birds and probably lost track of time. She is an obedient young lady, most of the time." The Emperor relaxed back in his chair trying to judge this man, without probing firmly. Time had changed him, time changed everyone.

The Count walked the length of the library reading the book titles. He could feel the Emperor's eyes and power on him, but there was another. He stopped in front of a shelf holding books of history that also emendated a considerable force behind it. He opened a book turning pages; he looked to the Emperor his right eyebrow was raised. This was a secret listening spot, perhaps a secret exit too. How much could he access? Belissa considered spying and cleverness an attribute, he was beginning to appreciate this man. He would have to tone down his powers and shields. Keeping the poison at bay and concealed would help. He replaced the book and walked back to the Emperor. "She has spirit, obedience is an excellent trait, but a good mind that can reason I find much more valuable. I am not all that acquainted with your social customs. However, in Diamante women are equal partners in a pairing marriage. Therefore, intelligence is valued, as well as spirit. You have a wonderful library."

The Maid walked in just then with his coffee, "Your Majesty, the Professor will be right down, and the Empress has arrived. She will be here soon as well. Can I get anything for you and Count Rakie?"

"Splendid, Marie. Yes, would you bring a pot of coffee and black tea for the Empress, and some wine. Perhaps some snacks too. I must apologize, we're normally more organized. I wasn't sure of anyone's arrival time."

The Emperor looked to the Count. "You look surprised Count. Did you think we were not serious about you or that we would insult you by not have a proper consultation?"

"No apologies, our schedules were all rearranged by the incident in Elk's Pass. I understood this would be an informal meeting, the presence of the Empress does surprise me." The Count came to sit in a chair to the right of Emperor.

"With any other country, you would be right to expect an informal meeting with just you and me. You will find when it comes to a marriage with the Empress only daughter nothing will be normal or easy, I'm afraid." The Emperor stood, "My Dear we were just speaking of you."

"I hope it was something nice. What are we afraid of my Dear?" The Empress Sorcerous entered the library. She was almost overwhelming, not only in her beauty but her power. She stood almost as tall as the Emperor, although her presence was much superior, long black hair hung to her knees. Her skin was flawless and a rich, creamy color. Her black highly arched brows and deep, lush dark chocolate brown eyes overpowered her perfect ruby red lips. Her midnight blue riding dress added to her stately demeanor. The Count understood completely how a man could fall into her arms and reveal every secret, grant her every wish. He was about to himself, the woman was calling him, how bold. She wanted to play with him, how fun this week would be. He looked away as he stood to gather all his power and revealing just enough to satisfy the Empress. He went to her and bowed deeply, then extended his hand as if to shake it, but instead, he took it in his and caressed it sending a few of the more exotic spells he had learned overseas. He looked directly into the Empress' eyes, holding her gaze he bent and kissed her hand. She was probing him deeply; he would share a few details. He put on his most charming smile and said, "Empress, this is a great honor and wonderful surprise to be in your presence. I will add a presence that is both stunning and commanding. Now I understand why the Emperor's description of you was so understated." The Count released her hand and looked to the Emperor they exchanged knowing smiles.

The Empress said, "I was not aware the Count was among one of your friends?"

"Oh, yes my dear, in our youth. The Count was invited to our wedding, don't you remember?" said the Emperor.

"Count I am sorry I don't remember you." The Empress said politically.

The Count turned to her and omitted a feeling of great sorrow. "You would not have met me, your Grace. I didn't attend." He deliberately paused, "It was not a happy time for me." He left it there.

Several people came into the room at once along with the Prince. "We have food. Thanks to whoever order coffee, Mags refuses to fix it unless it's breakfast."

Then an older silvered hair powerful Witch set down a tray of sandwiches on the library table and strolled over to the Count. She glared at him and said, "He only drinks a cup or two, and I have to throw it out, it's a waste. Hello, I am Maggie." With her hand on her hips, she stood firmly in front of him and continued, "You can call me Mags, everyone else does. If you need anything, ring for me. I will be happy to serve you and keep in mind…I am the only one around here that knows where everything is. We will get men servants to you as soon as we get extra servants." This time she glared at the Emperor, then without stopping she said, "You are very handsome, powerful too, not a bad choice at all. We'll see if you have the stamina to keep up with my young girl." She turned and walked to the door before the Count could address her. She stuck her head back in the library and commented, "Your men are very charming too and clean."

The Count couldn't help but laugh. "Is that the lady who only allows an animal that is for dinner in the Castle?"

Laughingly the Emperor said, "The very one. She is the only one who knows where things are in the Castle because she has been here since it was built."

The Empress said, "Haden, that is not true. Count, please forgive her for being impolite. She has been here long enough to be considered part of our family. We all just accept Mags as she is."

The Prince added, "I think she likes you. If Casandra likes you, we will all be fortunate. The food will be exceptionally delicious."

A very tall man with silver hair stepped up to the Count and extended his hand. "I am Professor McMillan. I teach at the Academy, and I advise the Empress. I am also a counselor; I hope you don't mind including me in this meeting. If you prefer, I can just be involved in the legal aspects."

The Count shook his hand and said, "I don't mind at all. I did bring my own counselor and advisor; would you like them present?"

"That is your choice, of course, but this meeting is a very primary one. We should begin, I am sure the young sorcerer is anxiously waiting to meet you."

The Professor went to the table and started filling his plate. "Mags sure knows how to impress everyone with food. Let's see if our young mistress can be ready on time to impress you." He looked to the corner of the room where the Count had felt the presence.

The Count felt two energies behind the bookshelf leave. It must be an exit, he thought. He hadn't met Casandra, and he already liked her. "Yes, this does look wonderful." The Count filled his plate. The food was at one end, and the Emperor was seated at the other end. He motioned for the Count to sit on his right, the Empress sat across from him, the Prince on his right, and the Professor across from the Prince. Henry hadn't thought this would be quite so intimidating. He took a bite of sandwich and remembered he had been in sticky spots like this before. His ability to read thoughts always helped. However, these people were all powerful enough to cloak their thoughts easily. He needed to win this one, he needed the antidote. "Your right young Prince, these are amazing sandwiches. I might have to charm that woman and snatch her right out from under you."

The Emperor set his wine down and said to the Empress, "Now you see why I was never truthful about you around this man. He is well known for snatching things."

The Count laughed, "You were right to keep me from the Empress. You wouldn't have had a chance with her."

"The both of you stop." The Empress said sternly, but she was smiling, "This is not about me. It's about Casandra."

The Professor interjected, "Yes. Let's not waste time with idle talk and get right to the main points. I would like to know your expectations, Count. What outcome are you hoping for?"

The Prince swallowed his cookie and said, "Outcome? Professor, you need to really get to the point. I want to know your exact intentions, Sir." Then he stared directly into the Count's eyes.

The Count read his thoughts, this young man adored his Sister he would defend her to his death. He saw real loyalty and love. "Allow me to get us more coffee." He poured them more coffee and gathered his wits. He needed to change his tactics immediately, "Your loyalty to your Sister is admirable, I will answer you first. I intend to get to know Casandra and see if we are compatible. If we are I will offer a contract, hopefully before I leave here. I have been widowed for many years. I find life is not as enjoyable without a companion. I guess you are not aware, I placed a bond on your Sister before her birth."

The Empress stood and stared daggers at the Emperor. "I was not aware Count, thank you for giving me that piece of information."

The Count said, "Well it was withdrawn when I married my late wife, Elaine. I wasn't aware I would still be considered."

The Prince said, "I see, now for the Professor's question."

The Count had the distinct notion this young man could read thoughts too or at least feeling. He would have to move carefully, lying would not be an option. The Count began, "My expectations, I do have those. I am not going to bother to lie to you; you would know in an instant. I am also sure you have checked into my past, and the Emperor knows some facts firsthand." He continued, "I am also aware you have been inventing what my expectations are. The Emperor thinks I will only use Casandra to remove myself from an uncomfortable situation with my family. The Prince is concerned I will do away with both him and his Father to take the seat of Emperor. The Professor, being a man of education, has quite a few theories about me. The most prevalent one is I am in financial doom, and the realms would bring me fabs. The Empress has not decided. She is willing to hold her judgment until she has more facts. I believe her ability to curb emotions gives her great insight. However, once she has made up her mind, I doubt anyone in this room could sway her."

He had pegged each one of them, by the thoughts going through their minds. He knew he had boggled them. "So, on to my best outcome." He drank some coffee and continued, "I am sure you know that my Father is seriously ill. My Brothers are hovering like vultures. I have three Brothers who hate me, we are unlike this family. They will confiscate my holdings and throw me in jail as soon as they dethrone my Mother. After a reasonable amount of time, they will hang me for some crime or another. I have two viable options; run to another Continent or gain more political power than them. Marriage to your daughter would give me that power. I have prepared for either, but marriage is my first choice."

The Emperor sat up in his seat. "I think I need coffee, the wine is having an effect on me. I think you are not lying. The Count I know would charm and sneak his way around these questions, and this meeting would end with all of us more confused than ever. Since you are in an honest mood, I have a few questions. What about your financial position and what kind of power do you expect me to offer you that would keep your Brothers from hanging you?"

"Ha, yes, the money. You have heard I am fabless, my business is failing, my only asset is my land. I do own over three-quarters of Belissa Villas, but taxes are appalling. I could lose that at any moment." He paused, "All that is a mirage, not for your benefit, for my Brothers. If I decide not to marry your daughter, or she takes an instant dislike to me, I will be gone from here by tomorrow. Of course, I cannot tell you where, but I can tell you I will live a lavish lifestyle for the next nine hundred years. It has taken me years to move my assets over the oceans. You may hold the most power in the world Emperor, but I am by far the wealthiest." He would let that sink in, "If we do marry my taxes will be paid, my business will prosper, and your daughter will be the richest Sorcerer in the world."

"You see Emperor I am a patient man. However, I don't believe it will take much time for my Brothers to fail miserably as King. Unless Dillion becomes King, if not, the whole Kingdom will fall into complete financial ruin. Richard or any other of my other Brothers would deliberately place Diamante in jeopardy to require your help. Your daughter will be holding a huge interest in my country you would have to step in to save it. What better way to keep the country free and open to trade for your Consortium than saving Diamante? Please do not name me King or Emperor, I have no interest in ruling anything other than my winery. Casandra may never be considered for the Empress position. Bryan and Katherine have that honor. Perhaps our children might be in contention for that job. I have no problem educating them at the Academy in preparation. In the meantime, I am sure you could use me in the Council or as a diplomat. I am at your disposal. I would welcome the opportunity to travel and expand my wine market."

The professor asked, "Count where was your education?"

"In Ablenea then at the University Sir." The Count answered.

The Empress chimed in, "There is the connection to you and the Emperor and would you explain the rumor of you being a part of your

Brother's death? Also, there is the matter of your marriage to Elaine ChiaChiaRom."

The Count sighed, how can he explain this? "That is a long story, your Majesty."

"Do your best, Count." The Empress sat back and crossed her arms then raised her eyebrow.

The Count was tired of this questioning, "Haden and I attended the University at the same time, Empress, we were friends. Elaine killed her husband, Jack. There was a lover's quarrel between my twin Brother Harry and my older Brother Jack."

The Emperor stopped him, "He wasn't your twin. I knew him, he was your younger Brother."

"By seven minutes according to my Mother. We looked alike but were complete opposites. He loved me but hated being a twin. Early in his life, he changed his appearance permanently. He loved the story about being younger. He was trouble, and always knee deep in it. I would end up there saving his butt, too many times. Elaine married my older Brother Jack, just after he was called to war. Jack asked that I stay a Belissa Villa to keep Elaine safe while he was gone. Harry came to visit, and Elaine fell in love with Harry while Jack was away. When Jack returned, he found out about their affair. He forced a duel and fought with Harry. Elaine came to get me to stop them, but we were too late, Jack had shot Harry. I tried to save Harry, then I heard the shot. Elaine grabbed the gun in anger and shot Jack."

Henry stopped and poured himself wine. "I took the blame for Jack's death. Elaine and I had a love of Harry and Jack in common. My Father forced the law of Brothers on us; I was the only Brother left to take care of Elaine, not that I mined. Somehow this tragedy has been turned around and misconstrued. The last rumor I heard I had murdered all my Brothers and Elaine. So, while it is uncomfortable to talk about, I understand your concern and need to ask this question."

Everyone at the table was silent, the Count hoped this was over. He still had the interview with Casandra, at least he could ask questions of her. Not all the pressure would not be on him.

The Prince broke the silence. "Count why did you take the blame?"

"In our land, the Lady would be prosecuted, stripped of her money and lands, perhaps beheaded. I knew too well what she would face. Besides if I were Harry's second no one would question my involvement, nor would I be charged with any crime. That one act of kindness was my biggest boon. Not only did I gain the women I eventually loved, but I was feared throughout my country and others. The fear men have of me everywhere is the principal cause of my great wealth. I am also privileged to many illegal and dubious sources. A worthy lesson for a young Prince, a bad reputation is not always a bad thing." The Count turned on his brilliant smile and placed his arm on Bryan.

"He is telling the truth, Father." The Prince smiled at the Count, "I am beginning to like him."

The Emperor stood, "He does grow on you, it's time you meet our young lady Henry. Come with me."

It was the first time the Emperor used his name, he had passed on to Casandra. So, maybe honesty would work on her too.

Everyone stood and walked to the next room where a little Sprite sat almost consumed by a large blue velvet chair. The Emperor made the introductions, "Count Rakie. May I introduce you to Marion Donnan, Casandra's best friend."

The Count walked to her and bowed. "It is my pleasure, Marion."

Then Casandra was standing beside him. "Count Rakie, I am so glad you could come for this visit." She curtsied in front of him he couldn't help but smile. So, this was the vision from the roof, these were the mice. He didn't want to stare too long or hard. No wonder Haden had questioned him extensively. This was a treasure worth all his wealth. He took her hand and sweetly kissed it, power was racing through it. She was polite enough not to probe him, he would return the favor. He would not even use his charms or spells; this would be or not. He would not force this, contrary to the fears of the Empress he would be authentic. Although she did have the same talent as her Brother, she was judging him. "I am speechless; I was told you were beautiful, but ...well the De Volt women have been highly underrated. You are stunningly gorgeous, I understand you have a brain as well, that is a rare combination."

Casandra was the one who was speechless. The Count was the one who was gorgeous, and who her family had underrated. All she could manage to say was, "Thank you Count Rakie."

Thank the Night her Mother stepped up, for her tongue was definitely tied. "Casandra, we have been bad hosts by keeping the Count cooped up in the Library so long. Get him some fresh air while the day is still warm. Count as soon as the sun sets the temperature drops, perhaps a walk in the garden or the path to the lake by the cottage. This will give you some time to get to know each other."

She took his arm and led him out the double doors onto the balcony overlooking a green garden. "What would you like to see, the garden or the lake?" Casandra waited for his decision.

He said. "Which is the best?" He looked down at her, she was an exact duplicate of her Mother but younger with her Father's aqua eyes. She had said something he missed, "I'm sorry Casandra, I wasn't paying attention. Which is your favorite?"

She turned her head, placed her hands on her hips and said, "Not even five minutes and you are already not paying attention to me."

He began laughing uncontrollably, "You do have spirit. I apologize, your eyes transfixed me. Did you pull me into a spell?"

Now she laughed, "If I had you would be in my arms, not trying to charm me. I say we walk through the garden out to the lake."

A bold young woman too; she was a fast thinker. He was having trouble following her thoughts. She was nervous, he couldn't tell if he was overwhelming her or if this was a real attraction between them. He held back his power and checked his hand, not much change. "Lead the way Lady De Volt."

As they walked through the garden, she named the trees and flowers. Henry held the gate open for her to pass and glanced up; every window had people standing and staring. They were making sure to make their presence was known. "Your garden holds many herbs I wouldn't mind owning. Did you do well with potions at school?"

She giggled, "Not really. I nearly blew up our class one day. Marion is a wiz at them, thank the Night she stepped in and recovered my mess. The Professor was never the wiser. That was my hardest class. I am an expert at plain, straightforward magic and spells of course. Marion got me through that class and the advanced. You have an interest in potions?"

"Yes. When I get to spend time at home, I am usually in my lab. I have a winery and distillery; those skills are helpful. Hardly any of my brews are without a touch of magic. It is a talent that has made me rich." He smiled.

"Are you trying to impress me with your wealth Sir?" He threw his head back and laughed again. She liked him when he laughed, he was even more handsome, if that could be possible.

"No, Casandra, I was trying to impress you with my talent. I have brought some wines; I hope your Father lets you try some for dinner." She was a delight.

"Well, I think I should try them before I tell you if I am impressed or not." He laughed again. He felt it again was she probing or was that intuition he was feeling. He couldn't help but gently probe. She stopped short, "I see we're are assessing each other."

He smiled, "That is what courtship is about; we get to know who the other is by testing. We use our eyes to see if we are attracted, and our skills to learn our strengths and weakness. We speak to understand each other and use our talents which are the reflection of our souls. Our minds are the most important of our assets. Without our minds, we would not have any of those attributes."

Casandra stopped and looked at him, "You believe we have a soul? You are a rare man. Tell me do you have feelings? I am sorry, of course, you have feelings. I meant to ask do you share feelings?"

The Count looked down into those beautiful eyes. "Casandra, you must understand a few things. We do not come from the same countries. The customs and traditions that are part of your world do not exist in mine. The Diamantes' handle pairing and marriage differently. Also, I have traveled to every Continent which has exposed me to many societies. Yet, the one constant among everyone is the belief in souls. Not all people share feelings or thoughts. For instance, in my land part of the courtship is called a Blood Spell. We exchange blood, in it, we place our thoughts, feelings, and experiences. It is a way of sharing memories."

They continued walking in silence. It was becoming more natural for Henry to read Casandra's thoughts. She was knowledgeable and highly intuitive and understood he was asking for a Blood Spell between them. He wanted to laugh because she was not willing to share some of her thoughts and memories. This young lady was becoming more interesting with each step. Finally, she turned and said, "You're right. A courtship is just like a test. Why haven't I seen this before?" She grinned she was so excited she uncover this notion. "I say we stop wasting time. We should each name a test, the rules, and then do it." He nodded in agreement. "Alright, I'll start. This one will be a fitness test. The first one to the boulders by the lake gets to name the next test." Off she ran.

The little lady thought he was too old to run a race! He was so astounded at her boldness, he was already fifty feet behind. He added a little magic and was running beside her laughing. She was fast, but he landed in the clearing just ahead of her. They were both a little out of breath but laughing. "I cannot remember the last time I ran a race just for fun. You thought I was too old to keep up with you." He sat on a boulder he felt happy. That was a feeling he hadn't felt in a long while. "So, it is my turn…"

"Wait, I must tell you something before you start. You spoke of traditions before. This place we are standing in has an ancient tradition. I brought you to it on purpose. My Father told me this place holds secrets. What we say here cannot be heard or known outside of this circle of these rocks. He had talked of great importance with his Father and Mother in this very spot. Just yesterday we talked about many things here, even if you. It has been used like this for as long as the Castle has been here. I wanted you to know because I expect you to be truthful while you are here with me, as I will be with you. In this place, only the truth can be told." Her face was severe and authoritative.

"I understand Casandra. The Diamante hold the truth dear as well. I know others think we are liars and sleazy, but we think of ourselves as clever and shrewd. We know that truth between pairing partners is essential. We call our marriage a partnership and everything is equal. That is why a small Blood Spell is done before marriage. Once a Blood Spell is complete, we can speak silently to our partner. Our thoughts are shared with each other whether we like it or not. Many deliberately chose never to do a complete Blood Spell. I would ask you to do a little

Blood Spell with me now. Before you answer, let me explain. We have such a short time to make the decision to wed, truth and honesty are qualities acquired over time. Time is not our luxury. A small drop of blood can hold many memories. I would ask you take memories you want to share with me and place them in a spell in your left hand. That hand is used for engagement the right is for marriage. However, if you agree, I request to see the faces of the men you lesioned with and your feelings about them. If you are comfortable, I like to see what happened in Elk's Pass and the night of the fire here, at North Castle."

"And you would give me a spell with your memories?" asked Casandra.

"Yes, of course, the memories that would help you to know who I am."

"I am trusting you Count. I want to see your wife and women who are important to you; feelings about them too. Also, anything you think I should know."

They both took a few minutes to create their spells. Henry removed his small blood bond knife of Belissa from his jacket. "Are you ready Casandra?" He sat down beside her and stuck himself in the middle of his palm. She held out her left hand, and he pricked her palm. He placed his hand in hers and closed his eyes.

Within seconds a picture of an Elf came to his mind. He loved her deeply, and she loved him and still did. There a young man she cared for, but she felt great sorrow as she left her child with the Prince of Tallia. Then a big man appeared all dark with sparks of sexual attraction but not love, and again there was great sadness as she left her child. A happy lanky boy emerged next, they each held deep feelings for each other. This was getting harder for her each time she made a liaison. Then he saw huge arguments with her Father over this practice. Then memories began rushing by; her Brother and her snow skiing, Marion and her hugging, then Professor McMillian teaching her martial arts, that was just today. The ride through Elk's Pass, Devon, and General Martin appeared, they damned near kill her. A man carrying her to a boat on this lake. Ah, the kidnapping, there were no faces but voices. He knew those voices. Her memories ended in blackness, pain, and fear.

Casandra was so dazed by the vivid pictures flying through her brain she felt herself falling into the Count's chest. Women were passing by and so many Brothers dying in the Great War. She saw his Mother, she was beautiful. Then a killing between men in a barn. His Sister-in-law killed her husband. No wait, this was his wife, he paired with his Brother's wife, but he loved her. There were children, but something was wrong with them, oh, no they all died. Were they all sick? She felt his deep depression and long hours working and working. Monks were helping him heal. There were only a few men he trusted; she saw their faces.

Then she was sobbing, and he was holding her rubbing her back. She looked up into his face; he had been crying too. "Shhh, Casandra it's alright I have you. You're safe, you have been through much for one so young. I will not make you leave your children, not one of them. They will all be yours. I promise. I was under the assumption High Sorcerers do not hold on to feelings. You surprised me."

"That is an art we must train for. You can see this is a skill I am still working on." Her eyes were smiling and bright, her body was electric, he was pulled to her lips. He kissed her so tenderly, their bodies quivered in unison. He stood back but couldn't resist touching her cheek.

Casandra felt shivers up and down her body with electric pulses and deep passion. However, then he stroked her cheek, and his hand was on fire. She grabbed his hand it was so hot to the touch. "Count what is wrong with your hand. Let me see."

He was up against a boulder and had no place to hide. He wasn't ready to disclose the poison, but this was a place of truth. "Nothing to worry about. You have perceptive probing skills."

Casandra held onto his hand, "This is poison. Tell me. Who did this? We need to return to the Castle now." She turned and pulled him along.

"Casandra I should probably wait until we are in your Father's presence to tell the story. This was given to me by the very men who stopped your carriage in Elk's Pass. Your memories show the faces; I know the names."

Angrily she said, "They were Hex, weren't they." She was practically running.

"Casandra, slow down. I have contained this poison for two days. It will be fine. I have a plan, and I am good at poisons. I can heal myself."

She was angry. "Well, I have someone even better than you at curing poisons. So, let's not waste time."

He was laughing again he thought she was terrific, "You really don't like wasting time, your memories were short, and to the point, your kiss was too." Such a soft kiss had both of them quivering passionately. Remarkable. "That kiss was what flamed my hand you have bewitched me. I wonder what a deep passionate kiss would do to us?"

Casandra made a dead stop. "Men, even dying men still only think of sex." Then she remembered all the women she saw in his memories. "You have had enough women to know how to kiss properly. I lost count of them." She started to walk away then returned he was smirking, "You didn't kill your Brothers why did you let everyone think you had? And Elaine, your children."

At last, she could push her anger into the ground. "I am so sorry; I can't even know... how devastating."

He placed a finger to her mouth, "Shhh. Most of those women meant nothing, but Elaine...well, now you understand why we share our memories. You and I are bonded more than many who have known each other for years." He placed his arm around her, "Let's talk with your parents and the Professor before this goes any farther. Please call me Henry, you have earned the right."

They walked silently up to the Castle. Casandra saw the Count was deep in thought, his brow was wrinkled. Mags was in the hallway when they entered the Castle, "Maggie I am asking for your help. Could you please send for my Chancellor Ski and Major Addison? Have them meet us in the library immediately, tell Addison to bring wine. Are the Emperor and Empress in the Castle?"

A broad smile crossed her face, "They are already in the Library Sir, along with the Professor and Major. Is this good news?"

The Count laughed, "Depends on your point of view."

Casandra put her hands on her hips and glared at him. "Mags get Marion and the Prince they should be there, too."

The Count smiled, "That is a provocative pose, Casandra. You care for me."

"Get in the library, Henry. You really don't recognize that is an angry pose?" Casandra pushed him forward.

The Emperor looked up when the two entered the library, "How was your walk?"

The Empress stood, she had been seated in front of Father. She cocked head and stared at Casandra, "Are you alright Casandra?"

The Count put his arm around her and said, "She's fine. She just got a little winded in our foot race."

Casandra put her hands on her hips again and said, "Who got winded?"

The Count put his fingers to his lips, to silence them. Then went to the windows and started closing the drapes, "Well, I did win my Dear Lady."

Casandra huffed, "Henry you cheated with magic! It was not a fair race."

The Empress said. "You two had foot race? And Casandra you just called the Count, Henry. What's going on here?"

"Yes. What is going on." said the Emperor.

The Count slowly paced the library, "Sir, we need to have a serious, very private talk. Is this room suitable for that?" Henry started pulling books randomly from the bookshelves at the back of the Library.

The Emperor said, "Let me call the Elves and have them check the room over." Chancellor Ski and Addison entered with bottles of wine from his winery. The Count motioned his men to the back corner of the library. He climbed the ladder to the top shelf, removed a book and brought it down. Addison cleared the table, and Ski put his glasses on and scrutinized it. The three turned and made a sign to be silent as Marion and Bryan entered the library all at once.

The Count began speaking nonsense. "Ah, good Addison, you brought our best wine. Professor, I think you will like this vintage. I hope to make this a celebration, everyone stand by Casandra. We will have a toast." Henry pushed everyone as far away as possible from the book. He went back to the table and opened the book quickly, a giant cobra stood up ready to strike the Count. The three of them sent flames from their fingertips, and the snake exploded into dust falling mostly on the Count.

The library door opened, Mags entered with wine glasses and behind her came two Elves. Mags stopped and said, "What was that and what did I miss?"

The Count smiled, "You didn't miss a thing. We were just reading a history book of Darnania. Please, come in with those glasses. I need a drink."

Addison opened and served the wine, then said, "Darnania, if I remember right their flags shows the symbol of a cobra."

Chancellor Ski added, "You are correct Addison, and it seems the Hex has at last educated themselves. Although I am not sure, they understood the irony. I would bet that was more of a coincidence."

The Prince took a drink of his wine, "Excellent wine Count. Would you care to explain the exploding snake?"

The Emperor looked to the Count, "We are just about to find that out, is the room clear, Eric?"

The Count looked to the Elves. Eric was the man who loves Cassandra. Henry watched the man as he came to stand in front of him, He smiled and said. "Gentleman, I no longer feel a presence in the room, do you?"

The Elves had magically cleaned up the room including the Count's jackets. Eric smiled at him and said, "No sir, we don't; we would like to take the ashes and see if we can figure out how we missed this. Can you enlighten us Count?"

The Count said, "Belissa are more sensitive to hexes like this. Your thoughts Addison?"

"Sir, I agree with you, but it may only be we have lived among hexes longer." Addison smiled.

Eric glared at the Count and said, "I believe we have a private room, Sir, for the moment."

Addison added, "Emperor, might I suggest a few cats and dogs inside the Castle?"

"Oh, you may, but I am allergic to cats, and Mags doesn't trust dogs." said the Emperor.

"They are filthy animals!" said Mags.

Chancellor Ski looked shocked. "You prefer snakes? Count you have forgotten your manners introductions."

The Emperor asked Eric to stay. Then the Emperor came forward and said, "Addison Leoreko Rakie, it has been a long while this must be your Father Ski Leoreko Rakie. It is a pleasure to finally meet you, Sir."

The Chancellor took the Emperor's hand and said, "You pronounce our last names well, but we have long ago dropped them. We got tired of people mangling them."

Henry said, "These two are my Counselors and best friends, and they happen to be my relatives as well. A rare combination, Ski is my Uncle and Addison is my cousin."

The Count introduced everyone; when Professor McMillan was presented the Chancellor went to him and extended his hand. "Professor McMillan Science Magi?" McMillan nodded. "Goodness Henry this is very fortunate for us. Professor, I hope to have some time with you. We have much in common."

The Emperor lifted his glass and said to Count Rakie. "Our thanks to your keen senses." They all raised their glasses and drank. "Count what is this all about? Please, everyone, be seated." The Emperor went to the head of the table and the Empress to the foot. Everyone else sat in-between. The Count sat next to the Emperor with Casandra on his left, and Addison to her left.

Everyone turned to the Count. "Sir, I hardly know where to begin."

Casandra drew in a breath, "Well I know where to begin Father, Henry has been poisoned. I believe by the Hex."

The Count stared at her then took in a breath and said. "Well, I personally would not have chosen that particular spot to start Casandra. You do like to get right to the point." Addison chuckled, and the Count gave him a stare.

The Empress said, "We should have a look. The Professor is one of our best herbalists he could help you."

"I will consent to this, your Majesty. However, first, we need to understand the situation we are all in." He turned to face the Emperor, "I have been able to contain it to my hand, and I will be fine for now. The explanation of the poison is first." He turned to Casandra and smiled, "We were also stopped on our way here, not at Elk Pass, but on the flats. We were detained by General Gate. I hadn't thought it that unusual at first. They offend stopped me to ordered wine or confiscate mine. I had sent the King a special brew, I thought he wanted more." He sipped his wine. "However, when General Brad entered the tent I became suspicious. I knew I was in deep trouble when I saw the face of the Prince. Brad stood in front of me and insisted I shake his hand. He told me to sit down and offered me food and wine. I forgot Martin, General Martin sat across from me." The Emperor squirmed in his chair. "I refused food and wine then General Brad promptly told me not to worry about being poisoned, I already had."

The Professor added, "The handshake, I suppose he had taken the antidote probably an alcohol base, very interesting."

The Count relaxed and looked to the Professor. "That is exactly what Brad told me, Professor. Also, when Casandra walked me through the garden, I touched some of the herbs. My hand was sensitive to the coriander and thistles. I find that interesting too. I dabble in potions myself."

"Good, find Sir. That will help us considerably." The Professor rubbed his head as if he was looking for answers. "I take it your antidote comes when you have gained them something."

"Yes. Something or perhaps someone, Professor to be exact, Casandra." Everyone grabbed a breath. "Well, that is what I thought at the time. After coming here, I have changed my assessment several times. Here is all I was told. They want me to marry Casandra as soon as possible. I am to leave here in five days with an engagement secured. Then go to the Engelton Castle with a contract; I receive my antidote, and I assume further instructions as well. Now, I only know I am to insist on our honeymoon and nesting take place on one of Diamante's northern islands, Azula. They assured me it is a paradise created just for the Sorcerer, a perfectly safe and private place." He looked to Casandra, she was hurt deeply he would have to explain this. "Well, if you didn't like hearing this, the next part will have all of you hating me. I only ask you allow me to finish before you kill me."

He reached for the wine and refilled his glass, the Empress crossed her arms and snarled. "Make it fast Count. I am having a hard time containing myself!"

He swallowed hard, "Casandra took me to the boulders today. She told me about the privacy there. She explained of only being able, to tell the truth in that spot and want to question me there. I agreed. I suggested, since our time was short and to become more familiar with one another, we do a Blood Spell."

The Empress stood slapping both hands on the table and screaming. "WHAT have you done! You fool! You have poison flowing through your blood. At least now I understand the intimacy between you and Casandra." She glared at her daughter, "I have raised you to know better!"

The Emperor was standing next to her. He put an arm around her and said, "Beatrice we must hear this out before you incinerate him. Please sit, breathe, have some of Henry's wine. It is excellent. This may be the last chance we will have to drink Henry's wonderful wine. Go on Henry, this better is good."

"Sir, since I have been stopped on the flats I have had no time to work this problem out. Crows were overhead all the time, you were relentless with your questions. I knew there were two presences here in the library. I knew I had to play their game with you earlier in our meeting and with Casandra. I had thought the two presences in the library were the two mice I had seen on the roof. Just in case it wasn't, I was not ready to reveal my plans." Casandra smiled, and his heart eased. He looked deeply into her eyes, "When one presence left, and one remained, I knew I had to be very clever."

He looked down the table at the Empress who was staring daggers at him. "Empress you pushed me into the garden. I knew I could not tell Haden of the truth until we could be assured of complete privacy. Somehow, Casandra was at the core of this, and I needed more answers quickly. Casandra had suggested a test to measure each other. A Blood Spell came to mind; I needed to know more about this young lady the Hex required. Why was she so important? I specifically asked her to tell me about the times she felt I should know. I compelled her to show me the memory of Elk's Pass. I knew she would give me the memories that she needed answers to as well. She gave me much more. None of you know what she has been through. She is much more special and braver than you will ever know, well Marion may know as much." Casandra had put her hand on his thigh under the table. He looked at her, tears were forming in her eyes. He reached down and took her hand in his.

"Speaking of Marion," said Marion, "I do not understand the Blood Spell, could someone explain?"

The Prince reached for the wine. "You're not the only one Marion."

Chancellor Ski said. "Allow me Count, it is a spell used by Diamante to gain knowledge between Warlocks and Sorcerer or Warlocks and Warlocks. There are relatively small ones like the Count and Casandra shared today, and complete ones like I, Addison, and the Count share. Partnerships, engagements, and marriages are the most prevalent use of the spell. Most Diamante refuse to do a blood spell at all, as Elaine had; that was Count Rakie's late wife. I personally believe the reputation for sneakiness came from the refusal of this spell. A small spell consists of a drop or two of blood transferred through a prick from left hand to left hand, it allows the two parties to only share specific memories of each other. In an engagement, usually, past lovers are shared. Complete discloser is done with the right hand and much more time and blood are involved. As it implies all memories are shared and after the ability to read one another's mind is a benefit. We can communicate with one another mentally."

"Or a deficit." said Addison, "For instance, right now there is a huge argument occurring that none of you are aware of. Well except for Casandra, I suppose having an ability to read hearts has helped her attain this telepathy."

"That explains your ability to win at cards; all those times at school you two robbed me!" the Emperor complained. "Tell me what's the argument, Casandra?"

"Father, I asked mentally why Elaine had refused the Blood Spell. Henry said he would tell me later in private. I asked was it because of the children, then Addison screamed you gave her information about the children. Henry said no he didn't. The Chancellor said she can retrieve the whole memory. Addison said, Henry, what were you thinking? Then Henry said, that is why we must not speak of this. I asked why not, and Henry said it will be too painful." Casandra paused, "I only saw snippets and pictures, flashes of his memory. But Chancellor Ski, you just said I can see the whole memory. How can I do that?" She stopped and waited. "Speak out loud, please. Father will only make me repeat this."

Henry put his face in his hands and said, "Casandra, you have enchanted me, I swear. However, this habit of honesty and integrity streaming out of you is completely devastating. You must learn to hold back pertinent information. You will be dealing with the Hex like it or not, and this will get you killed. I have grown too fond of you. I will not bury another love, do you understand?" Realizing his admission, and that he had raised his voice, he grew pale.

Marion jumped up. "The Count loves you, Casandra!" screamed Marion. "Ha! And you love him. I can tell this is amazing." All heads turned to her, and she sat back in her chair. Then squeaked, "It is really, ...that is if the Count wasn't dying, and your Mother didn't hate him." Something occurred to her. "Wait, what do you mean back in school, you all were in school together?" The Emperor, Addison, and the Count only looked at one another. Annoyed, she said. "Also Count I'll have you know Casandra is quite capable of being deceptive if you really had any of her memories you would know...." Then she stopped speaking and look from the Emperor to the Empress, "I can see why it is most common not to do a Blood Spells. Thank you for explaining it to me Chancellor Ski." She stared at the table.

After a moment the entire table burst out laughing.

The Professor shook his head, "I thought I had a time with Casandra, but this little Sprite is going to be my biggest challenge yet. If it is any solace to you Count this is not an unfamiliar conversation with these two."

The Empress raised her eyebrow. "Really Professor. You have not complained to me about this. Is that because I am the one there is concealment from?"

"Really Empress, I am your advisor all these years. When have I ever mislead you." The Professor smiled.

The Empress landed on her chair with a smile. "Hmm, I will think on this." Then she looked to Casandra, "Elaine and I were second cousins. We were at the Academy at the same time, we weren't close friends, but we spoke often. My child, I compel you to share with us. What is in this memory of Elaine that is concerning you?"

The Count's heart stopped, he heard Casandra gasp. He could feel her thoughts shifting to the memory of his about Eliana and the children, "Please your Majesty, do not let her go to the memory. Not yet." The Count turned to Casandra too late, "Casandra. Look at me." She was unresponsive, so he grabbed her hand and looked to Ski, "Can you stop this?"

"No, I am sorry Henry. The best I can do is lead the memory in truth, explain what she is seeing, that may help her. Actually, it may help everyone in this room understand what she faces. Addison observe Casandra, she isn't accustomed to this blood magic." The Count took her hand in his and kept watch on her face as Addison stood behind her chair, placing his hands ever so gently on Casandra's shoulders. Everyone could tell they were communicating with each other. The Chancellor came to her other side and took her hand.

"Would you like me to tell this Henry?" Chancellor Ski waited.

"Please Ski. Addison and I will do our best to hold her emotions."

Ski took a deep breath and looked at the ceiling, "It was during the Great War. Remember you sent for us, Emperor. You asked the Count to be a strategist for you. We even started investigating your circumstances here at the Castle and the Temple, and Casandra's kidnapping. The Count was sure he could talk Elaine into coming here to live. She had just had another miscarriage, and he felt your countries medical expertise would lure her." Ski put his hand on Casandra's brow.

"Yet when he told her she was cool to the idea. It took most of two weeks to convince her. That very day General Martin landed on our Belissa Villa Vineyard with a Medical people, of all things. Evidently, while we were investigating for you Emperor, the General had stopped in and inquired about a purchase of ale for his army. She had shared her sorrow over her miscarriage, and he offered help. He told her of the great strides and developments Engelton Medical people had made. Elaine accepted his offer immediately. We all understood her great sorrow, but now she had placed the Count in the King of Hex indebtedness. The Medical people took Elaine to check on her condition as we questioned General Martin. However, he overtook the conversation, telling us of your proposal to the Count. He implied Henry rethink your offer and consider the money our winery could make exclusively selling his wine to the King along with other information. The Medical people came to us telling us Elaine was pregnant. This was the first time we knew the extent of the King's spying. Martin insisted the Medical people stay to care for Elaine placing a convenient spy in Henry's house. Martin offered Henry anything he wanted to help the King win all of Marais."

Henry looked to the Emperor, "That was when I sent the cryptic letter to you refusing your offer. I could only hope you would figure it out and use our advice."

The Emperor gave Henry a smile, "I understand Henry, continue Chancellor Ski."

Ski looked hard at Casandra, her face had not changed expression she seemed in a trance. "Weeks before her nesting time she fell ill. The medical Witches insisted we move her to Engelton, we refused. Martin once again showed up to transport her. The travel to Engelton was hard on her. We rushed her into the Science building, but they could not stop the early arrival of the children, none lived. Elaine had lost too much blood and expired within minutes." Casandra's face was frozen, tears were streaming down her cheeks. Henry's expression was filled with pain, even Ski was silent.

Addison picked up the tale. "We were all present at the time of their deaths, I cannot find the words to describe the event or the sentiments. We were rushed from the room and found ourselves standing before the King. He offered condolences, and it seemed anything the Count wanted; lands, titles, a new Sorcerer to marry, or several just to have, along with children. The King seemed truly upset over the children. He wanted Henry to stay in Engelton and work on strategy but this time it wasn't an offer, it was a command. Henry begged time to grieve and asked to bury his wife and children before returning. That request he got. However, when we retrieved the bodies, we were given ashes. I had specificity asked they not be cremated. Our wishes were ignored."

Ski looked at Addison smiled and continued. "Fortunately for us, Addison always has the presence of mind to handle a situation. He had taken blood samples of all of them. The Count could see all of Elaine's memories. I ran a few tests on her and the children's blood. What we uncovered, only hinted at more questions. The decision was made to return to Engelton and work with the King.

Meanwhile, we would do some spying ourselves. Henry's strategy worked brilliantly to take over all of Walden. The King had confidence in him. Henry convinced the King an attack on Marais through Elk's Pass, or the flats would result in a long battle losing the war. He persuaded the King to take Marilla instead and cross the North Sea. An attack across the Flats and the North would crush you in between. The King loved the plan."

The Emperor stood. "Henry visited here enough. You knew no one could cross the North Sea...you divided their forces. Night, Henry... you handed me victory." Everyone was astonished.

The Prince said, "Count because of your advice you have been called an idiot, the worst strategist ever born, a buffoon, the world laughs at you. Why?"

The Count laughed. "Yes. I have an atrocious reputation. It has only helped me, my young Prince. It has gained my trust and has worked to my advantage until this issue with the poison. Regrettably, our plotting to uncover information on the deaths of Elaine and the children was fruitless." He tightened his hand on Casandra, "All we found was every person that had treated Elaine had also mysteriously died, no records were found. Our only evidence was found in the blood samples Addison retrieved. However, that showed definitive proof the children were not mine...or Elaine's."

Everyone looked to Casandra, her expression finally changed. A look of discerning then accepting what the Count had shared. She whispered to him, "Oh Henry, they don't want me. They want my children. That is all they have ever wanted."

The Count took her face in his hands. "Listen to me Casandra, I vowed to you I would keep all your children. I will die keeping that vow." She turned away from him and buried her face in her arms on the table. "You are making promises I fear you cannot keep, Count!"

He pulled her around to look at him, "Casandra look at me, look at me!" She opened her eyes and stared into his. "We will find a way, everyone in this room will work this out. You are too young to lose heart; you must trust me." She nodded yes, but her eyes exposed a heart of futility.

The Empress ran to her and pulled her into her arms, "Count you have laid a dismal picture of Elaine's tragedy, how do you conceive the same will not happen with Casandra?"

"Because your Majesty." He stood, "Casandra gave me two significant memories, the first was of Elk's Pass, the men who took down her carriage were the King's men."

Addison came to the Empress. "May I give her a peace spell to help calm her, your Majesty?"

The Empress released her and commanded, "My darling girl you are released from your compulsion." The Empress sat Casandra in the chair. "Of course, Addison." He handed Casandra a glass of wine and told her to drink it. The Empress sniped, "We all had come to that conclusion long before you got here Count."

The Count took the insult with a smile. "You did not know two of the men Casandra knew. Marion created wild costumes and disguises, but they would know your power anywhere."

"Impossible." The professor interrupted, "I covered Casandra's power, and Marion's disguise had all the men completely distracted."

The Count laughed, "It was a fascinating choice, Marion. However, one of the men knew all three of you."

Marion stopped him, "Count, now that I remember it one man did look familiar, but this was the first time I had ever seen anyone with emerald eyes. No! The Professor is right we fooled them!"

"Might I ask if you remember a personal guard to Casandra the third year at the Academy, named Walter."

Eric stood, "I fired him! He was no guard to these girls, Oh, no... what did I do?" He sat down.

All three let out a moan at the same time. Casandra shook her head, "Marion, Walter might not have recognized me, but I doubt he would have ever forgotten you."

The Count laughed. "No he did not, nor did he ever stop retelling the escapades of the Sorcerer and Sprite. Every time he got drunk in the company of myself or the King the stories would be told. I feel I know the both of you quite well."

Addison gave Marion a big smile and said, "So, this is Martin's Sprite. I am delighted to meet you, Marion. Is Grace here too?" Marion turned from pink to red in seconds.

Henry laughed and continued. "Walter is none other than General Martin. The man who stopped the carriage was Ernst, a Llianian Wizard. Over the past thirty years, Ernst has been the personal bodyguard of the Prince of Hex. Which makes Prince Devon, the young man who tried to probe you. You were right about one thing you almost had the

Prince in your power. Ernst was the one who stopped you. You are lucky Casandra; Ernst is one of the few who could have killed you. On the walk back from the boulders I kept asking myself if Casandra was the prize they wanted, why not steal her then and there? They had her right in their hands. However, the second memory was even more telling. It was the night she was kidnapped."

The Emperor stopped him, "Did you see his face?"

"No Haden, I didn't, but I heard his voice." Henry smiled, "A very distinct voice; it was King Hex."

Major stood and ran his hand through his hair and walked to the desk. "Casandra's memories were always of darkness and no voices, no sounds. I find this all implausible and deeply disturbing, how could you really see that night. Yet, I believe you are speaking the truth. Count you said Casandra knew two men who were the others?"

The Count turned, "Casandra do you think a retelling of that night would harm you? You could leave the room."

"No, I have nightmares, and I would like answers to what really happened. Maybe the dreams would stop." She reached for his arm.

He smiled, "Brave girl. The night of the kidnapping a tall, thin man dressed all in black came into her room, he wore a floppy black leather hat."

The Professor said, "Ernst, but she said his face was black. The man who stopped the coach was pale white."

"Yes. Casandra did, but keep in mind she was four. Ernst placed a hand on her throat with a speechless spell then carried her out to the balcony. The Castle below was already on fire, and as he dropped her to the arms of the man below, she saw his right cheek which looked black. Really it was covered with red blood. To a four-year-old, it would look black. A hooded man caught her and ran down to the lake. The only thing she could see was his jacket. There was a button with a scorpion insignia. Hex officers can show their allegiance to their land, I would bet again it was Martin. A scorpion is his insignia."

Casandra was beginning to shake. Henry looked to Addison, who placed his hands on her shoulders. Henry said, "The man in the boat was the only one to speak to her. Casandra turned and saw the Castle on fire. Fearing for her Grandfather, and Maggie flooded her heart she began crying and screaming. The spell Ernst cast was broken. The King soothe her with a song spell which lulled her into darkness. She woke several times over the next few weeks with pains in her abdomen; they always drugged her back to the darkness. I am assuming they removed some of her eggs." Casandra's face lite up with awareness, then rage, "She woke in the care of the Monks. Someone took these memories from her and healed her. I know this was done from love but Empress you suppressed these memories to stop the nightmares. Somewhere deep within her, she feared these men even as she stood defiantly against them in Elk's Pass. You have created a brave young woman, your Majesty. I am honored to hold her memories, and I will treasure them as I conceal them away from the Hex."

The room was still only the crackle of the fire could be heard. Major's voice of reason brought everyone to the present by saying, "Well we can learn from the past, but we cannot stay there if we want a future. You have made a compelling case that the Hex is only interested in providing themselves power. They want the power of the High Sorcerer to add to their genetic pool. They could feasibly create the most powerful Sorcerers ever, or a monster like those that were forced into the sea thousands of years ago. All our plotting and planning must be thrown into the fire."

The Count said. "Yes, but the fire is cleansing; it will give us a new view of the problem."

Mags stared into the fire. "I only heard the screaming from the house, I was so close to you. If only I had kept running toward the lake, instead I turned to the Castle. I am so sorry, Casandra."

This time it was Casandra that went to Mags holding her and rocking her. "No, this was not your fault, not at all." She turned, "Well, world renown strategist, what crazy plot do you see in that fire?"

The Count had indeed lost his heart to this Sorcerer. Seeing her smile with the light of the fire on her beautiful face, he would come up with something. "You're right, we need a plot, but first we need to explain why we have been held up in this room for hours. I am certain ears are pressed against that door."

The Professor said, "This is true. I have been allowing them to only hear the laughter, nothing else."

The Emperor said, "Excellent Professor. Now, I might not be a good plotter, but I know what we need; One, A cover for this meeting. Two, The Count healed. Three, a plan for Casandra, and four, dinner. I am starved, did we have lunch? My Empress, your ideas please."

"You left one out Emperor, we need these spies gone. I have a plot for that. Mags if you have a cat I can copy it. I will try for some non-allergenic cats, I need a dog too."

Marion stepped up and said. "Well, the excuse for being in this room all afternoon is simple, we will announce your engagement. Even if it is a fake one."

"That solves many problems Marion I should have known the stories of you were right, fast thinker," Addison said smiling.

The Empress put her right finger to her mouth and started barking orders, "If we do announce and engagement, we could have an excuse for the rest of week, along with the Counts return visits. Conspiring with him would be much easier. Yes, Mags go create an engagement celebration, with all the trimmings. What's left of the afternoon Major and Eric will take the ladies into town to shop and set appointments for the tailor, seamstress, baker, and scribe…several scribes. We'll need more than one to get the invitations out on time. Professor and Chancellor, we'll stay in the library and work on healing the Count. Haden go shuffle around in the Major's office bring us books on marriage contracts books. Well, start planning as soon as we can. Go."

The Count held up his hands and said, "No, stop! We need to think this through."

"Why?" said the Empress.

"Yes. Why?" said Casandra. Casandra raised her eyebrow and said, "The Hex plan is to have you marry me. You planned to come here to marry me. My parent's plan was to have me marry you, and I plan to marry you; this should make everyone happy."

The Count looked shocked. "You want to marry me, remember I hold your memories. Your Brother's estimation of me was not very favorable. Why would you have me if you thought so little of me? Oh no. Don't tell me you were to marry me and then what? Then kill me off? Tell me should we even bother to heal my hand Lady?" He crossed his arms and glared at her.

"Oh, don't give me that look Henry. It was Bryan's idea," she said smiling.

The Count turned and stared down the table at Bryan. "Prince I really liked you! I see you don't take after your Father. It takes a good mind to solve difficult problems. Tell me I am curious. How long did you give me?"

Bryan grinned. "Well a year, but I told her if she liked you she could keep you."

The Count began laughing and walked over and hugged the Prince. "I still like you Son, but I really don't think we should carry out a pretense. The Hex would know, more importantly, I would. This should look real, and I would like to make it real." He walked to Casandra took both her hands in his, "Casandra would you honor me by becoming my wife? I am captivated by you. I can't even imagine how much I will be in love with you next year."

She looked deeply into his eyes, they were filled with love, and she had learned he respected her in this room today. "Yes, Henry I will marry you. I will be the one honored." They embraced and sweetly kissed, she could feel the crackle of magic under it. Chills went up and down her spine. It was a little too much sexual power in front of family. Then she leaned back and said, "Well at least for a year, then we'll see."

The Count threw his head back and laughed, "And that my love, is why I adore you."

Addison slapped him on the back and said, "Congratulations Henry. Now I should be off to get the men together for the traditional song and formal engagement. Mags, could you possibly handle an extra thirty men for dinner?"

"Mags can handle anything Addison. Why just ask her. She single-handedly runs this entire castle. Right Mags?" The Emperor grinned at Mags.

Mags place her hands on her hips. "Of course, no worries. I can manage it glowingly; only forty more houseguests to feed and care for, and engagement dinner, the State dinner tomorrow, and a Ball. There is nothing too big for me to handle. I'll see how well you fair with the Hex." She stomped from the room.

"Come on Marion. We'll go shopping, What about a date? The merchants will want to know that." Casandra stood next to her Mother.

"We need Kathryn," Marion said.

Bryan whispered. "She is resting."

The Empress asked, "Is she feeling bad?"

Bryan smiled, "No. You are going to find this out soon enough. She is pregnant with our Princess. She has asked to be relieved of all the meetings so she can be present for all the parties. She will be thrilled for you Casandra. I am sure the sooner, the better for her to enjoy all the festivities."

The Emperor grinned. "More Grandchildren. This turned out to be a great day after all. I say at least a month for the wedding date."

The Empress bellowed. "We need at least seven months."

The Count sighed, "King Hex wants this done in weeks. How about three months? I can tell them you almost charred me when I mention weeks. They will understand your need to have a big fuss."

"Right." The Empress started counting on her fingers. "Casandra that would put it close to Empress Moon, an auspicious time for a wedding and totally acceptable. Also, Kathryn will be over morning sickness. Plan it. Now off with you."

The Emperor said, "Don't I have a say in this?"

The women all turned at once and shouted. "No!"

Mags opened the library door where almost all the servants were standing trying to hear their meeting.

Mags smiled, noted who was there and said, "It is good to see you all have nothing to do. I can use all of you in the kitchen now. We have just added forty more dinner guests, and this is a special dinner too. The engagement has been made with Count Rakie! You are nosey people, and we have work to do." She started barking more orders than the Empress.

The Attachment

A knock on the door woke him. Devon turned wanting only to spend more time in his comfortable bed. The cots in the barracks could not compare to these soft sheets and pillows. A voice spoke, "Devon, your Father sent me with breakfast. He said you were to be up early for an appointment at the School of Science with Professor Moondale. Mister Ernst said to meet him at the stables as soon as you are dressed."

His servant Graceson set breakfast on his desk. "Sir, the maid, cleaned and pressed all your uniforms, I will set out one and run a bath while you eat. It's good to have you home. I hope you will be staying in the Castle a while. Your Mother and Sisters have missed you, and so have I."

Devon saw his Mother's face always sad, and then he remembered her face looking at his Father's last night. That woke him. The memory of the scene in the hallway with his Mother and Father flashed into his mind. There would be no more sleep this morning. He bolted from the bed and fled to the bath. He wanted to wash that memory away.

He washed and dressed in his light green uniform as rapidly as possible. Looking in the mirror, he thought he could use a haircut. More white hair was appearing daily in his head of dark black hair. His Father's hair was completely white and silver with red undertones. The more magic Warlocks carried, the lighter the heads became. It was easy to see the most magical touting long silver-white locks. Yet, that did not make them the most powerful. Power could not be seen, only felt. No one was more powerful than the King. Devon swallowed breakfast and rushed to the stables. The sooner he could master power the sooner he would be out of his Father's house.

Ernst had the horses saddled when Devon came into the courtyard. "Good morning Devon. Enjoy that soft bed in the Castle?"

"Wish I was in the barracks, the beds aren't as good, but the Warlocks are less volatile. Ernst, do you think my Father even likes me?"

"Mount up Prince. That's a question which should not be asked in your Father's courtyard. Moondale will be upset if we are not there on time." Ernst pulled his hat over his eyes, mounted and trotted out of the courtyard. Devon knew his bodyguard well enough. Ernst must know more than he wanted to share. Over the years Devon knew Ernst better than anyone. The less he talked, the more he knew, and the day would come that Ernst would share his knowledge with him. Anything of importance he learned from him, fighting, magic, and strategy. Witches and Ernst were the best at reading people just by being in their presence. Of all the powers Devon could learn that was the one he would like to master the most.

Ernst was a Liliana Wizard from Arlequin a dying breed, and the only wizard he knew with the talent of judging others. He was intuitive and could not only accurately see a Witch or Warlocks gifts, but their personality and desires. He could cut to the truth which was most helpful in playing the games of love or war. His Father had enlisted his help during the Arlequin Wars in the old country of Hex. Ernst was his spy and acquisition expert. He was the one to acquire his Mother, the High Sorcerer of the North Castle. Ernst could have asked for fabs, lands, or titles but he was not a man of ego, he wanted only to serve. Ernst had once told him if he used his powers for his own gain they would be depleted in no time. His magical powers would be exchanged with illness. Thus the reason so few Llianian lived long. Devon's Father kept Ernst close to him. The King told him Ernst was his most valuable asset, a healer, and a powerful wizard with extraordinary powers. The King insulated Ernst from harm by assigning him to Devon. Also, Ernst had no kin left in this world. The King said giving Devon to Ernst to care for was enticing him to remain in his serve. Devon was grateful for that.

The School of Science was full of activity. Warlocks of all ages and levels were rushing through the doors. The military was present, not just as guards, they attended to learn the latest method of fighting and weaponry. They stopped at the stables, Ernst took the reins from Devon and said, "Son, I know you do need some answers. However, the King has not released me to speak to you about any of these matters. Until he does, I must be quiet. I live only at his pleasure. Go in there and learn as much as you can, spend this time wisely. I am sure many of your questions will be answered today." He walked away with the horses.

Devon was in shock, he had been under the impression Ernst served the King, not as a slave to him. Devon ran after him. "Ernst wait, stop!" Devon ran in front of him to stop him. "Ernst, you have always said you serve the King is that not true?"

"Master Devon, go to your lessons, what you are about to do next is important. Learn all you can

it will make explanations much easier when the time comes. When we are far from the Castle, you may ask me again." Ernst walked around him leaving him standing confounded in the middle of the stable door. Ernst stopped looked back and said, "Think back Son, when have I ever said I serve your Father? You are my master, no one else."

Devon ran his hand through his hair and walked on to the Science Building, trying to remember a time when Ernst had said he a servant to his Father. He could not remember one time. Devon only remembered his Father saying Ernst served him.

The building was built of large white stone excavated from the surrounding mountains. Windows were placed symmetrically across the front, and the building stood five stories high. On the second story there was an enormous balcony it could hold a hundred Warlocks maybe more. He wondered if they ever used it. He entered the main hall through sixteen-foot wooden doors. The map on the wall showed Mondale's office on the other side of the garden courtyard on the top floor.

The students paid no attention to him, but the military saluted him and stared at him after he passed. His rank was a major, higher than most here, but the crown on his emblem told his station. In his own company, all the staring and whispering had ended long ago. They knew his Father had insisted he be no lower than a Major. He was set apart everywhere he went, and he hated the division. Devon was still puzzling over Ernst's remarks when he entered the upper floors looking for room 498. Then he saw a sign on the wall reading Professor Moondale with an arrow pointing up, Devon climbed. At the top of the stairs were double doors with the flag with a snake curled around a staff pointing upward. When he reached the doorway, a guard stood at attention saluted and said, "You are Prince Devon?" Then he gave a suitable bow.

Devon saluted and answered, "Yes. I believe Professor Moondale is expecting me."

The guard answered yes and opened one door for Devon to enter. He introduced Devon to yet another two guards who saluted and asked him to take a seat he would announce him. The other guards watched him as Devon took a chair on his right. He wondered what was in this office which required three guards. A few minutes later the guard returned and told him to go to the right of the library room take the far corridor and turn left then follow it to the end of the room. The Professor office was on the right. Devon followed the instructions and knocked on the door with the professor's name. A voice said to enter, he found Professor Moondale climbing down from a ladder by the bookshelves. The professor crossed the room and hugged Devon.

"Ha, My Prince. How long has it been since we have last seen one another?" The Professor released him and stepped back to look him up and down.

"Don't you remember me? Of course not. It was well…let me think. You were about to go to school back on the old Continent. That was before Engelton was ever thought of, but I have been planning for you long before you were born." Moondale stood and smiled shaking his head back and forth.

Devon hardly remembered anything before being sent off to military school at The Oaks. He did, however, remember this crazy old Professor Moondale. Moondale would come to visit his Father at their

Palace in Hex and spin mad tales and wild stories. As a young boy, he hung on every word. At the Oaks, he was laughed and bullied any time he repeated them. It was easier for him to forget the stories and the Professor. This Warlock had to be every bit of nine hundred years old, and he looked at it as well. His hair was completely white, his skin was just a shade darker, his eyes were gray and black, eyes that could make a man cringe or heart go stone cold. They had a look of a wolf. Devon was always fascinated by his eyes, but many like Ernst couldn't bear to look at them. He was thin, but because his back was hunched over, he looked thick through the middle. His hands were more arthritic than Devon remembered, but the enthusiastic smile was still all over his face. The Moondale was old, but his spirit was anything but aged.

Devon sighed what could he do but like this crazy old silly man. "Professor Moondale, it has been forever since I have heard one of your stories. You used to scare me you know. All the crazy things you had me believe as a child almost got my head blown off at school. I had thought I would have you teach me at the University, but Father had taken you here to start the Engelton Magic Academy."

"Yes. Well, it seems we have come full circle. Please sit, let's start by catching up on our lives. Can I get you some refreshments?" the Professor walked behind his desk filled with books and papers all in neat piles. He pushed them aside and sat in his chair.

"Oh no, thank you, Professor, I just had breakfast." Devon sat in the chair across from him. The next hour passed with Devon doing most the talking and the Professor asking questions. He was exceedingly interested in his field of study at the University in weather magic, and his abilities as a Warlock with his small amount of Wizard. The Professor asked a few questions about his military duty and travels. He inquired about Elk's Pass and his encounter with the Emperor and Sorcerer. The King had not released Devon to speak about Elks Pass. He thought it better to be safe and not say a thing. Devon tried to change the topic by asking Moondale to share his last years at the Castle.

Moondale was evasive and quickly changed the subject. "Time has gotten away from us we need to get some work done, or the King will be upset. Devon, what has your Father told you about coming to learn here at the Science of Magic school?"

"Not much, just that I need to know how to control the Sorcerer and you can teach me and help me do my part in his plan." Devon sat back in his chair.

The Professor rose and walked to the window and looked out watching the students walking to their classes. Bright sun rays streamed into the room with dust mods dashing in all directions. He took a deep breath turned and gazed at Devon with his wolf eyes. Devon felt a chill go up to his spine.

"Where to begin with you? It is hard to know. I have asked the King to let me have a larger hand in your education throughout your life. Now he throws you upon me and expects me to teach you in days, what should take years, I am sorry Devon. I'll do the best I can and hope you don't end up hating me. I do need to know your experience in Elks Pass. However, I understand your reluctance to share that. I will speak to your Father and have him approve of speaking to me. Moving on; I also need to know of your personal experience with women; Witches, Sorcerer, and other magical creatures."

Devon cringed, "No worries Devon, I don't want intimate details only the power exchanges. I need to know what level you are working on." He shuffled through several books on his desk. "I would like you to begin with a list of those experiences; you can omit names. Just write down their classifications, such as Witch, Sprite, Sorcerer etcetera. Have a look through these first six books. Many will cover history you already know just skip through and read all the facts about the prorogation history and differences in culture. I won't test you. Yet, you will find it is in direct correlation to the powers and talents of each magical classification. I have put aside a room in my private library for your use. No one will be allowed to enter until your studies are complete, so don't worry about anyone looking at your notes. Also, all the books and materials even your notes must remain in the library. It will be locked by a guard when you leave. At your return, you should have a guard open it. Is that understood?"

Devon said yes, and the Professor led him from the office to a room next to his office. One door connected to his office and the other to the hallway into the library. The walls were made of light walnut wood panels. A small table and four chairs sat in the center with one large window across from the hall door which looked out over the courtyard. The Professor set the books, pen, and paper on the table. "I am going to the King. I need to have a discussion of the progression of your studies. I will have a guard come to get you for lunch. We can go over your list of personal relationships. You may want to do that first." He turned and left just as abruptly as he spoke. The man certainly got straight to the point Devon liked that.

Looking out the window, Devon was reminded of his years at the University, happy years without pressure from the King and country. He needed to get to work. The list would not make itself, and it would not be that long. He had no intention of compiling a complete list either. Moondale would get just enough to satisfy. He worked on that first, and Devon wondered if he should include the whores his Father had hired to school him in lovemaking. He decided he would since the Professor might have been the one to suggest it.

Finishing, he began sifting through the books, many were a repeat of his history lessons. Here and there he would run across a cultural custom that he was not familiar. He had known that High Sorcerers had sexual liaisons with Noble Warlocks to procreate children. He thought this was done to fulfill a political purpose to partner countries and people. He hadn't known it was also done to keep the bloodlines of the nobility powerful with magic. Without interbreeding, power was lost, and without magical power, their Kingdoms were doomed. It was done to mix talents and strengths. Each generation would become more talented and influential. The High Sorcerer gave her children to the Warlock; never to know them or love them. The Sorcerous would marry once to align with a Warlock of a high standard who would take on the job of Emperor or King, and they would have as many children as possible. Once the High Sorcerer became the Empress, there would be a forced divorce. Once again, she would give the children to her ex-warlock husband.

One book was entitled the 'Life of a High Sorcerers.' Devon became engrossed in it. The Sorcerer was taught not to feel any emotions whatsoever. He wondered how could that be? His Mother was a High Sorcerer and very emotional. Now he speculated if she had liaisons before marring his Father, did he have Brothers and Sisters out in the world he knew nothing about?

He needed to focus and not question everything in this book. Sorcerers were groomed to be the judge of all the people of the Continents using logic only, without emotions. It stated the life of the Empress was solitary and celibate, one of prayer and study. She would hold court; resolve disputes, garner agreements, marriages, arrange liaisons, proform blessings, rituals, and coronations. Her most important function was taking peoples souls at their death to the Goddess of the evening known as 'The Night.' She alone was the judge and jury of the soul of all beings.

The Empress was the single most powerful and talented magical entity in this world. No Warlock, Witch or Wizard could overpower her. In the hierarchy of power; Empress, the Emperor, was the most powerful. Wizards, High Warlocks, High Sorcerer, and Oracles were next in power. Then came Magi, Seers, Witches, Elves then Sprites and Fairies. The lesser forms of magic were long and most of the names he had never heard of including Banshee, ghouls, and leprechauns.

Devon needed a break he stood, stretched, and walked to the window. His Mother was a High Sorcerer; she was not at all like the description given in this book. He had never seen her powerful, and she had raised her children and loved them; he knew that. He couldn't wait to go home and have a talk with her about this. Would his Father allow that? He had control of everything in the family. His Sisters... he hadn't even thought of his Sisters. Were they considered High Sorcerer? Evidently not, they were only fascinated with gossip and news of the world. Were his Sisters hoping to have a liaison or marriage? He had never considered that or their powers. What of no love or feeling? They were nothing but emotions and talking, giggling and laughing.

He suddenly realized how little he knew of the world. He had gone off to military school at age twelve. He attended the University at age eighteen, and he entered the military at age twenty-three. At thirty he felt like a man, but this knowledge had shaken him. This, and the memory of his Mother and Father last evening in the library. He knew nothing of relationships or people. Was he that self-absorbed? He had thought he was different from the King, perhaps he was the King's son.

A guard knocked at the door. "Sir, Professor Moondale has lunch prepared. I am to lock up here and show you to his private quarters."

Devon turned and smiled. "I am ready for a break I always hated reading. I do need to take my list."

The guard chuckled. "I feel the same Sir, and he told me you would be bringing some notes." He led Devon out of the library and down a corridor to a pair of etched glass double doors. "Go right in, Sir. He is expecting you." The young man turned and stood as a guard at the door.

Devon walked into an entry hall two stories high with circular stairs going up to what he guessed were bedrooms. On the right was a parlor with fifteen-foot windows facing the eastern slope of Engelton Mountain. On the left was a dining room with windows equally tall looking over the Hex University. The walls were all plaster and held paintings depicting history, the furniture was elegant but from a time passed. They were what his Mother collected antiques; they were everywhere, all the rugs were the hunter green color of the Kingdom.

He heard a clatter in rooms just beyond the entry Devon called, "Professor, is that you?"

"Yes, Devon I am in back straight through the entry. I'm in the kitchen preparing us some lunch. I thought it would be nice to eat on the balcony. It is a beautiful day, and we could use some fresh air." He found the Professor opening a bottle of wine and a lady servant carrying a tray out from the kitchen through double doors.

"Can I help with anything?" said Devon.

"No, I think we have it. Thank you, Marie. Give us a couple of hours we need time to talk." The Professor nodded to the women, and she smiled and closed the doors. "Well, I see you have the list for me. Very good. Please sit and help yourself."

Lunch looked terrific it consisted of cold meats, bread, cheese, and some fruit desserts. He sipped the wine. It was excellent, it must be some of the Counts. The man had a talent for wine, but Devon seemed to drink too much of it. The Professor helped himself to wine after he finished reading over Devon's list. The skies were blue, and the view from the Professor's balcony was spectacular. The mountains on the left were glorious, and a bird's eye view of the Castle and University was right in front of the table.

"It is a beautiful day. Thank you for thinking to have lunch outside where we could appreciate it." Devon drank some wine enjoying it. "The wine is excellent as well. Count Rakie?"

The Professor laughed. "Yes. You can always identify his wines by the rose on the bottle. He is a scoundrel, but no one can create a wine to compare to any of his. It might be the only reason your Father has permitted him to live over the past few years." The professor relaxed and took in the view. "Your Father has blessed me with all of this. I know he views my work as essential to the Kingdom. When I asked if I could quarter here at the building and library; your Father said sure. One day he found me camped out on the roof and could not believe I was living out here. He sent men over the next day, and this is what he made me. I was happy with the lab, library, and office. This is a bonus. I will not forget his kindness."

He picked up the list and commented, "I see you have had some experience with Witches and Sorcerer, but you list the power you felt mild or very low, except for one Wizard woman in Mento…interesting. That reminds me…here is a letter from your Father. I went to see him while you were at work."

Devon opened it and read it.

> *Son, I was impressed; most would love to brag about their adventure with the young Sorcerer. However, I give you permission to share all the details with the Professor. He knows more about the handling of magic than anyone I know. He has counseled me all my life. He is to be trusted.*
>
> *Respectfully*
> *Your Father*

Devon folded the letter and placed in his jacket pocket. "It seems you have questions about Elk's Pass. What is it you would like to know?"

Moondale smiled and said. "First tell me what happened, as you would if you were reporting to an officer in your unit, from the time you created the snow until meeting with Count Rakie. Yes, I have had reports, but I want to get to know you and hear your mind working."

Devon recounted all his actions to the Professor. He ended with, "That is the accounting of the actions. I had not thought much about the power that I encountered until just today. Much like I had never thought about the power I felt with Witches or Sprites until you asked me to evaluate earlier. Professor the first coach I pulled down was the Emperor. I had told the Generals I wasn't sure it was the Emperors. Now that I have thought back to it, I chose it because of the power coming from it. It had a weight of great power when I touched the carriage. It challenged me, I found that fun and interesting. The Sorcerer's carriage was not the same. The Emperor's power was weighty, the Sorcerer was the opposite very dainty and buoyant but somehow more powerful. While I knew the Emperor immediately, I would not have chosen the Sorcerer's carriage as one of importance."

The Professor just gaped at him. "Remarkable, reports from your instructors held your ability to comprehend and adjust your thoughts quickly and report factually astounding. This is fascinating new information. Light, you say… tell me about the power of the occupants."

Devon shut his eyes and thought carefully before speaking. "Thinking back I had discounted the man he seemed to look and speak like a magician. I expected magic from him. Of course, the Sprite was exceptionally high powered, I don't remember any Sprites from our lands emitting that much magical energy. However, I assumed she was of an elevated level going to the North Castle. That is not a place for a regular Sprite in our society. The red-headed Sorcerer was equal to the Sprites, nothing to make me believe she was more than the whores they pretended to be. Until she opened her arms and took one step to me and began to speak. Her voice was soft and smoothly melodic wooing me to come to her. Her eyes pierced into my soul. If the men around me had not grabbed me I would be under her spell yet."

Devon stopped to drink more wine, "Professor, I have been trained to react as a soldier, not to use my powers to make observations of power or report them. This method opens all kinds of possibilities. Why hasn't someone taught me to do this before?"

"I have been trying to persuade your Father to do this for years. He has been reluctant. For someone who is immature, it can be dangerous. Using great intuition and the heart connection can make discerning judgments but often devastating decisions. Consider the concept of disconnection the High Sorcerer use, it is the main reason they hold the abilities to handle the great power they wield. This method can be used but only in conjunction with the other scientific observations and accurate methods. Never rely on it solely. Powerful magic can deceive, bend the truth, and defect facts. We can work on this, and you can practice this at home. You have four Sorcerers and two Warlocks to use as your homework. Tomorrow we will discuss at least two or three of your observations. The stop at Elk's Pass was your first confrontation with powerful beings. Now that you know you have the power to measure another's talent, use it. I wonder if living with Ernst for all those years caused some of his talents to rub off on you. I want you to use insight silently and see if you just understand this in hindsight, or if you can sense it in the present moment. For now, back to the books. Read and write down your questions for tomorrow. You can leave when you feel you are done. I have classes to teach in the afternoon so I will see you at my office tomorrow morning." He walked Devon to the door, and the Guard took him back to his room.

Devon spent the afternoon in the book 'Life of the High Sorcerers' He wondered how they created the rules for the Sorcerer. The list of what they could and could not do was enormous, archaic, and trivial. A Sorcerer could not vanish jewels; they would explode he questioned that one. Several of the rituals intrigued him, the Season was one of those. They had one Season to be free, to feel love, and to have fun. The time was at their discretion, most chose some time in their early academy years, but always before marriage. He wandered if Casandra had her Season yet.

Then there was a Moon Dance ritual to find the strength, talents, and fertility of a Sorcerer when they were young; at the time of egg retrieval. It referenced the ability to mate as well. He would ask the Professor more about that tomorrow. He examined a couple of other books and marked a few passages in a third discussing power base of the anatomy. He would need to know that. His part in the plan for the Kingdom was to produce heirs. He was to play the role of the Count.

The Medical would place three more eggs in her womb; a female for his Kingdom and two males for the crown of HexhH. At the time of birth, three children would be removed. The other would be hers and the Counts. The Count would swoop back on his Pegasus and fly away, no one is the wiser. Engelton would have royalty equal to other countries. The King was nothing if not patient. The Oracles had predicted Devon would change their world.

He would be the Prince that brought peace to the land. He had heard that every day of his life, he wanted it over with. He needed a Season of freedom. This was too much to read and think about, he much preferred to practice magic; he found all this plotting worrisome. He closed the books. It was time to speak with his Mother, but would she provide answers. Ernst would be at the stables pretending to sleep while gathering as much information as possible from everyone who entered.

As they rode through the streets, Devon turned in his saddle and asked, "Ernst, what rumors have you heard today?"

"Not much at the tavern but the stable was as full as the hay in the barn. The army is all talking about the maneuvers that are coming up. Full battalions are scheduled. They are sure we are headed for war, and it is nothing but a ploy to keep the Continental Council from knowing when. You are at the center of it, yes lad, you are leading the battle. The Prince that brings peace. Seems a contradiction to me."

"How disappointed they would be to learn I am only a stud to gain the powerful children who will wage the true war." Devon didn't want to be a Prince or a King, but what did he want? He would not think about that, ever. He had no choice in the matter.

Grayson met him at the side door taking his uniform jacket and replacing it with an everyday soft wool jacket. "Your Mother is in the garden waiting for you. Devon would you like me to bring you an ale?"

He almost hugged him. "That would be wonderful Grayson, thank you."

The garden was showing spring all over. Greens and colors of many shades of pink filled the flower beds with lilies and gardenia scents filling the air. His Mother had chosen a spot under an arbor of wisteria; green but not blooming and thank the Night, no bees were buzzing yet.

She looked sad up until the moment she saw him, then a smile spread across her lips. "Devon, I thought you had forgotten me." She leaned in for a kiss and hug.

"No Mother, I am just running late. There is much more to know and learn than I thought. You High Sorcerers are a lot more complicated than I thought." He laughed.

"Well, you should have just come straight to me. I would be glad to explain things to you. We are much simpler than that professor and King make up. What do you want to know?"

"You are willing to answer my questions?" Devon could not believe she would talk to him.

"Yes, just ask. I will tell you anything you want to know." His Mother padded the seat next to her and Grayson appeared with his ale.

"Thank you, Grayson." Devon waited until he left. "I have been reading about the role of High Sorcerer. I had assumed you are one. My Sisters all are Sorcerer although I don't know what power. The book says you learn at a young age to disconnect your heart. You don't love or feel, and you have liaisons before marriage. Yet I have never felt that from you or my Sisters. Will, they have liaisons or marry Kings from other countries? Why haven't you told me about all this before now?"

"How much do you want to know?"

"Everything you are willing or able to tell me." He waited as she wrung her hands. She waved her hands and continued.

"I have been waiting for this day I thought you would ask before now." The sad look came over her face again. "You are correct I am a High Sorcerer. I attended the Academy. I was fourth in line for Empress. I had graduated, and while it was not probable I would become Empress; all the traditions were observed. I made my liaisons and highest honors in my class. The Empress granted me the highest noble available. The Emperor's oldest Brother, Kenneth. In fact, we were married. It was rather a short marriage. Our coach was taken down over Brusel on the way to my home continent Aeirla, which no longer exists. It was the first day of the Arlequin War, lucky us."

His Mother looked to the sky as if she was looking at that memory. "I honestly don't remember much of want happened that day, just falling from the sky. I woke up in a bedroom in a small village with Ernst by my side. Kenneth had died instantly; I was badly hurt. Earnest healed me, you know Wizards are wonderful healers. After I healed, he concealed me in the village until we could leave. Ernst was wonderful to me. We...I felt for the first time in years. I fell in love with him. He was going to take me to his home, but the war made it impossible. Ernst was a friend of mine from the Academy, along with your Father. We all attended at the same time, of course, your Father was in disguise the whole time he was at the Academy. I had believed he was Landan. It wasn't until Ernst brought me to Hex after the war was lost by the Arlequin I became aware of the Kings true identity. The atrocities I witnessed firsthand of Llandia armies and the Hex, well... I never wanted to go back. They murdered every Wizard and every Dandan they could find; no one was left alive. Not a child, woman or old person was left to tell the tale." Her voice drifted like her eyes into the past. "Ernst was." She stopped to turn her head away she was crying.

Devon could hardly believe her tale. This was not the fairytale story of his parent's courtship, and marriage told over and over. From the time he was small he heard nothing but the romance of the Princess and the soldier. She was a Queen's only daughter from a land north. His Father was an ordinary Warlock from Hex. "Mother, I had not wanted to bring you sadness. Please don't cry." Devon took her hand, and she smiled.

"I owe my life to Ernst, and so do you. I was carrying an egg when the carriage fell. This is the reason I had wanted to see you in private. I needed to tell you this story."

Devon held a hand up "This Castle is not a place to discuss secrets."

"It is fine here, I have cloaked us. I still hold some powers. Only Grayson knows where we are, no one can hear. You can trust Grayson, but we must be quick so just listen for now. Understand?" Devon nodded.

"I can tell you more about gestation openly, but for now you need to know I had one unfertilized egg when the carriage fell. I had only a short time before I would lose it. I asked Ernst to help me, and he agreed. You are his Son, Devon. However, I told the King that you were

Kenneth's Son. I had lost so many children I couldn't lose another. I wanted you more than I wanted happiness for myself. Your Father wanted Kenneth's Son, so he wanted me. He has never loved me; he has only wanted my power and my children. He is evil, and he is bound to teach you to be evil too. I am so sad that I put you in this place. I love you, I did not want this life for you. Please be careful, if he discovers this, we will all be dead. Do you understand? He has a chain on me, he will teach you to do this too. You must be careful of this chain. Remember if I fall from a cliff that chain will pull him down as well. Therefore, I can never be free he fears my demise." She stopped and tilted her head. "I will meet you tomorrow in the stables after your return from the Science School he is searching for us, so we must be found.'"

Devon felt a veil lift and his Mother was holding his hand and speaking, "You see Devon when a young Sorceress is of age her eggs are removed and held by the Empress in the Temple. It is a special chamber that keeps them warm and safe. At the appropriate time, an egg or two is placed back into the Sorceress to be fertilized for a liaison or marriage. For some strange reason the powerful Sorcerer produces all their eggs at once, if they are fertilized and carry all at once, every one of them can perish. Years ago this was happening at an alarming rate hardly any women lived past the age of sixteen. The process of the Moon Dance ritual was begun by the Monks. They were the only ones who could determine the time and strength of the Sorcerer." His Mother looked up and smiled. "Well, I have a feeling I am about to lose you to your Father." She chuckled.

The King came out from behind the hedges. "Well, there you two are. I have been looking all through the garden for you. I see your Mother is giving you a lesson in Sorcerer history. Good, very good." He came to his Mother and bent down to give her a kiss, then caressed her neck she shuttered. "I am very pleased my dear. I hadn't thought you wanted to share any of this with him. It was hard enough for you to explain to me."

"Oh, my darling he came home from that Science school with so many questions about Sorcerer and was so confused. I told him Moondale always makes everything more difficult than it needs to be. He had a real one right in front of him why not ask me. You know he is much better at the hands-on type learning why are you torturing him?"

The King removed his hand from her neck and laughed, "He will have some hands-on to, don't worry. Did she answer all your questions, Son?"

Devon was in a state of astonishment. He had no idea how to answer that, and the man would know if he lied. "Father, I am overwhelmed with all this. I don't even know how to answer you."

"My dear you must have given him an earful."

He did not want anything to fall back on to his Mother. "No sir, not her. It was the Professor, the books, and the very private things he wanted to know. This whole day has been very uncomfortable."

"Well, I know one question you asked me that only the King can answer." She stood and turned to the King. "Devon wanted to know about his Sisters. He asked about their powers, their futures, their children, and marriages do you have an answer for that my husband?" The Queen placed her hands directly on her hips and tilted her head with a massive grin on her face.

"Oh, can a week not go by that you are not tormenting me with this? Devon did you really ask this or is your Mother using you to bring up the subject for the millionth time?"

Devon stood and put an arm around his Mother, "I did ask. I know it will seem selfish of me, but until I read the books of the High Sorcerer I never even thought of my Sisters as Sorcerer. I never thought they had powers or would need school or have children. They have always been my little Sisters, and it has been a while since I have been home. Father, they are not little girls any longer."

His Father came to the other side of his Mother and put an arm around her too. "Yes, I guess you are both right. I must consider their future too. So much has been put on Devon that is all I could think about. It is time I think about the three gigglers." They all laughed.

Devon took a deep breath. The King had been fooled, he hoped. "Well, I am starving could we find something to eat?"

"I am too." The King took his Mother's arm, "Come, my High Sorcerers, let's see if we can find the girls and have a nice calm dinner."

“If we want a nice calm dinner we should feed the girls in their rooms.” His Mother laughed as she said it.

Dinner was friendly and relaxed but not calm. Devon enjoyed himself and his family, perhaps for the first time. He had never felt like he fit in, but tonight that was not the case. Devon fit very nicely. He loved these four Sorcerous and his Father, just not the King.

Devon's Father

Devon thought he wouldn't be able to sleep, but he slept better than he had in a long time. He woke early, rushed through breakfast and dressing. When he walked to the stable, he wasn't sure how to be with Ernst. The road to the Science Magical School was long and quiet. Devon dismounted and handed Ernst his reins but keep a hold on them until Ernst looked at him. "She still loves you. I thought you should know." Ernst had tears forming in the corner of his eyes. "It explains why I have always loved you, and it is the first time in my life things have made sense to me. I am feeling great Father, how are you?"

Ernst shook his head. "I had thought this would never be known." He took the reins from Devon and put a hand on his shoulder and said. "Go learn something. I will be here for you when you're done."

"I know, you have always been here for me." Devon turned and ran into the school up the stairs and realized a huge mistake he had made. He should have never revealed he could sense powers; he would have to be careful from now on around Moondale. No one could know he was almost a full wizard.

The guard led him to Mondale's office and opened the door, Moondale was seated behind his desk reading a book, "Ah, good morning Prince; how was your evening?"

"Good, it was a good evening with my family we haven't all been together for a long while. I had forgotten how nice it is to be with a family; that is until we start getting on one another's nerves. How was yours?"

"The usual, nothing special. Did you have a chance to work on your homework?"

"I did. I am sorry I didn't seem to sense much. Father is powerful, but I have also seen his power. I wasn't sure I felt any sensitivity, maybe because I am so used to him. The same with Mother, she is so familiar I saw nothing new. I can feel a great power but discerning what that power is doesn't seem to be among my talents." Devon stilled himself and tried to see if he had convinced the Professor, "I will continue to work at this. Maybe I just need more practice. I could enlist Ernst for some assistance." That worked, the Professor looked persuaded.

"Good idea, Ernst might just be able to help you with this, as I said before you have been around him so long you may have just instinctively picked up some of his habits."

He needed him off this topic. "I did have a fascinating talk with my Mother, she told me quite a bit about Sorcerers and the Moon Dance rituals. All the secrets surrounding this is nothing more than a mutation. She is not sure if they have ever understood why all the Sorcerers eggs mature at once or if they ever will. All the rules and regulations are nothing more than to keep from extinction. The will to survive is powerful. I do not criticize, I am one of those survivors. I suppose it is no coincidence that my mission is the survival of our people." Devon crossed his arms and gave a big sigh. "In the end, it is the power that survives not the people."

"You are quite the young theologian Prince. I had not known you to be so cynical. Tell me do you believe in the Old God?"

"I know little about it, but a few things from my travels. While I cannot say I believe, I can say I discount nothing. There are some strange occurrences in our world, along with stranger people. Ernst has taught me. He said, you may not be wise, but that doesn't mean you can't act like you are. Believe in truth, have faith in only yourself, listen more than you speak, and never judge what you don't know." Devon leaned back in his chair.

"Well, that is good advice I must remember it for myself. I have a few more books for you to look over. Don't take too much time with them we need to have a common scientific language before we can work hands-on. I would like to begin that midmorning. This afternoon I will have some work for you in the library."

Devon left to his room and as he had hoped these books were on the anatomy of Warlocks, Sorcerers, Witches, and every other magical creature. He was captivated by them and had a hard time just breezing through the chapters. The throat was not the power source, but the release. The power source was in the woman's reproductive organs. Her power was controlled by sexual energy; things were becoming more evident. Thoughts brought the energy up, words created spells, and shoulders released spells through arms and hands. That was why the King was always touching his Mother's throat and shoulders. Sprites power was in their brains and released through their eyes. Men's magical energies were on their shoulders and discharged by tongues or sexual climax. Elves power was in their ears. Well, that made sense of those pointed ears and their magic were released through hands. Why had they not taught him this earlier? He wished his Sister knew this, they needed to know this.

The guard knocked on the door and told him the Professor was ready for him. This time he took him down the stairs out of the building and across the courtyard. He followed the man down some stairs and through a tunnel. The guard unlocked an iron door. Inside was the Professor and three others. The lights were dim. He could hardly make out the interior of the room, but off to one side was some sort of laboratory. The Professor motioned him to the table at the center of the room.

"Come in Devon. Now you have some idea of the seat of power for each magical creature and the release point. The release point is important for defense combat. The power source is the advantage of attacking in battle. However, we have developed a method to make both defense and attacking obsolete. You can control your opponent by Attaching. An attachment is an invisible skin attached to the source of release. It is created from your skin and the blood of the recipient; along with a spell, you will learn to make in this lab. The Attachment has a barb on one end. You must learn to attach to the release point and probe the barb into the source. To control the High Sorcerer you must attach to her throat and probe to her sexual organs. I know what you think this will harm her eggs. No. This will only stimulate her sexually, all the better for you. Let's begin to make your attaching patch."

Devon cleared his throat "But how does that control an opponent Professor?"

Moondale smiled and leered at the young man seated at the table. "Once your attachment is in place, you only need to touch it to take their power. A hand will take a little power; enough to subdue them. A kiss on the throat will pull major power, intercourse well… depletion. Don't look so worried it does not usually kill them and sleep builds their power up for the next day. You will grow more powerful daily. It works on men or women. Let me show you."

Moondale walked to the center of the room where a Warlock and Witch sat. Each had been placed under a frozen spell. He went to the Warlock seated at the table and put his hand softly over his mouth. The Warlock jumped, the Professor took something from his hand and put it on his shoulder. Moondale said, "I am carefully and steadily moving the probe to his shoulders. However, it will not be painful as I have been told subjects find it feels icy or sometimes warm. Others say it is hard, sinister or some say evil." The Professor stood behind the man bent down and pulled power from his shoulder. Then he turned to Devon with a leering smile.

They worked for an hour on Devon's spell. The Professor told him to go to the Witch seated in the middle of the table. She looked scared and was trembling. She was beautiful a full-figured Witch with green eyes and long blond hair.

The Professor stood behind her and placed his hands over her ears. "Devon, look her in the eyes she fears you. I want you to kiss her softly as seductively as you can. Take your time to seduce her. Then place your attachment when she does not expect it. Place your left hand on her stomach and work the probe slowly downward."

Devon turned her in the seat and sat next to her; he began soothing her. He assured her he would not harm her or hurt her. Then slowly the fear left her eyes. He kissed her cheek then moved slowly to her lips. He dipped to her neck, she sighed. He drew back her head saw her eyes half open, and she smiled. Then he kissed her parting her lips with his tongue. She opened her mouth for him to enter and he slapped the attachment to her throat. At the same time, he placed his hand on her stomach slowly working the probe downward. The Professor was in his ear giving instructions to set his mouth on the attachment and suck in her power. It was the most erotic sensation he had ever had, her power rushed into him. It was fierce; Devon thought he would explode. He lost all sense of time and presence in the laboratory. He could feel her resistance, but that only made him push into her stronger and push the boundaries. Her hatred, fear, and anger gave way to waves of ecstasy. This was not right, but he could not seem to stop, she overtook him. He felt hands pull him away while he only wanted to stay pulling more and more power.

"Devon…Devon slowly calm down. You must learn some restraint."

Devon came out of his trance. "I am so sorry Professor. You said there was power, but I certainly didn't know how much. I thought it gave me control, this power controlled me." Devon fell back into his chair.

"It's all right it takes patience to control the subject you just need some practice. Well, that's enough for today. I need to get to class, and you will not be able to sit still. All that power is racing through you. I suggest some physical activity. A sword fight at the barracks might just be the thing." The Professor walked him out.

Ernst met Devon at the stables, "You look mad. What happened?"

"Ernst I can't really talk about it right now. I need a workout. Let's head to the barracks for some swordplay." Devon hopped on his horse and galloped away. He sparred with three men before he calmed down. He won all three matches, something he had never done before. His commander was impressed. On the way to the stable, Martin appeared, he hadn't seen him since the encounter with Count Rakie.

"Devon, you were extraordinary today. I have never seen you maneuver so well, very balanced too. You seemed much more confident, powerful. I had never noticed how much you fight like your Father, you are fearless." He smiled with a chuckle.

Devon took a big sigh. "You are doing it again Sir, laughing at my expense. I believe you know exactly how I could be so powerful."

Martin placed his hand on his shoulder, and Devon quickly moved away. Martin roared with laughter. "I see your lessons are going well. You always were a quick study. Devon, I am your mentor, and I have no reason to take your power. That was a true gesture of friendship and love I have for you. I would never harm you. Your Father would kill me, very slowly I might add."

Devon shook his head, "I am sorry General Martin, things are changing in my world very rapidly. I am not sure of where I am headed with all this new knowledge; if we could call using an Attachment knowledge. It is just siphoning of power."

Martin put his arm around Devon's shoulder. "Come, I will walk with you to the Stables. I am going to the Castle with some news for your Father, it concerns you too. We'll ride together and talk."

Ernst had their mounts outside the stable. "The Lieutenant said you were coming along General. I take it there is news."

"Yes good news." The General smiled, and they were off to the Castle. "Ernst would you mind giving us some privacy. I have something personal to discuss with the Prince." Ernst rode ahead a respectable way.

Martin looked at Devon earnestly. "The first time I made an attachment I got into the biggest brawl in a tavern, you couldn't even imagine. Thank the Night your Father was there to throw me on a horse and rush me out of there. How he kept me from losing my rank, I will never know. We had both just become officers. We learned about this method during the Alia War. We were experimenting, and we were horrible at this. We kept journals to record our mistakes. I burned mine after the Professor took the best information from them. I never wanted anyone to know the stupid things I did."

Devon turned in his saddle. "Martin, why haven't I known about this. This is the power to control…well anyone you want. Does our military use this?"

Martin looked very seriously at Devon. "Think Devon, if everyone knew of this, everyone would use it. The incredible rush of power is addictive. That is something you must control. Remember this is the use of magic, and what is the first rule of magic?" Martin reminded him. "For every act of power, there is an equal force of static."

Devon stopped his horse. "So while I was feeling elation, she was feeling despair." The look on his Mother's face, he finally understood, the King had attached to her.

"Yes exactly. That is one of many reasons only a handful of the most trusted and powerful Warlocks know of this spell and are allowed to use it. You are in that handful. Use this power wisely and only when it is necessary. You have bonded with that Witch, she is now yours to command. Her life is literally in your hands. I'll wager that is not something the Professor told you. Not only that, if you would continue to take her power, you would eventually become bonded to her. Then her death would mean yours too. So be careful. Take your power when you need it but release your spells. I am sure that will be tomorrow's lesson, learn it well."

Devon's head was spinning, and they were at the Castle. "Ernst let the stablemen care for the horses. I am sure the King will want you to hear this." The three of them went into the Castle hallway to the King's office where the guards saluted them. "General Martin, the Prince, and Ernst to see the King with important news." Martin turned to Ernst while they waited, "I think we should suggest a trip to the isles after the young man's training. He needs practice, and we need to be close at hand." Ernst only shook his head in agreement.

"Go on in gentlemen the King is waiting." The guards held the huge wooden doors open as they walked through the outer room of secretaries to the King's office. He was standing at the large window that overlooked the garden and courtyard. The room was all wood with hunter green carpet, drapes, sofas, and chairs; all of the colors of the Kingdom. "Well... what is the news, Martin." The King looked nervous.

"Good news Sir we have an engagement." Martin smiled. "A family dinner is going on even as we speak. It is very private only the Castle knows of the engagement. Tomorrow they will fly the colors, but the official announcement will be at the State Dinner on Friday. He must have gotten the Emperor to agree to a shortened engagement period. They called three Scribes to start the invitations, that would mean months instead of the normal year. We will get all the details on Sunday from the Count, but we'll have the date by morning, from our spies."

Devon was in total amazement this crazy misguided plan was actually working. He couldn't imagine it. He would have the High Sorceress and all her power. Devon flopped on one of the couches and ran his hands through his hair, "Count Rakie brokered a marriage to the High Sorcerer in a matter of hours."

The King chuckled as he made his way across the great room to his massive oak desk. "That man could convince a man to fall on his own sword and call it a duel. I believe he did that with his own Brothers. I will give him credit; he is smooth; never trust him, Devon."

Count Rakie

"Addison stop fidgeting. You really should dress formally more often then you could dress for these affairs." The Count was laughing he loved to give Addison trouble. There was a knock at the door it was Ski.

"Could you help with my tie? Oh, I see you are already helping." Ski came in and shut the door. "You have a nice room with a view of the lake and a balcony. Is everything in this blasted Castle royal blue?"

Henry finished Addison's tie and turned to Ski's ascot. "It is the Emperor's colors, and I must admit, it offsets every other color. I think it's a wise choice. Think of the burgundy our Kingdom has; it is rather drab and dusty on the carriages and uniforms. It just doesn't have that clean, crisp look."

"You are in good spirits, Henry. You're critiquing the country's colors and styles now. Haven't heard you do that in a long while. I don't know why we didn't bring some man servants with us. One more dinner and a Ball to dress for. I am not used to this. We haven't partied in twenty years." Addison sat on his bed watching Henry fight with Ski's tie while trying to place his waistcoat on.

Henry dropped it and looked at Addison. "If you remember correctly, we were not staying here, and I don't relish parties. At least not parties where I am the center of attention. I much prefer being on the outside looking in, more interesting." There was another knock at the door, "Who now…does the Emperor need dressing? Come in."

Two men came in, one Henry recognized as one of the servants. "Sirs excuse me. Oh, I do apologize. I should have come up earlier. Here Count let me do that." He moved to Ski and began to dress him. "I am Walter, the Emperor's personal servant, this young man is Mr. Todd. We have him on temporary serve while you're here. We had expected him earlier. We haven't forgotten about you. Mr. Todd, I believe Mr. Addison could use your help."

Todd stepped up. "I am one of Count Madison's servants. I will have all your suits pressed and ready for the upcoming engagements. I look forward to serving you."

Addison said, "I am so happy you are here; you don't even know."

Count Rakie sat on the bed. "No I am the happiest, these two do not know how to hold still long enough to tie anything. I am surprised they can saddle a Pegasus."

"Sir, I see you are quite capable of dressing yourself. You will be a welcome asset to this household. We all welcome you to our home." Walter grinned.

"Thank you, Walter. I am looking forward to coming here. I do have a home of my own in Belissa, but I am sure the young lady will want to spend time here with her family." The Count looked out at the view of the lake and boulders where they kissed, a kiss that changed his life. "Tell me, Walter. What can you tell me about my young bride, any good stories?"

"Oh, I am afraid I would be in deep trouble repeating some of the stories I know. Let me just say we are all thrilled our young girl has found a good match. I will say you are about to have," He paused to consider and said, "much fun." He stepped back and looked at his work. "Excellent Sir." He turned to the Count, "Let's have a look; you must look your best for Casandra, wait till you see her."

The Count was laughing now. "Yes, Walter she is fun. Do you know she had me running a race this afternoon?"

"Oh, yes Sir, I did. The kitchen staff was gambling she would beat you." They were all laughing, but Walter said. "I would never bet against a Belissa, you are known for your speed and cunning."

"Well, I think this whole household is about to have fun," Addison added. "I will like to know that little Sprite; she looks like fun as well."

Henry said, "What is it about Sprites, Addison, you can never keep your hands off them?"

Addison laughed and said, "I don't know, Henry. I am drawn to them like bees are to flowers. I have never understood."

Walter laughed and said, "Well, be careful of Miss Marion. She is a favorite with the King. She is also the best friend to Casandra. Just between you and me…whenever our girl came home in trouble; Marion was partly the reason. She is a hand full Sir, you better watch yourself. The Emperor asked if you could meet him in the library before dinner, for a drink."

Ski said, "Great, now you have set a challenge before Addison. You boys and your games. This is going to lead us on a merry chase. I am getting too old for adventures of love, so keep this to yourselves boys."

Henry laughed and added "Ski, you love this, admit it. Addison, did you get all our wine into the kitchen for dinner?"

"Yes, he did, and I will make sure it is served all week. Your wine is exceptional." Walter added.

"Thank you, Walter. I think we will have a wonderful relationship."

The Count slapped him on his shoulder, and Walter said, "Take good care with our girl, Count, and you will be an honored friend here." Walter and Mr. Todd bowed and left the men.

The three entered the library where the Emperor, the Professor, and Major were already drinking wine.

"Count, your wines are wonderful. I believe we need to order some from you before you leave. How are you feeling?"

"I am feeling fine. Thank you all for your expert healing. I hope I can fake the symptoms well enough to fool the King. Thank you, Emperor, for the compliment of my wines. I put much of my life and all my passion for developing the vineyard. I hope you have a chance to visit sometime." Henry poured a glass for Addison and Ski.

Professor added, "I hope I am included in that invitation. I have always wanted to see the process." He stopped suddenly. "Oh, my Empress you are a vision." All heads turned.

The Empress sauntered into the library dressed in the elegant copper colored satin fitted dress with long gloves to match. It fell to the floor with a strapless neckline displaying a stunning topaz necklace and earrings. Her hair was swirled on top of her head in curls with hair clips of topaz interspersed with her crown. Every one of the men in the room took in their breath, the Count broke the silence. "Your Majesty I believe the Professor underestimated your beauty I would say exquisite." He gave a bow.

The Empress smiled and said, "Thank you, Count. You are healed very well."

The Emperor came around his desk and took her hand. "You are a Goddess, my dear. Beatrice your beauty is almost too much to bear." He kissed her hand and then moved to kiss her cheek. Beatrice took a step back but not before his lips had touched her sending sparks down her body, "Thank you, Haden. I have a gift for you." She removed her hand from his and gestured around the room, where at least twenty cats were milling about. "You seem to be breathing just fine, so my magical cats are working beautifully. You must praise Mags, she has been working so hard keeping your house together, as well as helping me."

"I will, my dear." The Emperor reached down for a yellow tabby that was rubbing his leg. "They really are pretty little animals; I have admired them at a distance." He cradled it and gave it a sniff. "How long will these last? I wouldn't mind keeping a few around the Castle."

"You can keep them as long as you like my Dear." The Empress grinned. "I almost forgot, a few of the State delegation arrived late this afternoon, so our party has expanded. I also asked the Mayor and the Councilmen from town along with their wives. I couldn't slight them; I hope no one minds."

"No, this is an engagement party, and it should be a proper one for my only daughter." The Emperor placed the cat on the floor and went to the doorway. He shut the doors and came behind the desk, looking again at the Empress. "Empress, gentlemen I wanted to have a word before the others got here. I am concerned, not only for Casandra but for all of us. I have an awful feeling about the plot we are about to uncover. Everyone here needs to take extra care; the King of the Hex has had years to organize. We are just beginning to uncover his motives. I have not felt right about the man since he didn't attend his own war. I can't get the memory of my Mother's and Father's murder out of my head, and I cannot help but think somehow their deaths are connected. Keep that in your minds as we work through this." He held his glass up to the portrait of his Father on the side wall, "To the Emperor." Everyone in the room raised their glass and said. "To the Emperor."

The library doors opened the Prince, and his wife appeared. Kathryn wore a stunning red velvet dress with pearls at the sweetheart neckline. The Prince wore a white coat and sash, together they looked the part of a royal painting. "Why are we hiding in the Library? Guest will arrive any time." Kathryn scolded. "Come on out to the entry to greet everyone."

The Emperor came over to her and kissed her on the cheek, "Congratulations. So, I will have a little girl to spoil."

Kathryn grinned, "Thank you, Emperor, but could we all keep this a secret this weekend. I told Casandra I didn't want to take away from her engagement. Bryan wasn't to tell anyone." She turned and glared at Bryan.

The Emperor hugged her. "You are the sweetest kindest most considerate Daughter-in-law I have. We will keep your secret."

She took his hand. "Emperor. I am your only Daughter-in-law." She grabbed his arm as he laughed.

They made their way to the main entryway when Marion and Casandra were descending the staircase. Marion was dressed in deep purple fitted silk gown that wrapped around her in a swirl. At the waist was a belt with amethyst jewels as well as her jewelry. This evening her skin was cream and her hair golden with amethyst eyes smiling at them. Marion was stunning, looking much older than she was.

Casandra followed in a satin gown of gold. The neck was as high as the torque she wore, it had long sleeves, and the skirt fell to the ground hugging her hips. As she made her way down the circular stairs, they all could see it was backless. Her black hair was woven around her crown. The effect was one of regal femininity.

The Count was astounded; he had run a race with a girl. Even the butler Walter called her their girl. This was no girl he was marrying; this was a sensual woman. Henry could not keep his mind from her beautiful back and how he wanted to caress her skin. He had to stop thinking of that dress and say something.

"Count, have you nothing to say to Casandra?" The Empress was standing before him.

Addison spoke for him, "I have known Henry for many years, and he has never been at a loss for words of compliment. Casandra, I think you have put my friend in a stupor. You are ravishing, not to be outdone by Marion. You have taken my breath away Marion. I love your violet eyes." Mentally he spoke to Henry. Don't make me throw water on you Count! Say something.

Casandra broke out laughing, "Addison you do realize I can hear your thoughts."

Addison backed away with a grin. "Marion, give me a tour before the guests arrive." He took her arm and walked down the hall.

Finally, the Count spoke, "Casandra I really am at a loss for words. I cannot even find words to express your loveliness." He walked to her; took her hand and kissed it.

"You look very handsome as well." Then mentally she said. I think I would like you to caress my back but not in front of my parents. Henry don't blush. Then she laughed.

The Count did blush. "You, my dear are enchantingly wicked." Mentally he added. A trait I adore.

The guests began to arrive. Henry was introduced to family, friends, Diplomats, the Mayor, and Councilmen. He, in turn, introduced his men and friends. He couldn't keep from wondering who among these people were the informants?

The formal Dining Room was set with white tablecloths and a vibrant blue runner down the middle of the table. White flowers in low crystal containers filled the center with white candles on mirrors reflecting the light. The Crystal chandeliers outnumbered the chandeliers of Winsette Castle, and that was a feat. There was a quartet playing soft music as they ate. Henry hoped they would have a chance to dance after dinner so he could touch Casandra's skin. The food was delicious and served superbly and elegantly. This really was one of the prettiest and delightful dinner parties he had ever attended. Everyone was joyous, laughing, and happy. People were making toasts to Casandra and him, making happy pronouncements of a long life with many children.

It was time he stood and proclaimed his right to wed her. He nodded to Addison and mentally told him to get the unique wine. Servants carried trays of tall glasses with golden wine into the room. The Count stood, and the room fell silent.

Henry took Casandra's hand and walked her to the center of the ballroom room where everyone could see her. "I have asked your parents the Emperor and Empress for a contract of marriage to you, which they have approved. A legal document is signed with an agreement between our countries and just like that you are my wife. It is your custom, we announce our engagement, attend many parties and Balls, then we marry at the Temple. In Diamentia we have customs of marriage too. First, the Warlock asks the woman to marry and to blood bond with him. Then if she accepts he gives her tokens of his respect and admiration, one of those tokens is a serenade." He took both her hands in his, "Casandra, it would be my honor to be your husband and care for you for the rest of my life. Do you accept?"

Casandra was almost in tears; this custom was so endearing. "Yes Henry, I accept."

"Casandra, will you blood bond with me as your husband?"

"Of course, yes I will." Casandra squeezed his hand and mentally asked. Didn't we already do that?

He mentally answered. Yes, but if I said that, the Hex would think you know of their plans, and you would be in more danger.

Addison appeared with a tray of drinks. Henry took one and handed it to Casandra, and then took one himself. He held up the glass and said, as the servants started handing out the wine. "This is a wine created from a particular grape I have given all my passion and love developing. As you can see it has a golden hue just as my Lady has worn this evening. It is effervescent like her, and a little sweet and sparkly. So, I have named it after her. A toast to Countess Casandra the most beautiful woman in the world, with Casandra's wine."

They all drank, Addison took their glasses and Ski appeared with a large black velvet box. The Count opened it and took out a waterfall necklace of diamonds, hundreds of diamonds fell into a V shape with the longest point at least ten inches long. Casandra had never seen so many diamonds in one place much less on one necklace. Even her Mother's crown didn't hold that many diamonds. The Count stood behind her to fasten it ever so softly caressing her back. Mentally he said. A caress in front of everyone, don't blush.

Casandra did blush. "Count, this is beautiful how can I thank you. I must say I like your customs much better than ours."

Henry threw back his head and laughed hardily everyone in the room loved that comment. Some of the ladies were in fact, agreeing with her. He thought I love this woman. He heard her mentally say, and I love you, Henry. He stepped back, and all his men surrounded her, and they began to sing. They sang in a chorus, and the song was enchanting. It was a song of love between two people and the story of how they lived; the children they had, the strength found in each other to overcome obstacles and after a long life how they died together in each other's arms. Casandra and every woman in the room were in tears by the time they finished. Then the Count knelt before her and said, "I vow to shield you with my life." Every one of his men knelt and repeated those words.

Something came over Casandra, and she knelt before Henry and said. "And I will defend all of you." She kissed Henry softly and mentally said a kiss in front of everyone. He grabbed her in an embrace, both were laughing. Then the Emperor and Empress were standing in front of them.

The Emperor grabbed Henry and yelled, "I think I picked the right man for my girl."

The Empress hugged Casandra, "You love one another, I am happy for you. May you have a long life together just as in the song."

Her Brother grabbed Casandra and Kathryn took the Count and started dancing.

"Casandra, I am so happy you have found love and a rich man at the same time. He pledged his life to you. I cannot tell you how wonderful I feel. I have always felt like I failed you, that I couldn't protect you and you would have an unhappy life. I love you, and all I have ever wanted was you to be happy. The Count has made that happen." Bryan kissed her on the cheek.

Casandra hugged him and sighed, "Yes he has, and I have fallen madly in love with him. You know you have always been there for me.

How many times did you bail me out at school? I can't even count the times. Does this mean you are not going to kill him?"

"No, I will not kill him." They both laughed.

There were more toasts and slowly people began to leave. All of them came to Henry and Casandra telling them the party was the best ever and they hoped for a wedding invitation. Everyone loved Henry's traditions. They were also surprised and happy to see Nobles marry for love and not money or alliances. The Emperor and Empress said their Goodnights.

Henry took her hand. "A walk before bed? I should be tired, but I am exhilarated."

Casandra put her arm in his, and they walked to the garden. "Alright, but just for a bit. I need to spend some time with Marion. I haven't had much time to spend with her tonight. I should probably find her."

"Oh, I don't think that is necessary. Marion has been kept entertained this evening. At this very moment, she is with someone in the garden." Henry winked at her.

"Addison… he was dancing with her all night! I thought you told him to escort her, did he want to be her partner?"

Henry smiled. "He has a particular attraction to Sprites. He also commented on how beautiful she was and surprisingly smart. It is nice to have his mind occupied and out of ours."

They were in the garden, and the night felt cool after the dancing. The sky was clear, and the stars were shimmering.

"Is this real Henry? I feel like I am dreaming." He took her in his arms and kissed her softly and tenderly, and she responded with strength. Soon they were in a passionate embrace with Henry's hands stroking her back. He broke the desire for her by stepping back and holding her by her shoulders.

"This is no dream Casandra; I am yours. I cannot believe it myself. I had given up on ever feeling a deep love and having a passion like this. I want you so, but this is not the place for us to confide our deep thoughts. Let's go to our rooms and leave the garden to Marion." They walked back to the Castle.

Casandra said mentally. I never thought I would marry and love my husband. Henry, I would never even dream of this happening because

I couldn't take any more disappointments. I stopped dreaming the day I went off to the Academy.

Henry asked, "Why?"

Casandra said, "I was told never to expect to love my husband, it would be a marriage for an alliance. The first day everyone found out I was the strongest Sorcerer there. No that's not correct. There is testing, and everyone saw I was the strongest ever. My fate was mapped. I would be Empress one day. My Brother the Emperor if my husband was not a strong Warlock. What man would want me, except as a trophy to show the world he was grand. Someday we will divorce you know, the Empress cannot be distracted by family or husbands.

Henry stopped walking and turned her. He said out loud, "First of all, your Mother is very young for an Empress, so we have time before that happens. Second, I am one hundred plus years old, you will outlive me for hundreds of years. By the time this all happens, we will be happy to live apart for a while. Don't divorce me we can just separate. I want to call you wife forever."

She looked deeply into his eyes and said. "I will always be your wife don't abandon me, Henry. Don't die and leave me. I want to die with you just like the song when we are old."

"Cassandra, you must promise me you will live beyond my death, you are so young to think thoughts of death. You must live for our children and our grandchildren. Promise me you will live every moment of your life with love." He tilted her head up and repeated, "Promise me."

Casandra smiled, "I will Henry, I love you."

He held her close. "Tomorrow let's take a ride and get out of the Castle for a while."

"I would love to ride one of your Pegasus." Cassandra nudged him with her hip.

Henry held her close with one hand on her waist and the other at her neck. Then slowly he moved his hand from her neck down her shoulders and across her back. He caressed her skin as far as the dress was cut. Casandra sighed and melted into his arms. "We'll see, first I want to see you ride a horse." Casandra pouted, and he laughed and shook his head. "That pout young woman will not get your way. Now we should go to sleep. I am sure your Father will have us up early planning." They went to their rooms.

The Empress

"The party was a success. Everyone is saying it was one of the best dinners ever." Mags helped the Empress from her gown and handed her night clothes. "It wasn't just our cooking; it was the flowers from the garden too. The musicians were wonderful. Oh, that song the Count's men sang, everyone was so moved. That necklace was stunning. I hope to have you tucked in soon so I can get a look at that. Do you think it was real? I wonder how many fabs that cost. Your Majesty, you are quiet are you well?"

"I am fine Mags, just remembering the evening with you. Yes, it was an excellent night absolutely perfect, right from a fairy tale. It just has me thinking back to an engagement party long ago. I shouldn't be thinking about my perfect night or weddings." She came out from the screen and sat at her dressing table. "Could you help me with my hair before you run off to snoop on Casandra."

"Snoop! I do no such thing. The girl freely tells me more than I usually want to hear. Well I mean, she can't talk with her Father she says it is uncomfortable. She says she won't burden you, she knows it is hard enough to contain emotions." Mags saw the Empress's face fall. "I am sorry your Majesty, I don't always say things right."

Beatrice padded her hand and said, "Mags it's alright. I know exactly what you mean. You have been a God sent to me. I know you are her

Mother too. She is right you know I would be all wrapped up in her problems, and the Temple would fall, well really burn." They both laughed, "Mags I know you are just as proud and happy as I am. I was so sure this marriage would be one of convenience, a good matching to her for children. That is why I agreed with Henry. To think they fell in love. I understand a young girl falling into the charms of an older handsome man. I did that myself. The Count, on the other hand, ... well he seems mesmerized with Casandra. It is real love, or the man is the greatest actor alive."

"Oh, your Majesty he is in love, for sure. I felt their love and attraction from the moment I stood in the room with them. Theirs is a great love, the kind of love that legends are made of, songs are written for their kind of love. Oh, and he is so good looking with those large deep brown eyes and thick wavy hair. He has a mysterious look about him. Most candidates come to this Kingdom to take our money, he brings riches. His wines are the finest I have ever had. You know he gifted me some fine liquor. I know he was trying to get on my good side, but he did let me probe him. He is powerful too I tested him, very worthy of her. Their children will be something to see." The Empress froze, and she shuddered. "Beatrice, are you alright? That is the second time you looked like you have seen a ghost. Start talking or I will not sleep." Mags stopped brushing her hair.

She looked in the mirror at Mags. "Oh, I am just a silly woman. It's that stupid fortune teller I went to when I was at the Academy. A group of us girls thought it would be fun, it was for some, not me. She asked the others to leave, then she told me things I did not want to hear. She wanted me to see The Hermit."

"Beatrice, you never told me about this what did she say?" Mags put an arm around her. The Empress stood and took Mags to the bed where they sat next to each other.

"I was told not to repeat things until after they happened. The fortune teller described Haden perfectly, our short marriage, even warned of the deaths of the Emperor and Empress. She told me our daughters would both be in danger, they needed the best training and protection. She said the girl who would be Empress must never marry for love. I thought to choose the scoundrel Rakie a nearly perfect match. Tonight, I found my decision completely wrong. Just as I was wrong not to share this with Haden until after his Mother was killed." They sat on the bed, silent.

"This explains so much about your marriage and the fighting over the children. You wanted them with you, he insisted they stay with him, the Temple wasn't safe...well, we all thought that. You knew they would all be in danger, didn't you?" Beatrice could barely answer a soft yes. "Did you go to The Hermit?" Mags waited patiently for her response.

"I am not brave like Casandra. I waited. I didn't want to hear the truth. After I cleaned up the Temple and sent Haden home with his Mother's remains, I flew to her. By that time, it was too late for me to make the choices to correct things. I pleaded, fought, and lied to get my children with me. I learned the hard way to never chose from the heart. I did, Hayden did, and so many are dead. Hating him and myself was easy. It was easy to divorce him and live away from him; to keep my remaining children safe."

Mags stood. "No Dear, I don't think it was easy or that it is now either. You two are still very much in love. I will have Anna bring you some seuling tea and think about this. There are always answers you know."

Beatrice stood and hugged her. "You are right. There are always answers. Just not always the ones we want. Go, I need to dance and pray." Mags smiled and kissed her cheek then left for the kitchen.

The Empress put on her robe and walked out on to the balcony to look at the beautiful starry night. Down in the garden, she saw two figures kissing, she could see the Sprite with Addison. On a bench below was her daughter and Henry, he was holding her so securely and lovingly. They were buried in a lover's talk. She remembered the discussions between her and Haden. The kiss Haden gave her in the library this evening brought back memories. Mags was right, they were still in love. Then there was the Major; his eyes bore into her as they danced. She could not let this happen. She pushed the feelings out of her body, out to the stars. That is the place that feelings and love belonged, among the stars where dreams are made. This world was a place where dreams are broken. Enough of this, she needed to leave this Castle as soon as possible. Would a visit to The Hermit hurt or help? She asked the Night to give her the right answers. Then she went inside to leave the lovers alone.

Casandra

Henry kissed her and said, "Sweet dreams, my love."

Casandra threw her arms around him and kissed him passionately. "Now that is a Goodnight kiss." He laughed, "I just love watching you laugh. You look so happy and so very handsome."

"I will remember to laugh often," Henry said while smiling at her.

"But only for me Henry. I don't want others to steal you."

Henry laughed again. "Others have had their chance. I am all yours." Henry pushed her in the direction of her bedroom, and he strolled happily down the hall to his.

When Casandra entered her room Mags was bustling around the room cleaning and turning down the bed. "Well let's get you into bed, and you can tell me all the juicy details. Starting with that necklace. Is that real? How much money did your Count spend on it?"

Casandra turned for her to unlatch the Necklace. "Mags, If I told you I asked what Henry spent on it you would thrash me for being so rude. You know I didn't even ask. It is beautiful. I will wear my white Ball gown on Saturday it will show off my tiara. We will do a spell to make my dress sparkle too, that will be stunning. Oh, Mags. Isn't Henry handsome and so kind and wonderful?" Casandra scooted out of her dress and into her nightgown. She sat at her dressing table and started to undo her hair. There was a knock at her door.

"Casandra are you awake?" Marion's voice was a whisper.

Mags opened the door. "Yes but go get your nightgown and you can talk with your friend into the wee hours, Ana is bringing you sleepy tea. I want to hear about your Addison. I saw you mooning over him and kissing in the garden."

Marion blushed and said. "Mags you shouldn't have watched. I'll change and be right back."

Casandra was chuckling "Don't tease her she has just barely gotten over her breakup with Frank, stupid boy."

"Hum, well neither Addison or your Count are little boys, they are fairly grown men. Both of you girls should keep that in mind. I would be worried about your infatuation with the Count, but I can sure tell he is deeply in love with you. What a surprise. All these years we have been bracing you for a loveless marriage, and he comes along. This really has all of us dumbfounded. It is almost too good to be true. Yes, he is handsome and very generous, kind, and happy. I am not used to happy anymore, not since...well, it has been a while." She stopped not finishing her thoughts of the family before the Great War. Mags took her brush and combed out her hair. Marion opened the door and flopped on the bed.

"I am back, Casandra this was a perfect evening! Just completely perfect! Your Fiancé is extraordinary. He is so romantic gifting you such a wonderful necklace. Oh, and the song that brought me to tears, it brought everyone to tears. You make a handsome couple dancing, you fit faultlessly. Mags the food was delicious and the decorations; how are you going to surpass that for the Ball? Addison was so impressed, he said he couldn't remember a party more magnificent. Addison said Henry is captivated with you, deeply in love, like he has never seen. Addison and Henry were boyhood friends, so Addison should know. Addison is so handsome and charming, and he dances wonderfully too. You know Addison graduated with high honors from the University, and he is partners in the wineries with Henry. Mags, you shouldn't have watched us but since you did... Addison wasn't using charms on me, was he? Ah, his kisses took me away to some other world."

Mags and Casandra were both just smiling at her. "Casandra, I do think this little Sprite talks more and faster than I do. I didn't think it possible. No, Marion. I saw not one charm used on you or Casandra. Any feelings there are true ones." They both took a sigh; Ana came in with their tea. "Okay Marion come exchange seats with Casandra, and I will brush out your hair, and you both can tell me everything. Ana pour us all some tea, and we will have some girl talk."

The Emperor

Haden woke earlier than usual the morning after the engagement dinner. He was worried about his daughter's sudden attachment to Henry. They were once good friends; he knew Henry as a good man. During the Great War, his opinion had changed of Henry with all the mess about his Brother and Wife. All the plans they made were now obsolete. Would they have to rearrange, he didn't like change.

Then there was the Empress. As long as she was far to the end of the Continents, he was a sensible, logical, Warlock. However, when she came into the room, he was helpless. A small kiss on her cheek, that was all it took, and he was lost to her. Life was cruel; he and Beatrice had so little time together, and both had lost so many they loved in the war. Now, his daughter was in the middle of this covert war with the Hex. He had felt this coming, which is why he wanted the alliance with Henry's country. He had no idea the Hex was this detestable or shrewd. He had known from the war they were evil, cruel, and manipulative but they had been illiterate and ignorant. It seems that was no longer the case. The Continental Council had thought they had destroyed them and left them in ruins; they had been fooled. The Hex was never ruined, never stupid, and evidently more inventive than he had believed. He needed silence to think and coffee to wake. He would go down to the kitchen and make it himself if no one was there. But of course, someone was there, the cook Allen was baking bread for the day.

"Allen, you are baking already?" The Emperor went to the coffee pot at the fire and helped himself to a large mug.

"Yes, your Majesty, with all the people in the Castle I have to get an early start. Besides, for me this is the best time of day; before all the women come in and start gaggling. There will be a lot of that today. The party last night gave them much to gossip about." He smiled and kept kneading bread. "You're up early yourself Sir. I suppose you have plans to make for the wedding and such. Can I get you some breakfast?"

"I am fine if you hadn't been here I would have made coffee, that is all I want for now. You know Allen, the women get the fun plans of parties, cakes, and gowns. I get the worrisome legal and financials to work out. Like you I wanted some solitude to think before everyone comes down babbling and insisting on this or that. I'll take my coffee to the garden and watch the sunrise and leave you to your baking. Have a good day, Allen." As the Emperor left, Allen told him to have a good day too then he bent over and rolled out more dough.

The Emperor envied Allen. All he had to do was bake bread and run the kitchen. It was hard work; it took a lot of planning, but at the end of the day, none of his cooks would be dead. The smell of war was not as pleasant as the smell of bread. As he walked in the garden, he smelled war, lies, treachery, and death. One war was enough for him for a lifetime; would he be doomed to another in his reign? Not if he could prevent it; too many loved ones and friends died in the last war. He would not be easily led into another.

He found a bench in the rose garden that had a clear view of the lake where he could contemplate. If he could learn from his mistakes and figure out these new developments maybe he could keep most of his people alive. He needed to keep all his children and grandchildren alive, not only for himself and the Kingdom but for Beatrice. Any more loss of children would sever their love completely. He had never held her heart entirely, he knew that from the first time they met. He watched the sun rise and with it, idea after idea came into his mind only to be rejected as reckless. He felt someone's presence beyond the hedge. "Henry, come forth; no need to sneak around."

“I’m sorry Haden, I was waiting for an invitation. I could tell you were deep in thought. I can come back later if you wish.”

“No, now is fine; my thoughts were just going in circles anyway. I see you couldn’t sleep either. Well, perhaps we should find a private spot. I’ll have Allen send someone with coffee to the library if you wouldn’t mind scanning the room.” The Emperor walked with Henry. “Henry, I have missed our friendship. I am looking forward to many years of friendship ahead. I know you are a good man, I see you are falling deeply in love with my daughter. I feel I should warn you loving a High Empress, which Casandra will be someday, is a horrible task. I wish it on no man.” He placed an arm around Henry’s as they walked back to the Castle.

“She still loves you. You know that, don’t you? Last night in the library a simple kiss on her cheek brought it back. The look on your faces when you came out to us after the song, well, that is the love I want with Casandra. Love that endures and never fades.” The Emperor’s grip tightened he had forgotten the size of him and his copious power. “Addison is sweeping the library seems his little Sprite had him up early too. Ah, what love will do to us Warlocks?”

The Prophecy

The Empress sat on her balcony hoping the fresh air would clear her head of her nightmares. The sky was still dark, and the fire had gone out a while ago it was as cold as her heart. Her dreams had repeatedly shown Casandra and Henry dead. No matter the scenario, in the end, they all died. She was grateful she was not an oracle, seldom did her dreams come true. However, this relentless dream had haunted her for months. The Hermit popped into her head. The damned Hermit nothing good ever came from her mouth. She was probably the source of her Nightmares. She noticed someone walking in the garden it was the Emperor. She fought the urge to go to him and disclose her dreams. She remembered the last time she confided in him; he did the opposite of her wishes. His pride and ego were the reasons two of her children were dead, and one was kidnapped. How and why Casandra came back to her alive, she never understood. After yesterday, she had more questions than before the Count shared his sights. Taking her eggs before the time. It is a wonder she lived through it, her poor little girl. Casandra did remember the pain, that was why she had given her spells to forget. Beatrice had thought she'd been sexually assaulted and that was the source of her illness. She was personally and privately going to kill the King of Hex nothing would stop her. The sun was rising, and it looked like it would be a beautiful warm sunny day. There was Mags at the door. She went into the room and called. "Come in Mags is something wrong?'

Mags entered with a note in her hand, "This just arrived for you. I felt its importance and urgency. I thought I would see if you were up yet." She handed her a letter.

"Stay Mags, I have a feeling I will need your help after I read this." The Empress opened and read. "Let's call some cats into my sitting room we need to have a talk, and it should be secure." Mags nodded and called cats, seven of them materialized immediately. They went to the sitting room both worked to clear out anything that was suspiciously magical. The Empress sat in her rose-colored chair, and a large white cat jumped to her lap. Mags stoked the fire and put a kettle on for tea. "I believe it is safe to speak now your Majesty, that note is from the Hermit, isn't it?"

"Yes, you've not lost your touch Mags. You never forget someone's energy, do you? Nice talent." Mags smiled, and the Empress continued "I will read it aloud for you, and you can help me with its real meaning.

> *My Dearest Empress,*
>
> *I was indeed surprised to feel your presence at the Castle. Yesterday a delivery man brought an invitation to the engagement party taking place last night. I knew you would not be comfortable to have me there in person nor would I be pleased to attend. I am a hermit for a reason. I am sure you understand all too well with your experience as Empress. I send my belated regrets. The love and joy emanating from the Castle last evening were awe-inspiring, giving hope where it has been forgotten over the past twenty years.*
>
> *It has been far too long since our last conversation; I do miss your thoughts. I am anxious to meet the young Sorcerer, and her little Sprite too. I am graciously extending an invitation for lunch this afternoon. I am sorry for the late notice. However, I am an old woman who knows how soon death could come. So, I can't afford to waste any of my time. I feel*

the great urgency in speaking with the three of you, and I have an engagement gift for the young bride.

There is no need to send a reply if I see the green smoke from your setting room chimney I will know you will attend. If you refuse, merely dunk this note in water. I will receive that message too.

Sincerely
Margaretta Savilla Southernland of Dorcher
The Hermit of the Crystal Mountain

"Well, well, well, she is as scullery as ever. The old Witch is clever indeed. I should have known; a tray of wild turkey and petit fours were missing last night. That Witch was here alright. Wouldn't be here in person, indeed. A couple of bottles of the Count's wine went missing too; I bet you will be served those for lunch. Oh, Empress, she knows they love one another. Remember her warning to not let Casandra marry for love. Do you think she is angry? This could be bad. The reference to death, wasting time, and urgency; I could feel that from just handling the note."

Mags poured them both tea while the Empress put the note down to receive her tea. She said, "Her comparison to the position of Empress and the Hermit is very true. Somedays I am as removed from the world as Duchess is, yet ever aware of every manifestation. What does she mean, far too long since our last conversation? I communicate with her often? I told her I was coming here through the crystal two days ago. More importantly the insistence of destroying the invitation, she knows foul play is in the Castle. I wonder if she can help us." The Empress threw the green stationery and envelope into the flames of her fireplace watching green smoke whirl up the chimney.

"I wonder if she is willing to help? I wish I could go along. She is too smart not to find me. You must remember every word exactly as spoken. We'll talk after your return. I will have the girls dressed appropriately. You will need to leave right after breakfast to get there in time." Mags left to get breakfast ready.

The Empress dressed and went down to the kitchen to see about breakfast in the dining room. "Where is everyone? We need to eat and leave."

Allen said the men were talking in the library he had taken coffee and rolls in earlier. Mags came in the dining room. "Empress, no one is sleeping around here, except the girls; I had to wake them. They slept together again, they are good friends. I need more time to get all these meals together. My magic is wearing thin. All these Warlocks have made my job harder. It's easier to herd cats than Royals. I think I will serve hard liquor and ale at the State Dinner this evening. These men need to sleep in, perhaps it will give me a little time to get ready for the Ball." Mags shook her head as she stomped out to the dining room.

The Empress followed. "Why not serve everyone coffee and rolls in their rooms tomorrow. Let them lounge in bed, and you can have the downstairs to yourself." The Empress hugged Mags. "It's worth a try, and it might work. I'll get the men, you get those girls." She headed for the library. She thought to knock, then realized how ridiculous that was everyone in there was magical and knew she was about to enter. She hadn't been able to surprise anyone since she was at the Academy.

"Good morning Gentlemen, breakfast is being served. I would ask that we all be especially respectful of our servant's time for the next two days. They have much to handle organizing the spectacular parties they are preparing. I am taking the girls to a luncheon date perhaps you could all dine in the village for lunch. It would be nice to spread a few coins their way as well." The Empress turned and walked out.

"Your Majesty," the Emperor called as he walked out of the library "who are you lunching with?"

"Why the Hermit Emperor." She kept walking knowing full well he was turning various shades of red. They all entered the dining room and sat as Haden's color was beginning to return. "My dear do you think that is wise. I have never wanted the children near her. That old woman can put strange thoughts into heads, as I know too well."

"You said she wasn't capable enough to put thoughts into anyone's head if I remember right." He was turning red again. "Well, too late for that; she was here last night."

"What I didn't see her!" He bellowed.

"Keep your voice down Haden. You do not want Casandra and Marion to hear you're ranting. Besides she may have some pertinent information for us." The Empress sat next to him and could feel the boiling from within him.

The Count sat across from her and asked. "Who is the Hermit?"

"That is a long story. Mags where are the girls?"

"Right here." Marion and Casandra's voices chimed in together as they each sat next to their men. Marion wore a very fashionable sunny yellow riding outfit, Sprites could change on a whim; it must be nice to have an endless wardrobe. Casandra was in a lovely teal riding outfit which offset her eyes that were already sparkling. Beatrice's heart opened and relaxed seeing the couples' love for each other.

"I am so excited Henry; we have been invited to the Hermits home. That is so rare. I know we promised to ride this morning, but could we put it off until this afternoon?" Casandra was bubbling.

"Of course, but who is this Hermit woman?" Henry asked again.

Marion popped up, "You really don't know? My goodness, she is the most knowledgeable High Sorceress of all. Not as powerful as you Empress, but certainly as great. She lives at the top of the Crystal Mountain, and it is believed her power keeps this world turning. It so amazing we have an audience."

"That is a fable. No one lives at the top of the mountain. Several of our men have climbed it, and they say it is barren, filled with only snow and ice." Addison laughed.

"Don't laugh she's there, alright. She hires Sprites to care for her and only Sprites. I have two cousins working there now." Marion sipped her coffee looking smug.

The Empress held her hand up, "No arguing about this you two. She is there, Addison. Years ago the Hermit got tired of all the men trying to climb her mountain and falling off. She said it was too much bad energy falling at her feet. She cloaked her mountain and created one a way off for men to fall from." Addison looked at the Empress with disbelief.

Casandra continued, "Marion is right she only surrounds herself with Sprites because they are honest. She doesn't turn the world, Marion. The Hermit is a prophet and holds all knowledge of the world.

She was to be the Empress years ago, she married and had ten children. The man she married was very possessive and greedy. He tried to use a spell to keep her for himself and gain all her power. He wanted to rule the world. It backfired, he died, and she gained all his power which was very evil. As you know, Empress's can only contain good energies that is why we try not to kill only punish. To hold our power, we must constantly release any disruptive forces."

The Empress said, "That is also the reason we cannot be married as Empress. Husbands have a way of creating disruptive and negative energies." Hayden glowered at her. All the women laughed especially Kathryn she continued, "She declined the position of Empress and sequestered herself to the mountain retreat. It took years to undo his spell. She makes a point not to go near Warlocks. I can't say I wouldn't feel the same. Her Warlock killed most of her children that's not something easily forgotten or forgiven. She has spent years building the structure. It is a fortress, and no one can enter except at her request. This is a request that is not refused. It is more of a command."

The Empress paused and took a drink of coffee as everyone stared at her. "One day someone must take her spot on that mountain. I have often wondered who it will be. I am her great, great, great, Granddaughter. That would make Casandra her great, great, great, great, granddaughter. I don't believe I have ever mentioned that to you." Well, that piece of information stopped them all dead in their tracks, everyone but Kathryn had mouths opened like flies. The Empress could only laugh.

"Mother you never told me this. Why not?" Casandra stared at her.

"Well, she is…let us say a bit eccentric. Generally, Warlocks become very uneasy knowing their offspring may follow suit. However, this wedding is the most eccentric I have ever known. I thought it would not hurt to share this with everyone at the table. As I said, I am hoping she can help us. So far things have not gone to plan." The Empress hurried to finish her breakfast.

"Going to plan; whose plan would that be my dear, yours or hers?" The Emperor sat back in his chair with a stern look.

The Empress sat back in her chair and returned that look more powerfully, then answered sarcastically, "Well my Dear…"

Marion interrupted giggling, and everyone turned their heads. She coughed and said. "Not everyone enjoys endearments I happen to appreciate the Empress's disdain."

The Empress nodded, "Thank you, Marion. It really doesn't matter whose plan it is if it works. Your plans certainly haven't Emperor." Everyone looked down at their plates which left the two staring each other down. The Empress turned away saying, "Please, everyone at this table had a plan, and they have all failed. This is not the time to blame anyone. Girls we must leave. Gentlemen, I believe you have some plans of your own to make." The Empress rose and threw her napkin on the table, signaling the conversation was over. The Warlocks all stood then sat quietly to finish their breakfast.

Mags came in. "It sure is quiet in here. I see the Empress and the girls have left for their luncheon date. Would you Gentlemen like lunch served in the library?"

The Emperor said, "We were informed by her Majesty to take lunch in the village today. We are to stay out of your way. It seems you have your Castle back Mags."

"Well, this is a first. Are you listening to the Empress? This is strange." Mags shook her head and laughed.

"Wait. Mags tell me did you know the Hermit was Beatrice's Great-grandmother?" The Emperor glared at her.

"Four times great I believe Sir. You look astonished. I know a lot of things you don't Sir. Of course, I am much older. After all, I was the one who changed your diapers." She smiled.

"You love telling everyone that don't you. You didn't think I would want to know of this relationship after my Mother's death?" Everyone at the table watched Mags.

"I couldn't speak then Sir. I am sorry. I shouldn't be speaking now. If you weren't the Emperor, I wouldn't be speaking now." She picked up his plate and started for the kitchen.

"Wait, you have met the Hermit, haven't you?" The Emperor grabbed her arm.

She stopped and gave him a glaring expression then he released her arm. "Why of course I have met her. Since the death of your Uncle and his Bride, every High Sorcerer has met her and every Sorcerer at this

Castle. That was a terrible wedding day. Both dead and on their wedding day it was a dreadful tragedy."

The Count stood "What did you say, Mags about the wedding day, how did it happen?"

"Why their magical carriage was pulled right from the sky on their way to the nesting." Mags stopped, and her face went white as a sheet. "No. Sir, you are not thinking. Surely..." she looked around the table every face was colored grey or white. The Count practically fell back in his seat. Mags sat in the Empress's vacant chair.

The Professor wiped his hands over his face. "I should have seen this, I should have known. The old King has been working his plan for over a century. That is why he is outsmarting us. The Empress and the Hermit should know this. Mags, can we get a message to them?"

"I can catch them on a Pegasus if I leave now." The Count stood to leave.

Both Kathryn and Mags said at once, "That isn't necessary." Then they stopped and looked at one another.

The Prince said, "Wait, Kathryn how would you know?"

The Emperor said, "Kathryn if every High Sorcerer has visited the Hermit that means you have. I watched your face when Beatrice told us she is related to the Hermit you knew this, didn't you?"

The Prince said, "Father, please she is my wife. Now Kathryn, did you know we are relatives? Have you seen the Hermit and why aren't you with them? Why do we not need to send a message?"

Kathryn smiled at him, "I am sorry Dearest, I cannot say."

The Prince was turning red now he started to speak, but the Count held up his hand, "Prince, she has told us, Kathryn and Mags. The Hermit gave you a speechless spell, didn't she? Just nod once if that is true." They both nodded. "The Hermit is also the Prince's great-grandmother too which makes your children also her grandchildren. I would imagine she loves children having had so many of hers die. You visit often, don't you Kathryn?" Again, she just nodded.

The Prince looked furious, but said, "Our children have visited her?" She nodded. The Prince took in a breath. "You are privileged to know much about this woman and how she gains information. However, you can't talk to any of us about it. The Hermit and the Empress remembered the fall of Uncle's Carriage." Kathryn nodded. "Well, I think we should go to the Library."

"Again, not necessary I forgot to tell you the Elves came in this morning and said every room is clear. The cats and dogs are working. Eric did say not to trust that to be true this afternoon after the deliveries are made." Mags stood. "Will there be anything else your Majesty?"

The Emperor stood. "I will feel better in the library shall we Gentlemen? Mags we will have a private talk later; make time for me. Could you bring some refreshments about ten? Also, make sure the door is locked no one is to go near the library door when we are in town. Sorcerers…nothing but trouble." He snorted and walked out the door.

The Hermit

Beatrice was on her way, and she could feel a commotion at the Castle. Kathryn and Maggie were both giving out too much information. Even a confirmation of a nodded could ruin her plans. She needed to go get the Warlocks in control. She couldn't leave them to their own devices. She would have to concoct a divergence for them, especially Henry, he would be the one to fool. She also wanted to make sure her Grandchildren were safe. Which was hard to do from the top of Crystal Mountain.

She sat in her Library patiently waiting for the women to come to her, remembering. Her thoughts returned to the day her beloved Warlock had tricked her into one last romantic dinner before she became Empress. Of all times to spell her, during their lovemaking. Thank the Night she had a mirror close to reflect his power. He was a strong Warlock but never had he shown that much strength. His ego revealed it by throwing her onto the bed while a halo surrounded his body. She had known then he intended to overpower her, she grabbed her hand mirror from the nightstand. As he worked the spell, he restricted his own powers and rendered himself unconscious. At the time, she had a terrible feeling about her children. She ran to the children's room and found them next to death. He had placed snakes around their necks which almost drained them of their life-force. She called for a Wizard for healing, but only three of her ten children lived.

Unbelievable feelings of anger and hate had enveloped her; she almost encircled herself in flame. Yet, she had the presence of mind to use those feelings to destroy the Duke. She stole all his talents, ribbed out every one of his powers, carefully keeping him alive to feel all the pain. Then she deliberately squeezed every ounce of his life force while he begged for mercy. She found indescribable joy in torturing him; that scared her more than anything. She personally delivered his soul to hell along with his beating heart.

She held so much negativity and heat no one could come near her. She had to remove herself from the North Castle. She retreated to cold air, in the Antilles of Crystal Mountain. She began to release the heat and evil melting the ice and snow. She cut into the crystal stone to build her fortress. Now she lived in comfort on her mountain. She still contained more skills, talent, and knowledge than almost anyone. Her power was the difficulty; unless she used the evil power, she would not live. The Warlock's life force had increased her life by the seven children he killed. Who knew how many lifetimes she would live or how long it would be before she could release all the evil. Little goodness was left in her. Some days she couldn't find a glimmer of decency, she hoped her plan would give her life atonement. With age comes wisdom and knowledge; she wished to share some of that with her Grandchildren today.

Margareta felt the guest's presence long before they reached the mountain. She looked in on her cooks about lunch. "Madame." William one of her newest Sprite came to her, "Would you consider allowing Mary and I to serve your lunch today?"

"I thought you would want to see your cousin." Margareta kept a straight face she had planned on asking them anyway. It was hard for a Sorcerer to keep the wickedness contained. "Oh, alright you can, they are near. Go get Mary and meet me at the cave entrance you can both greet her too. William bowed and thanked her then rushed off to find Mary. Sprites were so cute; she could never be mean to them. It was one reason the Hermit filled her home with them; the other was, they were incapable of lying. She went to her closet and retrieved a heavy fur cloak which was a luxury she missed up until the last few years. She was finally cooling off after seven hundred years.

Two stable Sprites were already stationed to help the coachman. She rubbed her hands together and let the heat waves radiate out melting the snow buildup on the floor. The House Sprites joined her Mary bowed and said, "Thank you, Mistress, for allowing us to greet my cousin. We are so excited; we have not seen her since she was accepted at the Academy that was a long while ago. She has esteemed all Sprites being the first of our family to graduate, and with honors too."

The Hermit raised her eyebrow and corrected her. "Oh, you are almost correct, Mary. Marion is the first Sprite to be accepted into the Academy, much less graduate. I've had my eye on her for a while now. She will go much farther, much farther indeed, just as you two will." They both looked at one another and winked. Sprites never held back the Night had blessed them, she envied them. The carriage slowed and entered. The Coachman jumped down and opened the door, out came three bundled up magical creatures. The only way she could tell who she was greeting was by their power emissions.

Casandra jumped out first, "Casandra, you are a mighty powerful young lady may I hug you?"

Casandra opened her arms, "Of course, but I am upset why have I not been able to hug you before now? I only found out today you existed."

The Hermit smiled. "I will explain everything at lunch. First, Marion, I have some Sprites here that say they know you." Marion squealed and jumped down grabbing William and Mary.

The Hermit turned to Beatrice, "Grandchild it has been too long since I have been able to hug you. I hope your trip wasn't too cold. Let's get all of you in by the fire to thaw."

They climbed into the home of ice. Entering into a hallway to shed their coats and cloaks then settled by the fire in the tallest room Casandra had ever seen. The walls looked like sheets of topaz and opal, which were at less forty feet tall on two sides. A window as high as the walls offered a view of the mountains and the valley below. They were really at the top of the world. A large rug covered the floor with intricate red, blue, gold, and silver patterns woven throughout. On the opposite wall was a floor to ceiling fireplace of rose quartz. Many chairs and couches filled the room in small intimate groups. They chose the grouping in front of the fire with a hearth taller than Casandra's height. Sprites entered with hot tea and set it on the table between them.

Casandra's first look at the Hermit scared her, she was tall and skinny. Her bones in her face were severe, much like a skeleton. Her skin was creamy white like Casandra's, but she looked tired and drawn from worry or maybe sadness. Her full white hair was brought back in an elaborate braid which made her face look austere. Her lips were ruby red and her lashes and brows black. She wore a plain black velvet floor length dress. The neckline was up to her chin and sleeves covered half of her hands. Casandra looked down to see black laced boots with a small heel peeking out from her skirt. She looked young for her age, but her straight poker posture gave out the sensation of wisdom, power, and knowledge.

"You are correct Casandra I am a great force." Margareta smiled.

A smile made all the difference she was beautiful when she smiled. Her voice quality was as smooth and thick as the velvet she wore. Casandra cowered. "I am so sorry; I have lost my manners. I looked at you and could not help probing; please forgive me. You are captivating, your power and wisdom just flow from you. You are rather intimidating."

Margaretta threw back her head and laughed just like the Count. "You are pointedly honest; a quality I admire. You carry a little power yourself, Casandra. I fully understand Henry's adoration of you. Any man could hardly help himself from falling in love with you at first sight. The Night has blessed you. I believe I should give you girls some background of my life and how I came to be on this mountain, then you will be able to understand why I have asked you here for lunch." Margaret spent about a half hour telling her life story, briefly, with the lightest touch she could articulate. She finished by saying, "Let's go to lunch I am sure they are ready for us. You may ask me questions as we eat. I am certain you have a few."

They walked from the quartz wall of the fireplace to a cozy dining room. The walls were green like jade. A round table with a white tablecloth was filled with white dishes and crystal glassware gleaming. There was a beautiful ice sculpture of multicolored roses in the center with candles glowing in small glass votives. It would have been a dark room, but the sunlight was streaming thru a hole in the ceiling exposing a cave. The effect was ethereal as each layer of stone and crystal sparkled, drawing the eyes up. The Sprites were serving hot soup and bread while the girls were awestruck. The table was filled with fruits, cakes, and wine. Beatrice noticed the Count's wine, along with small petit fours no doubt taken from the North Castle.

"Now is the time for any questions, ladies?" The Hermit proceed to eat.

Marion straightened. "I have two questions. How should we address you, and are these walls made of jade, and how did you get a hole in your dining room ceiling?"

The Hermit laughed. "That is three, but I will answer all. The hole is natural. It appeared as I was carving out space. All the stones, crystals and gems are all part of the mountain; they are real. If you would spend time here, you could generate unlimited energies from them. I use them in spells and to communicate with others. When I first came to the mountain, I lived off them for years. I was too volatile to have live creatures of any kind around me. You can address me as Mistress, or Duchess which is simple.

Casandra said. "Mistress, I have a question. However, it is personal, it is about your Warlock."

"Yes, Casandra go on." The Hermit sat straight in her chair.

"I noticed you never spoke the name of the Warlock and in all the tales of you and him, his name is never revealed. Is there a reason for that?"

"Yes Casandra, there is a reason." She breathed in deeply, "I banished his name. No one in the world can speak it ever again. They may try, but there will be nothing but silence. It cannot be written; the ink will bleed. It can't be used by anyone, and it can never be remembered."

Marion looked to Casandra as if she was trying to tell her mentally not to trust this woman.

The Hermit broke the silence. "It seems harsh to you Marion, and it may well be. However, in my defense, power drains are a piece of magic we know little about. This Warlock was a power drain. Somehow, he sucked the very life out of my babies. They only felt fear and anger as they died. The Warlock was filled with evil, greed, ego, and lust. I was uncontrollable at the time this happened. I did not make the most logical or sensible decisions. Most of the evidence of how he had done this spell was incinerated by me in my grief. Every time I used his name my power increased. He put me into a never-ending well of anger and grief it took me years... Well, I had a lot to release. Some days I still find it hard to let it all go. I was in love with him, and I felt betrayed and hurt. You, young ones have felt heartache but not as intense as this was. Not yet, at least."

"What do you mean not yet?" Marion demanded.

"So… we get to the reason for your visit. I have gathered many talents from the powers I stole from the man, one of them is foresight. I am an Oracle. If you are finished eating, we will begin."

Casandra couldn't eat another bite after that announcement if she wanted. "I am finished, Mother, Marion?"

Her Mother patted her mouth with her napkin, "I am quite full, Mistress."

Marion took a drink of water. "I am ready."

"Well…Then let us go back into the large chamber by the fire we can take our drinks and let the Sprites clear the table." The Hermit rose and walked back around the stone fireplace. "Make yourself comfortable I will explain how we will proceed."

Everyone settled in, and she began, "Beatrice has been here before, so she has some idea. Yet, Beatrice, you have not had others with you, this will be different. I will begin by speaking to all of you. I will tell you the simple explanation of how we got here and the possibilities of the future. Afterward, I will speak to each of you privately. I will place a spell over those who should not hear by touching you once on the right hand. I will release you from the spell by touching you twice on the left hand. The spell will render you blind and deaf but just for moments. Are you agreed?" They nodded yes.

"You will not stop me for questions when I am speaking, hold those for the end. Realize I may not be able to answer all your questions. I will begin." She closed her eyes and took several deep breaths, then chanted a song sweet and bright. The language was foreign, yet it sounded familiar. The walls seemed to glow as if there were lights behind the gem and crystal walls. She ended with thanksgiving, then a spell that only the four could hear her words.

"The world will be calm as long as the Highest Sorceress only marries for convenience, alliance, or lust. When love comes into a Noble marriage, calamity strikes. It must be avoided unless the pair is balanced in the dynamism of love and knowledge. Girls, you both must understand every choice we make will open more paths. Casandra, your Mother and Fathers marriage, was one of an alliance, but it turned to love. Beatrice tried to correct the path, but the Emperor would not walk with her. He would not trust the future. The path that opened was the one which led to the deaths in his family including that of your Brother and Sister. When you were taken Casandra, she came for my help. I searched everywhere for you. I could feel strong magic hiding you I followed it night and day. One night you were dropped in the forest by the Monks' dwellings. Had I known what they had done to you; taking children too early and not the proper way, the heathens, I would have acted earlier. I didn't understand, so I have spent these twenty years learning." The Hermit stopped took a drink of tea then continued.

"The children they placed in the Count's wife were Casandra's. They learned the hard way; only blood can carry blood, they are so uneducated. They had one of my children in their clutches, she could have carried your babies. The Queen of Hex is one of my Granddaughters Elisabeth, Kenneth's wife."

Beatrice shouted, "She lives how?"

The Hermit only raised her hand her Mother sat back in her chair but angry and pouting. "He brought the carriage down to start a war. He spelled her and has kept her that way for years. Even now she is under his power. Once I found out I tried to remove her, but she would not leave her children. His spell is strong, and I am sure he is planning one even stronger for you, Casandra. The King is an idiot. He has no idea his son the Prince is a full wizard and not the son of Kenneth. The family is doomed. How I cannot say, but I know the King, and one of his men named Martin will die. There have been many plans spoken between them. The path they are on now is to have the Count take you to your nesting then exchange the Prince for him. That is one plan; it changes daily. The gems, moons, and stars tell another outcome. Is everyone clear?"

Marion sighed. "Unfortunately crystal clear."

The Hermit smiled. "Funny you should say that. William, will you bring my crystal ball from the library?"

He entered with it, and the Hermit thanked him. "I will begin with you, Beatrice." She touched the girl's hands and their eyes closed. Then she held the Empress's hand. "My Dear Grandchild, I fear to tell you too much. If the future is known all the Warlocks will tamper with it. The less they know, the safer you all will be. Besides plans are rearranging so quickly even the night stars are having trouble moving in tandem. You must not tell all these things to your Warlocks, do you understand?" Beatrice nodded.

"Well, you did your best. I supported you with the choice of the Count. Who knew he would be her love. I consulted the stars, and those wicked things hid the truth. Only now do they reveal the universal plan to me. Henry and Casandra are Selected Actualities."

Beatrice almost fell from her chair. "No Margaretta, will they live?"

"This the Night doesn't speculate. The Night wants its way no matter what. The stars and moons need Henry's children to transform our world. If the Hex King makes Casandra's children, we are all doomed. The King of the Hex only has six of her children left to implant. If they live... balance can never be restored. I can barely hold it now; the pendulum must swing the other way. The King is so imprudent; my Warlock was one just like him. The Hex believe they are chosen, but they only read the stars they want; never moons. The men are the only ones with power in their country. They drain their women's power to be stronger. The idiots don't understand our energies must be in balance. When their power dies completely, they will probably kill the all the women by draining too much of their power. There will be no magic left in our world."

Beatrice shook her head in disbelief. "What can I tell the Emperor and how much should Casandra know?"

The Hermit sighed. "I am still deciphering the stars and moons. I can say with certainty reveal the Hexian plan. You can tell them how they drain their women and how it is affecting the balance in our world. Do not say that Henry and Casandra are the Selected Actualities. There is no need to add that burden; you and I can carry that. The only solutions the gems have offered is to make sure Casandra and Henry have a child together. Implant Casandra early and give them time alone they will accommodate you. She must be pregnant before the nuptials. This part of the plan I will tell her. She will co-operate as she loves him. Could you stop in after the Ball? I will know more by then."

"Of Course, Grandmother." Beatrice was fighting all her emotions. Her baby, the one she created for herself was the Selected One. She felt a touch on her right hand.

Then the Hermit touched Casandra's hand twice. "Casandra, awake." The Hermit waited until she was fully cognizant. "Well, your Mother and I had a wonderful talk. I explained that the stars and moons were being uncooperative. I have told her she may not share my words with you, or the Warlocks. The Night has its reasons; we must trust them. You and Henry have fallen in love; it is a wonderful feeling. The Night is happy about it. Although it has had to change course a few times to remedy the outcome. That you can share that with Henry. The gems have shown that you can rectify this marriage. You need to be sure Henry, and you impregnate one egg as soon as you can. Carrying one child at a time would be wise. If the King does have his way with you, he will implant more children. His child dooms our world." Casandra turned white. The Hermit handed her a glass of clear liquid and told her to drink every drop then she continued. "His children will doom us all. If Devon's child is conceived, he will become the most powerful wizard and wisest magical creature our world has ever known. You may not tell anyone there is a possibility the King will take you, or that the Prince may take you. The children of Henry's and Devon's must live, but not the King's. Do you understand?"

Casandra swallowed dry air, then reached for her cold tea before answering, "I understand perfectly but why can't I tell Henry or my Father?"

"My lovely Granddaughter, Warlocks act differently when they are Fathers. The stars have said Henry would risk everything to keep you and the children safe. Which is a wonderful plan, however, the moon tells of too many outcomes. The most important one is Henry's child must live. You will sacrifice anything to keep Henry children safe; even your life. You may not share you would sacrifice your life to anyone. Do you agree?"

She looked deeply into the Hermit's eyes. She knew she was spelled, but the woman was so intense she could not resist. "Yes. Grandmother, is there anything else?"

"Yes, there is one thing more. If you have the opportunity, you must kill the King. However, you may not speak of this either. Now, before you take your holiday I want you to visit, bring Marion with you. I will keep reading the stars and moons. I will know more then." She leaned in and touched her right hand and then Marion's.

"Marion." Again, she waited. "I do love Sprites they are honest, astute, and loyal. They have common sense the other magical beings seem to lack. I trust you with this secret, but you must tell no one. I mean not even speak it out loud or think about it. Never think about it. Don't worry, I will spell you when we are done. You are the most important person in this room. Now, are you willing to help Casandra and her children? Are you completely loyal to her?"

"What kind of question is that. Do you think I would have come this far with Casandra had I not loved her? I vowed to protect her while we were at school. Of course, I will protect her children." Marion said indigently.

"I know, Marion. I have watched you both over the years. I chose you for the Academy you know."

Marion's jaw opened. "No."

The Hermit laughed. "Oh yes, the stars and moons helped me pick you out from among the Sprites. I saw to it you had everything you needed to succeed. I put you together as roommates, gave you a scholarship and gifted your parents with fabs. You have done exceeding well; beyond what I had hoped for. Now it is time that you repay me."

Marion froze. "Repay you? How? Why? I never asked for anything from you."

"No, there was no agreement with me. However, the Night gave you your life. That life belongs to the Night, this is at its command, not mine. I wish you and Casandra had religious training this would all be so much simpler if you just understood the old religion. You take from the Night every time you use your magic. When have you replenished that power and returned that gift?" Marion said nothing to that remark. "Very well, here are your tasks. You will go with Casandra everywhere, even at her nesting. The lives of Casandra's children depend on you. When the hour comes, her children live first; they trump everyone else's life. Is that clear my little Sprite?"

Marion hoped her spell worked she wasn't sure she couldn't share this with Casandra or Addison. "Mistress you are asking me to choose the children's lives over everyone else?"

"Yes. I see you do understand, even if you do not like it." The Hermit decided to give Marion information, maybe that would sway her. "Marion, you have a long life ahead of you. You must train with the Professor after this event is complete. I will send you to study at the University, and I am going to have you learn with the Monks as well. You will become a Professor and an advisor to the most powerful Queen that has ever lived. You are the centerpiece of the change in our world. Without you and the children, nothing will live, and all the magic will die forever. Now, do you agree?"

"If everyone dies along with magic, I realize I have no choice. I agree. What will happen to Addison?" Marion swallowed hard.

"Very good." The old woman smiled sweetly. "Addison loves you. Take love when it comes to you, Marion. You will have many loves, enjoy them all. Keep working with potions and learn the law. I will commence with the spell. Marion, you are compelled to remain with Casandra as her companion until the birth of her children. You will protect Henry's and Casandra's children at all costs. You will bring those children to me at the time of their birth. When asked, you will tell others I said you will train with the Professor, educated at the University and study with the Monks."

"Beatrice, Casandra, and Marion…Listen. You will not remember any of these spells, only that you are consumed to follow these instructions. Nothing and no one will stop you from the completion of your tasks. You will not question your feelings or share them with anyone. You will not have any thoughts about this in your head. No one can read your mind. Nothing and no one will stop you. You cannot speak of any of this to anyone. You are compelled. Do you understand?"

The three answered in unison. "Yes, Mistress."

She touched each of their left hands twice. "My Dears, you will be at peace, happy and rested. Awake." They all stretched and smiled, "I think we should continue this at another time, it is getting late. You don't want to be late for the State Dinner. I loved having you. Girls remember to stop by before you take your Season. I will have more information then." The Hermit stood and walked them into the entry, the Sprites entered with their coats and cloaks.

"I almost forgot, there is a bag of gifts for all of you in your carriage. However, I wanted to give Casandra an engagement gift. It is a finder's bracelet. Do you know what that is?"

Casandra shook her head. "No Mistress I have never heard of one."

"It is a jeweled bracelet with hidden powers to find the wearer. The stars told me to have you wear this on your holiday. It has four gemstones, have Henry place a drop of his blood on a gem, and the stone becomes a beacon to the blood donor. Wear it on your left arm always. All you must do to call Henry is place your right index finger over the gem. You can add as many as four people; the same method is used to call them. Only use it in case you need help. I would do a faceting spell to assure you don't lose it or have it stolen. It was my Grandmother's wear it well."

"Thank you. This could be the answer to not wearing my torque and crown."

The Hermit held up a hand. "Please tell Haden any Warlock that is worth his salt can spot that torque vanquished. Don't wear it while in disguise." She hugged each of them and walked them to their carriage.

Gregory got them all settled in and took off for the Castle. Casandra could hardly tell it was him he was so bundled up. They raced down the mountainside flying into the sky heading homeward. Just as the Hermit had said, there were presents on each of their seats.

Beatrice smiled, "I hope we make it home in time, Haden will be furious if we are late. She took an extensive amount of time to say little. I can only speak of the King's plot to the Emperor. I am sorry Marion, but there are things I can only speak of with Casandra."

Marion leaned back with crossed arms. "I can't remember half of what she told me, then she put a speaking spell and a compulsion spell on me. I don't like her!"

Casandra said, "Me, too. I can only say some things to Mother and others to Henry. A compulsion spell; what has she compelled you to do?"

Marion sat thoughtfully, "I can only remember the part about becoming your advisor. Everything else is hazy. She foretold I would be the Professor's student and go to the University. She also wants me to learn from the Monks, what a waste of time. I was so happy when I was there, now I am just plain mad." Marion was turning red.

The Empress chuckled. "Marion do not hold red as your color, it is very unbecoming. Why don't we open our presents."

Marion opened hers first and perked up. "It's a tiara of green emeralds how beautiful. She must have known my ball gown is green. Of course, she did. She is an oracle. Oh, it's lovely." She put it on her head, "There, how do I look? There is a card. It reads; the wearing of emeralds gives luck, love, and long life. You will know all three."

Beatrice said, "You look like a Queen. I believe I have some emerald jewelry you can borrow that will match." Beatrice unwrapped a golden book of their family tree. It was filled with family pictures and spells. "It has a card too which says, it is time you know all about the family. It says, 'To know the past reveals the future. We can only hope in our family this is not true. Please feel free to share this with Casandra and Kathryn. It is an interesting history lesson.' Well, at last, she is giving up some secrets. I hate her crypt notes; they always have a double meaning. Casandra, what did you get?"

"Let's see." She unwrapped her present which was a large old book. The book was titled, The History, Talents, and Customs of Diamentia. The book was tattered red leather with brass hinges and clasp; on the top was ancient words in Llianian. Casandra opened it to the first chapter was written in Llianian too.

Marion looked at the book, "I didn't do that well with ancient languages, but I am pretty sure the first chapter title reads War Spells. If the inside is filled with spells how would you know what they were? The inside looks as ancient as the cover; they are probably too old to work, what a strange engagement present. Is there a card?"

Casandra took the book and found one. "Yes. It reads, knows your foes, as well as your friends. That quote is not mine, but the author of this book noticed it. I thought you might like this book to learn more about the culture you are about to enter. The spells are for Count Rakie, potions are his pastime, he will find these interesting and helpful.

Casandra turned to the front page. "The author's name is Prince Nicholas Rakie. This book was written in the year 500."

Beatrice sat back, "Mags is going over every inch of these cards and presents. There are two more presents in this bag. One is marked for Kathryn and Bryan, the other is for Count Rakie." She sighed, "Do not try to probe them, girls. They might blow up in our faces, the old witch is having a little fun with us. This is what comes from being held up on a cold mountain for centuries. We have a lot of time before we get home. Let's change the subject to something more cheerful."

Marion jumped up. "How about wedding plans?"

The Realization

The meeting with the King and Martin was dragging on too long. His Mother would be in the stables waiting. They had dismissed Ernst long ago he needed to find a way to leave.

"Devon! You aren't listening to a word we are saying." The King was standing.

"Yes Sir, you are right Sir. I don't know what is wrong with me my mind is racing, I apologize." Devon was embarrassed.

"Don't be too hard on him Sir, he did his first Attachment today." Martin smiled.

The King came around his desk and pulled Devon into a hug. "You should have said. That was quick. I should have known you would be a natural at this. Well, I understand completely. I remember my first I couldn't think straight for a week. You need fresh air and some action."

Martin said, "He fought with three men, and won all three matches. I was watched Devon fight as fiercely as you. You can be very proud of him your Majesty."

"I am, Martin I couldn't have asked for a better Son. This is only the beginning for you Devon; the things I will show you. Ah, the gifts and talents you will have, the world will be your Son. I will be supporting you all the way. Go get some fresh air take a walk or ride. We can go over our plans after dinner. Martin, can you stay?"

"Certainly Sir." Martin stood. "I will get Ernst to keep him company. Then I will return." They walked out to the Castle courtyard together.

"I will be fine by myself Sir." Devon was hoping to be alone. Ernst appeared, coming out of the stables.

"Ernst," Martin walked over to him, "Could you keep an eye on our Prince? He did his first attachment today. We don't want him running into any trouble."

Ernst nodded, "Really? Well, I think I can handle that. Besides, I have something to show him in the stables. A new colt was born. Come to see, Devon."

Devon was getting mad why they were all treating him like a child. He huffed off to the stables while Martin watched.

"In here Devon! Matilda had a beautiful new foal!" Ernst smiled, "Your Mother can never resist babies she is in the stall."

Ernst stepped back and closed the door to the barn, giving Devon and his Mother privacy.

Devon released a breath to try and expel his anger. "Mother, I must apologize again my days are not going as planned." He went to her and hugged her.

That one action gave Elizabeth all the information she needed. Her heart fell, was he lost to her already? Attachments were evil, the more Attachments made, the more goodness would be consumed. Then nothing but evil and power existed.

"Devon, I know what has happened to you. I will tell you what you are experiencing. You took someone's power, and it was exhilarating. That power wore off, now you are using your own power to stay in that euphoric state, and it is waning. You are beginning to weaken, and like all of us when we are weak, the negative powers creep in. You must learn to push evil down, imagine it flowing down your body and leaving your feet sinking into the ground. Close your eyes and do that now."

Devon did, and he could feel the anger and despair sinking beneath him. "That seems to work Mother, thank you. But how did you…" He stopped himself. The last thing he wanted to talk about was her Attachment.

"My Dear boy how do you think we Sorcerers remain calm. This is one of the techniques we are taught at a young age. There are others I will share. Devon, you must not leave a person attached to you. It is a double-edged sword. If you continue to use them for power and sex, the Attachment will grow into you. A bond forms that can only be severed by death. When one dies so will the other. Power is an addiction; the more you have, the more you want to attain. The first is one of the most powerful. Hopefully, you took a low powered person, the higher the power, the higher you will become. However, remember the fall. It can kill you, and them."

Devon stepped back and for the first time saw the fold. "They say I will learn to detach tomorrow it cannot come too soon. I did feel the overwhelming power at first, but the longer I am away from the Witch, the more I am drawn to her. Mother, I worry about you and my Sisters. I do not want this for them." He got down and petted the small horse as he nursed at his mother.

Elisabeth almost fell back into the stall. She clutched the boards to hold her, thank goodness Devon was paying too much attention to the colt to notice. What could Elisabeth tell him? What should she? It was time for truth. The King was out of control, and somehow, she felt responsible.

"Devon, I was so young when I married, I knew nothing of the real world. I fell from the sky and saw Ernst family obliterated. We saw all of Arlequin eradicated. I didn't know then the Hex had done the same to other countries. To keep my children safe I stayed. Your Father was happy to have a Prince for his Kingdom. He Attached me, he said it was part of wedding customs. After that, the King used me for power but more for information about Sorcerers and the secrets of the hierarchy. I think he knows Ernst is your Father, even though I told him I wasn't sure if you were his or Kenneth's. He attached to Ernst to try to find out. Ernst and I spelled each other to keep secrets from him."

She stopped and listened. "We have some time yet, the dance between Warlocks and Sorcerer is a delicate one. In Marias, we are taught to share the power to give and take which creates more power for both. A Sorcerer is the most powerful of all the magical creatures, it is our responsibility to control and dispense power. The King does not like that system; he wants the Warlocks to be the most powerful, and he uses Attachments to do that. He developed his own system of schools, reproduction, and all the customs and rules to support it. Your Sisters are lost to me, and you will be soon. We are all nothing more than his experiment to create his new world." She turned away from him never could she look into his eyes again.

Devon went to her and hugged her, "Mother you will never lose me I love you. I know I will never lose that feeling." He cupped her face in his hands. "My Sisters have already been Attached, that is why I cannot feel their powers or know their talents?" She closed her eyes and shook her head yes. "Who?" She turned away. "I will kill him." He walked to the stall door.

"Devon stop!" Ernst was in the doorway. "You will do nothing of the sort. Think! I have taught you to think, use your mind boy. Your Mother was told years ago by a Prophet you would find out all of this on your own and if that happened, it would only lead to disaster. The King is more powerful than you, he would only use an Attachment on you to control you. She told us our only hope of redemption is to tell you the truth ourselves and help you maneuver through all this. I am so sorry about this, Devon. I should have never trusted, never befriended the King." Ernst grabbed him into a hug.

Devon fell into Ernst's arms sobbing. "How will we be free and not lose all the ones we love?"

"I don't know Son. I only know, now you are still free. Your Mother and I will do everything to keep you that way." Ernst pushed Devon away from him and looked him in the eyes, "You must treat him the same, play his game for now. You have always resisted him; you can still do that slightly. Now you are an even player, you can manipulate him as he has you. He has sent me to care for you. So, we will take a long ride together and talk. Come with me, Son."

His Mother came to Devon and stretched up to kiss his cheek, she smiled at Ernst, and he took her hand and squeezed it. There was an exchange he was not privileged to. "The King summons me. He is going to tell me Martin is to marry Janet." Devon stiffened. "It will be alright Devon, she wishes it. Try to be happy and excited for her and your mentor." Ernst was there with horses. "Don't be late for dinner, there will be a party." The Queen hurried off.

As they were riding away from the Castle, Devon turned to Ernst, "How does she do that, be around him?"

Ernst smiled. "Very easily Son. She loves us. That is how."

"Ernst? I just realized you almost always call me Son. I can remember Father, I mean the King, being upset by that." Devon looked at Ernst.

"You must continue to call him Father, Devon. It does not bother me in the least. However, it irks him when I call you Son." He laughed, "That is why I do it. You will start to notice little things like that now. Your Mother always calls him King and I never spend the night in the Castle when he is there. You want to know if your Mother and I are still lovers? I think a simple yes is all you need to know." He smiled again.

Devon felt his heart lift a hundred times. Just to know they still had each other was all he did need. He loved them both so much. "Father, I am afraid I made a mistake with Moondale the other day. I told him I could feel the level and talent of some Warlocks and Witches. The Professor questioned me about it."

Ernest nodded and said. "I see; he is questioning your talents. You think he is wondering if you are my Son."

"Maybe. Part of my homework was to measure my family. I failed deliberately. He suggested I had picked up some of these talents just by living with you. He asked me to talk to you and see if it was possible. If that was the case, I suggested I would ask you for some personal training. He thought that was a brilliant idea."

"Good deflection, Son. I will think this over and talk with your Mother. I had always avoided teaching you. I thought the King would be outraged." He picked up his hat and ran his fingers through his hair. Devon recognized this as the same gesture he used when he needed to clear his head.

The Ruse

The Queen entered the King's office, and Richard walked to her and hugged her, softly touching her neck. She would have to tell the truth. "You smell like the stables."

Martin stood. "Ah, my Queen couldn't be kept away from that new foal. You are as beautiful as ever." He came to her and took her hand bowed and kissed it, "Even when you smell like stables." He laughed.

The King laughed too. "I should have guessed. You and your children, it doesn't matter if they are human, magical, or beast; you claim them all my Dear. But Martin, how did you know of this? A guess?"

Martin stood behind his chair and offered it to the Queen. "No, I don't have that talent, reading minds and such. I found Ernst at the barn when I took the Prince. Ernst said he wanted to show Devon a new foal. Do we have a stallion or mare, your Majesty?"

The Queen took his chair. "A beautiful stallion, of course, I should say handsome. It is good to see you Martin; you will stay for dinner. We must hear all your news; the girls will be over the moon to see you."

The King sat in his chair across from her while Martin placed another chair beside her. Richard could only think of Ernst and her in the stables together, he pushed down the jealousy. "Did you see Devon?"

"Yes. Devon came to play with the foal." The Queen looked squarely at him she could feel his anger.

"How was he?" Richard was speaking as calmly as he could and hoped no one could see he was still covetous after all these years.

She knew she had to be truthful or choke. The King would probably let her die if she lied. The only power she had left was Devon. He knew she could divide him from his Son, his sole heir. "I know King." He looked shocked, "I am not pleased you let him attach and didn't teach him to release on the same day." She was annoyed and let him know it. "If you must play these games at least be safe with him. He was tense, angry, and nervous. How did you think he would be?"

The King turned red, then Martin started to speak, but she stopped him. "I am sorry Martin; I should not have spoken like that in front of you. King, I am sorry, it was not even your fault. It's that blasted Professor. He just goes off and does as he please." That seemed to placate him. "Well, playing with the colt calmed him down some. Ernst came with horses and said he needed to ride. I told them not to be late for dinner, but with those two, they will be eating late. Is that why you called me here?"

Martin decided to step in between these two before the rug caught on fire. "No, If I may King?" He looked to the King, and he gratefully nodded. "I have extended an offer of marriage to Janet. With the permission of you and the King, of course." He was almost happy to have the attention brought to himself.

The Queen turned in surprise. "Marriage, good grief Martin. I am shocked." She saw his face drain, "Oh, no Martin. I am not upset just surprised. You are already like family now, and I do care and admire you. I could not have chosen a better match for any of my girls. It is just...well, I thought you were a confirmed bachelor. You will surprise the country with a marriage. So many women will die of a broken heart when they hear of this." He started laughing, "What I think matters little, what does the King think, and Janet?"

The King was laughing too. "I did not know of your reputation with the women Martin, perhaps I should rethink this. No, I think you are just fine for my daughter. I see how she listens to your every word. I think she will be pleased. Now that I know you are in such high demand with the ladies, she may even begin to like me as her Father."

Martin held up his hand. "Please the chatter of women, that is the only reason I have not married. Janet is the only one of your daughters who doesn't chatter. Of course, her beauty may have something to do with it. To your concerns my Queen; I am ready to slow down and have a home of my own. A comfortable place to rest at night in peace with a family of my own."

"Well you are in for a shock once you have children you will never have peace. They do give you a purpose, don't they my Dear?" The King looked at his wife, there were tears in her eyes. "Grandchildren!" She looked at the King and smiled as if he had given her the world. "I have to go! I need to...oh, my. I don't know where to start. Dinner first dinner. Now it will be late because I must make it very special. Oh, I will send Janet out to the garden alone to pick flowers. You may talk to her there." She started out the door then ran back and kissed Martin. "Oh, I am so happy! Welcome to the family Martin." She started for the door again then ran back to the King, "You are going to be a Grandfather!" She threw herself into his lap and gave him the best kiss he could remember having from her.

The King was laughing, "My Dear, if I knew you would react like this, I would have consented to marry the girls off long ago." She kissed him again, and she was out the door. "I am overwhelmed; my life is going to be wonderful." The Queen pulled Martin out of the chair, "You had better get out in the garden. Bring her back to the kitchen with you when you have convinced her." Martin only laughed.

The King sat back in his chair while thinking that went much better than expected. The Queen was happy, not something he had seen for a while. Martin was his best man and friend since the two joined the Hex army together. Now he could make Martin second heir to the throne. If his plan backfired, he was assured his country could continue to grow. Martin was privileged to all the countries secrets, and he had trusted him with Kenneth's son. Giving him Janet, his first child was easy for him. The whole day was a surprise. When he asked for advice on who he should consider for marriage for his daughters, the King had no idea Martin would recommend himself. Everything in his life was going perfectly; he was going to enjoy it. Yet the King had an uneasy feeling. He went to the window and watched as Martin made his proposal to Janet. She threw her arms around him, he could see smiles and tears. Well, his baby was one happy child. He knew she was his daughter, and she would give him many heirs with Martin. They were coming to see him he watched them make the turn to his office.

His young lieutenant knocked on his door. "The Prince and Ernst have returned your Majesty. They have requested to see you."

"Send them in Lieutenant." He was under the impression they would be late for dinner. Martin and Janet entered with them. Janet ran to him. "Thank you. I am so happy!" She threw her arms around him. She was so much like her Mother. He hugged her back, "I am too sweetheart. Martin is a fine man, and he will be a wonderful husband and Father."

Devon came to her. "What's this, you are marring Martin? When were you going to tell me?"

Martin came over to him and put his arm around his shoulder. "It was just decided today. Your Father asked who I thought Janet should take as a husband. I have waited years wondering if the King would agree to have me for Janet. I am as happy as her."

"Well, I guess I must endure you at home as well as work. What do I call you, General Brother-In-Law?" Devon laughed.

Martin hugged him. "We will just keep it, Martin, at home, General at work."

The King was elated Devon his daughter and best friend all loved one another. "Well, I have thought of giving you the Morris Castle. It will give you privacy, and it is still close enough to satisfy your Mother's need to spoil your children."

Martin stood motionless, the King knew he was shocked. He had always paid Martin well, but he wanted his little girl to have everything. The property was the best in the Kingdom, and the profits from it would make Martin one of the wealthiest men in the Kingdom.

"I am speechless." Martin could hardly react.

Devon hugged his Sister and whirled her around the room. "Well, this is the first time she hasn't been talking my ear off, Janet I love you. Congratulations. I hope you're up for this man he is very demanding." He turned to Martin. "This is my favorite Sister; you better take good care of her Martin."

Martin smiled and held up both his hands. "Don't you think I know that? Your Father has already threatened me." He reached for Janet's hand, "You have nothing to worry about, I happen to love her." As they looked at one another Devon could see he was in love with her and she with him.

Janet walked to him. "We have been in love a long while. Finally, we can show it." They held onto one another tightly.

Ernst walked over to them. "Congratulations to you both" He winked and shook Martin's hand.

"You better go talk with your Mother, Janet. Martin, you are about to be the center of attention, go let her show you off." The King sat in his chair as Martin and Janet walked out the door still holding hands.

"Ernst, you don't look too surprised did you know about them?"

"Yes, your Majesty, I accidentally caught them kissing one night. I promised I would not tell anyone. The General was afraid you would not approve." Ernst sat across from the King and Devon sat next to him.

"Well, he was wrong. I have always liked that Warlock he is a good man. The only one I trusted to mentor you, Devon. To know he loves her makes all the difference. Devon, is she really your favorite Sister?"

"Yes Sir, she is. I remember when she was born she was the first baby I ever held, perhaps that is why." Devon looked happy too.

"Your Mother led me to believe you would be late today. She said she saw you at the stables." The King wanted to ask more but would wait to see what this was about.

"Well, Sir Ernst and I were talking. I told him the Professor noticed I could sense power and talent. Moondale has been questioning me about it. He has this notion I picked it up from Ernst. He asked if I could have Ernst work with me."

The King sat quietly, one hundred things went through his mind. The largest one was wondering if Ernst was Devon's Father. The day he uncovered that nothing would stop him from killing Ernst. The only thing that stopped him now was his use as a restraint over Elizabeth. "I see. Ernst, what do you think about this?"

Ernst sat up straight. "Sir I don't know how that can be. That doesn't mean it could not be true. It may be a trait that is inherent to Llianians to pass on powers to those they live with for a long while. However, anyone who could verify this is no longer with us. It worried me, Sir. He gave Devon homework, it included testing his abilities on his family."

"What, do you mean? Devon, did you do this, test us?" The King was shocked. Just then there was a knock at the door.

"Sir, General Martin is back."

The King was relieved Martin could help sort this out. "Martin come in. You must hear this. Devon repeat all that you have told me to Martin."

Martin pulled up a chair and listened. "Did you experiment on your family, Devon?'

Devon thought Martin knew he was Ernst's son too. He hoped this plan was going to work. "Yes, I tried, but I couldn't really read much. I have always known of Father's and Mother's power, I am accustomed to it. I told Moondale maybe it isn't possible with Warlocks and Witches you always have known. He asked me to have Ernst work with me. I thought talents had to be inherited." His Father was taking the bait, now where was Mother?

Martin said, "I don't think it would hurt to try and work on these talents. I just find it odd you are thirty years old, and this is the first sign of them. Surely they would have shown before now."

The Lieutenant announced the Queen. "Why are you all locked up in here? It is almost dinner."

Devon stood. "Nothing much, I was just telling Father about the Professor."

The Queen came all the way in and shut the door. "You're not going on about the new talents he thinks you have? I told you that is preposterous. No one can gain talents from another. The only way that can happen is through blood." She turned to go then stopped. "Ernst, do you remember when Devon fell off that cliff and broke his leg?"

"Why of course, I would never forget that." Ernst looked at Martin.

Martin picked up the clue. "Nor will I, we rushed you to the healers, but still you had lost too much blood. Ernst gave up his. Do you think that would have done this but why haven't they showed up before?"

The Queen shook her head, "I have no idea our clan doesn't deal in blood, only Diamante's as far as I know do. Come, dinner will be cold."

"Wait this is perfect, the Count will be here in a few days we can find out from him." Devon looked pleased with playing his part.

The Queen cried, "Count Rakie is coming? No one tells me a thing around here. Yes, Devon, we can persuade him with a nice dinner. I like him he is so handsome and sexy." All the men crossed their arms and rolled their eyes. "You're all just jealous. Maybe we could wed one of our other girls to him?"

"Mother, he prefers men! Stop trying to marry everyone off. Am I to be next? Let's go to dinner just to end this conversation." Devon walked out of the room after his Mother, the others left laughing. They had done it; set the groundwork for the Count to test his blood. His Mother said she would handle the rest, he had no idea what was planned. All they told him; they were securing the throne for him and protecting themselves.

The dining room was filled with a hundred candles, and flowers were everywhere. Devon stopped as he entered. "If this is a celebration dinner what will the wedding look like? General, don't hold too still they will have flowers in your hair."

The King walked in, "I can't believe you did this all in a few hours, Elisabeth. I think I need to have you come to organize my army. We can't even break a camp that fast." He walked to her and kissed her.

Ernst was right behind him, "This is a lot of fuss for dinner, King."

"Don't let the girls hear that, let's pour the wine and get seated. Where are these girls anyway?" The King took his usual chair, and everyone else sat where the Queen directed them.

Janet walked in, and Martin stood. The King had never seen her look more beautiful. She was dressed in a pale blue shimmery gown which matched her eyes. She was the only one of the girls with blue eyes and black hair. He couldn't describe the dress but knowing Janet it had to be the latest fashion. She was a good student and a very powerful Sorcerous, but she was by far the most charming and popular girl at the school. She had been the Queen of the Seasons dance, every boy there clamored for her attention. He was glad those days were over he had run more boys from their door between his two oldest daughters than he had in any war. Jessica was still young, but this evening she looked every bit a woman. He wondered if Janet had dressed her. She was in a yellow gown which brought out her green eyes and blond hair. Jessica was his smartest and brightest girl. She could rule the Kingdom easily if she could learn not to giggle. He had thought her a pretty girl, but this evening she looked sultry.

Joan, his baby, was next to be seated. She looked the most like him with reddish blond hair and deep emerald eyes. She had a lovely pink dress, but she still looked like a little girl. They were still learning about her powers. He thought she would be the most powerful of all his children. It was hard to teach her anything. Like him, she would rather be up a tree or on a horse than anywhere, his favorite was Joan.

Devon had looked like Elisabeth, handsome with her beautiful features and her dark hair. He never understood his emerald eyes, if he were Ernst and Elisabeth's they would be black or if he were Kenneth's, they would be blue. Maybe it would be a good idea to have him tested. Unless the test proved, he was Ernst's son. The Generals would be there too; did he want them to know of his doubts? He would have to consider this carefully.

Martin stood held up his wine glass. "I propose a toast to the loveliest girl in our world, Janet. I will proudly call her wife. She has my love and my life, forever."

Everyone toasted and talked and laughed throughout dinner. Richard remembered times they were young, and everyone spoke of memories of the King's Father. Dinner went on for hours; everyone was so happy, no one wanted the meal to end. Joan couldn't stay awake any longer, so the Queen and Jessica took her to bed while Martin went off with Janet. The men went to the library.

Devon took a chair next to the fire. Ernst said his Goodnights and told Devon he would be there in the morning to escort him to school.

After Ernst left Devon said, "I think Ernst was hoping to have some direction as far as the Professor is concerned."

King poured them both a liquor, then handed one to Devon. "I am still thinking about it. I don't trust the Count, Son. Once we hand him the antidote, we have lost the only leverage we have. His life is something he values, not much else."

"Well, there must be something he loves. Threaten him with his life again, or someone he loves." Devon took a sip, "This is fine liquor."

"We had a hold over him with his last wife, I wish he loved this new one. We could use her, or maybe his Mother. Devon…I have raised a smart young man. What would you do to save your Mother?"

"I would do whatever I needed to do, for her or any of my family, even Ernst. After today I should add Martin to that list." Devon gave the King a genuine smile of love.

The King went to Devon placed his hand on his shoulder and said, "Son, I love you. I am so proud of you. I could not ask for a better Son you have gone beyond my hopes and dreams. We have a long way to go yet."

The Queen walked in just then. "I heard the last part, I think the only place Devon should be going is to bed, you have an early morning. Learn to detach as soon as you get there. Tell that Professor the Queen orders him as if that means anything around here."

"Yes, Mother." He chuckled and kissed her on the cheek. "I think you have some influence. Finish my drink for me. I have had enough alcohol, Goodnight Father."

"You to Son. Join me, Elisabeth." The King stoked the fire.

"That was a wonderful dinner everyone was so happy, but you were silent." She sat in the chair across from him. "Something is going on in your head do you care to share?"

"Oh, I think it was all the memories. I tried to remember a time with my family that was warm, loving, and enjoyable like tonight, I couldn't. Father was never warm or happy. My Mother died when I was so young I hardly remember her at all. We never had such an elegant and delicious dinner like the one you prepared. Tonight, I became aware for the first time in my life I have everything I have ever wanted. It is right here with my family; I am turning into a sentimental old fool." The King sipped his drink.

"If that is so, I happened to love old fools, so you're in luck." She sipped her drink. "This is delicious liquor; we should get more. We should have more nights like this." She looked at him lovingly.

"Yes, I agree." He had loved her with all his heart and never believed she would return that love. Now the way she looked at him, perhaps he had been wrong. Maybe controlling her love was wrong. He would not think of that now. She was here with him and still so beautiful. "You look gorgeous tonight did I tell you?"

"No, you did not, thank you. Come to bed with me my King?" She stood came to him and took his hand. "It's late."

He was so taken back, tears rose in his eyes, "Yes but it's not that late. Is it?"

She threw her arms around him. "No, it is not too late."

The Queen

It had been the first night in years that she had willingly made love to the King. She did love him; she just couldn't live with him any longer. At times, he could be the most charming loving, sweet, and sincere man. But that was rare, and when he overdosed on power, he was irrational, nervous, jealous, and angry. He could never just love her, he only used her. Now he would be teaching Devon the same addicting habit. She would not tolerate it. Elisabeth was never courageous, but the King had driven her to her wit's end she would need to find some bravery for her Son. She only prayed the Hermit could help. The Hermit had come years ago to offer her help, and the Queen refused. Her children were young, and Elisabeth held hope for them. What had she done to her darling girls, she should have taken her offer.

The girls were the King's daughters, in body and soul, he created himself in their spirit. Just before Devon returned from this last trip, her youngest had her eggs removed and her Attachment placed. Their powers and eggs were the King's. The poor girls weren't even aware of his control. The first time she saw she wanted to die. One night she awoke to find the King missing from his side of the bed. She tried to go back to sleep, but she felt something was wrong. Her first instinct was to check on the girls. A light was showing from under the door of Janet's room. She cracked the door to find the King standing over her bed draining power from an Attachment. She screamed and ran at him with all her energy. He subdued her effortlessly, that very day he created a jail in their bedchambers and concealed it. He still placed her there if she didn't follow instructions. He caged her when the girls were taken in for the ceremony. He had created a ritual for every young girl in Hex and Bezier to break and control their power. Soon every Witch in his Kingdom would be under his control. Now it would be Devon's turn to learn the Attachment spell. Her last child would find himself under an attachment if he didn't follow the wishes of the King. Devon was already questioning too many things. It would not be long until he would defy the King, as she and Ernst tried to do.

After the King fell asleep, she went to the garden and burnt the green note the Hermit had given her years ago. With the help of the Night, it would still work to summon her. She hoped that in all the commotion of the wedding and his nefarious plans for Devon, he would be too busy to notice much of what was happening. The Count was the one the Hermit said would help her years ago maybe he would help her now. She had done the best she could with the help of Ernst to give the Count the opportunity to do a blood test. She needed to make sure the King believed Devon was his son. If he did, no Attachment would be placed on him, and there would be a chance for Devon.

She came back to bed with the King, but sleep would not come to her. Her mind flew back in time. She had met Ernst at the Academy, he was dashing and charming, and he swept her off her feet. She loved Ernst long before she married; he was too low in the hierarchy for a liaison or marriage. Plus, he was a Wizard. She had thought the Night had blessed her when he was at her bedside telling her Kenneth was dead. At last, they could be together, let her family consider her dead. They only cared about the hierarchy, but the war ended that dream, and they were both captured.

Richard came and saved them both from execution. When he found out she was carrying an egg, he persuaded and spelled her. After the marriage and Attachment, the King had put a truth spell on her at least once a week and questioned her at length. He asked everything he wanted to know about Sorcerers power and reproduction. She like a fool told everything, including her love for Ernst. He was so jealous of

Ernst, as he should be, he placed an Attachment on him. Ernst loved her still even when she was utterly unattainable, he would not leave her. The truth spells never stopped. She learned over the years how to trick Richard and had become a master of omission. She hoped he would be too occupied to bother her for a few weeks.

She had been a coward for so many years; he would not expect an act of bravery. She remembered from school that battles were sometimes won by confrontation, but more frequently won by simple surprised. Well, this would be a surprise. She had suffered much but would continue to suffer to protect her children. She had failed her girls; she couldn't lose Devon.

The first principle of magic taught was magic was not a gift; it required payment, the Night would ask her payment. She was wrong to give in to the King; not once did she fight him until the evening she found him with Janet. She thought she repaid her mistakes with the loss of Ernst, but then the girls were lost to the King one by one. Admittedly, she had paid a large enough price; she deserved to win Devon's freedom. She hoped she would be redeemed by offering of help.

She was in the kitchen the next morning helping the cook when a crow landed on the window sill. The cook screamed, and the raven flew around the kitchen; he was flying into walls, the pots, and pans that were hanging. The King came in sword drawn. "What's all the screaming about?"

"One of your crows came in the window. I thought you had trained these nasty birds to enter your library window it nearly scared Cook to death. Could you catch it for us?" The Queen was ducking to keep from being pecked. "Don't you dare kill the thing and get blood all over my clean kitchen."

He took a towel and threw it and caught it in an instant. He inspected it and said, "This isn't one of my birds this is a common crow. I'll put it in a covered basket, have someone take it out to the field and release it. If you let it go close to the Castle, it will fly back in for food." He stuck the bird into a covered basket and set it on the cutting table.

"I'll take care of that chore myself. I need to go into the village for wheat and milk. Having everyone at home is expensive. I haven't cooked this much in years. We will need to send men to hunt as well.

Will you invite the Count for dinner tomorrow?" The Queen hoped for a yes.

"That will be entirely up to him, my Dear. He is an independent man. I never know what to expect from him. I don't trust him or rely on him for anything. It is hard to manipulate a man like him." The King frowned.

The Queen threw back her head and laughed. "Love, do you not remember your tactics classes at the Academy? Men are the easiest to manipulate. Henry is no different. Why are wars fought Richard?"

The King crossed his arms and started to turn red before he realized she was helping him. "Wars are fought for land, riches, religion, and righteousness. Oh, I forgot one, power. The man has all the riches and land he could want or need, he told us that. He holds no religious beliefs, and there isn't a righteousness bone in his body. He told my Generals he had no intention of becoming King or Emperor; we needed to find another incentive. Power, I wonder what power would be great enough to entice him."

The King looked intensely at her uncrossed his arms and walked to her, grabbed her and threw her into the air. "You are a genius, remind me to talk with you more often." He kissed her hard on her lips, then deeper.

She turned red. The King had never done that in front of servants. "Well, if I get kisses like that I will." She winked at him. "What time do you want dinner, Sir?"

"Make it after dark. I have a long day of meetings. I am going to have a surprise inspection of the soldiers as an excuse to visit the Professor. You were right in criticizing him, sometimes he goes too far." He released her.

The Queen reached up and caressed his face. "Thank you for talking to him, Richard. I know my lion nature comes out whenever the children are involved." She kissed his cheek. "I like seeing that quality in you."

She knew he could tell everything she said was the truth and hoped calling him by his name wasn't overplaying. She could only pray to the Night it was enough to convince him she was on his side. He squeezed her hand and smiled a broad smile. "I'll see you at dinner, but wait till we are in the bedroom to ask about the Moondale alright?"

"As you wish I need be off to the village."

The Queen turned to go, he grabbed her hand, "Take a man with you I don't want you to be alone in town."

Maybe he wasn't so convinced. "Of course, I was going to take Grayson, all the others are busy with all our children home. Would you rather I take a soldier?"

"Not at all. Grayson was attached to an Army General for years, he can handle anyone. I just don't want you traveling outside the Castle unprotected. Just now we need to be very careful." The King was being called by his Lieutenant meetings were starting. He kissed her again and left the kitchen.

Her insides were churning; she didn't know if she was strong enough to do this. Concealing from the King took power, and she couldn't use much, or he would become suspicious. Grayson was at the back door with the carriage. She picked up the crow and headed out. "Do you have the list, Cook? Grayson is ready."

Bernard had been their Cook for years; hired by the King and one of his reliable spies. It took him years to get close to the Queen, she trusted no one. He couldn't blame her; he would feel the same way if he were in her position. He had finally made some progress over the past year. "Yes, your Majesty, I have it right here. The King seems to be in a rare good mood today. He is treating you exceptionally well. All the years working for you I have never seen him kiss you. Today he kissed you often." He handed her his shopping list. "If the Count stays for dinner we should have some good wine. He is so particular."

The Queen gave him a big smile it was easier fooling one of Richard's spies than the King himself. "Yes, he is, and I am utterly enjoying it. Maybe things are going well for him, we can only hope. Serve him delicious dinners! I want him to treat me like this forever." She put her best look of being in love on her face and hurried to the carriage, so she could stop pretending. "I will see about getting wine for the Count."

Grayson helped her into the carriage, "Are you feeling alright your Majesty? I could go into town for you. I don't mind."

"No Grayson, I am fine. Let's go." Mentally she told him about the crow, and the Hermit was feeling claustrophobic in the small basket.

Grayson hurried through the Castle courtyards as fast as he could without arousing suspicion. Once out of the Castle, he trotted the horses to a place in the field where he knew no Castle Guards could watch them. "I think we are in the clear Madam, far enough away from the Castle but not too close to town. You should take her into the field and speak away from the road. We can never know who will be riding up and down this road."

The Queen took the basket into the field and opened it. The Hermit puffed out of the basket and began to arrange her clothing and hair. "I have forgotten how uncomfortable it is to be small. It takes a lot of effort to suck yourself in. I am so happy to see you, Elisabeth, you look well. I am surprised at the power you're holding. We must be fast the King still doesn't completely trust you. Also, did you know the Cook is his spy?"

"Yes Mistress, I have been learning how to hold back my power. I realized about the Cook last year and decided to gain his trust, he may be of use to me someday. Grayson is the only friend I trust, other than Ernst. I was going to contact you this summer. I had hoped to get Joan away from here. I was going to stage her death. The King took my baby earlier than the others. He placed me in my cell during her ceremony, and now it is too late for her. The Attachment has hooked into her. Only his death will release the girls now, but I don't know what the effect would be on them."

The Hermit stood up straight. "Elisabeth that would mean your death. You are not actually thinking...what are you thinking? Why did you call me?"

"I have decided I could die happily if my girls were free. You mustn't tell anyone, do you understand? Ernst and Devon would do everything to stop me, they don't understand. I can't live attached to him any longer. No one knows how depressed and hopeless it makes me feel. This is my choice, others would foolishly try to save me, and that would save him. Every Witch born in this country is under someone's control. It stops now, with me. I have been a coward long enough. Ernst and I have a plan, but we must act quickly, once my oldest Janet is married, her husband will have control of her too. If we don't convince the King that Devon is 99 percent his child and 1 percent Ernst's, he will place an attachment to Devon too. If that happens, Casandra, the Count, and all the countries are doomed." The Queen could no longer hold her tears, she began crying.

The Hermit took her into her arms and sent her comfort and reassurance in an attempt to heal her broken heart. "Tell me your plan Elisabeth, and I vow to do whatever it takes to complete it. If it is any solace, the Night has shown you succeed."

The Queen stopped crying, and looked into the Hermits eyes, "Thank you, I have been praying to her for thirty years, she has heard me. The Night has all my gratitude. Blessed be the Night."

The Professor

The day of the State Dinner not much was accomplished with the women gone. The men gathered to make plans, but mostly they argued. The Empress had said the reason so much had gone wrong in their world was the Warlocks failure to honor the Night. The Professor had spent years with the Monks healing, he was beginning to see she was right. What could be done now to remedy that? Mindfulness must be practiced daily to influence one's power and thinking. He knew of only a handful of Warlocks in the room who practice the energy of the Night, surprisingly it was all the Count's men. He would have to learn more about these Belissa. He was concerned about his training with Casandra and Marion. It was progressing slowly, they hardly had time for him. He did the best he could, but he was going to have a talk with the Emperor about it soon.

The State Dinner was beautiful, he had not been to an elegant formal dinner in years. He hated to dress for these functions but enjoyed the pomp and circumstance displayed. All the traditions and customs of history were exhibited, he hoped the youngster understood and appreciated the effort. All the young ladies were dressed impeccably, and Casandra and Marion were among the most beautiful. All the countries flags were displayed in the ballroom. The flag of double rings flew over the Castle with the Marais flag to the right and the Diamante flag to the left. The food was superb, of course, the wine too. The flowers were multi-colored; he had asked Mag where they came from, the Palace Garden had been depleted by the two previous dinners. She told him Wizards around the world had transported them for the Supper and the Ball. The floral perfume and exquisiteness gave the Castle an ambiance of joy and love. Everyone, there was celebrating love, it was infectious. The dancing and music went well into the night.

There were many young Sorcerer and Warlocks present from the Academy. They eyed him cautiously but were polite and pleasant. Marion danced with him and told him he scared the night out of most of them. Now that she knew him better, she didn't understand why. He was becoming fond of her, something he should be wary of. He knew his path with these girls required his patience, knowledge, and durability. He could not be objective and dole out wisdom while being emotionally involved. That was the advice he had given Students and Empresses all his life. He needed to follow that advice himself.

The Monks taught him the laws of the universe. The rule of awareness of power was the most important the Night would grant. The magical creature could not bring anything to the outer world that was not in their inner world. The private choices of the Warlocks and Sorcerers would be shown to the world whether they wanted it shown or not. The spiritual mind and heart can be one's worst enemy. When one's mind holds distorted and confused thoughts, the soul will create a biased chaotic world. The plotting on all sides was presenting its ugly face now. He had to teach his young apprentices to hold themselves to a higher standard than most nobles. Teaching young women to be mindful was not the most straightforward task, but that had been a requirement of the Hermit.

He had been shown his course years ago, by the Duchess. He was determined to continue the quest while holding the highest motives. He could feel the days of preparation fleeting by; he could not wait for the Ball to be over he needed time for these two young women. The Hermit could not foretell the outcome of his assignment; he had no idea if he would live or die, or of the fates of the girls. He only knew the future of the world if he failed. That was not a thought he would entertain.

He had found it difficult finding a place in the Palace to have a moment of peace, much less meditate. The Emperor would be in the garden, and the Count and his men out in the field and lake area. Today he made his way up to the roof of the Castle with the Falcons and pigeons. The stars were still out and the sun just on the brink of coming over the world's edge, his favorite time to meditate. The pigeons made a racket as he passed them, the Falcons just gawked from their coops. He found a suitable position on the wall by the Falcons and began to relax. As he cleared his mind, the birds began to serenade him. How beautiful nature was, it was as if they were in tune with his mind and heart. The Night was singing to him and the day was enlightening him. He flowed into a deep state of complete silence. The sound of a door at the end of the roof startled him, and the pigeons began to rant again. The sun was fully up, he had no idea how long he had connected to the Night.

"Sorry Sir, I didn't mean to disturb you. I didn't think anyone would be up here." Gregory wasn't sure if he should leave or stay.

"No, you're fine. I should be going on to breakfast. I just thought this would be a fine spot to contemplate this morning. With all the people in the Castle, it is hard to find a place of peace." The Professor stretched and walked to the Falcons. "They are beautiful birds. It is hard to believe they are so deadly."

"The way with deadliest things, don't you think? I spend a lot of time up on the roof with the birds, it is the most peaceful part of my job. I start and end my day here, the rest of it is rushing around in the stables and fields." Gregory opened his bag of feed and began to feed the pigeons.

The Professor started to leave then turned. "So the roof is empty after you feed the birds in the morning. What time do you return?"

"If I send the birds to hunt, the cook likes me to come up in the morning. Other than that, the roof is yours to contemplate in. I won't be hunting for a while we have just about consumed our forest with all the dinners." Gregory tilted his head as if wondering why.

"Well, that suits my needs very well. I need to use this spot for training if it is alright with you. I doubt I will get my young ladies up here today. I am certain the Ball will take priority over my will." The Professor chuckled.

"The Ball is all everyone is talking about, makes me wonder how bad the wedding will be. If you're teaching Casandra up here, she will be right at home. Her childhood was spent up here, she used to follow me all over the Castle. Hard to believe she is grown and to be a married woman." Gregory looked out the Castle buttress and smiled in remembrance.

The Professor left him with his thoughts and made his way to the dining room balcony for his coffee, where he found Beatrice.

"Good morning Empress. It will be a glorious day. I can feel the warm season coming, every day the temperature is warmer. I have just been on the roof meditating. I had a strong impression we would have an unexpected visitor today." He stirred cream into his coffee.

The Empress raised one eyebrow. "Good morning George. Yes, it seems we should be ready for an unprecedented visit from the North this afternoon. Mags has already informed me. I am wavering back and forth in a decision to tell Haden or not. Does he need to know? What do you think?"

"I don't think he needs to know; however, he might want to know. It would be more fun to surprise him. I remember none of us was ever forewarned. That is always the advantage of the Night." The Professor heard several voices making their way to the coffee pot.

"The weight of life around here has been heavy. I think I would like to have a little fun." She smiled wickedly and said, "I will tell Mags to keep this a secret."

One by one each member of their inner group made their way to breakfast. The conversation was light and mostly about the Ball and attire for everyone. The Empress was insisting they dress with elegance.

The Elves entered and gave their report on security, the library, dining room, kitchen, and parlor was free of eyes and ears. However, the Ballroom had been saturated. Eric, the Head of Security said they were working on all the rooms in the Palace it would take until the afternoon before they would be finished clearing everything. Eric said one of the carriage drivers had released hundreds of mice, rats, and crows on his several trips of transport to the State Dinner. They had him in custody, but he wasn't speaking. A spell was used, and they were working on that. He expected he had help and the same would occur this evening. One man could not have infested the Castle so easily.

The Professor asked, "Eric, what of the roof?"

"It is clear. I had my men check, with all the birds up there; rodents and crows won't enter that way. They are starting at the bottom and working their way up." Eric nodded.

The Emperor sighed heavily. "Thank you, Eric. I want you to know how much I appreciate your work here. We have invited you and your top officers to the Ball. Now, I think I would like all your women and men here as our guest. Tell them I will pay them twice their wages make sure they are dressed as Elves, not in uniform."

"I will, your Majesty. You are our Emperor Sir, there is no need to pay us extra. However, this is a wonderful idea, we can find considerable intelligence from the guests. It also makes our job easier to watch the many outside servants hired for this. Thank you for the opportunity." He bowed and left.

"I should have thought of that before last night." The major grumbled. "I had men all over this Castle. I had wondered, but now I am sure one of my officers is in league with the King. I need to find out who. Count, could you help me? I understand you have some mental powers that might narrow it down?"

"I'd be happy to, all my men are able to sense thoughts. They have been hand-picked by Addison, and they are in close quarters now; we could casually have a look. You could show off your men, maybe do a little sparing." The Count nodded to Addison they were mentally speaking again. The Professor hated when they did that.

"Excellent idea Count, when would we have time? There is a lot to do before you leave tomorrow." Major asked as he reached for more meat.

The Professor put his cup down. He decided he must start to play his part now before the winds from the North blew in. "Major, your Majesty, if I may be so bold to advise all of you. Yesterday we men spent hours hashing out many plans, none of which were sound. I think it is futile to continue meeting with the limited facts we have been handed. Eric used the word intelligence, I like that word, we do not have enough intelligence. Hopefully, the Count will return with plenty of intelligence, and we will have three months to plan. This does not need to be decided in a day. What does need to be decided today, is the contract between you Emperor and the Count? We must also have the method for the Count to appear sick in the King's presence. I have started a serum that will give him the appearance of the poison. I have also protected him from the antidote if he is forced to drink it in front of the King. I would like to use this morning to perfect it. Also, the girl's training has been sorely neglected. It is imperative they have some time to practice every day."

"Well, I must say I can't argue with the fact our meetings were fruitless." The Emperor looked somewhat sour. "However, I don't think our plans were that bad." The Major started to speak, but the Emperor raised his hand to stop him. "I will concede our intelligence, as you say, is limited. You make a compelling argument to postpone making any plans without knowing more." He paused and then said, "I also must agree to the contract between the Count, and I needs to be completed. However, I am not so certain I care to have the girls learn and rely on an outdated method of warfare and religion. It didn't help my parents or my dead children." The King crossed his arms as if to dare someone to start an argument with him.

The Count recognized he was the only one in the room who could convincingly argue with Haden. "Your Majesty, the Professor has made some good points, with which I agree. We do need more facts before proceeding with our plans. I don't see much to argue about as far as the contract. Casandra owns half of all my monies and holdings, as soon as we are married. I named her Countess Rakie, making her the seventh or eighth in line for the throne. I am sure Father will grant her a satanical particle of land in Belissa or in Winsette, she will be one of the richest women in the world. As for me, I expect nothing from you in return just Casandra, the women I love is enough to last me for a lifetime." He looked at her she was in tears he reached down and took her hand and kissed her forehead.

"However, your Majesty I would like you to reconsider your stance on her training." The Emperor was starting to redden in the face. "Just hear me out, your Majesty. She and Marion are going off on a holiday, which at most times would be benign, this one will not. Don't think the King will not have spies on her the whole time. If training helps her focus and concentrate, she should have that tool to use. Both Casandra and Marion need to be in the present not only for their holiday but for the trip to Azure. My men and I practice the religion of the Night, if she doesn't learn from a Master like the Professor, I will teach her myself after we are married. I would not go against your wishes. I do understand your faith was crushed by the deaths of your Parents and Children. Oddly, death was what brought me to practice the Night. After the Great War, I was devastated. Ski forced me to study with the Monks I thank the Night." He paused and looked to his bride, "I have been rewarded with Casandra."

The table was silent. Eventually, the King said, "Very well, she can never be too prepared for combat."

The Professor thought he had stepped out this far, he might as well jump off the cliff. "Sir?"

The Emperor grumbled, "Beatrice, George is your advisor, not mine; do something with him!"

"Hear him, Hayden, he is privileged to more information than I. Stop being difficult! No one wants to be around you when you are irritated!" Her eyebrow rose again.

The Emperor sighed again, this time exasperated. "Make your point Professor. I have other things to do with my day."

"Yes, of course, Sir. I will get right to the point. Our country and Kingdom will look like a beggar if we offer nothing to the Count. While Henry's gesture of love is noble, the Hex would use that information as a weapon to control him. He is to give the appearance of love here in our presence, but never to the Hex. It might mean his death and surely Casandra's."

The Empress moaned. "My Dear, you must offer Henry an equal portion to keep our enemies pacified."

"I would gladly Professor but remember this marriage makes him fourth in line for Emperor. We can place him on the Continental Council even make him an ambassador to any country he wishes. However, my Consulate will balk at that much wealth coming out of the Kingdom." The Emperor crossed his arms again.

"Emperor, you are saying if the wealth was not taken from your Consulate, a contract could be written today?" The Professor had him, this was too easy.

The Emperor uncrossed his arms and looked suspiciously at him, "Yes, Professor it would."

The Professor braced himself. "Then I propose the Northland, including Crystal Mountain. Its treasure of the diamonds and precious stones holds unmeasurable powers and uncountable wealth."

The table took a collective intake of air as Henry's mouth fell open. He could see the Emperor's eyes turn red as he screamed. "Are you crazy? That land is not mine to give it is the Duchess of Savilla's through perpetuity. I cannot do that! The wrath of the Hermit would be worse than the Consulate!"

Everyone at the table was screaming at him all at once. The Empress stood, placed her hands on the table and said. "Quiet everyone! I believe the Professor has more to offer."

The Professor releases his breath and continued. "I have the authority, given to me by the Duchess to grant Henry and Casandra the lands to use, as long as they live. They would revert to the care of her or her ancestors after Casandra's death that stipulation must be written into the contract. If you look at the contract written long ago; the wording states only that the land is held by her children or grandchildren. This is in accordance."

The Emperor turned to Henry, "You must permit our people the usage of the powers on that land as we always have. No gems can be removed without the permission of the Duchess she always says no... so don't bother asking. That will be in the contract. I will add in only Marais and Diamentia usage, if you violate it you will be barred! Is that agreeable?"

The Professor could see Henry was still dazed by this proposal. It was worth much more than his fortune. More than that, he sensed Henry knew it would be an advantage in maneuvering the Hex. "Perfectly your Majesty, I am in complete agreement. Professor you have just given me hope for the future, thank you, Sir. Feel free to advise me anytime." His smile extended across his face. "This little bit of news will stop the Hex dead in their tracks." He began to laugh and that had everyone at the table joining in.

The Emperor stood, "Let's write this up and be done with one thing. Professor, you have this morning with the girls. I would like to inspect my army after signing the contract. Major, let's give Henry a tour. This afternoon we will all work on Henry's sickness spell and talk a bit about the holiday security. Eric has some good ideas I would like to offer. If we can get all this done, I would really enjoy myself at the Ball this evening, and I am sure you all would, too."

The Prelude to the Ball

Beatrice followed the girls and Professor McMillian into the hall. "Girls go dress for combat and don't worry about your dresses for the Ball. I will see to them and have them waiting for you. Along with the High Sorcerer crown, no more tiara; wait till you see it. Casandra; you will love it." The girls giggled and ran up the stairs to get ready.

The Professor yelled at them. "Meet me on the roof." He looked at Beatrice, "Thank you for your support. I thought he might strike me dead for a moment. The part of my assignment I feared most has been carried out."

The Empress took a deep breath, "I hope you are right, Professor. I fear everything that is to come. So much is unknown the outcome could be disastrous or divine. I pray to the Night for the divine. You amaze me. I have argued with Hayden for years about training with the Monks. I can't remember a thing you argued that I had not."

"It was Henry who made him listen. He did not offer the training as religious but as a tool. I think the Emperor had never considered that nor did we. Henry is special, I look forward to knowing him." The Professor headed to the roof.

The Empresses morning went by quickly. All the last-minute details of the food, decorations, and dresses were demanding. The men were fed lunch by the Major, and she had a light lunch sent to her sitting room. After lunch, they would inspect the decorations together. Casandra and Marion were telling her all about the morning's lesson, they were understanding more about the Night and had many questions for her.

"Girls the Night and the Day are always here, being present to them and connecting to the land you stand on will answer all your questions. Practice is the only way to learn to connect. I can spend hours giving you explanations only your personal experience will gain the answers you seek. I know you're looking at me the same way I did my instructors. They would tell me to practice, meditate. That is not what you want to hear, I know. It is the truth, the more you practice, the more the universe will give you answers."

Mags came in, "Is it time yet?"

Casandra said, "Time for what Mags, do you mean to see of all the decorations? We'll go look now we are finished with lunch."

The Empress stood and said, "Not yet, Casandra. We have one other thing for you before we look at the ballroom. Come in and shut the door Mags." The Empress went to the window and closed the curtains then walked over to the wall where an ornate mirror hung. She swung one side outward to reveal a safe. "Close your eyes girls, Mags, keep an eye on them no cheating." She used a charm to open the safe, it was filled with gems from all the Emperors and Empresses since the beginning of the Kingdom. She reached in and retrieved the emeralds for Marion and the crown for Casandra, along with her Empress Crown.

"Open your eyes, girls." The both heaved a sigh.

"We only get to wear these crowns on special occasions, a good thing. You will find it wears you out halfway through the evening. Use a spell to lighten it, don't make it a permanent or the diamonds will fade." She handed Casandra the crown. It was entirely diamonds. There were twenty points on its scalloped band. Every inch was covered in rotating emerald cut and solitary cut diamonds. In the center of each scallop was a marquee cut diamond dangling, from the spaces between the peaks, were teardrop diamonds.

"Try it on for me," Mags said. Her Mother watched her placed it on her head it looked breathtaking. "I have waited so long to see you wear this I worked all week to shine it for you. I put extra energy into it. Between this, your diamond neckless and the earrings and bracelet of your Grandmother's you will radiate." Mags sighed.

The Empress handed her Haden's Mother's jewels. "Place all of this in your safe along Marion's necklace, earrings, bracelet, and ring. Don't leave this lying around we have too many unknown servants."

She gave the jewels to Marion. Marion had never had real jewelry to wear she always created fake. Now she could see the difference they all matched perfectly; each emerald cut stones were surrounded by diamonds. They laid side by side in a row the effect was mesmerizing. "Empress these are gorgeous. I am not sure I could wear them I can create a copy and…"

Beatrice stopped her. "No. You are worthy of wearing the real thing. I will not hear of any copies. Ever, do you understand?" Marion nodded, "Besides I want you to dazzle that Addison he would be a nice catch. Casandra could without difficulty persuade Henry to title him and you. You would be nobility and never again think of yourself as a little Sprite."

"I will tell Henry that is a marvelous idea, Mother!" Casandra was laughing. "Meet the first Sprite Duchess."

"No. Casandra, don't. You may ruin everything. I am falling in love with him, and his love must be based on truth. Please wait."

Casandra hugged her. "Of course my friend, now I can't wait to see the ballroom. Let's put up the jewelry and go see." They ran out of the sitting room.

Mags picked up the tray from lunch, "Actually, I can't wait for everyone to see the decorations. The Sorcerers I hired for this job have outdone themselves. As they should, if they want to provide decorations for the wedding, but I don't know how they will make the wedding more beautiful."

They walked out to the staircase, the landing and into the entrance hall everyone stopped and stared. The ceilings were bursting with white flowers hung in long straight strands. Candles were placed at different heights that would be glowing for the evening. The staircase was intertwined in greens and sparkling crystals. There were large arrangements of white flowers and crystals stationed periodically in urns in the great hall with stands of white candles in candelabras. The Grand Dining room had a series of circular tables draped in silver. Tall white candelabras held silver candles while long draping white centerpieces hung from the ceiling.

They entered the ballroom; the floor was a harlequin patterned of silver and white, they had changed it from the standard black and white. Silver bunting draped the orchestra area, over the walls, and at the doorways to the garden. Crystals hung from the ceiling at different heights, each holding a candle. Small white nosegays of flowers hung between the candles. Greens and white flowers swirled around the seven large crystal chandeliers that hung over the ballroom. There seemed not to be a place without a crystal, candle, or white flower. The aroma was intoxicating, joy and love filled the room. Seven sorcerers stood in the middle of the room. Casandra walked up to them. "You're hired for my wedding. However, how could you make anything more breathtaking than this?"

The Sorcerer in the center stepped forward. "Your Majesty, High Sorcerer, and Countess to be, your engagement is bright light and love to the Kingdom as reflected here. Your marriage will bring us an alliance and unbound treasure. It is only natural it would be golden. We'll start with invitations engraved with gold, it will give everyone a taste of your life to come. Your life will be blessed with the Night, and your wedding will reflect its color of blue for your country, also the shade of red, the Count's Country. Accents of the gold of the sun and silver of the stars and moons of the heaven will be suspended from the ceilings. While red roses are the symbol of love, the rose symbol is also used on the Belissa Villa Wines. Roses will be saturating the Castle.

Casandra sighed, "Oh, Mother this sounds wonderful she has convinced me, could we?"

The Empress laughed, "I love it. Mags, what do you think?"

Mags was crying into her apron. "Oh yes, but the Emperor already complained to me about the price of the Ball."

The Empress smiled wickedly. "Leave the Emperor to me. Ladies you may proceed. I will tell the scribes to use gold on the invitations this evening. Could you have something put together next week for us to look at, with estimates?'

The seven sorcerers smile, "I hope you don't mind, but we already told the scribes this might be a possibility. We can come on Monday with our plans."

The Emperor walked in. "There you are; you are needed in the library. Very gorgeous…over the moon really. Sorcerer, how much is this costing me?"

Casandra threw her arms around him. "No Father the sun and the moons will be for my wedding. I am your only daughter." And she smiled at him.

The Empress smiled and said. "We will see you at your convenience on Monday ladies. Please be our guests this evening, take all the compliments before The Emperor receives your bill." They all laughed.

The Empress and the girls followed the Emperor into the Library, where the men were already working on Henry. He was a shade of green she had never seen. "I think that is too much, Professor they will question why he looks so healthy this evening."

"You're right of course Empress. Chancellor could you help me tone the spell down."

They worked for an hour perfecting the spell then Ski said. "Tomorrow morning at breakfast we will cast the spell. In case Addison is not allowed to be with you remember to test the antidote before you drink it. If anything smells different, question it, and do not drink all of it. Let's try our antidote." It worked beautifully.

The Emperor returned to his desk, "Good, that's done. Now, all we need to do is sign the contract Henry, and talk about Casandra's protection on holiday. Major get Eric." Everyone took chairs around the room as Henry, and the Emperor signed the contract.

Eric came in, "Good afternoon, with your permission your Majesty." The Emperor nodded. "We have made some security measures for you while you're on holiday Casandra. I think you will not mind this. Several of your classmates have been accepted into our force one you know well, she is a good friend to you. She will be going on your holiday along with other women in my unit. They have been training for some time. I have been planning this unit for just this purpose, to guard our Noblewomen. They all will be at the Ball this evening."

Casandra looked to the door, Grace walked in. Casandra ran to her and gave her a big hug, "I am so glad you are here I have been trying to tell you about my engagement all week. Now I know why you haven't answered. Come in and meet Henry.'" She made introductions and then announced, "Grace will be one of my bridesmaids along with Marion."

Grace laughed, "Poor Count Rakie she has been planning this for years. I hope you don't mind."

Henry smiled, "Not at all Grace."

Eric continued. "We will disguise all of you on holiday. It is a common practice for groups of girls to holiday together this unit will not even be noticed. All of the women have undergone training with the Monks and combat with our Elves. Although Grace's training is not complete, she is still very good at detection. My men will also be nearby if they need to be called on. This leaves the matter of her torque and crown. Would you vanquish it for me, Casandra?"

She did Grace grimaced. "Even I can see it, I always could. I never said anything, but I was always trying to figure out what in the world you were trying to do with it. It was always flying above your head."

The Emperor said, "Damn, I was hoping we could at least have a signal to rescue you."

The Count said, "I know I am not welcome on your holiday of freedom and I need to be free to set up all the plans. However, I plan to have Addison disguised and be close by."

The library door opened Mags, and the Hermit walked in. Everyone froze except the Empress, and Casandra, who ran to hug her. "Are you coming to my engagement Ball, or just to meet Henry?"

The Hermit smiled broadly. "My dear I am a Hermit, they do not socialize. I came to meet your Henry. Now, did you bring the bracelet as I asked?"

"Yes, Mistress. Right in my pocket." Casandra pulled it out.

The Hermit walked to Henry. "I see you are as handsome as the reports of you. May I have your hand to examine your power?" Henry said nothing he gave her his hand and relaxed to show her his strength under duress.

"Very good," She turned to the Emperor, "Now you Hayden."

The Emperor looked miffed, but he extended his hand he did not want to look less than Henry.

The Hermit smiled, "Just as Beatrice had reported. Now it is good I have come just in time to help. I have given Casandra this bracelet to wear on holiday. The four gems in it can call if she needs help. I had adjusted the ruby to respond to Henry's blood, by placing a drop of blood on a gem you can add whoever you like. All she needs to do is touch the gem it will send a signal. Does that satisfy you, Emperor?"

The Emperor was apparently taken back. "It does Duchess, I am glad you stopped by. I have something I would like to clear with you."

The Hermit stopped him. "Hayden, you and Henry signed the contract correct? The Professor and I are old friends." She walked to him and placed her hand on his shoulder. "You look well George it is good to see you. After this is all done, please come for a visit. It has been too long. Did you show the Emperor the papers allowing you to act on my behalf?"

George smiled. "I didn't need to. He trusted me. I will come to see you as soon as I can."

"He trusted you! Hayden, I believe we are making progress. Beatrice, he isn't as bad as you said." Only she and Beatrice laughed, but the Emperor was turning red.

"You take yourself too seriously Hayden."

She came around the table and sat next to Henry. "If security is taken care of, I need a moment of Henry's time and his men. Casandra, Grace, and Marion, you need to start getting ready for your Ball. Henry will tell you what you need to know. Everyone else, please remain."

Casandra grabbed Grace's hand, "Wait till you see my dress."

Marion grabbed Grace's other arm, "Wait till you see my jewelry."

Mags came in with tea, "Just the way you like it Mistress don't ask me to stay. I have too much to do. Besides I will hear all about it later."

The Hermit smiled. "Thank you, Mags. Run along, the evening will be perfect."

Mags kissed her on the cheek. "Have a look at the decorations before you leave. It reminds me of your wedding day. I'm sorry I shouldn't have brought that up."

The Hermit kept her smile. "It's alright Mags that was the happiest day of my life. I should remember it more often. I intend to see that and the girls in their dresses, perhaps steal a little food and Henry's good wine."

"I knew that was you at the engagement dinner you can't-fool me. I will pack you a basket and have it in your carriage." Mags hands were on her hips, but she chuckled.

The Hermit laughed, "No one can fool you, it is a nice talent and the reason you are ensconced in this family."

She waited for the library door to close and sipped her tea then turned to Henry. "I have a favor to ask of you, Henry." Everyone took a seat around the table as she told of Elisabeth's circumstance. Beatrice was in tears, hearing of Elizabeth having an Attachment spell on her. The Emperor was immobile, and she could tell Henry was aware of much of the story. "You know some of this Henry?"

"I knew who she was. She confessed to me when my wife died. She asked for my help taking the Prince out of the country, then she changed her mind. She became pregnant and begged me to keep her secret. I had no idea Ernst was Devon's Father; the Prince's eyes are as green as emeralds. I had heard of this spell called the Attachment; I have no firsthand knowledge. I think you have Ski."

Ski nodded, "Sadly I do. I have had Witch's brought to me for healing, and most I could not save. All I know for sure is that unless it is removed promptly, it is impossible to remove."

"Ski is right. I know a Wizard who healed from this, but the Attachment skin remains. We could not remove it." The Professor took in a deep breath as if he felt deep regret.

The Hermit said, "I wish there were a way we could save the Queen. She told me the bond between her and the King had grown so strong that if one dies, the other soon follows. It is the reason he watches over her so closely. She no longer fears him; she is brave. She has found a way to conceal from him, and she has agreed to spy for us if we help free her Son. I believe she has some fool plan to commit suicide and take King with her. I can't say I would not do the same if I were her."

The room was silent what could anyone say Henry broke the silence. "What is your favor?"

The Hermit took a deep breath. "Henry don't tell the girls about the Attachment. At least not now; it will only frighten them."

She stood and stretched. "The favor yes; the Queen has set the seed that you know blood knowledge to the King. She, or he, will ask you to do a test to see if Devon's blood has some Wizard in it. If you agree you should see that it does, but also show the King's blood to be prevalent. Devon has only known recently he is Ernst's child. Unfortunately, he let some professor know he exhibits some of Ernst's talents. She is afraid it will become common knowledge, that would force the King to Attach to Devon, and he would be lost."

"I am confused, the Professor I know has the King's ear. The King must already know Devon is not his Son. Devon's eyes should be black or blue." Henry watched Hayden as he understood they were to help the man who took Casandra from her bed and probably killed his Father.

"The Queen changed his eyes at birth. Elisabeth told the King she wasn't sure if Devon was Kenneth's child or his. The King knows about Ernst love for her, they have loved one another since the Academy. He uses honesty spells on her and Ernst. The King trusts no one, and also holds Attachment spells on Elizabeth and Ernst, he uses the knowledge to control both." The Hermit let that settle in. "Devon was hurt badly when he was young, Ernst gave him a blood gift to heal him. Can you do this Henry, make the King believe he is Devon's Father and that Devon holds some of Ernst's blood?"

Henry turned to his men. "Can we Ski? You and Addison are the experts at blood."

Ski answered. "I can make it appear the King is his Father so can Addison. Addison, do you have some ideas about adding Ernst's blood?"

Addison smiled wickedly. "I do, and we will do it in front of the King. Oh, I am going to enjoy this."

"Not as much as I am. Ski, I want you to go home and work solely on the Attachment spell, we need to solve that spell. I have a feeling most of the Sorcerous in his Kingdom have one." Henry turned to the Hermit, "I am your man, Duchess." He took her hand and kissed it.

The Hermit blushed. "Henry it has been a while since I have been touched by a Warlock. You are very powerful, good thing you are spoken for." Then she laughed. "One more thing, the King is having thoughts about you. As I have said, he trusts no one. Elisabeth said the King is thinking of replacing you with Devon permanently. He sees you as having everything a man could desire. However, you have just given me an idea. The King regards power as the most import aspiration in the world. He would understand if you would have the same obsession."

Henry held up his hand, "Say no more, my lady. You are a smart one. I have great admiration for brains and beauty. I will ask for knowledge of the Attachment Spell." He laughed.

The Hermit laughed and said, "Henry remind me never to play cards with you. You have been ahead of me all the way. I like you, and I hope you and Casandra have a long and happy marriage."

The Emperor mumbled, "Really…Never play games with him."

The Hermit turned to him, "Emperor, do you agree with this scheme, helping Ernst and Elisabeth?"

The Emperor looked her in the eye. "I remember her, Elisabeth, she was beautiful. My Uncle was a special man I will honor him; I will help because I loved him."

She stood and took his hand. "You are a good man Hayden. Now, come show me the decorations you have spent much of your money on."

The Emperor laughed and took her arm. "It is my pleasure, and you know I have always wanted to meet you." They left the library, talking and laughing.

The Professor stood, "That went much better than I thought it would."

The Empress answered, "She is a High Sorcerer…and of Selvilla blood how could he resist her. It is said once a man tastes Selvilla lips they are doomed to love them. You are lost Count, you will come to love me too." She laughed and left them all to think over that.

The Ball at North Castle

The Hermit and Emperor were walking out of the Grand Dining room when the girls came down the stairs. The Hermit stopped, "Look at them, Hayden. All three of those girls will be growing up very fast over the next few months. We must give them all the help we can. Your decisions will put the world at war, or peace."

"I have felt the war in the air for the last year, tell me what to do. This time I will follow your orders." He turned her to face her.

The Hermit hesitated then said, "Remember the basic laws of magic. We cannot produce what we are not. Therefore, the King will fail. When making your choices look within and trust yourself. The future is very unclear Hayden, each day, and with every decision the outcome changes. I will let you know if I see a clear path for you."

Casandra came toward them, and she was luminous. Her hair was plaited within her crown, which glistened under the candle lights. Her eyes were sparkling as much as the diamonds necklace Henry gave her. Her strapless ballgown was white with crystals sewn into the netting which covered the entire dress. The skirt belled out a good two feet around her making her look as though she was floating across the floor. She wore white gloves that passed her elbows with a sash which laid from her left shoulder to her right hip. It was the colors of Marais and Diamentia; blue and red attached with a brooch of diamonds. It was striking. "She is beautiful Hayden, you should have her portrait made looking just like this, absolutely breathtaking."

Her Father went to her and kissed her cheek. "I will Duchess. Casandra, I have never seen you look lovelier. No one could outshine you this evening."

The Count was on the landing, and the Hermit noticed him staring at Casandra. Was he crying? She was too far away to know for sure, but she sensed he was. She loved Henry more and more. She would give him time to compose himself.

"Marion is that you?" She was in emerald green silk that shined like the moon on a lake. She was covered with emeralds and diamonds. Her hair was up in the color of pale blond. She wore white gloves with the tiara in her hair. "You look like a Princess one reads about in a storybook. I hope your young man sweeps you off your feet on the dance floor this evening." She incanted a small charm of irresistibility and placed it in her hand. "Just in case he doesn't see your beauty." And she winked.

Grace was a beauty all in gold, with her golden hair hanging down past her waist. Her Elf ears were covered, it made her beautiful face even more noticeable. She was tall and lean; she would have a few men after her this evening. "Not everyone can wear gold, but you are a vision in it. If you don't have a boyfriend, I will wager you will by the end of the Ball."

The Emperor said, "Casandra is spoken for, but you two must bring any men to me for approval. You are both a vision any man would be proud to have you on his arm."

A voice from behind the girls said, "I know I would." The girls turned, and Addison was standing there. "Emperor I believe I would like to spend the evening with Marion, am I an acceptable choice?"

The Emperor asked Marion, "Well, do you want a Belissa too Marion?"

Marion laughed, "Addison will do very well." She put the irresistibility charm in Grace's hand.

The Emperor laughed, "You are accepted Addison, treat her as if she was my daughter." He slapped him on the shoulder, "Beatrice is going to have my neck if I am not dressed on time. Duchess, you are always welcome here. I know you are a Hermit, but please visit us. This was your home once, and it still is. Think about being at the wedding it will be small. The Temple can hold only close family and friends, you are family. He kissed her on the cheek and went off to dress.

The Count came from the shadows and walked to Casandra, "I can find no words adequate to describe your beauty." He brought her hand it to his mouth then he bowed to her, turned her hand palm and kissed her. "I love you, Countess."

Casandra took the hand he kissed and raised his head and kissed him on the mouth tenderly, "It is hard not to be enthralled by your charm and good looks, Count. I might be jealous you're almost as pretty as me."

The Count grabbed her by the waist and spun around laughing. Casandra had been right when she told her how handsome he was when he laughed. The Hermit said, "It is time for me to leave. I am so glad I came and saw all you happy and beautifully dressed magical beings."

Beatrice walked up she was in a midnight blue gown that billowed across the floor. Her crown was of diamonds, and blue sapphires and her hair twirled through it. She wore white gloves and a silver and gold sash with a blue sapphire and diamond brooch attached at the hip. "I will walk you to the coach. The Emperor told me he wanted you to attend the wedding ceremony. Please say you'll be there. It will make our evening perfect." The Empress took the Hermit's arm.

The Count stepped forward. "Please, it would mean so much to Casandra and me." Casandra smiled and nodded.

"Alright, I will come to the wedding ceremony but not to the reception." The Hermit placed a hand on Henry's shoulder. "Good luck tomorrow." As she removed her hand, there was a gold coin. "Carry this in your pocket for luck." The Count bowed, took the coin and smiled. She had placed a hex on him he could feel it. It was a hex of protection. He couldn't help but think, was it necessary, then again, if the Hermit thought he needed it, he should be careful.

Beatrice and the Duchess walked out to her carriage. "Is there anything I should know Mistress?"

The Hermit stopped and took both her hands, "Now the future is more muddled than ever, every choice changes the outcome. The Count was ready to flee altogether, the game got too exciting for him to turn his back on. He is a very interesting Warlock, I hope to know him better. Come to the Mountain after the girls are off on holiday. Take care." She kissed her on the cheek and sprang into the carriage. She gave the impression of being an old, half crippled woman. Then, occasionally, she would do something like that…hop. She was wily.

Beatrice looked down the hillside she could see carriages coming up the drive to the Castle. The Emperor stationed his army along the driveway with lanterns it was a beautiful sight, yet she knew the real purpose, there would be no mice or rats tonight. She had better get in and gather her family for the reception line, before long the Castle would be filled.

Empress asked the others to see the guests in the dining room and ballroom. The dancing began, as the Emperor and she remained in the front hallway to greet the latecomers. Finally, the line had dwelled, and the Emperor took her hand, "Let's have a dance before we are bombarded with good wishes."

The Empress said, "Make the announcement of the contract as soon as possible everyone has been harassing me to tell them." He looked at her with an exaggerated face of disappointment. "Alright, a dance first, then the announcement." They walked through the Grand Dining Room to the entrance of the ballroom.

The Major was waiting for them. "Empress you have created heaven in our world this evening. Everyone is in awe and saying they surely will not miss the wedding. Is it time for the announcement?"

"A dance first with my beautiful Empress. I will not miss this opportunity to have her in my arms tonight." The Emperor beamed with the familiar look of love she missed all these past years. She smiled and held back the tears that were forming in her eyes.

The Major stopped the music, and the ballroom dropped into silence. He raised his voice to a commanding tenor. "To the mystical and magical creatures that attend this Ball tonight, I am honored to present the Emperor and Empress of our land in a dance."

The Emperor whispered to the Major, "Give us a turn or two then join us on the dance floor my dancing skills are not what they once were."

The Empress smiled she had heard him, "Thank you, Hayden, I don't like everyone staring at me. You look dashing this evening. This takes me back…it has been years since the Castle has vibrated with love and joy. I wish our future would hold more times like these, without the intrigue."

The music started, and he took her into his arms and wrapped her in a charm of peace, joy, and love. He thought she would object, but she threw back her head and laughed. To him, she was the most beautiful Sorcerer in the world.

Major had asked Kathryn to dance, the Prince was off talking. She wore a gown the color of ice, and she looked stunning. All the women had dressed like Princesses; it had been a long while since the last Ball he could feel their excitement. He was walking her to the dance floor when she pulled at his hand.

"Stop Major look. Father has put an enchantment on the Empress. How lovely I think I will cry." The Major was so taken back he could only watch them, mesmerized. He knew he should go out to dance, but everyone was caught up in the Emperor's enchantment spell. The Major stared at the two dancing in each other's arms and thought how wonderful his life could have been if he had married. If wishes were fishes, the sea would be full. He wouldn't bring that sorrow to this evening.

Thank the Night the Count broke the spell by taking Casandra to the floor and tapping the Emperor's shoulder, "Might I have a dance with this enchanting Sorceress?"

"You may and thank you for that. The Major was to come out here after a few turns where in thunder is he?"

"I am afraid your enchantment encompasses the room." The Count took Beatrice in his arms and danced away.

The Emperor bowed to Casandra. "Beautiful daughter, would you dance with your Father?"

She walked into his arms, "Tone down the enchantment. Dad, we have ladies about to faint."

The Emperor laughed, "I am not that powerful. Oh, that I could be, our troubles would be over."

Beatrice gave a sigh of relief. "Thank you Count that was awkward. I fell into that. I couldn't control the spiral he led me on. It has been years since I have shared such love and joy with him. I blame you, Sir. The love you and Casandra have shown has taken everyone here to happy memories."

"My Empress, please call me Henry. I do love your daughter with all my heart and soul, as much as Hayden loves you. However, I think the Sorcerers you hired flooded the room with enchantments." The music stopped, and the Emperor signaled them to the center of the floor.

The Emperor took Beatrice's hand. "Welcome to the Castle of the North. The Empress and I extend our gratitude for your attendance and wish each one of you an enjoyable evening. We will make a few announcements first. I believe this will answer some of the questions you have. First, the decorations. Will the Sorcerers who are responsible for creating this fantastic atmosphere please walk to the center of the ballroom."

They hurried out eager to be acknowledged. "Ladies you have thrilled everyone here, but most importantly you have delighted my two favorite women. I thank you. They are already contracted for the wedding which is scheduled for the Sorcerer's Moon, so don't even think of asking them for your parties on that day. I am to understand the decorations for that event are top secret. Meaning they are not telling the men, so don't ask us." He paused for the laughter to stop. "Regarding the wedding invitations, I have it on good authority if you are here tonight you are on the list for the wedding as well. Anything else my Dear?"

He looked at her, "Why yes, I have been asked who is paying for this, are the countries taxes about to be levied?"

He gave out a hearty laugh. "I don't know why I am laughing I haven't gotten the bill for this yet. Unfortunately, I am paying. I took care of Kathryn's and Bryan's wedding, however, this time the Count is furnishing all the wine. Thank you, Sir." The ballroom filled with cheers.

The Emperor held up his hand, "I want this evening to be filled with happiness. The Empress and I have decided to take a moment to disclose the contract of marriage only once this evening. Any questions about it can be spoken of in a private nature with us, but not this evening."

He motioned for the Count to step forward, "We have agreed upon extending the Northern mountain and countryside including the rights of minerals and powers to him and his people, in accordance with the contract with Duchess of Savilla. It will be held in partnership with

Casandra until her death when it will revert to the Savilla lineage." They started whispering; he held up his hands. "Your rights to the power and rituals remain the same. This is costing our country nothing and giving the Count and Casandra indescribable riches. It has been sanctioned by the Duchess, who was here today and left just moments before you started to arrive." They all applauded.

The Count signaled the waiters to enter the room with trays of Casandra's wine, they quieted. "In return, my Father has agreed to an alliance with all of the countries of Continental Council. You are free to travel and trade with Diamante. From this night forward, Casandra will be known as the Countess Rakie, with all the rights and privileges offered to that station, making her eighth in line to the throne of Diamante. On our wedding day, she will be my equal, all my properties, investments and interests are half hers. This includes the investments here and overseas, it is extensive. I would list those for you, but honestly, I have no idea of the worth. If you see my Chancellor, he might be able to give you some idea. Now I ask you to toast my beautiful bride with a special concoction I named after her, Casandra." He took two wine glasses from a tray and stood by Casandra. "To my love, the most gorgeous woman in our world." The room drank to her, then started chanting, long live the Count and Countess.

The music started, and everyone came forward to offer congratulations. The attendance was more than they had anticipated. Mags was frantic in the kitchen trying to keep the bowls and trays filled with food. The Count had extra wine bought in, thank the Night. He was contracted with hundreds of orders for the wine Casandra. The ice sculptures were glowing in the candlelight while the rooms were all filled with laughter and music. The essence of love and joy enchantments was intoxicatingly creating an evening of fun and romance.

The party and dancing went very late. No one wanted this night to end except the Elves. They were happy to have everyone out of the Castle. They had caught a dozen servants bringing in mice, and several of the servants were found wandering around the Castle. Four carriages were confiscated, thirty guests were marked as spies, with another twenty as potential spies. Henry's men were helpful in finding the double agents in the Emperor's Army, they would be dealt with the next week. It would take Eric's men until dawn to clear the Castle. It was a productive night, but Eric was happy to have it end. He had gotten to dance often with Grace, but only once with Cassandra. He only regretted he was interrupted in the garden by one of his men, just as he was about to kiss Grace. He was delighted to know she would not have stopped him from kissing her; she was attracted to him as well. She had used a love spell on him, but it was not needed.

It was dark yet but just barely. The Count was awoken by eyes staring at him. He laid still, waiting for the attack, but nothing happened. He slowly cracked one eye to find Casandra, in her nightgown watching him. He was so shocked he had no idea want to do, so he closed his eye and waited for her to make her move.

"I know you're awake Count. Open your eyes don't play with me." Casandra sounded serious.

He opened them and smiled, "Is it so bad, Casandra?"

She had a very somber look, "It is. I woke in the middle of the night and realized you're leaving this morning and we haven't talked. I know nothing about what will happen." She started pacing, "When will we be together again? How? Where? I already miss you." She tightened her fists, "We should have made love what if something happens to you, how will I live? I am so frightened." Then she straightened up as tall as she could. "I will not have it. You cannot leave without me at your side. I don't need a holiday. I need to be with you. I will not be safe or happy without you. Don't just lay there say something encouraging or laugh." She walked to the bed, "So, now you know you are about to marry a crazy Witch. There it is, what are you going to do about it?" She stood without a smile and her arms crossed with her one eyebrow raised.

He pushed up on his arms and looked at her with amazement. He didn't laugh or tell her charming lies to placate her. He just pulled her into his arms and loved to her. They were perfect lovers. He tried to be quiet with her, but she was too intense to be completely silent. He burst into her, and she held him so tightly he thought she would crush him. He gently placed her in his arms tilted her head up, "No one has ever spoken to me as you just did. Well, perhaps my Mother. I will answer you now, I would have spoken to you before I left. I did not want to ruin the magic of last evening." He kissed her and said. "I was enjoying the enchantment of love and peace." She smiled at him.

"I must go to the King alone Casandra you cannot be there, and you know this. I want you to have a holiday and have fun but be careful and always wear the bracelet the Hermit gave you. I will seek you out on your holiday. Trust me I cannot stay away from you that long. I must arrange my life in Belissa Villa and Winsette Castle for your trip there and speak with my Mother and Father. I will return here after I meet with them, and your Father and I will make plans. I am going to ask to take you from your holiday directly to Winsette Castle for your formal introductions. And I adore you. I wish I could give you comfort about our future together. However, the Hermit is right; every one of our actions can change the future. Look at me. Last week at this very time, I was packed to leave the continent forever, and this week I am lying in bed with the most wonderful woman I have ever known. Even an oracle has a hard time promising a future. I do not make promises lightly, Casandra. I will never laugh at you when you come to me in seriousness. Also, I am a Warlock that likes a little crazy, so you are a lucky woman. Is there anything else?"

She smiled at him and said, "Yes. Do we have time to make love again?" Her right eyebrow raised. He understood now why the Empress left the room laughing yesterday he was bewitched by the Selvilla Sorcerer.

The Morning After

There was a knock on the door, mentally Addison said. Henry are you ready?

Henry answered. No, I've only just finished dressing Addison.

Addison opened the door. "This is not like you. I felt you awake early, you haven't even packed." Addison stopped. "Oh, forgive me."

Henry laughed, "You were up as early as me? What or who kept you awake Addison. If you break that Sprite's heart Casandra will never forgive you and I will hear it for all of my life."

Addison leaned on the wall and crossed his arms, "Will Casandra care that much if it is my heart that breaks?"

Henry looked closely at him, "The Castle was filled with so much love, and joy; you shouldn't mistake charms and incantations as true love."

Addison straightened up, "Henry, Marion and I have been together several times this week. I am afraid I fell in love with her long before last night. You have been so obsessed with Casandra you haven't seen half of what has gone on around you. I hope you are ready for the King he is powerful and will not be easy to fool."

Henry looked to his friend how had he missed this, he really did need to gather himself. "I am sorry, Addison I am happy for you." He slapped his shoulder, "Let's go to breakfast and see our girls I can have a man pack for me." He asked a servant to take a message to his soldiers. They would have everything packed and in the carriage by the time breakfast was done.

Marion and Casandra were on the landing waiting for them, the Castle looked as dark and vacant as he felt without the decorations. They walked into breakfast together it was filled with the conversation of the Ball and enchantments. Too soon the Emperor stood and said. "Shall we go to the Library?"

The Professor gave him a potion to drink then they all worked the charm until he was sufficiently sick and shaking. He was glad he had given Casandra a proper goodbye kiss earlier he was in no condition to kiss her now. He said his goodbyes to everyone. Then the Empress gave him a hug with temporary healing, "Everyone out… let's give them time alone."

Casandra was standing in front of him crying.

Henry held her. "My darling, don't send me away with tears let me see smiles."

She tried her best to smile, "I love you Henry please be safe and send me a message to let me know you are safe."

"All you have to do is ask Addison his mind is in constant connection with mine, so he will know. Were you aware he has fallen for Marion?" Henry needs to know if she had noticed.

"Really? I know Marion is over the moon for him, but…well, I have been so busy with you we haven't had time to talk. That explains a lot." She raised that eyebrow again.

Henry stood back from her. "Do you realize you raise your eyebrow when you are considering something or being thoughtful?"

"I do not my Mother does that." She suddenly turned pale. "So, does the Hermit."

"Take care not to do that on your holiday even in disguise someone might recognize that trait."

He drew her into his arms and kissed her deeply before Beatrice's healing spell ended, he could feel himself sinking. "I love you, Casandra. I will make this work we will have all your children and live to be old and cranky." Then he laughed, and she smiled adoringly for him.

She walked him to his Pegasus, and he took time giving Ski his orders. Ski would take the carriage and all but six of his men back to the Villa and start work on the Attachment cure.

Addison and the other six would head to Engelton. He could feel Addison still saying his goodbyes. Addison appeared, and it was really time to leave. They mounted, and Henry leaned down for one more kiss. "See you on the seashore." Only three steps and he was flying, now if he didn't look down, Henry might stay mounted until he reached the King.

Beatrice met them in the entry, "Girls we need to do some planning, and we'll use my sitting room. Emperor, you may have your library back. Mags bring us tea." Marion and Casandra followed her up the stairs. In the sitting room, Grace sat, patiently waiting.

The Empress closed the door, "Girls, please come and stand by me. I would like to show you a spell. She took Grace by both hands. She created a ball of light between them and gradually made it grow until it encased them both. Casandra and Marion watched puzzled, they could see the Empress and Grace speaking but could not hear them. The Empress twirled her finger then popped the bubble. "Do you girls understand what I just did?"

"Was it a secrecy bubble?" Casandra offered.

"No, it was a silence bubble. It is a wonderful little charm to keep in your formula box. It would have been useful last night for the both of you. If I had not been in the hallway, the entire Castle would have heard everything you did with you men." Casandra and Marion turned bright red, as the Empress folded her arms and raised her eyebrow.

Grace chuckled, "So that is where you were, Empress. We were looking all over the Castle to ask you what you wanted to be done with the servants we suspected of spying."

Casandra put her hands on her hips, "First of all Mother, I hope you were not eavesdropping and why were you in our hall? Your room is in the other wing."

It was the Empress chance to turn a shade of red. "That, young lady, is none of your business. No, I did not eavesdrop. I merely created a spell to protect the two of you from prying ears."

Casandra grinned, "After the enchantment Father set on you at the Ball I am surprised you even left him last Night."

The Empress snarled, "Casandra!"

"Oh Mother, it is alright that you show him, love. After all, the only reason you are not together is that of your obligation be the Empress. I do not understand, nor will I ever, why you cannot be together and rule the world. It is ridiculous that one must be one at the top and the other at the bottom. There should be some kind of magic to change that."

The Empress sighed, "It is not the only reason Casandra, you know this. How often have we talked about this? The balance of magic must be held between us. I have stayed just about as long as I dare. I can already feel the Magic thinning. Mags will help you with the planning after today." She hugged her close, "I hope you never have to be Empress but maybe you can work on that magic for Kathryn she will be next. Speaking of Kathryn and Mags here they come. Work on that spell together and use it."

The Emperor sat in the library with Major, the Prince, and the Professor as Eric gave his report of the spies that were caught the evening before. He also had a list of suspected traitors. "Sirs, I know your instinct is to cut them all from you. However, I see value in using a few of them, especially your General Matthews. He is high enough to feed information which would manipulate the King."

The Emperor agreed, "That is excellent advice, Eric. My worry is how to keep a close enough eye on him?"

Eric gave him a commanding smile, "I have an idea which would benefit my efforts and achieve your demand. They are aware of all the spies we have found embedded in your forces. Now would be a wonderful time to take measures for higher security, it wouldn't even be questioned. If you were to address your commanders directing them to have an Elf officer devoted to each division your spies could be contained. We could help them secure their meetings and messages, then we would be implanted into their spy system. We would be able to watch the traitors and control the intelligence they have."

The Major smiled, "Emperor, I think we need to raise this gentleman's rank and pay. I would also like to suggest we include Eric in the plans for Casandra's holiday and the meetings with the Count. Eric, you have always been a good friend to me, now you have become invaluable to our country."

“Thank you, Major.” Eric gave a half bow to the Major.

“Eric, you have been Cassandra’s protector for most of your time at the North Castle. I think it is fitting you are with her on her holiday, your last time together. None of you need to say anything more. Bryan raise Eric’s rank and pay too; make him a General, put him at the top. Consider making him an Earl or Duke; with some land, also. I can’t remember the procedures for nobility, work on that today. I would like to have Eric at a meeting tomorrow. Major, have my officers at my conference room tomorrow afternoon, say two in the afternoon. I will announce your raise in rank and use this past week’s efforts as the reason. Now, gentlemen, I would like to have my office back. I need to work on the country’s business. Major, could you remain?

Eric bowed to the Emperor, “Thank you, Sir.”

The Professor shook Eric’s hand, “Congratulations Eric. Good day, Emperor and Major. I do have a few tasks I need to attend to.” He parted ways with Eric in the hallway, then headed out the doors to the garden. He had yet to have one private moment with Mags this would be his opportunity.

The Hoax

The small band of men surrounded the Count as they were flying to Engelton. Addison had to hold Henry on to the Pegasus he almost fell three times. The Count refused to stop and rest; he wanted this over. They landed in the afternoon, in the Engelton Castle courtyard and Addison helped Henry from his mount. They were immediately met with guards who seized the Count from Addison.

"I will take him to see the King," Addison announced.

"No Sir. The Count is expected, you may remain with your men in the barracks. We will escort him to the King." The guards helped Henry walked away while other guards escorted Addison and his men through the Palace courtyard.

The Count mentally told Addison he was alright, just be ready to come when he needed him. Henry decided to put extra weight on the two guards ushering him and trip a few times just to give them grief. He was feeling sick, but the height of flying had made it worst; he should have used a carriage, but that would have slowed them down considerably. He was taken to the King's office, the officers outside just stared in disbelief as they push him along. The Prince, Ernst, and all the Kings Generals were inside waiting. They threw him in a chair directly in front of the King. Henry had to fight to keep his power concealed he would not show these men how much power he had. He never trusted or liked any of them.

The Kings face grimaced, "Count you look sick. I would love to help you feel better. General Brad, the antidote please."

The General placed it on the desk in front of Henry, just out of his reach. Henry tried to straighten up but couldn't.

"Count, I will see that marriage contract." The General helped Henry to sit up. Henry reached into his coat to retrieve the contract. "I'll remove that Henry; we don't want to you to overexert yourself." General Due Bre reached in Henry's pocket, took the contract and handed it to the King. Henry just stared at the King with as much hatred as he could muster. He needed to play this part flawlessly.

The King finished reading, folded the contract and gave him a very smug smile. "My goodness Count you have far surpassed my expectations this is a handsome settlement. You own all the North Mountains, powers, and gems. I would venture to say you are most likely the richest Warlock in this world. A nice accomplishment for a man whose title has been stripped. To think not long ago you were one of the poorest Warlocks in the world. When I make you King, you will remember this and keep me as your ally, whether you want to or not. Of course, it would be better for both of us if you want to be my friend." The King paused. "Henry, I have never known you to be this silent. Don't you want to talk to me?"

Henry placed his hands on the desk, "I'll have the contract back, your Majesty."

"I think you should have a drink of antidote first Henry. You really aren't looking well." The King smiled the man was thriving on Henry's weakness. He was a sadistic idiot.

"The contract first." Henry leaned forward and took the contract from him, grabbed the antidote, and stood to leave. "I will be leaving now."

General Brad stood to stop him, "Henry you have gone long enough without the antidote it will start to cause you some serious harm."

Henry smiled at him, "Your concern warms my heart, General. However, are you even in your right mind? I wouldn't trust you any more than I would any of these others. All of you would stand here and watch me die, then cut me to pieces just to make sure I could not reassemble myself. I am leaving and testing this antidote before I drink one drop." He turned to leave.

The King stood, he could not let Henry leave without doing the blood testing. Life with Elisabeth had been wonderful he was not about to let this idiot ruin it. He could kill the Count anytime. "Henry don't be a fool, do as the General has ordered. You know I need you not only alive but healthy enough to marry the girl. The Emperor will not allow Casandra to marry an invalid. If I had no need of you, I would have killed you twenty years ago. You know that. Besides I have grown fond of you over the years."

Henry turned and smiled at him, "You Sir, are fond of my wine, and I am fond of your coin; that Sir, is our affiliation. Don't stand in front of me and make more of it!" He walked to the door. Where was Elisabeth she was to stop him? He could hear a commotion in the outer room he turned the door handle.

"Count, I am so happy to see you. I was just telling these officers I would wait until the meeting was over to see you. I wanted to make sure the King did not forget to bring you to dinner. Are you alright Count?" Elisabeth came to him with concerned eyes.

"Yes, my lady. I am just a little tired from the events of last week. I am engaged, did you know?" The Count bowed to the Queen and deliberately fell to the ground.

The Queen tried to catch him, but the Generals were already lifting him back into the room and onto a couch.

"Richard the Count is seriously ill let me call the Healers." The Queen went to the officers and started barking orders.

The King came around and canceled them. "Come in my Dear and listen to me. Henry has been poisoned, and General Brad has the antidote, but Henry doesn't trust it. He wants to take it home to his laboratory to test it first. He is foolish, please, come in and convince him to drink antidote. He will be fine in a few minutes if he will just stop being stubborn."

She went to Henry and knelt by the couch, "Henry stop being a Warlock! Take a drink. I know you and the King have had your differences over the years, but he really does like you. He has told me, on many occasions. I could force you I do have powers, I could compel you."

Henry threw back his head and laughed, "How could I refuse you. I have always loved you. If we could just think of a way to get rid of him, would you run away with me?"

The Queen blushed and kissed his cheek, "Henry really this is not the time for jokes or flirtations. Drink the antidote! How is that young woman going to handle you, or keep you? Drink!" She took the bottle uncorked it and put it to his mouth.

"Yuck, what is in this? It tastes like mint!" Henry made a face.

General Brad said, "Mint is my favorite flavor."

"I hate mint; couldn't you have made it taste like wine?"

"Just drink a little then Henry." The Queen tilted the bottle again. "Here sit up and drink as much as you can. Make him rest here a while. You are staying for dinner, that is my command. Oh, is that handsome Addison with you?"

"Yes your Majesty, he is along with me." Henry smiled at her.

"Well bring him with you, and I think it would be wise to spend the night you will feel better with a good night's sleep." Henry kissed her hand and said he would. "I would like clarification of how you were poisoned, perhaps at dinner." She glared at the King and left the room.

The King and the Generals took their seats. "Henry." King snarled, "From now on I think I'll have the Queen deal with you. We need to have an honest talk. You are a pivotal part of my plan coming together. The next few months you will be in heavy contact with the Emperor and his Council. You must understand we cannot give you information that would put the mission in jeopardy. It isn't so much we don't fully trust you, it is more the fact the less you know, the easier your part will be to play. Having said that, we do need a way to contact you if our plans change."

Henry took another sip of the antidote, discerning the ingredients it was very similar to the Professors. "You didn't think to ask me for help. You forced me into a situation that is very unappealing to me. Now you want me to be a co-conspirator without a morsel of knowledge. How do you know I will not inadvertently do or say something to ruin your strategies. I should at the very least know what not to do?"

The King sat back and looked at his friend Martin. Martin came to the couch and sat next to him. "You are looking better, Count. Please drink more of the antidote."

The Count raised his eyebrow if it worked for Casandra perhaps it would work for him. He took a liberal drink. "This is obnoxious. I can swallow no more just now it is burning my stomach. May I have some wine to wash away the taste?"

General Brag said, "No wine just yet, Henry. Ernst, could you get some ale for the Count that should help his stomach and ask Cook for a piece of bread. Henry, have you eaten today?"

"Not since breakfast I was sick afterward. I couldn't keep a thing down." Henry looked at the Prince he was almost a green as Henry felt. This boy was not the King's son he was compassionate.

"Henry, I have known you many years, and I have been your biggest supporter. Not only do I find you an entertaining fellow, I really enjoy your wines. We discussed bringing you into our plan and would have except we had nothing to entice you. You are a handsome man; you have your choice of women or men. For Night's sake, you had the Queen on her knees to you a moments ago. You have wealth beyond our means to match, now you have a Mountain of jewels. If you had a need, we could bargain with we would have used it. We promised you the Kingdom of Diamante; we do control your Brothers. However, you have never shown any interest in politics." Martin paused, and Henry took advantage of it.

"I hate politics, and the last thing I want is to be burdened with a crown. I hate all the requirements being placed on me now. I am now forced to deal with my loving Brothers to plan for this ludicrous pompous wedding. My Mother will force me to take her, and her court to the North Castle and Gods knows what other parties. I might add, everyone expects me to provide the wine. I have other interests! You have never bothered to inquire about those." Henry was feeling better, now he could control the path of this discussion. "If you have the influence over my Brothers, make them play nice with me, the Emperor, and Casandra. I don't need a battle with them. If you had paid any attention to the wines you say you love, you would recognize magic is my passion. All kinds of magic." He swirled the bottle of potion in this hand. "If I had a laboratory I could make this shit taste like a golden ale." He stared at the bottle but noted the looks that were exchanged between everyone in the room, he had them.

The King sat up. "We have a lab Henry, right in the Castle, and we also have an excellent school of science. I would be willing to take you there, and you could pick anything that interests you or all of it." Ernst came into the room with ale and bread. Henry took a piece of bread and drank a large swallow of ale. They started to pour some for themselves, but Henry stopped them.

"One moment gentlemen." He held out his hand and created a ball of golden light and dumped it into the pitcher and part in his cup. He took a swig and said, "That's better. You have my interest, see how easy it is to deal with me? It is best to know your adversary and your associates."

Martin drank his ale, "Henry you do have a talent with magical potions."

The King agreed. "If you are feeling up to it General Brad can take you to the laboratory. You can experiment on your antidote. Martin why don't you see that Henry's men are settled in for the night. We can take the Count to the Science School tomorrow before he leaves. Don't forget to tell Addison he is expected at dinner, then meet us at the laboratory."

The King came around his desk and extended a hand to Henry. The Count looked suspiciously at him. "No poison Henry. I believe we have a mutual agreement. I will draft a letter to your Brothers immediately, then I will meet you in the Laboratory. I have a small courtesy to ask you. If you can help me, I would be in your debt."

"What would that courtesy be, King?" Henry still did not take the King's hand.

The King sighed, "Well, I guess I can't blame you for being apprehensive of me. I have been given to understand you hold the ability to examine blood for qualities and configurations. Is this true?'

Henry tilted his head as if he were considering it, the King was leading himself right into his plot and in front of his generals. "It is the Belissa talent. We work a great deal with blood. We often do blood bonds with fiancés, partners, and consorts. Sharing our wealth equally one must not hold secrets. Casandra and I did one last week."

The King pulled a chair up and sat in front of Henry. "Is that so, did you find out anything interesting from your bride?"

Henry threw his head back and laughed. "Quite a bit actually; wouldn't you like to know some of that? What is the nature of the blood test you are asking for?"

The King crossed his arms, "I would like to test someone's blood to see what traits and powers they possess. Can you do that?"

Henry held an unmoving face. "Belissa's can detect all of that and numerous times more. I can do this for you, but it will take me some time, it is not my area of expertise. It is Addison's, though. If Martin can bring him to the laboratory, I believe we can accommodate you, King."

Henry extended his hand. The King took it and pulled Henry up, "Go on to the lab I will be along as soon as I draft a letter to your Brothers. They will give you everything you want knowing the crown remains theirs."

That left the King alone with the Prince and Ernst. "You two go bring the Queen to the laboratory I want her there." He gave Ernst a look of hate, which gave Devon a shiver that went up to his spine.

Addison was taken through the Castle to an upper floor to the laboratory. When he entered, Henry was working at a burner with a test tube. Henry turned and smiled. Mentally he told Addison the King had taken the bait. Now it was Addison's show. "Henry, you look remarkably better than the last time I saw you. I was beginning to worry."

"My Dear friend, the General's antidote works well; it tastes like shit. So, I am modifying it. It seems we have an agreement with the King." Henry smelled his concoction and gave it a taste. "Not bad would you like to try it, General Brad?"

The General tasted it. "That is remarkable, you should write that down for me. Martin is right, you do have a talent for tastes."

The Count drank the rest of the antidote; he had weakened it to a tenth of its strength. The spells were worn away, and he was thinking much clearer. The King entered with the Queen, Devon, and Ernst. The man was devious and cruel, he would humiliate and agonize the Queen in front of her own Son. Henry wanted to strangle the man. Instead, he went to the Queen and bowed. "Queen, you have an interest in blood tests?"

She turned to the King, and he smiled. "This one I do Count. You look much better."

"I am Madam, the tonic worked wonders." He held up the empty bottle of the antidote. "Now, what tests are we running for the Kingdom? And whose blood do we draw?"

Addison stepped up, "Your Majesty," he bowed to the Queen, "You look enchanting, I am pleased to attend dinner with you this evening. I took the liberty of sending you some wine for dinner. I understand Martin is engaged to Janet, your gorgeous daughter. I had a special wine chilled for a toast to her."

Henry sighed, "Well, well, congratulations are in order Martin. I never thought to see you properly married. What did I tell you about Addison, he is always taking liberty with our wine." Everyone laughed. "Addison, I told the King we could help decipher a blood sample for him. Since you are so much faster, I offered your services."

"Of course," He walked to the laboratory table and started lifting and reading bottles Addison asked, "What are you asking us to find and do you have the sample?"

The King said. "The sample of blood will come from the Prince and Ernst. It seems our Prince has developed some characteristic of an Arlequin, just recently. His Professor at the Science School has been raising questions. He had proposed that having Ernst, so close Devon has picked up his traits."

General Brad said, "I have never heard of such a thing what is he trying to do, upsurge you." The General was turning red.

The King was also getting angry. "I don't think so, General. I do know the man won't rest until there is an explanation. The Queen remembered Devon having a bad injury when he was young. Ernst provided blood for him. Addison, what do you know about this?"

Addison looked at Henry and mentally said. You set this up nicely my friend. "I do agree with the General, just having contact with a person would not be sufficient to pass on traits. However, if there are some traces of Arlequin in the Prince's blood, now that may cause him to acquire traits. Prince, we will need a good quantity of your blood, I am sorry. Henry, would you help? Ernst, I will only need a few drops of your blood. This really won't take too long let me get prepared." Addison went to work mixing and heating up potions while Henry went to the Prince.

"I could prick your finger, but it would take some time to get enough blood. If I cut your arm, it will be much faster. I can close the wound with magic, but it may leave a scar it is your choice."

"The arm then." The Prince met Henry's gaze.

The Count proceeded, he rolled up Devon sleeve and saw at least six scars. "I see you have enough scars no one will notice another." The Prince only smiled. Henry would take enough blood to find out more about this young man. He set the blood sample down next to Addison and mentally said. We need to save some blood to find out more about this Prince. "Addison, would you like me to get Ernst blood?"

"Please Henry, I am almost ready." Addison had his back to the others. "Would you all like to step closer? It isn't dangerous, and I can explain how I am doing this."

They all came around to the counter, and Addison put a blue liquid in a beaker, over a flame. "I will add the Prince's blood first." He poured almost half of the blood collected. It quickly bubbled and turned a light green, then he placed a drop of Ernst's blood and a black line spun through it and disappeared.

"It's not strong enough," Henry commented. "Ernst a few more drops please."

Addison said. "Wait, Henry, I may just need to make the base stronger." He poured all most all the Prince's blood sample in and the liquid turn emerald green. "Here it is Henry." This time a black ribbon spiraled to the bottom of the beaker, then Addison cut the flame off.

"There it is King, the black running through is Ernst blood. This is proof the Prince holds blood from Ernst in his body. The traits are limited; he won't have the strong powers Ernst has. Maybe not many of the traits of the Arlequin clan at all. I would certainly encourage training and see how far he can get. It never hurts to have extra powers in your arsenal."

Addison stepped back so all of them could take a closer look.

Henry came to Addison, mentally he said. You are a genius.

Addison replied. Oh, I am not done yet, watch. "Blood is amazing, it can reveal traits, powers, intelligence, and parentage. It can also measure the amount of power a Sorcerer, Wizard or Warlock can hold."

The King turned. "You can tell parentage? And how much power a Warlock holds?"

"Oh yes, and the strength of their powers. Fascinating, isn't it?" Addison admired his work, deliberately ignoring the King.

“How? How can you tell who the parent is? And the power?”

“Oh, that is easy your Majesty. I already know Ernst blood is foreign to the Prince.” Addison reached in with a tweezer and pulled out the spiral of black blood. It was as solid as steel. “If Ernst were Devon’s Father his blood would have mixed with Devon’s. There would be nothing to see, no particles or flakes floating around. The first drop did try to mix, that is why Henry wanted to add more of Ernst’s blood. That would have probably disappeared too, a common mistake. I needed to strengthen the solution with Devon’s blood. Look at that deep color green… your son is powerful. Did you notice how it turned the foreign blood to steel? Devon can stand up to great power. Magic always defends its power it is only natural, even in blood. What I find incredible is the color, such a deep color. Normally blood is just a shade of red blue to red-purple or red to orange like mine. This is as green as your eyes.”

The King looked like he saw a ghost everyone in the room was quiet.

Except for Devon, he was smiling. The Prince walked to Addison. “You’re saying if you added my Father’s blood it would mix in and disappear?”

“Absolutely.” Addison smiled and winked, “Smart man.”

Devon said, “Go ahead Father, just for fun I want to see it work.”

The Queen took in a breath, and the King glared at her.

Henry held out the pen knife for the King to prick himself. Henry said to Addison mentally. I am enjoying this.

The King took the knife cut his thumb held it over the beaker and released a few drops. Addison turned the flame back on, and the King’s blood disappeared. Not believing, the King added a few drops more, it vanished immediately.

Devon put a hand on the King’s shoulder. “Not a flake or particle. Can’t deny I am your Son.” Devon laughed, and the King smiled and hugged him. Henry could see the King look to Elisabeth, this time with compassion.

The Queen relaxed and breathed deeply. “Dinner is probably almost ready I will go see to it. Don’t stay here playing too long.” She smiled at Henry and left the room.

"I'll help you clean the lab, Addison." Henry went to the table.

"Nonsense, you two deserve some wine. I'll have my men take care of it." General Brad took the beaker off the flame. "When this is all over King I would seriously enlist these men to teach us some blood magic."

Henry looked at the General earnestly, "Dispose of the Prince's blood yourself you don't want that to get into the wrong hands."

They went off to dinner Addison mentally said. Did you palm some of that blood Henry?

Henry replied. You didn't see me you were a great distraction. Sleight of hand is in the realm of my expertise.

Ernst said, "I show you to your rooms you may want to clean up before dinner."

The King said, "Thank you, Ernst. You come to dinner too; understand?" He placed a hand on Ernst's shoulder. Addison could see a transfer of power from the King to Ernst.

Ernst turned quickly, "Follow me, gentlemen, I know a shortcut." Henry and Addison followed Ernst out the door and down the hallway. They crossed the central courtyard through an archway and into a garden. He walked to a vine-covered bench where the Queen was sitting. Ernst held up his hand and made the sign to be silent. The Queen held out her hands, an energy ball of silver appeared. She blew into it, and it encompassed the four of them, it was clear.

The Queen stood. "We don't have a lot of time. I just had to thank you both for your intervention in the matter. If you have an opportunity to talk to the Hermit tell her the only way I feel safe communicating is with green paper. Now that the weather is nice I sit in the gazebo every afternoon from the third to the fourth hour she can visit me there. I will do a concealment spell like this one, he leaves me alone only during that hour. I thank you for taking my Son out of this. Tell the Empress I owe her my life; she will have a payment."

She looked to Ernst, and he said, "If there is some way I can help, do not hesitate to enlist me. I have raised that young man, and he is not the King's Son in any way. I hope we are not too late the King has no heart, never did. He aims to make Devon's heartless too."

Addison said, "Ernst I saw the King give you power why?"

Ernst tilted his head and smiled weakly, "He does that when I please him. It's not his power he gifts me; it's a return of my own he stole from me." Addison frowned.

Henry said, "I am sorry, Ski is working on a reversal to the Attachment, we intend to help both of you. I can get messages to you Elisabeth we will help Devon, I will keep you informed. We better leave."

The Queen said, "Yes Ernst please take them to their rooms I will see you at dinner, you leave first."

Ernst turned, "He invited me to dinner, so I better be there. Please find an excuse to dismiss me, if you can." Ernst walked out of the bubble.

Henry kissed her on the cheek. "He loves you." He walked out along with Addison, they looked behind them no one was standing there. Addison said mentally. That's an excellent spell.

Ernst smiled and mentally said. Yes, it has always worked well.

Addison and Henry looked at one another with shock. They mentally asked Ernst. You use telepathy?

Ernst laughed, mentally he began to answer their questions. Yes, and yes, the King knows of this power. It is why I am showing you to your rooms and not some guard. He has me spy on you and reports your thoughts to him. I have been doing this for years. Yes, I can anticipate your questions, also one of my talents. I used to fight him, every time I did, he took more of my power and tortures my Queen and me. I don't fight anymore. The Queen and I wanted you to know because he ordered me to report to him before dinner. I will give you some time to decide what you want him to know, come to the stable soon, he will stop me before I get to the dining room. One more reason I don't want to be at the dinner. What I don't know I can't tell him. Yes, I do love the Queen, I always have.

They reached their rooms Ernst spoke out loud, "Is there anything else I can help you with?"

Henry held his hand out and said, "No thank you, Ernst." Then he asked him mentally. Did you take Casandra from her bed?

Ernst dipped his head. Then mentally said. Yes, I am ashamed to say it. The King put a hot poker to my face and compelled me to climb into her room. He said he would do the same to Elizabeth.

Addison mentally asked. Then you did not kill the Emperor?

He answered. No, that was Martin. He turned to walk away then turned back, "I will see you gentlemen at dinner." He added mentally. That is why I pushed them back into the carriage and sent it flying at Elk's Pass. I was hoping to make amends to the Night, and Casandra.

Henry mentally said, Thank you Ernst Gadwell of Arlequin.

Ernst smiled but walked on not saying or thinking anything.

Addison thought. This is going to be one exciting dinner. We better decide what to tell Ernst.

Henry thought. We better dress fast and head off the King.

They dressed quickly Henry told Addison, "I am going to talk to the King about that School of Science before dinner. I will see you down there." Mentally he said. Find Ernst and talk to him.

Addison said. "I think I will check on the men. I'll meet you there." Then he went to find Ernst.

Henry found the King in the library and began asking questions about the school. Not long after Addison and Ernst walked past together talking about Pegasus. The King stopped them, "Ernst, excuse me Henry, Addison. I need to have a word with Ernst in private, Castle business."

Henry took his glass from the table, "Of course, I will go out and have a look at the garden we passed through so quickly on our way to our rooms I didn't get a good look at it."

He left going into the hall, and Ernst shut the door. Henry thought. Can we trust him?

Addison thought. We have no choice.

The Queen found them walking down the hall, "Henry, Addison join me in the parlor. The girls are waiting for you they have a million questions about your engagement party."

They followed the Queen, the girls swarmed them. Addison and Henry could hardly keep up with the questions.

The King and Ernst joined them after a while. Ernst mentally told Henry and Addison he reported of their interest in the Science School, and particularly about the Attachment spell. As Addison suggested, Ernst also said they had made speculations about the blood tests. The King laughed when Ernst said you were wondering who in the room might be Devon's Father. He wasn't pleased that you picked Deu Bre as your first choice because Deu Bre is so handsome and the King is a jealous man. He was pleased with the information. Dinner was announced, and the party moved to the dining room.

Henry offered a toast to Janet and Martin, he worked hard to keep ill feelings about Martin to a minimum. He knew Ernst could feel his antagonism. Grayson came into the dining room just as dinner was to start. He told Ernst he was needed in the barn; a mare was about to fold. The Queen smiled, and the King excused him. Dinner was filled with talk of weddings and engagement parties. Janet innocently asked Henry to bring Casandra to the upcoming engagement party.

Henry used this opening to give the King a little information he didn't have. "I am sorry Janet; my bride is taking her holiday. I expect not to see her until after her return. Then we will go to Diamante for a series of parties and such in my Kingdom. Your wedding is a few seasons away. I am sure she will love to see you on your wedding day. I guarantee we will both attend. I would be delighted to be here for your engagement party."

Janet answered, "With all the preparations for a wedding how can she vacation?"

Henry took a sip of wine, "Oh it isn't a holiday like a vacation. My understanding is it's more of a reward for the hard work of finishing school. Many in the East give this gift to the Sorcerers."

The Queen corrected him. "Henry, you have it all wrong. High Sorcerers are granted a season. Casandra has not been free to do as she wishes since she was eleven years of age. The schools she has attended, the boys she has had liaisons with, even the clothes she wears, and her friends are chosen for her. Of course, Henry was too; no doubt for being a good alliance with Diamante. Henry's money had more to do with it than his looks, or how she feels about him. Henry, she had no choice about you. Lucky for her you are a handsome man if you weren't, she would still be forced to marry you anyway. Her holiday is her payment; one season to do as she wishes and go where she wants. She can do everything she wishes or nothing at all. Freedom for a season, a cheap payment for service to her country for the rest of her life. A season should be months, not weeks, you have cut that short. Tell me Henry do you even like or appreciate her?"

Henry was taken back, "Your Majesty I hardly know how to answer. She is beautiful, brilliant, and sweet. I suppose I do like her."

Devon said, "What? You like her?" He was visibly upset with Henry.

Joan said, "She is your bride, you should love her."

Henry did not want the King to know he loved her. "Joan Dear, customs on this Continent are different from yours. Marriage as your Mother said, is for alliances. I hardly know her; it's only been a week. Your parents married for love, they are the lucky, as you girls are. Who knows with time, we may grow to love one another."

The King sat up straight, "I am surprised Casandra is being allowed the holiday. I heard there was trouble there with rebels, where is she going?"

Henry said, "To Sigal and some islands in that area, that is the fashion this year. I understand it is very exotic and filled with revelries. Many of her friends will be there. I have never been; it is known to cater to youth, not my preference. Of course, we have been the Plains to acquire our Pegasus."

Jessica said, "Father I think you should institute a season for us we always follow your orders." Everyone laughed.

The Queen took the Kings hand "I am sorry Richard, I should not have spoken about this in front of your spoiled children."

The King laughed, "I might have stopped you had I really know what a season was, but I take the blame for my spoiled children. I remember all those boys I have chased off, none of them were of my choosing. I hardly tell you what to wear or what to study or how much of my money to spend. I allow you to marry for love. Look to Janet and Martin. Henry, did you know they have been seeing each other secretly for years. I gain only a son-in-law; he comes with no monies or title. However, I have called him a good friend for years, now I get to call him family. I couldn't be happier. Young ladies, I think you have it good. Do you want a season? You will save for it, and you will be on an allowance starting tomorrow." The table was silent. The Queen was trying not to laugh.

Joan spoke first, "Father, I am perfectly happy with my life. Well, you could send Jessica away. She always causes trouble." The King threw his head back in laughter, along with everyone. Henry had never seen the King so happy.

The King said. "My beautiful Queen, I have enjoyed this evening, and I would like to have it last. However, our guests will be leaving in the morning, and we have some business to discuss. We'll go to the library. Will the ladies excuse us?"

The Queen stood, went to the King and placed her arms around him. She gave him a tender kiss, "I'll say Goodnight love we must be up early tomorrow. The girls and I have appointments to plan Janet's wedding. We plan to spend much of your money, so go find more fabs." Then she laughed.

The King actually said nothing just looked surprised as she left the room.

Henry said, "I see your daughters are not the only ones spoiled, King." Addison mentally said. Play this close to your chest Henry, we must make him believe. That surprised look he gave the Queen shows his suspicion.

They settled into the library with after dinner drinks and a roaring fire. It was making Henry sleepy. "Your Majesty, I hope this business can be concluded quickly I am suddenly exhausted."

General Brad said, "That is to be expected Henry you have been fighting back the poison all week. You should really head home and rest a week or so."

Henry replied. "I have too much to do in too short of time. I am sorry rest is not on my agenda."

"I will keep this to the point, Henry." The King sat in the chair opposite him. "I must ask, my sources told me you and the Sorcerer seemed very much in love. At dinner, it seemed you are indifferent to her."

Henry looked to Addison. Henry knew the King believed them lovers for years. That was why he always gave them a room together. Addison would still play the part with Henry. Addison turned and pretended to look at the books on the shelf, giving off an equal amount of disgust and hurt.

"As I said she is beautiful, and we seem to be compatible. It will not be an unwelcome marriage. However, love is something that must grow and be cultivated." Henry looked at Addison and mentally said. You are looking a little too forlorn. "Am I mistaken? I was told to do all I could to make this match and convince the young woman to shorten the courtship. The Empress almost seared me when I mentioned weeks."

Addison started snickering. Henry gave him a look. "I was forced to create a charm of love. Did I not give you want you wanted?"

The King looked at Addison. "Yes Henry, you gave me exactly what I wanted. I was not aware of how good you are at deception, Addison does not do as well. Now, this holiday, when does she leave and how does she travel?"

Henry said, "She leaves sometime this week. They do have preparations for a wedding to settle. Being the concerned groom, I have insisted Addison be a part of her guards. I thought you would be interested in her plans, so I placed him in a convenient position for us. He flies back to North Castle when we leave."

The King sat back in his chair and smiled. "Well, it is nice to have you on my side for a change. I have always enjoyed your devious mind, just not when used against me. You are an easier man to deal with when you get what you want. Now is the time to tell me exactly what that is."

Now, Henry smiled and lifted his empty glass to Addison, who came with the wine bottle to fill it. "Not just me King; Addison as well. Magic, any magic that can give me power. Tomorrow I will see what you can offer us, and I am very interested in a spell I have heard of, it is called an Attachment." The Generals took in the air; they were not happy about this. "I see not everyone here is fond of letting that spell fall into my hands. I wonder why? You General Brad want me to hand over our secrets of blood spells this would be an equal exchange."

The King smiled and shook his head, "Henry I am sorry. I have deeply underestimated you all these years. The lust for power is the one motivation I can understand. We will see what we can do to give it to you."

The King drank his wine, "I will give you some information about the Attachment now, and more when you deliver your Countess with the final portion when you leave Azur with your child and Countess. I will compensate you for your knowledge of blood. I must apologize Henry you will become Emperor, like it or not."

Henry had a bad feeling, "Don't look so worried Henry you will be recognized for bringing all the Continents together in world peace. I will join the consortium and be your right-hand man." He gave a wicked laugh. "Martin will be your advisor; Casandra your Empress and you will have all the time you need to pursue your passions." He looked to Addison. "One last question, you eluded to have some interesting information about Casandra. I know you would like to share that with me, you will sleep so much better."

Henry could not express his deep feeling of hatred he held for this man, he would destroy him if it was the last thing he did. "King I not happy about that. Let us leave becoming Emperor on the table for now and see if we can't find a more suitable candidate for Emperor, like your Son." He looked to the Prince, "Something to consider."

Henry stood and stretched, "When we spell a blood bond we can ask the partner for certain memories. I had always been curious about her kidnapping." Henry went to the mantle and stared at the fire he could no longer see this man's face, "Lucky for you, her Mother could not stand all of Casandra's nightmares. She masked her memories, I got to see the unmasked memory. I saw her memory from the time Ernst took her from her bed, dropping her to Martin, who gave her to you in the boat. I saw the Professor taking her eggs and felt the pain. You came close to killing her twice, Casandra must be watched by the Night. She was in darkness a long time before she was taken to the Monks." Henry let that settle in. "If not for the kindness of others, you gentlemen would be without a donor to carry your infested eggs. Oh, Yes King. I have a good idea of your strategies. You have underestimated me, in so many ways." He set his empty wine glass on the desk. "There is more. Perhaps when I know more about the magic you promised, I will be able to remember it." He sighed, "I really can't go on this evening, I must retire, please excuse me." Henry bowed to the King, waiting patiently to be dismissed. The King stood and walked to Henry and placed a hand on his shoulder, pulling power from him. Henry closed off his source of energy, making sure the King could not access it. This was not what he wanted, a pissing contest, let the King think him weak. Henry slummed to the ground.

The King said, "Don't antagonize me, Henry. I can destroy you. Martin help Addison take Henry to bed. I am sure by morning he will be thinking much clearer. Good night, Henry."

They began dragging him down the hall. The Queen watched from nearby cloaked in a disappearance spell. She went to her room to dress in her most alluring nightgown. Henry had come close to finding out first-hand about an Attachment spell. She would need to placate the King, or his anger would be used on her. She could do nothing to help Henry she would pray to the Night for him.

The Prince went to his Father, "King I know you are angry at him. Think how you would feel if you had been poisoned, forced to marry a person you did not love or want, and told you were to become exactly what you hated. He has been under a great deal of duress. I know I would get a little sarcastic if I were him. He is playing games and trying to keep some of his pride. You just took the last bit of his vanity."

The King let out a breath, "My Son, you are wiser than I thought. I will give some of that vanity back to him tomorrow. Besides nothing can ruin tonight, with my family, and my Son." He hugged Devon, "You are more compassionate than I, but that can be a double-edged sword. There are times to show strength and times to be benevolent. Henry has a large ego, he would overpower me if he could. I needed to show him I will always be more powerful. I will teach you how to do the same." He slapped Devon on his back giving him some power. "We need to get some sleep tomorrow we will make Henry happy."

Martin helped take Henry's boots off, "The rest of his clothes are your problem, Addison. Henry, you are hanging on a slippery slope. I know you are mad at the King for manipulating you into doing his bidding but being sarcastic and flexing your power is not the way to sway the King. Behave yourself he does like you, he just doesn't trust you. Try to be nice to him."

Henry looked up, "He wouldn't believe me."

"Okay, Henry, how about just being civil" Martin shook his head, "You are a good fellow. I will try to help you tomorrow. Just be… well just let me handle him."

"You're doing this for wine aren't you Martin?" Henry laughed, "I am joking Martin that is the real problem… you Hexian's don't know what a joke is."

"You're right Henry, so don't joke tomorrow. Goodnight." He left the room.

Addison added mentally. You almost came undone, Henry. Martin was right, you need to be more congenial tomorrow, or we will both be dead. The King was not playing with us.

Henry added I know, you are right.

The next morning Henry and Addison met the Queen in the hallway. "Henry." She shielded them, "Please be careful. He will think nothing of killing you or worse, giving you an Attachment."

Henry said, "You spied, well, I agree with you. I promise I will be careful. This is too dangerous for you. Release the shield."

She did. "I'll walk you to the dining room. Henry, you look much better today. I will send the engagement invitation to your Villa or should it be the North Castle?"

"It doesn't matter Madam. I know the day, and I will be here. I will send some nice wine for the occasion." They entered the dining room where Martin and the Prince were with the King.

The Queen walked to the King and kissed his cheek, "Gentlemen, you will serve yourselves this morning everything is on the sideboard. We are leaving now for the town. Count thank you for the gift of wine for the engagement party it is very nice of you. I will see you at the party Count. Now I am going to have a look at our new Pegasus."

The King stood and kissed the Queen, "I can't keep you from babies, no matter what the type." He went to serve himself, "Yes Henry, thank you for the gift."

Henry bowed, "My pleasure, King. I feel I owed it to you for my bad behavior last night, please accept my apologies."

"Of course, Henry. I would like to apologize to you as well. I was not expecting you to have known my plot… well, not the details, not even the general plan. It put me off, and I did not handle it well. However, it did give you an idea of what I would do to you if I thought I couldn't trust you. Let's have a pleasant breakfast we can leave for the Science Schools right after."

Henry looked out into the hall and men were already carrying Addison's and his bags out. He was in a hurry to get done with them.

The Science School was very interesting, and Henry was impressed professor Moondale had made some strides understanding talents and how to magnify and enhance them. Addison mentally said. He is not sharing anything about the Attachment.

Henry replied. My anger has done this.

The King said, "Prince would you be willing to give Henry and Addison a sample of your newest skill?"

The Prince looked shocked, but recovered, and said. "If that is what you wish Sir."

The King said, "See Henry, even my Son doesn't trust you. You are right my boy Henry isn't to be trusted quite yet. Yet a demonstration is not an instruction. It will wet his appetite for power that will keep him in our hands." The King looked at Henry, "I keep my bargain in all things."

That was a threat if Henry ever heard one. Henry replied, "I would be in your debt, King."

The Professor led them from the Science building across the courtyard down the stairs, and through a maze of corridors in a basement. Henry had always been grateful for Addison's ability to remember everything in pictures and words. Henry could too, this is what had brought them together in school. Between them, no Professor could stump them. He would remember the way down here. They walked into a dark room to one side a table was set up as a small laboratory. Along the wall bottles of chemicals and charms stood one next to the other. Henry said mentally. You take the wall, I will do the table.

A door opened, and a young Witch was brought in and pushed into the chair in the middle of the room. Someone raised the lights, and the Witch started to protest but the Prince waved his hands, and she froze. He tied her hands to the chair cut her arm and took her blood. At first, Addison thought they needed help with blood work. However, the Prince healed the wound and went to the table and took blood from his own arm. Now Henry understood the scars on his arms.

The Prince worked a charm with the elements and incantations. Henry concentrated on the mixture and Addison memorized the words. The Prince put a glove on his hand and poured the concoction over the glove. He went to the young Witch and began to woo her kissing her and holding her tenderly. As she fell under his charms, he placed his hand on her throat. Henry could see the enchantment enter her body, the Prince dropped the glove and put his lips on the spot and his hand on her abdomen. As the spell and elements worked their way down her body, she threw back her head enjoying his touch. Then the Prince began sucking her power from the Attachment. The spell shot down to her loins and hooks sprang from it piercing her, then she started screaming. He was draining her life force and taking her to near depletion. When Witch fell forward, Henry could see the attachment on her neck from it a ribbon of energy extended to the Prince's mouth. The Prince turned and looked at Henry. He said an incantation and wrapped his hand around the power and pulled it firmly out of the Witch. Her body writhed. Henry couldn't tell if it was sexual pleasure or pain at first. Then the hooks tried to grab on as he pulled it up through her body her screaming was pure torture. Henry watched the Prince cherishing every moment of pain he was creating. His eyes had turned from green to red, and he was himself in the cloud of passion.

Addison told Henry mentally to look at the men in the room. Their eyes were red as Devon's, and there was a greedy sinister look in them as if they wished to take part in this display. Henry thought to Addison. They have all experienced this.

Addison mentally added. Often, I think.

The King stepped to the Prince, placed his hand on Devon's shoulder and began to remove some of the energy streaming out of him. Martin called in two guards, and the Witch was removed. Then Martin and the Professor pushed Henry to the Prince. The King placed Henry's hand on Devon's shoulder.

A shock of energy pulsed into Henry's body. It wasn't a pure, clean white energy of a Witch. It was dark and heavy, like a storm. It was harsh and very sexual his body responded uncontrollably. The passion was overwhelming and evil; it burned him like the sun. He pulled away and fell onto the table he used it to keep standing. Addison was coming to help him, and he mentally told him to hold back, this was sinister.

The King calmly said, "Professor take Devon to work off some of the energy and come to visit me tomorrow when you have time." They left the room, and Henry was finally able to stand straight. "Well, Henry you look overwhelmed. The first time is remarkable, isn't it? Wait until you can do this yourself you will come to find it addicting."

Addison could feel Henry's anger building. He mentally told Henry to tread lightly they needed to know more about this. They are watching you like a hawk. Your every movement and expressions are being scrutinized.

Henry took in a deep breath, shook his head and ran his hand through his hair. "That was unbelievable, had I not seen and experienced it, I would never have believed you. The power was massive and the sexual energy...well, I have never felt anything so erotic." Henry put on his best card playing face and a wicked smile.

Martin slapped him on the back, "Did I not tell your Majesty when it came to sexual linkages Henry would be open to all manner of experimentation."

Addison came around the table and said, "You are willing to give us this great power in return for handing over the Countess to Devon. It seems too big of a bargain to me. With you being on the short end. There must be more King."

The King glared at Addison, "Oh, don't worry, you will learn too. Both of you will be able to control every Sorcerer in your life. We do expect fair payment you will both do as we wish, one way or another for the rest of your life."

Henry said. "Give me a moment with Addison." They moved to the side of the room and whispered then walked back, and Henry extended his hand to the King, "We are your men King Hex."

The King took his hand and shook it, "Good, I am glad to have you on my side Henry. Now before you leave, we will need some of your blood. The Professor will fashion a spell for you to use on Casandra you will find it helpful in controlling her. It will be ready for your use on your wedding day. I suggest you use it on your carriage ride to Azul it will make it so easy for her to accept Devon as her lover."

Henry said, "Devon almost brought that Witch to her end. I hope he learns some self-control before my wedding. I would like to keep Casandra for my wife and have some children of my own someday."

Martin said, "Elaine told me you really wanted a family. Come, Addison, I will take your blood as the King takes Henry's then you can be on your way. Henry, you will have so much energy, you will fly straight to Diamante."

Henry mentally said to Addison. This asshole was attached to Elaine. I know it.

Addison mentally said. Henry stop and think, do not use your heart right now. Think about the fact they have Casandra's blood.

Just then Henry felt a cut on his arm and felt his blood flow. Addison said more to distract Henry than anything, "Martin I know we are to get this information in installments, but can you tell me where in the world you first come across this spell?"

Martin looked at the King who nodded. "We first saw it done in a remote village in Parragon during the Alia wars. We went back to the village at the end of the war to learn it from the tribe. Then we spent many more years of experiments perfecting it. You both should practice before you perform this spell, as Henry mentioned it is hard to release from the Witch. Many Witches and Warlocks gave their life to our efforts. Devon is doing well, having only learned this last week."

The King said, "Henry when you come back for Martin's engagement party we will have an attachment for you to practice with. We will need to observe you at first. It is too easy to inadvertently kill Witches and yourself."

The King healed Henry's arm and said, "You are good to go on your way." They all walked out of the basement room and into the sunlight, it was blinding.

The Wedding Preparations

The Empress and all three girls were in the Parlor with Mags after breakfast. The dressmaker had come with samples and sketches for the wedding dresses.

Casandra handed her Mother a sketch of the dress for the Temple with a hood. "I like this Mother, but to make it look right, it would need to be satin. The weather will still be too warm for that."

"Yes, I agree with you dear. What about this one?" She handed her a dress that was sheer with beading covering it from the bodice down to the floor. The Temple dress would be the most difficult to choose. It needed to cover her body from the neck down to her feet.

Marion took the sketch and created a three-dimensional copy about a foot high. "Look Casandra, your Mother has chosen a good basic line. If you use the deep blue of Marias and sheer fabric with crystals instead of beading, you will shimmer. The skirt falls in folds from the hip down. Look what happens when the skirt unfolds, and a train is added. That is sleek you would look like a Goddess."

The Empress said, "Marion you have a talent for this. What do you think about it, Casandra? It is simple but elegant."

Casandra said, "I love it but is this possible? There is a lot of crystal on it."

The dressmaker Leroy said. "Your crown and jewels would look fabulous with this, Casandra. Normally I would say I could make it work but our time is so short. Also, you need two dresses this one is gorgeous for the Temple formal wedding, but the reception will call for a dancing dress. Then there is the going away dress, time is our enemy."

The Empress said, "Leroy hire a few extra seamstresses and send them to me. I will enhance their skills so it can be done. I will send you spells, as well."

"Thank you, Empress, I do appreciate it. So, that is the choice for the Temple." Leroy wrote down the selection, "Marion. Can I keep your model to work from?"

"Of course, I can make a model of all the dresses for you." Marion handed it to him. "Do we all wear our countries colors to the Temple?"

Leroy said. "It is tradition to wear the countries colors of the Bride and Groom. I have some dresses for you girls too, but first the Bride. Would you make a model of this dress? I spoke to the Sorcerers, and they said the ballroom would feature gold and diamonds. This is a strapless dress made of silver crystals and gold sequins covering the bodice, from the waist to the floor it is layers of gold and silver tulle. I will add magic to make it sparkle. Of course, gold ballet shoes to make dancing easy. As for jewelry, I think a simple gold diadem for your crown and your hair with hundreds of crystals. Crowns are too cumbersome to dance in; you want to enjoy your reception; this dress would be cool and still beautiful."

"That is true Casandra. I wish I could do without my crown. That dress is beautiful Leroy." She stopped and looked at her daughter who was crying, "Casandra? Do you not like this dress?"

"No Mother, I love it. It's the dress I have always dreamed I'd wear." Casandra hugged her Mother who was crying too along with Mags and Grace.

Leroy stammered, "I love it when I can make the Bride cry over one of my designs. That is a yes. Now for your going away suit, I thought it would be time to show the Count's colors. A black skirt and boots with a pure white crisp blouse topped off with a hooded cloak of the wine red of Diamante. What do you think?"

"Leroy, you are making this easy it looks so comfortable. I love it." Casandra was having fun doing this.

"Almost perfect," said Marion, "I have something for you I designed. It's a patch, a design of both crests from Marais and Diamante. Leroy, you could you use it on her cloak pocket."

"Marion that is wonderful. I can add it to her attire she will be creating a new fashion statement. Every woman on this Continent will be asking for this. I will give you a commission if you help me design these, Marion." Leroy was so excited.

"I have a job! Casandra, you told me I have nothing in my future." Marion teased they all laughed.

The Empress stood, "Well, I see you have all this decided. I must return to the Temple, enjoy making all your choices."

Casandra stood too, "Mother don't leave we need you here for this."

"Nonsense, Casandra you are making wonderful decisions. I will love everything. Mags and Kathryn are here to help, and I really just wanted to see your dresses. Marion, thank you for the samples, which made it easy to see."

The Empress gave hugs all around and a kiss for her daughter and daughter-in-law. She was grateful to have an excuse to leave all this was bringing her to tears. That was not what she wanted for her daughter, she smiled and said, "Besides, you will soon have seven Sorcerers to contend with, they have very definite ideas. Good luck with them. Leroy, you are marvelous as usual. I want a cloak like that one made for me in deep blue with the Temples Crest on it after the wedding is finished of course."

Leroy bowed, "Yes your Majesty. Speaking of the seven Sorcerers here they are. I sure hope they don't want to change everything."

The Empress walked to the hallway, "Ladies, I have to return to the Temple today, and I have approved of the dresses for Casandra. Casandra is in charge now; she has let me know her wishes. If you wish changes on the dresses, you must bring them to the Temple for my approval. In fact, I would appreciate you coming to the Temple at the end of the week for final approval of the plans." She turned and winked at Casandra who mouthed, thank you, Mother. That should make them all worry about pleasing Casandra.

The Emperor was standing at her carriage. "You were leaving without saying goodbye to me."

The Empress sighed, "That has been our life, saying goodbye to one another." She had tears in her eyes.

The Emperor said, "Each time I think it will be easier, it never is."

She paused, "Help your daughter with her wedding plans since I must return." She entered the carriage, then poked her head out the window. "Keep her safe Hayden I cannot lose her. I am not sure my heart could stand it."

The Emperor jumped in the carriage and closed the doors, then pulled her into his arms and kissed her deeply and passionately. Holding her, he said, "I love you, as I always will. I promise I will do everything in my power to keep her safe. I believe Henry will too he is a good choice. I had wished they didn't love each other like us, it makes life so difficult. They aren't starting off well. At least we had the first years of our marriage. As I watched them on the dance floor, I saw us…years ago. They are so in love, seeing that has made me so much more aware of what we have sacrificed for this Kingdom. Has it been worth it Beatrice?" Hayden held her tight.

Beatrice pushed away from him, "I am not so sure it has been worth it, and so many seem to be against us. We have spies in our households and in the Nobility. The Kingdom needs to change Hayden, or we will lose it. Power rules our Kingdoms and magic needs to be as it was in the past, free to everyone. We once talked about these things and how we would work to change them; our children are inheriting the same problems we did."

Haydon released her, "I will think on these things my love; go balance the power. Know I love you as no Warlock ever has." He kissed her and left the carriage, nodded to the driver. He could not stop himself from standing in the courtyard until he could no longer see her carriage. Once again, his heart was numb, this was his way of life. He drew himself up to face the brood of Sorcerers in the Castle. He would rather face a battalion of soldier's head on than wedding planners.

The Impressions of the Spell

The band of Belissa men didn't fly far before the Count landed on the flats. "I am hungry, and I have too much nervousness to sit a Pegasus any longer. We need to talk to all the men, Addison can you take care of camp? I need to work this energy off."

The Count did not wait for an answer; he took off running across the flats. Addison remembered Henry running when they were in school he always came back from it with definite ideas. So, Addison organized the camp and food for the Count's return. He told his lieutenant Sutton to put up one large tent to shade them. Then he worked at placing a concealment spell over it. He finished just in time to see crows flying over trying to look like scavengers waiting for a meal. Lunch was cooked and served before Henry made it back to the camp.

Henry was soaked with sweat and red in the face from the desert sun. "Good job on the tent Addison, from a distance I could not see it at all."

"Come in out of the sun and drink. Thanks, Henry. I used a new spell they will be able to see us from the sky, but the words will be in different languages. Henry, you are acting strangely; tell me, how can we help?"

Henry guzzled the water. "Addison, I am not sure I can explain, but a run always helps to clear my head. This evil essence that ensconced me took a while to be released from my body. I apologize for taking off like that."

Henry turned to all his men, "Gentlemen we have all had a blood bond, so I trust you with my life, and you trust Addison and me. What I experienced today is too difficult to explain, and we don't have the time for long explanations. I have decided to give you my memory of this experience. I am sure this is what they did to my Elaine and plan to do the same to Casandra. We will need to work together faultlessly to keep Casandra safe." He pierced his finger with a knife, "You can give me a memory if you wish or not. I ask nothing but that you understand and give me any help and your suggestions." He walked around the table giving and receiving blood.

These men showed him all pictures of Casandra and him over the last week. They all loved him like a Brother and wanted Henry happy and married to Casandra. Then he realized the tent was quiet. He looked around at his men's faces they were filled with pain and anguish.

Paxton looked up, "Henry this is pure evil. I have never felt this, debauched."

Henry sighed, "That is a perfect word for it, Paxton. I have been searching for a description since we left Engelton. All the negativity Sorcerers place on the ground for us is drawn out by this spell. These idiots have no idea what they have unleashed. They play with this power like it is a toy and they think they control it. They are lucky they have only a few Sorcerers under this Attachment Spell. What will happen when they control the Witches all over the world?"

Sutton and Paxton looked at each other, "They will destroy this world. They plan to unleash nothing but negative powers." They looked to Addison, "Are they all crazy?"

Addison swallowed, "Perhaps, I was on the outside of this scene. I was struck by how entranced they were. I couldn't get the picture of their faces out of my mind. They said it themselves, they are addicted. I am not sure we can help Prince Devon, Henry. Unless we can get Devon away from the King soon, he will not want to leave at all. I believe he is lost, if not yet, soon."

Henry pulled his plate of food to him and started eating heartily. "I am afraid you are right Addison. We will plan for that as we come to it." He continued to mindlessly eat when he pushed back from his empty plate, he was himself.

"We need to plan a course of action. As I said before, anyone that has any ideas speak up." Everyone sat silent. "Think carefully about this gentleman. Addison will take Sutton, Jake, and Bowen to Belissa Villa and tell Ski everything we know about the Attachment Spell; then go to the North Castle you four will disguise and protect Casandra on her imprudent holiday. Keep in contact with me mentally so I don't worry about any of you and her."

Henry turned, "Paxton you and I will face my Brothers. Don and Perry, you will be our guards trust no one at my Father's Castle except my Mother. I have been away from Winsette Castle too long, it will take me time to know who to trust. When I return to the Hex Castle for the engagement party, I will only take one man to assist me. I want the King to feel I trust him with my life. I will leave it to you to choose who will come with me. If things turn bad, we might not leave alive." He looked at them, and they all raised their hands. "Gentlemen I said one. And I refuse to choose, you have time to work that out yourselves. Let's break camp and separate. We have much to do and little time to do it."

Addison smiled, his friend was back, always attacking, and defending only when forced to. He loved Henry, he had a master's mind with a heart of a warrior. Addison always felt safe and protected with him.

The North Castle

The Emperor walked into the parlor to fifteen Sorcerers and Warlocks. "Casandra your Mother just told me to come to help you with your wedding plans. How can I help?"

Mags stood, "By leaving your Majesty. These proceedings are top secret, and I know how you gab to your advisors. You'll have it all around by morning."

He scolded but winked at Mags, "I should be angry at you Mags, but I see all of my girls in here having fun. Don't spend too much of my money." He was happy to go to his library, in peace. He found the Professor looking through books spread out on the table.

"I'm sorry your Majesty, I will leave. I was just looking for a little information." He took pieces of ribbon out of his pocket and started marking his place in five or six books. "Could I leave these out? I can come back later."

The Emperor walked to him and looked at the books. "What are you reading? And there is no need to leave we are both able to work in here. Wait, I thought you would return with Beatrice? Casandra doesn't leave until the end of the week."

The Professor smiled, "You remind me of Marion, she manages to ask at least ten questions before I can answer one. I am trying to find out more about the Attachment Spell. I remembered something about it. I just haven't been able to put my finger on it."

The Emperor picked up a book and read, "The Magic of Parragon; I was there during the Alia wars, briefly. The place was decimated by the time we got there. We chased King Hex, well he was just a General then, we pushed his army all the way through Parragon and back to Hex. It was a rough trip up the mountains, he pillaged and burned out every village on his way. I knew then he was ruthless and cruel. My men almost starved thank the Night we crossed into Antico, they were happy to see us. They fed us well and asked we stayed on their borders until they could rebuild it. They are wonderful people. I was happy the Empress arranged a liaison between their Prince and Casandra, my grandchild will grow up happy there."

"Do you remember any of their traits that were unusual." The Professor keeping browsing. "Anything about power draining? I have that stuck in my mind. It would be close to an Attachment."

The Emperor stood still and turned pale. "The Antico had a ritual they did with men and women. Those who got out of line would have hands laid on them to remove power. As a reward for good actions the tribes would do the same and give power." He moved around to look closer at the books. "I had asked, but they never revealed how they did it. They just said that it was learned by the Priest; he was the only one to know the spell. That was one of the reasons they welcomed us. It seemed several of their Priests were kidnapped by the Hexians; they feared more would be taken. So, you think the King has this knowledge, and maybe these two tribes shared it, or was forced to?"

"It is a logical conclusion, Emperor. I would like to find some facts to support it." The Professor kept reading, and the Emperor helped. At least in this, he would get lost, and he wouldn't overthink about Beatrice or the danger Casandra was in.

The Emperor said, "This reminds me, Professor, I had wanted to question Henry about the book of Darnania History, the one that snake came out of. All three of them seemed to have knowledge of it."

The Professor looked at him and said, "I had forgotten all about it, but you are right. I will put it in my notes and ask." He pulled a notebook from his pocket then he added, "Snakes are known for the poison they carry I wonder if that has anything to do with the Attachment Spell."

They worked until noon, then went to lunch on the balcony with the Major, Bryan, and the girls. The Professor reminded both Casandra and Marion lessons were to start promptly at one. He told the Emperor they were to study every afternoon, even during Casandra's season.

The Emperor wanted the Major and Eric to join him in the library after lunch. The Emperor asked, "Professor, would you be offended if I had Major and Eric look at some of the books we were discussing this morning?"

"No at all Emperor, they may have some insight we didn't. Girls, I will see you on the roof." He left the lunch.

Grace looked to Casandra, "What kind of lessons are you having on the roof?"

Casandra sighed, "He has had us up there every day, and it seems all we do is meditate and do strength exercises, using mindfulness, that is what he called it."

Marion chimed in. "I don't see the value myself it seems crazy, then we hold magic above the Castle. What that is for I don't know. We hold out our biggest power, then make our power disappear into nothing. I wish he would get to the fighting part. That's what I want to learn."

Grace took another spoon of pudding and said, "Oh, he is working on your balance. That is something Elves learn too. You must be in the present to fight Marion. I am learning that in my lessons too."

Eric said. "Grace is correct. In fact, I believe I will have Grace join you in your lessons she could use the practice."

The Major smiled at the Emperor, "You are lucky to have a teacher like the Professor. You have had sword training, and both of you know how to spell and throw power but in a fight Marion, knowing when to use your power is more important. There are times when fighting is advantageous, other times not displaying power will win you the battle in the end."

The Emperor added, "The Major is right, sometimes you will not know your enemy's motives or tactics. Just as we do now with King Hex. To win a war, it is imperative to understand your enemy as well as you do your friends. In war, Casandra, information is supreme in making judgments. Leaders cannot allow emotions or falsehoods to enter their minds. Facts are needed to plan an attack or suppress one. The

Professor is teaching you how to be in touch with your senses; to know fact from fiction. Another most valued tactic is surprised. Holding power from a Warlock can save your life one day, to fight again on a more important day."

Casandra thought about that for a minute. "You did that Father when I was taken, and Sarah and Mark were killed. You waited until you understood the King tactics then fought on your terms and won."

The Emperor looked straight into Casandra's eyes, "Yes I did, I paid a very high price and lost many friends. It was very hard not to go running out into the fields after the King's army. Until this week I have never understood your kidnapping. Had I known the Kings scheme earlier this whole mess would never have happened. I am so sorry, my darling girl. I regret this with all my heart. I have only wanted your happiness and now…well, now."

Casandra went to her Father and threw her arms around him, "Father, if not for this mess I would not have Henry. How happy would I have been? I thank you for him. I will take the training seriously from now on. I will work on my powers. I will learn about this King of Hex. If I have the opportunity, I will kill him myself."

Tears were rolling down the Emperor's face, and he hugged her and buried his face in her shoulder. "I believe you would." He raised his head and kissed her on both cheeks, "I love you, little girl. You will always be my beautiful little girl. I am so glad you and Henry are in love, and if I am obliged to personally kill every Hexian in the world to give you a long life with him? I will. Now if you want a holiday go to your lessons. I need to feel confident that you and Marion can take care of yourselves before you leave."

Bryan came over to her and hugged her, "Don't forget this evening, we need to do a little scheming ourselves. It is time to start working on your children." Casandra winked at him. She, Grace, and Marion left for the roof. The Prince put a hand on his Father's shoulder, "Thank you, Father, she really needed to hear that from you. I don't remember seeing her this happy."

The Major added, "I know that to be true; she has always been a quiet child not anymore. Henry has brought out the best in her. I never gave her credit for her bravery. I don't mean to meddle, but I would like to suggest the original plan to have her carry all three eggs at once be reconsidered. If the King hopes to add children that could make pregnancy difficult for her."

"I agree, Bryan. I also feel Major, and I should not be a part of this negotiation with Casandra. You and Kathryn will handle it with much more discretion. She needs to feel comfortable with her decision." The Emperor threw down his napkin, "If we are done with lunch I need to show both of you something in the library."

The lessons on the roof went by quickly, and they also learned a few new fighting moves from the Professor. These exchanges were close contact using their bodies. They learned to balance and use their hips weight to push against the Warlocks. They were also taught the strengths and weakness of the Warlocks and their power sources. They were working on the fencing moves when Pegasus circled overhead, it was Addison.

The Professor said, "Alright that is enough for today now that he is here, I will not have your attention anyway. Go on, go."

Marion turned, "No. We promised the Emperor we would do well. We will stay as long as you like."

The Professor stood back, "I see. Now I know the reason you have both done so well today. You have finally taken this threat seriously. This is good to know. However, we are truly done for the day, so Marion, go see your boyfriend."

She and Grace put up their swords and ran to the stairs, "Come with us Casandra, Addison can tell you how Henry is."

Casandra just smiled, "Henry is safe. If Addison is here, Henry is at Winsette Castle. Go, I will see you at dinner."

Casandra lingered and asked the Professor, "Professor, you have been teaching us defensive tactics all these days. Will you show us attack exchanges?"

"I haven't spent time on that because I feel you will not need to know that, just yet." The Professor placed his sword away and closed the fencing case. "Why do you feel you need an attack move? I thought your first choice of attack would be a spell or straight out power. You know how to do that."

Casandra paused, how could she phrase this question without showing her intent was challenging. Then she just asked, "If I am standing against the Prince of Hex or the King of Hex, and my powers have been stunted or removed, how can I kill them?"

The Professor stood shocked, but took in a breath and said, "I see." He continued to pack up the books and weapons they had used. "I am thinking about this carefully… your question is valid. You intend to kill them, one or both if you can?"

Casandra sat on the ramparts and said, "If I could cut the head from the snake, the war would not tear our countries apart. It would not be necessary at all. How would I do that without my powers?"

The Professor came and sat next to her. "The problem is not killing the snake, my dear. The problem is cutting the head off the one snake does not guarantee the nest of snakes will not appear to take its place. You would have to go into the nest and destroy them all at once. I can't give you a method to do that without using a massive power. If not yours because yours had been taken, then somehow harnessing theirs. You and I do not know enough about their powers to make a connection. I also cannot fathom your Father or Henry allowing you access to them. They will be protecting you with all they have, and you will not go into the layer of the King. That is a certainty. We should go get ready for dinner." They both stood to leave.

Casandra stopped, "Professor, what if I find myself in the nest? I should be prepared for anything. Nothing should be left to chance."

The Professor stood toe to toe with her, "You are right. However, I do not have an answer for you at this time. I will consider this and let you know when I do have answers for you." They both sighed and went to their rooms.

Casandra decided to wear a dress for dinner and put her hair up. She wished Henry was there. She missed him already, how could she wait weeks to see him again? Casandra wanted to forget about her season of freedom. She went down for dinner feeling lonely, a feeling as she was accustomed. She was alone most of her life. Marion and Grace were her only two close friends. As she stepped off the last stair, she heard someone yelling Countess, then realized that she was the Countess. Coming in the door was Addison.

"Countess, I wanted to speak with you before we were with the others. Henry has been in my head all day, and he will not leave until

I deliver this." Addison bent down and kissed her cheek. "He loves you and wanted you to know he can't wait to be with you again." He reached into his coat and pulled out a ring, "He wants you to wear this daily and remember him each time you see it." He raised her hand and place a ruby surrounded by diamonds on her right-hand finger.

Casandra was astonished, "Tell him it is beautiful and outrageous. Tell him he needs to stop giving me jewels. I would much prefer him holding my hand than this ring. Tell him I don't need this to remember him all day and night. I will do that anyway." She wasn't going to cry. No, she wasn't going to feel sorry for herself. She was the High Sorcerer and a Countess, everyone expected better. "I am sorry Addison, don't tell him that. This is incredibly thoughtful and romantic. I love him, and I miss him already. I was just thinking how I wish we would marry now. I don't need this silly holiday, I just need him."

She gazed at the ruby, it reminded her of her eggs. She once snuck into the Temple room to look at the eggs they shined like this ruby.

"Countess come back. Your thoughts took you miles away. Perhaps you're not used to being called Countess." Addison was smiling down at her. "Don't worry Casandra, I will tell him you love him. I would like to tell him you are happy and well. You aren't happy this evening."

"No, Addison, I don't suppose I am. I feel bad about that too. I should be happy about planning a wedding and traveling on holiday to an exotic land. I love the man I am to marry. It's just this feeling of hopelessness I have. I can't explain it. I am sorry I shouldn't burden you, we should go to dinner. I want to do another blood bond with Henry so I can speak with him long distance like you do." Casandra turned to walk away.

Addison took her arm and walked her to the entrance of the door where a Guard stood. "We are forgoing cocktails tonight. The Countess and I have business to discuss before dinner. Let the Emperor know we won't be too long." They walked out to the front courtyard. The Castle walls were bathed by a full moon, and the stones on the path glimmered white.

"Countess, Henry and I have been bonded together for well over a hundred years. I have only known you a week, but because you have bonded with him, I have insights into your mind. The expectations of you are high, insurmountable, for one so young. Over the next few weeks, your life is going to change extraordinarily. You will holiday, no doubt you will confront the Prince, which may not go well. You are going to be introduced to the Kingdom of Diamante, and all of Henry's family. Trust me that is not going to be pleasant. Then there is your wedding and keeping you, Henry, and your children out of the clutches of the King. This is not my idea of a normal wedding. I think you have a reason for concern, worry, and doubt. Happiness is not going to be on the top of the list for you, and it is completely understandable." They were walking arm in arm around the side of the Castle.

"I am concerned, Addison." Casandra stopped. "My Mother has had premonitions of danger and evil. I had dreams of a battle we lost. I am silly, maybe it is all these choices I am having to make, or just feeling lonely. I am sorry, I don't want to worry anyone. Please don't tell Henry, he will feel miserable that he can't be with me. I am a woman now. I should be able to handle this right?"

Addison pulled her into his arms and hugged her. "You are a woman, but even for a woman, this would be difficult. I am here for you Countess. I want you to know I am Henry's friend, but I feel more like he is my Brother. I love the man, I will do anything for him. He loves you like he has never loved anyone trust me. I am here not because Henry asked me. I am here because I want the best for him, you are the best. You are beautiful yes, but more than that… you are strong. You are smart, giving, and selfless. When you said, you would rather have Henry than that ring, well… that was proof of your selfless love. Once you learn to answer to the name of Countess Rakie, you will find things easier to handle. You are deserving of more than that simple ruby ring." He was laughing as he spoke. They were walking back to the courtyard of the Castle.

"You're right. I was hearing someone say Countess and I thought, we had no Countess in this Castle." She was laughing now too. "When I was young, I heard everyone speaking about the Empress's eggs. I was curious about them, so I went on an adventure at the Temple to find them. It took me two summer holidays, but I did find them." She stopped at the front doors of the Castle, and the light from inside exposed the ruby ring. "They looked just like this ring, the same color plus almost the same size. It was the first thing I thought of when you put it on my finger, Addison." She paused and said, "I am choosing my child tonight after dinner. Will you come with me? Can you know what Henry would want?"

It was the first time in many years Addison was stunned. "Countess, Henry and I can communicate almost all the time. We intentionally block thoughts and conversation that are personal, like the one we are having now. He will feel the general frame of mind, not the details. I am sending him this conversation. Yes, Countess. It will be my honor to help you chose your child for Henry." Addison smiled and had tears in his eyes, "He is pleased, he wants to tell you more, but in person."

The Castle door flew open, and Marion was standing there. "You two have one minute to get into that dining room or your Father is going to have a fit." Both Casandra and Addison started laughing, "This isn't funny! Come now, and you better have a good excuse for Mags and me too Addison."

Casandra put Marion's hand in Addison's, and they all went to the dining room. She held out her ring and said. "Look what I got from Henry today." She made her way around the room and ended with the Emperor. She kissed his cheek and said, "I am sorry Father I had to have a little privacy to tell him thank you through Addison. Isn't it lovely?"

The Emperor grumbled, "Casandra do you realize Henry has given you expensive presents almost every day for the last week?"

"What, don't you think I am worth it?" Casandra sat by the Professor and winked.

"Yes you are worth it, but he is spoiling you. What will you do tomorrow when there is no present?" The Emperor drank his wine.

"I hadn't thought of that. Addison ask Henry if there will be a present tomorrow." Casandra laughed. "I am just teasing don't ask."

"Too late. Henry said perhaps the next time he sees you. Also, that depends." Now Addison was laughing, "I really can't say the rest." Being late for dinner was forgotten.

After dinner, everyone went to sit by the fire and have wine. The Emperor said, "Casandra, we will leave you and your Brother to discuss the details of your children. I do not want to influence you on this; you have my support with whatever you chose. Would you like others to help you?"

Casandra said, "Yes Kathryn, please stay, and Marion. I would also like Addison, he can tell me what Henry thinks. Is that alright Father?"

"I believe that is a perfect choice. Please remember to crystal ball with your Mother after, or we all will be in trouble. Also, come to tell me." He went to her and kissed her on the forehead, "I love you." That was the second time today he said that she was floored.

"I love you too." And she hugged him.

Bryan began, "As you know Casandra, you have three eggs to use one must be a boy, one must be a girl, and the other will be your choice. We must begin incubation now, and there are characteristics you can choose too. Are you relaying this to the Count, Addison?"

Addison said, "Yes he understands."

Casandra looked at her ring and said, "I want only one child at a time. So, I will choose one child. What does the Count say?"

Addison took in a breath and held up his hand, "Henry said that would be fine, but he wants to know what made you decide that."

"He knows why? As everyone in this room knows if our plans fail, and I fall into the King's hands at least not all of my children will be in jeopardy." Casandra was mad they were all thinking it. Why couldn't they be honest?

Addison took her hand, "Henry says thank you for being honest and realistic. Now a boy or a girl? He would like a little girl just like you."

"I want a little boy just like him." Casandra folded her arms.

Bryan shook his head, "This is going to be a long night."

Kathryn said, "No it isn't. They can have both, but who will be first? Think about this Casandra. I chose boys first because they must lead. The youngest is more cuddled, not a good trait for boys. The girls last, to give them more time to develop before being sent off to school. You know the pressure you felt. If you had not grown up as the only future Empress, your life would be different."

Marion said, "Casandra, Kathryn is right, you cannot choose from your experience of the station. This will be different. Your children will have a normal progression, not at all like you."

Casandra turned to Addison, who was laughing. "Sorry, Henry just reminded me he and his Brother were the babies of his family. So, if you want a boy like him, have him last." Everyone was shaking their heads and chuckling.

Casandra said, "It is just like he is in the room with us, being sassy. Alright, we will have a girl first. Now to the traits." After hours in the room, they had the final outline for their little girl some of Henry's Mother, some of her Mother and Grandmother, but mostly Casandra. He insisted on their baby having blue eyes like Casandra. Casandra wanted to include Henry's ability to remember and work out puzzles and strategies. Their child was chosen; the engineering would begin in the morning. Both her Mother and Father were pleased with their choices.

After the choosing, Marion and Addison went off on their own. Casandra had a feeling they were in the next room making love. She tried to sleep, but slumber would not come. At first, she was excited about their little girl. Then her mind began to worry. Would her baby even live? What about the Prince of Hex, what were his plans? Then the nightmares took over as the night before plaguing her. She had lied to Addison; her dreams weren't only about a battle; they were about her standing before the King of Hex. He had won, and she was in a dungeon chained to a wall. She was stripped of any powers, of Henry, and her children. The King was showing her the children he had implanted they were evil and filled with hate with eyes of red. She couldn't stay up all night, tomorrow would be more wedding plans and map out her holiday. Then there was training with the Professor. Meditating might help her sleep, at least meditating was peaceful. That's if she could meditate.

Casandra began as taught, relaxing her body, starting with her head. She slowly relaxed every muscle in her body, then she began to concentrate on her breathing. Slow intakes, slow releases of breath, while continually bringing her attention to her breathing. Her eyes were closed, and the room was dark. She noticed she could hear her hearting beating and she felt as light as air. Between her breaths, she heard a whisper saying. Excellent Casandra, just pay attention to your breath, listen to your heartbeat.

The voice sounded familiar, "Can't you sleep sweetheart?"

She answered, "No I am worried."

The voiced said. Keep your attention on your breaths, Casandra. Tell me why you are worried?

"Who are you? You sound familiar." Casandra returned to her breathing.

"I will tell you if you keep in this meditation. Can you do that?" Her eyes flew open she swore the voice was coming from someone in her room. She turned on the light, but there was no one there. Casandra closed her eyes and began again, but it was becoming more difficult to concentrate. She relaxed after a few breaths, and once again she could hear her heartbeat. The voice returned, "Last night I sent you dreams is that what has you worried?"

"Yes," Casandra almost lost her relaxation and had to work a few minutes more to hear her heartbeat. "You sent me dreams are they premonitions?"

"Just relax Casandra, listen for your heartbeat. I sent you the problem, tonight I will send you the solution. When I leave you in a little while, you will fall to sleep immediately. When you wake, you will know what to do the moment your eyes open. Do you understand?"

"Yes, Mistress. I understand thank you for sending me the solution." Casandra finally placed the voice of the Hermit.

"Ah...So you know me, that is good. If you want to hear me, learn the old ways, Casandra. We are all connected, but only through peace. I am always here with you, just listen. Keep practicing your meditations, learn from George. Come back to me tomorrow night we will talk. Henry wants to see you. I will place you in his dreams."

Casandra was standing by Henry's bed in a Castle somewhere. She bent down to kiss his cheek, and his eyes flashed open. He grabbed her and said, "You're here, you're real." They kissed, and she fell into his arms. Then sleep overtook her, into her dreams, she floated, and Henry was gone.

The Castle Diamante

Henry woke alarmed. Where was Casandra? He swore he had made love to her when he found her standing by his bedside. What was Henry thinking, she was at the North Castle, not here in Diamante at Winsette Castle. The past weeks were taking a toll on his mind he needed to spend more time with his spirit and meditate. He would do that this morning before everyone and everything took over his life. Henry and his men came into the Castle late the evening before. He had not wanted to stop and camp out where the King could see him, and he also wanted to avoid meeting his Parents or Brothers in the strange condition he was in. After he mediated and dressed, he felt more himself.

He gathered his men for breakfast. "Gentlemen we must go to my Mother and Father as soon as we finish. I am sure they are already waiting for us." The guards had given Henry his old apartment, but it had been redecorated for guests. He wondered where his old furniture had gone. The rooms were ornate and busy with patterns. The small dining room off the kitchen was more baroque than he remembered making it hard to eat breakfast.

The Castle was built of onyx floors, the walls, and pillars of red jasper veined in black. The baroque rugs and gold guiled accents seemed repellant. Henry was glad he didn't have to live in this Castle.

The paintings of war and sculptures of warriors filling the halls were too ornamental and grotesque for him to relax in; he would be happy to go to his Belissa Villa.

They headed to his Father's suites. Before they entered the last hallway there stood his Mother. She looked thinner, and her eyes showed the stress of her husband's illness. Her blonde hair had turned white at her temples. Her blue-grey eyes showed tears being held back, but her mouth could not hide her broad smile showing beautiful teeth. She was still a beauty, and her soul was as sweet as Casandra. Henry was sure that was the attraction he initially had to Casandra. He had Mariette's face and smile, his coloring and build came from his Father. All his Brothers had the chocolate eyes and brown wavy hair, but each facial feature was different. This was not surprising since three different wives produced them. Mariette was his Father's fourth wife, Henry and Harry were her only two children. His parents loved one another, that was the only reason she had lasted so long as Queen. It was also the only reason his Father had permitted him to live after his Brothers' deaths. The King stripped him of his title of Prince but had replaced it with Count when he had learned the truth. Henry walked to his Mother and scooped her up and spun her around in the hallway.

"Henry Marshall Rakie put me down before you hurt me." He set her on her feet, and she tried to straighten her hair. "If that is an indication of how you are feeling, I am happy too." She grabbed him and hugged him, "How I have missed you, my darling boy."

"Mother I am over one hundred and fifty years old. You really must stop addressing me like your boy." Henry laughed. "How is Father?"

His Mother took him by his arm, and they began to walk toward the King's chambers, "I thought he would leave us last week, then news of your engagement came. He perked up and has even started walking about his chambers. It's remarkable. Your Brothers simply don't know what to make of it."

Henry snorted, "I can only imagine their disappointment. Sorry Mother, but it is the truth. I need to talk to him will he see me this time?"

Mariette laughed. "He said if you are nice. Can you not belittle your Brothers or make fun of your Sisters-in-law?"

"Hum, you are asking a lot of me, but you are in luck. I am in a good mood. I have a beautiful bride, as sweet as my Mother. With what I already own, and the dowry of Casandra, you are looking at the richest Warlock in the world and the most powerful one." Henry grinned. "I love you, Mother if you were not in my life, I would not have recognized those lovely attributes in Casandra. It has taken a long while, but I now know she is all I have ever wanted, the rest of it means nothing. We are going to have a daughter first; we chose last night. I asked for many of your attributes. Casandra wants to give her your name as your true name, Sarah, it was her Sister's name too. She said it was a sign from the Night. Would that be alright?"

Marietta stopped right there in the hall, this time tears were streaming down her face, "Henry, Casandra agreed to this?"

Henry hugged her, "Hell Mother she thought of it."

The doors to the King's chamber opened, and there stood the King. He was stooped over, but the stern face Henry had last seen was still plastered there. "So, you have been in the Castle for less than a day, and already you have your Mother in tears. Henry, you will never change!"

His Mother stepped forward now a good five inches taller. "Winsette really, these are tears of joy. We are to have a grandchild, our first girl." She took him in her arms and kissed him. "I am so happy. I will truly spoil her. Casandra has chosen her name…it is Sarah. Can you believe it? Henry said it was her idea." She walked him into the chamber and sat him in the comfy chair by the fire.

The King looked at Henry and pointed his finger, "You talked her into this, you're trying to gain back your title."

Henry moved a chair across from him and sat down, "Father, I do love you, mainly because you never change. I can count on you to always look at the bleakest sides of life. I don't understand how you got my Mother into your bed was it that opposites attract?"

The King sat back in his chair and crossed his arms, "You look exceptionally happy. What are you up to and what do you want?"

Henry called Paxton over, "Could I have the contract and see if we have any of the good liquor left. I believe Father would like it."

Henry opened the marriage contract and handed it to his Father, "Let's start here."

The King took it and called his servant to get Henry's older Brother. This did not surprise Henry. None of them trusted him any more than he believed them.

Dillion Rakie must have been in the next chamber because he was in the room in less than a minute. "Henry, you are up early. I hadn't expected you until late in the day. I understood you arrived late last evening."

Dillion was his only Brother who was taller than Henry. He was the oldest and the heir to the throne. He had the same muscular body, chocolate eyes, and brown wavy hair. His face was handsome but longer and thinner then Henry's. The only feature that marred him was his bushy eyebrows. Henry stood and gave him a half bow. "Dillion, you look remarkably well. I have brought the marriage contract for the Kingdom to approve. I believe Father would like you to read it."

Dillion forced a smile and brought a chair over to the King sat and began to read the contract out loud. "Henry, it says here you have already given the title of Countess to her that is a little premature, don't you think?"

"Perhaps, but it is not unusual. Since Casandra will be Empress one day it rather demeaning." Henry crossed his arms. If Dillion were going to object to everything in this contract, it would be a very long day.

Dillon nodded and kept reading he ran through the ordinary wording of every marriage contract. Then he stopped and started paging back and forth through the pages.

The King said, "Well what is the matter, Dillion?"

Dillion stood and walked to Henry, "You have given your half interests, which is custom but where are the pages of our gifts?"

"Dillion, I did not feel I had any right to give her anything which was not owned by me, that is quite a lot as you know. If you wish to gift her anything, it is your prerogative. I did take the liberty of the title, but I thought you would not mind that, considering there are not monies attached. The Emperor does expect some land to come to her. However, an apartment at the Castle would be acceptable too, again, this is entirely up to you."

Dillion said nothing and turned to the last pages as he walked to the fireplace mantle which was taller than Dillion, he stopped reading and looked to Henry, "Sir," he turned to the King, "I can hardly believe this. Henry owns the use and mineral right of the Savilla. The Northland and mountains, the most powerful place in the world." Dillion's face was filled with astonishment he was lost for words.

Paxton walked into the room with glasses and the liquor. Henry stood, "Ah, a drink to my good fortune." He poured and handed the wine around the room.

Henry held his glass to his Father. "Sir, I toast you. You have been the best Father I could have had. You have given me freedom from the throne so I could find my own way. If you hadn't have done that I would not be the richest man in the world. To my Mother, who showed me what kind of woman to look for, to love and to marry. I am truly the luckiest man in the world." Henry threw his head back and laughed and drank down his glass. His three family members just looked at him dumbfounded.

His Mother stood, "I would like to toast our first Granddaughter, and the first High Sorceress this Kingdom has ever known." She drank down her glass.

Henry laughed and hugged his Mother, "You haven't heard her full name, Sarah Winsette De Volt Rakie." He held up both hands, "I swear I had nothing to do with it. I chose a girl like Casandra, she wanted a boy like me. I won, so I had to completely give in to the name. I told her it would look like I wanted my title back. I don't!" He smiled at Dillion. "Why would I want to be a mire King when I can name my position in the Continents? Plus it will be fun to lord it over you Brother." He laughed again and poured more drinks.

The King said, "Winsette is not a girl's name. What is she thinking?"

Henry said, "That is exactly what I said, along with everyone else in the room. However, she insisted, she will call her Winnie. She thinks it's cute, of course, she has never met you. I will call her Sarah."

The King drank his glass, "When will she be here, I will have a talk with her. That is a terrible name for a strong Sorcerer! Winnie, I have never heard of such a thing." He held out his glass, "I toast this Sorceress who put my Son on the right path for once in his life. I hope this means you will not be consorting with the dregs of society. Henry respectable, I cannot even believe it." He downed his drink.

Dillion drank his liquor. "Henry could I have more, it seems I will be drunk before lunch." He held out his glass, "Henry, to you. You have been thrown to the bottom, and we Brothers have worked tirelessly to keep you there. Stubborn man, you wouldn't stay there. I, like Father, can't wait to meet this magical woman who tamed you." He raised his glass to him.

Henry laughed, "I am proud of her she is amazing. I can't wait for her to come here you will all be charmed, without a spell. She is the most beautiful Sorcerer in the world, her power is overwhelming, she is smart and loving, and kind. I think I am drinking too much myself."

The King looked at him. "Son are you truly in love with her?"

Henry looked at Dillion and raised his one eyebrow would it work on him? "I will tell you honestly. First, I need to know is this room free of spies?"

Dillion eyed him and said, "What is it you're after Brother?"

The King said. "What are you talking about?"

Dillion walked to the door opened it and found servants loitering. He walked to the adjoining door to the sitting room, opened it and saw several lieutenants waiting. "I will be a while with my Brother, you are dismissed." Dillion whirled his hands and covered them in a secrecy bubble. "That should hold us, make it fast or we will be discovered."

Henry sat down. "Yes. I love Casandra, and I need your help to keep her. King, you need to know of this plot. The King of Hex is a cruel, murderous man whose vision is to rule the world, and he intends to use Casandra to do that. He means to start with your Kingdom. His has offered me your crown by killing you, Father. I told him I was not interested in this Kingdom then he offered to corrupt me with power and place me as the new Emperor. In fact, he is insisting on it. He intends to rule through me, I am just to be his slave. He told me he plans to use Casandra to breed his children. Dillion, I know you have gotten in too deep with him; he uses you now. Are all my Brothers working for him?"

The King said, "Dillion what the hell is Henry talking about?"

Dillion grabbed the bottle and poured another drink, "Father, I am sorry. Samuel and Richard were the two that had black market dealings with him doing his banking and covering up his monies. I only found out two seasons ago, when the King began threating us. Those two have us in so deep, the rest of us have had to play his game. We've been working on plans to remove ourselves from him; then he came to us and said whatever Henry wanted we had to play along. I wanted to tell you Father, but the others felt it would kill you. So, we have been hiding and skulking around. He has spies everywhere. He knows our moves before we have a chance to make them. We don't even trust our own wives."

The King threw back his head and laughed, "More liquor Henry. I knew something was wrong. I thought you were poisoning me and wanted me out of the way. I told you, Mariette, they were plotting."

Henry filled his glass. "Sir, I was the one poisoned by King Richard of Hex the madman is out of control. I will tell you about that later now we three need to plot our own way out. I do have an excellent plan. Well, the start of an excellent plan. It begins with you giving the throne to Dillion and making him King. He needs to run your Kingdom while you and I mastermind the downfall of King Hex. What do you say, do you want to play with me Father and you too, Dillion? Can any of our Brothers be trusted in this?"

Dillion held his hand out to Henry, "King Hex has used this throne and the collapse of the banks to maneuver our Brothers and me for years. I don't trust Samuel or Richard, and I am not too sure about the others, but I would love to help. Father?"

The King rubbed his chin. That was always a sign he was thinking, "So, Juliet's boys are the traitors, I should have known. Lavinia was always loyal to me. Forgive me Mariette but had she lived, I would have only had one wife even though we did not love one another." He held his hand out to her. "Bernard's Mother was a cheat; he will choose the side he thinks will win, use him but never trust him. Henry, I knew you were smart when you build your own wealth from nothing. I was so proud of you, but I couldn't show it; you understand?" Henry nodded. The King sat back in his chair, "Dillion you have been running the Kingdom for years. You have always been my choice for King. I say you can have it. I have a better life to live playing a game with my Sons. Hell, it sounds like fun!" He smiled for the first time.

Dillion rubbed his Father's shoulders, "I do love you, Father, thank you for having confidence in me. Now, spies will know we had a secrecy circle. I can tell them Henry confessed his collusion with King Hex, then he and I can speak openly to our traitor Brothers."

Henry slapped Dillion on the back, "You have always been my favorite Brother, besides Jack that is, both of you are very smart. Maybe we can keep Father's illness to have meetings in here. What happened to your dogs you loved? They would sleep with you, they are a wonderful way to keep the spies out."

The King said, "Richard said the dogs were giving me a cough he had them removed along with my cat Smoky. I want them back, tell that bastard it is my dying wish to have them here! Marietta, you get them for me, and I want you back in my bed too. That was Samuel's idea, he said she was too sad to be around me. I haven't had this much fun for hundreds of years. Dillion shall we play?"

Dillion smiled. "Yes, Father we will play." Dillion took Marietta's hand and said. "And you madam, if you play with us, I will see you live a long happy life here in the Castle, or wherever you wish."

Marietta laughed. "Dillion, I will play. You don't have to promise me anything. I have always loved a good game."

Dillion dropped the circle, and they were all laughing. They began making the arrangement for Casandra's visit. Henry gave his Father the medicines Ski had made for him. It was the most delightful visit Henry had had with his Father and Brother in years. He was looking forward to these days with them plotting and planning it was the way of life for the Rakie men. Dillion was so pleased that Casandra had included strategies in Sarah attributes, it surprised Henry. He wondered if Dillion had secretly wanted girls but felt the pressure of only producing male heirs, as all his Brothers had.

Dillion suggested to the King they gift the Delta of the Diamante to Casandra this was the origin of the Warlocks in Diamante. It was the most potent land the Diamante had; it was used for ceremonies of all kinds. He wanted to name the land Sarah Winsette's Delta for his only niece and Diamante's only High Sorcerer. I told him we would be honored, but they were spoiling my little girl. He said I would have to get used to it he and Audrey always wanted a girl. He was claiming bragging rights to having Rakie blood in the line of the hierarchy. His niece opened the doors to free trade with the Continents, brought riches and power to the Kingdom, along with raising the nobility of their lands. When she was of age, he would name her Princess of Diamante. His Father clapped his hands at that announcement. Henry was sure his Father would live to see his only Granddaughter because he was looking healthier than when he had entered the room an hour before. The highs and lows of his heart over the last week had gone from despair to elation he could hardly believe it.

Marion

Marion was fighting sleep. The endless meetings and lessons they were forced to attend were taking a toll on her. She couldn't wait until after dinner when Addison would steal her away to find peace and love in each other's arms. Marion had her share of infatuations and heartbreaks at the Academy, but nothing like her experience with Addison. He was not only handsome and smart but kind and giving. If this was true love, she never wanted it to end, except she would like to concentrate better. Keeping her mind off his kisses and caresses was nearly impossible.

Today they were going over the security and itinerary for Casandra's Season. Casandra's crown and torque would be removed. Eric, Grace, and Addison would add their blood on the stones of her bracelet. Magical carriages would be used to transport them from the Marais to West Coast where they would spend one-day shopping and sightseeing in the city of Grandeurs, the largest and oldest city in Marais. Marion couldn't wait to see it. Although flying in the Magical Carriages was not her favorite, she didn't trust magic to propel them through the air. The horses didn't appear to be a better choice either, she feared them. Pegasus liked the atmosphere but refused to fly over Oceans, they couldn't swim. Horses loved swimming, but horses wanted their feet on the ground. After her last fall from the sky, Marion couldn't blame them she was even warier.

They would fly along the coast to Sigal, again sightseeing and taking in the history of the countries of the South Seas Continents. Then they would visit the Mountains of Paldao where they would stop off at the Plains of Paldao where the wild Pegasus lived and maybe see a Unicorn if they were lucky. After several days in each country, they would spend several weeks in exotic Traza. It was known for its many-colored beaches, bright aqua blue waters, and flowers of all types. The country was overflowing with foods that were tantalizing and of course, parties, dancing, music, shopping, and fine liquors. Theaters were built on the beaches for plays and concerts which overlooked the ocean and opened to the starry sky. Marion attending Casandra privileged her to travel in the best and most exclusive manner. The best part was Addison would be with her, even though he would morph and look like someone else, he would still be there. The Emperor was renting a home owned by a friend, the King of Ceilo called Winter's End.

Marion and Casandra had not spent much time together outside of meetings. Casandra looked worried and miserable. Marion knew that look. She wasn't feeling like a good friend, she would have to spend some time with her and have a long talk. She was probably just missing Henry. The meeting ended with a review of the security again. Marion was tired of the constant security issues. She was beginning to understand how constant worry had formed her friend's personality. She was seldom light-hearted, always working to improve and being perfect. Marion realized it was not a choice for Casandra but a demand of her station. She wished Henry were here at least she could retreat into his arms and forget the gloomy days coming to them.

Marion worked hard at the fighting stances and lessons the Professor gave that afternoon, but the meditations were difficult for her. Sprites were not suited to sitting still and being present. She knew she would just fall asleep again. So, she placed her fingers under her thighs as she sat on her mat. If she wiggled them, she could stay wide awake.

"Marion! I see what you are doing. Really, I would just once like you to concentrate and feel the effects of meditation before we leave. We only have a few more lessons." The Professor stood shaking his head.

Marion sighed, "I am sorry Sir, but you do not understand Sprites are about movement, not stillness. This is impossible for me, especially on top of a roof on a mat. Perhaps I could call down a cloud and float on it or hang from a tree. Flowers, of course, flowers they can take you into a dream world."

The Professor looked at her confused, then he smiled, "Of course, I should have guessed. The Monks used this method to heal me. Girls, there are many ways to meditate, and Marion has just given us an advanced one." Casandra and Grace looked confused. "We are going to the woods." He waved his hand, and they were standing in the courtyard. The Major came out of the stables on the far end.

"Professor, you wanted me?" Major walked toward them.

"Yes, today I am taking the girls into the woods. I think we should have an escort, just to be safe. Not Addison. I need Miss Marion to concentrate." The Professor gave her a stern look.

Major unsuccessfully suppressed a smile, "I will have a guard here with mounts in a few minutes. Thank you for informing me. You may want to tell the Emperor."

"Of course, girls, you may have a small break be back here in a quarter of an hour. I will talk with the Emperor." The Professor walked off.

Casandra turned and headed into the Castle, Marion and Grace followed, "Wait, Casandra, could we talk?"

She didn't stop walking, "Sure, I am getting my riding boots. You may want to do that too." Marion and Grace followed.

Grace caught up to her first, "Casandra what is going on with you? You are so distant; what world are you in?"

"Can we just get our boots?" Casandra didn't want to talk about her thoughts and feelings, so she began running up the stairs.

Marion stopped Grace from following, "Leave her, she will talk only when she wants to. We just need to be present for her now. There is something she is not telling us, and I have a feeling it is essential. We can try again after our lesson."

Grace put an arm around Marion, "You are a good friend. I am glad you're my friend too."

They retrieved their boots and went to their lesson. They rode off to the woods on the west side of the lake. The forests were tall, and the undergrowth was filled with the first wildflowers of the season. Marion was enchanted with the fragrances it was intoxicating. She dismounted and walked into the shade of the forest, the others followed. Marion carefully pushed her hands around one of the flowers at the foot of a tall tree then raised it up without disturbing the roots.

The Professor came to her. "Marion, would you like to share this ritual with the girls?"

Marion gave the flower to the Professor, "Here Sir you take this one. I will find three more for each of us. We can't disturb the roots; we will replant them after they have given us our dream." She found flowering plants that had shallow roots. Then a butterfly perched on Marion's arm. "There is a perfect hallowed spot deeper into the woods. Follow the butterfly she knows."

They walked to a clearing with sunlight streaming into the center. The ground was covered with a thick green moss, small white flowers completely surrounded the clearing circled by tall white pine trees. "We are going to call a sacred circle, this is a perfect spot we're in a Faery Circle. Hold your flower out in front of you and shadow my dance and song." Marion began chanting in a Sprite language, slowly dancing to the left.

The Professor said, "In case you don't know the language, the chant declares; Beloved is our Mother's ground. The Spirit of love fills our forest. The Father of light illumines the miracles, and the deep springs feed our souls. The Night has blessed us we are alive in spirit."

"Outstanding Professor." Marion continued.

They sang and danced, steadily increasing the pace and rhythm. Before long each was dazed in the sunlight that had become so brilliant they were blinded. Creatures seemed to enter the circle which could not be seen but only felt and heard. The aroma of flowers suspended each of them in the air. Marion told them to smell their flower, then look deep into the heart of the bloom. For each of them, a dream would unfold, unique only to them. Time stood still, and no one knew how long they were held in their thoughts. Slowly the light dimmed, the music of the animals softened, and each of them became aware of ground firmly underfoot. Marion observed everyone, they had an aura of peace and a glow that radiated from within.

In the center of their circle stood a wolf, a bear, a fox, and a large cat. No one was startled or afraid, they all just watched as the wolf walked to Grace, bowed then stepped between Marion and Grace, and ran into the woods. The bear bowed to Marion, the fox bowed to the Professor, then the cat bowed before Casandra and purred; each left the circle peacefully.

Marion understood she would tell them later. “It is best to have a period of silence. We will not speak until we are back on the roof of the Castle. Then I will explain more, for now, please contemplate your dream.” They quietly replanted their flowers and left the meadow, mounted and rode slowly back to the Castle.

Marion was concentrating on her dream. Addison was telling her how much he loved her. Yet it was wrong Addison was leaving. She couldn’t put all the pieces together; why was he going? She had seen Casandra giving birth, but again there was sadness where there should have been a joy. She was forcefully removed from her thoughts as they entered the Castle courtyard. She wondered how much she should share.

They dismounted and silently climbed to the roof then sat on their mats. Marion began. “We are all connected to one another, the circle pulls us even closer. Each of us has been shown a piece of tomorrow. Mine was not a happy dream. These visions show possible outcomes. At any time, we can change that depending on our choices. The image shows us where and what we need to do. Addison and Casandra were in my thoughts. I understand I am to clear my relationship with Addison before this trip begins. Casandra, I was with you when you gave birth. The bear came to me because he is the fiercest animal in the woods. That is what I need be for you and Addison, to be intense and aggressive.

Professor you do not need to tell us your dream, but the crafty fox is your answer to it. You will need to use more of your intelligence than you ever have. Grace, a wolf is a member of a pack whatever your dream, you are to remain faithful to your pack. It also represented your fierce powers and loyalty. Casandra, your symbol is a cat; you will protect us all. You must become the predator, and not be the prey that you are now.

The Professor said. “I need to think about what I saw and carefully understand it. Tomorrow we will discuss this in our lessons. I think it would be wise to keep this information within our circle, for now, it is important. Marion, thank you for this, it must have been the will of the Night to show us these dreams.”

Marion stood. "I had no intention of creating such a serious dream circle. I had only wanted to experience fun or happiness. That was my purpose, to create some fun. We have all been too serious. I am sorry, I feel we all have been shown our tomorrows are much weightier than we thought. You're right; we should all interpret our visions and talk tomorrow."

The Professor stood up and said, "Let's prepare for dinner we must not show our concern to the Emperor. Let's keep this meditation as vague as possible if they don't ask, don't mention this."

They went to dinner Casandra sat by her Brother, away from her Father. One look at his face and she knew they were about to be interrogated.

The Emperor adjusted himself in his seat, "I heard about your outing to the woods today. Professor, would you like to enlighten me?"

The Professor took a drink of wine, "Your Majesty, Marion was having issues meditating. I thought of the Monks who connect to nature to meditate. Marion shared a moving meditation rather than a still one. We went into woods and Marion lead in a sacred circle."

The Emperor began eating. "That's all? Nothing more?"

"What more do you want to know Emperor?" The Professor squinted at the girls, they all had their eyes on their plates. They were looking guilty, this was not going as planned.

"Major, please tell everyone here what you saw in the forest. I am sure we will all be entertained by it, and others may have some question to ask these four." The Emperor pointed his knife at every one of the girls and continued eating.

Major set his fork and knife down. "I can only tell you what I saw. We escorted the Professor and the girls into the woods. Marion collected some flowers, and they all followed a butterfly into a glen. My men told me a glen had not been there the day before, so we surrounded them. They started to chant and dance. A star appeared in the sky and came down to the center of them. We were blinded, but we could hear animal sounds. We couldn't see anything, we moved forward to find them but ran into a wall. After a time a wolf came running out of the circle, followed by a bear, fox, and finally a large cat which might have been a leopard. The bright light disappeared, and they came walking out of the circle. They replanted their flowers, mounted, and said nothing on the way back to the Castle."

The Prince turned to his Sister, "Casandra what magic did you play with?"

Casandra smiled at him and raised her eyebrow. "Just a circle." She started cutting her meat.

Addison set down his fork, "Marion, you are usually quiet. Normally you are jumping in defending Casandra like a loyal dog. What in the world went on?"

Marion looked at Addison and swallowed. How she could tell him about her vision, "Nothing unusual happened it was just a simple dream circle." She looked down at her plate.

Addison crossed his arms, "Nothing unusual; a Bear, Fox, Wolf, and Leopard walking in a circle with you is usual. Were they real or magic?"

Marion looked at the Professor then at Grace. "I'm really not sure. Addison this has never happened to me before."

Eric watched Grace, "I feel covertness, I could order you to reveal this, Grace."

Grace sat back in her chair. "Are you ordering me, Sir."

Eric was shocked, "I should. Yes. Tell me why you all are being so evading? A good reason please." Eric sat back in his chair and crossed his arms over his chest and glared at Grace.

Grace looked around the table. "It was as the Professor said. It was a moving meditation. There was a bright light. Then we each had our own vision; a very personal vision. Then the animals appeared, one before each of us. The animals simply walked out of the circle. Like Marion, I am not sure what was real. I have never experienced anything like that."

Eric look deeply at her, "Too personal to share with us?"

Grace looked to Casandra. "I have my concerns, Sir. My vision was not a positive one."

Casandra shook her head, "Go on Grace, tell him. I know Eric, and he is relentless. He will not be happy and will interrogate us until we share this. This is sad because none of us have had time to process the visions ourselves."

The Emperor sat back in his chair crossed his arms and took in a deep breath.

Grace sighed. "I was holding one of Casandra's children. An eagle swooped out of the sky and took the baby. I jumped on a Pegasus and chased after it. I had nearly caught it when it turned and struck out with one of its talons and ripped open the throat of my Pegasus we both fell to our deaths."

Grace had gotten everyone's attention. "Marion told me that the wolf represented the pack and loyalty. I need to acquire the aspects of a wolf. I am not sure what this all means. Would you like to analyze this for me, Sir." Eric turned his white eyes on her and glared. He was mad but said nothing.

The Emperor said, "Wolves in a pack are invincible you went off on your own to chase down the baby, are you a lone wolf Grace?" Grace looked frightened and then glared but said nothing, the Emperor turned to the Professor. "Professor. Do you think this is a premonition?"

"Sir I can't say… my vision was not nearly that clear. Faces and pictures of places and things. I have no answer for you. It may be, or it might just be the Night telling us how to defeat the King. Grace needs to remain in the pack, mine would be to figure out this puzzle. The crafty fox was my animal."

Addison said, "Marion what was your vision?"

Marion looked at Casandra. "You left me, I was trying to understand why, and then I was in a Castle in the sky with Casandra while she was giving birth to her babies."

Casandra said. "Babies, more than one?"

Marion nodded yes. Everyone at the table began talking at once. Casandra looked at her hands and went directly to her vision. She was in the dungeon chained to the wall, cold, drained, hungry, and in pain. Now, what was that meaning?

Addison asked, "What was your animal, Marion?"

Marion said, "The bear. A strong animal, fierce."

Bryan took Casandra's hand he could see she was in her vision, "Casandra, where are you? Tell me your vision. Casandra, I know you can hear me, tell me."

She regarded his face. "I was in a dungeon chained to a wall…my animal was the large cat." What would he say of that? He was stunned. She stood. "I absolutely know the meaning of my vision. I have been dreaming about the same thing every night since Henry left. Marion said the cat was a predator. I have not felt or reacted like a predator for the past weeks. Indeed, I have felt like prey. I'm sick of feeling this way. Please excuse me, I have no appetite this evening." She threw down her napkin and stomped out of the dining room.

Marion stood, "I am sorry, Emperor. I have done many circles and never once did anything like this happen. I have lost my appetite, as well, and I need to talk to Casandra." She moved her chair back to leave.

Grace stood, "Please excuse me as well." They left and found Casandra walking out the front door and followed her, all of them were upset.

Grace said, "I am sorry, I should not have spoken. I thought if I shared it would be enough. They are a bunch of nosey men. Eric made me mad he ordered me! If I had not worked so hard for my position in the unit, I would have walked out. Thank you, Marion, you gave me a good excuse to leave. Besides I want to talk to Casandra too."

They all kept walking Marion continued, "My vision had a lot more about Addison. You were right Grace, it was too personal to share. I couldn't wait to leave. Thank Casandra she walked out first."

Casandra kept walking, "I am so tired of all this plotting, and people in my head with questions, and decisions. I would be happy to leave and go anywhere but here. I don't care about sightseeing, security, or wedding plans. I want to drink a bottle of wine and sleep until noon."

Grace agreed. "Casandra until this week I have not understood your life. I looked at you and thought, Oh, she is pampered with all these people around her caring for her. I didn't realize they were keeping you safe for them, not for you. You have never had a day alone or were free to choose what you wanted. It is always about your station and about your country, your safety or how many children of power you can give them. I am so sorry it isn't fair."

Casandra finally stopped walking away from the Castle went to Grace and hugged her. "Thank you. Just having you understand means so much to me. I am just so mad. I hate feeling this damned helpless. I just want to hit something. By the way, Eric is in love with you; that is why he gave you such a hard time."

Grace stepped back, "What are you talking about he is my Commander, and he cannot be in love with me."

Marion stepped up, "Yes he is. I could have told you that at the Ball he can't take his eyes off you. Where are we going?"

Casandra said, "I have no idea; just away."

Grace said, "I understand your feelings of helplessness. My Father is a very mean man, as a child, I felt helpless. He would beat my Mom. I think that is why I wanted to go into the squad. I wanted to learn to defend myself and her. Now, I am going to lose my position, I know it. I wish I were a man they just go out get drunk start a fight, and the next day they laugh about it."

Marion and Casandra stopped and said, "Alright that sounds like fun."

Grace said, "I have no idea where we could go to do that; we are women. Women drink tea and sew."

Marion said, "I don't sew. Let's get a bottle of wine from the kitchen and figure it out."

Casandra and Marion looked at one another and giggled, then they took Grace's hand and turned the other direction.

Off they went to the kitchen, Casandra distracted the chef while Grace grabbed the wine. They opened the bottle and began sharing it. Soon they were laughing and giggling. Grace said. "The girls in my unit would love this wine. Charlie loves wine."

Casandra said. "Let's get more bottles and visit Charlie." The game began as they dodged the Emperor's guards and Eric to steal more wine. Not long after they were pulling several of the girls out of the barracks and into the stable to drink wine. Grace told them about their dinner and the meditation; also how Casandra felt like prey. Charlie suggested they test out the skills the Professor taught them. Casandra agreed. One by one each girl chose an opponent, and the fighting began.

Casandra took on Charlie and within six moves had her on the ground. "Charlie, you let me win because I am High Sorcerer. I want a real fight." Charlie swore she didn't and all the others took a turn fighting Casandra. Casandra fought very well with all of them, but she felt they were not giving her a good enough fight. "Come on someone hit me."

Grace took a swig of wine, and said, "I'll give you a fight Sandi, watch this." She ran at Casandra and hit her below the waist and flipped her over her head. Casandra was flat on her back she looked up, "Oh you are going to get it now." She leaped to her feet and threw a kick that landed on Graces face. She went down, and the two tumbled around the stables.

Marion became worried the two were going to get hurt she stood up and said, "Casandra stop!" She grabbed Casandra by her arm. Casandra threw Marion into a horse stall.

Charlie and the girls were laughing Charlie said, "The high and mighty Sorcerer is not that easy to defeat! Ha."

Marion and Grace got up from the floor and attacked Casandra, Marion hit her eye, and Grace took her down at the knees. They were all in a pile in the stall laughing when Eric walked in. Charlie and the girls came to attention. Grace got to her feet and stood at attention in the horse stall. She had hay in her hair and blood was dripping from the corner of her mouth.

Eric couldn't believe it. Many times he broke up a fight among men but never among women. "What is going on in here?"

Marion stood and helped up Casandra who was on the bottom of the pile. Casandra smiled at him and said, "We're having fun, Eric. Would you like to join us?"

Eric could not even think. "No Countess. I don't think this kind of fun is allowed in my unit."

Casandra walked up to Grace and laughed. She pulled the hay from her hair and wiped the blood from her mouth smearing it. "There that's better. Well, maybe you should allow a little fun. Everyone around here is too damned serious." She walked to Eric, and he could smell the wine on her, "What do you see in him, Grace?"

Grace pushed Casandra's shoulder, and Casandra fell over. Grace bent to help her up and said, "We should probably take her to bed now. She's had a little too much, fun tonight."

Eric took in a deep breath to compose himself, so they were drunk and fighting. Well, at least he could understand that. The stable door opened. Addison walked in, "You found them." He looked at the scene, "What in the world is going on here?"

Eric walked over and picked up an empty bottle of wine and said, "They were having fun, Addison, can't you see that?"

Addison took the bottle of wine, "Ah they are having fun with one of our best wines. These young ladies have excellent taste."

Marion said, "We were just leaving, Charlie, Linda, Janet, Margie, Kathy, and Ann thanks for a wonderful evening." She, Casandra, and Grace began backing out the door.

Eric blocked the door, "Your evening isn't over yet. The Emperor has been looking for you, Casandra."

Casandra waved her hand in the air. "No worries, he is always looking for me; wanting me to do this or that, say such and such. I am tired of him he can wait." Casandra crossed her arms and raised one eyebrow. Eric's jaw dropped while all the girls started giggling.

Eric rubbed his hands over his face. "My unit may leave, but Grace will remain here. You will all report to my office at six in the morning now you can go directly to the barracks."

They all said. "Yes sir" and left swiftly at the same time. He looked to Addison for help.

Addison came to Casandra, "Countess, Henry would like to talk to you this evening, and the Emperor has said you can use his crystal ball. He sent us to find you and bring you to the Library."

Casandra had a silly smile on her face, Grace was looking wobbly, and Marion was holding herself as tall as she could, but she was beginning to sway. Casandra said, "Why?"

Addison took in a deep breath and said, "Why, I don't understand the question."

Casandra stopped leaning on the other two and straightened her tunic. She stood tall and said, "Why does the Count want to speak to me? Does he want to tell me everything is going to be wonderful? Why Addison, is he going to be another person wants to appease me."

Addison said, "He just wants to hear your voice Casandra he misses you."

Casandra's smile disappeared, and she pushed the hair from her face. Addison could see she would have a beautiful black eye in the morning. Marion grabbed Casandra's arm, "Let's go, Casandra. These people are in a mood." Marion took Grace's arm and began to drag both from the barn.

Addison stood three feet taller than Marion, and in one step he had his arm around her waist. "The only place you are going is for coffee in the kitchen." He lifted her with one arm and took Casandra's hand, "You too. Eric, can you handle Miss Grace?"

"We'll be right behind you. My young soldier and I need to clear a few things up." Eric had both his hands on his hips.

Addison continued out the door, and both girls turned and gave Grace a wink.

Eric shook his head, "Grace, I know you are good friends with Casandra, but she has a position in this Kingdom. We must keep her safe to fulfill it. You of all people, can't let her go unchecked like this. You three, drunk, fighting, and allowing our unit to see it, also deliberately involving them. You have put me in a challenging position. I will be required to discipline all of you. We are about to take those two on holiday to a country that is... Well, the culture is open, questionable, and some say immoral. Can you even imagine what could have happened if you three had done this in Traza? This could have been disastrous. I should not even let you go." Eric paced around her in a circle. "Well, what have you to say for yourself?"

Grace just stood there and looked straight out the stable door she said nothing. Eric walked to stand in front of her. "An answer please." He looked straight into her eyes.

Grace said, "I was mad, you forced me to betray my friend; you and the Emperor. Casandra is the position of High Sorcerer, I understand we are here to protect her position. Yet to me she is my friend first. Casandra is scared, but her position doesn't warrant fear. She is tired, but her position does not allow for rest. She is chained to that dungeon wall, but her position requires Casandra to remain attached to the wall until some Warlock comes in to save her. She has managed to stay in her position for twenty-four years. All she wanted was to be free one night Sir. We all know this holiday will not give her any freedom. She will have us on top of her every day, all day. So, I will gladly take my punishment for allowing my friend one damn night of drunken freedom, Sir." Grace looked past him out the barn door into the night.

Eric tilted his head smiled, picked a piece of straw from hair. "Grace, I hope I can have you as a friend, what am I to do about you?"

He reached to her mouth to rub the blood from the corner, "She really socked you in the mouth."

Grace smiled. "Yes, but did you see her eye?" She started laughing and wobbled again. Eric caught her before she fell and pulled her close and kissed her. Softly at first, then she pulled him even closer, and they locked in a long passionate kiss. She opened her eyes and said, "Is that my punishment?"

Eric laughed, "No we are going for coffee. Be in my office at 6:00 A.M. tomorrow."

Mags was pouring coffee down Marion when they entered the kitchen. Eric asked, "Where is Addison?"

Mags moaned, "He has taken Casandra to the library to use the crystal. The Emperor found her in here with a black eye. These girls, I think he will be glad when they are Henry's problem. He was not happy."

Eric said. "Well, here is another one for you Mags. Where is the Emperor now?"

"Out on the balcony." Mags shook her head.

Eric went out to the balcony, "Sir, I apologize my unit was involved in a fight with the High Sorcerers. They will be dealt with in the morning."

The Emperor said, "Sit down Eric; this was not your unit's fault. Don't be harsh with their punishment Casandra took the wine to them. She and Marion have gotten into their share of parties in the past years. I had hoped this was over."

Eric said. "Sir, if I may, your young Sorceress has not had a normal life. She is afraid, and we haven't been able to alleviate her fears. Casandra has arranged a huge wedding in days and is marrying Henry in three months. I might add she hardly knows him. She is being hunted, and it is as if Casandra has her own personal war with the King of Hex. She is remembering her past for the first time; if I were her, I think I would drink a little wine too. I just hope this evening has helped her to burn off some of her troubles, better here than in Traza."

The Emperor smiled, "You're a wise man Eric. I am happy you are going with her. I am so sad that this has fallen on my little girl. You are right, she has not had a normal life."

Addison walked out on the balcony just then, "Henry is talking to her Sir. He understands the pressure she is under, she is young. I remember a few times you and I were at odds and had a little too much to drink. I recall I was the one with the black eye." He laughed. "This is the same thing, Sir. You know what she told me? We men are too serious. You have to admit our conversations over the past two weeks have not been joyous."

"No, they have not." The Emperor smiled, "Do either of you know how well she fought?"

Addison said, "I'll have Henry find out. Wait he is asking her now." Addison listened, and he started laughing so hard he could not stand up straight.

The Emperor and Eric began laughing just watching him. He finally stopped and said, "Oh, how I wish you gentlemen could have heard that conversation along with the thoughts in Henry's head. That was priceless," He was wiping tears of laughter from his eyes. "It seems a young woman in your unit, Charlie, suggested they all fight Casandra to test her skills without using powers. So, that is what they did. She took them all down, except for Grace. You Sir," he pointed to Eric, "in Casandra's words, ruined their fun. Marion tried to stop them and was thrown into a stall. I assume she thought they were getting a little too rough."

The Emperor stood taller, "That was not a bad idea. She won them all, hmm." He smiled, then laughed, "I am sorry, but I can't help but feel proud of her. It relieves me that she can defend herself. I must tell the Professor his training is working."

Eric stood, "It was a good idea, just not drunk and unsupervised. Someone could have gotten seriously hurt."

Addison added, "You might want to know, Eric, the hour or so we were looking for them, they spent sneaking around us and stealing wine from the kitchen. Henry has suggested I make a potion for their hangover. Excuse me, gentlemen."

Eric looked at the Emperor and shook his head. The Emperor just laughed, "I hope you send Charlie and these girls with her on holiday. It seems you have trained them so well; they can even elude you."

Eric could only smile.

Henry's Headache

"Casandra, I understand you have been getting drunk and brawling." Henry looked into the crystal she was deliberately turned to one side. Casandra was hiding the black eye that Addison had told him about.

"Well, I wouldn't call it a brawl, exactly." Casandra wanted to look at Henry, but she didn't want him to see her black eye. Her Father had thrown a fit when he saw it.

"Show me your black eye Addison said it is a good one." Henry wanted to laugh but knew better.

Casandra turned to the crystal, raised her eyebrow and said nothing.

Henry asked, "I have only two questions, first and foremost who won the fight?"

Casandra couldn't believe it he wanted to know how well she fought. "That is what you want to know, how well I fought?"

Henry laughed. "Yes that and why? Did what happen in the woods prompt this?"

Casandra sighed, "Partly...it was all connected. Henry, I am assuming Addison told you about our visions. I have been feeling like a target since Elk's Pass. Every day since has been filled with ugly memories, uncovering depraved facts we will face, and pressure to make life-altering decisions in a matter of moments. The only happy moments have been with you. Grace suggested wine. Marion thought wine was just the thing to raise our spirits. Grace mentioned Charlie, and some of her friends in the unit loved your wine. We all partied in the stables, out of the sight of the Emperor and his men. We went back and stole more wine, it was great fun. We had such amusement hiding from Addison and Eric."

She grinned at him and began giggling; then started using her hands to talk, "Addison, Eric, and Major were all searching for us. We fooled them!"

She was smiling and giggling. Henry realized she was still drunk. "I see if it was all for fun, which I understand perfectly, how did the fighting start?"

Casandra looked straight at him, "That's the thing, Henry, it wasn't really fighting. I mean it was… but not really." She hiccupped, "Charlie, one of the girls, women I mean, in the unit. She wanted to know why we were having a party in the stable." She started laughing, "So we told her."

Henry asked, "Sweetheart, can you stop laughing and tell me what you told her?"

Casandra gave him the eyebrow. "I already told you, Henry, aren't you listening to me? That's why we fought."

"I'm sorry Casandra I don't understand." Henry was losing his patience with his drunk bride. At least he knew she was a happy drunk, he would remember never to question her while inebriated.

Exasperatedly Casandra sighed, "Charlie. Charlie asked if I had ever had to fight someone physically without using powers. I hadn't Henry, and when I did fight with powers, at school…well, I think some used to let me win. Charlie said I should fight them. Everyone agreed it was a splendid idea. So, I did." She hiccupped again.

Henry couldn't believe it; she couldn't have fought all of them. "How many did you fight?"

"All of them." She hiccupped again and giggled, "Well, not Marion. She was trying to break up the fight between Grace and me. I threw her over my head into a stall. Henry, we must teach her; I swear she hasn't listened or learned a thing from the Professor. All she does is day-dream of Addison's kisses. Wait till you see the two of them together it is sickening." She hiccupped again, "I took them all down, but not Grace. She was giving me a good fight then Eric came in and ruined our fun. He is in love with her, did you know that?"

Henry was astonished. "No I didn't know about Grace and Eric, and it seems Addison has blocked quite a lot from me as well. That is probably a good thing. Well…then, Congratulations my love, well done. You have put my mind more at ease. I will not worry so much about you. It is also good to know you don't go around starting fights. Please see Addison after our talk he will give you something to help with the hangover you will have in the morning."

"Henry, why don't you create wine that gives no hangovers?" She hiccupped again.

Henry laughed, "Because my love wine like all things in nature, has a positive and negative aspect. The positive is how you are feeling now. Laws of nature cannot be broken without a consequence. Remember the third rule of magic." Henry had a thought, could the third rule answer his questions about the Attachment, he would put it back in his mind now he wanted to talk with Casandra. They talked for a while, and it only made him want her with him. He was careful not to speak of anything that spies would use. He knew he was being watched even in sleep. They ended the call, and he talked with Addison then went straight to his Father's chambers. His Father would love Casandra's story of drunkenness and fighting.

Henry, his Mother, and the King were laughing when Dillion came in to see what was so funny. Henry told Dillion about Casandra, he was holding his sides. "This is all very funny, but there is a lesson Father. Have we neglected to teach our Sorcerers to defend themselves? It is something we should consider."

Henry looked at him seriously, "Father you have chosen the right son for your crown. Dillion is always thinking. Professor McMillan has taught the old way of combat fighting. After things settle down, I am sure we can commission him to come to the Castle to teach our women."

Dillion smiled, "Excellent Henry. Are you ready to meet your Brothers they are waiting outside? I know it is late, but with the spies in the Castle I felt this could not wait."

The King said, "You are right, Dillion. Let's get part one of our plan going. Stop smiling at Henry remember you don't like him."

"Yes, Sir." Dillion slapped Henry on the shoulder and went to get the Brothers. "Come in Brothers." They all came into the King's Chamber looking bewildered.

The King stood and laughed, "I see you all thought you were coming in here to watch your Father take his last breath, sorry to disappoint you. Come in, take a seat around the fire."

Dillion had arranged chairs in a semi-circle around the hearth. The King's favorite dog, a big black Dane was curled up in front of the fireplace. He raised his head and growled as the Brothers came forward.

The King said, "King down." The dog laid his head down. "I have felt so much better having my dogs around me again." Three more dogs came over to him as he sat down in his wing chair. "It is late, so Dillion take over."

The Brothers looked to Dillion, while Henry stood at the back of the room.

Richard spoke up first, "I take this little meeting is about Henry. Why are you lurking in back? Come up here where we can see your murderous face."

Henry walked up and took a chair, "I will oblige you, Richard. However, this is not about me." He stared hatefully at Richard until he looked away.

Dillion waited, "Are you children done with the staring contest?" Richard looked up at Dillion standing by the King. "There are some issues with Henry and his engagement you will undoubtedly want to be answered we can address those briefly. However, as Father said it is late. We will meet tomorrow morning in my office at ten am and go into details about Henry's engagement. The reason for this meeting is to announce the King is retiring from the throne. He wants to spend his time enjoying his dogs, wife, and Grandchildren, not especially in that order. He has selected me as the new King."

The room was quiet Henry went to the door and had Paxton bring in a tray of sparkling wine. He handed them around the room then raised his glass to Dillion, "To my Brother Dillion King of Diamante, and to my Father. May you live long and enjoy your life." All the Brothers stood and raised their glasses and drank to Dillion.

His Father said. "Henry, what is this wine? It has bubbles of happiness. I love this."

Henry laughed, "It is my new concoction, and I call it Casandra. When you meet her, you will understand why."

Bernard went to Dillion to shake his hand, "Congratulations this is unprecedented I can't remember choosing a King while one still lived. How will this be handled?"

Dillion beamed, "That is the reason for this meeting. It has never been done, so we must make decisions on how this will be managed. The burden of power will move from Father to me starting now."

The King took the ring of power from his right hand and placed it on Dillion's finger. "We will give him a proper Coronation of course. I think we should let the wives plan that they are good at giving parties. They should arrange for the parties, parade, and Balls for Casandra's visit too. Dillion thought we could make it at the same time she is here. Henry can give the women dates and Casandra's needs. I would like Dillion to wear the crown this week, while Henry is here. Is anyone against this? Speak now."

Samul spoke, "I am not against this Sir. Dillion is the natural heir. I don't mean to sound condescending but what do we do with you? I mean to say, well this is the King's chambers, and what do we call you and the Queen? Why is Henry even a part of this?"

The King asked the Queen to stand by him. "Do you care where we live my dear?"

Marietta said, "As long as I am with you Winsette, I have no preference."

Dillion went to the door and brought in his wife Audrey, she walked to the King and kissed his cheek. "I told Dillion I would not be comfortable in your chambers Marietta. You should remain here, even after Father's death I wouldn't want to stay here. This will always be the place you two lived and loved." Henry thought it seems Dillion has chosen a gracious Queen, as well, even if she was half Wizard.

"I would imagine you boys and your wives would call me Father. I am still that. I am a husband, Grandfather, and I do have friends. My name is Winsette Rakie that has always been good enough for me. Let's use that if it is good enough for my Granddaughter it will be good enough for me, don't call me Winnie." He laughed.

Henry and Dillion laughed while the other Brothers looked lost. Dillion said, "Henry is giving us our first girl of the family, he and Casandra are naming her Sarah Winsette De Volt Rakie. I hope I remembered that correctly."

Richard stood, "So, you have come after you title! I knew you could not be trusted!"

Henry sat down, "Richard, I seek no title. I am ecstatic Father has left me out of the family squabbles. Besides, I am the Emperor's diplomate and fourth heir to the Emperor's throne. As soon as the engagement contract is signed, I will outrank all of you." He threw back his head and laughed heartily.

Dillion stood and sighed heavily, "Sadly it is true Brothers. Now for what you will all really hate. Henry brings us a contract that not only opens our borders for trade and business with all Continents but costs us nothing more than naming Casandra Countess. The right for minerals and jewel of the North Savilla Mountains are open to our people. Of course, we must find some lands to grant her. However, that is our choice. I have suggested we name the Warlock honor grounds in name only to be transferred only to Henry's heirs. That will not take any of our lands, or our nobles. They will praise us for our wisdom. Henry has made all of us look the hero to our people. We have a contract which brings us great wealth and peace." Dillion held his glass up to Henry, "To Henry, our unlikely savior, and don't think this means any of us to trust you."

Richard was the only brother without an outraged look on his face. Henry thought he knew every detail of the contract, how fascinating.

The Addiction

Every day Devon practiced Attachments and releases. Every afternoon he went to the barracks to fight, and every evening he went into town to find a whore. His power had increased tenfold, and his cravings more than doubled. He knew the Attachments were morally and ethically wrong, but the need and thrill were irresistible. He could not stop himself. One night he went to the King after dinner to speak with him. He found the King and Martin in the King's study having a drink.

The King waved him in, "Devon, get yourself a drink. We were just talking about you. Martin thinks you deserve a holiday you have exceeded our expectations. I think he is right it is time for you to rest. Casandra will be in your possession soon. You look troubled…come in."

Devon closed the study door and poured himself a drink. "I have some questions Father."

Marin stood. "Devon, would you like me to leave and give you and your Father privacy?"

Devon held up his hand, "Actually could you stay, I am hoping to have some light shed on some questions about the Attachments. Well… Not attachments but more the feelings they produce. I don't know how to put this. I am feeling nervous…No, angry. I find no peace anywhere, I have such cravings, and I can hardly think straight. You both have done this I don't see this in you. There must be something wrong with me."

The King stood, "Devon, sit here, both Martin and I went through this. It is only that you are doing so many. When you have your own Attachment, a constant one this will end. Until then you must learn control. I think your time of practice has ended, you need time apart from this. Martin, what do you suggest?"

Martin went to refill his drink, "Well, I had to lock your Father in the dungeon for weeks, literally. He drugged me, we were in a military engagement at the time. You can learn control, Devon. You must understand we were at this for years before we understood and started controlling the urges." He took a drink.

The King said, "His Mother will have a fit if we use the dungeon or drugs. I am just getting along with her I don't want to do anything to upset her."

Devon smiled, he never heard his Father care about her feelings before. "Then I should leave the Castle."

Martin said, "Excellent idea you and I could go on a small trip. I will watch over you and keep you drugged until the urges subside, but we need to be back for the engagement party. Then your Father and I think it would be good to seek out Casandra on her holiday. We have her itinerary; we could leave right after the party. How does that sound?"

"That sounds great, but where do we go and what excuse?" Devon asked.

The King said. "I have it, Belissa Villa. We need to get the wine for the engagement party, and it would not hurt to check up on our ally the Count. Add to that, it is a suitable trip your Mother and Sister will not worry about either of you. The King clinked his glass with Devon's and Martin's. "To the Count, who has given us an excuse for almost everything."

Belissa Villa

Henry was happy to be in his home, his sanctuary. His bed was big, and just the right softness and his laboratory was a small walk down the hill.

The Villas were just that: homes all built of the same materials, but with an individual look. They were connected by walkways and drives, nestled in the rolling hills of the Belissa countryside.

Ski's home was the first on the roadway, with a view of pasture land for the horses and Pegasus to the north. The east side was a field of hops and barley. Southwest was Addison's home; his view was vineyards and hillsides with natural caves and a spring that fed the lake. Henry's house was the original home of the first Count of Belissa Villa and Jack's his older Brother's. It was due west where the vineyards cascaded to the lake and sunsets were picture-perfect off his terrace. All the homes were built of clay brick and plaster, with red clay tile roofs. The stable was central to all of them with barracks to the North. The first Count fashioned them after the homes he had seen in Paldao where the wild Pegasus herds live.

Henry's was a two-story, he was always the one to have guests. However, Elaine was not fond of guests in their house, so he had a guesthouse built down the way. The inside of Henry's home was plastered walls and wood floors with tall ceilings. Elaine had decorated with colors of the sunset soft, earthy, and peaceful. The furniture was traditional; it would have been an ordinary farmhouse if not for the expensive touch's Henry added of priceless paintings, and antiques from around the world. Substantial brick fireplaces filled each room, and brass candelabras with crystal glass shades hung from the walls. Large cut glass windows and doors brought the magnificent views of the landscapes inside. His fine china and glassware in his dining room gave his home an elegant feel. His collection of items handmade and rare throughout the house showed his appreciation for detail.

Henry and Ski each had their own lab. Ski was working on the Attachments, and they had stayed up late the night before working out new theories with the information Henry brought back. Henry was always working on the wines and brews, he would spend days creating new blends. The servants that worked for him were all his friends he had collected through the years, loyal and loving. Ruth cooked and cleaned, her husband Bob took care of the stables. Henry had built them their own house nearby on the land.

Henry had a late breakfast out on his patio overlooking the lake when Bob came around the corner of the house. "Henry, sorry to disturb your breakfast, but the word has come through the animals that we're about to have visitors. They are on the road, down in the village, looks to be that Martin of Hex."

"Thank you, Bob, your animals, are never wrong. I had expected someone from Hex this week Martin is engaged. The party is next week; they will want wine. Would you tell Ruth I am finished with breakfast? I will run up to Ski to let him know." Henry wiped his hands with the napkin and placed it on the table.

"I can go up to Ski's you finish your breakfast Ruth will be mad you left so much on your plate." Bob turned to go.

"No, Bob knowing Martin is coming has ruined my appetite. I need to speak to Ski anyway. Tell Ruth to expect guests we will put them in the guest house. I hope they don't stay long."

Henry walked around the house, crossed the lane and began running up to Ski's house. Belissa Villa was filled with trees and gardens, a sprawling village of friends with delightful paths to run on. He was so happy Casandra had raced him, he always loved to run. It freed him, and his mind would think up the most bizarre and beautiful things. He went straight to the lab he knew Ski had woke early and started his work. He knocked on the door but didn't wait for an answer and walked in, "Ski, it's Henry. Where can I find you?" Ski's lab was not neat and orderly like Henry's. It had multi-levels and was cluttered.

"I'm up top, come on up." Ski was hiding the Attachment research at the top, smart man, he could mask that easily if someone got nosey. Henry climbed the circular iron stairs and walked to the back, finding Ski working on an attachment.

"Well, Henry, I just don't know how they do it. I am getting closer now that I know they start with blood. Addison gave me the exact spell, so I must not have the chemical mixture right. I wish I could get my hands on one, then I could dissect it. Think you could get one Henry?" Ski finally looked up from his work. "You are running again?"

Henry was leaning on his work table, arms crossed, "I ran here it helps me think. I will try to get you an Attachment, but they are being clever and letting me know as little as possible. Bob just told me Martin is on his way here, he is in the village. I thought I would let you know. They will probably want to spend the Night, I hope no longer. You must hide all this. Could you come to dinner?"

Ski chuckled, "I wouldn't miss it. You never know what kind of knowledge I might glean out of them. Relaxed men speak carelessly, especially when the wine is involved."

Henry grinned, "You are right about that, and you are a master gleaner. Come down when you want. I will take them to the winery, and if there is the time I might show Martin my lab. That should keep them occupied this afternoon. We'll have drinks on the patio if it remains nice. I would like to eat dinner there too. I miss this home; I guess I am getting old. I would rather be here than anywhere."

Ski put his hand on Henry's shoulder, "It shows you are mature and wise. When a man knows where he belongs he creates. My Father told me when a man is young he wants to see the world and gain its riches. Old men want to watch the world spin by; he is the wiser one. He knows the life that unfolds before us is the one we get to keep. You get your bride here Henry, and your world will unfold splendidly."

"That was beautiful you should write that down. However, I do not feel wise. While running up here, I felt it would be best if I just stole

Casandra and ran off to another country. Unfortunately, we would be hunted by everyone. After my talk with her the other day I don't think she would go along with me anyway." Henry paused, "Ski, she told me she felt like a target. What could I say because she is; I feel like the arrow about to plunge into her."

"And the King is the bow. Good analogy, Henry." Ski sat on his stool, "The only thing we can do at this point is to remove the target. The question is, how can we move the target and make the King think he has hit a bullseye?"

Henry and Ski were deep in thought Henry said, "Well nothing is coming into my head, and our visitors are nearly here. I had better go play nice with the boys. See you at dinner. Thank you, Ski you always keep me on the path."

Henry ran home and found he was feeling physically excellent. He was going to run every morning and meditate. Henry would meditate now while waiting for Martin. He went to his study and made himself comfortable on his cushion. He relaxed and released all his tension, surprisingly it didn't take long for him to feel the floating sensation of meditation. He could feel the hum of the land, and nature in his ears. He also knew when Martin's men were coming up to the stables. He thought the Prince was here and he felt Ernst. He slowly opened his eyes and eased himself into his world.

Henry walked outside to meet Martin, and sure enough, there was the Prince and Ernst. "Good afternoon Martin and our Prince. This is a surprise." He shook hands with them and asked, "Are you hungry?"

Martin said, "No thank you, Henry, we stopped for lunch in the village. They have your ale there, and that is Devon's favorite."

Henry said, "I have my ale here, too, young man. Well, you will spend the night and have dinner with me I insist. Bob will have your things taken to the guest house. There is plenty of room there for you three. Your men can stay with mine at the barracks."

The Prince looked around, "Do you have a whole town here Count?"

Henry laughed, "It looks that way, doesn't it? We call it the Villas because they are a collection of homes built for all of us. They look similar, but they are different to suit each person. Really, we all just can't get along living on top of one another, so this was an excellent solution, to live peaceably together." They all laughed, "Now, what would you care to do first, visit the lab, see the winery, or just sit and admire the view and drink?"

The Prince said, "All three if we have time."

"Very well, let's start with the winery. We can investigate and drink at the same time." Henry led them down the road to the path that led to the winery. The Prince asked many questions about the process of winemaking, and where Henry got the barrels and bottles. Martin had never known Henry manufactured it all, at the Villas and in different places he owned. They tasted some wines and then moved on to the brewery. Henry showed them the new bottling building and how the ale was bottled. He told them it made it more portable for traveling and would send some for them to have on their return trip. Then they walked back to the lab where Henry gave them a demonstration of how to infuse magic into the wines and brews. He was sure they wouldn't understand it, but just in case they did he gave them the wrong spell and formula. It was better to lose a little wine now, than all of his secrets.

He walked into the house and found Ruth setting the table outside. "I thought you would want to have dinner out here the sunset will be beautiful this evening and the weather is fine." Ruth went on about her business.

Henry replied, "Thank you, Ruth, you read my mind. I will get us drinks Dear you worry about dinner. What will everyone have?" The Prince and Ernst wanted ale, Martin wanted wine. Ski came in and said he would help. Finally, when they all had drinks in hand, Martin handed Henry a list.

"That came from the Queen, she gave me strict orders to hand to you, and not to change the order on her." Martin laughed.

Henry laughed too. "I wouldn't dare disappoint the Queen. She is my most discerning customer."

Martin added, "She also told me she would not hear of you giving her the wine. She expects to be billed. However, if you had any of Casandra's drink available she would like that added."

"Ah Casandra wine is limited to your engagement party, my Brothers' coronation, and all the wedding festivities. I hardly have enough to go around." Henry smiled, "Don't worry I have set aside enough for a toast at your party that is my gift to you, Martin. You have always supported my winery and me over the years. I am making more it will be ready for your wedding. Tell the Queen there will be no charge for that; it is my gift, and I want no arguments about it."

Martin smiled, "Thank you, Henry, it has been easy to support you. You are likable, and I find you amusing. I would like to keep you as a friend, you are coming to my party?"

Henry knew he meant that. "I always have like you Martin, as well. Maybe it is the fact you have the best temperament of any Hex I know. I would not miss your party; however, I will not get there until the day of. I may be late. I have been gone too long, and with Addison off with Casandra well…things are falling behind in the winery. I have shipments to deliver, and with all this wedding nonsense I hardly have time to make them. I have had to reschedule everything. Just you wait till your wedding gets closer the demands are endless. You should hope for a nice war to take you away until the wedding day." They all laughed.

So, Henry's suspicions were on target they were here for more than wine. Nothing like a good game to keep his mind from Casandra, "Another drink, Gentlemen?"

Casandra Punishment

Something moved, Casandra woke to someone staring at her. She opened one eye hoping it was Henry, but her Father was sitting on the bed.

"Good morning sleepy head. It has been a long time since I have woken you. This reminds me of when you were small." He was smiling at her.

Casandra tried to raise her head, then she thought better of it. Oh, what a headache she had. "What in the world are you doing here?" Looking at the window morning light was not even showing, "And so early. Please don't yell at me I will die at any noise." She laid back and shut her eyes.

The Emperor laughed. "I know very well what you feel like. I have been there. Trust me you will not die although you might have wished you could. I do need to speak with you, but I promise I won't yell. At least open your eyes." She did and even that hurt. "Didn't Addison give you a tonic last night?"

"Yes he did, but it was dreadful I couldn't drink it." Her tongue had fur on it, and she could hardly speak.

The Emperor looked around the room found it on the dressing table and took it to her. "Drink! It may not taste good, but it will help get the illness out of your system." He pulled her up to sit, and she groaned, but she took the tonic and drank. "I trust you have learned a lesson about drinking too much wine. It will be a while before it tastes good. Henry's brews are particularly potent, keep that in mind." He took the empty glass and set it on the table. "Casandra, I came to tell you how proud I am of you. You have been working hard, and the combat lessons are helping you. Spells and powers thrown in a fight can be defended, but used with combat whether, with a sword, gun or hand can defeat anyone. I feel much more confident about sending you out on your own. I only wish I had done this years ago. It seems your Mother was right again, just wearing the torque and crown is not enough protection; at least not now."

Casandra swallowed, the fuzziness was gone. "Father about the Torque." He started to speak. "Let me finish. I know you said you would remove it for my holiday, but I think I should wear it. I will need to hide it of course, but I would feel safer with it on. I will leave the crown at home."

The Emperor shook his head, "When did you grow up on me?" he sighed. "I want you to know something about the Torque and crown I had never allowed anyone to know. The Wizard Gadwell helped me fashion the Torque and made the crown. He, Eric, and I know when you vanquish either one if you remove them we worry. As we discussed from now on, we will use that as a sign you are in distress." He picked up the crown from her nightstand. "The circles match perfectly. If you remove them and match them, they become explosive. A hazardous one. The Wizard said you may only have few minutes to get away from the explosion, perhaps less. When it explodes, it will take down an area half the size of the Castle, or more. He wasn't sure since we never tested them, they were hard enough to make, to begin with. Funny isn't it, when two objects are infused with our power they become explosive when placed side by side."

Her Father looked off into the ceiling. Casandra didn't know what to say to him. "Father, this is good information I am glad you told me. I could have accidentally blown myself up." She was feeling better.

Marion was yelling from the next room, and her Father laughed. "That is Addison telling Marion what is next on her agenda. Eric came to me this morning to tell me about Grace and her friend's punishment for the little escapade last night, they are to clean the stables today. I thought that was fair. However, it is not fair that you and Marion are not included. After all, you two led those women into the barn, with lots of wine. Now you have enough time to dress and have some breakfast before cleaning the barn. You should be done by lunch then your practice on the roof should fill out your day. I'll leave you to it." He was laughing as he left.

Casandra did not find it amusing, but she did feel guilty about getting Charlie and the others into trouble. She dressed in an old tunic, pants, and boots then knocked on Marion's door.

Marion screamed, "Go away!"

Casandra opened the door, "Please don't scream. Come on let's get this over with. I need coffee before I can face piles of horse shit. Get dressed I will meet you in the kitchen. I am not ready for another lecture or being laughed at right now."

Marion found Casandra with a coffee mug in each hand. She handed her one and took a swig from the other. Marion looked at it and moaned, the cook laughed. They both stared daggers at him as they walked out the back door. They sauntered to the stables in darkness. Marion finally spoke, "You realize this could be done in the afternoon."

Casandra shook her head, "Lessons are this afternoon."

"You are joking? They wouldn't do that to us." Marion sighed and drank the coffee.

"Oh yes, they would, and I know they will be enjoying every minute of our pain." Casandra saw Grace, Eric, and the woman from the night before walking to the stables they met at the stable door.

Eric smiled, "It is wonderful to see you this morning Countess have you come to help?"

Casandra crossed her arms and raised her eyebrow to let him know he was walking a close line. "It seems only fair since I was the one to launch the drunken brawl. That's how you all refer to it? Drunken brawl?" She was sick and mad. She could not contain the flames escaping from her boots.

His reaction was a step back with a very solemn face. He had no way of knowing the Emperor's words to her this morning. He would try to be stern and brief, "I suppose men do have drunken brawls. Am

I not sure of the correct words for women drinking and fighting? I had not seen it before last night."

"Well, perhaps you should invent some words? The Night knows there is always a separation between the sexes. I am sure there is in this too. Could we get started?" Casandra was finding it hard to contain her powers.

"Of course, have you ever cleaned a stall Countess? My unit has." Eric opened the doors to the barn.

Casandra just glared at him, "Unfortunately this is not my first punishment, and I believe you know that. However, I find it interesting cleaning stables is the first punishment men choose to give a woman." She had more to add, but she saw the color rise in his face, so she kept her mouth closed. This day would be hard enough, and she didn't need another lecture.

Eric saw her mouth closed and was sure she wanted to add something more. He could not let the Countess belittle him in front of his unit he was glad she stopped herself. "Then you are knowledgeable. That is good. Marion, since you are Casandra's lifelong friend I will assume this is not your first punishment either. I will let you women get started. Ask my unit if you have any questions." He started to walk out and then turned back. "I might add, this should take you until noon if you finish early and I smell any magic we will need to find some other place to clean, perhaps the toilets."

Casandra placed her hands on her hips and said, "Well for that I would need more wine!" the women snickered, then she smiled and bowed to him.

Eric turned and stormed out he was just about to lose patience with this woman how was he going to spend weeks with her.

She went to the barn door and closed it and sighed. Grace came to her and gave her a hug, "Casandra, that was very close, you are his superior, but he is mine. He almost lost it at the wine remark. Please try to be civil to him for all our sakes. I do not want to clean latrines."

Charlie stepped up, "Grace is just trying to tell you we are in trouble. We should not have fought with you last night. We are supposed to be defending and protecting you. Now, none of us know if we are going to be allowed to go with you. This assignment means a lot to our careers. It is not easy for women to move up in the ranks. This assignment would really help us."

Casandra said, "What, he can't do that! I was the one who talked you into it. I fought back. It is half my fault, and I am here, aren't I? What do these men want? When we act like helpless women, they take control of everything. When we act like men, they get mad and retake control. I will never understand them, and right now I feel too bad to even try."

Marion walked up to the group. "Well, I think you were right about needing more wine. I just had a swallow, and I feel better. Want to try?"

They all started laughing and decided, why not, it didn't take much before they were all half drunk and cleaning away. Mucking out the stalls wasn't half so bad after a few swigs. They had finished up almost on time. Charlie passed around mint for them to chew on before Eric came. They were throwing the last empty wine bottle in the barrel when Eric walked in.

His unit stood at attention, so Casandra and Marion thought they would too. He walked around the barn and looked in every stall. Then he walked up to Casandra, "It seems you all did a fine job. Countess, do I smell wine and mint?"

She smiled sweetly. "Yes you do, Commander. We couldn't stand the smell of our own breath, we ate mint. We also found quite a few empty bottles while cleaning. I accidentally knocked the barrel over, and wine dregs spilled on the floor, I am sorry. I am surprised we are feeling this good after drinking so much last night." Casandra kept her face straight and tried not to raise her eyebrow.

Eric smiled suspiciously at her and said, "I am too. Your Father wants to see you, Marion, and Grace in his library after you clean up. The rest of you may clean up and go to lunch. I will speak to you after." He walked to the barrel to look at the wine bottles. The all left quickly and quietly, the three girls practically ran up the stairs to clean up. They washed, and Casandra found more tonic on the dressing table. Well, Addison was kind. There was a knock on the door, and Grace and Marion stuck their heads in.

Grace walked over and handed Casandra the tonic. "Addison left you some, too. This stuff helps, drink it, I'll do your hair. You were great Casandra covering for us. I am not sure Eric believed you, but you were so sweet and lied so honestly, he could say nothing. You wrapped him around your little finger. That was phenomenal."

Casandra laughed and said, "I did do well, but I don't feel very good about it. He is a good friend to me and was my protector as a child. He is a good commander and a nice man. I put him in a bad spot earlier. I should not have made him look bad in front of his unit. I will apologize for it the first chance I get."

Marion said, "Don't tell him we were drinking again!"

Casandra gave her a look, "I am not that dumb. I just think he needs to know I am sorry for being sassy to him. I don't feel bad about lying to him. That sounds horrible. I don't think I should drink. I say the stupidest things. You know last night Henry couldn't even understand me when we talked."

Grace said, "I have to agree with you. I have learned the hard way to not speak if I am drunk. Just say yes and no to your Father; don't elaborate or we will be cleaning the toilets. Got it?"

They all walked into the library and food was set out on the table with coffee. Casandra said hello and raced for the table. If she kept her mouth full of food how could something stupid come out?

Her Father came over and helped himself to some lunch. "Eric told me you did a fine job this morning, ladies. I guess you are wondering why I called you here for lunch." He waited for someone to say something.

Marion swallowed and said, "Why? Yes, we are wondering."

He continued, "I got this little green note this morning from the Duchess." Everyone turned and looked at his hand holding the note. "It is a request for the three of you to visit the Duchess for dinner." All three of them just looked at one another. "I see you knew nothing about this either. Well, that is a long carriage ride, and I don't like you traveling at night alone. I spoke with the Hermit and asked if you could go tomorrow morning instead. She was not content with my suggestion and insisted her plans be followed. You will leave as soon as you finish lunch and pack an overnight bag. She can only have a few guests, so I am sending Eric and Addison with you as an escort along with Gregory. Casandra, do you have any idea what this is about?" She just shook her head no. "Why are you so quiet?"

Casandra looked down at her plate and sighed he was forcing her to speak, “It is not unexpected, she said she wanted to speak with us again before I left on holiday.” She kept putting food in her mouth.

He looked at her carefully, “About what?”

She swallowed, “She didn’t tell me. She just said she needed to do some calculations, whatever that means.”

The Emperor tilted his head and said, “Are you alright you are acting strangely. I have never seen you eat like that.”

Eric walked into the library just then, fantastic two of them inspecting her. Marion kicked her under the table. She was starting to get mad emotions were hard to control under the influence of alcohol. She put down her plate and stood to keep Marion from kicking her again. “You think I am acting strange? Well, how often have you seen me hung over? None of us could stomach breakfast; then we worked all morning in the barn. We’re hungry. I am not in the mood for long conversations and accusations. Please excuse me I will go pack. Perhaps that will please you.”

He crossed his arms and said, “Casandra!”

Bryan interrupted him and took her arm. “I will help her pack. I haven’t had any time with my Sister. Come on we’ll have Mags make sandwiches for your trip. I’ve mucked out plenty of stalls, and it makes me crabby and hungry too.” He winked at her and walked out the door.

Grace and Marion looked at one another Marion said, “Well if there will be sandwiches in the carriage we will go pack too.” They both left the room rapidly, and Eric went to the library doors and closed them. “Your daughter is a happy drunk, but sassy the day after. Addison, you may want to warn Henry. I was just about to smack her this morning at the barn.”

The Emperor said, “What happened?”

Eric went to get coffee, “Did you know we have a whole different language for men and women, men get drunk and have brawls. She asked what it is called when women do it, and it seems the only punishment we hand out to women is mucking barns. When I threatened her with cleaning the latrine she said she would need more wine then she bowed to me, all this in front of my unit. I was dumbstruck.”

Addison started laughing, “I am sorry gentlemen. I find this funny. Henry said he would need wine to clean the latrine too, and he thinks she is right. He says you should tell her when women get drunk and brawl, it's called getting sloshed and scuffling."

Eric looked shocked, "I would be afraid she'd hit me." They started laughing.

Bryan walked with her, entered her room and fell on the bed laughing. "Oh, my dear lovely Sister… I could hardly contain myself." She gave him a look with the eyebrow. He laughed even harder, "You forget, I have seen you drunk and disorderly, like now, how many times have I gotten you and Marion out of some scheme? It is a good thing you are going to be gone for a day, maybe you will be more yourself by tomorrow afternoon. Really you are impossible after you start to sober up, and you can't contain your power. Honestly, it is dangerous."

Casandra went to her closet and got her traveling case and started packing. "Bryan you're not telling me anything I don't already know. Be helpful… tell me what I was to do? I tried short answers and not looking at anyone. Smartypants, what do you do? Stop laughing! I am so aggravated at everyone laughing."

"I am sorry Casandra, but you are so funny and indignant. I think because we see you so calm no matter what all the time. When little things aggravate you, we are shocked. I guess I don't try to cover up being drunk." He watched her.

"Bryan those little things aggravate me every day. I am sure they bother Kathryn too. I have a hard time managing my emotions when I am drunk. Maybe I should get drunk more and practice." He was laughing again, "Then there is that! Words just come out of my mouth I can't stop them." She sat on the bed about to cry.

Bryan put an arm around her, "I love you, drunk or sober. I can't imagine not being able to feel but even as Prince I must contain my thoughts, words, and emotions. Just try to remember not to look at your feet it says you're guilty. Always smile when you speak, especially when you lie and relax your body. I try to envision Father naked that really works." They both started laughing. Bryan pulled a green note from his pocket, "I got a little green note today myself. The Hermit wants me to take your egg to the Monks I finished it late last night. How does she know these things I am astonished. I was only going to tell you. I love you, sweetie. Are you ready for all this my baby Sister?"

Casandra threw her arms around Bryan, "I love you too with all my heart. Thank you, Brother." She kissed him on the cheek, "It begins, I can only pray to the Night it ends well. Promise me if anything should happen to me you will take good care of Sarah Winsette Rakie?"

Bryan hugged her, "I will not lie to you my Casandra. You and I have a difficult road ahead I wish Father would let me go with you. I would protect you with my life, and Winnie."

Casandra gave Bryan a solemn stare, "That is exactly why you must stay here you are more important than me. I am not hurt or angry about that Bryan, it is just the way it is."

There was a knock at the door their Father walked in. Bryan whispered in her ear to practice seeing him naked, they both started laughing uncontrollably.

The Hermit's Game

The carriage for six landed in the courtyard, and they all climbed in. Casandra sat next to Marion, Addison sat next to her. Grace and Eric sat across from her, with Eric staring directly at her. She had to admit he was as beautiful. Like Grace, his hair was platinum, and his eyes were a piercing white with gold edges. She understood why he was effectual at gaining information. He was the most intimidating man she had been around. They shared the sandwiches and talked. Every time the carriage bumped Eric and Addison stiffened.

Casandra commented, "I guess you and Addison would prefer to ride a Pegasus to the Mountain."

Eric tilted his head looked directly at her and said, "They would not be able to fly this fast, and the temperatures are too cold for them. If you are inferring I am uncomfortable not having control, I will admit I would prefer to ride on top. I like to know what I am heading into."

Casandra held his gaze, so he wanted to continue assessing her. Well, she was too tired for this game. She reached over to the side of the coach and pulled back the curtain. "We have windows for that. We have a long ride I think I will try to sleep." She laid her head back and closed her eyes she could no longer look at him. She will fake sleep if need be to avoid staring into his cold inquiring eyes. In no time at all the sway of the carriage and her full stomach put her to sleep.

Marion was pulling on her arm. "Casandra we are close to the Mountain. That was a fast ride the sun is just setting."

Casandra stretched and looked out the window. The North Mountain was purple against a sky of pinks and oranges. She sat up, and there was Eric still staring at her. Had he stayed in that position for hours? "Was I snoring?"

Eric sat back, "No Countess not once." He smiled. She could not help herself she raised her eyebrow, and he looked out the window. They landed and was greeted by Marion's Cousins who hustled them in and took their coats.

The Hermit stood in the entry. "Ladies, Gentlemen welcome to my home the North Land Mountain of Savilla. Come to stretch your legs it is a long ride. She led them into the main room. Casandra enjoyed watching the awe on the men's faces as they gawked at the opal and topaz walls. She walked to the window to catch the last of the sunlight which was spilling colors on the crystals of the walls, floor, and ceiling spreading a rapture of color and light everywhere. "Mistress, this is spectacular do you have this view every evening?"

She joined Casandra at the window. "Mostly, if the weather is good, not during the winter soleus. Of course, then we have the Northern lights."

The Sprites came with a tray of drinks, each in different glasses and different colors. The Hermit took one from the tray and handed it to Casandra.

Casandra held up her hand looking directly at Eric she said, "I think I have had enough to drink for this week." Eric smiled.

The Duchess sternly said. "I have made a drink especially for each of you. This will cure you and open your mind. What do you gentleman call it…horse hair?"

Eric laughed, "Do you mean the hair of the dog that bites you?"

The Hermit grinned, "Yes I believe that is it." She held the glass to Casandra and said, "You are compelled to drink this."

Casandra looked wearily at it but took it and tasted. She felt the ill effects of the hangover fall from her body, and the liquid strengthened her, it warmed her soul. She tilted the glass and emptied it then giggled. Eric glared at her.

The Hermit set the empty glass on the table and said, "Leave the tray and get Casandra another." Eric started to say something, but the Hermit held up her hand and stopped him, "You realize I have allowed only one man in my home since I built it. George was the first, you two are only the second, you are both privileged."

She handed him his drink he took it and drank it. "Thank you, I am sorry I do not know how to address you."

She handed Addison his drink and said, "A common problem since I hardly have visitors. Mistress or Duchess would be fine whichever makes you comfortable." She handed out the other drinks and gave Casandra a second. "As I was saying, I never have males here my experience of men is they can never be trusted. However, three men play a critical role in my Granddaughter's life."

Marion objected, "I know Marion, Great, grand, grand…too many to say. I will just say Granddaughter; you know what I mean." She glowered at Marion, and she sipped her drink, "You two, and Count Rakie are important to Casandra. Casandra, you will bring Henry to me after you visit his land."

She looked intently at Casandra, and she nodded, drank her drink in one gulp. "Yes, Grandmother." The Hermit snapped her finger and Casandra glass was replaced with a new drink. "Drink up everyone, you are all compelled."

Everyone drank, "Eric your family is all dead correct?" He said yes. "Both your parents were soldiers, and you had an older Sister there are questions of loyalty surrounding her. You have many questions about your family." He was dumbfounded.

She turned her attention to Addison, "You are an Orphan Addison, you have no idea who your parents are. Chancellor Ski adopted you, and he raised you; then saw to your schooling. You are not sure you want to have answers to your questions. Well, gentlemen, you are both in luck because I believe anyone who will be facing death should indeed have all their questions answered."

Grace took a noticeable deep breath. "Grace, I didn't forget you were in the room. You are alarmed I am so blunt. My last statement includes you and Marion as well. All of you will face death, be prepared."

She paused and took a drink, then everyone was handed a new glass, "We will have a nice dinner together; both of you gentlemen will go to your rooms. Setting on the dresser is a potion; if you chose to drink it, you would sleep a deep slumber like you have never experienced. You will wake feeling one hundred years younger, with energy and a clear head. You will have all your answers. I will speak to both of you separately in the morning. I will speak with the girls separately after dinner." She held her glass up and said, "A toast to a long life for us all."

Then she noticed Grace, "I am not scary Grace I am eccentric. There is a great difference, and yes, I can read minds, Addison. Is Henry here with us this evening, tell me what he is saying?"

Addison smiled and said, "Henry wishes he could be with us, but he is entertaining the Prince of Hex this evening. Then you probably already know that. Yes, he does think you are an eccentric but a beautiful one."

She raised her eyebrow, and Addison chuckled, "Henry said he has learned the eyebrow trick too. He finds it a very effective form of intimidation." Eric snickered.

The Hermit turned to Eric, and he stared into his drink. That had Casandra laughing hysterically. "Oh I am sorry Grandmother, but Eric has no room to talk when it comes to intimidation. All he needs do is look at someone, and they fold. He has the most incredible eyes."

The Hermit smiled, "I have noticed that. I believe dinner is ready. Shall we?"

She showed everyone to the dining room, and Eric went to the walls. "Is this really jade?"

The Hermit replied. "Yes, there was a deep vein running through the mountain. I hope you enjoy dinner. The Sprites love cooking wondrous dishes. I like plain food. They get frustrated with me. Cassandra, say grace."

Casandra had not said grace for years but knowing she would soon have a daughter she felt blessed, "We thank the Night for the good food we eat, the friends we have at the table, and we are grateful for the blessings you grant us. We ask we all be together again at this table with our Duchess, the holder of the High Mountain. Keep her safe, keep her warm, keep her loved as we are. Blessings." She opened her eyes and looked to the Hermit her eyes were deep in sorrow. Would she not be with them long? Casandra had an eerie suspicion this might be her last dinner party on the mountain.

Dinner was filled with laughter; the food was delicious, and their glasses were never empty. Casandra felt light headed and happy but not at all drunk. Her Grandmother whispered in her ear that the drink was an antidote to wine. "You will be able to drink as much as you want on your holiday and never get drunk." Casandra gave her a hug and stood up and danced around the table.

The Hermit held up her hands and said, "It is getting late we must get to our business before Casandra starts singing. Gentlemen, you are excused."

Casandra clicked her glass with her spoon. "Grandmother I need to have a private conversation with Eric. Can we go into the living room."

"That's fine. I will start with Grace, and I am sure Marion wants to kiss Addison Goodnight. Tell me Addison has Henry talked you into drinking the memory spell?" The Hermit looked slyly at him.

Everyone looked at Addison who smiled politely. "He wants to talk to me about it. Goodnight Duchess." He and Marion left.

Eric stood, "Thank you, Duchess, for a lovely dinner Goodnight."

"Casandra please shut the door after you. Grace come here and take Marion's seat." The Hermit's face transformed to a solemn appearance.

Cassandra whispered as she passed, "It will be fine." She shut the doors and walked Eric to the living room.

She motioned for him to take a seat by the hearth. "Eric, I want to apologize to you for this morning. I should not have spoken discourteously to you in front of your unit. You have always been kind and protective of me in all the past years. I should not have disrespected you. I promise I will behave better on our trip."

Eric was shocked once again today by her. "Miss Casandra, I was more shocked than anything this morning. I have known you for many years, and I have never seen you behave like this. This morning and last evening are out of character for you. We all care about you at the Castle, and we are concerned. It is my job to protect you, and I must anticipate your actions to keep you safe. Erratic behaviors make protection twice as difficult. I do appreciate your apology and accept it.

However, you should be extra careful." She started to say something he stopped her. "Please allow me to finish this is a difficult conversation for me. You are not a soldier I cannot order you; I take orders from you. I do understand the need to test yourself with your newly acquired skills, but I wish you would have come to me. I would have gladly arranged a competition. However, I can't with a good conscience not bring up the drinking."

He sat back in the chair and looked at her. "Eric, I am well aware of my bad actions while drinking. I hold a great deal of energy back and all my emotions down all the time. I rarely relax, and when drink relaxes me, I can't hold the emotion back. I am the first to admit I have poor judgment and fear nothing. This evening my drink was an antidote it will keep me from being drunk on my holiday. That is why I was so happy just now. It is one thing I won't worry about, of course, I may not relax. Which is the whole point of the holiday, I don't know why I have to go. I would just as soon stay up here on the mountain for six weeks." Casandra stood and put more wood on the fire.

She sat back down with Eric scrutinizing her. "You have too much burden on you for such a young lady yet, it is the way it has always been. Every piece of information we learn about the King is worse for you and me. The warning the Duchess gave us tonight didn't help any of us. I watched as you said the blessing, who will sit at that table next year. I might not, or Grace, maybe Addison we are all in jeopardy." He sat forward and put his elbow on his knees, "It is good you have told me about the drinking not being a problem, but there are so many other things to take in consideration. Frankly, I would love to keep you on this mountain until you are an old woman. I believe Henry and your Father would love it as well. Is that a life for you Casandra? I looked at the Duchess she is not happy, nor will she ever be. She hides up here from men, from the world." He took her hand, "Casandra, I would rather have only a few years of love and excitement and happiness, yes throw in some danger too, even mistakes; than to live to be hundreds of years alone. I have protected you for twenty years. I only want the best for you. I…I care about you, Casandra."

Casandra smiled and said, "I know, Eric. I love you too." Eric turned his head and stared into the fire. Casandra asked, "My drink had healing protection from alcohol and wellbeing for me. What was in yours?"

Eric flashed his perfect smile. "Love and truth. After feeling all the warmth from it; I was wondering about the drink I have waiting. Do I really want to know the truth?"

Casandra raised her eyebrow and said, "Love and truth that is a wicked combination. I think the drink waiting for you is the truth part, and Grace is the love." He started turning red, "If you believe what you just told me about life as truth, and you wish to live your life filled with love and excitement what are you waiting for? I think you understand this mountain because you have been living on your own mountain for a long time." Casandra ran her hand down Eric's cheek. He was a handsome man and once she so loved him.

Grace walked in just then and looked a little befuddled. "Hi, Casandra, she wants to see you next."

Casandra stood and gave her a hug, "Can't talk about it, can you?" Grace looked at her feet. Casandra turned to Eric, "She normally puts a spell on people to keep them from talking. Don't bother asking her questions."

Casandra left them in front of the fireplace as she secretly sent them a charm of love and communication. She went into the dining room and sat by her Grandmother. "She is as white as a ghost. It's just a comment I am not asking."

Her Grandmother poured green liquor into her glass. "I saw that charm. You shouldn't mess with your friend's hearts. They have their own learning to do without your interference."

"What kind of wonderful news do you have for me?" Casandra took a drink while the Hermit sent one of her compelling charms.

"My dear, you are turning cynical. I know you have had one bad thing after another over these past weeks, but where is your spunk. You will not be able to win this game if you don't keep a clear head and use it wisely."

"Is that what this is about a game, my life amounts to a game." Casandra couldn't believe this.

"Me, me, me that is all you consider. The Night has given you everything; your life has been wonderful and fun up to this point. She provided the best of food, wine, education, beautiful homes, the latest fashions, exotic holidays, good friends, a powerful lover in Henry, great power, and beauty. Now she asks for recompense. You want all the good, but just like mucking out the barn today, you don't want to do the actual work." That hit Casandra right in the heart; she was right. "Yes… I saw today and last night too; standing up to the men, fighting, putting yourself in their arena. Today you called them on it, you showed them they are the ones who suppress women. You have been truthful to each of them and showed them a strong woman. Now you want to stay on the mountain and hide. What is worse, you all believe that is what I am doing. I have tirelessly worked my entire life to uncover and undo this hideous plan. If the King wins this game, all women will be powerless. He taps into the evil that we Sorcerers work so tirelessly to keep buried in the ground. I thought you were the one to stand up to evil maybe it isn't you. Maybe it will be your daughter."

Casandra was horrified and angry. "What about my daughter, I will not have her fight this."

"That is what your Mother said after it was too late. Your Mother was so scared she wouldn't come to me. Her Mother died by drinking herself to death for fear of it. How many of my daughters do you think have died with this knowledge? None of them did a thing about it when they could have stopped it. Right now, the King's wife, one of my daughters, is under an Attachment Spell to him. Even his children have an attachment on them they have no idea how powerful and wonderful they are. It is too late for them. He wants you, he wants you attached to his power too. He is so evil he addicted his only Son a wonderful weather Warlock Wizard to this debauched behavior. If Prince Devon, captures you, his Son will become the most powerful Wizard yet. Do not fear Devon, the King is the one who will drain your powers. He would use an Attachment on his own Son to have you. You must kill them all for your children to live."

Casandra was jolted, "What have they not told me? What are my Father and Henry leading me into." she just wanted to run.

"I compel you to sit down and hear me out," she poured more wine, "Warlocks are under the misconceived notion they must fix all the world's problems. They believe they are stronger and smarter than us.

Warlocks are drawn to us like a moth to a flame, but down deep they fear our power. They should. If you chose not to fight the King... if you are not the one to destroy him your daughter will have the same fight. I read the crystals each day and with every one of your decisions the future changes. I can hardly keep up with it. Casandra your will to fight must be strong. The crystal shows the King's death, but every time you run or back down from a fight your death shows. It isn't just your death; it is everyone who sat at that table this evening including me. Some scenarios show Henry, your Father, and the Prince die. It has flipped and flopped so much I am afraid to predict the future. I no longer know what to tell you or how to help you."

Casandra downed her whole glass of wine and poured more. "Well, that is wonderful news Grandmother this was a great sermon. I am really motivated to go out there and slay a King. Evidently, I am not in any position to have a choice. I don't know why that upsets me. My entire life has been lived without a choice." She drank more wine, "You do realize I didn't ask for this beautiful face, or power, or any of the hundred other blessings the Night has bestowed on me."

Her Grandmother stood and stretched, "Last evening you said you were tired of being a target, a victim. This evening it looks to me like you are enjoying it."

Flames came from Casandra's feet and ears, and the Hermit had flames coming out of her hands and head. They both looked at each other and began laughing. "That looks ridiculous." Casandra was no longer mad. "I am sorry, that is another thing, all I have done is apologize to people. Everyone finds my objections and reactions amusing. I am tired of being laughed at, I am tired of being afraid, I am just plain tired." Casandra put her head on the table.

"I understand that. So am I, Casandra. You will sleep well with all the spells you have drunk. Sleep and dream, Casandra. We will talk again in the morning you will make a clear choice by sunrise."

The Hermit opened the dining room doors and went to the living room, Eric, Grace, and Marion was talking around the fire. "Good, you're still up Eric. Would you and Grace help Casandra to her room? Marion come along."

They walked into the dining room, and Eric stared daggers at Casandra. Her head laid in her hands on the table. "I can't believe this, not again."

"Eric, she is not drunk I have put her under a spell. She must make decisions tonight; the Night can wait no longer. Have faith my boy, we need her and you to be filled with optimistic views. Do you understand? One never wins a war if they think they are defeated before it has begun." The Hermit waited.

Eric took a step back, "Those were my Father's words the day he left for war." He went to Casandra and lifted her up. "Show me her room Grace."

Chancellor Ski

Ski had made some real progress on the Attachment Spell, and he wished these guests gone so he could speak with Henry. Poor Henry was having a difficult time not strangling Martin. Ski could hear his thoughts, Henry was sure Martin had put an attachment on Elaine. They both could listen to the conversations of the Hermit, through Addison. Ski wanted to know more about her, but that could wait. There was too much going on this evening Ski needed to direct it better.

Ski was seated next to Ernst, "Ernst tell me more about you. I know so little of Arlequin and its people."

Ernst looked at Martin who smiled as though saying go on speak. Ski and Henry knew Ernst was under an Attachment. Ski looked at Henry; he had his elbow on the table and his head on his chin with an intense look of concentration on his face. Ski knew this was his cue to question while Henry observed.

"I am sorry it must be difficult for you. So many were lost, and many must have been your friends and family along with the land. I can't imagine a whole country decimated. I have heard tales really I had just wondered the truth of them."

Ernst only stared in his glass of ale but said. "It is difficult to remember Chancellor. Since the day the King pulled the Queen and me from the ashes I have preferred to not think of it at all. After I healed, I returned to see my country for myself. The stories are mainly true, perhaps exaggerated. The land was still smoldering, and I found no one. I took a magic carriage we only landed for a few minutes. So, I could see my old home, my powers were drained very quickly. I took a locket of my Mother's as a remembrance. As the carriage lifted, the locket disintegrated right in my hands. It was the most beautiful country I had ever seen, I loved it dearly. The Wizards created such a horrific spell it may be another hundred years before any magical person can walk on the land. I understand Parragon sneak on the land. I heard stories they did not live long. My country has been expunged." Ernst took a drink of his ale, "Although I do wonder, I could not be the only survivor. Surely some have lived beside me. What do you think? You are a knowledgeable man. Surely, I am not the last Arlequin. Wizards must live among us."

Ski gave Ernst a smile and sent a wave of compassion to him. Ernst looked surprised. "Sir, I think you are right. There are others, and I think they are among us, or maybe just so changed from the spell they no longer appear to be Arlequin. I know of at least one Lillian Wizard. I am a scientist I believe their powers have changed we all evolve, and we have since the beginning. Have you thought of marrying, at least creating children to give the world your unique traits?"

Ernst smiled, "I have Sir I have just never gotten around to it."

Martin said, "Ernst, I never knew you want to marry. I will tell the King you are highly valued by us you can have anything you ask for. Why have you not asked?"

Ernst put his arm on Devon's shoulder and said, "This one has kept me busy. I am sure a wife would not appreciate a husband who spends all his time with the Prince."

Devon had been quiet all through dinner and Ski was picking up illness and high emotions. Devon turned and said, "Ernst once I take a bride I will release you. You deserve your own life and a family. I promise I will help you find it." Ernst swallowed back tears, and Henry could see the outline of the attachment on his neck. Ski said mentally to Henry, look at Martin; he wants to kill Ernst. Ski look to the neck of the Prince. He had a high collar on, but Ski detected bruising.

Henry said, "Tell me, Martin, why are all we confirmed bachelors wanting to be tied down and have children we must be mad."

Martin quickly put a smile on his face and raised his glass, "Love creates madness Henry, to madness."

Ski said," I will not drink to that. I have had two wives and nineteen children I want no more, I will live in peace. Thank you very much."

They all laughed Ski mentally said. We need time with Ernst. Martin and the Prince must get the spell.

Henry replied mentally. I want some time with the Prince too.

Ernst mentally said. Henry, you are doing an excellent job of blocking me this evening, but I know you are talking about Devon and me. We need to talk.

Henry grinned at Ernst and mentally answered him. Don't worry. Trust me; we need to remove Martin from our party first.

Henry stood, "Gentlemen I have been working on a new brew. Would anyone here like to test it out?'

Martin raised his glass, "Henry, do you really think I would not be willing to be your lab rat for liquors?"

Henry laughed, "Well I was counting on you. I just thought the others might like a choice."

Ernst said, "Not me I will stick with my ale."

The Prince looked at Martin. Martin said, "Go on Prince, Henry will be careful with you. He would not offend the King or you. Would you Henry?" Martin gave Henry a look of warning.

Henry looked straight at Martin, "I would do nothing to create ill will with the King, at least not intentionally." Then he smiled.

The Carriage Ride

The next morning Addison was up early after the night of dreams he could hardly wait to speak with the Duchess. When he walked into the main room, she was sitting there waiting for him. One Sprite was stoking the fire, and the other poured him coffee. She motioned to him to be seated across from her. "I see you drank your potion last night how do you feel this morning?"

Addison drank some coffee, "As you predicted, I feel wonderful physically." He drank another drink of coffee and added, "Mentally I am unsure, in disbelief would be a good word to describe it. Can you answer a few questions for me in private?"

The Hermit stood. "I have a small office bring you coffee and come with me." She walked to the wall and waved her hand the wall disappeared, a hallway led into a small room filled with books from floor to ceiling with tall windows looking out on the mountains. Two chairs faced each other in front of the window. "Please sit Addison we have complete privacy here what are your questions?"

Addison sat and looked out the window it was a sheer drop down. He could not even see the bottom of the mountain. "We are high up, aren't we? Do you ever worry about falling off?"

The Hermit laughed. "Not since I built this place and moved inside, it took a few years, but I think it was worth it."

Addison knew she was telling the truth. "He really hurt you, didn't he? I'm sorry, that is none of my business. I really wanted to ask if what I dreamed was the truth. I want to know what is going to happen not just to me but to Marion, Casandra, and Henry."

The Hermit waved her hand a pot of coffee appeared on the table, and the door closed to the office. "Addison you have a right to know the whole story; about me and about what you will face. Drink your coffee. First, your dreams about your parents were absolute fact."

Addison let out a deep breath then shook his head in disbelief. "My Mother was Arlequin, and my Father was Henry's Brother Richard? I hate him. Does anyone know about this? I mean, Henry or Ski? Surely someone had to know. Who was she, my Mother?"

"Henry and Ski do not know. No one on this Continent knows except Richard. However, even he doesn't know you are, his son. I think your Mother's family know you exist, but they haven't been able to find you." The Hermit settled back in her chair. "Well, as far as I can understand, Richard knows he had a child. He thought he was dallying with a peasant girl. Little did he know he was with a wizard, much less a Queen and a Gadwell." She watched his face go white.

"Gadwell? Not Antioch's family? Ernst Family?" Addison drew in a deep breath.

"In the coming months, you will find more family than you think. However, I believe you need time to understand your relationships on your own. Your Mother was Ernst's Sister, Antioch's Aunt. When she showed up on his doorstep two years after your birth with demands, he strangled her and dumped her in the river. He looked for you, but never found you. This is your good fortune your Mother was smart. She had premonitions about you fathering a vital child. A girl who would become a hero in our world. She prearranged your adoption, keeping you in the Rakie family. I think she hoped you would grow up looking just like him. Fortunately, you must take after her you are much better looking. The only thing you inherited from that family is their brains and the ability to see something once and remember every detail. Richard can do that too... ironic...you and Henry are the same age, but he is your Uncle. What do you think he will do when he finds out?"

"I am worried about that. I am not sure. I mean to say Henry and I are like Brothers we love one another. I just hope Henry doesn't kill Richard."

Addison sat back and listened to the Hermit tell her life story and paint a gloomy outlook for their futures. This was not the time to hold back any information, she could not know what might keep them alive in the future. Eric came in next, and his session was a close version of Addison's. She had put a silence spell on each man and a little something extra for Eric. Casandra came in last, dressed in a blue tunic and black pants with tall black boots; she looked regal.

She gave her Grandmother a kiss on the cheek. "Grandmother, I have decided." She sat in the chair across from her and placed her hands in her lap. "I will fight to the death if I must. If I fail and leave this to my Daughter, she will know I did everything I could. I am counting on you, you must not fail me. I swear I will come back and haunt you if you fail me."

The Hermit smiled. "Excellent I am so proud of you. You understood all your visions and all the possible outcomes. Do you have questions?"

Casandra smiled, "I understand everything clearly, Grandmother. Do you understand me?" Casandra glared at her.

The Hermit chuckled, "I promise you I will not fail you, ever. Now let's go have breakfast and I will tell your group about the Monks, and you can be on your way."

Everyone joined together in the dining room. The Duchess looked at each one a long moment then she said, "I free all of you of the compulsion to not speak. You are all free to share the information you have learned. However, if anyone feels it is too personal to share, please allow them the right not to speak. You are a special group of people who love one another deeply; respect each other."

Marion sighed, "Thank the Night. I was about to bust holding all this inside." Everyone laughed.

The Hermit said, "One other thing: I have arranged four days with the Monks at their Monastery at Monk's Mountain for the three young ladies, starting today. I have already sent a message to the Emperor, so don't give me that look Eric. George will accompany them, you can pick them up on your way out to start the holiday."

Marion protested, "But we have to pack?"

The Hermit raised her eyebrow and said, "I said I had arranged everything Marion. You are already packed for your holiday and the trip to the Monastery, you really must trust me. Casandra has something she would like to tell this group."

Casandra looked around the table, "I have made my decision. I will fight the King."

Addison and Eric began objecting at one time.

Casandra stood, put her hands on the table and leaned in, "STOP! I said I will fight the King! I plan to kill him. This madness ends in my lifetime, or it will end my life."

"Henry is fuming said he will not hear of this!" Addison hit the table with his fist.

"Tell Henry this is my choice, and I am a free Sorceress. I have a right to my choice. If he doesn't like this Sorceress, he can go find another." She sat back down, and they all stared at her. "You will help me accomplish this, or you will stay out of my way. That is the only choice any of you have or Henry. Is that understood?" Casandra crossed her arms and raised an eyebrow. Everyone knew she was serious.

She looked to the Hermit who was smiling from ear to ear. "Well said, Casandra. You can argue about this in the carriage; we will have our breakfast in peace. Keep a pleasant conversation, or I will compel you back into silence. Marion, you like to talk; it is your turn to say the blessing."

Eric looked at Addison, they were already plotting a way to stop Casandra. Everyone was silent eating quickly. They were all hungry, and the food was terrific. However, all of them wanted to be in the carriage and on their way to the North Castle. Marion went into the kitchen to say her goodbyes to her cousin. While the others all said their goodbyes and climbed into the carriage. They returned seated as they had on the trip up to the mountain. Eric immediately sat, crossed his arms and stared at Casandra.

As soon as they were up in the air and away from the Mountain, Casandra said, "Go on, get it over with. You and Addison can start to command me, compel me, and whatever else you would do." She crossed her arms and raised her eyebrow.

Eric took a breath in and pressed his lips together. “Miss Casandra, you are unreasonable, just like when you were a child. We are here with you because we want you to live. Tell me how do you propose to kill the King of Hex? Are you going to walk up to him and spell him? Throw fire at him? Stab him?”

Casandra replied, “I am the only one in this carriage that could get that close to him. All of your options are a valid manner of death I will consider those. However, my vision gave three possible deaths of the King. I suggest we discuss all three.” She shared her visions, and ways they could defeat the King. Addison was informing Henry of each one.

Addison bent forward so he could see her, “Henry and I do not like any of those. He wants to think about it before we rush into action. He would like to know what Eric thought.”

Eric said, “I am totally against turning her over to the Prince on her wedding day. I am sure they would kill Henry and take Casandra to some other location; we may never find her again. Assignations are always a bad gamble, not many are successful. Henry, unfortunately, I am not in favor of any of these plans. All of us had visions. I think we should share those before we take one plan to the Emperor.”

Everyone shared the information the Hermit had given them at least what was not part of a compulsion spell. Casandra looked to Grace, “Grace has the clearest and most helpful information.”

Grace told them of a battle on Azul the day after the wedding. Henry and Casandra land and the Marias Army converge on the island attacking the Hex, destroying everything. Grace sighed, “Unfortunately, I couldn’t see the outcome.” She looked at Eric, “I die, and I have no idea what happens to anyone else. Any other alternatives?”

Casandra looked out the carriage window. “There is a fourth one, but we have no need to discuss it.”

Addison asked why. Casandra answered, “You really don’t want to know, and I am not telling you.”

Addison sat back and said, “It must be awful.”

Casandra leaned forward and looked at him, “Why don’t you tell us about your parents?”

Addison leaned forward and said, “Not before I have a chance to discuss it with Henry.” He sat back, and Marion crossed her arms giving him a pleading look. "No, not to you either, Marion. I want to see Henry in person before I even think about it. To answer your question Henry, yes, it is that bad." He looked at Eric, "Why don't you tell us about your experience, Eric."

Eric looked at Grace, "I am not sure I even believe the story she told me. I don't know that I believe anything she said. I want to get back to convincing Casandra to give up this crazy idea she can kill the King." He looked at Casandra who was about to cry, and her hands were shaking he wondered why.

Casandra glared at him, how could he think the Hermit lied to them. "You think she lied? Maybe it is because little pieces of truth slide into her words; like her words last night of your Father's." Casandra glowered at him. "No one ever wins a war if they think they are defeated before it has begun." Casandra waited patiently.

Eric said snidely, "You heard that? I thought you were drunk."

"Eric, how long have we known each other?"

Eric answered, "I don't remember you were my first assignment."

Casandra took in a deep breath ready to let him have it.

He Quickly said. "I remember not being happy about following a little girl around the Castle and woods." He looked out the window not wanting to go on, "I was just out of the Academy and won a position in the elite unit of the Emperor's guard. Then they made me your babysitter." He laughed but kept looking out the window as if he was considering the past. "Your Father was not in the best way, after losing his parents and the Empress. You seemed to not notice any of it, running from one piece of trouble to the next. If I could not tell him where you were or what you were doing, he screamed at me. You would order me around and hide from me every chance you got. I finally started hiding from you, but I was always there in secret, always watching." He smiled, "I couldn't wait for you to go off to school…when you did I missed you."

Casandra looked at her hands in her lap they were shaking, and she couldn't seem to control them, so she put them under her legs. "Eric, why are your eyes that color? I have never seen eyes like yours. Most Elves have gold, gray or blue eyes; yours are white with gold rims."

Eric tilted his head, a habit he had when he was gauging people. "My parents were assigned to the Embassy in Ezzguar in Arlequin.

They were both in the same unit it was a peace assignment so they could take their children if they were over twelve years of age. I was not born yet; my Mother was pregnant with me, and my Sister Sophia was sixteen. Sophia fell in love with a young Arlequin; he was in the hierarchy, and part of the forces stationed there. There was an attack on an outpost. Someone had given the Hex and Parragon vital army positions and key information. Everyone accused Sophia, and her affair with the Major was exposed. My parents almost lost their commission and were forced to leave the assignment. Before they could leave the country, the war started. They were lucky to get out with their lives. My parents told me I was born on the ship in Bezier Ocean." He was observing Casandra. "Evidentially this whole story was a lie, this morning I learned Sophia was not their natural daughter but adopted."

Eric looked directly at Casandra's. "Today I found out I am Sophia's child. To the point, about my eyes, I had always wondered the same thing. Years ago I learned I was half Wizard and half Elf. I assume my parents changed my eyes permanently from black wizard eyes to the opposite." He turned his eyes to Grace. "That crazy story she told, I can't believe. If I did, I would have to acknowledge my Parents never let me know Sophia was my Mother."

Grace asked, "Your Sister's name was never cleared is that why she killed herself?"

Eric said, "I don't know. The Hermit said it was because they wouldn't let her be my Mother, but I was young only three years old when she died. I don't think anyone ever knew why she killed herself. I surely will never know now. All of them are dead, and I don't even remember Sophia." Everyone was silent, and Eric looked at Grace. "And you? What did she tell you besides the battle?"

Grace turned her head, "It was very private I am not willing to share any of it. Marion, you?"

Marion crossed her arms again and said, "No one else is sharing, why should I?" She looked to Addison.

Addison said, "Pouting will not make me speak. So, Casandra, we have more than an hour left on this ride. Entertain us with the fourth vision?"

Casandra turned her head and looked out the window. No one spoke for a long while. Eric kept looking at her, and she could hardly keep her hands under her legs any longer. She removed them and concentrated on making them still and telling them to relax, soon they stilled.

Eric shifted and asked Casandra if she remembered the day she ran off to the lake. She just nodded her head and said, "The day the bear came out of the woods?"

He said, "Yes, that was an exciting day. Do you remember what I told you?"

Casandra said no. Addison said to tell them the story. Marion and Grace agreed, so Casandra nodded but kept looking out the window as Eric shared the story.

"It was a pleasant early spring day. Casandra was maybe six she was eluding me like every day and headed down to the lake. As you know, the grasses are short in the meadow, and I had a time not letting her know I was there. She was playing with cattails at the water's edge when I saw a shadow in the woods to the side of her. I walked out slowly from the grass and stood behind one of the few trees, to get a better look. It was a black bear fully grown and looking for dinner. She turned and saw me first then she set her little hands on her hips. I gave her the sign to be silent, and to my surprise she obeyed." Casandra turned and smiled at Eric, "The bear had noticed her when she turned to look at me and began a slow prowl forward. Then she saw him. I told her to stand perfectly still and to step slowly back to me."

Casandra said, "I told you I couldn't move my feet. You told me to just move one foot at a time."

Eric sat back with a big grin on his face. "See you do remember, and you did just that. I grabbed your hand and pulled you toward me. I put you on my back and climbed that tree as fast as I could. Good thing it was big and tall. We sat up in that tree for hours, while the bear scraped every piece of bark from that tree. It was practically empty of bark by the time the Kingsmen got around to searching for us." He was laughing. "It's a funny story to tell now, but at the time I was scared, and so were you. Your little hands were shaking so badly you almost shook us out of the tree. Just like now, Casandra. I think Addison is right, you need to tell us about the fourth vision. Just talking about it can make looking back at it funny, just like the story of the bear." His eyes were piercing hers, and her hands were shaking again.

She could no longer look at Eric only at her hands shaking. How could she kill the King if she could not even keep her hands still thinking about it? She would start with what she knew was right. "My Grandmother told me the reason we have not been able to defeat this Hexian spell is the fault of the Sorcerers."

Addison said, "Henry and I have seen this spell, and it is of no fault of the Sorcerer. It is the creator of the spell."

Casandra leaned forward and gave Addison a look with a raised eyebrow. "Would you like to know what I know Addison?" he smiled and shook his head yes. "Well then be quiet and tell Henry to listen."

She turned back to Eric, "Throughout the years the Duchess's Granddaughters have had many opportunities to end this madness, but none have believed the Hermit or her predictions. She includes my Mother and Elisabeth in those who did not believe her until it was too late. My Father's Mother, who was not even of her blood, believed her and tried to get the men around her to listen. You know that outcome."

Casandra realized she had been almost shouting, she looked at her hands still shaking and lowered her voice, "The Night has faith in me, but told me it had to be my decision to fight or run. Since the carriage falling at Elk's pass, I have been vacillating from wanted to fight back and wanting to run. The Night needed an answer to help us. The outcome cannot be predicted without out it. If I choose to run, all Witches will fall to this spell, and the battle would fall to my Daughter to continue." She watched Grace who wore a sorrowful face, "Even with my choice made many of us will die. The fourth vision shows almost all of us dead." She looked at Eric, and his eye was whiter than ever. "Eric our talk last night helped me immensely. You said you would happily protect me on the Mountain until I was an old woman. We stayed hours up in that tree for hours, so I have faith that you are a man of your word. However, you also said I need to live my life short or long. I refuse to waste any more of my life not living every moment in as much happiness as I can drink in." She smiled at Eric, "And for the last time… I was not drunk last night Eric, she put me in a spell."

Eric smiled at her and took her hands which were still shaking. "I know you were not drunk I just can't help but tease you. It is perfectly fine if your hands shake in anticipation of killing the King. He will only think you are afraid of him; up until he feels the poison close his throat. I take it you think it would be wise that I tell Grace I love her; before one or both of us die?"

Casandra smiled and looked at Grace she was as red as Henry's colors, "Yes, but it would be helpful if you looked at her… when you said it."

Eric turned giving Grace his beautiful, perfect smile and said, "I love you Grace Stafford do you feel the same." She didn't answer but threw her arms around him and kissed him.

Marion clapped, "I guess we know what Grace's very personal private vision was." Addison put an arm around her, "I am not telling my vision until you share yours."

Casandra looked out the window, "Look we are almost home what will we tell the Emperor?"

Addison said, "I don't know Casandra. You still haven't shared the fourth vision."

Casandra smiled and said, "Tell Henry that is for another time. I will not kill the King today."

Love at a Distance

Even though it was late by the time everyone got to bed, Henry couldn't sleep. He tossed all night, he felt Addison shut down their communication after he drank the Hermits brew. Before daylight, Henry was up and dressed; he went to the winery and packed the King's order himself. Henry wanted Martin out of his house, and Henry wanted to be free to know what was going on at the North Mountain. He didn't trust the Hermit and didn't want to visit her ever.

Ernst was very helpful the night before he told them every detail they wanted to know. The King had no intention of teaching Henry the entire Attachment Spell. The King intended to put Henry under an Attachment when he delivered Casandra the day after his wedding. Henry thought the King would outright kill him that day, maybe death would be preferred to an Attachment to the King.

However, the information that worried Henry most was the Prince's addiction. This little trip was an effort to curb his compulsion and check up on Henry at the same time. The evening before, the Prince was out of control and killed a poor Witch in the village of Karrington. Martin had used an Attachment Spell to control the Prince on the rest of the trip to the Villa. At Ernst's insistence, Martin removed it before they arrived, but Ski worried that Martin could tell Devon was Ernst's son. The Diamante understood the more blood drawn, the more memories were known and information. Then the little magic trick Addison had performed would reveal they were all traitors. If the Prince could not be controlled except by using an Attachment they would be found out fast. They needed to find a way to help the Prince cling to control. Ski was going to concoct something before they left. Henry put a spell on all of them to sleep late. Henry finished the Kings order and walked back to the house.

Ski met him on the trail. "Henry I am glad I caught you. Martin is up and drinking coffee at the guest house. I had Bob tell him to meet us on the terrace for a late breakfast. We should hurry there. Anything from Addison?" Henry shook his head no, "Hmm…I have not been able to connect with him either, but he is in a safe place. He just doesn't want us to know about his parents, whoever they might be."

Henry smiled, "You're right. I am just so used to him in my head that I feel a little lost without him. I could not lose him or you my friend. How is the potion for Devon going, is that it?"

Ski put an arm around him, in his other hand was several bottles of liquid, "It is, and my friend it is complete. I am excited about it. I made it exclusive to Devon it will take years for the King's scientist to unravel. I have even thought of a fabulous story to accompany it. Just let me explain I have it all in hand, Henry."

"Well let's get them on the road. I want to speak with Addison as soon as he opens up." Henry sped his pace to reach the terrace where Martin was already there. "Good morning, sleepy head. Where is Ernst and the Prince?"

Martin looked the worse for wear, "Ernst is having a time getting the boy up and out this morning. I think he and I had a little too much to drink last Night. I had wanted to get an early start, we have business in Talla on our way home. We need to get there today."

Henry loved this part of the game, "Not taking a long way home, then. Martin before Ernst and Devon get here we need to talk. Please sit." They sat around the table.

Bob came out with coffee, and Ski said, "Bob. Would you please take this potion to Devon. It will help him with the hangover he is bound to have," He placed another flask in front of Martin, "This one is for you it will help immensely."

Henry sipped his coffee, "Martin last night after you passed out, Devon was distraught. He told us what happened in the village the night before. I do not know if you have business in the village of Karrington, but it is best you do not return to the young Witch's village. I got up early to get your order ready; you will be ready to leave after breakfast. I took the liberty of having your men pack while we eat." Henry held up his hand as a signal to let him continue, "As I saw at the Science Building in Bezier, this spell is addicting, and Devon is having trouble handling it. It is something I recognized because we have had to deal with an addiction to our liquors for years. I would like the King to know, I will not be rushed into attaching many to learn this spell, we will go slowly. I am methodical in my studies; this will be no different. I will only do what I am comfortable with and can handle. If the King is not happy with this new turn of events, we must renegotiate. Please take him that message. He and I will speak after your party. Now Ski has developed something for you, and I would have him explain since it is his development."

Martin drank his potion and Ski began explaining, "Martin, you know most brewers add magic to their brews, as we do. Addiction to liquors has long been known. However, there is an addiction to power as well. Many of our friends have come to us complaining about our use of powers when someone in their family becomes dependent. We have worked for years at formulating a blend to counteract the effects of alcohol. Recently we have developed a brew to help with power addiction. Unfortunately, every magical person is at different levels and has unique requirements. The antidote needs are made for each individual. I want you to understand this potion may not even help Devon, or he may have to be on a dose for life."

Martin looked devastated, "Well it would still be better than other methods. I will just say they are crude. I would not like to have to use them on Devon the boy is suffering enough. How is it administered?"

Ski silently said to Henry, I told you I had this one. "It is just a potion, a few drops in a strong drink once a day will keep the nerves down. You should understand that I make no promise this will work. Then again, we have had those who only drank it a week or two and never experienced the problem again. It really depends on the individual. One thing you should know is while he is taking this he is very susceptible to emotions, he may be angry or despondent. You need to watch him. I have made several bottles for you to take along, and I gave him a drop in the hangover potion. I wanted to see if it worked. We will see if he is nervous, the young man was about to jump out of his skin yesterday. It can be modified if you feel the potency is not right."

Henry stepped in, "I included the hard liquor Devon liked so much it would be a perfect way to administer the potion at the end of the day. I have also decided on a name, and had it labeled, Devon's Brew clever wouldn't you say?"

Just then Ernst and Devon walked onto the terrace. "What is so clever Count? Oh, Chancellor Ski thank you for the potion I feel better than I have in weeks. I don't know what was in it, but I would like to have you make me some. I always drink too much when he is around." Devon pointed to Martin and poured himself coffee then smiled, he did look healthier and calm.

Martin grinned. "We shall have Ski make some for you he has been generous enough to give you a few bottles to tide us over. You look well Devon. You should know Henry is calling his new liquor you enjoyed so much after you Devon's Brew." Then Martin laughed.

Devon laughed. "Well that is an apt name; this morning I felt like I had drunk poison. It tasted wonderful, but I have learned a little goes a long way."

Henry could hear the Hermit release the vow of silence. Addison and all the company were well. He relaxed and laughed at the Prince's remark. "Good, you have learned. Balance in all things young man, remember that." They began their breakfast.

Monks Mountain

Their carriage landed on the edge of a small cliff, not more than twenty feet from a sheer drop off the mountain. They were met by Monks in robes, each wore a colored denoting their station, from red at the low end, to white. Violet, gold, and silver were reserved for the fully enlightened like his Eminence. They were shown into a large entry hall three stories high with stairs carved out of the mountain circling up on either side. The floor was the color of red jasper, and the walls were streaks of multi-colored stones. A woman with black hair and emerald green eyes greeted them she wore a deep blue robe.

"Good morning ladies, Countess, Professor McMillan, it is wonderful to welcome you back. My name is Moori I will be your mentor and accompany you in your lessons. The Duchess has asked for a private room for the girls. She wanted the Countess to feel a sense of privacy while here. Professor I would like to introduce you to Achille who requested to be your companion."

Achille bowed and said. "It is an honor to serve you."

The Professor bowed to Achille, "It is my great pleasure to consent Achille. Please, lead the way. Ladies, I will see you later."

Moori said, "We will need time to acclimate the women; they will see you at Thorns serve. Ladies follow me. Casandra has been to the Temple many times. Marion and Grace, I will explain as we go along."

The three followed her into a changing room for women. It had benches and hooks with red robes on the wall, beneath the robes were white sandals. Moori stopped and said, "There are stalls with curtains if you are uncomfortable changing in front of one another. No one is allowed to enter the inner sanctum, or Temple, with the negative partials from the outside world. Your clothes will be washed and stored in your lockers while you are with us. Red robes and sandals are worn at the beginner level. There are three baths in the private bathhouse. The first is clear running water for cleansing with soap, it is the pool of red unakite, the one in the middle. The pool of sodalite blue water is a soaking pool it restores the soul and removes any negative thoughts or feelings. I recommend all of you using the blue pool. The pool of quartz crystal with green water is the healing pool. Casandra, you must spend ten minutes at the minimum in it. Marion and Grace, you may not want to use it at all, or spend very little time in it. If there are no questions, I will leave you to change and go into the bathing area. When you are done place your sandals and robes in the basket at the door. There are fresh ones on the wall for you to use after bathing." Moori waited to see if the girls had questions.

Casandra thanked Moori then told her she would explain to her friends. "Girls, I do not need a stall; besides, I can't wait until I get into the baths. I think it is the best thing about this place."

Marion started undressing and then sarcastically said, "They take being clean very seriously. Moori is very formal. This is not going to be a fun four-day adventure."

Grace was undressed faster than any of them and was putting on her robe, "Why did she say Marion and I might not want to go into the healing pool? I feel like I could use a little healing."

Casandra put on her robe and hung up her riding clothes on the hook, "The healing pool is great, and you can take a dip, it can heal almost any hurt. It restores fertility, and I will need that to produce my little girl. I understand that when you entered the army, they temporally sterilized you, Grace. The waters may restore that. Morri doesn't want you to have an unwanted child or you Marion."

Marion said confidently. "Oh, I can't have children until I am released. I have told you about that before; it's very complicated, and that won't happen until my wedding day, I want to try it."

Grace sat down and waited for the others, "The procedure we have done lasts until the medicals remove it. Isn't it funny how we all reproduce differently? Marion, I have heard Sprites take over a year to produce a child. Is that true?"

Marion laughed. "Fifteen months, my Mother has reminded me of that fact often. I have never really understood all of it, we are so small, yet we take the longest to make. Grace, do you have to be implanted like Casandra or do you carry your own eggs like me?"

"I am like you Marion; eggs just don't grow while the procedure is in place. Why do Sprites have such large families, I would think the women would be sick of being pregnant for so long?" Grace walked to the door and peeked inside.

"To hear my Mother tell it, once a Sprite gets pregnant, they just can't stop the process. I know she complains enough about all of us, I have twenty-three Brothers and Sister."

Grace whistle, "Wow, I knew there were a lot of Donnan's at graduation, but I thought they were your Aunt's and Uncle's."

They all filed into the bath area bathed and washed each other's hair, laughing and talking. Then they went into the blue pool, and there they all sat on the shelf provided on the side. They inclined their heads back and relax in silence. Casandra got out and entered the green pool, like the last time she had children, she would come to the baths three times a day to prepare for insemination. Marion and Grace both went into the pool to join her. They dunked their heads under the water and floated on their backs.

Finally, Casandra said, "You both need to leave me and go back into the relaxation pool or go get dressed. I need to be in here for a while. I will be bathing three times a day. I would not stay here this long. Do you both want to have children with me?"

Grace said, "I don't but this feels so wonderful I haven't felt this great since I was a child. Alright, I will get out. Come on Marion the way you carry on with Addison you will be pregnant before Casandra."

Marion splashed her with water, "Really, Grace, you know nothing about Sprites."

Grace climbed out. "No, but how much do you know about the Diamante men and women? That might change your abilities some. I bet you haven't even asked."

Marion jumped out and got a towel, "Casandra Grace is right. Tell me about the Diamante."

Casandra swallowed, "I hadn't even thought if breeding with the Diamante was different. Henry and I never discussed it. We need to find out about this. I do not want to ask Henry. I can just see him throwing back his head and laughing at me. Although he does look wickedly handsome when he laughs. Still, it would be embarrassing."

Grace said, "Well there are a lot of people here on retreat maybe we can find a Diamante who would be willing to tell us, or do you have that red bounded book your Grandmother gave you? Maybe we can find something in it?"

Casandra said, "I did pack it. I wonder if we can bring it in here? I will ask Moori."

They all dressed in their robes and entered the next room. Moori was there waiting for them, "I will show you to your rooms Ladies follow me." She led them up a staircase through tunnels that twisted and turned; they walked in circles so many times that Marion was dizzy. "Here we are." She opened an old wooden door, and they entered a small sitting room with a round hearth in the middle. The smoke trailed up through an opening in the ceiling, with some sunlight coming through, "There are four small bedrooms exactly alike choose one, ladies. There is a toilet room over here, you will share." She opened the door to show them. "We will eat in a communal dining room. You are welcome to bathe downstairs or up here, but please do not leave the room and wander around on your own. You can see how easy it is to get lost."

Casandra was accustomed to the dull light wood furnishing and nothing fancy decorating the walls which were pink. Pure wool rugs lay on the floors, the beds were covered with clean soft and comfortable pillows and blankets. All the colors blended from a creamy white to deep pink tourmaline. The rooms were well lit for not having a window, and with all the plainness it was still warm and homey. On the bedside table was a lantern with a vase of colorful fresh flowers and the master's Volume One. Each time Casandra stayed at the Monastery she would read the book, and every time she left the mountain, she would forget every word.

Marion and Grace came into her room, "All the rooms are just alike, and they all have this book." Marion held up her book. "You have one too, Casandra."

Casandra smiled and said, "I know it is a wonderful book. I have read it each time I have stayed here."

Moori asked, "Have you ever remembered it, Casandra?"

Casandra replied. "No, my Mother told me the words don't come away from the mountain until the person is ready to live them. I guess I was never ready."

Moori said, "I think sometimes that is the reason I have never chosen to leave since attending school; I must, one day soon. My mentor says I don't leave because I would have to wear clothes that bind again. I don't know, maybe she is right. I do like the comfort of robes. Let's get an early lunch then we can go to the lesson room and study before the service of Thorns. Follow me."

Moori took them to the dining room, "We do not serve any animal here. However, you can request it, but it must be eaten outside of the inner sanctum."

Grace chuckled, "Well, Casandra. You will be right at home. I have rarely seen you eat any animals. Do eggs, cheese, and milk count?"

Casandra said, "Yes I do eat some meats, but it won't hurt us too fast. Think about how healthy we will be."

They all ate and talked. Grace asked about Diamante women, and Moori asked why, so the girls confided in her. She said she would try to find out. Their day passed quickly, the lessons were spiritual in nature which Grace found fascinating.

Then Moori took them to a meditation room. "I lead a meditation class every afternoon. I will have you join us it is an hour long, which can be difficult for beginners. If you can't stay in meditation that long feel free to just sit and relax quietly." There were white pillows on the floor they each sat on one, then fifteen more students came into the room, and Moori began. Marion and Grace thought they would not be able to meditate that long, but every one of them did.

Afterward, Marion said. "I don't understand I have such a hard time meditating at the Castle, but here it was easy. I feel so calm, at peace."

Moori smiled, "Many find it easier to meditate in groups the energies of the experienced student transport the group together into the universe."

Grace said, "So that is where I went. I could feel myself leave the room. Strange, I can't tell you where I was."

Casandra was very experienced at meditation; however, she had only used it to study and perform at the Academy. "This was different for me too. What's next?"

Moori said, "Now that we are connected, and in balance, we fight, of course. You will have private lessons with Casteglion he is one of the best here on the Mountain now."

They were taken to a room with polished wooden floors and padded walls with one large window. The door opened, and a man walked in. He had only loose pants on; he was naked from the waist up and was nothing but muscle and dark bronze skin. All of them had seen naked men, but nothing like the man that stood before them. This was a god; his body was all muscle and power, his head was covered with sable ringlets, his face was rugged and chiseled with a broad smile and white teeth with aqua eyes that were mesmerizing.

He walked to the girls and bowed, "It is my honor to instruct you, ladies."

Casandra bowed and said, "It is my pleasure to be your student." Grace and Marion mimicked her.

"I understand you have been in training with Professor McMillan. We will begin with a challenge so I can evaluate your level. I will start with you, Casandra. We must be family you have my eyes, but your skin is lighter." He pointed to the floor, told her where to stand and they began to spar. Fifteen minutes later Casandra was panting and sweating. Casteglion almost looked refreshed. "You are terrific considering you have trained only a few weeks."

He turned from her to Marion she was on the floor in less than five moves. Casteglion reached down and swung her back on her feet with one hand. "Marion, you will have lessons with me three times a day while you are here. I will make time for you."

Then Grace fought with him. She had him sweating at the end, but he did take her to the floor, "Excellent, Grace, you gave me a good workout. When you learn to combine the movement of the universe and agility, you will be a talented adversary. Now we will practice."

They left the room, exhausted. Moori was waiting in the hall for them. "How was your lesson?"

Marion rubbed her back. "I don't think I can do another lesson with him. I need to sit in the healing bath for hours, he tried to kill me."

They all laughed, "I thought you might want to clean up before Thorn's service. The Duchess has a surprise in your room. There is a masseuse to rub away the soreness."

Marion squealed, "Me first."

After they bathed and had a short massage, Moori took them through the maze to the Temple. They stopped before the main entrance of the sanctuary and entered a side entrance that separated them from other people. Each person took a candle from a box and filed in.

"Before we enter I would like to explain the service." Moore reached into the basket and took out four candles. "Each day there is a service called Thorns before dinner. The lesson is taken from the Master Volume One, a lesson for each day of the year. Today is the lesson on the Rose. I will lead you to the visitor section where the Professor sitting, we will listen in silence and darkness. At the end of the lesson, the teacher will light the candle of the first person in the Temple. If that person understood the lesson and is willing to live it, his candle will light with flame. He passes the flame to the next person. Do not feel disappointed if your candle does not light, it takes time to comprehend. Come."

There was barely enough light to follow Moori across the room which was circular with dark polished stone on the floor and walls. A large altar in the center was brightly lit from beneath the floor which was clear crystal. The seats were nothing more than white cushions set on a shelf cut out of the mountain. They were taken to the right side of the room next to the Professor, they nodded and sat quietly. A Monk in a shimmering white and silver robes walked to the center of the altar. Everyone in the room took in a breath. Casandra looked to the Professor, and he smiled and pointed to the man as if to say… Listen.

The Monk bowed to his audience and said, "I am honored to speak to you precious souls."

The audience replied, "It is our pleasure to listen your Eminence."

He began, "There are no roses without thorns. There is no task without problems. There is no goal without obstacles. This is the way of the universe. This is the way of our life. The rose thorn will prick our fingers when we take the rose from the plant. However, for the rose, the thorn prevents insects from climbing its stem and eating its precious flower. The thorn will keep us from picking the rose. When we pluck a rose, we stop the natural unfoldment of its life cycle. When we cut the rose from the plant, we remove the seed that will bless us with more roses. We thank the Night she has given us a multitude of roses to fill our life with many blessings.

Some see the thorn as an obstacle that they call evil or injustice, or perhaps abhorrence. The Night does not recognize the barrier as bad, it sees only a thorn.

A man excavates a well for the village. This is a good thing; the villagers all help him dig. They are all excited to have fresh water from the well. However, it is not long before they run into a large boulder. Some quit working, saying it is too complicated, impossible to lift the rock out. The man continues to dig, and he thinks, this is only a thorn. He knows anything of great worth and beauty requires work and diligence. He explains this to his friends and villagers, "It is not the size of the boulder, but the mental picture we have of raising the boulder. If we work together, we can move the boulder."

He was looking straight at Casandra as he continued. "My friends it is never the difficulties themselves that are the source of our alarm, but the destructive way we interpret them. Our minds, when connected to the universe can remove every boulder and all thorns."

He stepped from the altar and lit the first candle, before long almost every candle was flaming. That included the Professor's, Casandra's, and her friends. The rest of the service comprised the most beautiful choir and musicians that played music that soothed her soul.

They had dinner together. The dining hall was windowless with oblong tables covered in white tablecloths, flowers, and candles. The room held at least twenty crystal chandeliers and beautiful white china and crystal glasses were at each place setting. Monks came to each person with warm damp towels to clean your hands, and the food was scrumptious.

At the end of dinner, Moori said, "It was wonderful to have his Eminence speak. You must be some special visitors. He was looking directly at you Casandra."

Casandra had felt that too. She usually would discount that comment, but here in the Temple, she could say nothing.

Moori just smiled, "I see. I was not the only one who noticed you must be facing enormous thorns. Which explains the intensive training and my mentoring you. Marion, you have a 6:00 A.M. appointment with Master Casteglion we need to get you to bed."

Marion groaned, and Moori smiled than turned to Casandra, "Casandra you need to go into the healing bath before bed, can you find it by yourself?"

"Yes I can, but I don't think I can find my room." Casandra laughed, "How early do we need to rise?"

Moori said, "I will get you from the baths in an hour, and I will see that you all make your lessons over the next four days. Goodnight Professor, I hope to spend some time with you before you leave."

Professor said, "Yes me too. Ladies this young woman was my student at the Academy. One of my brightest and best. I am very proud of the work she is doing here. Tomorrow after dinner would work for me." Moori nodded to the Professor and left. The Professor turned to Casandra, "Moori has lived her whole life for the opportunity to mentor you, Casandra. She will help you with the boulder. Let me walk you to the private baths, and we can talk."

The next two days were a repetition of the first, but they went by quickly. Grace asked Moori a million questions about the faith, and it opened lengthy discussions with Casandra genuinely understanding the old ways. Everyone found their balance in the practice of ancient fighting. Marion had thrown down Casteglion in lessons, and she was very proud of herself. Grace and Casandra tried to tell her bragging would only bring a more laborious practice the next lesson.

Marion came dragging into their room after her last lesson of the day. "I will never fight again. I cannot feel my hands and my legs burn. I swear the man hates me. I would so love to hate him, but he is so good looking. You were right; Casteglion said I was too proud and until I learned not to bring emotion into a fight I would lose. If he weren't a Monk, I would flirt with him shamelessly."

Her hair was wet, and Casandra said. "Have you been going to the healing baths after your last lesson, Marion?" Casandra shook her head, "You know what Moori said."

"Yes, but I only take a short dip, don't give me that look. Casandra my body is in pain. I couldn't function without it. I will be careful trust me." Marion went to her room to pull her hair up.

Moori stepped into the room. "I have a surprise for you ladies. After service, you are taking dinner with his Eminence in his private dining room. That is a privilege. Are you ready to go to Thorns?"

After Thorn's service, Moori took them to a double doorway with two Monks in deep purple robes, the highest level of Monkhood before High Eminence. Moori bowed and said, "Ladies have a wonderful dinner. I will return when you are finished." She nodded to the Monks then turned to leave.

The oldest Monk smiled and said, "Moori where are you going? You are expected for dinner as well, please enter." The Monks held the doors open for them to pass. Moori was shocked but walked with them.

The room's floors were wood, the walls were alabaster, and candles hung from the ceiling and in stands around the room. The Professor was already seated, along with his Eminence, Achille, and Casteglion. They all stood and bowed to the young ladies.

His Eminence said, "Please, have a seat, ladies. Achille, would you offer a blessing?"

Dinner was beautiful, but Casandra felt the girls were in an interrogation.

Achille questioned Grace about what she had learned about the faith of the Night. Casteglion questioned Marion at length about the ancient arts of fighting, and poor Moori was asked about everything from all three. Casandra looked to the Professor; he was unusually quiet, and he ignored her glances. She wanted to stand up and tell them to stop badgering her friends but felt it was not appropriate. They hadn't asked her one question. Finally, she could no longer take it.

She interrupted Achille and said, "Excuse me but I must ask you why are you interrogating my friends?"

His Eminence just stared at her, was he trying to intimidate her. Well, she was going to stand her ground. She crossed her arms and sat back in her chair and of course, raised her eyebrow.

His Eminence set his napkin on the table, a sign dinner was finished. "Countess tell me are all three of these women your friends?"

She didn't hesitate. "Yes, and the Professor."

He said, "And Achille and Casteglion?"

She felt like he was leading her into a questionable area as the Professor had many times. "They are my acquaintances, and teachers that I respect."

He sat back in his chair, "And myself, what am I to you?"

Casandra knew it. There it was… if… she said she hardly knew him he would tell her they are all one. If she said he was her friend and teacher, he would call her a liar because she hardly knew him. She was pausing too long she must speak. What was it her Mother would tell her, "Everyone has a place in the tapestry of life. Some people are woven together throughout the pattern. Others only connect to our pattern for a small distance. All are essential to the perfect pattern of life. You, Sir, are here for a short distance but you are just as important to the pattern of my life as Marion, Grace, and the Professor. You have given me the awareness to overcome my obstacles." She uncrossed her arms. "What is it I am to contribute to your tapestry?"

He smiled at her, "Casandra you are the reason I will live. You have not realized it, but you give everyone on this mountain the opportunity for life; a long and abundant life. We thank you, and we will be in support of you and your children; forever indebted, forever grateful. I was wondering how long it would take until you stood up and fought for your friends. You waited until you were sure we were unfair, and you held your temper. You also thought long before answering and carefully using your words. You will do well standing before the King."

He clapped his hands twice, "Moori, you have moved up a level you are now green. You will leave the Mountain tomorrow morning with Casandra and travel with her until her wedding. You will return here, enlightened. We will speak again then." Monks came and handed her the green robes.

He turned to Grace, "Achille has told me you expressed an interest in studying here. I would welcome you. First, you have a choice to make about your service to the Emperor and Eric." Grace gasped. "Not to worry Grace, the Night will accept you with whichever choice you make."

He then spoke to Marion. "Casteglion told me you had moving meditations and had a fascinating one about the four of you. Would you share that."

Marion told his Eminence of the bear, wolf, fox, and leopard.

He then said, "The universe provides." He turned to Casteglion nodded and Casteglion left the room.

The rest of the dinner was pleasant and relaxed. The Eminence said goodnight then everyone went off to bed. Moori took the girls to their room. Then she took Casandra to the healing bath, on the way there she stopped at the door and knocked. "The Healers have your egg, your Brother delivered it this morning. I will wait here and take you to the baths after." Moori gave her a hug.

The next morning, they were told to go to the Temple before breakfast. His Eminence was standing there with a group of Monks. "I came to say goodbye and bless you. He placed his hands on each of them and said a blessing to the Night.

Casandra thanked him, "I will give you a long life your Eminence, pray that the Night gives me the knowledge of how."

He smiled. "The Night has already put your plan in motion, now you have a visitor." He stepped back and behind him and the group of Monks stood Henry.

Tears immediately filled her eyes she could not even see him clearly. He came to her, and she fell into his arms. His Eminence watched as they left the Temple.

A Wizard appeared next to him, "Well, Antioch what do you think of our savior?"

"She is going to have a difficult time, your Eminence. However, I will do my best to support her. It is as the Night wishes." The wizard disappeared.

The King's Qualms

He stood at his office window watching the squirrels playing in the garden. Martin was giving his report on Henry and Devon. He was worried; if Devon couldn't be trusted his plans for Casandra might fail. He had planned for years, now lack of control could ruin everything. "Martin, I wanted to send him off tomorrow after your party. If he is that unstable that he needs to be drugged, we could have a serious problem. I should have listened to Elisabeth she has told me Professor Moondale is nuts for years. She says he is just experimenting on her, the girls, and Devon. All those years he had me believing Devin was Ernst's son. As soon as that girl has my Grandchildren get rid of him."

Martin sighed, "I have to agree with you King, and I think the man is becoming manic. He drinks too much wine and is addicted to his Attachments. One of my soldiers refused to take his class because he heard everyone in it gets an Attachment. Of course, his Attachments are loyal to him and will not confess. I haven't come to you because I have no solid proof. Moondale could benefit from some of Ski's tonic."

The King walked back to his desk and sat. "I can't trust Devon to be alone. I wanted him to have more experience I pushed him too hard."

Martin could see his friend was hurting, "Richard, we have been friends forever. This is not your fault we trusted that idiot with him.

He is the one pushing Devon to do five and six a day, even when we were young we could not even attempt that. If we had two a day, we were running around fighting everyone we knew. Besides the tonic seems to be working beautifully. Unfortunately, we are once again indebted to the Count. I can't wait to attach to him, I can't wait to find out what goes on in his mind. Richard, I simply do not trust the Count. Your Son needs time, he needs a season like Casandra." he chuckled.

The King looked him, "The Professor had him attach six in a day, then he is an idiot!" the King hit the desk with his hand. "A holiday, that is a wonderful idea, you're right; he needs a vacation. He needs to relax for a few weeks. I had thought to send him chasing the Countess and try to attach to her. Now, I think we should talk to him. It is time he makes his own choices. I think that will be better for him than ordering him around. If he wants to follow that Witch, fine. But, I do not want him to attach to her, and you must go with him and protect him with your life."

The King went to the door and barked orders to have the Prince come into the office. "If he wants to follow her he can, but he has to go somewhere and relax for a while. I can make up some trivial reason for you to be gone for a few weeks. You, Ernst, and a few men; we will keep this small; you will go unnoticed."

There was a knock on the door. The King answered, "Come in."

Devon came in, "Father," he came to his Father, "Sir I am so sorry, I know I have disappointed you. I just don't know what happened to me. I was fine...the Witch was fine then she just dropped."

The King said, "Sit Devon sit. Son, I understand. I know exactly what happened I have done the same. Did the Professor not tell you young Witches are easy to outpower. This is common with a young Witch from the country with little experience, with a small amount of power." He walked around the desk and put his hand on his shoulder. "Martin pour us some wine. I understand the Count's tonic is helping you with the cravings. I think you need some time off, and I mean more than just no school, no army; I mean no more Attachments. I know we planned to send you off chasing Casandra, but I am not so sure that is the best for you. We have months until their wedding; you can just go to Azul and relax or somewhere of your choice."

Devon stood and walked to the window. He looked out at the garden. How had he gotten into this mess? Devon had not made his own choices since he was eight years old. How could he make his own decisions now?

The King handed him wine. "It is good to think about this, drink a glass of wine. You don't have to decide today. You can decide after the party. If you do want to chase that Sorcerer, you should leave sometime this coming week. If not, well you can stay here a while. I would welcome some time with you." He put his arm around Devon, and Devon just smiled.

The Season Starts

The seven of them sat around a table in the outside courtyard of the Temple having breakfast. Henry wasn't eating he was just looking a Casandra.

Addison was speechless. Marion looked radiant and somehow stronger. "It has only been four days, but Marion, you look so different. What have you been doing?"

Grace started laughing, "This little trip has changed all of us more than you know." Eric looked at Grace, he believed her, she was not the same. She looked at peace and confident. Grace shook her head, "Well, she has been spending a lot of time with the Master in Ancient Arts of Fighting." She smiled.

Addison looked at Henry and said, "Would that be a man named Casteglion?"

The three of the girls just looked at each other and smiled. Casandra said, "You know him?"

Addison said, "Casteglion trained both Henry and me. He is an amazing warrior, a very charming, and handsome man." He looked at Marion. Just then Achille and Casteglion walked up to the table.

Marion said, "Oh yes…that is what I thought at first. He," she pointed at Casteglion, "he is a sadistic and cruel taskmaster, who almost kill me." She crossed her arms and glared at Casteglion.

Casteglion roared with laughter, "There will come a day you will thank me, Miss Marion. Addison and Henry, it is good to see you. Henry, you look fit. Have you been training again?"

Henry stood, "Master, I have. Thank you for noticing. You look well. Tell me how did our girls do?'

Casteglion said. "I would hardly call them girls, Henry. Casandra is a voluptuous woman, and she is an excelled fighter. Marion, as beautiful as she is, has had a difficult time. Professor you would do well to continue with her daily practice. Grace," He turned a gave her a loving smile. "Well, Grace is my prize student. I have complete confidence she could take down any man here including me." Eric crossed his arms and glared first to Grace than to Casteglion. "This man sitting with you must be Eric, it is a pleasure to meet you. Grace speaks highly of you." Casteglion bowed.

Eric stood and returned the bowed the tension between them was evident and said. "You must be new here. I don't remember you."

The Professor changed the subject and went to Achilles and Casteglion, "Don't worry, the girls will be practicing at least once a day throughout the journey, by the Emperor's orders." He looked at Marion, "I am glad you came to say goodbye to us. I have made a commitment to return after next year's classes. Marion will be coming with me; you'll have plenty of time to train her."

Marion sat up, "Who said I will be coming back here? I have not even been asked."

The Professor looked at her, "You have already forgotten your promise to the Duchess?"

Marion swallowed, "You know about that, how could you know about that? I have told no one."

Professor just smiled. Casteglion said, "Wonderful, Marion you have been a challenge to me. Training one with such a spirit is not an easy task, but the Night has sent you to me. I am honored to take you on." And bowed to her.

She stood, "Casteglion, maybe by next year I can honestly say it is a pleasure to be your student." She bowed to him, and they all laughed.

Achille stepped forward, "Casteglion and I have made you gifts for your journey." He brought out a beautiful silver chain with a crystal hanging from the end. "For you Miss Marion."

Marion took it and looked into the crystal, "Master Achille is there something inside the crystal?"

Achille smiled, "Very observant. Only you as enlightened ones can see into the heart of the crystal. Your bear is in there."

Marion looked deeper, "I see, but he is breathing and moving he could not be living. But how in the world did you do this?"

Achille smiled, "You may have had a challenging time with Fighting Arts, but you excelled with me, your awareness is keen. He is alive, in a resting state until the time you need him most. You just need to break the crystal and command him. He will do the mission he is given."

Marion looked up to Achille, "How will I know when to call him?"

Achille smiled gently, "You will know or ask me. I am always with you." He handed out the two other Necklaces. "Countess, here is your leopard. Grace, your wolf and of course, the fox for the Professor. Please wear these when you are out on your journey. Do not let others see them. They are a great value to those who can recognize what they are."

Casteglion said, "Yes please, do not lose them. It took us half the night to capture those animals. It took fifty Monks the other half the night to subdue them and place them in the crystal. If you lose them, his Eminence will have us doing it again, I am sure."

Moori came up to the party, "We should be leaving I will miss the both of you. Hold me in blessing."

She gave both her friends a hug and Casteglion said, "You are ready Moori, you will do wonderfully I am sure of it. We will see all of you at your wedding Countess."

The Professor stepped up and took Moori's arm, "We will take the small carriage we have a lot to talk about." They walked out of the courtyard to the cliffs landing spot.

Eric said he and Grace would be riding mounts to the city. Addison said he and Marion would wait for Casandra in the second carriage, everyone left Henry and Casandra alone. Henry waved his hand, and a privacy charm surrounded them. He grabbed Casandra and kissed her deeply, "I have missed you. For the life of me, I do not understand how you have gotten so deep into my soul. The thought of not seeing you for weeks depressed me so much, I had to taste your lips before you left on your holiday."

Casandra kissed him softly, "Henry come with me. I don't care about freedom or even the sights we are going to see, not if you are not with me to share them. I love you with all my heart."

Henry smiled at her and kissed her again. "I can't Cassandra, there are things I must do to put the plan your Father, and I made in motion. I also need to find out more about the Hex spell, and I must make a place at my Father's Castle to receive you. I have not had a home there in years. I must see to that along with some details with Dillion. Not to mention our business; I am assuming you would like to remain the richest women in the world. If I work really hard, I can meet you in Traza, if you would like?"

She hugged him tight and screamed, "Yes! Yes! I love you, Henry."

Henry held her and looked deeply into her eyes he needed to release her. The pull of love was drawing him in. "I do not doubt your love, or I would be extremely jealous. Addison was right; these four days have changed all of you. Hard to believe, but you are more beautiful. I think you almost changed Casteglion from being a Monk." he laughed, "You even smell better, taste better, I cannot resist you. You must go now before I take you right here in the courtyard before everyone."

Casandra gave him a long kiss, knowing precisely what was enchanting Henry, she was carrying Sarah Winsette Rakie. No man could resist a woman ready to make a child.

The Engagement Party

Henry and Paxton took a coach from Harbor City to Bezier, after making all his deliveries. Paxton drove; Henry wanted him because he was an expert burglar, that talent might serve them in bringing back an Attachment for Ski. As they dropped to the Castle courtyard, Henry saw Joan playing in the side yard she was his favorite of the King's daughters. The King was mad to have an attachment to his own daughter of ten or eleven years. Henry felt sorry for her, and he wondered who she would mate with at the pleasure of the King. She must have seen Henry she ran out the gate straight for the carriage.

Joan was jumping up and down, "Henry you're here. Martin said you might be late. I told him no, Henry will be here early. I just knew it."

Henry climbed out of the carriage, grabbed her and threw her in the air. Soon he would have his own little girl, and he fully intended to spoil her. Joan squealed, and the Queen was out the doors to see who was there. "Henry, I am so glad you could make it. Martin had us worried you would not get here. Are you really that busy?"

Henry put Joan down, "If people would stop having engagement parties, weddings, and coronations, I could rest. Now Paxton and I can drop off some packages and bunk in the barracks."

The Queen said, "I will not hear of it. However, you will not have your normal room this stay. I have a small single bed in the Castle for you, and your man has a place above the stables. Is that suitable?"

Henry stood still while Joan stood on this side pulling his jacket. "That is wonderful. I know you have many people to accommodate, and I will do anything to make your life easier. What is it you want little girl that you're pulling on my jacket?"

Joan stuck out her bottom lip, "Henry, you forgot me. Last time you told me you had a special present just for me."

Paxton stood on the top of the carriage. "Henry, would that be the basket that has been making all the noise?"

Henry smiled, "I don't remember. Toss it down here and let me look."

Janet and Jessica came out of the gate, with Martin and the King behind, "Henry, what have you got there?"

Joan was jumping up and down, "Henry, hurry up open the basket. Is that the one for me?"

Henry was laughing, he slowly lifted the lid and out jumped a sizeable black puppy with a green bow around its neck. Joan squealed, and the puppy jumped up and licked her face. She was giggling and screaming at the same time. Henry said, "Well, I can see you don't like him much I can take him back home with me."

"No, no, no Henry! I want him, Henry! I love him!" She threw her arms around Henry and kissed him. Henry could feel the Attachment on the sweet girl's neck. "Thank you! Thank you! Thank you, I think I will call him Henry just like you. Is that alright?"

Henry hugged her again, "My sweet girl you may call him whatever you like. He is an Antico Water Spaniel, and he will grow to 180 to 200 pounds. He is the best guard dog in the world, he will always protect you. My man Paxton is excellent at training animals; I brought him along to help you learn. Would you like that?"

"Yes Henry, very much. I have never had my own dog." Joan looked suddenly very seriously at Henry, "I really need him to protect me. Bad things happen, Henry."

Henry looked at the King, and he looked sad. "You spoiled my Daughters Henry, by always bringing presents. Girls you cannot expect Henry to do this."

Henry patted her on the shoulder and said, "Oh, well then Paxton keep those other presents up top and hand me my suitcase."

Jessica ran up to Henry, "Father if Henry has gone to the trouble to get presents it is rude of you to refuse them. Is there one for me Henry?"

Henry laughed and said, "Paxton is there one for Miss Jessica?" Paxton began handing down presents, and Henry handed them out.

Jessica ripped open her box. It was a beautiful lace shawl with roses embroidered on it. "Oh, Henry this is beautiful."

Janet opened her box with hand-blown fluted glasses that shimmered in the sunlight. Henry said, "You cannot have a proper engagement toast without a stunning glass."

The Prince and Ernst came out, "Prince this one is for you. I haven't bought a gift for you in a long while. Also, my Queen, Ski sent this to you." He handed out the packages.

The Prince opened his. "A silver flask, with my initials on it and the crown insignia. Now, this is a useful gift. Thank you, Henry."

The Queen opened a small bottle of pink liquid, "Henry what is in this?"

"Ski made the box from the bark of the ginkgo tree from the North Castle, and the perfume from the white lilac trees in their garden. I didn't ask him how he got it. It seems you mentioned you missed the perfume of lilacs on his last visit." Henry winked at her and told Ernst mentally to have her look for the hidden message of the Hermit.

"Ski is so thoughtful; I am so surprised. Richard smell this perfume. Do you like it, lilac was one of my favorites as a young girl." The Queen grinned.

The King took a whiff, "That is nice, an intoxicating aroma. You must wear it tonight make all the others ask what perfume you're wearing."

The Queen smiled smugly. "Yes, I can say it was made just for me." Then she laughed and kissed the King on his cheek.

"Henry, I take it back; you can continue to bring gifts. You have made all my girls happy." He laughed, but then his face turned very stern.

Henry followed his gaze. Professor Moondale was dismounting close to where Joan and her dog were. Paxton jumped from the carriage and handed Henry his suitcase. Mentally, he said, the dog doesn't like that man I had better go to Joan.

Moondale walked over to Joan. "Joan come to see me." Joan just looked at him. The dog stopped playing and ran between Joan and Moondale. "Joan, what is this a dog? I hate dogs get him out of here now!"

The dog held his ground and started a very low growl, "But he is my dog. Henry gave him to me. He is my very first dog ever, and he is mine. He will protect me always."

Moondale took a step toward the dog, and the dog bared his teeth. Henry could tell Moondale was going to spell the dog. Paxton grabbed up the dog and stood between Joan and Moondale.

Paxton bowed and said, "Sir if you were thinking of spelling this dog, you should know they are immunized to magic. They can take magic and turn it back on the Witch or Warlock. This dog was raised with young Joan's scent, he is her dog." Paxton turned his back on the red-faced Moondale. "Joan, we should take the dog in the garden. He can run, and I can teach you how to give commands. Would you like that?"

Joan took Paxton's hand and said, "Yes Paxton, I would like that very much. Mother, Father, can I go with Paxton?"

The King walked to Joan and kissed her head, "Yes sweetheart, go on. Paxton, thank you. I will have my men put up the carriage and place your things in the stable bedroom." He looked at Moondale, "Come in Moondale we need to talk in my Library. Henry, meet us there after you have settled in." The two of them walked into the house.

Henry looked at the Prince, he was ready to kill Moondale. Ernst said mentally. That is precisely what Devon is thinking Henry.

Henry walked forward, "Prince would show me to my room?"

The Queen stepped up, "I can have Grayson do that."

Henry smiled. "Yes, but I really want to talk with Devon."

Devon tilted his head and looked puzzled, "Talk to me Count, why?"

Henry laughed, "I like you, Prince, come for a walk with me. You can bring Ernst and Martin if you're afraid of me?"

Martin spoke up, "Well I am curious I want to go along."

The Queen asked. "Do any of you three know where you're going?" They all looked at each other. "I thought so, Ernst you better help them find the way."

Ernst grinned, "Yes Queen, that is my daily job with these two." Martin and Devon protested, but everyone else laughed.

The Queen turned and walked away speaking, "The party starts at seven. Do not be late, gentlemen. Come on, girls we have a lot to do this afternoon."

They walked a few yards when Devon turned, "What did you want to talk with me about Count?"

Henry smiled, "Your tonic, how is it working, Ski can adjust it, but you have to be honest with me."

Devon heaved a sigh and continued walking, "I suppose it is working well enough. I am not nervous like I was. The cravings have subsided." He looked to the ground, "Sometimes, like just now with Moondale; I have a hard time controlling my emotions of anger."

Henry stopped, "I don't like that man either, Devon."

Devon said, "Well, I hate him! He has." He stopped and looked at Martin, "I would not be on your tonic if he hadn't pushed me. I don't want him near any of my Sisters. Martin, you can tell Father I said that Moondale is a madman."

Henry stopped and looked at Martin, "Devon, your Father thinks the same thing, but he is going to be difficult to get out of our lives."

"Just kill him! I would be happy to do it for you." Devon stood his ground.

Martin said, "Son, we should not be burdening Henry with our problems."

Henry replied, "Martin is right. I am sure the King would not like me knowing all this. But Martin, I am not a stupid man. You and the King must realize I know much more than you like. For instance, I know Joan has an Attachment spell on her." Martin started to protest, and Devon looked shocked.

"Henry, that is part of the ceremony for Sorcerers in this land, when they come of age. This is our law and now custom." Martin looked to Devon, and he looked heartbroken. "Devon, it is for their own protection. Your Father and I will keep them safe." Devon just turned and sprinted.

Henry walked fast to keep up with Devon, "Devon, I will talk with Ski and see if he has an answer for your emotions running high. Martin and your Father are right in this. Think carefully, how many people has Moondale attached to? How many will die when he dies? Has he taken power from Joan? The way he approached her today, so brazenly in front of all of us. I felt certain he was going to pull power from her while we were standing there. I think you did too that is why you were so mad. I was ready to pull his head off myself." Henry put his hand on Devon's arm, "Did you look at your Father's face? As soon as Moondale arrived his face told the story of his feelings. He hates him, too."

Martin came up to Devon, "Son, we had to make promises to Moondale to get him to cooperate with us. Unfortunately, he is expecting to become part of this family."

"No, never, over my dead cold body, Martin!" Devon's hands were clenched.

Martin stood in front of him, "We would never have kept those promises. The King has a plan. You must trust your Father and me."

Devon said, "Moondale has to be kept away from her. We need to speak to the King now."

Henry laughed, "You don't have to worry about Moondale coming near Joan as long as she has that dog by her side." Henry put his arm around Devon's shoulder. "Paxton has trained that dog; he will not let Moondale near her. Joan has always been my favorite; a lovely free spirit. I will help protect her."

Devon said, "How did you know Henry?"

Henry started walking again, "Addison brought my attention to Mondale's erratic behavior on our last visit. However, I could feel it when she hugged me, the last time I was here. I saw Moondale with her in the hall, taking her power. At that time I didn't know about the Attachment spell. After I learned of it, I figured Moondale was using her. That is why I gave her the dog."

Martin said, "Why didn't you say something at the Villas about this?"

Henry stopped walking again, "Martin, I didn't know until I saw the look on the King's face and Devon's that you all hadn't approved of it. I didn't even know of your law or custom. I just have always loved that little girl, and I didn't want her hurt. I know I am on thin ice with you and the King. You almost killed me, remember. You don't trust me now, and I don't trust you, getting a dog for Joan couldn't make our relationship any worse."

They walked to Henry's room, and he cleaned up and met them in the King's library.

"Henry, come in here, we need to talk shut the door behind you." The King poured wine for them all. Martin, Devon, and the King were all seated. Henry took a glass and sat next to Devon. "Martin and Devon have just told me of your talk about Moondale. We have not always seen things eye to eye. Sometimes our cultures and customs have been polar opposites. One common thing we do have is we love our families sometimes to a fault. I have not given you credit. I knew you were smart, but I did not think the Belissa clan had any morals. Diamante is known as unscrupulous and cunning. You have integrity; I can hardly believe it. Well, at least when it comes to women and children. I always thought that charm was put on for the ladies; all this time it was real. What am I going to do about you, Henry?"

Henry roared laughing, "How about let me live."

The King laughed too, "Oh I think we can promise you that you will live. I like having you around you make life interesting. The last time you were here at dinner with us, Joan told me she was so happy Martin was marrying Janet because that left you for her to marry. When she found out you were marrying Casandra, she was heartbroken."

Henry sat up in his chair, "What she is planning her marriage to me?"

Now Devon laughed. "Yes Henry, she told me about that years ago. You are the only man she wants. You play right into her hands with all the gifts you bring."

The King agreed. "You don't want to hurt her, but you have."

Henry stood, "How can I remedy this? She is too young to think this way. She will have more men than she can count, better men than me." He walked to the fire and stared into it.

Martin said, "Well there is one way we can make everyone happy. You can have a loving marriage after all Henry. You can marry Joan when you become Emperor."

The King stood and put his hand on Henry's shoulder. "Yes, I would have never dreamed my baby the Empress of the world." This news stopped Henry's heart the only way that would happen is with Beatrice, Kathryn, and Casandra's death.

Casandra's Season

They left Monk's Mountain and landed in Emerius to get the larger overseas carriage. Grandeurs was the first City they would spend time in. Addison and Marion were sitting across from her with Marion working on the disguises for them. They would be in Grandeurs by dinner too late to sightsee, but early enough to go dancing. Casandra wished Henry would be there to dance with her. She looked out the window thinking, this was not the holiday she had looked forward to for years. She and Marion had mapped out a vacation in Antico and the Alia Islands, it was not as flashy but more beautiful with lots of magical places.

"Casandra, what do you want to do?" Addison felt she was miles away. "Casandra? Come back to us?" Addison reached across the carriage and shook her hand.

She jumped, "Addison." She saw his concerned face, "I'm sorry, what did you say?"

Marion said. "We were trying to decide on where we will go dancing after dinner, the Planet or The Music Box? Which one do you want to go to?"

Casandra smiled, "It doesn't matter, you chose." She turned her head and looked out the window.

Eric took her hand, "Casandra, this is your holiday you should choose we are just here for the ride, so to speak."

Casandra wanted to cry this was not her holiday she wished she was back at the Castle in her room. Her life was more about making others happy, never herself. The King had decided where she should go on holiday. Now they wanted her to make the decision where to go dance; find time to ask her opinion. She would need to answer something so they would leave her alone. She said, "The Music Box."

Marion sighed, Casandra said, "Well, then the Planet. I truly don't care, Marion."

Eric said, "Why don't we try both I have never been to either. You girls are the ones who go dancing."

Casandra knew they were not going to stop placating her, "That's a good idea." She would make sure to ride with the Professor carriage over the ocean. He wouldn't force her into the conversation. She let go of Eric's hand and reached into her bag for the book Achille gave her. It was a brand new book with no title, and the cover was plain. She thought it was a journal, but when she opened it she realized it was the Master's Volume 2; she could read every word.

Eric looked at the book and said, "That is a pretty journal is it a gift?"

Casandra shared that Achille gave it to her and passed it around. No one in the carriage saw the words.

Dinner and dancing were an effort for Casandra, but the next day would be shopping. She found beautiful gifts for her wedding party, and dishes and linens. The girls wouldn't let her buy anything saying she would have plenty of wedding gifts. She wanted something to give Henry but could find nothing. Addison told her Henry had everything he needed, not to bother. The Professor came into the shop to tell them they needed to get to the carriages for Segal. They were walking to the station when she spied a glass shop. In the window was a pair of beautiful crystal fluted glasses. She darted into the shop, pulling Addison with her. "Addison does Henry have wine glasses like that?"

Addison inspected them, "I have never seen glasses like these, Henry would love them. I can see him serving his wines in these."

The shopkeeper took her order, and she had them sent to the Belissa Villa as a wedding gift for Henry. She had each engraved.

At the station, she told Addison she needed to speak with the Professor, so she jumped into the carriage with the Professor and

Moori. "Do you mind if I come into this carriage? I have things to talk to you about."

After they were in the air, the Professor asked. "Do you really have something you need to speak with me about or have you just had enough of the babysitting?"

Casandra started laughing, "Both. I know they are well-meaning, but this season is nothing that I wanted and everything my Father wanted. I should have just let him have his way and stayed at the Castle. They all keep badgering me about what I want, then when I tell them, they say 'Oh no you don't want to do that.' I think this Holiday is for them."

The Professor smiled knowingly, "That is the way of the world, my Dear. We go through life thinking if we only had this or if only that person would go away, our life would be perfect. When you were at Monk's Mountain, did you feel this way, Casandra?"

"No Professor, I never thought about it on the Mountain." Casandra sighed.

Moori smiled. "You were engaged in life on the Mountain, but here in the carriage, or at the dance room, you were the watcher. You watch like most unaware people, not seeing." Casandra looked puzzled, "You must be engaged in life to really see what is happening before your eyes. We can do some exercises here in the carriage to help you if you like."

The Professor said, "The power of the negative force can only fill empty spaces. I know I have told you many times."

Casandra said before the Professor could finish, "The negative force is like the fog; shed pure light on it, and it will dissipate."

The Professor smiled, "You did listen."

Casandra reached into her bag and pulled out the book, "I would like to know what you think of this book."

The Professor took the book and shuffled through the pages, "Moori, why does Casandra have this book?"

Moori opened it and said, "What do you think this is Casandra?"

"You two are no help! Eric, Addison and all the rest think I have a pretty journal. I think I have a book filled with words. Not only that, it is a book I never knew existed. Now, will you answer me?"

Moori laughed. "I should be upset, it took me five years to get to this book. How did you get this in one session?"

Casandra was dumbstruck. The Professor said, "You finally get to take the knowledge away from the Mountain. Your Mother will be proud, I know I am. I was beginning to question my teaching skills. You should know there are dozens of more volumes Casandra; evidently, you will need this information for your mission. You should start reading, and we will help answer any questions."

The next leg of the trip was to a small island in the Traza Ocean, and it was over an eight-hour journey. They stopped to eat and rest in Jaunante Islands. Casandra read the entire time, and her mind was swirling.

Marion came up to her, "Casandra, are you mad at me or the others? Why are you riding with the Professor?"

Before she could answer the Professor was standing there giving Marion a stern look, "Marion you are nosey. But if you all must know she is using this time to meditate and learn. Something the rest of you would do well to do yourself." He looked at the others, and they cowered. Casandra had to stifle a laugh she could remember well the times he had done that to her. "Marion, I believe it is time to put on our disguises."

Marion said, "Follow me." They walked out to a cove by the ocean; hidden from the view of the few people who worked on the small island. "Addison, you can morph, so I will start with the Professor." She worked just a few minutes and changed his hair, eyes, and skin color. He became a blonde, blue-eyed man with a beard and one hundred years younger. Grace wanted curly red hair with green eyes and without the Elf ears. Eric asks to look like a Wizard. Marion turned his white hair and eyes black and removed his Elf ears too. Marion changed her face to an oval shape then added blue hair and eyes. Addison had changed his hair and eyes to match Marion. "Casandra since you were not on our carriage ride we couldn't discuss your changes."

Casandra sneered, "Oh this time you are going to let me decide? How unusual." Marion gave her a nasty look, "Alright I want a longer nose with white wavy long hair and eyes like Eric, white with gold rims. Don't forget the Elf ears. I will like intimidating everyone."

Eric shook his head and said. "You will not have so many men flirting with you, looking like a half-breed. It is not all you think it is."

Casandra took his hand, "You are so wrong about that Eric, most women are staring at you all the time. If you are right and I am not attracted to men, it should make your job easy. Go on Marion change me."

Marion made the changes and Eric took in a breath, and Addison laughed. Casandra said, "Is it that bad?"

Addison said, "Henry wanted to know what you looked like. I told him you are as beautiful as ever."

Eric said, "That look is only going to make my job harder. You will stand out in a crowd."

Casandra said. "It is done; I need to get back to my lessons, let's go."

They landed in Sigal in the middle of the Night. Casandra and the girls didn't wake up until the middle of the afternoon the next day. Addison and Eric went out to scout around the city, they had a late lunch and then went out to sightsee the town of Mardit, a very colorful city. The buildings had spiral roofs, and each was a vibrant color. The winding streets were made of green bricks lining the coastline. The harbor was filled with ships from all over the world. Casandra loved the brightly colored flags and banners which hung from all the restaurants and shops. However, by the end of the second day, she had her fill with shopping and museums. After lunch, on the third day, she spied a fabric shop and headed for it. There was a bolt of sparkling dark blue material in the window. The light seemed to emanate from it, and it was the perfect color for her Temple gown. She wondered if it could be flown to the North Castle in time to add to her dress. She grabbed the bolt and went to the counter, where Marion and Grace were waiting.

Grace sighed, "That is beautiful, but I bet it is too late for you to use for your dress."

That was the final comment any more objections to her choices would result in a fire. "I will need dresses for Balls and other parties. I am buying this, and no one will tell me no." Smoke was coming from her feet, the girls walked quickly away. She bought the whole bolt and spent too much on it. She also hired a wizard to take it to the North Castle immediately. When she left the shop, Eric was watching her judiciously. Then they went off to another museum this one was about the Great War in Arlequin. The battle on the sea was depicted in dreadful details. It did nothing but bring back memories or seemed to predict the near future.

She was happy to leave the museum for dinner at a harbor restaurant. The Professor, Addison, and Eric got into an in-depth conversation about the Great War and all the conflicts. Even Grace and Marion had thoughts to add. Dinner was appetizing, but Casandra couldn't eat or enjoy it. She was still pushing down anger about her awful holiday, and fear for the lives of everyone at the table.

Moori said, "I enjoyed the museum, being on Monks Mountain all the years of the war I didn't know much about the outside world. Casandra, what did you like most about our day?"

Everyone at the table stopped and looked at her. How could she give an honest answer and not disappoint everyone there? She took a breath and said, "This time now, here with all my friends by the sea. It is relaxing." There, she wasn't telling a lie.

Addison looked at her as if Henry was asking something. "You didn't like the churches we visited? I thought you would."

"They were beautiful, and the architecture was astounding." Casandra could see his concern. "What is it that Henry wants to know Addison?"

Addison wiped his mouth with a napkin and coughed, "Well, he is concerned you are not enjoying this holiday. In fact, I believe we all are."

Casandra took a breath and pushed down emotions, "It is wonderful, aren't we all enjoying it?" She looked to Moori who knew she was lying her face was filled with compassion. "Moori you seem to love all the churches, and Marion I know you are dazed with the shopping. Gentlemen, you are all engrossed with the rich history."

Addison said, "And you Casandra have you been dazed, engrossed, or in love with anything we've seen?"

Marion, Grace, and Moori looked down at their plates they knew better than to push her like this. The emotions started creeping up her body, she was ending this. "Addison, I will try to be as civil with you and Henry as I can, only because you do not know me well yet. You are about to learn what happens when I am pushed too hard as everyone at this table can attest to, it never ends well."

She pushed her plate of unfinished foods away from her and looked at Eric he was ready for anything. "In truth, no. I have not enjoyed the museums. I might remind you I have just finished sixteen years of studies. I have found the museums repetitive and a constant reminder of what we may face shortly." She took more breaths to relax, "The Churches are a reminder of my station, a life I will live all too soon at Bayonne Temple. Just to let you know shopping involves occasionally buying items, which no one at this table has allowed me to do. I know I need to wait until I open my wedding presents." She held up her hand and took more breaths, "It has always been customary for the Sorcerer to plan her own holiday. This has been nothing of what I wanted. I am trying my best to accept it for what it is, a token of love. Oh, let's not forget the assembly of friends dogging me at every turn and some fifty or so Elves eyes tracking me." She stopped, and just concentrated on her breathing and pressing down her emotions.

Eric said, "Casandra the whole trip will not be like this. I knew you would hate this. I tried to tell the King and Major this was not what you'd enjoy." He came to sit next to her and took her hands. "Sweet girl in two days we will be in beautiful mountains with stunning scenery. I have planned a special night on the high range camped in treetops of the prairie. We will see wild horse herds, Pegasus, and hopefully unicorns. Then we will move on to Traza, it is filled with beaches and exotic nightlife. I promise I will not drag you to one church, market, museum, or battle site."

Casandra looked around the table with tears in her eyes, "Why didn't they just once ask me what I wanted? No one but you Eric has ever asked what I wanted. I would not even be in this Country. Why didn't they listen to you, you know me better than anyone."

Eric hugged her, then saw Addison and Grace both giving him questioning looks. He dropped his arms and said, "Casandra was in my charge from the time she could walk I am like a Brother."

Grace crossed her arms and scowled at him then Addison said. "Henry said he wants to do a blood bond with you, Eric."

Casandra stood, threw her napkin on the table and said, "Grace and Henry are jealous. Henry wants to know about you Eric, well he should. Tell Henry he may want to have a talk with..."

Eric stood turned her to face him, and the look he gave her stopped her from speaking. "Miss Casandra that is enough. I compel you to stop speaking.

Addison said, "Casandra he was just teasing."

Eric sternly said, "Tell Henry she is in no mood for teasing. Casandra, take a walk, now. That is an order my men will follow."

Casandra turned and left. Eric looked at everyone at the table. "I was assigned to her from the age of four, I should know her well, and yes, I do love her. I raised her, she is my girl, and always will be. It hurts me to see her so hopeless. I thought we could take her mind off this enormous task. If I could take it from her, I would. Grace, I love you, but you must give me room to love her too. Good evening."

Casandra walked along the main street by the bay she was so mad. At first, she had not even paid attention to what direction she walked. Eric's men were following, there was no way she could get lost. Now, she was sweating, and the sun was setting. The day would cool off soon and hopefully, she would too. She couldn't even scream. Eric had compelled her before, and it always made her rage. However, thinking back he also kept her from getting in a lot more trouble by speaking sarcastically to the Emperor. He had forced her to learn restraint. She remembered her life with Eric. For many years she thought he was her Father; he was undoubtedly more loving than the Emperor. In her teen years, she had a massive crush on him. She was cooling off; this was a big city, how far had she walked. She stopped on a bridge and looked across the bay, the restaurant was far on the other side. How would she find the hotel, she had walked two hours; now she would have to walk two hours back. She wished Eric had come after her.

A horse stopped behind her, "Your wish is my command." Eric looked down at her from his Pegasus. "You ordered me to say that after Mags read you that fairy tale, you were just four. It doesn't seem that long ago to me. I see you are calmer; I release you to speak."

"I am sorry Eric; it seems all I ever do is apologize to you." Casandra took his hand, and he pulled her up behind him. "Do you forgive me?"

Eric said nothing, "Eric, you must forgive me." She almost commanded him to forgive her. She could never stand for him to be mad at her.

Eric finally said, "I told Grace and Addison I thought of you as my little girl."

She wrapped her arms around him and laid her head on his back, just like when she was little. "I just remembered when I was a little girl. I thought you were my Father."

He laughed, “I can remember the day you called me that in front of the Emperor. I almost got kicked out of the army.”

Casandra giggled, “I told him I would never speak to him again if he took you away from me.”

“I know he told me. You were always opinionated and stubborn. Thank the Night you grew out of it.” They rode in silence for a while.

Casandra said, “You really must forgive me. I promise I would never say anything about the crush I had on you or kissing you or…”

Eric stopped the horse. “Casandra that is it…right there. We can never speak of that.” He turned in the saddle to look at her. “That was a mistake on my part, but Henry and Grace may not see it that way.”

Casandra was smiling she would use this to get Eric to accept her apology, “It was no mistake. I enjoyed it. You were the only one who could explain and show me what was expected of me on my liaisons. I couldn’t have handled that without you. I used to wish I was not a High Sorcerer but an Elf.”

Eric looked at her thoughtfully, “Well, you are not Elf, even though you look like it now and you are a betrothed Countess speaking this way is completely inappropriate and useless. I love Grace, and you love Henry, and that was long ago. Do I need to place you under a lifelong compulsion? I can do that, you know.” He turned in the saddle and signaled the pegasus to continue.

Casandra put her head on his back again, he was right she was no longer a girl. She did love Henry but holding on to Eric she felt safe. They reached the hotel, and one of Eric’s men helped Casandra off the Pegasus. Eric dismounted and handed his man the reins. They walked together inside. “Thank you, Eric, for everything, but mostly for being my friend.” She turned and walked away.

Eric grabbed her arm. “I forgive you, and I thank you for being my friend. Tomorrow, how about we try hiking on the trails by the sea. Would you like that?”

Casandra leaned up and kissed him on the cheek. “Your wish is my command, General.” Then he smiled.

The Curse

The engagement party was beautiful, but the King was stalling. He wasn't even mentioning the Attachment Spell, and Henry couldn't waste another day. Henry needed to leave, there was a schedule to keep if he wanted to meet Casandra in Traza. He was worried about her. Addison had told him how she was withdrawn; off in another world and didn't participate with them while sightseeing or shopping. Henry went down to breakfast early, hoping to find the King. Grayson told him he left early but would be back to get Henry by noon.

The Queen came into the dining room. "Henry I am so glad you came down early. I was wondering if you would join me after breakfast for a ride to the town. I want to get something for Casandra and you for your wedding."

Henry said. "I would be happy to walk you to town, but it is not necessary to get us a present we will be inundated I am sure."

"No, Henry I spoke with the King, and he insists. He said he wanted you to take it home with you. He knows the Emperor would probably burn it." She laughed. "I need to take care of a few things. I'll come back to get you."

Henry had a feeling this was just an excuse to be alone with him maybe he would learn something new from the Queen. He had his breakfast, and the Queen came back to the dining room, "Grayson is bringing the carriage now. Are you ready?"

Henry smiled, "What do you have in mind for a gift. I really don't know her well. I am not sure what she will need."

The Queen took his hand, "You are another man who hates to shop, well, I have a pretty good idea of the needs of a newly married woman. Come on, Henry."

They drove out of the Castle grounds and towards the town. Almost halfway there the road dipped. At that point, the Queen put a secrecy bubble around them. "Henry, I was afraid you wouldn't come. We must talk here but before I forget." She handed him a note. Henry vanquished it and put it in his coat pocket. "It is from the Hermit, I am to tell you that you will need everything on that list. Now, Ernst took Devon to Traza they are looking for Casandra they left this morning, but that trip takes a while. The King is starting to trust you, but Martin plans to put an Attachment on you. He doesn't want to wait until the wedding he is trying to talk Richard into doing it now. I would not trust him."

Henry took her hand. "I know about the Attachment; Ernst told me. Elisabeth are you aware of how addicted Devon is to the spell?"

The Queen looked to Grayson. "I fear he will be lost. I was too late for my daughters, now Devon. Thank you for helping me. I will do what I can to help. I can no longer tolerate the King. I will be happy to end this life. Please tell Casandra, I wish her success, and I pray to the Night for her. She must kill the King at all costs. Will you give her that message?"

Henry swallowed he wasn't going to tell her "at all costs," but he agreed. She removed the bubble, and they continued to town and shopped for a wedding gift. When they returned to the Castle, the King was waiting for them.

"Henry, I have come to rescue you from the Queen. Has she worn you down with shopping yet?" The King smiled.

Henry helped the Queen down from the carriage. "She has been spending your money on me, so I have not minded at all."

The King came up to the Queen and kissed her cheek and stood behind her. "Well, do you like my present?" He leaned down to her ear like he was going to whisper to her but placed his lips on her neck exactly where her Attachment was. "What did I buy him, my Dear?"

She leaned back and looked up at him. "A beautiful silk comforter and pillows with large embellished roses. Henry is going to have it on their bed in the Diamante Castle. He is taking it with him when he leaves here. He is buying furnishing for the apartment in the Castle. I ordered them a little surprise gift too."

The King smiled, "When are you leaving Henry? I had hoped to spend some time with you."

Henry smiled, "I should have left this morning. I need to leave as soon as possible. I have duties at Winsette Castle with my Brother's Coronation, and Casandra's visit to meet my family. Of course, I must return home first to get more wine. Weddings are expensive."

The King put an arm around him, "You do not have to tell me that. Give me this afternoon can you leave later today?"

Henry said, "Of course that would be fine if it can be home by tonight." Henry mentally told Paxton to pack and try to follow him to the University.

The King said. "I have a horse ready for you let's take a ride we can talk."

They rode to the University with only small talk. The King took him down to the same cellar he had been in the last time he was there. Moondale was waiting for him, along with two guards and a young Witch.

"Henry, I have it just about ready for you." Moondale turned back to the table and poured a green liquid on his hands. "Here, pour this on your hands. It helps to keep the attachment from sticking to you. We need to get Henry a pair of gloves, King. Now, I have put a spell on our Witch, so she is still. It is best to get her into a receptive mood. When the subject is relaxed, the Attachment easily slips on the throat and into and out of the body."

Henry just looked at him, "Moondale, you make this sound so easy and clinical. How would I do that, and how do I handle the Attachment that it doesn't stick to me?"

The King chuckled, "Come on Henry, should we have gotten you a Warlock, kiss the Witch. Here, place the Attachment in your right hand like this." The King picked it up he practically drooled at the touch.

Henry took it. It did not feel strange but almost like it was a part of him. He turned to the young Witch, she was scared. Henry smiled and softly touched her cheek as he leaned in and whispered, "I will not hurt you." He smoothed her hair and began to kiss her face from forehead to mouth. He slowly moved down to her neck, and smoothly softly placed it on her neck. He immediately felt the power coming from it and bent down drawing her life force. He started whirling lost in an erotic dream. He pulled back then and looked at her, she was right with him. He stopped and returned some power back to her and slowly he tried to bring back the Attachment to his hand. The King was in his ear, instructing him on how to release each hook carrying it slowly upward. The poor Witch was screaming, Henry spelled her to be silent so he could concentrate. The Attachment came off in his hand. Henry wanted to throw it across the room he was so repelled by it. It was more important to save it if he could. The Professor grabbed it; he was only able to snag a piece of it. He wiped his hand on his jacket to remove the green matter and palmed a small piece of Attachment in his jacket pocket. He was so disoriented he could hardly stand so the action looked normal.

The Professor came around with a wet cloth, "Here Henry you do not have to dirty your fine jacket. Here wipe your hands."

The King held him up while Moondale wiped his hands. "Gentlemen I am sorry; I seem to be a little dizzy. Is this common?"

The King chuckled. "Dizzy yes, and in a little while, you will have so much excess energy you will want to fight or have lots of sex. I think you will like it, Henry. However, it is also the reason you cannot go back to the Castle. I would not like you to taking advantage of one of my Daughters or Queen. Your bags have been packed, and your man is waiting outside for you. You did very well for your first time. You listened to me, and nothing went wrong. Look, our young Witch is fine." Henry tried to focus on her she was smiling like she was enthralled with him. "Would you like to have her you could burn off some of that energy with her."

Henry looked up at him, and he realized the King was cradling him. "What I am sorry, I don't understand I think I need fresh air." Henry was trying to follow Moondale and the Attachment he put it in a copper pot and placed it over the flame. "What is happening? I am getting hot, King."

The soldiers came over to him and helped him out to the courtyard. The King said, "Help him in the wagon, the Witch too." The King brought the Witch out and placed her next Henry, "She is my gift to you; do as you wish with her. She will be loyal to you from now on anyway, even without the Attachment." The King said, "We will have another spell manufactured. You will have questions after your head clears. Martin will deliver it to you in four to five weeks; it will work much superior to this one. Do have anything to ask now?"

"You have to make an Attachment every time?" Henry tried to focus.

Moondale came up to him, "No, but they only last a limited amount of time. It takes weeks to make one, we must plan this out carefully when you are clearheaded." Someone slapped the Pegasus, and they were up in the air while Henry tried desperately to hold on to the wagon.

Paxton used magic to keep Henry and the Witch from falling out. Paxton mentally called some of Henry's men to help him after they crossed into Diamante. They managed to get them to the Villas in one piece. Henry fell to Ski's feet, feeling like the energy inside him would burn him up. He threw his jacket at Ski, "There is a piece of the Attachment in the right-hand pocket, along with some green matter that I can't identify. I need to get away from all of you, I am running. Oh, the Queen has a note for you and a list for in the left-hand pocket."

"Henry, it is the middle of the night and what about the Witch?" Ski looked at him strangely.

"I don't care. I don't know if the Witch is loyal or a spy, think of something." He turned and ran as fast as he could.

Pegasus of Paldao

Eric had been right, Paldao was pure magic. Spectacular Mountains shades of blue and purple stood majestically against the deep blue skies. Trees with pink moss stood tall on the tops of the mountains, and creatures she had never seen fluttered all around them. They were all riding Pegasus, and Casandra was dazed and awe-struck to feel flight. With the sun on her face and wind in her hair, she could fly like this forever. Casandra had not felt this free since she was a child.

Casandra was laughing, "Marion what are these flying creatures?"

Marion was not happy the Pegasus frightened her, "They are fairies, we used to have fairies in our land, but they all disappeared after the Great War. They are beautiful, but they are very tricky, do not trust them. They can see behind our disguises, and they say they will tell others if we do not pay the price. I am negotiating."

Casandra laughed and flew to Eric, "Thank you, I love you, this is what I wanted. It seems Marion can speak with these fairies she is negotiating. I have no clue what she is saying."

Eric was smiling; she was happy. His girl Casandra was delighted. "Marion the fairies have already been paid don't let them fool you."

Marion yelled, "Money you gave them money! They don't care about money. What are you thinking? They want information that is what they can trade for magic." She turned back and spoke to them. By sunset, they were in a small inn at the foot of Pegasus Mountain. Marion had managed to give the fairies the information they wanted, and in turn, they would bring them Pegasus on the flats.

As far as Casandra was concerned, this was the best meal she ever had. It was a meatless vegetable stew and bread that melted in her mouth. Grace and Eric were speaking quietly in the corner, and Marion and Addison were in a world of their own.

Casandra got up and went over to Moori, "Come outdoors and stargaze with me." Moori grabbed two mugs of ale, and they went out into the courtyard and looked up to the sky.

Moori pointed to a bench on the opposite side. "Let's sit, the stars are brighter here. I have never been anywhere so exquisite."

Casandra took a drink of ale she could taste magic she wondered if it was Henry's. "Yes, it is brimming with magic, even the ground pulses with it. The heavens are so close I feel like I can reach up and touch the stars I have never felt closer to the Night."

Moori sighed, "Me neither, and I have had some close touches."

"Moori, how did you come to be a Monk? Isn't it hard to give up everything and devote yourself to the Night giving up marriage and children." Casandra sat and relaxed.

Moori kept looking up to the stars. "Not for me, I do not want either." Moori was silent for a few moments and then continued softly. "When I came to the Monks I was a young girl, traumatized, badly beaten, and very broken. They tell me I didn't speak for almost two years. All that time is blank…just darkness. I was found washed up on the shore of Bezier. I hardly remember much of what happened. I don't like talking about it. When I have worked at remembering, it only brings on nightmares. His Eminence has told me I must understand all of myself before I can advance to Level 8. In my dreams, when I do remember, you are with me. I am not here to help you, Casandra, you are here to help me."

Casandra put her arm around her and poured love into her, "Then we should get to know one another… let me tell you about me." They talked for hours until Eric came out.

"Casandra, Moori, it is a beautiful night to stargaze, but it is getting late. We will be out under the stars for the next two nights you should share a tree then you can whisper all night." They all went inside to their beds.

The next morning Casandra couldn't wait to get back in the air. They flew over the top of the mountains and found the flat plains on the southwest side. They picked out the trees they wanted to sit in for the night, Moori and Casandra shared a tree. The trees had a full trunk, and the canopy was low and full. Each tree had wooden platforms in the upper branches where they could stare at the stars and watch the grass fields below. The leaves were sweeping and fleecy and the color of the night sky, a dark blue and green. Light pink and coral moss hung from the branches to the ground.

Eric and Grace were about two hundred yards away, while Addison and Marion's tree was almost twice as far. The Professor said he preferred sleeping in a tent at the campsite, with the guides and Eric's men.

A dinner of strange fruits and vegetables was served at sunset, then the six walked to their trees with lanterns as evening covered the plains. The grasses which had been light greens and golds turned to a fluorescent color, so they glowed. The few trees that bordered the plain had changed to radiant blue and orange with luminous pink and purple mosses. The clouds in the sky matched the vibrant color of the flat plains. Everything in Paldao had changed with the stars into a brilliantly colored world. Florescent birds and insects buzzed around them as they as they walked to their trees. Casandra stopped watched the ground, she could not only see the magic under her feet but feel it rise up her body. "Eric this is the most beautiful and magical place I have ever seen. I want to stay here forever."

Eric smiled warmly, and Addison said, "Yes that is the way everyone feels on the flats, but the natives know that only shortens their life. That is why they live off the mountain and limit their visits. Some creatures find the magic so strong they cannot even stay on the plains overnight. Remember to whistle if you need anything, no talking. Pegasus has a very keen hearing, and they are skittish."

Casandra and Moori climbed the tree, spread out their bedding and turned out their lantern. They could see the campsite in the distance and soon the sounds and light from there disappeared. The evening sky sparkled with stars appearing like diamonds propelled through the darkness.

Moori and Casandra laid on their backs and watched as the universe spun before them. Moori whispered, "Casandra, I can feel the world move, can you?"

Casandra answered softly, "I always do when I look at the evening sky. Sometimes I feel I can reach out and touch the stars. Have you never felt that, the motion of our world, or the pull of the moon?"

Moori didn't answer she was quiet for a long while, Casandra knew she was remembering. Intuitively Casandra allowed Moori her thoughts and the time to unfold them, Moori needed that most. Casandra saw a shooting star and followed it with her finger, "I use to dream that a star just like that one came down right in my hands. Then it exploded, and it flung me out into the night sky. I felt like I was falling, but I was falling up. I just kept going and falling until I was at the sun. Then I would wake up. It was such a real dream, but crazy. How could I fall up?"

Moori turned her head and said, "In Masters Volume Five there is a passage about that. Falling up, needing to hate to find love, finding laughter in tears, and fighting fear to be forgiven. I will find it for you. It says; When the universe reverses, we are home."

Casandra said, "Well, that doesn't make any sense. It's irrational."

Moori chuckled, "Well, your dream sounds irrational too, it seemed to fit." This time it was Casandra's turn to reflect on how many times she had that dream as a little girl, then it stopped while she was at the Academy. Now she was dreaming about the dungeon and catching stars in her hand almost every night.

They both fell to sleep, then Eric was shaking them and held his hand to their mouth he whispered, "Girls look out into the grassland." He pointed and said, "A large Pegasus herd." They both sat up and watched as the herd ambled by their tree. At least sixty Pegasus of all different colors pranced under their perch, there were babies with no wings and adults with large silver-white wings. After they passed, Eric went back to his tree with Grace. He had told them they would probably not see any more. The guides had said the Unicorn didn't appear anymore.

Casandra and Moori rearranged the bedding several times but could not get back to sleep. Finally, Casandra said she was getting out of the tree and going back to camp to sleep on a cot. Moori said she should not go alone and she would go with her. As they started down, and fairy poked its head over the platform. She blinked several times, "Casandra and Moori you must hurry. They are here and waiting. You need to come down, hurry." Then the fairy disappeared.

Casandra looked at Moori, "Should we whistle? I am not sure." Moori let out a low whistle, and the fairy was back. "We put them to sleep they can't hear. The unicorn King wants to speak privately with you, hurry."

They climbed down their tree when they got to the ground, they were dumbstruck. Each could only gawk at the magnificent creature that stood before them. The Unicorn was pure white with wings tipped in silver. His eyes were so deep purple they were almost black and the spiral horn coming out of its head was covered with crystals that burned like the stars in the heavens. Behind him stood at least twenty more just as beautiful, but in varying colors of whites, silver, and golds. The King unicorn walked to them and bowed.

The fairy said, "Casandra you must bow and place your hand on his mane; he will speak to you mentally. Casandra and Moori dipped, walked to him and put their hands on his mane.

He mentally said. I have been standing here for a long while waiting for you Casandra, Moori, good daybreak to you. They both wished him a good day, and he shook his head and thought. My name is Lucius you have been sent here for my blessing because you will need our magic to defeat the King. We have created a Pegasus especially for you. You will be introduced to him tomorrow his name is Shelton.

Casandra said. "Moori and I are grateful to you for your blessings we thought you were only a legend. The Paldao told us you never appear to them and we should not expect to see any unicorn. We are surprised and honored to meet you."

Moori said, "Yes King, we are honored. We are going to the Pegasus plains tomorrow. Our guides have told us the Pegasus no longer land for them how will Casandra find her Pegasus?"

The King whinnied and thought. We no longer land for them or work for them. Soon not one Pegasus or Unicorn will be visible to anyone. The Unicorn will be the first to leave. We own this land, we agreed to allow them to live in the mountains and take small amounts of magic, but the plains and flatlands belong to us. Nothing can be removed from the land without our approval. The Paldao have found a way to swindle us. The Paldao Royals have sold the rights to hunt us to the Hex, they take our magic. The people of this land have turned greedy and hateful. So, the Night has taken their magic away, and now she will find us a new home far away. We have only waited for you; by aiding you, she will assist us.

Casandra asked if this was the only way, to hide and leave a land so beautiful.

He mentally said. Place your hand between my eyes. Casandra did, and pictures flew into her mind of the atrocities the Hex had done; she understood everything. He mentally said. Casandra, you must kill the King, or we will all die. We will give you extra powers. We will be grateful, and as your compensation, we will protect your children. You and Moori must whisper my name to them when they are born.

Then he told her to rub her hands up and down his horn she did, to her surprise, the horn felt soft like velvet. White sparkling light shot into her hands and quickly moved down her body. Sparkling white dust covered her hands. Then he told Moori to do the same she also received his blessing. Lucius stepped back and thought. The morning has come we must leave. Your friends are waking up; you can say you saw us and we blessed you, but not that you spoke with us. It would be best not to tell your friends about this meeting until you are off this land, for we will be gone that very day. Your Pegasus awaits you, Casandra. He was made especially for you by the Night, and you will be able to communicate with him, this blessing has done that.

They watched as the herd ran off to the hills. Eric jumped down from his tree and ran to Casandra. "Was that a Unicorn herd?"

Moori said, "Yes I whistled, but you must not have heard. I have never seen an animal so beautiful, I don't think I ever will."

Casandra said, "I petted one, the magic was powerful and majestic. At least you saw them, did Grace?"

Grace came up from behind them, "I did, this is the best part of the trip, Casandra. I am so glad I am here, thank you for including me."

They all walked back to camp for breakfast. Addison and Marion had also seen the herd run by. The guides were ecstatic about the unicorn sighting that was the conversation throughout the meal.

They flew almost all day before they came to a village. Cabins were huddled along one side of a river with a campfire centered in the middle. The guides told them they had to stay on the right side of the river and not to bother the Shaman. Paldao Shaman lived on the hillside only they could communicate with the Pegasus and Unicorn.

The group settled down for dinner, and the guides explained what they would see. At sunset, the Pegasus would fly. The visitors could watch from the riverside. They couldn't enter the river; it was sacred, and no one could pollute it, nor could anyone take a Pegasus from the other side of the river. The Shamans were the only ones to negotiate between the customers and the Pegasus. When the parties were satisfied, the Pegasus would cross the river. Then the Shaman would release the magic to the owner. Pegasus could only be borrowed. When the owner died, they would return to the herd because they lived for thousands of years. None had traversed the river in months. Addison said it took he and Henry months and much money lining the Shaman's pockets to have the herd they have. Eric said the same thing that was why the Pegasus was so uncommon and the Emperor only had one small pack.

Casandra asked Addison, "Are you going to buy Pegasus?"

Addison chuckled, "I doubt a Pegasus is going to offer itself to us we are just sightseers. They do understand us magical beings; they are bright. Besides I don't have my international banking credentials that is the only payment the Paldao take as trade."

Casandra said. "Are you negotiating Eric?"

He shook his head, "Casandra negotiating and banking has to be arranged months in advance. We can't just walk in here and take a Pegasus home."

The sun was setting, they all followed the guides down to the river. There were several groups, all sightseeing standing along the shore. It wasn't long before they could see a small bird like horses flying high above the plain. They circled and made lazy eights in the sky, continually coming lower and lower to the ground. When they started to land out in the field, the guides started talking and yelling. A few men ran to the hillside huts to get the Shaman. The herd slowly walked to the riverside. They crossed the river and walked to the spot where Casandra stood. She could hear their thoughts; they had come to greet her. They said they all wanted to see the girl who would kill the King. Eric and Addison became very curious but said nothing.

The Shaman walked down to a small pier that jutted out into the river and began singing to them. Casandra was surprised she understood the singing and the whinnies of the Pegasus. A substantial black Pegasus landed and walked into the water to stand in front of the Shaman. He said he was to go with the girl in the blue tunic. The Shaman came and got Casandra and asked the Pegasus if they had the right girl.

Eric stepped in front of the Shaman, "I am sorry, gentlemen but we are just sightseers and are not prepared to buy a Pegasus. Besides that Pegasus is a large size, do you really think this young lady could ride him?"

Casandra pushed in front of him, "Eric, I can decide if I want a Pegasus or not. I am willing to negotiate. I do have my own money."

Eric looked shocked, then Addison stepped up, "Casandra I told you that you must have an international account and it must be in place and accessible."

She stood up taller and said, "What makes you think I don't?"

Addison glared at her and said, "Did you remember to bring your credentials with you?" Then he crossed his arms.

He thought he had there, but she waved her hand, and an international letter of credit appeared. She walked to the Shaman and started negotiating while the two men just stood there, flabbergasted. She came back to Addison and asked what she should pay for the Pegasus. He told her this was exceptional Pegasus; she would have to spend at least ten million fabs. After only a few minutes, she agreed on eleven million and handed the Shaman her letter of credit.

The Shaman walked back to the river and spoke to the Pegasus. He returned to her and said they had a deal then they walked to the office to finalize the transaction. When they returned, the Pegasus walked across the river. Shaman went up to the Pegasus to give his magic to Casandra.

The Pegasus stopped him and told the Shaman. This is not necessary I was made for her she is already mine. He walked past the Shaman and up to Casandra and bowed. I am honored to be of service to you, my Sorcerer.

She bowed to him and said, "It is so wonderful to meet you, Shelton. You are the most handsome Pegasus I have ever seen, and probably the tallest. How tall are you?"

He mentally thought. I am twenty-nine hands tall I was made to help you; the Night knows what my size should be, I was made black. But you are not black, you are white. You smell like Casandra, but you look wrong.

She grinned and mentally said. I am in disguise so the King cannot find me it is not time to fight him. I have black hair and aqua eyes; my skin is usually a creamy color we will look beautiful together. Eric and Addison walked over to them, and Shelton jumped between the men and Casandra.

She said, "Shelton, these are my friends who here to protect me." Shelton shook his head. Eric and Addison stood still. Casandra came to the side of the Pegasus, leaned on his shoulder she said, "These two will be traveling with us they have also put on a disguise. I will introduce you. Shelton this is Addison he is the best friend of my betrothed, Henry." Shelton bowed his head, and Addison nodded. "Eric I would like you to meet Shelton, Eric is my oldest friend."

Eric bowed, and Shelton mentally said. "I know him he has been here before and tried to buy me. He is a fair man."

Eric said, "I remember this Pegasus he was here last year. He is large for you Casandra; we must devise a saddle to hold you. I will take him to our herd."

Shelton shook his head. "Tell this Eric he knows nothing you will not need a saddle to ride me. You will take me to the herd. I want to be with you tonight you should sleep with me." Casandra laughed and thought. Oh, Shelton, I wish I could talk like you. You say what you think.

Addison said, "Casandra are you mentally speaking to him?"

Casandra said. "Yes. I can't really explain yet. Shelton said I need to sleep with him and I will not have a problem riding him. Come on Shelton I will get my bedroll from the cabin, and you can pick a place for us."

Eric said, "I will come with you. Tell Shelton if he has you out in the open. I will be with you."

Shelton led them to a grove of trees with a bed of moss under it. He laid in the grass, and Casandra was told to settle beside him. She curled up by his chest. She placed her head on his shoulder, and they dreamed together all night.

In the morning, Eric woke first. He had slept the best night of sleep ever. The moss was firm, just right for a good night's sleep. No insect bothered him, and he woke feeling full of energies of love and peace. He was only five feet from the Pegasus, he laid still to watch the two of them sleep. A thin, silver web weaved between Shelton and Casandra. He had never seen magic weaving Sorcerers and Pegasus. Shelton was not an ordinary animal, but what was he? He was worried that he had let Casandra be touched by magic, without knowing its origin.

Shelton opened his eyes they were aqua, just like Casandra's. Eric stared directly into his eyes thinking if this beautiful animal hurts her he would be forced to kill him. The thought came to Eric as if Shelton was talking with him. Eric, I am here to protect her and help her find her way. I have been sent by the Night created for her and her children. You would do well to trust me, the day may come I will carry you. We must work together. Last night I knitted us all together. Now you may hear me too. Eric looked down, sure enough, the silver light was woven through the three of them. He said, "What is the light that enfolds Casandra and me?"

Shelton mentally said. It is the energy of the universe, Eric. The Night uses it to heal, bind, enlighten, travel, and give peace. How did you sleep?

Eric smiled and thought. Best night of sleep I have ever had. Did you say travel?

Casandra raised her head. You are talking too loud in my head Shelton. What are you telling Eric?

Eric said, "What do you not want me to know?"

Shelton said mentally, Eric you will know when the Night wants you to know, trust us. We must be up, and gone men of Hex are on the way here.

Casandra jumped up and gathered her things, and their party was ready to leave in less than an hour. Shelton extended his wing, and she used it to pull herself up on his back. Eric could see the white netting Shelton had knitted the night before wrap around her. Addison told Eric she needed a saddle. Eric shook his head no. "She will be fine.

Shelton has a hold on her you can't see. We need to trust him, Addison, he told us men from Hex are on their way here, let's leave."

They all mounted and rose to the sky; Casandra's heart flew with Shelton. He was magnificent, and she laughed with joy as they soared.

The Attachment's Influence

Henry ran all night into midmorning. After the sun rose, he was acutely aware of eyes on him. Henry knew it was his men watching out for him. He ran into the lake to cool off and sprinted to the back terrace where Ski and the Witch were waiting for him. Ski handed him a towel and a glass of water.

"Do you want to change? What can we get you, Henry?" Ski smiled at him and mentally spoke. This Witch you brought with you isn't very informative. I think she is a spy, so be careful.

Ski handed Henry the towel. "I will change later. Ski can you get me food and coffee? Tell Ruth I will stay outside. I wouldn't drag water through the house. Madam, what is your name?"

She smiled at him, and he could see the connection between them, "I am Gretchen, but my family calls me Grady. I was a tomboy that's how I ended up in the King's Army. I am happy you took me with you, Sir. I will serve you well."

Henry eyed her she was very young to be a soldier, but the King liked them young and stupid. She had short red hair and green eyes, he hadn't noticed that in the Moondale's basement dungeon. He sat at the table, "Come here and sit with me, Gretchen." He did not want to use her nickname; he had already been personal enough with her. "I apologize for using the Attachment on you Gretchen. I hope you will forgive me. I did not choose you, nor do I feel that you are obliged to me in any way."

Gretchen cocked her head and looked oddly at him, "I don't understand, why would you apologize to me? Soldiers all volunteer for service; that includes the Attachment Spell. The King has attached to me as Martin and Moondale have, it is part of service. I follow orders, the King gave me to you." She smiled and said, "We should get you a bath and have sex, then you will be thinking better." She stood and walked toward the house.

Henry yelled orders. "Stop, get back here and sit down. First, I want food and an explanation. Why do they use perfectly good soldiers and drain the power from them? Your powers can be used for so much more."

She stood shocked, not even knowing what to answer. "I told you I am a soldier under their orders. I am ordered to be yours; beyond that, I do not know. I do not know what you want Count. Do you not want to use me? I can't return, they told me they would drain me to death. I have no place to go."

Ski came back with food, and they sat down. Henry said. "I understand Gretchen. However, my household is full here at Belissa. Give me time to consider this. In the meantime, go to the barracks. See a man named Paxton, he will give you duties. Follow that trail it will lead you right to him."

Henry devoured his food with Ski watching. Finally, Henry asked, "What did you find out while I was running off steam?"

Ski sighed, "Not too much. We have all been playing babysitter with Miss Gretchen, and I was hesitant to do much at the lab with her eyes on me. Henry, I need the details of how this affects you too. Gretchen gave me some idea of how she feels when the Attachment is made. She was not clear about the removal of it. I believe they drugged her or used some type of mind control."

Henry kept drinking water, "What makes you think that?"

Ski said, "When you ran off she was acting like she was drugged she didn't make much sense. I cleaned up her neck and then she began answering all my questions. As she became more lucid, she stopped talking altogether. Another thing, Ruth washed her uniform, the name that was sewn inside is Phobia Davenport, not Gretchen. What to do with her; which is the question?"

Henry pushed back from the table. "She can't stay here. I acted kindly to the King's young daughter he is using my sympathy for young girls with Attachments spells to his advantage. I think it would be best if I kill her."

Ski dropped his jaw, "Henry, you cannot be serious. I am beginning to think this Attachment Spell has gone to your head."

Henry smiled, "Ski, relax. She seems amiable to orders, and the King said after using the Attachment, she would be loyal to me. I wonder how deep that loyalty goes. Have you given her a thorough exam on her throat yet?"

Ski said, "Not yet."

Henry said, "Good, we will start there. I need a bath I will meet you in the lab office in twenty minutes."

Ski and Henry invited Gretchen for some wine, then drugged her. They had plenty of time to examine her and ask some questions about the spells. Henry asked her about what she knew of the King, Moondale, and Martin. They gathered beneficial information about the working of their minds. The most critical piece was Moondale used magic from Paldao to make the Attachments. It was a small thing she overheard one time. The Queen had told him Devon and Ernst were headed to the Paldao. Henry wondered if it was to get more Unicorn dust. Casandra was going there next; he would have Addison to get her out of there.

Ski created a spell that clouded her mind, giving her the illusion she had slept with Henry. Then Henry sent her out with Stephen to guard an order going to the East and Parragon. She happily obeyed, this trip would keep her gone for months; long after the Kings death. She would die with the King if she were attached to him, and if not, Henry would decide what to do with her when she returned. He would enjoy watching the King's reaction to the fabrication he planned to tell the King; he had accidentally killed her in a fit of lust. That thought amused Henry for the rest of the day.

He worked day and night getting the orders together for his Brother's coronation. He did not want to spend time constructing the apartment at the Castle, so he decided to have Ruth go with him. She hired locals to help her decorate and remodel. Henry was on the road in less than two days. He took orders to be shipped by sea to Mento just to cut his stay at the Castle short, he could not wait to get to Traza to see Casandra.

Winter's End at Traza

Shelton's wings were more prominent than any Pegasus Eric had ever seen, his wingspan extended over forty feet. When Shelton would glide, Casandra laid on his neck, together they looked like one large bird. Eric had never seen anything so remarkable or graceful.

They landed for lunch in Fuga a village on the shore of the Bayonne Ocean; from the outside tables of the Inn, they could see the Bluffs of Traza which was less than twenty-five miles away. Eric noticed the color of the sea was a match to Casandra's eyes. As he observed her from across the table, he realized she had never been more animated or engaged in life. She was genuinely alive, authentic, and in the present.

They were served fruity drinks and trays of fresh exotic vegetables with spicy sauces. Soft bread and platters of fish were passed around. The girls loved it. Eric had a feeling the men wanted meat.

The Pegasus grazed close by; occasionally Casandra would look to Shelton and smile. Eric smiled to himself she was in love with that animal. He said, "Casandra what will you do when we reach Tzuha we rented a house for the next few weeks, and your Shelton must sleep in the barn."

Casandra laughed, "Perhaps I will sleep in the barn with him."

Marion scolded, "Casandra I know you love being in nature, but speaking for those of us who were forced to live all the time outdoors; I prefer a bed with clean sheets and a roof over my head. I do not miss my life growing up in the glen. Do not expect me to sleep with your Pegasus."

Casandra sipped her drink, "Marion, I expect you to continue sleeping with Addison like you have ever since we have left Marais." Everyone laughed, but Marion turned red. Casandra leaned into her friend and said, "I am only teasing you, Marion, I can't say I blame you for choosing Addison over Shelton or me."

Addison looked at her, "Should Henry be jealous?"

Casandra recognized she had not thought of Henry all day. Where had her thoughts been she was just filled with happiness and joy. Was this mindfulness? If so, this was the first time in her life she had felt mindfulness since she was a child. Suddenly her heart fell, she missed Henry. She leaned forward to look at Addison, "Addison can you speak to Henry?"

Addison set his fork down, "Not very well, Casandra, we are too far apart. I did get the thought that Martin and the Prince were either in the Paldao Plains or soon to be." Her face fell, and Addison could see the weight of her circumstance fall on her shoulders. "I actually can't wait to see Henry's face when he sees Shelton he will not believe it. We spent months here, at least a half of a year, negotiating for our herd. It took Henry and me weeks before the Pegasus would let us ride them. Now that I think of it, Henry is going to be jealous of you. Probably Shelton too you love him way too much."

Casandra pushed her plate away, "I hope you all understand that the match of Sheldon and myself is not normal, he is more than an ordinary animal. He is my connection to the Night, Eric knows." She glanced across the table at Eric, "When we leave for Diamante I will explain until then, everyone should trust Shelton."

Grace said, "That is why you fly freely with no fear. I have never seen you happier or more at peace then gliding on his back."

The Professor smiled, "I agree, Grace. You are in the moment while you fly, enfolded in mindfulness, bursting with the presence. Enjoy it but learn how to control it. To succeed with your plan to defeat the King, who thrives on the negative, you must command the presence. Do you understand what I am saying to you, Casandra?"

Casandra looked at the sea she understood him correctly. "Yes Professor, I am only the vehicle for the presence, just as Shelton is the vehicle for the Night." The table had quieted she hated the solemn mood she had brought to them. "I was wondering about that as I was in the air today. I was going to ask you about in private."

Marion said, "My friend your fight with the King is not today! We are on holiday, and I suggest we continue having fun." She lifted her glass, "To Sheldon, the biggest, most beautiful Pegasus ever."

Eric said, "I will drink to that. Casandra, this is your time of freedom you have the rest of your life to resolve the world's woes." He raised his glass. "To the Countess, I wish you a long life filled with love and many children."

The table all toasted her, and she felt the love and support around her. Addison added, "One word of warning to all of you, Pegasus hate ocean waters. The salt water naturally hides magic; they have a hard time getting their bearings over the sea. When we fly out, we must stay over the buffs or beaches."

Eric added, "Thankfully we haven't far to fly, but be careful over the bluffs as there are updrafts and currents in the air that can clutch us and bring us careening down to the rocks."

Shelton was suddenly standing next to them. Eric heard Shelton say. He knows nothing, Casandra, I can fly over water and never smash into anything.

Eric turned to Shelton, "I heard that Shelton. If you are an exception to this rule, tell me. Do not ridicule me!" Everyone but Casandra was at a loss to what had made Eric explode.

Casandra snickered, "Shelton don't be rude apologize at once, Eric is your friend."

Addison's head cocked, "Eric, you can hear Shelton too. I was wondering about that; you both communicate with him mentally. I wonder if I can?" Addison got up from the table and went to Sheldon and placed his hand on his head. He said out loud, "Shelton you can fly out over the sea this is wonderful news. However, the trip over the Bayonne Ocean is long. It would be best if you could sail on a ship for most of it, can you do that?"

Shelton laughed. I can do anything Addison Rakie, I am pure magic.

"Yes, I can see that. I am sure the King's men will too. You and Casandra will need to cover that while we are in Tzuha, your beauty and size will attract enough attention. This is all wonderful news we had to hire Shamans to take our herd to Belissa this takes much off my mind. Thank you, Shelton."

The Creation of the King

Henry and his men landed in the courtyard of the Castle and were met by his Brother, Richard. He walked to them. "Henry, we have been expecting you. I have been delegated to showing you to the new quarters assigned to you. Please follow me."

Henry climbed from his Pegasus, "Paxton. Please, take care of the delivery to the Castle and go to the barracks I will find you later. Ruth and Bob, bring your workers. We will see what my good Brother has given us for living quarters."

They walked into the Castle and followed Richard through the entry and down the first corridor to the outer ring of buildings around the Castle. Richard stopped at the last apartment and handed Henry a key to the door. Richard said, "Henry, here are your apartments they have not been used for years. Dillon had assigned better for you, but I thought the Emperor would be insulted if we put him in the outer ring. This is all that is available, you can move to the inner circle when the festivities are over. It seems so many are coming for the Coronation we could not spare the expense to renovate as many as we need. You have unlimited monies I am sure this will be no burden to you." Richard stood smiling like a cat that swallowed a giant mouse.

Henry took the key and said, "Thank you, Richard, this is fine. So, the Emperor is not only entering the land of Diamante but the inner

Castle as well. I wonder how many thousands of years since an Emperor has attended a Diamante Kings Coronation?"

"Three thousand, five hundred and seventy-eight years. I bet you expect some kind of boon from us that you got the Emperor here. Well, not from me, Little Brother." Richard snarled at him. "I know this is just some of your game playing. I will not play with you. I don't trust or like you, and I never will." Henry gave him his best-wicked smile, and Richard turned and walk away saying, "Dinner is at seven you are expected, do not be late."

Henry opened the door to a room with an entrance that was very familiar to him; his Brother's apartment. When Harry came of age, he requested an outer apartment because he wanted freedom of the watchful eye of his Father and the Brothers. Henry knew his Mother had closed and sealed Harry's apartment after his death. She had unlocked it for Henry, or they would not have been allowed to walk in. The outer walls of the Castle were built of black onyx, known for repelling magic and protection for the inner Castle. However, the inside of the apartment was made with red jasper floors and white porcelain walls. Usually, the effect was like walking from night into day, but Harry's home was nothing but grey. Cobwebs covered the walls and doors, he pulled them down and walked into the main room. Its magnificent stone fireplace reached up to the three stories of the apartment. Two comfortable chairs sat opposite each other in front of the fireplace. He remembered all the talks they had sitting there. He wanted to fall down and cry, he felt all the pain and sorrow as if Harry had just died. Richard did this on purpose he wanted Henry to feel pain every time he came to his Castle home.

"Henry…Henry, don't let him do this to you," He heard his Mother's voice. Henry turned to see her standing in the entryway. "I sealed this thinking someday I would come back and find my Son, and that the tragedy ever happened. When Dillion told me the Emperor had accepted our invitation, I knew this was the only space left to accommodate you and your friends. At first, I protested, but then I had a dream of Harry, I knew it was time. I came yesterday to clean, but I could not turn the key. I am so sorry I could not clean this up for you." She just stood in the doorway looking as pained and broken as Henry felt. He went to her and pulled the Queen into his arms, and they both cried.

Henry spoke, "I am happy to be here Mother, I practically lived here with him. I never liked my apartment at the Castle. He and I certainly got into a lot more fun here away from Father." They both laughed. "Harry was the one full of fun never serious or thinking ahead about a thing."

The Queen stepped back. "Yes. That is exactly what killed him, he never thought about his actions. Unlike you who has never made a move without thinking three moves ahead. I do hope you are doing that now my darling boy."

Henry smiled at his Mother. "More than three these days. Unwittingly Richard has helped me out immensely. Harry and I spent a lot of time placing charms and alarms in here, if they are still working, this will be an ideal place to make plans and have conversations of importance. Mother, can you help me decide how to fix this place up? I brought workers, and I know what I like, but I want Casandra to be comfortable here too."

His Mother smiled, "I will Henry. I have time now if you are willing, but I don't know your Bride. Tell me what she is like and perhaps I can recommend some changes besides a good cleaning, this place is dirty." She touched the chair, and the fabric fell from the chair. "Well, we need new furniture. How does she dress and what does she like?"

Henry smiled, "She loves the outdoors, animals, and books. She doesn't eat meat often, and she is devout in her belief of the Night. She wears mostly greens and blues but looks the best in white and diamonds. I would like to see her in red. I think that would be a wonderful color for her. Although she is not flashy, she does radiate. I know that sounds strange, but I see brilliant energy when I look at her. I can't take my eyes off her. Her eyes are aqua the color of the Bayonne Ocean, and her hair is as black as a raven. Her lips are the color of the deep red rose of our Crest." He stopped and laughed. "I am not much help, am I?"

His Mother hugged him, "No Henry, I can see exactly who she is. You are truly in love with her don't let your Brothers see this. Now we need to get to work."

Ruth's crew came in, and they all used magic to clean and go through his Brother's belongings. Henry and the Queen decided what to keep and what to store, and the Queen and Ruth gave recommendations of how to decorate. It was agreed they would all shop together the next day.

Henry had forgotten what a fantastic library Harry kept and worked all afternoon to restore it. To his delight, Henry found the charms he and his Brother enchanted were still working. He updated them and added a few new ones along with conjuring a big white Dane to guard the place, and a black cat with aqua eyes to hunt down mice.

Henry bathed and went to dinner at the Castle. He spent the evening with his Father and Dillion planning the next moves of their plan. On his walk back to the apartment, Henry noticed nightingales on the balcony of the bedroom. He would check on that in the morning. Henry wanted to leave now for Traza, but the Hermit had sent him detailed instructions of a shopping list. He really was not looking forward to the visit with her. Henry hoped he had gotten the international account open in Casandra's name in time. Although he had no idea why Casandra needed twenty million fabs. What would she buy for that amount of money and how in the world did the Hermit have millions of fab in her back pocket? All questions he would ask Casandra when he saw her.

The Enchantment of the Cliff of Winter's End

Casandra soared over the sea as Shelton dove to the waves then swooping her high in the air. They spun and twisted through the air while she squealed in delight like a child of five. All her friends and Elf army laughed at her childish behavior, but they also felt the great magic she was producing. Not one of them had ever been healthier, happier, or more at peace.

Before they knew it, the Winter's End sign was on the cliffs overlooking the Bayonne Ocean. The three-story white wooden house was perched on the end of the cliffs just before the land dipped down to the sea. Eric had chosen it for the security, two sides dropped sixty feet to a jagged rock bed. No other home came within five hundred yards of the house which was surrounded by eleven-foot stone walls. It had a barn, barracks for the men, and ten bedrooms. The Emperor had used the house on many occasions, it belonged to a good friend. It was the King of Cielo's winter home hence the name Winter's End. Cielo was noted for brutally cold winters, anyone with fabs would leave for warmer locations. The season of summer was not quite there, but the beaches and home were filling with students and partiers.

Their party dropped to the lawn that sloped to the sea while Addison took the girls to the house and Eric took the Pegasus to the barn. Eric set up his men and the schedule for the guards. Then he returned to the house. Eric had always loved the home; it was what he had chosen for his own home, although he rarely got to use it. The floors were natural wood, the walls white, and the furnishings were simple straight lines made of beech. The patterns and colors were the blues of the ocean, the bright colors of birds and greens of the tropical plants and trees. The relaxing sounds of the sea and the smells of the white waxy flowers of the Hybirdiea brought the tropics indoors.

Addison came down the stairs. "This home is beautiful. It is like a hotel every room has its own bath and sitting room. Marion is taking a bath; she could not wait. She will be happy now, nature is not her friend. How is the security?"

"It is great, no one can climb up the cliffs, and the stone fence is easy to monitor with charms and men." Eric went to the bar and fixed a drink. "Can I get you something? The servants will be here in the morning; we are here early, so dinner will be up to us this evening. Some of my men went out to get food for them."

Addison said, "I remember a restaurant on the beach that served the best-broiled sea fish. I think we could walk."

"I think I know the one; that is a great idea. When will Henry be here?" Eric stopped and looked at the stairs, Grace was coming down in a white gauzy dress that hugged her body. Addison turned and looked at Grace.

Addison said. "Henry will be here before the end of the week perhaps in a day or two, he is at the Castle today. Grace you look lovely, can Eric get you a drink?"

Grace walked to the bar and said, "Yes something refreshing please."

Marion came running down the stairs. "I am starved. The bathtub is wonderful, but where is everyone?"

Addison walked to her and gave her a kiss. "We are going out for dinner. I haven't seen the Professor, Moori, or Casandra we should go get them." They both left to find them.

Eric came around the bar to Grace and handed her the drink he made. He said, "You are beautiful, Grace. I can't wait for Henry to get here so I don't have watch Casandra so closely and I can look at you more."

She smiled took his drink and hers and set them on the table then took him into her arms and kissed him. "I have felt guilty sleeping with you every night when we should have been watching Casandra."

Eric said, "We have always had eyes on her if not us, Addison or the men." He hesitated, "Except the night on Pegagus Plains, in the trees. I don't know what happened to me. I never fall asleep while standing guard."

Grace hugged him. "Something happened that night, we were all put in a spell. I overheard Casandra and Moori whispering, there is something they are not sharing. Now that Moori is here, she is keeping Casandra to herself. I don't like it."

Eric looked to the stairs, "Henry is coming soon, and then we will all be divided from them. They are in love. This land is the land of love."

The Preparations for Casandra

Henry woke early and went up to the attic to investigate the birds, as he thought, they were the King's spies. He chased them out and told the workmen to attend to that first. After a quick breakfast, Henry told Ruth he was going out to get his errands completed so he could leave by evening. She reminded him to meet the Queen and her at the Roupart furnishings at one, and he was to have tea with his Father before he could leave. Henry came into the kitchen with a large painting. "Ruth, I found this painting of Belissa in the attic could you clean it up. Harry had it hanging over the fireplace in the living room. I would like it to return there. The frame is broken too. I wonder why it was up in the attic. Oh, there is some furniture up there too. We may be able to use it in one of the guest rooms. I will see you at Roupart."

Henry left the Castle and made his way to the streets of Winsette to fulfill his list. He needed to order paper for himself, bottles for his lab, and materials for Ski's lab. Then he would begin on the Hermit list, purple ink made from lilac, green vanishing paper, a gold chain thirty inches long, and snakeskin gloves. Hours later Henry felt lucky he found the ink and vanishing stationary at the parchment store. Now he was in the jeweler getting the gold chain when he spied a black and white cougar pendant with ruby eyes if it only it had aqua eyes he would buy it for Casandra.

“I am Dennis may I help you, Sir?” The attendant was standing in front of him. “Pardon me, but are you a Rakie?”

The Count grinned, “I am Henry Rakie, and yes, you may help me. I need a simple gold chain thirty inches long.”

The man tilted his head and said, “Yes Count, I saw you looking at the Leopard brooch I thought that would be your purchase.”

Henry laughed, “I thought it was a cougar. I wish it had aqua stones for the eyes.”

The man reached in the case removed it and placed it on a black cloth. The Leopard held a red rose of small rubies in its paws but had eyes of aqua quartz. “Is this more to your liking Count?”

Henry stood up straighter, “Do you know my Bride Sir?”

He smiled and said, “I fashioned her a crown. I worked for the jeweler at the North Castle.”

Henry grinned and said, “I will take it, the pin and the gold chain. Maybe you could suggest a wedding ring. Also, Dennis, do you know where I can find snakeskin gloves?”

Dennis chuckled, “I can help you with everything but the gloves. I have no idea where you will find those.”

Henry had just enough time to have a quick lunch before meeting the Queen. Then he walked into Roupart just as the Queen drove up in her carriage. “My darling Son, you are just on time, ready to shop?”

Henry laughed, “No, I have had my fill of shopping. I told you to pick everything, I meant it.”

“I refuse to pick the bed that is personal to you and Casandra.” The Queen grabbed his arm and took him through the door where Bob and Ruth were already inside waiting.

The Queen and Ruth began choosing couches and chairs, tables, and beds. Henry didn’t care for one bed he saw. A salesman approached his Mother and recognized her as the Queen. He pardoned himself and returned with the owner who began showing them more furnishings.

Henry was bored, he told Bob to decide on the beds and began to wander around the store. He was drawn to a piece of furniture that fascinated him, it was put together like a puzzle, with inlaid woods.

The owner came to Henry, "Count, you don't remember me, Brandon Roupart. Well, it was a long time ago. I furnished your apartments when you were young, and I went to school with your Brother.

I am looking forward to the Coronation and Ball and of course meeting your bride. Congratulations."

Henry wondered which Brother. "Thank you. Yes everyone is excited about the coronation. I am sorry I do not remember you, which Brother attended school with you?"

Roupart reluctantly said. "Richard. I find it interesting this piece of furniture caught your eye. Richard admired it just a month ago himself." Brandon kept a straight face, looked at the piece, and said no more.

Alright, Henry would play he was bored with shopping anyway. "Really. I was just trying to figure out what this is. It appears to be a very old and an odd piece to have in here."

Roupart smiled, "Yes, it is old. I bought it from an estate sale a few months ago. I often buy pieces that hold history or an interesting story. This piece is both, it is a secretary, look." He began pulling out pieces and folding down hidden shelves soon it turned into a bookshelf with a built-in desk. Drawers and nooks opened with hidden little crannies. Henry was fascinated. Roupart pointed to the desk. "See this?" In the center of the desk was a carved cat, it looked like the leopard pin he had in his pocket. "This piece was handmade, a wedding gift for the Duchess of Savilla. Commissioned by your Grandfather Henry Rakie the first, the Father of King Winsette. It is a sad story that she killed her husband the Duke then ran off never to be heard of again. The story is; Henry bargained for her as a liaison when that failed he courted her, but she married another. Then again so did your Grandfather. The tale says he loved her to his dying day. He was your namesake, wasn't he, you should talk to Richard about it. He knew the whole story when he came in here and insisted I give him this, saying it belonged to your family."

Henry said. "You didn't, did you? This belongs to the Savilla family, not him."

Roupart laughed, "I made him pay. He returned it after two weeks, saying his wife hated it. Royals often do that. They take furnishings and return them after their parties and guests are gone. Of course, that makes him the second Rakie to swindle me, which brings me to the uncomfortable subject of payment."

Henry held up his hand, reached into his pocket handed him a piece of paper, "My letter of credit. My bank is just across the street, please take it over there and check it. I understand, Roupart, most of my Brothers are unscrupulous. Myself, I don't like most of them and trust even fewer of them." Henry flashed his wicked smile, and Roupart bowed, took the letter and headed out the door to the bank.

Henry turned his attention to the desk, he studied it carefully. The whole desk was a puzzle, Richard knew it. Henry began to move parts and pushing on the wooden inlaid when suddenly the oval carving of the cougar popped open. Henry reached in and found an envelope. It was addressed to the Duchess but never opened, sealed with wax that was cracked and aged. He heard the front door to the store open and quickly put the letter back and closed the compartment.

Roupart handed Henry the letter and bowed, "It seems you can buy my entire store. I am sorry Henry, I hope I didn't embarrass you." Henry started to say something, but Roupart stopped him. "Richard is a bastard, and I hate having to deal with him. I thought he sent you here because of your interest in the desk. I apologize could we start over?"

Henry threw his head back and roared laughing, "Roupart, you are funny. I thought you were playing games with me; not that I don't like games or what kind of Diamante would I be. Here you were protecting your livelihood as a businessman should, which is what I am."

Roupart reached out his hand, "I like games too, but let's do business first. What can I sell you?"

Henry shook his hand; he could feel Roupart's energy of honesty and friendliness. No wonder Richard couldn't deal with him. Henry said, "My Mother is picking the furnishings, whatever she decides will be fine. I do need a bed, but what I really need are snake skinned gloves for a woman."

Roupart smiled and said, "You have come to the right place. I told you I buy things of historical interest, that is historic." Roupart grinned, "Snakeskin gloves dates from about the time of this desk." Henry was surprised, Roupart was a fascinating man. Roupart took his elbow then walked him through the store to the back, through double doors into a room stockpiled with everything. It was the biggest warehouse of things Henry ever saw.

He stopped dead and said, "Roupart you lied, I don't believe I have enough money to buy your store. Good night man how much is back here?"

Roupart laughed heartily and strode down an aisle filled with furniture. "You're right Henry, sorry again. I did lie. I don't let everyone know about this. I will just say, I have many clients I deal with, and I cater to their tastes. Much of this is sold, or soon to be." They stopped at a four-poster bed that was made from bones.

Henry had touched it before he realized what it was made of. "Roupart is this what I think it is?"

Roupart chortled, "It has bones of every species of Witch that has ever lived. It is sold, Henry. Sorry, you can't have this, and please don't ask who bought it. Now to the gloves. I know I placed them here for the client to look at." He opened drawers and finally came up with two pairs of women's gloves. "Here we are. This Henry is a piece of history. These gloves were worn by young Sorcerers to keep from being overcome by the charms of Warlocks. Of course, now they have all learned ways to combat the charms and spells in the Academy. However, the gloves are beautiful and ingenious. They conform to any size hand, they shrink to fit like skin. Best of all they change color to match any ensemble. What more could a Sorcerer want." Roupart put one, and they practically disappeared. "I have two pairs; these are the best the others are worn."

Henry just looked at this odd man. Roupart was so enthused about his historical things. "I will take both." Henry smiled.

"Excellent. Oh, I have one more thing to show you, follow me. Henry, all the people of the city and country, are so excited about the pairing of you and the High Sorceress. Open trade is going to make us all rich, and it has already started." He kept walking around boxes and crates, then they came to something covered in cloth. "Here, Henry here is the bed for you." He pulled off the cloth, and a stunning wooden canopy bed carved with vines and roses appeared with unicorns carved into the headboard. "This bed is carved from the petrified wood of the North Woods. It is said to be the bed of Queen Hezebala, she traveled with it. It was left here on this continent during the Great

War. It recently came into my possession from a brothel in Cielo. Nice history, to think of the things that were done in this bed. Hmm."

Henry did not know what to think of Roupart, but he did like the bed. "Best of all Henry, it has your symbols. Look, roses and vines on all four posts and look inside. Through the vines, you can see a leopard spying down at you."

Henry saw the leopard but what were they doing in the canopy? Mating, they were mating. "Roupart the rose is my emblem but how is leopard my symbol?"

"Oh, Henry I am sorry that was to be a surprise. The women and businessmen are making little flags to wave at the parade, with the symbol of the rose for Rakie and the leopard, for the De Volt family. It's the same symbol that is on the desk, that is where we got the idea."

Henry ran his hand through his hair, "We are having a parade? This is too much Roupart, I am only a Count. My brothers will not like a parade for Casandra and I."

"Dillon thought it was a wonderful idea, now I do like that Brother of yours. It's a parade for his Coronation. We felt the flags would be a wonderful way to honor the Emperor for consenting to your match with the Countess." Roupart stood, smiling.

Henry couldn't help but like this odd man. "Well, I guess I must take this bed. I have new bedding, and whatever you do; do not tell anyone it came from a brothel. That history is to remain between us."

Roupart laughed and said, "As you wish Count. It has matching tables, chest, and wardrobe."

Henry threw back his head, laughing and said. "Yes Roupart, I will take the set and some chairs. Let's go see what my Mother has picked out."

Henry approved of all the purchases and went to Roupart's office to make the payment. Henry closed the door and said, "Roupart, would you like to play a game with me?" Roupart smiled, and Henry continued, "Add that secretary to my bill. I want it sent to the Hermit of Savilla, secretly."

"Richards wife Suzanne comes in here regularly, he will notice." Roupart smiled.

Henry said, "I am counting on it. When he does refuse to tell him who bought it. Infer that for a price you might reveal the owner. When he has paid handsomely enough, tell him I bought it. However, tell him you delivered it to Belissa Villa. Can you do that for me." Henry opened his pocket and pulled out twenty gold coins.

Roupart stopped him, "Henry I have taken enough of your money today; besides you are just doing this to aggravate him, aren't you? Henry, you found the hidden drawer, didn't you?" He slapped the desk with glee.

Henry laughed, "You did too and didn't open the letter?"

"What, and spoil the next person's fun, never." Roupart got serious, "Does that letter belong to the Duchess?"

Henry nodded and said, "I believe it does Roupart."

"I would be most pleased and honored to play with you Henry, but I will name my price. I would like introductions to your Sorceress at the parade in front of your stupid Brother Richard." The odd little man, half bald and as thin as a rail, crossed his arms and stared at Henry.

Henry glowed, and said, "It's a deal, but I think you and your wife should come to the Coronation Ball to play this out. I will see you get tickets this afternoon. I have a feeling this is the beginning of a great friendship."

Roupart opened his top desk drawer and pulled out one of Henry's best wines. "Henry, you have just given my wife the best present of her life. Come to think of it probably me, too. She will love me for this!" Roupart poured, and they had a glass, or two.

The Beaches of Traza

The restaurant on the beach was delectable, and afterward, they found a bar with exotic drinks. Along the shore, musicians played bizarre instruments of strings and drums which made erotic music. Both Eric and Addison knew the dances, and they taught the girls the moves and steps. They danced and drank well into the night. Casandra walked with Moori back to the beach house. Everyone was drunk except her; she didn't think the spell the Hermit gave her as much fun. She waited for Moori to sleep then went down to the barn to sleep with Shelton. Eric's men woke him to tell him Casandra was sleeping in the barn. He was still drunk but went to the barn; curled up next to her and went to sleep.

The group spent the next day's strolling the beach and shops that lined the boulevard. Marion was in heaven again, shopping. However, this shopping trip had Casandra's attention. The pottery, jewelry, and fabrics were all so different and colorful she had never seen anything like it. She bought gifts for everyone, but the tea set she found for Mags was her favorite. She wished she had bought one for herself.

They stopped for lunch at a seaside inn and watched the boats in the harbor and the beachgoers while they ate. A small sailboat caught Casandra's eye. Addison noticed, "Casandra, have you ever sailed?"

Casandra said, "No, I have been on large boats, but never a small sailing ship. That one is bouncing around on the sea, it looks like fun."

Addison said, "It is. Eric let's go see if we can charter a boat tomorrow."

Eric agreed, "That is a great idea, what do you want to do this afternoon. Can it please be not shopping."

Marion answered, "I want to swim."

"The water will still be cold, but you are welcome to try." Addison gave her a questioning look.

"I'll try, but on our way back I want to stop at the teashop. I want a tea set for myself." Casandra smiled.

Marion said, "Casandra, let me get it for you. I have been searching for a wedding gift, and I would like to have you pick it out."

After lunch, Eric and Grace went off to see about chartering a sailboat. Addison, Marion, and Casandra made their way back to the teashop. The Professor and Moori wanted to return to the house. Casandra picked out a lime green teapot with the white waxflower that was everywhere on the beaches. It would be an excellent way to remember this trip.

The sales lady said she had cups to match and Marion pushed her outside saying, "I want something to be a surprise, find something to look at, nosey."

Casandra and Addison walked to a hat booth just outside the teashop. Casandra started trying on hats, and Addison teased her about everyone she put on her head. Casandra noticed a young man staring at her. Marion called Addison, she was having trouble with the money exchange. They walked back into the shop, and Marion told her to stay up front and not to look at her purchase.

Casandra was looking through some glassware when the young man from the street said from behind her, "Beautiful choice, just like you."

Casandra spun around, the voice was familiar, but the face was not. "Do I know you?"

He said, "I don't believe so. If I had ever met you…you would have remembered. Are you on holiday?"

Casandra said, "I am. Your voice sounds so memorable, you remind me of someone."

He said, "By your curt answers, I believe you do not like that someone. I am not him, but I will apologize for any hurt he has caused you. May I have your name, and perhaps a dance this evening on the beach?"

Casandra touched the ruby of the bracelet the Hermit had given her. Addison was immediately by her side. He said, "Is this man bothering you, Dear?"

Casandra took Addison's arm, "He was just flirting with me darling, good thing I do not have a jealous boyfriend."

The man bowed to Addison and in a very different voice said, "I am so sorry, the young lady did not tell me she was taken. Madame." He turned to leave, and the glass Casandra was holding shattered in her hands. She stood still in shock while watching her hand bleed badly with a large piece of glass protruding. How could that have happened? The young man grabbed her hand in both of his. He waved his hand, and the glass shards were removed; another hand wave and the blood disappeared. He rubbed his hands over her, and she was practically healed within seconds, her hand looked normal.

Casandra looked at Addison he was sizing up the man. "Sir, who are you?"

He smiled and said, "I am a physician, Doctor Malcolm, here on holiday."

Casandra said, "Thank you, that was the quickest I have ever been healed. Where are you from?"

He said, "Alia Islands." Their conversation was interrupted by the Shopkeeper and Marion rushing to see what happened. The Doctor handed the shopkeeper some gold, "Allow me to pay for the broken glass for bothering you two on your holiday. Good day." He turned, and Addison followed him out the door. Marion was finished with her purchase they followed and found Addison down the street looking in all directions. Marion wanted to know everything that had happened.

When they reached Addison, Marion said, "That was weird, and you two played boyfriend and girlfriends, I don't think I like that."

Addison gave her a look of aggravation. "We were playing Marion. I don't like this, he disappeared faster than he healed you. He is a strong healing wizard. I am glad you called me, but what prompted it, tell me your conversation."

Casandra had a shiver run up her back, and she told Addison she called him because she had a strange feeling about his voice. She gave him word for word their conversation, and how he had changed his voice.

They walked back to Winters End and there the event was repeated for Eric and the guard. They all listened and, in the end, they all fell silent. Casandra couldn't help but to look at her healed hand. Then she said, "I can't get over how fast he healed my hand. Also, why would that glass just break in my hand like that? I saw the cuts, they were deep? Look, now my hand appears as if it never happened."

The Professor came to look at her hand closely. "He must be a powerful wizard to heal that fast. If he is indeed a physician, I can find him in the directory. Casandra play the man's voice back for me."

Casandra sat down, closed her eyes and the Professor stood behind her, placing both hands over her ears. She imagined the first conversation again, but this time she heard who it was. Her eyes flashed open, she looked to the Professor, and his face was grim. He shook his head yes. Casandra covered her face with her hands. Eric stood and practically screamed, "Who was it?"

The Professor quietly said, "The Prince of Hex, Devon."

Addison stood and started pacing, then screamed out loud. "Henry, hear me! Get here fast! Devon has Casandra's blood!"

The Invitation

Henry had gone with his Mother to the Kings chamber after the shopping trip, Dillion was there with his wife, Audrey. Henry relayed the shopping experience at Roupart's furniture store. When he told them of the little trick he was playing on Richard; Dillon said he would have his Page get an invitation for Roupart and his wife out that very evening.

Henry's Father said, "I want that man seated next to me at dinner. I want to see Richards face. I might just think of something to add fuel to the story about the Secretary."

They were all enjoying a laugh when Henry got the message from Addison, something was wrong. He stood and started pacing the room.

Dillon said, "What is wrong Henry?"

Henry looked at him, "I don't understand all of it, Dillion. I am too far away from Addison. I need to leave now! They are in trouble."

Dillion said, "Can I help?"

Henry said, "Devon has Casandra's blood. Can I use your overseas carriage?"

Dillion went to his door and told the Marshall to have the carriage brought to the courtyard immediately and get a travel bag from Ruth.

Henry's Father said. "What does that mean, Devon has Casandra's blood?"

Dillion said, "Unfortunately I know exactly what that means. Henry, I will walk you to the carriage. Father, I will return and explain."

They ran down the stairs taking them two at a time. Audrey, Dillion's wife, stood at the carriage with an oblong black box. "Here Henry, I pray to the Night you will not need this but take it just in case."

Dillion opened the door and shoved Henry in, then sat next to him. "Henry that box contains a very sharp knife used by wizard physicians to remove intricate spells. That knife was used to remove an Attachment Spell someone put on my Daughter-in-law."

Henry looked in disbelief, "You know about this."

Dillion said, "Some, but not enough. The wizard that helped us knew much about it and is now dead. Get to her fast if they put an Attachment on her you only have two days to remove it. We will talk in depth about this when you return. Get back here in one piece. I need you, or I will be dead." He grabbed Henry and hugged him. "I have always loved you, brat."

Henry had tears in his eyes, "Me too."

Paxton opened the door holding the travel bags, "I am coming with you." Dillion jumped out of the carriage and Paxton jumped in, ordering the driver to Traza.

Knowledge of the Curse

Casandra held her hands in tight fists and walked to Addison. She glared at him and asked, "Why would the Prince need my blood?" She waited, but Addison only stared back, in a lower voice she asked, "You know why Addison what has he planned?" Addison immediately shielded himself, as he knew she would command him at any second. She was burning inside why was there a secret? She turned to Eric, and he looked away. The Professor went to the bar to get a drink. Grace swallowed hard and clamped her mouth shut. Marion quietly left the room.

She turned to Eric, "Does everyone here know but me?" Eric took a deep breath and stared back at her crossing his arms, the typical stance he took while acting like her superior. She was enraged, but she pushed the anger to the ground and calmly raised one eyebrow and said, "You know better than try to keep a secret from me. This will not end well." She turned and walked toward the stairs. She would find out from Marion she was easy to squeeze out the truth.

Eric came after her, "Casandra where do you think you are going? Get back here this very moment!"

Cassandra was standing on the first stair, Eric was below her, she glared at him. "You do not want me near you at this moment."

He stepped up to her and said, "I compel you to stop right there Casandra!"

She stopped and turned to face him, "I am not five years old Eric! And you are not my Father! DO NOT SPEAK TO ME IN THAT VOICE, OR I WILL HAVE YOU REMOVED FROM YOUR STATION!"

Eric thought he had to be careful, or she would put the house on fire. He didn't remember if he had ever made her this angry, but he could not let her know what she faced. Eric loved her too much for that. In a soft voice, he said, "Sweetheart, you must trust me. You will know when the time is right. None of us are sure about the spell or how it works. When Henry has a definitive remedy, we will include you, I promise. I know you did not mean what you just said to me, but my darling little girl, that was something close to what you told me once before. Remember the day with the Witch in the woods, the woman in the tree?"

This did not endear Casandra at all, she said, "That day. Oh yes, I remember it well. That day was a poor choice to use on me today! This day… today is nothing like that! Childhood memories will not appease me." She crossed her arms and tried desperately to release herself from his command to stand there. It didn't help everyone in the room was intently watching.

Eric took her hand, and sighed, "Very well I compel you to come with me and sit on the couch. And no speaking!" He took her arm, they walked to the couch, and she sat without speaking. Inside she was using all her power not to ignite all of them. He took both her hands and said, "I will have that flame you are holding you will be at peace in the count of three. One two three." A ball of fire the size of a man flew into his hands, "Grace open the door and help me." They walked outside and extinguished it with a water spout from the sea. He came back and sat next to her, "Here is what will happen. We will work out a plan, and you will sit and listen. You will also obey us. I compel you to follow my instructions. Breathe Casandra, slowly and deeply. He waited for her breath to return to normal, "Now you may move and talk."

Casandra felt better, the Professor handed her a drink she just stared at it. Eric kept an eye on her but spoke to Addison. "Addison, I think we are safe in the house when do you think Henry will be here?"

Addison was too stunned to think he had never witnessed anything like that compulsion before, how did he do that? "I must ask…"

Eric just said, "We can talk later, we need to decide what to do next. Drink you drink sweetheart; I know you are thirsty." He raised the glass to her lips.

Addison wondered who gave Eric that much power over Casandra. Addison said, "We know it does take some time to make the Spell." He stopped himself because Casandra looked at him and took a drink. "However, Devon's talent is Weather, he could have us trapped easily. Henry is on his way; they are pushing the carriage. Henry thinks he will be here sometime in the morning. He also said they are about to go out into the ocean. They won't have any communication with us until he is closer. Henry loves you, Casandra."

She just looked at him and said nothing, she returned to staring into her glass.

Eric said, "Tell Henry his Bride is very stubborn, but she does love him."

Casandra looked up at Eric who smiled. She looked around, everyone had a grin on their face. Casandra wondered why they all thought this was so damned amusing, she returned to stare in her glass. After an hour of debate, nothing had been decided, and Casandra was weary. Holding back emotion was the most stressful of all for a Sorceress, and power was building again. Henry was still talking to Addison and Eric had sent men out to find a carriage to take them to a safer place. Grace had gone to see about Pegasus, they had returned the ones they leased, Shelton was the only one in the barn. They discussed finding a ship, but that would take time. They sent someone out to find out about that. They were hoping it would at least take a day for the Prince to make a Spell.

Eric's men informed him there were no carriages that were not booked, and no ships were sailing for two days, Grace could not find one Pegasus for rent or sale. Henry thought Devon's reach was no more than a mile or two. Maybe if they could rent a sailboat large enough to take them a mile or more out to sea Henry could pick up Casandra with the carriage. Casandra was fighting the overwhelming feeling of being a target. Now they wanted her to be a target on the ocean for Henry to find. She continued staring into her glass.

Then Eric came to her and retook her hand and said, "Tell us what you think, Casandra. Please, sweetheart, talk to us. I released you to speak you still say nothing." She just glared at him.

The Professor came over and sat down next to her, "Casandra, put into practice the Master's laws and help us solve this dilemma."

She closed her eyes and took a deep breath, and in her mind's eye she saw the Hermit, even she was smiling at her. She heard the Duchess say mentally. Tell them exactly what you are thinking girl, stand up to them. There is no one as powerful as you. You have forgotten who you are.

Casandra opened her eyes pushed Eric's hand away. She stood and walked to the bar and poured water into her glass. She gathered her power and turned to throw water over all of them and said, "I Casandra command silence, and be still!" They all looked at her surprised. "Be careful what you ask for Eric you are about to get it! I Casandra, release myself from all compulsions. You three smart gentlemen and Henry along with my Father, have been planning my every move. Not only on this fake holiday but throughout my life. Well…look at the fix you have me in now. I have been plotted and pushed into a nice cozy corner with no exit."

Eric tried to speak but could not. Casandra laughed and said, "How does it feel to have to hold your tongue General, be careful not to struggle too much, or you may swallow it. If I have had one day to myself in all my life, I will count myself grateful. Yet, the Night gave me just a few minutes with the Unicorn King on the plains while you all slept. For that one Night, I am eternally grateful because of this gift, I will discharge my life to the Night. It is for her to decide, not me, and definitely not any of you. I will tell you what I am going to do. I am dropping this stupid disguise and going to go soak in a tub of bubbles. You may stay down here and continue playing games with my life."

She took a full bottle of wine from the bar and walked to the top of the stairs and turned, "I release all of you from my spell. Now play nice." She ran to her room, took her robes and went to the bathroom. She locked the doors and placed a secrecy spell on it. Then she dropped the disguise and felt immediate relief, that was what she needed. She turned on the hot water, took off her clothes and got in holding the wine bottle.

Eric jumped up and shouted, “Guards, with me.” He ran to her room; her door was locked. He waved his hand and unlocked it.

Addison was right behind him. “Henry stop shouting. Eric, maybe you should give her a little time to think.”

Eric ran his hand through his hair, “I have been in charge of her for years. Never have I seen her act like this. I never saw her do that, command like that. I need to see her and know she is alright.” The Professor started to say something, but Eric stopped him. “You don’t understand the Empress has me spelled to take care of her, to know her, to love her. I cannot stand outside this door.” He pushed open the door and entered the sitting room, then the bedroom and finally, he went to the bathroom door. “Casandra, I know you can hear me come to the door and let me know you are alright or just speak to me. I will not leave until I see you.”

Casandra would let him stew, but then a voice quietly said, “You have all you need to know everything right with you Casandra look to your wrist.” She saw the bracelet and knew what she would do. She got out of the tub wrapped a towel loosely around her, so she could embarrass them a bit. She walked to the door and flung it open wide. All the guards, Addison and her friends looked away. Eric did not he had seen her naked before. She smiled and said. “Well, what do you want? Would you like to climb in the tub with me, Eric? It wouldn’t be the first time. Remember the day…”

Eric was fuming, “Casandra stop! I needed to know you were alright. I am posting a guard on your balcony and one in the sitting room and one at the door. I will send up dinner, and Moori will sleep with you tonight. I understand your need for a secrecy spell, but I will tear that down in two hours. Get your ranting over with by then because I will be attuned to you for the rest of this trip. Your holiday is over!” He slammed the door and started assigning his men.

Casandra smiled to herself, her plan worked. She would not need two hours, but she would make Eric tear down her spell just to aggravate him.

Devon's Desire

Devon ran to the house they had rented in a disappearance bubble. Martin was there with people he had gathered to party with. Some Devon knew, most were strangers, one young Witch would probably be Martin's Attachment for the Night. Devon said hello and ran to his room. Moondale had given him a small kit for making an Attachment if he happened to run into the Sorceress. He had thought he wouldn't be able to use it. Luck was with him today.

Ernst came in and pulled Martin into a private corner. "Have you seen Devon?"

Martin chuckled and patted Ernst's back, "Don't worry he just came in and ran upstairs. Did you lose him again?"

Ernst didn't think it was funny, "Yes in the marketplace. I hate it when he doesn't tell me what he is up to. He isn't in Hex or Bezier; he could find himself in real trouble here. There isn't much the King can do here to save his hide from the jailer."

"Let me talk to him; this tonic of Henry's may help with the addiction, but he is not acting right." Martin handed Ernst his wine glass and marched up the stairs to Devon's room. He opened his door to Devon mixing a potion. Martin went in, "What do you think you're doing Devon, are you taking your tonic? That kit is for Casandra only!"

Devon looked at him with disbelief, "I know that! Martin, why do you think I am using it? I am not stupid so stop treating me like I am." He returned to his work.

Martin sat on his bed and said, "We have to find her first, and we need her blood. The blood we retrieved at Elk's Pass is being used on the eggs. You can't make an Attachment without her blood." Devon set down his kit, put his hand in his pocket, and pulled out a bottle of blood. Martin said, "You think you have Casandra's blood in that bottle?"

Devon set the bottle on the dresser and said. "I know I do. I went out today to look for them. The Shamans gave us a good description."

Martin interrupted him. "It was vague at best, a girl with white hair and gold eyes, a red-haired girl, some guy with green eyes. That description fits hundreds of people here." He folded his arms and watched Devon he was getting mad.

Devon pulled up a chair in front of him, "What if you saw a group that matched, one with red hair, one with white, a man with green eyes like mine and a woman Monk."

Devon watched as Martins' eyes lit up. He unfolded his arms and sat forward, "Tell me, young Prince, what did you do?'

Devon told Martin the group was eating lunch in the same restaurant he was in. He paid his bill and changed his appearance. He returned to the restaurant and asked to sit in at the table next to them. Overhearing the conversation one of them slipped and called the white-haired woman Casandra. He remembered Addison was to be with her, but he couldn't tell which man he was. They split up after lunch, he followed the white-haired woman. They went to the shops on the Boulevard, two of them went to the back of the store leaving Casandra alone. Devon told Martin he felt the luck with him and approached her. He recounted the conversation and how he broke the glass to get the blood. Devon thought it was her the moment he stood next to her. However, when her blood touched him, he knew it was her.

"Martin, I disappeared myself and ran here. I am certain she is Casandra. I am not addicted like you, and my Father says. I am obsessed! Obsessed with her! I must have Casandra. I can't explain it, Martin, it is as if she spelled me. I will not rest until I taste her lips."

Martin believed him, “If you are right, what a boon this is! You will do more than taste her lips son…but where is she now?”

Devon laughed, just like Martin had always done to him. “I am a part wizard Martin, and I have her blood. That is all I need.” Devon pushed his chair back and went back to work.

Martin smiled and thought he and the King had underestimated this boy. They would have to be more careful with him. Martin said, “I will get those people out of the house then send Ernst for dinner. I will be right back to help you.

Over the Bayonne Ocean

Henry was so frustrated. Flying over the sea, he could only get pieces of what was happening at Winter's End. The Prince was there, and Henry had heard most of the ordeal at the teashop. He fully understood Eric had unusual powers over Casandra, and he thought Addison said she was firing him from his job. Anything that was screamed, Henry could understand. Especially the part about Eric taking a bath with Casandra and her standing in only a towel. It was clear he did not know his Bride. Who was this woman? Odd, he thought he should be jealous, but it only made him want to know her better. He looked at Paxton, "What do you think of my bride Paxton, who am I marrying?"

Paxton laughed, "Well, let's look at the facts, Sir. She is beautiful, rich beyond measure and she is a powerful Sorceress. She can drink and fight like a man, she is bold and speaks her own mind. And…she can spell a room full of Witches and Warlocks with a glass of water…" He stopped to laugh again. "I wish I could have seen that, and her standing in front of everyone in only a towel. I will have to advise you, Henry, if you do not marry her I will steal her away. She is my kind of women." Then he laughed again.

Henry grinned, "You are right Paxton, I have myself one of a kind, a precious jewel. I need to rest, as we get closer, I will be able to read more of Addison's thoughts. Wake me when your power weakens, I don't want to waste any time getting there."

Memories

Casandra dropped the towel, grabbed the wine and a razor from the drawer. Then she got into the tub and took several swigs of wine while she considered how to go about retrieving Addison's memories. Then Casandra took off her bracelet and wondered how to remove the blood from the jewels without calling them. The bracelet had called Addison quickly at the tea shop, she didn't want them to know she was using the bracelet. Maybe if she were careful and barely touched the bracelet with the razor, it wouldn't call them. She drank more wine and decided she would try Grace first, if she came busting in she wouldn't mind. She kept drinking and tried to recall what Henry has done at the boulder.

She carefully placed the bracelet in the soap dish using cloth, then she stuck the jewel holding Grace's blood with the razor. She quickly sealed the jewel then she waited. She drank more wine and waited… nothing happened. She carefully gabbed the blade into her arm and sat back closed her eyes and visions of Grace's childhood flashed before her, and of school then Eric kissing her. Then she saw Eric and Grace making love in the tree on the plains. Oh, that was not something she wanted to see! She sat up and splashed water on her face.

The water had cooled, that had taken too long. Casandra drained the water then added more hot water. Then she decided Addison was next. This time Casandra would ask a question before she stuck herself, the question about the Attachment Spell. She was standing in the dungeon of her dreams watching Devon place an Attachment spell on a Witch. Henry was there, and Addison's mind was taking pictures of bottles, formulas, and the Attachment. She watched Addison, as the King pressed power into Henry and saw the lecherous expressions on the faces of the men in the dungeon. Henry closed Addison off to the feeling of the Attachment spell, telling Addison he loved him too much to feel this awful spell. Again, the water was cold.

She had no idea how much time that passed she had to do Eric's fast. This time she asked to be shown how Eric really felt about her. The memory was of her Mother compelling him to protect her and love her. She made him love her! She saw how frustrated he was at first, and he had changed her diapers; now that she never knew. She saw the fights he had with her Mother and Father and his sadness when she went off to school. When she was just sixteen, Casandra asked him to help before her first liaison. She felt the compassion, respect, and love he had for her. Then she saw the tender kisses they shared and how quickly it got out of hand. He had not wanted that; it was the compulsion her Mother had on him that forced him to make love to her. He loved her, like a Father, a Brother, a friend, and a lover. How could he contain that? She was not the only one who lived a life controlled by others he was no freer than she was.

She ran hot water for the fourth time, washed and changed into her robes. She combed out her black hair and wiped the razor, placing it back in the drawer. She took another swig of wine; it wasn't helping to ease any pain. Grace, Addison, and Eric loved her, and they only wanted the best for her. There was a knock on the door she knew it was Eric, how could she face him now. Eric softly said. "Casandra if you are still in the bath, you are looking like a prune. Take down the spell and come out we need to speak."

She drew in a breath and released the spell. She opened the door Eric stood there filled with such compassion she wanted to cry. She grabbed her wine and walked past him, to the windows. Seagulls were flying over the house she hauled the curtains closed and plopped into the soft reading chair in the corner.

Eric walked to the bed across from her and sat. "I brought you dinner it is in the sitting room. You should have something to eat if you are going to drink that whole bottle of wine."

She got up and walked to the sitting room, maybe if she just obeyed him he would leave. He followed her and sat across from her. She looked at the food, and her stomach flopped, it was covered in exotic spices and smelt of fish. She picked up a fork and shoveled whatever strange vegetable was in the dish in her mouth. Only three swallows later she started to feel the food coming back up and ran to the bathroom. It was odd how this made her feel much better. She looked up, and he was standing there watching her. "Eric, can I not throw up in private? This is too much even for you."

She stomped out of the bathroom and crawled into bed. Eric stood there in his Father stance, arms crossed with the intense stare. All these years she would get so mad when he looked at her like that. Now she knew how angry and frustrated he was with her. She couldn't help herself she started to giggle. The more she tried to stop the harder she laughed. He was fuming now, and he came to the bed.

"YOU THINK THIS IS FUNNY?" He was right by her side red-faced and yelling.

Her heart was pounding, and she couldn't look at him tears filled her eyes so fast she turned her head away. He took a deep breath and said, "Casandra look at me."

She wiped her eyes then knelt on the bed to be able to look him in the eye. It surprised him, and he took a step back. Casandra sighed, "It seems to me, all I ever say to you lately is I am sorry. I think I will make a sign and just show it to you every morning and every evening. Then all this confrontation in the middle will just disappear. I am truly sorry Eric, my friend." She looked him straight in the eye.

He was lost for words. He ran his hands through his hair and said, "I can't imagine being you. The older you get, the worse it gets. I don't know how to protect you from this or take care of you any longer. I had hoped Henry would take care of you but...Well, I tried to give you freedom, and I have failed. I have failed you."

Casandra put her arms around him and said. "No you haven't, look where you are now, here with me. I wish you, and I could take Shelton and run to the other side of the world and hide from everyone." She released him, and he smiled, "The Prince has my blood he will find me where ever I go."

Then Eric looked somber again and said. "We can stop him."

She sat on the bed and patted it, "Sit, Eric." He sat beside her, "This game we are in is not going to end well. Who knows who will live or die, perhaps the Prince, perhaps me, maybe both of us." He started to object, and she put her hand to his mouth. "No, don't lie to make me feel better. Don't think you are the only one to protect me, and stop being responsible for my happiness. The Night has the ultimate game plan, not you or Henry. I have been so mad at all of you because everyone expects me to blindly follow and obey. Eric, I trust you with my life but when will you trust me?"

Eric looked away, and she knew he was crying he stood and looked away from her. "This is difficult for me Casandra I am older and stronger." He stopped and look at her she was no longer a little girl. "Do you remember when Mags read that silly fairytale? The one with the Princess that made everyone tell her your wish is my command? You made me say that to you before you would do anything I asked." He smiled, "Here you are all grown up, and I still see my little girl." Eric straightened up and bowed, "Your wish is my command, Casandra. I will trust you, how can I show you?"

She threw her arms around him and kissed his cheek, "Just tell me the truth, tell me what I face. Tell me about the Attachment Spell."

He stepped back dumbfounded. "How do you know what it is called?"

She smiled and said, "You have forgotten the vow I made so soon. I swore to you I would find out."

He took her hand, "We really need to speak with Addison he is the one who knows the most." They walked from the room, and he said, "Henry is not going to like this, we promised him we would not tell you anything."

She laughed and said. "You didn't. I found out on my own, and Henry can only blame himself for that."

Martin

He was amazed they had actually done this, Devon found Casandra. Martin worked on the Attachment using Devon's and Casandra's blood. Devon was right this was more than luck, this was the heavens opening and blessing them. It was times like these he wished they hadn't taken Ernst ability to transport away. The King would need to know this. Martin had sent Ernst and Devon out to find the Sorcerous. Which gave him the opportunity to place a few other blood spells into the Attachment. When he was finished Henry, the King, and Martin would be able to use Casandra. Since he felt her power while he carried her to the boat years ago, all he wanted was to taste her power. Martin had almost taken her while serving as her guard, but the Elf stopped him. He was looking forward to meeting that Elf again. If Devon was obsessed with kissing her, then he was obsessed with taking her power.

Devon returned and told Martin she was at a house named Winters End. Martin felt if they moved quickly their chances of success would be greater. Martin said, "We need to put a plan in place now. I am sure they have figured out you were after Casandra. Before they remove her from the island, we need to grab Casandra. Your Father never wanted to play games with Henry, he is a dangerous man. If we can take her back to Bezier, the game would change significantly. We would have the winning hand. I only wish we had more men with us."

Devon beamed wickedly, "I have it handled, Martin." Devon walked to his bag and brought out this rapacious protractor, "We are in the tropics no one would think anything about a tropical storm popping up over Winters End. I only need one person to go with me to get her out. Their stupid men put a guard on one balcony, they might as well have posted a sign saying Casandra sleeps here." Devon laughed. "We need to take her out to sea immediately they will not be able to track her out there. We need a ship. I noticed one of ours in the harbor this afternoon. Can you commandeer it, Martin?"

Martin was amazed, "Son, I am proud of you, and after this, you will deserve a raise in rank. You want to finish up the spell. Ernst and I will see the ship. As soon as the vessel is in place, we will move. You and I should go into the room they probably have someone with her. Ernst will stand outside with the Pegasus; we will fly to the ship. The storm will create enough confusion among the guards to slow them down. However, Devon, you must place the Attachment and drain her power quickly. We cannot have her fighting us, we only have five to ten minutes to get her out of there and on the ship."

Devon beamed. "I will be quick," Devon turned to the spell. "She will be mine, not Henry's."

Martin and Ernst went to the harbor, all the while Martin worried. What would the boy do when he found she would be common property. Perhaps the King should show him the advantages of mutual Attachments.

The Wisdom of the Blood Spell

As predicted Henry was furious that Casandra knew about the spell. He was close to Traza now, he and Addison were in constant communication. Casandra was asking detailed questions. Henry and Addison did not understand how she would have known what to ask, it was as if she had been at the Science building. Henry asked Addison if he had done a blood spell with her. He said no mentally and told Henry the only blood he spilled was for the bracelet back at the North Castle.

Addison looked at Cassandra's wrist, her bracelet was gone. Addison said, "Casandra where is your bracelet?"

She looked surprised. "Oh it came off in the bathtub it must be upstairs."

Eric ordered Charlie to retrieve it, and then he said, "The Hermit told you not to take it off, why did you do that?'

Cassandra said, "I didn't Eric, I told you it came off in the tub. I just forgot to put it back on afterward. You were knocking on the door." She sat back and raised her eyebrow.

Addison told Henry mentally. I think she is lying. I will have a look at the bracelet. Charlie came down with it, and Addison went to Charlie to handle the bracelet before Casandra could do anything magical. Addison said, "It is still wet I will dry it." Addison ran his hand over it and found scratches on three gems. He sighed, "What kind of gems are these Casandra they are already scratched."

Casandra had to think fast, "I don't know Addison, the Hermit said it was her Grandmothers. I am not even sure they are real gems." She got up and took the bracelet from him, "I hadn't noticed, you're right, they are scratched I can fix that." Before he could take it back she waved her hand, it was on her wrist, and the scratches were gone.

Henry spoke mentally to Addison. She is covering her tracks how could she get blood out of those stones without alerting you? Addison only sighed. Henry said mentally. Try to connect with her if she's blood bonded, you will be able to speak to her.

They both returned to the table, and the conversation continued. Addison started softly calling her name mentally. He thought she is getting very uncomfortable. I think she can hear me.

Casandra said, "Excuse me, I need to use the restroom." She went into the restroom downstairs. Addison was trying to get into her thoughts. How could she block him? She couldn't think of a thing, except to get away from him and she knew she was in the bathroom too long.

Marion knocked on the door and asked if she was alright. "No Marion, I am sick. Please go away."

Casandra couldn't stay in the bathroom all night or could she. She looked in the mirror and gave herself a spell with a greenish tint in her skin, then she created illness in her stomach. It was simple to develop a disease, she was already light headed and fuzzy. Also, she had thrown up earlier in front of Eric. Marion had taught her this spell when she needed to get out of class. Marion would know but would she tell Addison? She had to make this good when she opened the door, and all of them were standing there.

Addison stepped forward, "Let me have a look. I know medicine I can help you."

Casandra said, "Addison, I think it is nothing more than all the events of today. I just want to go lay down for a while I don't want to be sick when Henry gets here." She turned to go to her room, Addison followed calling her name mentally. She just kept thinking I am sick thoughts until he left.

Addison went to his room and returned with a tonic for her. She took one drink and could feel the spell unwinding, he was on to her. She ran to the bathroom and forced herself to throw it up, but when she peeked over her shoulder he was standing there, "Why do Warlocks love to watch me throw up? Addison, please leave, let me rest."

Addison grinned, "Forgive me, Casandra. I will leave, but I will still be talking to you."

She walked out of the bathroom, and Moori was there. Moori closed the door after Addison, "Go on, take a nap we have a few hours before we need to get out to sea. Eric wants me in here for your protection. I will put a sleep bubble around you if you drop the act of being sick." She kept a straight face. "What are you hiding Casandra?"

Casandra dropped her spell and got in bed. She pulled up the covers, and Addison said mentally to her. I know you are faking Casandra. I want you to think about how you released my blood from that gem.

She said out loud, "Go away Addison, get out of my head. I did not give you permission to be there."

He mentally said. You didn't ask for my permission to steal my memories! Show me what you did.

She looked to Moori, "I dropped the illness spell; put me out." Moori ran her thumb across her forehead.

Casandra dropped off to sleep. Before long she was dreaming, and it was a lovely dream. Henry was there and bent over her while she slept, kissing her and telling her he loved her. Casandra put her arms around him as he began kissing her face. She closed her eyes and relaxed as he slowly moved from her face down to her neck. The room was spinning then his face went out of focus. There was screaming, she tried to pull back and open her eyes, but she couldn't open them. Then she felt it. A pleasant warmth on her neck that slowly seeped into her skin and rushed down her body. In a few seconds, it started to burn, and the heat twisted in her throat and stomach as if a thousand needles were being pushed to her. That was when she could hear her own screams. She opened her eyes, and the man from Elk's Pass was taking her off the bed, the Hex Prince. He carried her to the balcony then handed her to a man while he got on a Pegasus. It was the same man that took her to the King the Night she was kidnaped, he bent down and kissed her on her neck, then began pulling power from her. Blazing pain shot down to her legs she could feel it coil around her bones. Where was Eric? She tried to touch the bracelet but couldn't move. Casandra writhed and screamed, but the winds and rains were tremendous. She was sure no one could hear her. As the man threw her over his shoulder, she saw Moori curled into a ball on the bedroom floor. They were up in the air in a moment.

The house was being torn apart by the sudden storm. Eric tried to make his way to Casandra's room, but a force lifted him and threw him against the wall. Addison was holding on the banister to pull himself upstairs when the railing pulled away, he was taken with it. By the time Eric got to Addison, the winds had subsided. The storm ended as quickly as it had begun. His heart fell, he knew he would not find Casandra in her room.

Devon was pleased with himself and flew to Martin to take hold of his prize. He took Casandra in his arms on his Pegasus and kissed her deeply. He smiled at her and said, "I told you I would be back for that kiss. Don't look so scared, my sweet lady I will take good care of you." Devon bent down and took power from her, and she felt a wave of burning heat surge down her body. He turned her in the saddle and placed her face down on his legs over the wings of the Pegasus.

Casandra tried to move but couldn't. He must have tied her with a spell. She couldn't move her arms, but she noticed she could shift her weight. She mentally screamed Shelton's name. She had to time this perfectly and hoped Shelton could catch her. She watched for him and told him mentally to fly below her. The shore was getting farther away, where was Shelton? She watched below her and finally could see only flashes of him, he had made himself invisible. Casandra wiggled and pushed, then fell. As soon as she was away from the saddle, she could feel Shelton's white threads weave around her. She landed on his back but still couldn't move. Shelton had tied her to his back and was flying back to Winter's End. The Prince and his party tried to turn their Pegasus, but they refused to cooperate with them. They flew out to the sea.

Shelton said. I made you disappear, then told their Pegasus to take them far away, they will think you fell to your death in the sea.

Eric's men ran into the house, "General, you need to come out here and see this."

Addison and Eric walked outside. There in the middle of the yard was Shelton standing with Casandra tied to his back. Eric ran to her and cut her down and took her into the house.

The furniture was toppled everywhere, Addison turned over the dining room table "Place her here so I can get a look at her." Addison created a light and began to look for injuries. She had been tied up with a spell that was quickly dissipating. He pulled back her robe and saw the Attachment. He thought and said. "Henry get here fast, and we need a doctor."

Moori came to his side, "Don't try to remove the spell yet. When she comes out of that spell, we will need to hold her down. She will be screaming if we don't stop that, she may end up with a voice as low and gravely as mine. If she screams too long, she may never be able to speak. It took me years."

Henry was standing next to her, "How do you know this?"

Moori jumped a foot. "Count. You frighten me."

Addison noticed Moori was bloody and hurt herself. She opened her robe completely; her upper body was scarred with what looked like Attachments. One side of her neck was open and bleeding. "Trust me, I know."

Marion and the Professor walked up to the table. Marion looked at Moori and fainted. Addison caught her and laid her on the couch then waved his hand over her and said. "She is fine, just fainted. I will keep her like that. I don't think she will be any help to us. Moori what do you suggest."

Casandra started to moan, and her arms and legs were shaking violently. They all moved to the table. Henry placed his hand on the Attachment and Casandra screamed and struck out at him. Moori took her hands, "I am here Casandra you have helped me to remember all of my past, now as in accordance with the Night, I am here to help you. Trust us. Eric now would be a great time for you to use the power you hold over her."

Casandra had broken free of the spell she was now screaming and fighting to get off the table. Eric held her down and climbed on top of her. He sat on her legs and tried to hold on to her arms. He screamed "Casandra, I compel you to stop screaming! You may not speak or make a sound." She immediately stopped, but her face was red. He said, "Casandra I compel you from moving, you will hold still." She was getting redder, "My darling sweet girl listen to me. I want you to take a deep breath and release it." She did and began to pant. "No baby, no panting. I want you to control your breath slow deep breaths. I will breathe with you, follow me." She began following his breath, but now she was crying; he knew that could choke her. "I compel you not to cry! I love you, and I will not watch you drown in your own tears. Do you understand me?" She stopped crying. "I know Cassandra. I see you are in great pain. I wish I could take it on for you, my lovely child."

Henry stood back in a jolt, what was this man to her, he felt very jealous but knew he could not show it now. Eric was calming her, and Henry needed him for now. Addison thought to Henry. It is not what you think I have watched them together, he is more her Father or Brother. Be patient Henry, think...what will we do?

Eric was watching him. "Henry I will explain later we need to help her first."

Henry came to her head and looked down at her then he kissed her forehead. He had tears in his eyes she was in great pain. He said. "I love you, and I will remove this from you. Addison, please ease her pain. This will hurt Casandra." Henry placed his hand on the Attachment and began bringing it slowly up her body just as the King of Hex instructed but he could barely get it to move. The harder he pulled, the deeper the Attachment sunk into to her. Her body was shaking uncontrollably.

Addison stopped him, "Henry this isn't working. This is Devon's Attachment, and I don't think it is responding to you."

"It is, this Attachment must be different somehow. Moori tell us what we need to do." Henry moved back.

Moori said, "When they experimented on me several men could use my power. However, it is the Professor who helped me." The Professor stood at the table with the sharpest kitchen knife he could find.

Casandra's body started to shudder. Eric held her down and said, "I am sorry, sweet girl. I compel you to keep your eyes and ears closed, you may not hear or see any of us." He gave Henry a patronizing stare. "She is scared."

Henry said a little too sharply, "I know that. Professor, I have a scalpel that would work much better." Henry took the scalpel out of its box. "Where do I start?"

The Professor said, "With Moori, going slow and methodical was best. My eyes are not the best do you have a steady hand?" Henry answered yes. "Moori please connect and direct us. I will talk you through this. Eric, we need a strong man to hold on to the Attachment and pull it up as Henry cuts it away. I know from experience this will take a while. We will need to relieve one another."

As Henry's hand neared Casandra's throat, she writhed and moaned. Addison said to Henry, "They must have used your blood or at least some of your blood. I can't keep her still when you touch her."

Henry reached into his pocket and took out the snake skinned gloves; he forced them on, they clung to his hands and wrists. He retook the knife and touched Casandra this time she had no response.

The Professor asked, "Are those snakeskin gloves? I haven't seen those in eons." Henry just smiled and nodded yes, the Professor said, "Well, then, let's begin I will lift here you must cut as I lift."

Eric called some of his men and ordered others to stand guard. They all shared time holding the Attachment away from Casandra's throat. Moori guided Henry. Her talent was going into the body and healing cell by cell.

One hour into the procedure wind whipped around the house. Henry asked, "We need Marion, Addison wake her."

He did, "Marion we need your help. Put us in a peaceful bubble. I think Devon is brewing another storm. Do not look at Casandra." Marion said nothing, she gazed at the table, but too many were around it to see Casandra.

Addison returned to the table then placed his hands on Casandra's head. Moori stopped short. "She can't breathe, Henry she has lost too much blood."

Before Henry could react, Casandra's body lurched forward, and the scalpel cut open her chest. She was bleeding badly. Addison grabbed the knife and cut his palm and pressed into her chest. Henry said, "You can't do that, Addison, you need to keep the pain down."

Paxton stepped up behind Henry. "Henry the Doctor is here."

Henry was relieved he had sent Paxton to get the Doctor and a ship. Dr. Marlez pushed Henry to the side, "Let me see what we have." He took a moment to evaluate Casandra, "Henry give me the scalpel, I need some clean towels. Young lady come over here. Press as hard as you can on her throat." The Doctor cleaned her up as well as he could and sealed the slice in her chest, "I will heal that later. Professor McMillan nice to see, you hold on to that thing. Henry sit down. Paxton bring Henry a chair." Henry was relieved to sit down, "Addison I need you to relieve the pain." The Doctor waved his hand, and Addison's hand closed. Henry, is this your Bride?"

Henry said, "Yes, I have never been happier to see you."

"You have done a good job on her throat; the chest wasn't your fault she was choking. I saw her body jump but Henry she has lost too much blood. You are about to do a full blood bond, like it or not. Sit."

The Doctor cut both Henry's and Casandra's palm and bonded them together. "Addison, she is going to see everything in Henry's life be prepared to put her out if I tell you. Who are you?" He looked at Eric who was still straddled over Casandra's stomach.

Eric said, "Simply said I am her protector. I have some control over her, she is under a compulsion spell."

The Doctor smiled, "Good hold on to her; it may not be enough. The last part of the Attachment is the most difficult to remove. Can you control her breathing?" Eric said yes. "Henry is giving her his blood, and you will be giving her your breath. I need you to open all her vocal chord with every breath. This is the only way I can remove it without damage. Understand?" Eric said yes, and they spent another hour taking the Attachment out.

Devon at Sea

Martin and Devon reached the ship. The Pegasus had refused to turn back to get Casandra. Martin had never experienced Pegasus refusing to obey. The Pegasus set them down on the boat and then pulled away. Martin said, "I have had some unruly beasts, those are the worst animals ever. Look, they are crazy flying out into the sea they will be dead by tomorrow. Devon did the Sorceress go into the ocean, it was so dark I couldn't see a thing."

Devon gawked off to the land, it was still night the only marker was the white surf in the moonlight. "Martin, I had her balanced and tied on my saddle the next thing I knew she was gone. I looked down, but all I saw was black. I had so many clouds in the sky I couldn't see more than thirty feet. I have a feeling something down there pulled her off. I saw a web of some kind. The whole thing was strange and fast. My Pegasus had a mind of its own, mine would only fly forward. I will try to reach out to Winter's End and see if I can sense her." Devon blew a strong wind to the shore, sweeping around Winter's End. She wasn't there, but some people were. Where could she have gone? He kept searching but after a half hour nothing had changed, and they were moving too far out from the shore to keep up the search. He went below deck and found Martin. He told him that he could sense nothing and was giving up the search. "Martin, did I kill her? Is that why I can't sense her?"

Martin patted Devon on the shoulder, "We will know soon enough; we have only a few weeks until the Coronation. If she lives, she will be with Henry."

Henry's Memories

Henry sat perfectly still and watched as scenes from Casandra's past came into his head. He knew better than try to understand it, he needed to let it flow past, and he would be able to decipher the details later. He hoped Addison was helping Casandra with his memories. She did not know this kind of magic; she would need his help. Eric was there buried in her memories, every day, and all day. He was beginning to understand their relationship. Henry laughed to himself as he saw Eric bath her and change her diapers. He had been foolish to be jealous. The Empress had spelled the man, he was forced to love her. Henry saw he would have fallen in love with her without the spell.

The Doctor pulled him back by removing the bond. He told Henry to just stay seated. Henry watched helplessly as Eric lifted Casandra from the table and placed her on the couch. He looked at the table filled with blood and towels soaking it up as two Elves lifted him under the arms and took him to a chair that had half of the stuffing torn out. Henry was looking directly at Casandra, sleeping peacefully, but white as a sheet. He tried to stand, but hands pushed him down.

Addison hung light balls from the ceiling so they could see, and Eric handed him some cheese and a bottle of wine. "Here Henry, the Doctor said you need to eat, that is all that is left in this place. We need to get out of here. I am having my men try to find clothing and getting us packed. Henry, do you hear me?"

Henry nodded and took a bite of cheese and drank wine. Henry grabbed his arm and said, "Eric, I understand your relationship with Casandra." He drank more wine, "We need everyone here in the living room, we have to organize. You're right we need to get out of here." Eric called everyone together as Henry became more lucid.

Addison came over and sat by him. "Addison, did you put the Attachment in alcohol?"

Addison put his arm around Henry. "I did. Our girl is something else she has had some life. I hope I guided her safely enough through our lives."

Henry asked, "What time is it?"

Addison said, "It's about four in the morning we need to get her out of here before daylight."

Eric sat down by Casandra and helped her sit up. "Casandra you wanted to know what is going to happen. Wake up, we are deciding." She opened her eyes saw Henry and smiled. They were fully connected, he could hear her every thought. Addison laughed and said mentally. You are going to be just fine sweet girl. I know Eric calls you that, it fits I am calling you that too.

Eric said, "Henry, I need to get back to North Castle and inform the Emperor. He needs to know what has gone on."

Henry said, "Yes Eric you do, and I do have a plan." He looked to Casandra, "Casandra, I am sorry…I am sorry about all of this. We need to leave before the sun rises. Do you like sailing?" She mentally said I don't know.

Henry said, "Would you like to find out because I have a ship right out there about a mile offshore. We can take it almost to Diamante." Henry turned to Moori, "Moori, I need a favor from you and the Professor. Would you be willing to go to Belissa Villa and help Ski discover more about the Attachment? Addison has it in alcohol, and Ski really needs to have a look at a whole one. Moori if you could give Ski any information I would be so grateful."

The Professor said yes, but Moori asked, "He just wants information?"

Henry remembered the conversations between Moori and Casandra. Since her youth, she trusted only a few, the Professor and Casandra were among those. "Yes, Moori. I promise he won't touch you just tell him what you know. Then my men will return you to Monk's Mountain or wherever you want to go. You would be my guest." She looked skeptical. "Every one of my men and women trained at the Monastery you will know most of them." She shook her head yes.

Henry smiled, "Good. Paxton, did you hire that driver?"

Paxton said, "I have drivers for both carriages. The Doctor was kind enough to lease us his, they are outside waiting. The ship is ready too they just signaled, there is also a Pegasus. Eric told me we are taking him with us. I need to take food and hay out to the ship; our Pirate Captain is not going to like this. We don't have time to hire a Shaman; I will need to go along to care for him and connect with him. Roger, I mean the Doctor has agreed to come with us."

Casandra squealed in her mind. A pirate, really, a real pirate let's go! I am so excited.

Henry and Addison both looked at her. Addison chuckled, "Casandra you are a little too excited to meet a pirate; I hope we don't disappoint you." Addison noted Eric's solemn face, "Eric he was all we could get this quickly; besides he is an old friend."

Eric said, "You have pirates for friends."

Casandra said mentally. Well, I know a few of his unsavory friends as well, I could tell you a few things about him!

Addison said, "Cassandra, I can't tell anyone that. Please settle down we need to finish here."

Henry continued, "Thank you for coming so fast, and for coming with us to Belissa. I will owe you for this one Roger."

The Doctor laughed and said. "Henry, I have fourteen children, any time someone offers me a job, on the ship and a vineyard for weeks, it is like giving me a vacation."

Everyone laughed. "Alright, here is what we will do if anyone has a better idea tell me, don't complain later. Moori and Professor McMillan, will go to Belissa and take Ski the Attachment and tell him everything we discussed. Take my Brother's carriage then have one of my men return it to Winsette Castle. Eric, could I borrow Grace and Charlie for a special message to my Brother. They can stay in my apartment at the Castle until the Emperor arrives for the Coronation. You will be at the Coronation?"

Eric nodded yes. "That works out perfectly they can scout out the Castle and city for me. Perhaps they can keep the Emperor's lodgings clean of spies. Not all my men can fit into one carriage, can I send six to Belissa and they can go on to the Castle? We can meet up at the Coronation. Henry, I also need to take Shelton to the ship he will not allow you or Paxton on him."

Henry agreed, "Besides you will want to see the Casandra is safely aboard." Eric gave Henry a surprised look. "The Doctor and the rest of us will take the carriage over you can come back and get the rest of your men."

Eric shook his head, "We are going to have to do a little work around here before we leave. A little magic and it will be as good as new, we should get started."

Henry looked around for the first time the place was a mess. "We all could help."

Eric stood, "No she needs to be out at sea; we don't know where Devon is."

Casandra told Henry mentally that Devon watched her fall from his lap into the sea. She hoped Devon believed she was dead then he would stop perusing her. However, she could feel he was nowhere near.

Henry grinned wickedly. "My sweet Casandra, you have given us our plan. She said Devon watched her fall into the sea, and now he would relinquish his search for her. I think we should accommodate him and have them think she has died, or at least lost at sea. It would give her time to heal. Do you think the Emperor would go along with this plan? I can keep her in the ocean where they would have a hard time finding us until the Coronation."

Casandra mentally protested. Wait! I am not going anywhere covered in dried blood and torn clothes. Also, I am under a compulsion still, tell Eric to release me.

Addison and Henry laughed. Addison turned to Marion, "Marion, please help Casandra clean up and dressed in some traveling clothes."

Henry stood, "Eric, she is still under a compulsion she would like for you to remove it."

The Doctor stepped up, "Eric, it would help her throat heal if she doesn't speak, is there some way you could see to that?"

Eric took Casandra's hand and said, "Casandra, I compel you not to speak or try to make a noise with your voice until the Doctor tells you to. I release you from all other compulsions."

Casandra smiled and kissed Eric on the cheek. She stood and wobbled Eric held on to her and said, "Grace, Charlie, help Casandra. I want all my women and Sam to go to Belissa the rest will stay with me to clean up. Sam can take the carriage back to your Brother. The women of the unit are still assigned to Casandra as her personal guard by the command of the Emperor. I realize ship space is limited, so Henry you will take that duty until you are at Diamante in Winsette Castle." Marion and Grace helped Casandra up the stairs as Henry was grinning at Eric.

Eric gave Henry his fatherly gaze and said, "Would you like to share your amusement."

Henry said, "Casandra just told me mentally, how nice it was that she could show you love and not have me upset. Then she said. Watch Eric, he is about to give orders just like a Father does his children. That is why all his men love and follow him."

Eric turned his head and watched as Casandra disappeared into a bedroom. "So, you can hear her thoughts, and you gathered all her memories from childhood on?"

Henry said, "Yes I am still sorting through them they are all there. She didn't have time to take all mine, but she has much of my life too. We will have time on the ship to work through most of it. You changed her diapers?"

Eric slapped Henry on the shoulder. "Oh, good Night, your poor soul. You do not know what you have done to yourself. Look back to her childhood. Mags was already getting too old to chase her down it was just faster for me to change her diaper than drag her back to the Castle." He shrugged. "It took me years to teach her to hold her tongue. I had to put her under a compulsion every time we had guests. I promised her she would have freedom with her thoughts only. Only the Night and I know what goes on in that pretty little head. Now, of course, you and Addison do too. You will find she squeals when she is happy, and curses when she is upset." By the looks on their face, he knew they had already experienced that Eric started laughing, "Help me clean this place up while we wait. By the way, remind her I am her Father's General it doesn't look good, kissing me and hugging me in public. Besides she knows it hurts her Father deeply that I can touch her, and he can't." Henry gave him a questioning look. "Henry, just think into her past. Better yet just ask her she wants honesty."

Casandra was bathed and dressed by the time the carriages were packed and the downstairs put back together. Her rooms were gone entirely. Eric's men were working on them when she walked out. She was feeling very weak; she couldn't believe how hard it was to dress even with help.

Downstairs she gave Moori and the girls a hug and kissed the Professor on his cheek. Henry said. "She says to have a safe trip, and Moori she wants me to remind you about the wedding arrangements at the Temple. She told me I couldn't look at that memory, so I hope you know what she means."

Moori bowed to her and said, "As you wish." Then laughed.

Henry helped her into the carriage, and they were off to the ship. Henry leaned out the window and asked, "That huge Pegasus is Shelton? Eric is riding without a saddle." She told him that Shelton doesn't need a saddle and only people Shelton wanted could ride him. Henry brought up the memory at the Shaman Village of Eric and her bonding to Shelton, he understood. Now he also knew why he needed to place 12 million Fab in an international account and have all the paperwork delivered to Fairies on Pegasus Plains. Then Casandra held his hand and Addison's. Now that she was off the Continent she could share the memory of the morning with the unicorn. She told them she had promised to tell Eric the story when she was free to speak and asked them to explain before he left the ship.

They landed on the ship and was introduced to the real pirates Casandra was mentally squealing.

Eric came over to say goodbye, he pulled Addison and Henry aside and said. "She is squealing again, isn't she?" Addison and Henry said yes and shared the memory of the Unicorns with Eric. He said. "I dreamt of Unicorn that night."

Marion said she had, too. They hugged, and Eric got into the carriage with tears in his eyes. Casandra looked away she would not cry.

She and Marion went to pet Shelton. Marion whispered to Casandra, "I am sorry I fainted. I was not any help to you. I can't believe that I keep fainting. I never do that, I don't know what is wrong with me. I am moody and anxious; I am not myself. I am sick to my stomach. I don't think I can take the rocking of this ship. I think it was the Monks' Monastery, and you and the Professor with all the meditation and exercise. Really I just don't think that is for me." She waited for Casandra to answer, then she remembered, "Oh, I am sorry, you can't talk to me. Moori has been with you, and I have been with Addison; we haven't talked in a long time. Hmm, I really need to talk to someone. I can't talk to Addison about this." Marion looked away to where the men stood talking. Casandra pulled on her dress and shook her head no. She was trying to tell her she didn't know how to keep Henry and Addison from reading her thoughts yet. They were becoming suspicious, and Casandra didn't want them to pick up her thoughts. She turned away, and Marion pulled her back. "Where are you are going, I need to tell someone. Do you have that book? The one the Hermit gave you? I need to read it…Casandra, I think I might be pregnant." Addison was standing right next to them.

The Emperor's Rage

Eric landed in the courtyard of the North Castle with the Emperor standing at the gate to the Castle. "Why are you back here so early, and where is my daughter?"

"Eric flew out of the carriage and gave the sign for safe they had used in the war. Eric said, "We need to go to the library."

The Emperor virtually ran through the Castle, with Eric and Major following. Eric detected spies instantaneously when he got to the library. He went to the windows and saw that crows were flying across the meadow, he closed the drapes and held his hand up, signaling Major and the Emperor not to speak.

He walked the room and said, "Sir what happened to your cats and dogs?"

The Emperor said, "They are on top of me demanding petting and attention. I can't get any work done. So, I kicked them out about an hour ago. Things couldn't have changed that fast."

Eric stopped and quickly pulled a book from the shelf with one hand and grasped a mouse with the other. "Major, would you be so kind to open a window, and see if you can get a cat in here."

Major did just that, and the dog and cat were back in the Library. They had three mice and one rat found in only a few minutes. The Emperor was astonished, he called the dog to him and petted him then the cat ran to him as well, "Well done Princess and Thor. I will not push you out again, even for a few minutes. Now explain."

Mags came busting through the doors, "What is wrong?"

Eric said, "Mags sit down. She is alright and with Henry. Everyone, sit and let me explain." Eric recounted the story from the day at the Tea Shop, until he left her on the ship. He explained the Attachment spell. However, not giving the details of how difficult and painful it was to remove. He told the Emperor Henry had brought Doctor Marlez to Winters End and he was with them on the ship. He also explained to the Emperor that Henry requested the Empress come to the Coronation. Her presence there would give Dillion the backers he needed to stand against the King.

The Emperor paced the room while Eric gave his report, then all three questioned him at length about everything from the Pegasus to the ship. Eric was exhausted he had not stopped from the time he left Traza. The Emperor stopped pacing and looked at him. "Eric are you certain she is alright?"

Eric just looked at him, how many times did he need to tell him. "Sir, she was walking and smiling she even gave me a hug before I left the ship." He regretted that as soon as he said it. "I would not leave her unless I was sure Sir." He sighed and looked at the floor he couldn't see the hurt in the man's face.

Major said, "I believe you, Eric, so does the Emperor. Mags, Eric looks tired, and I think he needs some food. Please bring him something and us some wine. We need to think about this new development."

Eric stopped her, "Mags not a word to anyone, do you hear me? This could mean the matter of Casandra's life. Henry and I agreed we needed to keep her whereabouts secret for now. We have a strong indication the Prince and King of Hex believe her dead. We need to keep up that pretense, or at least that she is missing."

Mags said, "Why, Eric? What have you not said to us?"

Eric told them Marion held them in a bubble while a wind swept through and told them she could feel the Prince's touch on it. "I returned to Winters End to get my men and clean up. At sunrise, there were spies all around the house and over the ocean. I decided to spend some time looking for her out in the ocean and in the seaside town, just to make them believe I didn't know where she was. I wanted to give Henry more time to get out to sea. I flew out to Henry, and he told me the Doctor said Casandra needed rest and quiet. Henry was going to keep her out at sea for the next weeks to give her that. He said at sea their magic would not be detected; she would have peace to heal. I think we should give her that. Of course, the decision is up to you." Then he told them the crows had been following him and his men on this Continent from the time he got to Peroba.

Mags stood up and said, "I wish we could pretend she was dead and let her hide away somewhere. Let her have true peace!" She turned to the Emperor and said. "I told you years ago to give her to Eric he loves her, and she loves him! He could have taken her away, and this would not be happening." The Emperor's face had fallen she had hurt him. Well, she thought fine, how he had hurt that child, then thinking twice she said, "I am sorry Hayden, I should not have spoken that way; it just came out. I will bring back food." She left the library, and Eric didn't know what to say.

Thank goodness Major smoothed things over. "Emperor forgive her, she is upset. Mags has always stood up for all her children, which included you. She had some spirited words with your Father over you, right in this very room. Her idea of pretending is not a bad idea at all."

The Emperor straightened up, "What, pretend she is dead?"

Major said, "No, no or yes, at the least...pretend she is missing. They evidentially went chasing after her on holiday. If they believe she is missing the Hex will give up the chase for the moment. As Eric said, it would give her time to heal and gain back her strength she will need that in the weeks to come."

The Emperor said, "I will think about that. Eric, I consented to attend Dillion's Coronation. It is the King's duty not the Empress. An Emperor has not been present for Diamante Coronation for thousands of years isn't that enough? Besides, I doubt I could persuade her to attend."

Mags came in with food wine and coffee. Eric couldn't hold out any longer he dug into to it while talking. "Sir, the King holds Hex and Bezier with Diamante, Talla, Mento, and Machinto as allies. Parragon, Strella, and Antico swing with whoever has the power at the time. Most of the time they just do as they damn well, please. He holds great influence on the world now, with fear. With a strong show of support for Diamante, Talla who is wavering will feel strong enough to stand up to King Hex."

Major went to get some coffee, and said, "Eric has made a good point. Henry is a wizard at strategies maybe we should trust him on this."

The Emperor fell into his chair at the end of the table and said, "Yes, you have finally said something I can agree on. Why did I not see this before? Wizard, we need a Wizard!"

Major dropped his jaw. "Oh no Sir, not that old Wizard of Arlequin. Remember the trouble we had with him the last time, even his own country kicked him out after the war."

Eric said, "No one will work with him, Sir. If anyone even has an inkling he is involved, they will protest."

"Well, then no one will know. We need Casandra alive and well. I will use any means to do that, even underhanded ones. Let me think, gentlemen, if I ever get the opportunity to face that King of Hex I will kill him with my bare hands."

Eric told him, "You will have the opportunity, Sir. Henry told me the King of Hex will be in attendance as well."

Hayden walked to the window and peeked out into the garden. The birds were sitting on the garden wall, and squirrels were climbing the trees. How could he know which was real, and which an illusion? It was all very confusing, and it was hard to think straight or make a decent decision while confused. He turned and said, "It is hard to think clearly with all this deception going on; now Henry wants to create more of it. Even I have stooped to hiding and plotting. The King of Hex is going to be at the Coronation, well the Empress will not be impressed by seeing the King knowing he has her cousin Elisabeth under a spell. Henry doesn't realize the Empress's strength or power, or he would not ask."

Eric said, "Henry told me not just the King will be there but Prince Devon, all his Generals, and the Queen as well as her daughters. Henry thought that might entice the Empress."

The Emperor got this mischievous look on his face, "Where is Mags?" He marched to the door and had the guards get her, "I want her to be in on this."

Mags came in the Library, and the Emperor told her to be seated, "Listen, everyone, we are going to play one of Henry's games, and everyone here has a part. I will explain the general plan, and you all will help me plot it." Then he laughed. Two hours later, with much argument, they finalized their plan.

Mags said, "I will go prepare everything for all your trips. I will start by telling the Prince he is going on a rescue mission to find Casandra. I will spread the gossip that we are beside ourselves with worry, all while keeping the wedding plans on track. I will go get Bryan in here to speak with you at once." She got up and left.

Major said, "I am leaving to speak to the Empress in person about Casandra being missing. I know you want to talk to her, but that is our protocol. It is important it all looks authentic. Then I will go to Diamante Castle to plan for us and scout things out. Good luck with the Wizard. I am not sure he will agree to any of this and be ready for Henry's criticisms." He left the room just as Bryan came in.

The Emperor said, "I wish you luck with the Empress and not a word to her about the Wizard. She never liked him."

Bryan shook his head and crossed arms with a raised eyebrow. "Not that Wizard Antioch again." They explained the plan to Bryan. He would contact the Wizard Antioch and set the meeting with the Emperor at Monk's Mountain, where else would a worried Father go but to the Monastery to pray for his child's safe return. Then they would all go pretend to search for Casandra, meeting at Diamante Castle for the Coronation.

The Emperor told Eric to go rest until everything was in place and the Prince was ready to leave. Eric turned to the Prince, "Bryan, be careful, tell no one of these plans. I mean no one, not even your wife. Understand?"

The Prince said, "As you say. I will just tell Kathryn Casandra is missing and I am going to look for her."

The Emperor said, "Send her to the boulders. I will tell her what I want her to know. She must run the Castle in our absence. I want her innocent of any of our plans. If we fail, ...she will not be to blame." Then the Emperor put on his serious face and took a walk to the boulders to speak with his Father. He could not afford to make a mistake in this, he would not lose one more of his children to this King.

The Discovery of the Curse

They landed at the barn in the middle of the Night. Sutton was there to greet them, along with Ski. "Professor, it is good to see you. I just wish this was under different circumstances." Ski took Moori's bag, "Mistress Moori, you and the Professor will stay with me at my Villa. First, we will go to Henry's home where the rest of you will stay. Ruth, our housekeeper, came home to pick up some items for Henry's new apartments at Winsette Castle. Lucky for you she has fixed you all some snacks. We all can talk there privately and make our plans."

Sutton and Ski put them under an invisibility charm as they made their way up to Henry's Villa. After they were all inside Sutton closed the drapes and called the dogs and cats inside. They were starving and very tired everyone ate and talked at the same time.

The Professor told everyone what happened at Winter's End. He said, "Henry's last words were to tell you everything, but I am so tired I am not sure I have. He also told us to act like Casandra was missing, at least until we heard from the Eric. After he speaks with the Emperor, he will send us a messenger with instructions."

Sutton said, "That will at least give them a little time to rethink the plan. The King is bold, going after her while she is in disguise it shows his capabilities. I will feel better when they are in our country."

Ski agreed, "We should let you and Moori sleep. I will take you to my Villa, and Sutton would you get everyone settled in here. We will have a late breakfast, here at Henry's."

Moori said, "Chancellor, Henry used strange gloves on his hands to remove the Attachment, I think the Professor forgot to tell you."

The Professor said. "Ah yes, Henry had a pair of snakeskin gloves like the old-fashioned one's young ladies would wear when I was young."

Moori said, "The Attachment was digging in deeper when he touched Casandra, the gloves seem to keep that from happening, here." She reached into her pocket and handed him the gloves.

Ski took them and grinned, "That boy is a wonder this might be the answer we were looking for. Sutton…"

Sutton was standing next to Moori, "Father I will have my men hunting water snakes as soon as the sun comes up. I wish Paxton were here he would be better than me at that." He bowed to Moori, "Mistress, I was privileged to take one of your classes when I did my training at the Mountain." Moori smiled and said, "I remember you, Sutton."

"We all take the training. Our lady patrollers had their robes, while they are not the right color they wanted you to have them. Paxton told me most of your clothing was lost. It is my honor to serve you, Mistress."

Moori relaxed Henry was right she would be received here. "It is my privilege to accept your kindness, please express my gratitude to your young ladies. I do miss my robes, really the color means nothing to me, only to others." She stood took the robes and bowed to Sutton.

Ski asked Moori if she would like him to attend to her wounds, she declined and said she would manage by herself. He showed them to their rooms and put a healing spell into Moori's room.

The next morning they all met for breakfast in Henry's Villa. Moori had slept better than she had on her travels with Casandra. This place was filled with magic, she could feel it, coming right from the ground.

Ski asked if the Elves had anything else to tell him before they left for Winsette Castle. Sam shared the strange plan Henry had laid out for them to follow. Sutton and Ski laughed and said, "Henry and his games, he loves to stick to his Brothers. Sutton perhaps you should go with this group to ease their way to the King's Court. Ruth needs to get back there to organize Henry's household hurry back. I will need you here too."

Everyone left. Moori and the Professor went to Chancellor Ski's laboratory. Moori had never in her life seen so many bottles and jars filled with unrecognizable substances. At first, Ski only asked the Professor his thoughts and questions, but soon he turned to Moori.

She answered with clarity, and it surprised her that she could remember all of her past without deep emotions. "I was ten years old when the Hex army came into our village in Scorpio. They killed my Father and took my Mother and me. I watched as they slowly sucked the life force from her, of course, I didn't understand then what they were doing. I only knew she was near death. They put us in an animal cage on the back of a wagon as we traveled from village to village gathering women and girls. I never knew where we ended up just that it was far from home."

She gave detailed descriptions of Martin and a man named Moondale as they removed her eggs and experimented with them. Then she described the spells and the Attachments they laid on her, and how they felt. She detailed the final one at throat lunging down to her female organs. She was the first they succeeded with. Most of the other women and girls in the cells died at their hands. One day they took her Mother out, and she never returned. They used Moori again and again. Every time they would take her farther and farther to the edge, until one time they had pulled almost all the power from her. That was the night they merely threw her in the sea, like garbage. She would have drowned if not for the Monks from a nearby Monastery fishing. They pulled her out and gave her their powers. They were the ones who took her to Elk's Mountain, to heal.

Ski was silent along with the Professor while she told her story. He couldn't believe what this woman had gone through or the strength it took her to come back from death. They all sat still when she finished her story. Ski spoke first, "I would like you to know it is my honor to be in the presence of one so strong and determined; blessings to you. I will also do anything in my power to help you heal and continue in the dynamism of the mindfulness." Ski bowed to her, "I think we should have some lunch, then we will come back here. I shall tell you everything I know about this spell. You can question me then."

That is what they did, and Ski was as honest and straightforward as he could be with them. They both deserved the complete truth. Moori was surprised at how many questions she had for him. Ski said they needed to make their own dinner since Ruth was away, so they went to his kitchen. They were working together in the kitchen when she thought of another question. Moori asked, "Ski, you didn't tell us about the snakeskin gloves. Why did you send men out to find snakes?"

Ski grinned, "Excellent question. I think you would make a good scientist, your questions this afternoon have been very impressive. Let me explain; the snake skinned gloves were used by young Sorcerers to keep them from being charmed by Warlocks who would place spells on them for unsavory advances. Anyone of means would have their girls wear gloves, as in everything we progress. Sorcerers learned how to teach girls to ward Warlocks off. Only water snake skins were used for these gloves because liquids would not enter the skin, or spells, or charms. How Henry thought of it, I don't know. The snakeskin is impenetrable and can keep the Attachment Spell from digging into the skin of the provider of the spell. This discovery has opened new avenues to look for answers to a treatment for this spell. After dinner, the Professor and I will pull apart the Attachment Henry sent back. Hopefully, we will learn more. If you don't want to be a part of that, I would certainly understand. I have a lovely library you may enjoy."

Moori answered immediately, "No, no. I want to know everything I can, I need to see it. I need to understand completely, it is part of the seventh level. I have been too many years in a dark cell, cowering."

Ski smiled, and Sutton knocked on the door, "The Elves and Ruth are safely at the Castle, just wanted you to know." He turned to leave, but Ski told him to stay for dinner. They had a very relaxed and happy meal while Ski shared how Addison came to the family. Ski had adopted him as well as Sutton and Ski's nephew Jack, took Paxton. They were all roommates at school, and Ski said he always thought they were more like Brothers than cousins or friends. Sutton, Paxton, Henry, and Addison were all inseparable in their youth and now. After dinner, Sutton pushed them out saying he would do the dishes they needed to go to work. It was after Midnight before they finished up, and Moori began to understand the strange spell known as the Attachment.

They were walking to the house when Moori asked one more question, "Ski, help me understand why the people who use the Attachment Spell over and over get addicted."

Ski said, "Let's get into the house." He held the door for Moori, and they went into the living room Ski opened a bottle of wine, "Have a seat Moori. You know the rules of the universe. When one uses magic, a price must be paid. Stealing power required an even larger payment. Magical power in large doses gives a feeling of being invincible and boundless. Stolen powers cannot be retained it evaporates like lake water on a hot day. Remember law fourteen we can only keep talents we earn; all else will be given back to the Night. Men like the King have learned this the hard way. They now keep their Attachments to themselves and use only what they need when they want it. Unfortunately, they haven't realized they are playing into the hands of the dark. The one insatiable emptiness that will swallow all and never be satisfied. They are pulling from the ground the very powers witches and sorcerous bury to keep our magical energy flowing. That vacuum never shuts down and can never pull enough power in."

Moori sipped her wine and said, "Ski, you mentioned the King protects his Queen because if anything happens to her, he will die as well. The connection grows stronger over the years, does Martin have that connection to me?"

The Professor said, "Martin has not used you in years. I believe his connection to you is so limited now, that his death would mean nothing to you. You would not even feel it."

Moori scrutinized her glass of wine as she said, "The other day, when they entered the room, Martin came straight to me, leering. I froze at the sight of him." She stopped talking, and Ski and the Professor just waited patiently.

"The first thing he said was; I thought I killed you little bird. I could smell you from the road." She drank her wine and held out her glass for more. "He opened my throat in seconds and drank my power. When he tried to take me with him, I fought him with all my might. I thought this hideous thing was dried up and dead. Now I find it alive and pulsing."

Ski gave her more wine, and said, "There is only a short time to remove the spell. Until just now… I had thought as you did. It would die on its own."

Moori drank her wine and said, "Tomorrow you can use me. Make me a snakeskin that covers this thing. I will test it out. I will not be used by Martin again."

Ski said, "Moori, no, we will find another way."

Moori laughed, "Will you and be in time to help Casandra. I wonder if Henry and the Doctor got it all out of her. Can she still be used? We don't know do we." She set her glass down. "In the morning I will go to the lake and ask a snake to give me his life. You may place his skin on me. Maybe Sutton can take me there?"

Ski stood and said, "Sutton said he will meet you at the lake in the morning."

Elves and Their Riddles

Sutton returned the carriage to Winsette Castle stables then took the Elves and Ruth to Henry's quarters to freshened up. He walked the Elves to the Throne Room and asked the guards to announce them. The guards said Elves were not permitted. Sutton said they had a critical message for the King and needed to see him immediately. They waited fifteen minutes before Sutton was allowed in the room where all of Henry's Brothers and the King himself sat on the Throne.

Sutton bowed and said, "Your Majesty, Henry sent me with news for you. Only you."

Richard stepped forward and said, "We will find out soon enough just tell us all at once."

The King nodded, "Go on, I know it is about Casandra I can feel it in my bones. Henry and I still have some connection."

Sutton straightened up, "Casandra is missing."

They all started talking at once shouting questions and making accusations. Dillon came to Sutton whispering in his ear. "Is this the true message?"

Sutton said, "The Lady Elves are the key."

Richard was right there, "What are you two whispering about."

Sutton said, "Dillion asked me how I know the truth. Henry sent the Elves who traveled with Casandra. They are outside this chamber the guard refused them entrance."

The King clapped and said, "We have Elves bring them in."

Dillon called them in and instructed them to relay what had happened to Casandra. As they had planned, they told them of the abductions of Casandra from her room, the search for her and the group splitting up to report the kidnapping. Sam said his orders were to tell King Winsette and prepare a place for the Emperor, then wait for orders.

Winsette said, "Well we are to have Elves attend the Coronation too. How wonderful Dillion! This new law I enacted should be permanent it is so much fun to see this play out when I am alive." He started laughing and said, "I still remember my Coronation, I had to kill every one of my Brothers to gain the crown. There was so much blood on the floor it took hours before we could dance, you boys have it easy." The boys were cringing, which only made Dillion shake his head. Dillion mentally told his Father Sutton said that the Lady Elves were the key.

King Winsette asked Sam, "Is it true Elves can sniff out a spy at a hundred yards?"

Sam smiled, "Some are able to, your Majesty; most only have a hundred-foot radius."

Dillion asked, "I see you employ women in your guard do they fight or just sniff?"

Sam said, "They fight your Majesty." He was deliberately holding information to let him know this message was not for all of them.

Richard pushed his way forward, "You are a man of few words. Tell me, Sam, do you only work for the Emperor, or can you be hired for a price."

Sam said. "We swear allegiance to the Emperor only on his orders can we share our services or the information we learn. A price does come with the service."

Richard asked, "Sam are you always on duty?"

Dillion said to his Father mentally. We must get them alone Father.

The King answered mentally. I have a plan.

The King laughed, "Let the poor Soldier alone, Richard. Of course, he is on duty all the time, or what good would he be to anyone. Come closer Son and bring those young ladies with you."

They all walked up to the King. He said. "I bet you have smelled a rat right here in this very room." Then he laughed. "Don't worry Sam, I wouldn't ask you to tell me. Dillion, you should talk to the Emperor, see if he could spare a few Elves. Maybe we wouldn't always be at the mercy of that damned King Hex. I want the women to come closer, young ladies let this old man look at you."

The girls stepped forward and curtsied. Grace spoke, "I am Grace, your Majesty we are all pleased to meet you."

The King said, "Are you Casandra's Grace?" Grace said yes, and the King hollered, "Is Charlie here?" She raised her hand. "This is exceptional luck, Dillion! We have the fighting girls right here in our presence. Come Dillion we must take them to the Queen straight away. She has never even seen an Elf this is going to be such fun." He took Charlie by one arm and Grace by the other and walked them from the room.

Richard said, "The man is insane Dillion stop him. It is one thing to be old, dimwitted and senile, but now he has added lecherous."

Dillion laughed, "Let the old man have fun, Richard. He won't be with us long, and he is in the Castle who will find out?"

Samuels said. "What in the world was he talking about fighting girls. Richard is right; he has really lost his mind."

Dillion ushered Sutton and Sam out of the chambers then returned. "Think before you speak Brothers! I am more concerned about finding Casandra we must help Henry search for her. We need this alliance, think how it will look to the world if we sit on our hands and do nothing." They all looked to one another. "Alright, I will get the Elves out of the Castle, but you think of a plan which makes us look good to the Emperor while I am gone."

Dillion walked out to the hallway and said, "Sam, Sutton come with me, and we will retrieve your soldiers."

Dillion ambled slowly as the girls gave the King Henry's message in the King's private chambers. He heard every word. When the three of them walked in, the King was in his chair at the fireplace, with the Queen across from him. "This keeps getting worse and worse. I told you about the King Hex offering to make me an Attachments. I am sure Richard has one on his wife. King Hex will drain the world dry of magic, we should name him King Ass." Dillion was furious.

The King sighed, "We cannot make sound choices while madmen rule, Dillion. We need to train our wives to defend themselves. I don't want the King or his Generals near my daughter-in-law's, not one of them. I happen to like them more than most of my sons."

Dillion turned to Sam, "You are one of Eric's men; can you help us?"

Sam bowed, "I have been ordered by Eric to do all that I can for you Dillion and the King. But…not for your Brothers, and you must swear not to let them know we here to help. Of course, if this comes out… we will deny everything and blame you. No offense Sir."

Dillion stood tall, "There is none taken. I would do the same to you. I need to get back to my Brothers before they become suspicious. I suggest Queen, you and my wife take a personal interest in these Elves. We need them in the Castle to find the rats. Sutton, you better leave, and tell me the moment my Brother Henry shows up."

The Queen laughed, "I have a perfect excuse; these women are to set up the Emperor's apartments. I should help them along with your wife maybe we could work on Addison's Apartment too."

Shelton's Dream

The tall ship cut through the ocean helped by the magic of a full breeze as Henry sat in a chair by Casandra's bedside. This was the second day the Doctor had kept Casandra mostly asleep. He would wake her in the morning hoping the pain in her throat would subside enough that she could stay conscious. The Doctor, Addison, and Henry took shifts. Henry took the late nights and spending time sifting through her memories and wrestling with their future.

The night before Casandra was restless with dreams which were difficult to follow; this dream was no better. Henry sat on the bed watching helplessly as Casandra tossed and turned. There was a knock on the door he opened knowing it was Addison.

Addison walked to Casandra, "She is dreaming again, it woke me. I couldn't get back to sleep. I thought you and I could talk."

Henry gave him a weak smile, "Marion is still not talking to you, this is not your fault. Casandra and Grace warned her not to sit in the healing pool, the little Sprite wouldn't believe."

Addison said. "I wished she had been truthful with me from the beginning now we have a mess. First, we had the biggest argument I have ever had with a woman. Now…now she won't even look at me. I wish she would do a small blood bond, at least then I would know what she is thinking. Maybe Casandra can get her talking." He walked to the bed and looked at Casandra her face and neck was healing, but when she woke, the burning was almost too much pain for Addison to tolerate. He didn't know what else they could do for her.

Henry patted his arm. "Addison. Your healing skills are superb, you and the Doctor have done all you can. I have been thinking, this Attachment was meant to be permanent. Perhaps that is why I couldn't remove it, and maybe we didn't eliminate all of it. Back to Marion, tomorrow I will talk to her. Sprites can be totally unreasonable. Margaretta your little Sprite at school certainly was. She was so jealous she didn't even want me to talk to you. They have been mistreated over the years they all have chips on their shoulders. However, once you are claimed you have friend or foe for life."

"Margaretta would have been my friend if she had lived." Addison sighed.

Henry took Casandra's hand it felt so lifeless, "I don't want to turn our minds maudlin. You never told me about the dreams the Hermit gave you, now would be a good time."

Addison leaned against the wall of the small room. "With all this going on I had forgotten all about that." Addison sat in the chair. "So many years I wanted to know about my parents, strange, once I found who they were, I totally forgot about them. Well, sit back Henry this is a story that will interest you." Henry was silent while Addison shared his dream and the conversation with the Hermit.

"Your Brother Richard strangled her and threw her in the river. He never knew she was a high blood Arlequin Wizard, he thought she was just a whore. I have never liked him, now I hate him. If my dream was true, she knew one outcome might be her death because she had already paid the Village Witch to take me and fabricate the story for Ski. I can't be certain, but I think her Brother was Ernst, which would make her the last Queen of Arlequin. Henry…tell me what you are thinking you are going too fast for me."

Henry stopped and walked to Addison. "You are my nephew. Ski is my Uncle by marriage, so he is your Grand Uncle. Addison, do you know what this means?"

Addison said, "We are all blood related which explains so many things about our blood bond and life together. I have no proof the dream is true."

Henry said laughing, "Addison you have blood, and your memory is just like your Father's, thank the Night you are mostly like your Mother. Ernst, you say, that accounts for you healing abilities and your knowledge of powers and talent. All that is important but what really matters here is you are in line for the throne! Think of it... you are a Prince."

Henry started pacing. "Oh, this is rich. Three of my Brothers will be furious. My Father, on the other hand, will have another Princess, by the way, your child is a little girl. He told me he is sick of little boys; he likes girls better. If you and Marion are smart you will let Father pick the name, then you can have anything you desire from him. Oh, this is going to be fun. Addison, you should marry her before we get to Diamante. Then you can introduce her as your wife the Duchess, Marion. Addison that is your answer!"

Addison sat dazed trying to keep up with Henry. "What is my answer?"

Henry stopped pacing and placed his hands on his hips, "To Marion of course, think man. Sprites are the lowest form of magical creature. They have never been allowed an education or title. They do not allow intermarriage unless it raises the level of Sprites. Like the Doctor and his wife, she was only released to him because he was respected and an educated man. Marion was raised up in her society by being educated, which is why she was not allowed to breed until she was married. Her parents were expecting a great deal from her life and probably a respected marriage. Here she went and got herself pregnant, imagine how she has been feeling. Maybe she is not mad at you Addison but at herself."

Addison smiled for the first time in days, "I think you are on to something, if I could make her a Duchess she would be elevated higher than any Sprite ever has."

Henry grinned, "Of course if this is the truth, the downside is you are a direct relation to Antioch Gadwell, the most annoying Wizard the world ever produced."

Casandra jerked, Addison and Henry were taken to her dream. She and Marion were at a fair and wanted to ride a roller ride, but the man said they could not be seated together, they didn't weigh enough. Casandra called her Elf guards and told them one had to ride with Marion, the other with her. She got in with Martin. Wait...Martin was an

Elf, the ride started then Martin placed a charm on Casandra. He started kissing her then he bent her head back. Eric ripped Martin off the roller-ride.

Addison pulled himself from the dream and went to Casandra. He knew this dream would end as badly as the others she had been having.

Henry stayed watching the dream. Suddenly he was drawn into her memory of the abduction at Winters End. Martin was ripping power from the Attachment, and the burning was excruciating. Henry grabbed his own throat in pain.

Addison was trying to ease Casandra's pain; her eyes flew open. She was fighting with all her might to release from him. Casandra managed to push herself off the bed and throw Addison against the wall. She ran over Henry and opened the door. Henry grabbed her to throw her on the bed, but Casandra counterbalanced her weight against him, and he ended up in the bed instead of her. She ran out the door and up on deck. They ran after her but by the time they reached her she was mounted on Shelton flying into the night sky.

Henry ran to Shelton, "Let her down Shelton we will take care of her."

Shelton shook his head and flew higher. Paxton came running, putting his pants on at the same time. He yelled, "Shelton, come back here! Casandra needs medical attention. Henry is not hurting her."

Shelton flew over them and mentally told Paxton. Silly Warlocks, she is dreaming. She needs me now. We are an exact match. I will take her and her dreams to the moon there she will heal. Wait here I will return before dawn.

They watched helplessly as Shelton carried her to the stars.

The Wisdom of Wizards

Devon stared out the window of the conference room of his Father's Castle as his Generals sat around the table bickering. General Gage had followed the Emperor's Major to the Bayonne Temple. He said, "Sir, that procedure is only used in matters of grave importance. They would use the crystal to communicate if they felt she was alive."

Devon held his tongue, he knew she was still alive, he could feel her breath. He knew she was out to sea, with her Pegasus. The winds didn't lie to him. These idiots would not believe him.

General Due Bre said, "I tell you she is not dead, they are still searching in the Bayonne Sea my reports are true."

General Brad said, "Well so are mine! The Emperor has gone to the Monks no doubt to pray for her safe return. However, it is more likely they fear she is dead!"

Devon turned and asked one question, "Where is Henry?"

They all turned and looked at him. He walked to the door turned and said, "Find Henry, and you will find her living and breathing. I can feel every one of her breaths." He walked out, he could not stand another second in the room with any of them. He would go to the garden and think back to the kiss they shared in her bed, that is what kept him breathing.

The King looked worried, "I have never seen anyone so possessed as my son. He is linked to her by more than an Attachment Spell.

Swearing he can feel her breath and find her in the sea. I think he is going mad."

General Martin said, "Well, he is related to her." They all looked at him stunned. "Our Queen his Mother is the first cousin to the Empress. Perhaps that has something to do with it. I will go to Moondale and ask him about this."

The King stood, "I hate dealing with that man. You go ask Moondale, Martin, we need to know if we can trust Devon. We need to control him, we are so close."

The Night Over Bayonne Sea

Casandra felt the healing threads Shelton had spun around her as she dreamed. These were not nightmares but sweet memories of running through the fields at the North Castle chasing butterflies. She sat at the edge of the lake dipping her feet in the water; if she held very still, little tadpoles would swim by and tickle her toes. All were lovely memories of being whole, healthy, and happy. She felt the warmth of the sun and opened her eyes to see a sliver of light across the ocean's horizon. She woke to find she was flying on Shelton. Beneath her was the ship, Henry put her on when they left Winter's End the deck was filled, and everyone's eyes were on her.

Shelton mentally said. They are all waiting for you. You dreamed a long while, but now you are healed. Your wounds were severe, the Mother of the Moon worked with you all night. I can take you back to Henry or out to sea, it is your choice. You should know Devon knows you live.

Casandra said mentally. I know, the Prince knows more than I would like we are connected somehow. Shelton, I love Henry; I wish you would bond with him. You would find you like him too.

Shelton grumbled. I don't trust Diamante they are manipulators and cheats. Playing games, that is all they care for. I like the Elf better, and he loves you. I know you love him, he is good to me.

Casandra sighed having Shelton was a lot like having a child. "Shelton set me down on the ship and bond with Henry as a special favor to me. I love you the most."

Shelton flew to the ship and mentally said. Henry smells funny can I bond with Paxton, he is a good man, and I like Paxton. Shelton set down gently on the ship, and Henry came to lift Casandra off. Shelton turned his head and gave Henry a sneer, Henry backed up. Shelton extended his wing, released the ties that held her, and Casandra slid down his wing like a sliding board.

She stood before Henry and said mentally. Do not yell at Shelton I am fine, and I feel good.

The Doctor came to her, "Alright, young lady down to sickbay. We will check you out and see how magical your horse really is."

Shelton thought to Casandra. Tell that idiot I am a Magical Pegasus, not a stupid horse!

Casandra answered him. As soon as he releases me to talk.

Paxton walked to Shelton and said, "I heard that. Really, Shelton, you should learn manners, horses can hear too. You'll get kicked if you call them stupid to their faces. Casandra is right you should bond with Henry. You would know a lot more, Henry is brilliant. We all have an important role to play in the days ahead you are part of them like it or not."

Shelton answered him. I don't like games.

Paxton said, "I don't like being undermined. You went behind my back to get Casandra up here last night. I told you I would go to Henry and explain, and I would bring her to you. You are a liar and can't be trusted."

Shelton thought. I am not a liar, and I can be trusted! Paxton!

Paxton smiled and said, "Then show it! Bond with Henry, show him what you are here for."

The Doctor couldn't believe her throat was almost healed on the outside. He took a light and shined it into her throat, which was still red, but so much better. Cuts and bruises on her arms and legs were almost healed as well. The scab on her chest and throat would be there a while. "Casandra, you are much better. However, I still want you getting plenty of rest. Sleep heals, your horse showed Henry that. We need to take off the bandages on your neck and chest. They need air now to heal. I will give you an ointment to use on them. Use it three times a day and keep it clean. Now, I am going to have you to speak to me, and I want you to know you will sound and feel like you have a very sore throat. Hopefully, it will only last a few days. Casandra, I release you to speak, now say something for me."

Casandra swallowed and said, "Doctor, Shelton is a Magical Pegasus, not a horse. He asked I tell you that."

The Doctor chuckled. "Well, I will remember that. Let me have another look down your throat." He did that and listened to her heart, he said, "Your voice is scratchy. I think it will return to normal as it heals. Henry told me you do not eat meat. You haven't eaten much in the past few days. You will eat fish and soup of fish, or I will hand feed it to you myself. You need to build your strength back, and I wish I could get you into the sun's light, but Henry is afraid of spies. Resume your Marshall exercises as soon as you feel up to it that will help too. I will put up a shield of privacy, and you can ask me any questions."

She said. "I have a few." The first thing she asked was about having sex with Henry.

He laughed and said. "As soon as you would like." She asked about Marion he told her, "Casandra she is fine, but Marion won't be if she doesn't take care of herself. She needs to eat right and exercise, and all she does is moon around, and she won't talk to any of us. Addison is counting on you to help her."

Casandra said she would as soon as he answered her last question. "Why are the Prince and I still tied together. I can feel his breath, and I am sure he knows I am alive."

The Doctor said. "That is a much harder question to answer. It might be that you are related, or he may have unwittingly blood bonded with you as he used the Attachment Spell. You should ask Henry's Uncle Ski; he would be the one to answer that question better than I. If that is all I will release the shield and know unless you say the question out loud, neither Henry nor Addison will know what we spoke of." He released the bond and helped Casandra down then opened the door, Henry and Addison were standing in the hall. "Well, well, well, what a surprise Casandra. Can you believe we would find these two out here skulking around." He laughed while they glared at him, "What will it be first food or cleaning up?"

Casandra laughed, and Henry and Addison's face beamed. "I think I would like to clean up first. Addison, would you ask Marion to come to help me I still feel a little wobbly." Addison kissed her on the cheek and ran to get Marion.

Henry held out his hands, and Casandra leaned on him back to the cabin. He closed the door behind them then pulled her into his arms. He kissed her long and hard then pushed her back and gazed at her then said. "It is wonderful to hear your voice. What did the doctor say, will it be sore sounding forever?"

She giggled and said, "No, he said it will heal back to normal in a few days. I may still have a sore throat, but the burning is entirely gone."

Henry pulled open her blouse, "The scabs on your neck and chest, will they go back to normal too?"

She said, "Oh, I forgot to ask about that, but he did say we can have sex as soon as we like."

Henry was flabbergasted, "Casandra you did not ask him that, did you?"

Casandra raised her eyebrow and said. "Henry, you are not embarrassed by that, are you?"

Henry swallowed, "No. It's just well, men don't really ask questions like that. We have not really discussed that subject ourselves, remember I know everything. You carry an egg. I would like a few memories made clear before sex happens."

Casandra said, "Alright what memories?"

Marion opened the door and ran to Casandra, giving her a big hug. "Casandra I am so glad you are alright; I have been so worried. I am not ready for all of this. You must not leave me not ever, I can't do this on my own. Do you understand?"

Henry wondered what that meant, he would find out later. "I will go see that something is ready for you to eat when you are finished. Thank you, Marion, for helping her."

The Wizard

The Emperor waited in a secret room the Monks kept for meetings on the side of the Mountain where he would not need to go through the cleansing ritual. Achille had taken him to the room blindfolded. As he closed the door he said he would come back for him when the meeting had ended; his Eminence Zareb wanted a meeting with him. The Emperor could not help to think back to the last meetings with the Wizard. He was losing the war with the King of Hex. He hired the Wizard to help him. In the end, things worked out but getting to that point Hayden had almost lost half his army and most of his support from his allies. The Wizard had opened the ground that swallowed the Hexian Army as they made their way across the Northern Pass. All these years he thought the Wizard was solely responsible for the victory, now he knew he had Henry to thank. He led them into the trap as the Wizard opened the globe.

When he came in Hayden didn't know the Wizard was sitting right in front of him. As his eyes adjusted to the light, he saw the Wizard grinning at him, and he looked younger than the last time he saw him. His long black hair was tied back in the Arlequin way. His black-purple eyes sparkled, accented by the shiny snakeskin jacket, pants, and hat. He had a black beard that was closely shaven which peaked at his hairline giving him a look of a perpetual grin.

Hayden shook his head, "All the money I paid you and you still wear the same old clothes Antioch."

The Wizard took off his hat and laughed. "You are the only one I allow to call me Antioch. Don't ever do that in public, as if anyone sees me in public anymore. Also, these are new clothes I just acquired these snakeskins last month. It is good to see you, my friend, you look well. If not for you I would have been an outcast for centuries. I owe you, Hayden."

He leaned forward, and a bottle of wine appeared then two crystal glasses. He poured and then continued, "The word about your daughter Casandra is everywhere. She is well and fine, with Henry. You really have given her to him? He was the biggest pain in my ass over the North Mountain. You have no idea how hard it was to put that plan in his mind. He is a stubborn man, handsome though. You will have some pretty grandchildren, powerful too. What is on your mind Hayden?"

The Emperor shook his head, "I have missed you, Joseph. I don't understand why I am so calm in your presence. I haven't felt this relaxed since the Continental Council came to me demanding something be done with the King of Hex. I wish we could have killed him the last time, the coward didn't even go to his own war. I want my daughter to live, Joseph, and I will do whatever it takes to do that."

The Wizard sighed, "The Hermit's hand is in this deeply. She has her agenda and has planned over a thousand years." He stared into his wine glass, and it filled to the top. "This will not be easy, and I wish I knew her objective, Hayden."

The Emperor said, "All I know is Casandra is to kill the King. How I don't know, the damned Hermit puts compulsions on all of them. I think the Duchess has more in mind. Henry is sifting through Casandra's memories, but so far, he has found nothing. Let me tell you what has happened so far." The Emperor told the Wizard everything that had happened, and all he knew about the Attachment Spell. "What is your price, Joseph?"

The Wizard waved his hand, and the wine bottle and glasses disappeared. "Arlequin, it is time I have my home back."

The Emperor's mouth opened like a fish; his friend could not be considering this. "Antioch, Arlequin is still uninhabitable. What in the world would you even do with it?"

The Wizard smiled, "Hayden, you hold the title to it. The Continents gave the land to you to hold for the betterment of man. It is my home; there are others who call it home too. The Parragon and Hex are stealing right from under your nose. We want to return to our home. I can make the land whole again and I will."

The Emperor said. "My little girl lives, you have Arlequin."

The Wizard held out his hand, the Emperor shook it. The Wizard said, "You are not the first to ask me to watch over Casandra, his Eminence has a stake in her future too. You will need to speak to him before you leave, and I will need a few things from you. Then I will be off to Belissa Villa they will be surprised." He grinned devilishly.

The Emperor guffawed, "I plan to surprise the whole world before I am done Antioch Joseph Gadwell. What is that poem about revenge? Well, no matter, revenge has come."

The Night Sky

"Marion, what is your problem, do you love Addison or not." Cassandra was trying to shower and talk some sense into her friend. She stepped from the small shower and wrapped a towel around her. Marion helped her dress.

"Of course, I love him. That doesn't mean I can just marry him. My family hasn't even met him. Sit down before you fall down. I will brush out your hair. I can't believe Henry did not comb your hair; it is so tangled. He is not a Sprite. I can never marry Addison no matter how much I love him."

Casandra said, "That is not true. Henry tells me the Doctor married a Sprite."

"The one with fourteen children? That sounds like a wonderful life for me, tell Henry I said that. Oh and don't forget to let Addison hear that too. I thought I could talk to you privately I should have known better." Marion pulled her hair so hard she almost screamed.

"Marion, you are pulling my hair out of my head, are you mad Addison or me?" Casandra took the brush away from her.

"I think I will be mad at all of you! I can't believe you haven't said anything yet. Go on say it." She fell into the bed.

Casandra sighed. "Say what, Marion, what is it I am supposed to say?"

She lifted her head and said, "I told you so, that's what! Stay out of the healing baths how many times did you tell me?" She rolled over and started crying.

Casandra came to her and pulled her up and held her. She said. "Henry and Addison, you may not listen to any more of this conversation. I don't know how to block you so… I am trusting you." She heard them say they were going up to talk to Shelton they would not listen.

After an hour of talking, they decided she was a free Sprite and could marry who she wanted. They started out the door when Marion turned and said, "Casandra, Addison hasn't actually asked me to marry him. What if he doesn't want me to marry him?"

Casandra laughed and opened the door. Addison was standing in the hall waiting with a very unusual flower in his hand. He said. "Shelton took me to an island, and I found this. Casandra, could you give me some time with Marion alone."

She smiled and walked out to the hall. Henry was standing at the end of the hall, smiling. "Thank you, Casandra, at least she is talking to him. That is a start." He kissed her softly, "Cook has some fish soup made just for you." Her stomach flipped; she hated fish.

Belissa Lake

Sutton stood over Moori as she sat on the ground chanting a song to ask a snake to join her body. So far two had come to hear her story but turned away. He wasn't sure what his role was in this adventure; was he to kill them or just stand by a watch them commit suicide. He assumed she would tell him when the time came. He thought it a silly notion of asking permission to kill an animal. Although Paxton would have understood, he was a man who knew all animals. The sunlight faded on the lake, and at first, Sutton thought it was cloud crossing the sun. However, as he looked up he was blinded, a spell froze him in the place where he stood. The Wizard stepped gently to Moori's side and whispered. "Moori that is the right tune but the wrong chant."

She jumped three feet and backed up against a large rock. A very tall smiling handsome man stood there with black hair tied back, a trimmed black beard, and black eyes that were sparkling. "Who are you? Where did you come from?" She then saw Sutton frozen in place. "Release Sutton. How did you know my name?"

He snickered and said, "That is quite a lot of questions all at once. Which would you like answered first, Mistress?"

Moori turned to him and stood in warrior poise and said. "Release Sutton, now."

He crossed his arms and said, "I wouldn't normally do this, but Sutton and I are old school chums. I am sure he will want to know why I am here before he tries to kill me." He waved his arms and Sutton was free.

Sutton brushed himself off and said, "I don't mind being frozen Antioch, but really you didn't have to make it that damned cold. Excuse my cursing Mistress. Why can't you walk up to a door and knock like any other normal Wizard?"

"Where's the fun in that? Not my style, you know I must make an entrance. Please do not call me Antioch, you know I hate that name. What are we doing here enchanting snakes?"

Sutton said, "Yes. That is exactly what we are doing. Now, what do I call you, Gadwell the great?"

The Wizard glared at him, "Wizard would suffice. Why are you enchanting my little friends?"

Moori started to say something, and Sutton stopped her by holding up his hand and saying, "That Wizard is none of your business, go away."

"What you want me to just go away, without knowing why I've come for this visit or answering any of the Monks many questions. You, Sir, have gotten cranky in your old age."

Their attention turned to the Professor and Ski, running down to the lake. The Wizard turned and smiled, "A welcoming committee, how thoughtful."

The Professor stopped in front of the Wizard, "Gadwell why are you here?" Ski almost ran into the Professor he was running so fast.

The Wizard sighed and crossed his arms you, "You both look well. I am so happy to see you again. Thank for inquiring about how I am. I think living out in this wasteland has caused you both to lose your manners." He laughed and said, "I was just about to enchant a snake for this young Monk Moori…but first we have some nosey neighbors." He spread his fingers, and a green light buzzed across the lake then several crows fell from the sky. They heard some thuds in the tree line on the side of the lake where green smoke circled up from where an animal body should have been. "Now then, back to the snakes, how big would you like them Moori?"

Moori stood astonished, then she thought to herself if she could not stand up to this Wizard how she would stand up to Martin. She tore her robe aside and said. "Large enough to cover my scars." She closed her robe; now he was looking at her with astonishment.

His face became severe then he walked to the water to speak to several snakes in a chant. They all swam forward, he reached into the water and pulled one out. He placed his forefingers between the snake's eyes and the snake fell dead. He handed it to Sutton, then repeated the process four more times. Then he turned and walk up to Henry's Villa, and they all followed him without saying a word. He sat at the outdoor table then motioned for all of them to rest as he placed a silent shield around them and a bubble to shield them. He began explaining, "Moori, I know your name because the Emperor told me of you. A man we both know named Eric holds you in high esteem he requested I help you. The Emperor has commissioned me to keep Lady Casandra alive. He sent me to help you develop your remedy for the Attachment Spell. I am at your service Chancellor Ski until the Coronation; the Emperor is expecting me to be in attendance."

Sutton laughed, "The Emperor wants you at the Coronation, whatever for, and does Henry know this?"

The Wizard waved his hand, and a bottle of wine appeared along with five crystal wine glasses, he slowly poured the wine then said, "Sutton I am the entertainment for the Coronation, and Henry has not heard just yet. He is wooing the young lady at sea and is much too busy to worry about me. Shall we get started? Don't waste daylight my Father would always say."

The Pirate's Erudition

The cook placed the steamy bowl of soup right under her nose, which caused her stomach to lurch. Henry snickered and waved his hand over the broth, and the best aroma filled her nostrils. How he did that she didn't know, "Thank you, Henry." She tasted it and could not detect a bit of fish in it and ate the whole bowl, along with a glass of white juice that was sweet and milky. The cook brought her a muffin for dessert, and while it was an ordinary dinner, she thought it was one of the best she ever had. As she finished, Marion and Addison came into the galley to share the news they would be married as soon as possible.

Henry suggested a wedding at sea with the Sea Captain, Marion had a fit. Sprites had to be married by a Monk or hand-fast with a Priestess. Civil marriage was utterly unacceptable. Henry shook his head and said. "You can be handfasted by a Witch in a glen but not a Captain at sea?" Marion began to turn red.

Addison stopped the argument before Marion could go on a rant, "We could go straight to Krete we could be there in five or six days, there is a large Temple there."

Henry said, "That would put us early on shore, if the King's men find us before Prince Bryan meets us, I would have no reason not to hand over Casandra. I am not even sure the Emperor went along with Eric's plan."

"Bryan is coming? You need to tell me about this plan." Casandra asked for more juice.

Henry poured more juice and explained that they were to meet Eric and Bryan on a small island off the coast of Celia, Santé Graneia which was two days away. If they were not there, they would have to go to plan B, which was not one Henry liked. Go to Krete.

Casandra said. "We should stick to the plan and then go to Krete for Marion's wedding. There it is settled. I want to see Shelton, and I want to meet the Pirate Captain."

Henry glanced out the porthole, "The sun is almost down, my favorite time of day at sea." They all four went on deck and watched as the sun dropped from the ocean's horizon into the sea.

Henry gazed at Casandra as her face filled with wonder. "Henry that is the most wondrous sight I have ever seen. I think I would be happy being a pirate, sailing all day and night."

Henry smiled, "I think I would too, as long as I had you to share it with. Perhaps if things don't work out, we should buy a ship and sail away."

Her face turned grave, "If wishes were fishes, the sea would be full. Of all the endings to this venture, that has never been one of them."

Henry said, "I tried very hard to look at the memories with the Hermit. She has you under a strong spell." He put his arm around her and looked out over the sea, "Well, now I know being a Pirate is not one of them. Only a million more questions to go. I know, we could learn to cook and open an Inn. Is that one of our ends?"

Casandra smiled and kissed him, "No, that is not one of them. Can I meet the Captain now?" Henry took her to talk with the Captain who took her on a tour of the ship, while she asked questions. So many questions Henry was starting to get impatient and was surprised the Captain was not. Finally, Casandra said, "I have one last question for you, is this business profitable?"

The Captain let out a hearty laugh, "My Dear girl, I have never had anyone so interested in Pirates. I think you are going into this business, and I will never give information to one of my competitors. However, I will give you some free advice. Before you buy yourself a ship, you should know it is hard work. In between good paying customers like Henry, and the cheaters we have to save every penny to tide us through. I think it is like any other business, except this one holds us in peace on the ocean. Look to those stars." They all looked up, "Not a sight like that in all the world but at sea. She rocks me to sleep every night and carries me in the day to every port in the world. That is a boon, not every job has. She has already captured your heart. I can see it on your face. You have come home Casandra, to Mother Sea. I need to go back to work. Enjoy the stars for me."

She and Henry walked to Shelton, without speaking they both picked up brushes and started currying him. Shelton had bonded with Henry and Addison when Casandra was deep in conversation with Marion. Casandra laid her head on Shelton's chest, while Henry leaned on his wing. Henry watched as wispy white tendrils spiraled out and whirled around them. Henry could feel the healing as a deep peace came over him. As the skies darkened, more stars grew in the heavens. Henry was so satisfied; he wanted to be out with Shelton all night but knew Casandra needed a bed.

Henry mentally thought. I would love to stay here all night with you, but it is getting late. Casandra, we should get you to bed, you need your rest.

She answered, "I feel so peaceful here I want this to last forever. Henry, I need to ask you something." Henry waited for her to formulate her thoughts. She said out loud, "You looked at my memories of the visit to the Hermit. Henry, she said it was important that we consummate our mating immediately. Our daughter needs to be firmly affixed to me before we are confronted by the King. She told me if we didn't the scenario would be none of my children would live."

Henry went to her and said, "She put all of your visits under a compulsion, how are you able to speak about this now?"

She let go of Shelton, "Shelton is connected to the Universe, and she knows what has happened. She released me to speak to you. You can now look back to that one visit."

Henry walked to the ship's railing and went back in memories. He saw clearly the Hermit and the entire visit. The more Henry knew her, the less he liked her. Casandra touched his hand, and he returned to the ship. "Do you believe her? Or trust her?" Henry looked at her.

"Henry, Elisabeth didn't follow her wishes look where she is. My Grandmother and Mother had orders from her, the Warlocks wouldn't listen to them, and you know what happened, my Grandmother and Grandfather died. My Mother blames herself for not acting on what the Hermit wanted which led to the deaths of my Brother and Sister and me being kidnapped. I am afraid to kill the King. I am more afraid not to."

Casandra looked at Henry with fear in her eyes, he kissed her forehead and said, "Let's go to bed, we can talk more there."

Devon's Madness

"She lives, Martin, she has been seen on a ship. I have word today." The King laughed. "We need to get her before the Emperor does. Martin go bring me that Witch."

Martin was with Moondale when he was summoned by the King. He rushed to the Castle and ran to the King's office. He was pacing and shouting at the top of his voice, "Martin, I want that Witch! I want her now. Go! Go get her for me."

Martin said, "I will get Devon and leave immediately."

The King shouted, "No! Leave him here I do not trust him. What did Moondale say?"

Martin didn't want to tell him what Moondale said. What he explained to the King was, "He is unsure of him. Moondale said he had never seen anyone react as Devon has. He thinks perhaps Devon was put under a spell by the Sorceress, that might explain his actions. He is possessed, not obsessed, and not addicted. He suggested using Henry's tonic to keep him in check."

The King handed Martin a dispatch and said, "I will see he takes it. Go! Here is the location."

The King watched as Martin walked out. It must be worse than he thought, Martin was usually more definitive. What was Martin keeping from him? The King couldn't have Moondale to the Castle he would go to the Science Building himself. It was almost dinner; he would do that tomorrow.

Devon found the King in the courtyard on his way to the dining room. "Father, where is Martin going, I saw him leave the garden?" Devon ran to him.

The King said, "I had a small errand I needed him to do."

Devon stood in front of him and glared, "What errand?"

The King roared at him, "That is the Kings business, Devon. Do not speak to me in that tone, take yourself to your room and calm down. You are expected for dinner, do not upset your Mother."

Devon stood his ground. "She's alive you know it, and you have had a word. Admit it, you know where she is."

"Stop it, Devon. I will not tolerate this behavior from you. What is the matter with you?" The King took a deep breath and said, "Listen to me Son, that Witch must have spelled you for you to act this way. You must take your tonic; you were better when you took your tonic."

Devon almost fell over, they thought him mad. They could not believe he could just know things...Devon understood more than he ever had. He was having premonitions and hearing voices. His voices were telling him the truth, his family's views were the crazy ones.

The voice told him to agree with his Father. He said, "Alright Father I will go take my medicine."

He turned and walked to his room. The voice said, leave Devon. They don't trust you; they will use the Attachment on you, go quickly. He took the bottle of medicine and packed a bag then put up a shield and left the Castle.

It wasn't hard sneaking out of the Castle but hiding from Ernst was near impossible. Ernst knew he was up to something, Devon knew he had to be quick to fool him. Ernst couldn't be trusted either he had an Attachment too. Devon knew the King could know all their plans through the Attachment. All his life, he wondered how Ernst always knew what he had done or said, now he knew. It had only taken a few months for Ernst to teach him the wizard ways. He understood why Wizards were always in high demand and so sure of themselves, it was instinct to just know everything. How Devon wished Ernst had taught him to transport. The King would never find him.

Antioch's Assistance

Antioch worked on the snakeskin charming it from the meat and the bone. He asked, "Ski would you like the meat for food or chemical use?"

Ski asked, "Chemical use, I think. Is it good to eat?"

Antioch said, "I like it in a stew. However, I will use a different method to clean the skin if it is for food. I wouldn't want you all poisoned."

The Professor added, "If you have enough, my lab could use some fresh snake, I would appreciate it. Would one of you two come over here and look at this, my results are so close I am having a hard time deciphering whose blood was used in this Attachment."

Ski tried to see the difference in shades of the specimens but was having a hard time too. The Wizard could see the variances. The Wizard said, "Show me your samples of blood. Hmm… I can see the difference, there are four here." He looked through the samples, and when he thought he had a match, he held it up to the light. Several minutes later he said, "Here, these are your matches." He turned the sample cards over, and they read; Henry Rakie, Martin Merdock, Richard Bertrand, and Devon Bertrand."

"Well, that cannot be correct." He looked to Ski. "Richard is the King and Devon his Prince?" Ski said yes. The Wizard squinted and held his hand over the two samples again.

He announced, "These two are not related, Devon is Arlequin, most likely a siphon, possibility a Wizard."

Ski laughed and said, "You are right, but don't tell anyone. Henry and Addison went to a lot of trouble to have the King think that Devon is his son." Moori asked why. Ski told her they had promised the Queen they would try to save her son. He explained that Devon, was Elisabeth and Ernst son and they were helping Henry in return for Devon's freedom. "Although now it seemed impossible, the young man was addicted to the Attachments. He was turning rogue according to Eric's reports. Casandra told Henry he had a mad look in his eyes they had almost turned red."

The Wizard sat down on a stool, "Ski, you are sure Ernst is his Father?"

Ski said, "Why yes, he is. Did you guess or is this your wizardly knowing again?" Ski looked closer at the Wizard. "Are you alright Wizard?"

Antioch asked, "You say they had him doing Attachment Spells?"

The Professor walked to him and placed a hand on his shoulder, "Wizard, tell us what you know. I can compel you."

The Wizard looked up at the Professor and said, "No Professor you cannot, I am stronger and smarter than most. Lucky for you…we are working together; I will gladly share for the mutual benefit of our cause. How much do you know about the Arlequin Llianian Wizards?" The Professor said not much, and the others agreed. "I will try to keep this simple; young men and women of my ancestry hold levels of powers you call them talents. Low levels read others' powers or the energy fields around the body. In using this power, they can do minor healings, fortune telling, and every once in a while, they can mind read. Most of our people could do that much. Intermediates can do all of that and do it well. However, they merely know and can siphon, draw off energies of others or add to them. They are the real healers and were in high demand around the world. Wizards my caliber can do all that and more, all knowledge is ours, which is why I command my price anywhere."

Moori said, "You are equal to his Eminence with great power and great responsibility."

Antioch just looked at her strangely and tilted his head, "I have never compared myself to him; he is Lorarsian." He started to get up, then stopped, "Every day I learn something new. The universe continues to astonish me. Today I learned our mission of keeping Casandra alive is becoming more challenging than I had thought." He walked back and continued cleaning snake skins.

Moori walked to him and said, "Why won't you tell us Wizard, what is it you don't think we need to know or is it simply you don't think we can handle it?"

He grinned at her, "I see why Martin chose you and why he wanted you dead. Intuition is not a normal power a new wizard wheels; that takes immense power. Young lady, you don't even know how powerful you really are." He put his snake down. "Very well, I suppose you should all know what you are up against but where do I begin." He grinned at Moori, "You are a Wizard Moori, do you know why you have never married?"

"After being imprisoned for years, I never wanted to be controlled again. That is why I chose to become a Monk." She stood back and crossed her arms definitely.

"You were so young when you were taken you hardly know what it is to be a Wizard, that might be a blessing for you. Most Wizards don't marry, some chose to but not often; because we marry for eternity. Both Wizard men and women are drawn to others that are powerful. Many times, we deliberately choose a mate that is much more powerful with talents other than our own. We produce one offspring and move on, we protect our race, constantly improving it. Casandra is most likely the most powerful Sorceress in our world, other than the Empress. Therefore she is the prize for the King of Hex to promote his power and improve his Warlock and Sorcerer bloodline. Devon is another matter; he is a Liliana Wizard it is in his very blood to want Casandra. He is driven by a force that he can hardly control. Having him drain power with a spell has only opened his drive for power and knowledge to an extreme. Wizards forget nothing, we build on every experience, and we grow slowly and naturally, we outlive everyone by tenfold. This young man is absorbing the world at an excruciating rate. I have no doubt these spells have driven him mad, and it is certainly reckless and careless. I am equally disappointed to find that my Father has allowed this behavior. His Mother is the Queen, no doubt. Ernst is a mighty Wizard; he has bred many fine Wizards."

Ski said, “Ernst is your Father? Well, well, well, the King of Hex has an Attachment Spell on Ernst and Elizabeth to control them.”

“Well, that makes sense. The King takes Ernst power, this Attachment is not made to take the talents. My Father can’t even help Devon, only watch him blow up.” The Wizard noted the silence in the room and found all of them staring at him intently, Oh, they wanted to know his feeling about this. “Powerful Wizards hold little esteem for our Fathers, it is the Mother who teaches and nurtures us. He probably never stayed long enough to watch me be born, Devon is my half-brother, but I have never met him. So, stop looking at me like I have three heads. Understand Devon can take Casandra with or without the Attachment. He will also be insanely jealous until he has impregnated her. Mating in Arlequin was never particularly romantic or refined.”

The Wizard's Strategy

The Ocean was smooth and the air cooling in the evenings. The group would meet on the deck and gaze at the sea, moon, and stars. Tonight they were discussing going to Krete early, Eric and Bryan were not on the designated island. Addison thought they should stay on board a few days more until they knew where Devon was. In the end, they decided Paxton would take Shelton into the city and scout it out. Each evening, one by one, they would go to their enjoyments. The Doctor and Paxton would drink wine with the sailors and play card games and dice. Addison and Marion would make love and plan for their wedding and future.

Henry and Casandra would make love all night and sleep most of the day. Henry was worried about Casandra; she was still not eating well because she couldn't swallow, and her voice was raspy. It was a New Moon this evening, and Henry was feeling uneasy he insisted she go down to bed early. However, when they got to the cabin, Casandra let down her hair and asked if Henry would brush it. Soon, he was entranced by her soft shining black hair, and his hands began to rub her neck and shoulders. That was all it took for Casandra to turn and kiss him softly on his lips working her way across his face and down his throat. When she reached his chest, they were pulling clothes off, and soon Henry would explode inside her. Then as every evening over the past weeks, they would talk into the deep hours of the night.

This night at the witching hour Casandra felt someone probing her strength and talents, then staring at her. She opened her eyes to see Ernst looking down at her. Casandra flung him off, and threw a blast to his head, then used a white electric chain to wrap him. He was laughing at her. The more power she used, the larger he grew. Was this a dream? Where was Henry, then the door to their small cabin flew opened, and Addison and Paxton were pushing her aside and piling on top of him? They had heard her thoughts and knew what had happened and were there in seconds. It wasn't a dream, and she realized she was naked, she quickly released him and cover up with her robe. Henry was still asleep or was he dead; she rushed to him to see he was in a daze.

Addison created a light sphere, and the room was as bright as day. Paxton and Addison had a lock hold of magic on the man. It was not Ernst, but a handsome young man who could be related. Addison and Paxton screamed at once, "Antioch!" Addison immediately told her he had been their instructor at the University, and how they never found him amusing. All four of them could hardly fit in the room together.

Casandra yelled, "Antioch Gadwell the Wizard? How dare you come in here! What have you done to Henry, un-spell him at once, or I will tear you in pieces and feed you to the fish!"

He gave her a wicked smile and said, "I have made a grave mistake. I should have asked for you."

Paxton said, "Antioch, really, when will you learn manners you don't come barging into rooms. You don't lay spells on people, probe them, then proposition them and expect to be liked. We have warned you; you are lucky we didn't kill you. You're an idiot. Wake up, Henry! Now!"

They released the Wizard, and he fluttered his fingers, and white stars floated to Henry which woke him. Henry stood straight up hitting his head on the ceiling, and he was livid, yelling at the top of his voice. The Doctor and Captain were both pushing their way into the cabin. Marion was standing outside the door, she pulled Casandra out. They hauled Antioch to the galley where they all gathered to understand why he was there with everyone talking at once.

Antioch raised his hand, and everyone stopped talking. He took Casandra's hand and sat her across from him, then sat at the table. She tried to speak, but like everyone else, the Wizard had silenced her. He straightened his black shirt and brushed off his snake sleeves. Only then did he speak, "Now that you all are quiet, I will speak. I have been commissioned by the Emperor to see that Casandra lives, she is the only one I am concerned with. By the look of her, I have gotten here none too soon. Henry for the love of Night what have you been doing to her?" Henry was pushing his way forward with a face filled with anger.

Antioch sat him down next to him, "Stop being so dramatic Henry, sit and listen for a change." The Wizard reached across the table and placed his hand on Casandra's forehead and closed his eyes. Casandra felt him enter her mind and the memories of the past few weeks from the night with the Unicorns was revealed. Her thoughts rushed forward quickly and out of her control when he released her, she sat dazed. "I see, my dear this must be remedied. I will explain quickly, then I will release you all to ask questions. I have been in Krete for two days. I met your Brother Bryan and Eric there. We have been staying in a hotel, with all your family. If asked you will all tell this lie, Casandra, you have been ill and not able to come out of your rooms until this morning. Your family is waiting for you. I will transport you there as soon as you are dressed for travel. Martin is already there and has attempted twice to get in to see you. I feel Prince Devon is not far behind."

He waved his hand, and a bottle of gold liquid and crystal glass was produced on the table. He poured the juice and took a sip, then placed it in front of Casandra. "I want you to drink that. I only took a sip that you would know it is not poison. Ski, Professor McMillan, and Moori, along with myself have been working on the way to keep Casandra from having an Attachment put on her. The beauty of this..." He raised his hands and pulled a box from the air and opened it. Small iridescent snakes were crawling around in it. "is it will give the illusion you have a working Attachment. These snakes have agreed to live on you, my dear. They will take a small amount of your power and increase it exponentially, giving the illusion to the King and Devon they are sucking power out of you. Ingenious, right Henry, if they believe the Attachment is there and working, why keep chasing her down. That part of the battle is won, the rest we will talk about later."

He poured more liquid and told Casandra to drink again she did. "First you need to get dressed in traveling clothes and meet me on deck in ten minutes. I will heal Casandra up there where there is more room and place the snakeskin on her. Then we will leave. Now questions?"

They all started yelling at once, he held up his hand again and said. "One at a time. I will call on you first Casandra."

"What makes you think I will wear a snake!"

He said, "Oh you will and more than one. Four to be exact, one for each of your dominators. Don't worry Moori said she didn't even feel them after five minutes. They will not show up on your skin, and they will completely close the wound and heal it. It is uncomfortable to place them; that is why I will put you to sleep first. Moori said it feels just like the Attachment spell. However, the beauty is everyone who is connected to your Attachment will see and feel it as if it were real. Now go to the cabin and get dressed to leave. Henry?" Casandra obeyed the Wizard.

"I have many questions for you; why does Casandra obey you blindly, why are we to trust you, prove you do not work for the King of Hex, do not tell me it is because you are a Wizard and you know everything!" Henry gulped for a breath, and his face was red.

The Wizard tilted his head and, in all seriousness, said, "As I have always told you, I do know everything. Believe me or not I couldn't care less. She is in my care Henry. She will follow my orders, as well as listen to me. For now, that is all you need to know." He raised his hand to stop Henry from speaking. "Addison, where did you learn to control light spheres?"

Addison sarcastically said, "You have no need to know that."

The Wizard smiled and said, "This is serious business gentlemen. I have no time for Diamante games." He forced his hand to Addison's forehead and retrieved his thoughts. Others tried to stop him, but he froze them in place with a blue light that hung over their heads. He released them all but kept them in silence. "Marion come forward! I know you are hiding in the doorway now, just as you were at Henry's cabin. Did you think I did not see you?"

Marion timidly walked to the table with eyes on the floor. She looked and felt very much like a little girl about to be punished. Addison reached out and pulled her to him. He wrapped an arm around her, and he glared at Antioch.

The Wizard asked, "Are you planning to marry this man Addison?"

Addison was shocked he had retrieved his thoughts. Marion looked at Addison then Henry and finally to the Wizard, took a huge breath and said. "Yes Sir, Master Gadwell, that is the plan, as soon as we reach the Temple in Krete." Then she stared at the table. Henry and Addison looked at each other wondering how she knew him.

The Wizard tapped his fingers on the table and said, "Sit. You were going to do this without the permission of your Master, or Parents? But of course, you didn't ask permission to have your body restored for mating. I suppose now that you are an educated Sprite, you don't have to follow the laws and rules. You don't even have to show up for your scheduled appointments with me any longer. You just go off and decide you will be an advisor, study law, and cavort with that Hermit. Is that how it is to be?"

Marion's mouth opened, but nothing came out. Finally, she stammered, "I…I am sorry. Oh, I did forget my appointment with you. We have been traveling and I…I have not committed to any of the studies the Professor…well the Professor just took things over. As far as the healing baths, and the Hermit that was a mistake. I should have listened to Moori. You are right to be angry with me." She sighed deeply and returned her gaze to the table.

The Wizard leaned forward and took her hand, "Did you know Moori is half Wizard?" Marion shook her head no. "Look at me, Dear." Marion looked at him her eyes were filled with tears. "The universe made us your protectors for a reason. Your powers are wonderful and special but limited. We are the strongest, and we know what is best for you. Sprites are such free beings; it is hard for you to be wise. I just wish you would listen to others when they give you advice. The Professor canceled your appointment, and he and I have talked for years about your studies. I have argued your inability to listen would not make you a good advisor. He has seen that too, which is why you will go back to the Monks and learn to relax and listen. You are a very significant Sprite, Marion. Stop messing up and learn! You are a Mother for Night's sake, no doubt your little daughter will be as stubborn as you! Do you understand?"

Marion's eyes were as large as suns. She said. "Yes, Master."

He folded his hands, and his long, bony fingers made a triangle then looked at Addison and said, "You will agree to help her, Addison?" Addison looked at him and shook his head yes. "Well, then this is your lucky day, Marion. Unknowingly you have matched yourself up with a half Wizard. Although I do not know how wise he is." Everyone still could not talk, they just stared at each other. "I will send a fairy to fetch your parents, and we will proceed to schedule your wedding to my cousin. As your Master, I grant you permission to marry Addison. Now we really need to leave. Everyone get dressed and meet me on deck." He stood and walked out and up the stairs to the deck, where Casandra waited.

He walked to her and said, "Casandra, you must remember me?"

She looked at him and said, "You remind me of Ernst, you remind me of the kidnapping."

"As I should my dear." Henry was standing right next to him, pointing to his throat. The Wizard waved his hand, and all of them started talking at once.

"Oh please, you are so tedious. Do you all want to never speak because I can easily arrange that." The Wizard put both hands to his face.

Henry went to Casandra and put his arm around her waist, "No, Antioch of Gadwell, help us we will listen, and you can explain later. If Martin is out there, we need to act fast."

"Well, this is a welcome surprise. For that respect, I will give you an explanation when we are in Krete. Casandra come here by Henry. Henry take a place behind her about three feet back. The rest of you take five paces back. As soon as she is healed, I will take four back with me, Henry, Casandra, Marion, and Addison. Doctor you and Paxton will stay with the ship, and I will use some wind to get you docked by early morning."

The Wizard stood in front of Casandra and extended his arms. It was as if they reached to the sky and brought stars into his hands. Small flecks of light began to swirl around them. At first, the light randomly flittered everywhere, but then it started to organize traveling in one direction. The lights twinkled in various colors then almost at once they all congregated in like colors. Red and orange light specks churned around Casandra's head. They were extracting black beads from her. Blue and green floating light particles entered her head. Gently the colors of light moved down her body until she was encased in the spinning lights. The Wizard bought both his hands together, and the encasement turned golden. He walked to her side and place one hand on her back and one on her forehead. Methodically he moved her into a floating position about waist high. He waved his hands over her head and neck then closed her eyes with his right hand when he removed his hand she was asleep. He opened her shirt and laid his hand on her neck a brilliant white light burst into her throat. They all looked away it was so bright then he did the same on her chest, where the scalpel had cut.

He pulled Henry forward and said, “You will place the snake bandages on her neck. It will only stay with your touch, for your blood made the Attachment that is why you could remove it. I will help.” He waved his hand and produced the box of snakes. The Wizard placed Henry’s left hand under Casandra’s back to support her, and then he gently took her by her hair and extended her head back to expose her neck. Then Antioch took Henry’s right hand, reached in and got four snakes. He directed Henry on placing and smoothing the snakes over the exact opening of the Attachment.

When he finished golden specks burst into a million of lights all aiming one direction, toward Krete. They found themselves standing in the sitting room of Prince Bryan. The Wizard was holding Casandra, and he placed her in the Major’s arms.

The Major

Major flew over the deep blue Bayonne Sea and the coast of the outer circle of light. He could not keep his memories submerged deep inside while the magic of the land, and its light brought every detail clearly to his mind. This was his home for so many years when his Mother ruled the Bayonne Temple with his Father as Emperor. It had been hundreds of years ago, but he still remembered the day he buried his Mother, the Empress, in the tombs of the Bayonne Temple. His oldest Sister and her husband Maalik De Volt became the new Emperor and Empress. Major went to the Monastery at Tookuith where he trained to be a High Monk, he was already a Monk, but he wanted to be an instructor. He had been his Mother's child, unique only to her, and free to do as he pleased. The Major took advantage of that by traveling the world and learning all he could, then he met Beatrice. As he watched the darker blue ice of the middle circle, he closed the drape of the carriage, that was enough for one day. He knew too well those thoughts only led to regrets.

He felt the carriage slow and start to lose altitude; only then did he open the curtain. The Empress was waiting on the stairs of the Temple which was made of pure white stones, with one hundred or more steps to the top. That was necessary to keep the temperature warm enough to be habitable because the Temple sat on a cap of stable blue ice thousands of feet thick. She was as strong and fierce as his own Mother had been. He respected no other woman like he did Beatrice De Volt. He jumped from the carriage and ran up the stairs kneeling at her feet and said. "My Empress I bring news of your daughter we need to speak privately." He turned his eyes upward to the hawks that had followed his carriage to the Temple.

The Empress bowed and said, "You address me in full prodigal I do not like this, follow me." He followed her into the Temple across the Sodalite blue floor of the vestibule then to a side door which would open to her private chambers. Major remembered the entire Temple, the white marble walls, and columns, the clear sparkling crystal lights suspended from the ceiling that would light as they entered and go dark as they passed, this was the most efficient Temple in the world. It was also the humblest and at the same time the most elegant. The chamber was as he remembered it, but the furnishings were different. The furniture was simple lines covered in the color of ice blue, of course. Two couches sat opposite each other with two chairs at the fireside of the large cut glass mantle, he remembered many evenings being transfixed by the fire's light shimmering in the glass. In between the couches was a glass table with a pot of white orchids. He couldn't help but touch them to see if they were real.

The Empress sat in one chair and motioned to him to sit in the other, "It is safe here; I have made it so. Speak."

He sat up and said, "Casandra lives and is well, but she has been hurt. Please take a breath Beatrice you are turning red. I will tell you everything. Can I get you some tea or perhaps wine?" He took her hand in his, all these years and his heart was still hers. She pulled her hand away and told him to tell her every detail. Major methodically gave her every aspect he had, and the plan to dupe the King into believing she was lost. When he was finished, she stood and gazed into the fire. Major let her be silent; he knew her well enough to know she would need to process this information, and she would have questions.

She turned crossed her arms, raised her eyebrow, and said. "You Sir are not telling me everything. This plan…Hayden would never allow Henry to be alone with her out in the middle of my ocean. So, do you think I do not know what they are doing now?"

Major stood, as well, "Madame, I would never presume you do not know everything that is going on in your ocean. The Emperor commanded I not tell you one thing. However, I have a feeling it will not be long before you find it out for yourself anyway. I might as well tell you. If you say I told you, I will call you a bold-faced liar."

The Empress let her arms drop, smiled at him, and said. "Jasper, I have never betrayed you and I never will."

He took her hands and this time she held on to them, and he said softly, "He has commissioned the Wizard, against everyone's advice. He sent him to Belissa Villa to work on the antidote to the Attachment spell; Ski and the Professor are with him."

"Antioch? I should have known." She gazed into the fireplace, a fire lit from nothing. "So, it begins, my premonition is happening." The Empress sighed, "You will stay for dinner. I will tell my attendants, what will you have to drink?"

The Major was taken back; he thought having the Wizard involved would upset her. I seemed to have the opposite effect, interesting. "Wine, your Majesty. I believe I need wine."

Dinner was served in the dining room where he had spent many hours with his Mother. The table was still the same cut crystal one, but the chairs were soft and covered in white fabric. She had added paintings on the walls, and white drapes covered the windows that overlooked the picturesque ice and circles of power glowing with color and mystery. Again, there were fresh flowers on the table, not something he remembered his Mother enjoying. Also, the food was all crisp vegetables and fruits cooked to perfection. He had to ask, "This is a wonderful meal and all of it is so fresh. I notice you have beautiful flowers everywhere, how do you do it. I remember it being impossible to have anything here which was fresh."

She laughed, "I know, that was the one thing that I could not stand. I hired a Wizard to fix that. He created a hothouse, where I can grow my foods and flowers. The hard part was getting insects to agree to live here in this climate. Gadwell is a good Wizard Jasper. He is abrasive but will do everything he promises, or he will tell you ahead of time he may not be able to fulfill his commitment. He has been judged unfairly."

"You know him, well?"

She just smiled and took the coffee pot and cups on a tray. Then she dismissed the servants and placed a privacy spell around them. Beatrice walked them back to the fire and served coffee to the Major. She settled in then spoke, "The Wizard has spent much time building and improving the Temple. He is exceedingly inventive, and his work is impeccable. We have become terrific friends over the years. I would not tell many about our friendship they would not understand, especially Hayden. I trust you to keep this to yourself. I could not be happier that Hayden enlisted Antioch's help, I just wish I could be of some help in this mess."

The Major replied, "I won't say a thing about your friendship with the Wizard, if you say to trust him then I will. I am going to see him next after I leave here. I hope they have a solution for the spell. Then I am to go to Krete to meet Bryan and Casandra."

Beatrice sipped her coffee and stared into the fire, "I wish I could be the one to go see my Daughter. Hayden has made every decision for my children. Where he has taken them? If not to their deaths, to their imprisonment with the crown and power. Not at all what I had planned for my Daughter or Son. At least your Mother let you be free. I never understood why you saddled yourself with the duties of Hayden's advisor, why not just stay free?"

Major smiled at her and said, "You really don't know?" She shook her head no, and he stared into the fire, "To be near you; ironic, isn't it? You were thrown into duty at the Temple, and I strapped into duty on the other side of the world with Hayden. I ended up as far from you as possible." He looked at her; tears were rolling down her face. It warmed his heart to know she too remembered the love they shared so many years ago, long before her marriage. "No, Beatrice, no tears. The Night has done this for a reason, trust in the Night. Of all the things, I have learned in this world, my faith has never been shaken. I owe my Mother for that. I would never ask you to disobey your order. Please understand me, I only needed to be near and know you were alright. I would do anything for you."

He smiled and wiped her tears away with his hand. She kissed his hand and said, "I wish I had kept a boy for my special child. Your

Mother was wise, men truly have freedom. My Casandra must live by men's rules just as I do. I wish I were a man too."

He laughed, "I am glad you are not." but then stopped he had an idea. "Beatrice, I lived here many years, I know this place as well as anyone. I ran this place for almost a year before Hayden's Mother came. I could do that for you, and if you would really like to experience being a man, I believe I could work that out too."

They both began laughing, then she stopped, "You think you could?"

Beatrice in Krete

Henry's head was spinning from the transportation, and he was not happy about the Wizard being a part of this game. "I will see Casandra." He reached for her, but the Wizard froze him, and Bryan pulled him into a chair. Henry looked up to see the Major crying. The Wizard waved his hand over Casandra, and she woke. They helped her to stand. Antioch said. "Casandra, how is your throat, try to speak to me?"

Casandra swallowed and spoke clearly, "I am hungry. My throat feels good. No, it feels wonderful you healed me!" She was smiling ear to ear, she looked at Major and said. "Major I am fine, see. I am famished but fine. Mother?"

The Major hugged her, then turned into herself, the Empress said. "I knew I would never fool you or the Wizard. Henry, you will answer to me for this disaster! What have you done to my girl ripping out her throat?"

Henry tried to stand, but the Empress kept him frozen. "Speak, Hayden might like you, but I am not so sure of you. So, speak! Convince me not to place you in a tomb for life at Bayonne Temple."

Henry took in a breath but notice the Wizard grinning. "Empress, it was all I knew to do after the Prince placed the spell on her. We did the best we could with our resources. I would never hurt Casandra, I love her! I would die for her! Had the smug Wizard you enlisted let his talents be known I would have hired him myself!"

Casandra stepped forward and said sarcastically, "Wizard, please tell us how would you have removed the spell from my throat?"

He stood motionless, and Ski walked up to them, "Empress, Henry was the only one who could have removed the Attachment, for his blood made it. Isn't that so Wizard?"

He nodded, "It is true. Henry did the right thing Empress, and he is right again in saying he was unaware of my talents. After all, we have never told anyone of my relationship to Casandra."

Henry crossed his arms and said. "What relationship is that, Wizard?"

"Why, Henry...are you a jealous man. I told you I would give you an explanation of my power over Casandra, now I will. This is not the first time I have been commissioned to keep her alive. The first time was after she was kidnapped. They did not call me soon enough, by the time I reached her Moondale had all but killed her trying to remove her eggs. My Father brought her to me, I could not return her like she was. It took days of healing to mend her broken little body. I used my own blood, my own skin, and bone to heal her."

Casandra took his arm, "It was Ernst that took me from the dungeon. I remember your voice, not your face. I am so sorry, I remember stabbing you and fighting you."

He laughed and pulled her into a hug, "That was a good sign; you were fighting all the way. I knew then you had the spirit to come back from death. I still have the scar, it reminds me of our connection." He opened his shirt a faint blue line came from his throat to the center of his chest, "I also had to place some restraints on you to heal you, they are permanent. I was the one who took you to the Monks. I knew she needed all their power to recover. Then the Empress, Emperor, and I devised a way to track her with the torque, which she wears now. Then I saw that one of mine was by her side always." He looked to Eric he was standing at the doorway ever watchful.

Casandra felt, and sure enough, the torque hung around her neck. "But when did this happen? I thought only my Father could place this and remove it."

The Wizard said, "Your Father and the maker, me. Oddly, I am also your Father. There is enough of me in you to give your powers enhancement. I placed it on you while you were sleeping on the ship, which is what woke you. I must commend you on how well you reacted to my touch. You had me on the floor in seconds, keep up the training and meditation." He smiled.

Ski said. "The past is past, we need to plan for the present. We have food in the next room I would suggest we all discuss this over breakfast. Casandra, it is good to have you back. Please come with me, and we'll fix that hunger problem."

They all went into the next room where a large table had been set with as much food as Ski, and the Professor could find early in the morning. They all took seats Henry sat next to Casandra and Addison next to Marion. The Empress poured coffee and said. "Henry, you love Casandra. I will concede to having you as my Son-in-law. Addison, you plan to marry Marion is that correct?'

Addison looked at Henry and thought. She is up to something Henry. He said, "Yes, that is the reason for heading here to Krete. I will go make arrangements for our wedding after breakfast."

The Empress chose some fruit from the tray and passed it to Henry. "That is handled, Addison. It is just as easy to have a double ceremony; the arrangements are all made. Casandra, Marion, your wedding is at seven o'clock this evening on the island of Izle in the Temple of Mazic. The reception is planned, and your hotel is booked, it will be beautiful. Wizard have you heard from Marion's family? Will they make it here?"

While the four of them sat unable to speak or think the Wizard continued the conversation. "Let me ask my son." He waved his hand, and a man with long blond hair and blue eyes stood at his side. The Wizard smiled. "I would like to introduce Arron, my apprentice, and fourth son. Tell us what you know Son."

"Wait, wait…wait. You have arranged everything. How? Are we to be married today? This is not possible, we have parents to think of, and contracts to write." Henry was in astonishment.

The Wizard grinned and said, "Henry how many times do I need to remind you. Wizards know everything, trust us. Your parents will be here. Surprise! You're getting married today. Now we have a few details we need to work out. When I need your input, I will let you know. Eat, relax, enjoy your breakfast. Continue Arron."

Arron smiled and bowed to the Empress, and she said, "Good to see you again Arron."

Arron smiled and peacefully said. "The same to you your majesty. Marion, your family, is on their way. However, there are no more rooms on Izle, I have booked rooms in this hotel. You have thirty people coming, and your Father has demanded a judgment, it is at two o'clock this afternoon in this room. I have my Brothers and Sisters transporting everyone around, and I am also ready to take Eric to the Island at his convenience. The Emperor is about three hours north of here, he is expected this afternoon on Izle. Henry's parents will be here this afternoon as well, perhaps one or so. I have placed the young lady's trunks in your room Empress as you instructed, and I will transport their belongings myself to their rooms on Izle. Demetra is handling the reception. Everything is in order. Is there anything else I can do for you?"

The Wizard smiled, "Ah, my daughter Demetra, well your reception should be beautiful. Excellent, Arron, as always you have everything in hand. Thank you. There is one thing before you leave. Please have a seat, next to me, you will find this fascinating." He poured coffee for Arron and said. "Eric, would you please come over here?"

Eric looked around and walked over to the Wizard. "Yes, Sir want can I do for you?"

"Not what you can do for me, but what I can help you with." He smiled, "I understand you and Addison went to see the Hermit?"

Eric said, "Yes many weeks ago now."

The Wizard said, "Ever wonder why I chose you at the Academy, or why I put that bond on you to Casandra?"

Eric smiled and said. "Yes, I have often wondered, and I have even asked you many times. You have always refused my requests. So, you have information for me and today you decide to tell me. I find that very discerning."

The Wizard just grinned more full, "I am a Wizard Eric. You of all people should understand the withholding of information until it is absolutely necessary to reveal it. Now is the time, are you aware that Addison's Mother was Ernst's Sister."

Eric said nothing and looked at Addison then back to the Wizard, "That explains much."

The Wizard chuckled, then said, "I thought you would find that fascinating. He is part wizard, just like you. What I found from Addison's memories is you, and I also share a parent, Ernst." He stood quietly, then he drew up a chair for Eric and poured him coffee. "I have my cousin back and learned I have a half-brother in one day. I am sure there are many more…Ernst and Athena were both very prodigious. I have memories of Addison as a toddler. Athena must have changed your appearance, Addison. Although I have always thought you were part Arlequin. Eric, you are the even mix of Elf and Arlequin a very handsome combination. You and Addison have been berating yourselves for the events at Winter's End. I want you both to know the Prince is a practiced Wizard, Ernst has been training him for years. I would not doubt he knew every action you both would take, and where you were at all times. I wanted you to know this, as he will be counting on using your thoughts to get to Casandra."

"That is good to know. I will not be guarding Casandra; she has her women's guard here. I will assign them." Eric smiled "Does this mean Addison and I can detect Devon too?"

The Wizard grinned. "Yes, you can, especially now that you have had a sense of him. Though, Casandra is the one who knows where he is at all times." He looked directly at her. "Where is he Casandra close?"

She took a drink and noticed all of them looking at her, "I can hear him breathing. He is close, that is all I know for sure."

Henry stared at her and said, "You can hear him breathing. How?"

She looked around and said, "Could I have more bread? And I don't know how. I just hear things, people breathing, sometime heartbeats. I hear your heartbeat almost all the time."

The Wizard said, "She is audio, hearing is one of her great powers, don't even try to whisper around her. That is why she knows my voice is different than Ernst, and she knew Major was not Major but her Mother." He handed Henry more eggs and fruit. Henry filled Casandra's plate. "Casandra, remember Elk's Pass, Devon put a hex on you in the carriage tell us what he said?"

Casandra sat thoughtfully. "I don't remember him hexing us, I put a charm spell on him to distract him from the questioning. I was probing him and listening to his thoughts, I was so close to reading them when Ernst pushed us into the carriage." She started eating more eggs and slices of melon.

"That is all? He surely bonded to you at some point, or he would not be obsessed with finding you. Think, Casandra, what happened next?" The Wizard poured her more coffee.

Marion said. "He pushed his way into the carriage and threw money at us."

Addison said. "Why did he throw money at you?"

Marion shyly said, "We... I mean...well they assumed we were going to the Castle as ladies of the night." Several people said WHAT all at once. "We didn't say that; they did."

Casandra said, "Wait, Marion. He did remember. Ernest pushed us back into the carriage. Devon threw me a fob and said I will find you for a kiss. No... he said exactly; May the heavens willing, I will find you again, and I will get that kiss. This is the truth. An enchantment spoke to the heavens. That is when he bonded me with the money."

"Correct good, Casandra, I knew you could remember the words. He saw your power and craved you, typical wizard behavior." The Wizard grinned.

Henry snarled, "Really, craving is typical behavior for you?"

The Wizard glared at him, "This is important Henry, Wizards rarely marry; it doesn't end well. When we find someone with the great power, we are drawn to procreate. The only exception is when we truly love, and we never bed a married person. Do you happen to have the money he gave you?"

Casandra said. "No, I don't."

Marion said, "I don't even know what happened to it."

"I know," said the Professor, "I picked it up; it was very unusual. I put in my suitcase. I was going to research the coin when I got back to the Academy. Would you like me to get it?"

"Yes. Thank you, Professor. That coin and your marriage may be enough to satisfy Devon's cravings. We must remember he is not all Arlequin. Arron, do you have the potion ready?" The Wizard turned to his apprentice. He said he would check and be right back; he vanished.

Henry said, "Well, that is what has pushed up our Temple date." Casandra noted mentally. Henry, we are getting married today, I don't have my dress, my plans.

He took her hand and thought. All I need is you. I am just trying to follow the plans everyone has made for us. Henry inquired. "Tell us what else will we do today, Wizard?" Henry sat back and crossed his arms and raised his eyebrow.

The Wizard grinned. "Henry, you do realize I can hear you as well? To answer you we have a lot planned. First, you and Addison will go out to do errands for the wedding and run into your old friend Martin. He is down in the street now waiting to waylay you. You should like this part; tell him you refuse to play with him any longer. He has backstabbed you for the last time, then renegotiate handing over of Casandra on his terms. Tell him the Emperor has refused the Island of Azula for nesting. We need to have more control over the time and place. We also need to have access to him and the King."

The Empress said, "He has gone too far this time with this Attachment Spell. It will be the end of all of us. The coward that he is…he will be hiding at home while he sends us on a merry chase. His men are like wasps, stinging here and there, enough times stung causes death just the same. We need him gone."

Casandra sat up straight in her chair and demanded, "We need more than the King gone; we need all his men gone, especially Moondale. If it is the last thing I do in this world, I will see them all dead. I will be hunted no longer." She stared at the Wizard with the determination of a cat on the hunt.

The Empress watched her daughter, how could this little girl kill the King but the fire in her eyes she believed Casandra would. "Casandra needs to rest, and we need to work this out with the Emperor."

Eric stood, "Casandra go lay down, Charlie and Grace, please stay in the room with her and stay alert."

The Wizard pushed out his chair. "I will bring you a potion to help you sleep. Henry and I need to speak privately to you before you sleep. Marion, you and I will prepare for your judgment you may use my room to rest. Addison, please stay with her. Eric are you ready to secure the island?"

Eric said, "Yes, will you be here with Casandra? You and I are the only ones tuned to the torque."

"Yes Eric, I will be here with her. When I am not Henry or Bryan will be with her." He smiled. "Go on to the Island we need that secured this evening. Henry, we need to speak with Casandra, would you all please excuse us?"

They walked into the bedroom, and Casandra sat on the bed about to collapse. She had never felt so weak and tired. Henry came over to her and put his arm around her. "What you said before was very brave, but don't forget you have many who will be at your side to kill the King. You are not alone in this."

She turned and smiled kissed him softly, "I know, Henry, I know. Wizard, I must ask you, has it been your voice in my head all these years?"

He gave her a sweet smile and said, "Yes, although you have rarely listened. At the most important times, you have. You only need to think about my name, and I will be there. I have been present for some of your fun moments, and serious too. I have been with you at every birth as well. I couldn't leave that to just anyone."

She stood and hugged him, "Thank you, it seems I have been blessed with every advantage. I am beginning to trust the Night with my life."

Wizard said, "For now I would like you to trust Henry and me. First to the both of you, when you are around the King and his men, don't act like you are so in love. If he finds that out, he will certainly use it against you." He walked to Henry and said, "I formally asked for your daughter's hand in marriage." Henry was stunned. "Before you say no, which is what you want to say, hear me out. Your daughter will be the most powerful Sorceress in the world; mated with me her powers will increase. She will have the added protection of all the High Wizards and my protection from this moment on. I am very wealthy, and I will soon rule Arlequin. Don't worry, by the time she is old enough to wed, it will be restored and more beautiful than ever. I would be bonded forever to her, she would be protected for eternity and Casandra would be bonded to me while she carries her. I do not need your answer now; just think about it."

Henry looked at Casandra with her mouth hanging open and said. "I was among five on the list to wedding Casandra; things change Antioch."

The Wizard seriously said, "This won't. Since you and Casandra announced your marriage, the future has changed twenty times. Casandra will need my help to birth and raise this child. I can only believe I must be bonded to her before birth. That bond can only be a marriage bond; the Night wants me to marry. Please do not ask me questions Casandra, I cannot tell you outcomes. I can only acknowledge the ways that I see working. There are many paths and every decision you two make changes the outcome."

Casandra grabbed Henry's hand, "The Hermit said the same thing."

Henry said, "I can't wait for my session with her. I dislike her already."

The Wizard's face reddened, "THAT DAMNED HERMIT, YOU MUST NOT LISTEN TO HER! She is the reason this is such a mess, medaling in affairs of the Night is madness. There is no one more insane, her bitterness keeps her alive, and her hatred fuels her agenda. Believe me when I say...she has no regard for her family. She has sacrificed generations of her daughters to fight this spell. The stupid women cannot see rendering the spell useless is the only path." He was pacing the room shaking his fists. "Henry promise me to let me know the information she tells you before you act on it."

Henry said, "I will. I promise, but she lays a secrecy spell that darkens the thoughts so well I have not been able to read it in Casandra's memories. I may not be able to tell you anything."

The Wizard said, "I will think about this. Now for the bad part. What you need to do next you both may not like. Henry, you can't go to the meeting with Martin without smelling like you have used Casandra's power. Henry, you must take Casandra, but not too much she is not strong enough for that. I will stand with you Casandra and lend you my powers."

Henry stood up and said, "No, I can't do that to Casandra; not on our wedding day. I hate how I feel after, I am nervous and hateful. I can't. I can't even imagine how it makes her feel."

"Henry we must. I need to see if this process even works. We tried one on Moori, but none of us are part of her Attachment. We are hoping because you are one of the donors it will work much better."

Casandra stood, "How many donors?" Before Henry could stop his mental list, she had the names in her head, she almost fell back to the bed when she said, "The King! I must know if this works, Henry. If he thinks I have a working Attachment, maybe they will leave me alone. It isn't just me anymore. Henry, it is Winnie too, we must give her a chance."

Henry took her hand and said, "I will do as you wish."

She stood, and they both looked at the Wizard. He asked, "Her name is going to be Winnie? I think you need to change that."

They both laughed. "My Father agrees with you. I plan to give my wife the freedom to choose things for herself, so good luck convincing her."

The Wizard shook his head, "Well, we need to get started. Casandra and Henry face one another. I will stand behind you."

Henry said. "This is very awkward, could we do this alone?"

"You are lucky not to have the Professor and Ski in here. I persuaded them to give you some privacy. So, begin." Henry stepped forward to Casandra and looked at her. He put both hands on her cheeks and tilted her head left then dipped his lips toward her neck.

She jumped a foot in the air and then threw him across the room. She was laughing when she went to him and extended her hand to help him up, "Sorry, it felt strange, maybe I should close my eyes."

Henry accepted Casandra's hand and said, "Good idea. I am not sure your power is all that low. It must be the third helping of eggs that did that."

The Wizard was trying not to laugh. They took their places, and this time Casandra tilted her own head and closed her eyes. The Wizard watch Henry as he beheld Casandra's face, he had never seen such love emanate from a man. He wanted to know that kind of love if he could. The Wizard placed both his hands on Casandra's arms and radiated power into her.

Henry closed his eyes too and placed one hand on her hip the other cupped the left side of her neck. He kissed her softly on her lips then on her cheek over to her ear. Slowly he made his way to the patch on her neck where he tenderly began to suck power from it. Henry opened his eyes and looked up to the Wizard, then closed them and pulled harder at Casandra's power.

Casandra was enjoying the kissing Henry was giving, but when he pulled power from her neck, she flashed to the memory of Devon slapping on the Attachment and the strange sexual power he held over her.

At first, she was tingling from her ears to her toes and warm, then it changed cold and evil. The feeling of ice and helpless overtook Casandra. She needed control…the Wizard said she would have power, but how. She was panicking, in her mind, she heard the Wizards voice say relax and listen to me, Casandra.

The Wizard watched as Casandra's mouth opened and her head fell back in ecstasy then just as quickly, she stiffened and began shivering. Mentally he said. It is me, Casandra, the Wizard, relax and listen to me. Relax, I want you to remember the night you watched Pegasus run below your tree. Remember the colors of the trees, and stars spinning, think about the Unicorn and remember their golden light. Now take that light into you and share it with Henry. Softly, slowly, allow the golden light to raise to your neck and in your mind's eye, see it pumping into Henry.

Henry pushed his love into her as he touched her neck, but soon the draw of power was too high, and he drew her strength faster and faster. He needed to stop, but he couldn't get enough of her why didn't the damn Wizard stop him. Then the sweetest nectar filled his mouth and heart. He felt golden and as light as a feather. He was full, he released her and stood back astounded. She was bathed in a golden aura, she radiated gold. He had never seen anyone look that beautiful and bewitching, he had stopped breathing. He gasped for air with a breath filled with gold. In almost a whisper he said, "What was that, what happened?"

The Wizard gave out a hearty laugh, "How do you feel Henry nervous?"

"No, not at all I feel unusually calm and happy." Henry smiled.

Casandra put her arms around him "Good, now I will not worry about you. I am happy too, but tired. What did happen Wizard?"

The Wizard pointed to the bed, "Let's get your boots off and I will tell you. Arron are you here with Casandra's drink?" Arron stood before them with a gold cup. "Very appropriate choice of container, extra points for that young man. Have her guards come in. Thank you, Arron."

Henry helped her off with her jacket, and the Wizard explained, "Do you remember being cold, so cold you were shivering?" Casandra answered yes. "While Henry pulled out the negative energy you had no control over how much power to give. I almost had to stop Henry he was drinking way too fast. You remembered the Night at Winter's End. However, when I had you shift thoughts to the plains of Peroba, you could control the outflow of energy. You need to train to shift to a pleasant memory; you two should practice that. I need to talk to Ski and the Professor maybe we can come up with other ideas. Now, drink this juice it will help you sleep, and I will place a healing and protection bubble around you. I will wake you to get ready for the ceremony." Grace and Charlie came in, and the Wizard instructed them to stand on each side of her bed. Then he placed her in a bubble of emerald green, "That should hide you from the Prince, do you know where he is Casandra?"

Casandra's smiled faded, "He is in this building. I am sorry I can't stay awake." She closed her eyes and fell to sleep. Henry just stared at her. Casandra appeared so drained of life and power, her face looked translucent. Encased in the bubble sleeping, she could have been dead; dread hit him so hard he almost fell to his feet.

The Wizard grabbed him by the arm. "I'll have none of that Henry. You have control over the power Casandra gave you and how you use it. Use it as she gave it…in love and with promise. Now, it is time for you to be a performer. Convince Martin you no longer require him, show him your true power. You keep that hidden even from your Bride, but I see."

The Wizard called Prince Bryan into the room. "Prince, would you watch your Sister for a while?"

Bryan walked up to Henry and said, "She looks so pale, Henry we need to keep her safe. Sleeping like that she looks like our Sister Sarah. They resemble one another. I will watch closely."

Henry Demonstrations

The second Addison and Henry reached the lobby of the hotel, Addison could feel the Prince. He was hiding behind a pillar in the seating area just before the doorway. The hotel was built of local quarry stone, granite with an onyx mix. The reason Winsette Castle was built with onyx was Diamante's only needed a touch to know the presence of friend or foe. Addison walked out the door, and Henry walked around the pillar. Addison turned they had the Prince standing between them.

Henry gave Devon a pleasant smile and said in a low soft voice. "Have you come for our weddings, young Devon?"

The Prince only glared at him. Addison said, "We have errands to run come with us where we can speak freely." They each took an arm and towed him through the doorway and out into the street.

They walked several yards before Devon spoke, "Let me go, I need to get a room in the hotel. Why are you dragging me along with you?"

Henry said, "Good thing we found you that hotel is full if I remember right, there is another down the street. We'll take you there, but first, let's get a drink to celebrate our upcoming nuptials." They found a tavern quickly and took a seat in the far corner; Henry ordered an ale. "What brings you to town young Prince?"

Devon looked extremely tired and nervous, like a man driven mad. The Prince gaped at the table, "You have used her, and I can smell her.

I feel her power all over you she is mine, I will not share her." He turned his head to Henry. "I will not stop; you cannot stop me."

The drinks came Henry took a deep swallow, "Devon I promised your Mother I would help you. Tell me how can we help you?"

Devon said, "My Mother wants to help me?" Devon chuckled and looked at the ceiling. "Henry, she is more lost than I am. There is no help for me, but maybe if you kill me, I can release Casandra. Try that. I will surely kill anyone who stands in my way." Devon glared at him.

Henry was taken back by his honesty and brutal thoughts. He asked Addison mentally if he could do anything to help him. Addison put his hand on his shoulder and pressed calmness, and rational thoughts into his shoulder.

Devon quickly grabbed Addison's hand and removed it, "Stop placating me. I am not a child. What do you mean you are going to weddings, two weddings?"

Henry looked up, and there stood Martin and Ernst. Henry said, "Please join us, gentlemen. Look who we found wandering in the hotel, looking for a room. Did you lose him, Martin?" Henry had never seen Martin look that stern.

Martin pulled a chair out and said, "Ernst would you get me an ale and one for yourself." He handed him coins and sat, "Ernst just came from the Castle, it seems our young Prince decided to go riding out on an adventure. You have had your Mother and Father worried. I will send word of your safety as soon as we get you to your rooms at the Renincess Hotel." The Prince cheered up at that, he would be staying in the same hotel as Casandra.

Henry would keep him thinking that, and Addison mentally added. I think we should change the ceremony too. Henry said, "Oh, the same hotel we are staying in." Ernst came with the drinks. He looked concerned with Devon. Henry could not help staring at Ernst to see the resemblance to Eric, Antioch, and Addison.

Addison said, "We were just telling Devon we are on our way to run some errands for our upcoming weddings. We need rings, Henry, you know how women are about jewelry. Do you think we will need to get presents? I have never done this you need to instruct me."

Martin said, "Addison you are getting married? When did this happen? Henry's is months away yet."

Addison took a swig of his ale and said, "Try a day away. Tomorrow morning, bright and early at 7:00 A.M. the only time available. We had to take it, everyone needs to be at Winsette Castle tomorrow afternoon. I would have thought you all would be there already. I blame you Martin for my demise."

Martin laughed, "Me, what did I have to do with it?"

Devon sat with his mouth open, "Who are you marrying, it's just you who are getting married, right?"

"No, Devon, it's a double wedding; Henry and Casandra, me and the Sprite Marion." Devon looked devastated. Addison glared at Martin and continued, "I wouldn't be here if it hadn't been for the brilliant plan of your Father's, throwing all of us together. I don't understand; if you wanted to kidnap Casandra why the hell didn't you take her and be done with it? Why involve all of us, poison Henry, then chase us all over creation. You want to ruin your life that's fine with me, just leave me out of your stupid plans." He drank his beer and stared at Martin.

Martin laughed, "How much have you been drinking, we did nothing to you. Why are you marrying that Sprite?"

Addison leaned in. "She is pregnant. Normally Sprites do not have children until they are married, then they have their tubes opened, because the young Prince botched the Attachment so badly, we had to go to the healing spas. Who knew Marion would become fertile?" Henry mentally said I have forgotten what a glorious storyteller you are Addison, your narrative skills are stunning. Mentally Addison thank him.

The Prince said, "That is why we couldn't find you, Holy grounds are difficult to detect Witches, and Warlocks for that matter."

Henry said, "Martin your boy is upset with me, he wants Casandra for his own. Did the King not tell him she would be shared between us four. I know he forgot to tell me. In fact, this is not the first time he has devised plans and not shared them. I believe we have had many an argument on this point. Have I ever told you how I hate having to tell people the same thing, repeatedly? I need to know the truth, to work the plan."

Martin said, "I told the King that, Henry; almost every day. Look at Devon, she has put a spell on the boy. This is Casandra's fault, not ours. We had to do something he craves her."

"I don't believe you. This was your plan all along. My turning Casandra over to you on Azulu was just a ploy to get information out of me. You needed to know where she was going on holiday then you drop in and take her. That was clever; we spent weeks playing nurse then you would take her and not have paid me for my use. Well, I am done with this game. She will not be going to Azulu for her nesting, and tomorrow I will have my wife. I will have all her power, and you will have nothing for your trouble. I am perfectly happy being an Ambassador for the Emperor. It will help promote our winery and making me even richer and the most powerful Warlock in the world. Personally, tell the King thank you."

"Wait, Henry, we had a deal. We taught you about the Attachment. You owe us, don't forget that." Martin leered at Henry.

"Idiot! You poisoned me. I deserve knowledge of the Attachment just for that. Not to mention the cost this has had on my business. I have had to spend all this time wooing this silly girl and healing her. You damn near killed her dropping her in the ocean. No, go back to your King, tell him I am done with his plan. The next offer he will get will come from me." Henry stood, and Addison followed. "They will be my terms, and I need time to think of what I want from him. I will let him know when I am ready."

Martin stood, grabbed Henry's hand squeezed and pushed electric power up his arm. "Her eggs are processing now we have no time, Henry."

Henry took the golden power of Casandra's and gently pushed power back down his arm. Then he pushed gold power up Martin's arm into his neck to his head. Martin started sweating, and his throat was turning red. Martin released his grasp and stood back bewildered.

Henry gave him a wicked grin, "Her power is sweet, is it not? See you at the Coronation. Good day gentlemen." Henry and Addison turned and walked away without even looking back.

The Judgement

Henry and Addison finished up the errands and hurried back so Addison would be there for Marion. When they walked into the room of suites Marion was pacing she went to Addison, and he held her in his arms. "Sweetheart, there is no reason to be so worried. What can your parents do now?"

She pushed him out of her arms and said, "Kill me. Oh, Addison, they are going to be so mad. I don't think I can even look at them. I am their biggest disappointment."

Addison took her by the shoulders and said, "You are not a disappointment, and you have nothing to feel bad about. Life happens, and that is what this is…life."

The Wizard opened the door to Casandra's room. "Oh good. Henry, you are here. I want to have a word with Marion before her parents get here. Would you sit with Casandra? I don't trust Devon.

Henry said, "I will, however, Addison had a great idea. He told the Prince the wedding is at seven in the morning. I am sure he believed it, so maybe we will have an easy time."

The Wizard said, "I hope you are right. I only know too well the craving he feels; he would stop at nothing to get to her. I will send you some lunch as soon as it comes. After this meeting, I will sit with her you need to rest before tonight." Henry wanted to refuse him but knew better than to argue with a Wizard.

"Marion and Addison, please have a seat." The Wizard sat and poured water for himself and the others. "Alright Marion I have looked back in your files, and nowhere do I find any disciplinary notations; not while you were at home in early school or the Academy. Other than some rumors of wild behavior on your summer vacations, I don't see anything. I hope this is true it would make your story of using the healing baths a plausible excuse. Is there anything I should know before your judgment begins?"

Marion looked at him turning red and said, "I would not have been allowed at the Academy if there were any issues. I was chosen because of my record of good behavior and grades. Of course, I am telling you the truth. Casteglion was brutal in his training. I was so sore I couldn't even move. I had to have healing for my muscles. You know Sprites don't have large muscles he was having me throw him. I couldn't even lift anyone Look at me, even for a Sprite, I am small." She stood to prove her point.

The Wizard said, "It is not about how tall you are Dear, it is about momentum."

Marion crossed her arms, squinted at him and started turning a deeper shade of red. "That is what Casteglion said, I didn't believe him."

"Just like you didn't believe Moori about the healing pool?" Addison watched her as she turned several shades of red, then white.

The Wizard said, "There is a lesson to be learned here, Addison. As you see, Marion is a true Sprite they operate on fact alone. Everything is clear-cut for them, it is, or it is not. Anything thing that falls in between or needs interpretation causes room for mistakes. As her husband, you must be clear with her and make sure she understands any directions you give her. Never assume she knows the facts."

Addison nodded, and Marion was turning red again. Before she could speak, they could hear a commotion in the outer entry. Arron appeared, "The Sprites are here Father. They are hours early, and there are over thirty outside. Did you want to have them all come in?"

The Wizard sighed deeply, and Addison wondered how bad this was going to be. "No, thank you, Arron. I will go out into the hall Addison wait with Henry until I need you."

Addison said, "I want to stay with Marion."

The Wizard and Marion said at the same time. "No. Bad idea."

"This is a judgment for Marion she will be fine, and they will not hurt her. Please, let us handle this. Sprites are…well they are emotional. I will have you come in and speak at the appropriate time."

The Wizard went into the hall, and Addison kissed Marion. She said, "I will be fine, I will blood bond with you later tonight, and you will hear everything." She hugged him, and he went to join Henry.

The noise died down, and only two Sprites came into the room with the Wizard. The Wizard went to the Empress Chamber and cracked the door just enough for Addison to listen. Her Mother rushed to her and hugged and kissed her. She was red as a beet and full of negative energy. Her name was Cynthia, and she was an older version of Marion except shorter and thinner, her Father had said it was because she was always flitting around. Her Father stood behind a chair, and he was sickly green shade. The Judge was tall for a Sprite and very handsome with sharp features and well built. All her friends thought her Father was very dashing for an older man. He was also the head of their clan, which made this predicament shameful for him. All she could do when she looked at him was cry, then whimper and say she was sorry.

He folded his arms and said. "I hate when you whimper. Stop that at once and tell me how in the world you became pregnant!"

The Wizard raised his hands and said, "Please Mr. Donnan have a seat. This is a formal hearing, and we will record every word for the archives. Arron are you ready?"

Arron appeared. "Yes Sir, Margaret is seeing to Marion's relatives and settling them in their rooms." Arron sat opposite the Wizard at the end of the table. The Wizard motioned Marion's Parents to a seat to his right, and Marion sat opposite them.

The Wizard said he would begin by questioning Marion. She retold the story for her Parents, and the Wizard made sure she recounted it precisely as it happened. He had her explain the itinerary at the Monk's monastery, and he asked in great detail about the combat lessons and exercises Casteglion had her do. When she was finished, the Wizard turned to her Father and asked if he had any questions for her.

He said he did. "Marion, the healing waters are the exact thing we use to restore a Sprite's reproductive abilities. In your thirteen years of training, you were required to know this, and you were tested on it. All female Sprites are given specific instructions on reproduction and the care of a child. This is something you knew; how can you lie to us?"

Marion's mouth gaped, "Father in my thirteenth year I was at the Academy. Instructions are given midyear. I was not even in the Glenn at that time to take the lessons. I don't remember being tested for this at all. Wizard was I tested?"

The Wizard looked in his papers as if searching, he knew they were not there. He searched for it earlier and found this had been neglected by her parents. Using details were the only way to show a stubborn Sprite at fault. "I find no confirmation of testing Marion on this subject, and she is correct in that she was at the Academy during the instruction period in her thirteenth year. Marion, did you have instructions at the Academy?" She replied she had not. "Mrs. Donnan, did you give her private lessons in this subject?"

She looked dumbfounded, "Well…I can say with certainty. I must have told her. I think."

Robert Donnan, screamed, "Cynthia…you think? You either did or didn't! Which is it?"

Mrs. Donnan hung her head and stared at the table, "Really Robert…I can't say one way or another. I simply don't remember we have twenty-four children, after all. I can't be expected to remember everything, you don't even remember all of their names!"

The Wizard stared but under the table, he patted Marion's knee, and she gave him a slight wink. Arron coughed and said, "Sir, as you requested I went back in the files and found this document." He passed it to Mr. Donnan and asked him to hand it to the Wizard. Mr. Donnan looked at it before he handed it over. He started turning red in the face.

The Wizard read it and said, "It seems I have a document excusing Marion Donnan from the instructions on reproduction it is signed by the both of you. This clearly releases Marion from any fault in her pregnancy."

Robert Donnan said. "Cynthia, I did not sign that paper! She always forges my signature on things and never tells me. I swear this is the last time…what is done is done. However, that does not account for dallying with a Warlock. That is forbidden! We gave you every opportunity to succeed and look what you have done...shame us."

Marion was staring a hole in the table, and the Wizard knew Addison was about to come bounding through the door. The Wizard stood, "Sir, your daughter feels bad enough about disappointing you and she did not entirely have a Warlock for a companion. He is half Wizard and my cousin. I can vouch for his character and integrity. He has also planned a wedding for this evening, that is why you were called here. If you had understood my instructions, we would not even be having this judgment. I have chosen you as the wise counsel for your clan. I do hope you are more level-headed when handling the affairs in your woods. I give you an exception because I know Marion is your beloved daughter, which you have based many hopes and dreams on. I am here to tell you she had not disappointed you, but that she will be the greatest Sprite of all. Addison, will you please come out here."

Addison came out smiling and greeted Marion's parents. He sat next to Marion and took her hand.

The Wizard asked him to state his name, profession and tell Marion's parents how he would take care of her and the children.

Addison took a breath and said, "My name is Addison Rakie. I am a winemaker, and I am a one-third partner in Belissa Villa."

Marion's Father stood, "The Rakie of Diamentia? The fine wines everyone loves, you are a Wizard? I can't believe it." He almost fell into his chair.

Addison smiled, "Yes. One and the same. I would like to live at Belissa Villa after we are married and raise our children there. However, before we live there, Marion must complete her training as an advisor. That means a degree in law at the Academy, along with training from Professor McMillan. I will, of course, support her in this, lucky for her my Father is a Chancellor and can help her with her studies. She is committed to Countess Casandra De Volt Rakie as chancellor and advisor. It is a Godsend we will live just down the road from the Countess. I don't foresee any problems in our marriage except deciding what school the children will attend. I would prefer the University; she wants them all to go to the Academy. Also, you should know the law in Diamentia guaranties women equal to men. After tonight, she will own half my lands, holdings, and monies."

Both parents just sat speechless except Cynthia Donnan, who started crying. Addison took both her hands in his and said. "Mrs. Donnan, please, do not cry. I love Marion with all my heart. I intended to come to you both and ask for her hand. However, the Wizard decided to help us. I am so sorry if you have suffered, that was never my intention."

This time the Wizard coughed, "We need to proceed. Mr. and Mrs. Donnan, do you accept Addison Rakie for a son-in-law?"

Mrs. Donnan was laughing and crying but said. "Yes, we do!"

Mr. Donnan stood extended his hand and said. "Welcome to our family Son. Do you have any idea what that means?"

Addison stood up and said, "I believe it means I have twenty-three Sisters-in-law and Brothers-in-law. I am afraid I will never remember all their names."

Marion grinned, "Don't worry they are in alphabetical order, I'm number thirteen. For the record, you don't have to ask me Wizard. I will definitely marry Addison. I love him."

The Wizard smiled, "These proceedings are concluded you have my permission to marry. Now I will leave you four to get to know one another. Don't be too long, Marion needs some rest before the ceremony. Arron will see to refreshments and get you all settled in. Addison have her come in to rest with Casandra when you are done."

Apprehension

Martin had not liked the power the Count had pressed on him. The energy made him feel different somehow, he wondered why? He would have to talk to Moondale about this. It took Ernst and Martin both to calm Devon and get him in bed. He was sure he had not slept since he left the Castle. The boy was possessed; they had not wanted to use an Attachment on him. Yet, every day he was like this it seemed to make more sense. They had to control him somehow. If Ernst was with him, Martin knew he would not be able to spell him but how could they get through the Coronation with Devon this unstable?

He poured some wine for himself and Ernst, "Ernst, this is not going well. If we can't control him, well, I don't know what else to do. The King will not like this. Why did you promise to let him have one more try at her in the morning?"

Ernst smiled, "I was hoping it would satisfy him enough to relax and sleep. I have no intentions of allowing him out of my sight. I told him it would be better to try for her in the morning before the wedding. I will sit with him; he will go nowhere."

Martin said, "After I finish my wine I will get a message to a spy and let the King know he has been found and is alright. I can't wait until this is over and I am a settled down old married man. I have no energy to run around like this. We need to have him married off as well.

You and I should look for a wife among the nobles at the Coronation. He needs his mind off Casandra."

Ernst said, "I agree wholeheartedly. He needs some stability and children to occupy him. That will take a little wind out of his sails. You don't have to tell me about following him around. I feel I have done that most of my life, and to think it has only been thirty years." Ernst gazed into his wine cup.

Martin laughed, "What will you do with your life Ernst, if not for following him around?"

Ernst said. "Knowing the King, I will be following Devon's children around." And he laughed without mirth.

Wizards Wisdom

Henry sat by the bubble covering Casandra and stared with his head balanced on his hand. His elbows were leaning into the bed, but as instructed, he did not touch her. He only turned his head when the Wizard came into the room.

The Wizard smiled, "I do not believe you could get any closer to her if you tried. Henry, you need to get some rest. If the Prince has not tried for her yet, they have subdued him. That means they believed your lie about the time, or he is picking a good time to surprise us. Either way, I need you sharp. Go get some rest I will watch over her, Marion will be in shortly. Addison needs to rest too."

Henry stood and stretched, "You are probably right he would have come straight away. How did things go at the judgment?"

The Wizard laughed, "Why, exactly as I planned. She and Addison have permission to marry, I found Marion not at fault. She really didn't know about the healing waters, but that also means she really doesn't know anything about pregnancy, childbirth or parenting either. Addison is not going to have an easy time with her she is a handful. You and Ski will have fun dealing with her too. She will need your patience and care, Sprites are beautiful, lovely and stubborn. I often wonder why the Night gave us the charge of them."

Henry slapped his back and said, "I would never believe you had patience with anyone, not until I saw you with her today. I don't think I ever really knew you. Don't worry about Marion, I will protect her and so will Casandra. I think she loves Marion as much as she loves me. They really are more like family than friends they have lived together for fourteen years. I will go try to sleep for a while. Make sure I am up to get ready for my wedding. That seems surreal."

The Wizard smiled and gave him a cup of wine to drink, "This will help you sleep, I will wake you."

"Before you leave Henry, I want you to know the torque Casandra wears will fall from her neck the moment you bond in marriage. The Emperor, Empress, Eric, and I will no longer have any way to track or help her. Eric and I will always be connected to her, but it may not be enough to track her. Before you ask, it took years to make that torque for her and no, you do not want to create one for her. Henry, to place the energy into the torque consistently you would have to send her all of your love. That has damaged her relationship with her Father. It would not be a good way to start a marriage. That is why I offered the bond with your daughter. I would always be able to protect her."

Henry sighed, "I see. I just wish I knew where the Prince was."

The Wizard looked at Casandra and said. "I do too."

Addison and Marion walked in. Addison said, "That went better than I had expected. Marion, you need to sleep sweetheart; I will see you at the Temple." He took her to the bed kissed her, and she laid down then she said. "I can't sleep I have too much to do. I need a dress and gifts for the Temple and my Parents." She barely got that out before the Wizard put her in a sleep bubble, and she slipped into a slumber.

Addison said, "I didn't have a chance to tell her I took care of everything today."

"She will find out when she wakes." Henry took Addison's arm, and they went to their room.

Devon

Devon woke and found Ernst looking down at him. He said. "You are becoming a strong and clever wizard, but Son you cannot leave my side now. If they get any hint of your intent, you will be under an Attachment so fast. Sleep Devon, you have not slept enough you are not thinking straight."

Devon was fast asleep but for how long. He was fighting every move Ernst, and the Queen tried. Could he not see they were only trying to help him.

Donning for Marriage

The Empress was standing at the foot of the bed with the Wizardwhen both girls awoke. Casandra stretched and tried to speak, but her throat was dry. The Wizard came to her and placed his hand on her throat. "My Dear try again, you can speak."

Casandra said, "My throat is so dry could I have water?" Charlie poured a glass for her and Grace was on the other side of the bed handing Marion a drink as well.

"It is to be expected, I had both of you under a healing and energy replenishing spell. It is nothing to worry about both of you are just a little dehydrated. Drink slowly and get up slowly. I will leave and let you both get dressed. Our carriage should be ready in about one and a half hours. Please be diligent the Prince is staying here in the hotel. However, he has been put in a deep sleep, for how long we don't know." The Wizard turned and left the room.

The Empress said, "I think Casandra should bathe first so I can get her hair done in time. Cynthia are you ready for the last fitting for Marion, I can help you make the alterations while Casandra bathes."

Casandra got out of bed she had not even noticed Marion's Mother in the room; she needed to be more aware, and more awake. "Mrs. Donnan I am so glad you could make it here for Marion's wedding. Isn't it wonderful we will share the day forever, best friends forever."

She hugged Marion and asked, "Is there any way I can get coffee? I feel dull-headed."

Marion said, "Coffee sounds wonderful. Mom how in the world did you get a dress ready?"

Cynthia smiled and said, "It's been ready for a long while, the Empress told me this would happen at the end of the school last year. I didn't tell your Father a thing. Can you imagine the hard months I would have had to live through with him? I want you to know I am very proud of you and I love you very much." She hugged Marion.

The next hours flew by getting ready for the ceremony. Henry and Addison were taken to the Island of Izle to rest and dress for the service. They met the King of Diamentia at the Hotel Mazic, along with the Queen and Ski. Ski had told the King and Queen everything, even about Addison being his Grandson.

When they entered, the King said, "Addison I have always wondered about your Parents. I liked you and was happy you were Henry's good friend, but now I understand why. I want you to know I intend to name you Prince. However, for now, I would like this to be our little secret. We are planning a family dinner tomorrow evening. I want you and the Wizard to be my guest, and with your permission, I would like to have the blood proof to show Richard at that dinner. I only have to say it is a good thing you turned out more like your Mother than him."

Henry started laughing, and Addison really didn't know what to say, but he agreed. The Queen pushed them both off to sleep while they prepared for the evening. When they woke, they bathed and dressed in the Noblemen's attire of Diamentia. Their pants were black with a black silk stripe going vertically down the outside. The jackets were the deep ruby red of the Belissa clan. They wore white silk shirts and black ties, with the sash of Diamentia colors of gold and black running cross-wise attached with a red ruby pin.

The Queen straightened Henry's jacket and pulled at Addison's tie making it perfect, "Very handsome the both of you. I am very happy for you and having a double wedding with your best friend. You are both blessed by the Night. I can't wait to meet your brides. Let's go."

The King agreed. "The Sprite has already left. Addison you are going to have countless relatives. I met some of them this afternoon, this is only the immediate family, and they didn't bring their children. There are twenty-three of them, really, I hope you are not planning that many children. I can't remember all my Great Grandchildren's names now, much less twenty more. That brings me to a subject I must discuss with your brides, names for your children. We must come to a consensus on names. These will be my first Princes; they will have a beautiful name. Do you both understand." He said that firmly.

Henry and Addison laughed and said. "I believe I will leave that matter up to you Father. I think Addison will too."

They took a carriage to the Izle Temple up to the highest point of the island. The Temple's exterior was stone, covered in plaster and whitewashed. The roofs were shiny copper which devotees kept polished like a mirror. At least twenty other buildings surround the massive complex. The courtyard was stone; the same color as the walls and held a four-tier fountain in the center. There were four Temples around the yard with many-columned entrances around the square. One was for the daily worship, one for the novices, one for the service of deaths and sorrows, and one for celebrations. Each had elaborate symbols carved into the copper double doors, depicting scenes of the events held within. They headed for the door which had a couple holding a child in their arms in a field of flowers. The sun was above the man and the moon above the women. Stars and rays of light burst from the center.

Before they entered they could hear the commotion of people inside; the Sprites, no doubt. The doors opened with three Monks standing before them. They bowed and said, "We are humbly blessed to receive the Night's children enter and follow us." They were led to the front of the Temple on the right side. Marion's family were on the opposite side. When they entered the Sprites had become silent; now they were all staring at Addison and whispering.

The Temple was a round theater style with rows of benches at the back of the circle, there were cushioned chairs arranged in a semi-circle for the wedding party. Henry was fascinated with the interior of the build. He could not figure out what kept the ceiling up; there were no supports or columns anywhere in the circular room. The floor appeared to be glass, but as Henry looked at it he realized it was a solid piece of clear quartz, and he could feel the magical energy radiating up from the floor. He wondered how many years it took to move it to the Temple, it must have come from the North Mountain. Hundreds of candelabras were placed around and down the center aisle, illuminating the room. Only as his eyes adjusted did he notice the center of the roof over the altar was open to the sky. Then he also saw the walls of the Temple were semi-precious stones, mosaics of the life of a man and a woman from birth to death. The floor of the altar depicted a figure of a Goddess with her arms held out to the side and a crescent moon and star directly above her head. How could they have done that, magic, of course?

The back doors opened, and Addison and Henry jumped up, everyone in the room stood. His Eminence came down the aisle and stood in the center of the altar. He was dressed in robes that changed from gold to silver to white. He asked the Monks to bring Henry and Addison forward. He faced Addison on the left side of the altar facing the door and Henry on the right.

The doors opened again, and Marion came into the Temple followed by her Mother and Father, with the Wizard behind them. Marion wore the colors of her clan, silver and blue. She glowed in her gown of silver, covered with beads and crystals sparkling from the candlelight. She wore a silver-blue cloak edged in pearls and crystals. The dress covered her from the neck to the floor, even her hands. That was the traditional gown worn by Brides to the Temple on their wedding day. She carried the blue hyacinth arm bouquet that Addison had chosen for her earlier in the day. Henry could smell them from halfway down the aisle; she was beautiful, and his friend was hypnotized by her. Henry couldn't help but wonder how she could have gotten a dress so quickly.

Addison walked to stand in front of her as Mr. Donnan came forward and handed his Eminence an envelope with a donation. Then her Father and Mother kissed her on the cheek with tears in their eyes.

The Wizard walked forward and handed him the marriage certificate and said. "Your Eminence everything is legitimate Marion Donnan is given permission to marry Addison Rakie." The Monk nodded, and the Wizard took Marion up to the few stairs and placed her hand on Addison's waiting hand. The Monk motioned for them to step to the left of the altar, then he asked Ski to come forward, and Ski handed him the donation and marriage certificate and said, "Addison Rakie is legitimate your Eminence." The King of Diamentia stood and said he had given him permission.

Then the doors opened again, and Henry could hardly wait for Ski to move so he could get a clear view of Casandra. She looked dark against the opening of the door, but as she stepped forward, he saw she was wearing her Crown of diamonds and the necklace he had given her the night of their engagement. The light fizzed off the stones as if they were illuminated by themselves. Her dress was dark blue lace with encrusted crystals that looked effervescent in the candlelight. The dress fell gracefully to the floor, but as he looked closer, he noticed while the lace was covering her from her neck to her feet, the lace only covered the obvious places. However, between the spaces was nothing but the sheer blue material which she had purchased on holiday. She was carrying the gardenia bouquet he had bought for her, a flower of Belissa. As she came closer, he thought to himself, this was the sexiest bridal dress he had ever seen, and he was about to fall off the altar. Casandra smiled and snickered then thought. Hold on darling you have a few hours before you can tear this off. Addison thought the same get married first, Henry. Henry walked to stand in front of her.

The Emperor, Empress, and Prince Bryan came forward to give the donation and kiss her. To Henry's surprise, Eric was behind them, and he brought forward the marriage certificate and papers. Then Eric went to Casandra and kissed her on the forehead; it was so sweet and touching it brought tears to Henry's eyes. Eric reached around her neck and removed the torque that laid under her necklace, it turned from gold to black, and he said. "She is yours to protect now, Henry. Do not fail or you will deal with me." Then he smiled at Henry as Henry's Mother came forward and kissed him and his Father gave permission for the marriage.

Everyone took their seats, and the two couples turned to face the four Monks that stood on the altar. All the candles in the room flickered and went out; the sun had set, and the night sky was above them. The doors opened again, and a choir of children entered carrying candles singing a chant. Their candles went out as they stood around the perimeter of the room when the doors were shut and bolted. The song was joined by musical instruments from around the Temple that Henry had not even noticed. As the tempo increased the stars from above seems to come closer; four stars entered through the open ceiling of the Temple. One star came and hovered over each of the brides and grooms, illuminating the room to that of daylight. Casandra thought she saw the Hermit behind the Monks, but she disappeared as quickly as she observed at her.

A tail of energy from each star came down over each of their bodies and encircled them with a stream of silver golden ribbon. One Monk and his Eminence went to Addison and Marion first; took the bands and entwined them together joining their left hands and arms together. Addison reached into his pocket and retrieved two rings handed them to the Monk then he wrapped his arm around Marion's waist. A blessing was said as his Eminence place their rings on their finger.

The same ceremony was repeated with Henry and Casandra. Then the Eminence said. "You have been bonded by the Night with your stars from the heavens nothing can separate you from one another until death. Go in peace and live the way of the Night. Teach your children the way of the Night, and the Night will carry you home to the heavens where your stars are now united as one, for eternity. Blessings."

As quickly as the stars entered they receded up to the sky. However, this time there were only two stars. All the candles lit in the room, and a celebration song was blaring out along with hundreds of bells ringing throughout the complex. The ribbon of light that bonded them vanished, but each could still feel its connection as they followed the Monks from the Temple.

They lead them from the Temple to a reception room in one of the buildings below the Temple. Long tables covered in gold tablecloths sat opposite of each other in the room. One was filled with foods and sweets on the right of the room, and a table was filled with presents along the left side. There was a present for each person on that table from the groom's family.

Round tables with gold and silver table coverings were set with white china, and crystal goblets sat on every table. Chairs covered with silver surrounded the tables which held white candles in tall silver candlesticks. The tables encircled the outside of the room, and each table carried beautiful white gardenias floating in water bowls with silver moons and golden star crystals at the bottom. At the far end of the room was a band playing music while light orbs hung from the ceiling spinning patterns of the night sky across the ceiling and floor. A golden chest was set on the table of each bride with their new coat of arms. Everyone there would place a gift of money and a blessing in the chest for the newlyweds to start their life.

Henry and Addison walked their brides to the dance floor for the traditional first dance.

Henry couldn't wait to have his arms around Casandra, and he knew Addison was thinking the same about Marion. Henry was beaming, "I can hardly believe this is real, you are mine at last. I love you Casandra, and I don't know how I will make it through the evening without ravishing you. I could take you right here on the dance floor. What you do to me, I can never explain. The very first time I touched you on our walk I have wanted you."

Casandra threw back her head and laughed. "Henry, I feel the same. I want to skip all this and go to our room. Although, I must find Antioch's daughter Demetra to thank her. She did a wonderful job with our wedding, it was as if she knew my wedding dreams."

Then Henry laughed. Casandra loved to watch the man laugh, "You are so handsome when you laugh I just want to kiss you." So, she did, and their viewers applauded. That brought them back to the room and the reception.

Henry said, "Look at Addison he didn't even notice us, I think my friend is happy."

"I know Marion is. All she talks about is Addison; they are well matched. I am hungry when do we eat?" Casandra smiled.

"Is that all you can think about now that you can swallow. I would think you haven't eaten in weeks." Then he laughed again, "Because you haven't."

They walked to the food and Casandra said, "We are eating. I am hungry."

Marion's Sisters said, "I am so glad we haven't eaten since breakfast we are starved."

Everyone ate and drank, and then the guests went to the table to get their presents. There were squeals and shouts as they opened their gifts, Henry and Addison had spoiled everyone. Henry had gifted both parent's cases of wine and two of his prize dogs trained in spy erudite and beautiful crystal wine glasses for everyone. He gave Eric a trained Pegasus; Eric came to the table to tell Henry he could not accept it, but Henry said it would be insulted if he didn't take it.

Addison was just as generous with wine for the men and jewelry for the ladies, he knew how to win the heart of a Sprite. People were coming to wish the couples well and giving their blessing and gifts. They all started dancing, and the party grew. Casandra did get to thank Demetra and found out the Wizard had share Casandra's dream of her wedding day.

The King was campaigning for his choices of names for his Princesses. The Emperor was giving his ideas as well. Addison and Henry were in a conversation with Eric and the Wizard. Mrs. Donnan, the Queen, and Empress were all at a table discussing the upcoming Coronation which the Queen had invited all of Marion's family.

Marion came to Casandra and said she needed to go to the restroom, and Casandra excused herself and said she would join her. They asked a server where it was and grabbed Charlie and Grace to go with them. They all piled into the stalls, but Casandra was finished first. Casandra was standing at the mirror fixing her hair when she felt the breath of the Prince. She tried to speak, but her lips were sealed. Grace opened the door to her stall, but she froze in place with the door slamming shut and locked. Marion tried to scream when her door wouldn't open, she was stopped short and frozen in place.

Casandra could feel cold steel wrap around her body and knew the Prince had captured all of them in a spell. Watching in the mirror, she saw Devon materialize before her eyes. He was standing behind her and pressing her head to the side. He bent down and began to suck her power, Casandra pushed down the fear and tried to remember what to do. Think a pleasant thought, she went to her childhood and the field by the lake where she would play hide and seek with Etic. She could feel herself weaken and she began to panic. How could she concentrate on overpowering him, she needed help, she would remove her torque. Wait, she had no torque, think; call the Wizard. She couldn't think or speak; he was draining too much power. Devon released her and fell into a trance drunk with her power.

Casandra remembered her lessons from Casteglion and gathered all the strength and pushed her weight against him tossing him into a stall behind her. Casandra was temporarily free, she turned to radiate power against him, but he was faster. He threw her against the counter with the mirrors, and Casandra fell to the floor. She could only think of Eric; it was Eric she called.

Devon pulled her to him and kissed her, and whispered, "You have married, how could you do this to me, Casandra, you are mine. You have no right to marry Henry you are to be my Queen."

The door to the restroom banged open, and at least six men stood there, Eric was the first to break down the spell, then Henry, Addison, Ski, the Professor, Bryan, and the Wizard entered. The Wizard told them to do nothing Casandra was helplessly caught in Devon's embrace.

The Wizard said, "Devon, release her! I compel you to release her! Now!" He did, and she dropped to the floor. All at once Devon was dragged out of the room, and Henry grabbed Casandra. He felt for broken bones or injuries he only found some scratches and cuts, but she was weak from the power drain. Addison was pounding all the doors of the stalls looking for Marion. Eric began breaking down the stall doors. Marion, Charlie, and Grace were all standing at the doors frozen in place. Addison ran out to get the Wizard who forced Devon to release them all from their frozen state. The girls all started apologizing at once they could hear her cries but could not move to help her. Addison was holding Marion and ranting about how he would kill the Prince, while Ski made sure all the women were alright.

They went to the sitting room to find the Wizard and the Professor holding down Devon with a spell, also preventing Bryan from choking him.

Addison ran at Devon, but the Wizard stopped him, "Let me handle this Addison. Devon, first I will relieve you of the spell you placed on Casandra at Elk's Pass. Professor the coin?" The Wizard took the coin waved in the air and placed it back in Devon's shirt pocket. Devon closed his eyes and inhaled a deep breath. The Wizard yelled, "Father, get in here. I know you are waiting just outside this room. I compel you to reveal yourself! Now!"

Ernst appeared at the doorway; he looked solemn and stoic as Antioch had always remembered but a scar sunken and tallow colored on his face marred a once handsome wizard. "Antioch, it has been a long time since I have seen you. I see you have grown into a fierce Wizard. You can command Devon. I lost that power a year or so ago. He is a cagey and spirited man who often reminds me of you. I thought he had a coupling spell on Casandra, thank you for releasing him, maybe he will get back to normal."

The Wizard said, "It will take more than this to get him back to normal."

Only then did Devon seem to be aware of his surroundings; he immediately started to fight. Ernst held him down. He said to Devon, "Son settle down. These people around you could help you get away from the King. He will kill you if he finds out the truth about you. Devon, you are bleeding." Ernst turned Devon's head and felt a lump on the back when he pulled his hand away, it was full of blood. "How did this happen?" Ernst pulled ointment and bandages from his pocket and began to clean the wound.

Devon smiled and looked at Casandra "She did this. She picked me up and threw against the stalls in the restroom. You are a powerful Sorceress Countess, I underestimated your power. You were bound... I would be interested to know how you did that?" Everyone looked at Casandra, as Henry beamed.

Casandra raised her eyebrow just like her Mother. "I am sure you would. Well, now what do we do with you now that we caught you?"

The Wizard glared at Devon, "Yes Casandra, that is an excellent question. If it were up to me...I would strip him of his powers for a few hundred years. However, he is in a predicament being a Wizard pretending to be a Warlock... that might just mean his death. I must ask, how stupid is the King and his men not to know this? Father, have you been misleading people again?"

Ernst scowled back at Antioch, "We had a plan; to free Devon from the King...Henry was part of it. Devon was obsessed with Casandra; I couldn't explain it away." Ernst hung his head and returned to cleaning Devon's wound.

The Wizard scowled pushed out his hand and held it on Ernst's head. Light flashed down his arm to Ernst's brain, and Ernst slumped. Devon started to protest but the Wizard's hand flew to Devon, and he did the same with him. Both were out cold, the Wizard said. "Professor would you mind finding a Monk, ask if we can take these men to bath in a private healing pool here." The Professor nodded and left the room.

He turned to Casandra and placed his hand on her head and cocked his head looking at the ceiling as if seeing what happened just a few minutes ago. He then said, "Nicely done my Dear. Henry, Casandra could use an input of your power, it would be good practice for you. Also, a little wine wouldn't hurt. I would bet she is hungry again too. You both need to go back to your wedding. Eric and I can handle things here."

The Wizard then held his hand on Marion, "You are fine my dear, and the baby, stop worrying. Addison, I think you both should return to your party. Later this evening she needs to go to the healing pool for about twenty minutes." Addison started to protest, but the Wizard held up his hands. "Eric and I will clean up this mess. Ski will you take the girls back to the party and tell the Emperor to meet us at the healing pool, discreetly."

It took only a few minutes to put the restroom back in order. Eric threw Devon over his shoulder, and the Wizard took Ernst. The Monks showed them to a private healing pool, he removed their clothes and put them in the water. It wasn't long before they both awoke.

Devon jumped and said, "Where are we? How did we get here? Who are you?"

The Wizard stood on the side of the pool with his arms crossed, and Eric had taken the same position. "Let me make introductions. I am Antioch Gadwell the Wizard, just address me as Wizard. I am the most powerful wizard in the world at least right now. Arron?"

Arron appeared, holding towels and robes, "Yes Sir, I am here with all you need."

The Wizard smiled, "Devon, this is Arron my son and your nephew, he will surpass me someday. This gentleman to my right is Eric one of the Emperor's generals, and he sees to the protection of Casandra. Eric is my half-brother, son of Ernst. That makes him your half-brother as well."

Arron handed Devon a towel, and said, "Uncle dry off, and I will heal your head, sit over here. I brought ale for you and my Grandfather."

Arron handed a towel to Ernst they both looked at each other in complete disbelief, but they dried as Arron gave them each a robe.

Eric and the Wizard followed them to a table in the corner and sat while Arron worked on the back of Devon's head.

Eric glared at Devon and then Ernst. Ernst watched Eric and remembered the beautiful young Elf he had loved, then said, "I suppose you have some questions for me."

Eric used his white eyes to penetrate Ernst's black eyes then said, "Really, only one, who was my Mother?"

Ernst straightened in his chair a look of pain crossed his face, "You did not know her?" Eric only shook his head no. Ernst took a long swig of his ale and said, "I am sorry for you, you missed knowing a beautiful albino Elf, and daughter of the High Priestess of Arlequin. She was powerful, intelligent, talented, and gorgeous. More importantly, she was to be saved for nobility, not a plain Wizard like me. The Wizard obsession got to me. I found her so powerful and beautiful that I placed a coupling spell on her. She could not deny me, no one can, surely you have felt that."

Eric thought of the Night by the lake with Casandra and pushed that memory deep inside of him, he could not remember that.

Ernst asked, "Do you know what happened to her?"

Eric said, "I was adopted and removed from Arlequin while I was still a baby. My Parents died when I was young they told me they adopted her, this is the first knowledge I have of her. Do you know her parents or their name?" Eric poured himself a glass of ale.

Ernst swallowed, "Not even she knew who her Father was, someone of great importance I am sure, but I am certain you know her Mother's name. Adrienne Ryder, your Mother's name was Airlie Ryder." He took another drink, while Eric sat with his mouth open.

The Wizard looked at Eric, "Eric, I should have guessed…you are so talented. Your eyes are natural; all this time, I took it your Mother disguised you. She was an oracle and a powerful Elf. Your skills at interrogation and intuition are natural. Eric, I am sorry, I just realized what I did you to. I bonded you to Casandra you heard her calling tonight; you are still bonded to her?"

Eric stared a death stare at Devon's eyes, he coldly said. "I am bound to kill anyone who would hurt her, Brother or not. Although I do not truly understand why."

"Because Son, you do not know much about being a Wizard. Your instincts are exceptional knowing your talent is raw yet, who knows how powerful you will become, I am proud of all my sons."

Ernst gave a rare half-smile and touched Eric's shoulder. Then he sighed and set his ale down, "All these lies, I hardly remember all of them anymore. The King and Martin will take my memories as soon as we are together again, along with Devon's. Martin already tried to place an Attachment on Devon to control him. I made him remove it. Now…"

The Wizard said, "He didn't completely remove it. I could feel the remnants in his loins."

Ernst stood up, ready to attack when the Emperor came into the pool area. "So this is the young man that threw my carriage into the mountainside, and you Sir, must be the notorious Ernst, kidnapper?"

All heads turned to the Emperor. Eric stood and offered the Emperor his seat. "Your Majesty meet my Father Ernst, and my half-brother Devon, the Prince of Hex."

The Emperor stood next to Eric, "Is that how you knew Casandra needed help, Eric?"

Eric said, "It looks like I am still bonded with Casandra. Perhaps the Wizard can explain, I have no explanations for it."

The Emperor turned to the Wizard, "I will explain later, now we need to attend to these two. What would you like done with them? They are both threats to your daughter."

Before the Emperor could say a word, the Empress stood before them with fire extending out from under her dress. She took Ernst and threw him to the ceiling with an electric charge. With her right hand, she pushed the Prince into the pool and held his head underwater. The Wizard was smiling, admiring this beautiful Sorceress. How he wished he could have mated with her, still making love to her now might be interesting. Eric stood back crossed his arms trying to figure out what Antioch was smiling wickedly about; did he want her to kill them or did he just want her?

The Emperor went to her and placed his hands softly on her waist and said in a whisper, "My darling if you kill even one of them we will be in a huge war. A war I must send your son into."

She turned her head and glaring at him with hatred. She dropped Ernst on the chair and pulled Devon from the pool. Then she pointed at Ernst, "This man kidnapped my daughter and stood by while the King and his men did horrible things to her." Then she bent down to stare into Devon's face, "And this fool thinks he can take my daughter for himself." She screamed. "Idiot! I will see you dead first! I compel you to tell me the truth. Why are you after my daughter? Why will you not stop? Speak!"

Devon was spitting out water and shivering, "I placed a coupling spell on her at Elk's Pass, Casandra had been promised to me. The King promised she would be my Queen, she is beautiful and powerful, and I love her. I have carried a picture of her for years. She is mine! Not Henry's! She married Henry, I can't believe she married him. He is old! How could you give her to an old man!" He locked his jaw and was making a fist as he slowly stood like he would run.

The Wizard softly said, "Continue, Devon, I compel you to sit down and finish, tell us everything."

He looked to Ernst for help and the Queen placed her hands on his cheeks turned his head, and said, "Speak."

Looking directly at her, he said, "He promised her to me, I love her. I didn't want her hurt, like my Mother, I was going to take her away. We could hide. I know a lot of safe places, secret places." Devon sighed, and the Empress released him.

He began, "Then when Henry came for Martin's engagement party I overheard the real plan. It is Moondale's plan for Casandra and me, Moondale, he is an insidious mad devil. He already has Casandra's eggs fertilized, only one of her children will be mine. They know I am not the King's son, they are playing with all of you, just like they play with me." He grabbed a towel and dried his face and arms, and then continued, "Her children will be the King's. Two sons and they split an egg to give them two Sorcerers which they have already placed an Attachment on. The girls, they are an experiment. Moondale said he doubts the girls will live, the King said it didn't matter women are disposable. Casandra is only the vessel to birth them, and I am to be the pretend King until my pretend Sons grow old enough to rule. She and the children will be the token to keep you and the Emperor in line and from attacking them. The King will step back to run the world quietly and safely, just like the coward he is."

The Emperor stood before him and said, "Why Devon, why will he not step forward and fight?"

Devon looked up to the Emperor and said. "Power, that is all he is concerned with and because he is Attached to so many. If they start dying, the King will lose half his Kingdom. When he leaves, he places my Mother in a secret cell he had built in their room. She is imprisoned, and always guarded so he will not worry about losing his greatest power source. Martin has started doing that to Janet as well, I found that out the day I left. I mistakenly found the new tower he is building. It is for Casandra and me, with a cell for both of us. He rules by fear because he lives in fear."

"But what of Henry." The Empress asked.

Ernst said, "Henry is a dead man, now that you have pushed him into marriage, I imagine. They had plans to use him, but he is too smart they will never trust him or Addison." Ernst placed his head in his hands and said, "Ironic…if we live you all die. If we die and you get to live. The King must die. I would be happy to do it, but with this Attachment, it is impossible for me to kill him. Devon has a partial Attachment; I doubt he could kill him any longer. Martin will know everything that has happened here at the Temple the moment we enter the room. We are all doomed, you should have killed me when you had the chance."

The Wizard said, "Yes, I know everything is impossible, it is all horrible. I know you both live with evil, but I would remind you Father negative emotions drive the evil side of magic. You two will remember nothing, and now that we have the truth, it will be easier to find a solution. I suggest Emperor and Empress you go back to the wedding celebration and keep this to yourself. We can tell Henry and Addison about this tomorrow. Let them have this night to think all is well. Eric and my children can take care of these two. Save some of that sparkling wine for Eric and me we will make short work of this. Demetra, Enola, Sage we need you at the healing pool."

Old King Winsette

He told the Queen to keep the party going while he looked for Henry, he was well aware of what transpired with Casandra and the girls. Addison walked into the room just then, and the King went to him. "Addison is Marion alright and where are Henry and Casandra?"

Addison said, "They are fine Sir. Henry is healing her before bringing her back here. I guess you know we have the Prince. Although I have no idea what they are doing with him, I'd like him dead. But it is out our hands, and they are evidently not sharing that information with us. We got kicked out."

"Well, I will find out. I cannot sleep without knowing. Come to sit with the Queen and me. I would like to talk to you." The King returned to his seat while Addison pulled Marion from her family, snatched a bottle of wine and went to the King's table.

Addison said, "I don't think you have been formally introduced to Marion, meet the King and Queen of Diamante."

Marion bowed, smiled, and sat across from them.

"Well now Addison, we are only King and Queen for two more days, thank the Night. Also, I am a bit more than just a King to both of you. You are my Grandson, and tomorrow morning when you land, I wish you to have a blood test immediately. Richard will want the proof, and we want both of you at the family dinner tomorrow evening. Dinner is a six in the evening, I get hungry early. You, my beautiful Sprite Granddaughter-in-law, are carrying my little Princess. Now, to the important thing, we will discuss names. A Princess must have a name of beauty strength and intelligence. I also want your parents over here for their input."

Addison said, "Marion go get your Parents I would like a word with the King." She left, and Addison said, "Sir, I do not need to be a Prince, nor do I care to be a Prince. I am content to know who I really am. I also have no intentions of calling Richard Father. Perhaps it would be best to let this dog die right here."

King said, "Addison you are half Diamante, and I have always been suspicious of your ancestry. Ski and I have had long talks about it. It is one reason you were paired with my boys and given every opportunity to raise up in class. I have also always liked you, and I am very proud of the man you have grown into. I ask you to do this not for yourself but for me. I have several children that have chosen the negative side of magic. You can help me to believe not all of my offspring will divert to evil. Although I sometimes wonder if the Night is punishing me for my evil past deeds with my evil boys. Your children may be the ones of the legend, the very ones who will advance us all from the depths of malevolent. If your child is one of the Princess Sorcerer that bring our world to prosperity, I certainly want my name attached to her. That means young man, one of Dillion's first duties will be to name you Prince Addison Ski Rakie, fourteenth heir to the throne of Diamante. I doubt you will ever be King, but your Daughter may very well be its ruler. She must be protected for life; I like that bonding the Wizard does with Sorcerers. I think I will hire him, he is now a relative too. Bring him along to our dinner tomorrow." He turned to the Queen and kissed her, "This is going to be ever so interesting, I haven't had this much fun in years. You were right my Dear, I still have a lot to live for."

The Queen put her arm around him. Addison was touched at how they loved one another. "Yes, my King. Now, Addison, you must agree, you would not want to be the cause of the King's death, would you?"

Addison laughed, "Oh, no not me. I will call you Grandfather, but I refuse to call Richard Father, deal?" He held out his hand to seal the promise. The King shook Addison's hand and smiled.

Henry and Casandra walked up just then Henry said, "Watch out Nephew, he is a tricky old man. He will have you promising things that you may not want to do. He can't be trusted, he likes games, but he is always loyal and loving. I will give him that."

The King threw back his head and laughed, and Casandra knew where Henry had gotten that trait. She smiled and fell in love with the King. Winsette said, "Good to see you look well, Casandra. Sit; we are about to play a game, names for the Princesses. I need to straighten you out about not using my name for your baby. Really the ruler of the world cannot be called Winnie? No! We cannot have that! Here come your parents let's have them play as well. I have a list…",

They all sat together, and before long Ski, the Professor and all of Marion's family were drinking and playing the name game with the King. Marion's family liked it so well they thought it should be a part of every wedding reception. They had never heard about the weight a name had on the personality of the person.

The King told them Henry's name meant ruler of justice, Casandra's meaning was from the Night, and Marion's was a child most wished for. Everyone laughed when he said Addison's name meant Father of Warlocks. The King shared his list of names; Hannah, Carian, Etheria, Fabiana, Glynda, and on it went.

However, when Casandra found out that Winsette meant bringer of peace, she was even more determined to have Winsette in the Princess name. Henry liked Nanette, 'Daughter of the heavens.'

Prince Bryan told King Winsette if he would have a daughter he would name her Sarah, after her Sister that died too young. The Empress began to cry and walked away. Henry said he loved the name Sarah; it was also his Mother's middle name. So, they all agreed on Princess Sarah Alexia Winsette De Volt Rakie as their little Princess name.

Addison loved the name Zahrah, meaning 'Blooming flower.' Marion and her Parents liked Roselyn, meaning 'Beautiful rose.' So, Princess Zahrah Roselyn Donnan Rakie was created. By that time, the Wizard and Eric had returned. The Wizard told them in Arlequin Sarah meant 'Ultimate power' and Zaharh meant 'Great warrior.' That was all the King needed to agree to his Princess' names. Henry opened the sparkling wine and they all toasted to the wedding, love, family, and children.

Henry asked the Wizard to come to their room after the reception was over. Henry questioned him on what had happened with the Prince, but the Wizard would only say Ernst and Devon's memory had been erased. They would remember nothing of what happened, and he had transported them back to their room. The Wizard said they would have a meeting in the afternoon the next day to go over the details, and the Wizard assured him the spell to mate with Casandra was entirely gone. Then he looked at Casandra, "May I fix your aura, Casandra? You look a little off."

She agreed, and he began to move the energy around her in balance. He told her to go get ready for bed; he needed to speak with Henry, "Henry come over here, she has been badly bruised all over her back. I will give you an ointment to apply tonight but wake a little early and have her go to the healing pool. I will ask the Monks to reserve a private one for you. I will slip a note under your door with the time, you need to be out early before Martin comes to check on you."

Henry was taken back, "I will; thank you, Antioch…I mean Wizard. Will it be alright to make love?"

The Wizard smiled, "Carefully yes, and to answer your other questions, I will tell you all about the bond of Eric to her tomorrow at breakfast, is that all?"

Casandra came out of the restroom, "Wizard, Henry and I discussed your proposal to marry our daughter. We would be most honored, with one stipulation. You must love her, and she must love you and agree with your union, no spells or enchantments."

He tilted his head with a half-smile on his face. "May I touch your stomach?" Casandra nodded yes, and he walked to her and placed his hand on her abdomen and closed his eyes. He took a step back and with a blank face and said. "Thank you, Sir, and Sorcerers, I will serve, protect, teach, and love your daughter with all my heart, soul, and mind. She will be in love with me when she matures, which is only natural. I will agree and have papers for you tomorrow at breakfast. I will do a bond there at the pool."

Casandra asked at what pool. The Wizard asked, "How is your back feeling Casandra?" Her eyes widened, and she took in a deep breath, "The healing pool then, for breakfast; I will see you there."

The Wizard left, and Henry gave Casandra a wicked smile. "So, you were not going to tell me about the bruising and just suffer through lovemaking? Was that your plan?"

She sighed and rolled her eyes. "It's my wedding night, and I want you, Henry. If I let you see my back, you would put me to bed and not touch me."

Henry took her to the bed and said, "That Wizard is a pain and a know-it-all too. He will never marry our Daughter; she will not put up with him." He smiled and held up a jar of ointment and said, "But, I was given a cure by that Wizard, so I guess he is not all bad. I intend to make love to you, and I will be cautious and gentle. You get to take off your clothes, and I get to rub this all over you. Lucky Sorcerer." He threw back his head and laughed, and she smiled and complied.

The Healing Pool

Henry and Casandra both got into the pool at the unheard-of hour of four in the morning they had just gotten out and dressed in their robes when Marion and Addison came in. "Are we taking your time in the pool?" Addison asked.

Casandra said they were just leaving, but the Wizard came through the door with Arron pushing a table full of breakfast food. "Ah good, you are all here. We'll have breakfast, and we have a few things to discuss. Henry and Casandra need to leave soon, so Addison and Marion join us for breakfast and be a witness for our contract."

They all sat and had a breakfast of toast, eggs, and fruit with lots of coffee. The Wizard handed Henry the contract of marriage and explained the details. Addison asked Henry if he was sure about this Henry had always complained about pre-arranged marriages. However, Marion told Addison she thought it was an excellent idea and wished her child had protection from a Wizard.

The Wizard laughed, "Marion, I am your child's guardian she has my protection. As a matter of fact, you have the protection of any Wizard because she is part Wizard herself, it is handy you have married one."

They signed the contract, and then the Wizard stood and took Casandra's hand. "Please stand Casandra." She did, and he knelt before her sending out light from his hands to hers then slowly to up her arm to her heart and to the child she was carrying. "I vow to love, protect and care for you in every way, Sarah Alexia Winsette De Volt Rakie, beginning today and ending never. I marry you for eternally, vowed before the Night and the Sun no one will separate us." He stood and looked in Casandra's eyes she was baffled. "Did I forget to tell you Wizards never marry but once, and it's forever." He gave her a big grin, "She will love me, Casandra, no spells and we will be happy. I hope as happy as you and Henry."

Henry stepped up, "Wizard, congratulations I know you will make my baby happy because I will come back from death and tear your heart out if you hurt her. Eternity is a long time, Antioch." Henry held out his hand and gave him a wicked smile. They shook hands then they all realized, Addison and Marion had done a blood bond on their wedding night. She was crying and thinking that was the most touching ceremony she had witnessed. The Wizard sent Henry and Casandra on their way and Marion into the baths.

Henry and Casandra dressed quickly, packed and walked out to the carriage, in the courtyard. The King and Queen were waiting for them. Henry smiled he was wondering what the old man was up to.

The King stepped forward. "Here is your wedding present Son. We thought you should ride in style in your own carriage. An Ambassador of Diamante should be well represented. Look, your Belissa coat-of-arms, and it has seats that turn down into a bed, along with food storage. It has a globe of the world that even shows you where you are, and a crystal ball for communication. You can fly twenty-four hours straight, except for the bathroom stops." Henry opened the door and lifted the seat on the right it was filled to the brim with food. The King laughed, "I remember when Margaretta was pregnant I could not fill that woman up."

Henry grabbed his Father and gave him a hug. "Father this is an extremely kind generous gift, these costs a lot of money, I thank you." Casandra gave the King and Queen a kiss and hug. Then got into the carriage to see it, the King and Queen followed.

The Queen put a privacy spell around them and said, "I have something too." She reached into her pocket and retrieved a ring with a dull oval black center stone, and smaller stones surrounding it. It looked ancient like it was made of iron. "This ring was given to me by Winsette when we wed it holds many magical powers, but I could not wear it. I am not sure of what those powers are or if the legend surrounding it is true."

The King took the ring and gazed sadly at it, "I can verify it once was the property of Esmeralda the great Sorceress and the ring will only be worn if the Sorceress is strong enough to use the powers. The legend says it reflects the colors of our world as seen by the Night when it is worn by a chosen one."

The Queen took a deep breath, "After Henry told me of your marriage, I began having dreams. The Night has chosen either you or our Princess to wear this, or maybe both. It is not very clear to me I apologize." She handed her the ring. "See if it fits you."

Casandra took the ring and placed it on her right-hand ring finger. A white light flashed inside the carriage that temporarily blinded them. When the Queen looked down at Casandra's hand, she gasped. The iron had changed to pure white gold, the center stone was a deep purple multi-faceted diamond, with white and gold diamonds sparkling around the center stone.

Henry said, "That makes the wedding ring I bought you look cheap. I only gave you one dirty diamond. Let me see it?" He took her hand; the moment he touched it a spark burnt him. "Well, I don't think anyone will be stealing that!"

His Mother laughed, "Henry, your one diamond is the size of a boulder. I wonder if all the tales are true. My Dear, come to me at the Castle when things have settled down, and I will tell you every one of them. So, this is what the Night sees when she looks at us...deep sparkling purple with gold and silver stars around us. How lovely our world looks to her. I wish we were as lovely in person."

The King took his Queen's hand, "I agree. Now, we need to be on our way. We hired a carriage, and we will leave you to kiss in private." He laughed, "We will be riding with the Emperor and Empress, Eric and his men are with us. The Wizard and Addison will follow with my men after they set Martin straight. I am a happy man Henry, I gained a good man in Addison, and I have you back. Don't ever leave me again."

Henry gave him a hug, "Not likely King, I have too much fun with you around. You need to stick around for your Princesses." They both laughed, and the King and Queen left the carriage. Henry tapped the ceiling hauled Casandra in his lap and said, "Let's find out how to make this into a bed."

Martin's Folly

The Prince and Ernst were both still sleeping when Martin was ready for breakfast. He went into their room to find both of them smiling in their sleep. He touched Devon on his shoulder, "Devon, wake up; you wanted to take your Sorceress this morning, and I find you sleeping through it."

Devon opened his eyes he didn't want to move or speak, he hadn't felt so comfortable and relaxed in years. "Martin, I want to stay in bed go away." He rolled over and covered his head. Martin shook Ernst. "Ernst, what in the world is wrong with Devon what happened here? Are you both spelled?" Martin bent down and pulled energy from Ernst's neck and held it to see what had happened. "You took him to the healing pools! The old religion, the King won't like this. You know how he feels about the Monks. What were you thinking?"

Ernst sat up and rubbed his head and neck where Martin had drunk. He detested the man. Ernst hated anyone who would violate him like these crude men did. "I did what I had to do to heal him. That is what you wanted. Devon spelled that Witch, the only way I could remove it was with the healing waters. It looks like it worked, he is in no hurry to catch his Queen." Ernst stretched and got out of bed. "What time is it?"

Martin said, "It is about six in the morning the sun is just coming up. We should rouse him and get going. Casandra will be leaving for her wedding in a few minutes."

There was a knock on the door, "Sir, your guard is here, he needs to speak with you and says it's urgent."

Martin walked out to the room speaking. "Get Devon up and dress Ernst. Yes, what is it?"

"Sir they have left the island." The soldier stood at attention.

Martin said, "We have an hour until the wedding we should still make it."

"Sir, they are on their way to Diamante. Our informants told us Henry and Casandra were married last night, and most of their party have left for Winsette Castle."

Martin stood speechless, it had been a long while since he had been blindsided this neatly. It was a good thing his orders were not to stop the wedding, or there would be hell to pay. At least the King would not know how badly he had been duped. "Ernst get out here, with the Prince! Now! We are leaving!"

They mounted their Pegasus and headed out to the Island of Izle. They landed in minutes. Addison and Marion were entering their carriage to leave. Martin walked up, opened the door and sat next to Marion. Martin said, "Congratulations on your marriage, it seems we keep meeting in carriages Dear Marion."

The doors on both sides of the carriage opened. King Rakie's men had swords pointed at Martin's neck. Ernst, Devon, and all of his soldiers were disarmed and laying on the ground. A soldier said, "Step out of the carriage Sir, very slowly and carefully." Martin did as he was told, they took his sword, and the Wizard stood outside, holding him in a solid block.

Addison came out, as well, "Had we known you wanted an invitation to our wedding we would have sent you a message."

Marion stuck her head out of the carriage and said, "I wouldn't have." Addison turned and gave her a despairing look. She closed the door and stayed quiet. "Excuse my Wife's manners, Martin. She is young and of course a Sprite. What do you want Martin?"

Martin said, "I want an explanation, and to be released along with my men. The King will not like this Addison."

Addison crossed his arms and said, "Afraid he might kill the messenger?" He snickered, Martin started to turn red in the face. "Oh, don't worry, Martin, after all, you are his Son-in-law to be. Attached to his daughter, so to speak. Don't blame us, we are on the timetable... of the Emperor. Meet one of his new advisors, the great Wizard Antioch Gadwell."

Martin almost broke his neck to get a look at the man holding him. The Wizard smiled at him and said, "I finally meet Martin, the great general of the King of Hex. Odd, I never saw you on the Battlefield, of course, I never saw any general or the King of Hex on any Battlefield. I suppose you are all too important to get bloody you sure bloodied up plenty of others. Tell us what information do you want from Addison?"

Martin just glared at him, "What, no words for me? I could compel you to speak the truth, but then holding you this close I already know all I need. Young Prince Devon, I would like you to see what fear does to a general when he faces it alone." He shoved Martin to look at the Prince. "Addison is not your man, not any longer. So, go find another, dreg up some poor soul you have forced your will on." He released Martin, then brushed his hands like he was trying to get dirt from them. The Wizard added, "One thing more, Marion is my charge...meaning, she is under my protection. If I ever hear you disrespect her, I will close your mouth permanently. Understand?"

Martin said nothing and helped up the Prince then gathered all his dignity and said, "Addison this has only been postponed." They mounted and left.

Addison looked at the Wizard, "I am impressed. You do realize you have made an enemy for life?"

The Wizard just smiled, "He would be that by next year anyway. I have evil plans for the country of Hex."

Addison laughed and shook his head. "Can you teach me to do that? Hold someone in irons and read their minds?"

The Wizard slapped him on the back. "Cousin we will see what your talents are and start from there. I am so pleased you want to keep learning. My Grandfather taught that; an open-minded Wizard has unlimited powers. The answer is yes, what you can learn it is up to you. I do not have the time to teach you now, but I have many who would jump at the chance to teach you. Teaching helps apprentices advance. We will talk more at the Castle."

Martin's Memories

Martin was relieved the cold air was hitting his face as they rode to the Winsette Castle. He had not been overpowered in many years. Now he had twice in the past two days, it was humiliating. He needed Janet for more power, and he wished he had completed the Attachment on the Prince. The Wizard drained him, how he managed that without using an Attachment he couldn't understand. However, even if he had the extra power Martin wondered, could he stand up to Antioch or Henry; he exerted extreme power the day before. He did not want to report any of this to the King they had severely underestimated the capabilities of these religious zealots.

The Night, he had never believed the Night had any power. His Mother practiced the religion of the Night. Look where it got her and all his family. His mind went back to the day his Father, Mother, and six Brothers and Sisters were torn apart, limb by limb, in the games. They died just for the fun and entertainment of the King of Hex. Only after he was made to watch their deaths and shown the Night could save no one, was he released into the middle of the desert. He was the youngest, a witness for the King who forced him to pledge to Olgin who was the only true God.

The Night did not help him in the desert or the god Olgin; only a cranky old man. No one lived to exit the desert, but he did. Of course, having the old man's body to feed on helped. The gods didn't help the King of Hex either when he a Richard hacked his body away bit by bit. He would have his revenge and that Wizard's power too. First, he would take Addison and Henry. The Night, Oglin, Oglan, and the Woman in the Tree, all of them were nothing but legends to make the weak follow the strong. Maybe they needed a myth, a religion, for their Attachment Spell and have everyone clamor for it.

The Dynasty

Dillion and Henry were standing on the roof of the Castle to greet them. Dillion opened the door to the carriage and helped Marion out. "Marion, I am Dillion, and you are as beautiful as my Father said, he has an eye for a beautiful woman. The other women are having afternoon tea with my wife. Would you like to join them, or go to your apartment and rest?"

Marion smiled up at him. He looked like he could be Addison's Father and just as tall and handsome. She stepped out of the carriage and said, "Thank you, Dillion. All the Rakie men resemble one another you are all very tall and handsome but to be fair, to a Spirit, everyone but a fairy is very tall." Dillion gave her a big smile. "Oh, I would love to have some tea."

His Father had been right; she was beautiful, honest, and charming also, tiny. He already liked her she would spice up the family. "Henry will take you to my apartments and then join Addison and me."

Dillion turned to Addison, "Nephew, are you ready for this, war will ensue by evening."

Addison said, "I am not sure, Dillion. I have always been part of this family on the edges, I rather liked it there. I would not be doing this at all except for your Father. It is his wish I must comply."

Dillion chuckled, "I understand completely, why do you think I become King tomorrow, he is strong-willed. I hope to rule as well as he has that is due to that very determination. Honestly, you are helping us to root out the evil in our family, for that I am grateful." He turned and saw Antioch. "Wizard it has been a long time. You look well and much more powerful than the last time we were together. Father told me we have commissioned you, have you decided if you will accept?"

The Wizard said, "I have not heard all the terms of the agreement, I will decide then. Dillion, you look well, and now you are to be King. When was the last time we were together…so long ago. In school, wasn't it?"

Addison said, "You went to school together?"

Dillion smiled. "Yes, he was my roommate and friend. We argued constantly, he stole my food, clothes, and books. We were best friends… it has been way too long." Dillion grabbed the Wizard and gave him a hug.

The Wizard laughed, "I intend to do the same here in your Kingdom, eat your food, use your library, and have time with my friend. However, I prefer my own clothes. Why did we land on this roof might I ask, is something covert going on?"

Dillion took him by the arm. "Yes. We need to get inside before we are noticed, there are spies everywhere. You two are my big secret, and I don't intend to share the secret until just before dinner. I did not want to have you land in the courtyard or walk through the Castle; it too chancy. Also, Queen Elisabeth and her daughters are having tea with the Empress, I am keeping the Empress a secret too. Henry thought once the King of Hex found out the Empress was in the Castle, he would not allow his Queen any time alone with her cousin."

The Wizard looked concerned, "Politically you are placing yourself in a dire situation with the King, is that wise?"

Dillion said, "The way I see it, Henry and Addison have already headed our country in that direction with their marriages. For the first time in a millennium Sprites, Elves, and Marais will attend a Coronation all we need is a fairy and a Strella to make history."

The Wizard laughed, "I could provide that for you if you like."

Dillion led them through a hallway into a secret passage and into his office. He held up his finger to his mouth to signal them not to speak. A guard was standing at a door, he opened it and sitting in a wing chair of red, was the King smiling. They walked through, and the King said, "You made it through undetected we won't have that advantage for long. Addison, this is my new Doctor Eneida; he will test your blood right here. The new age is remarkable, isn't it?" They were all in the Kings chamber.

Addison was instructed to sit, and the Doctor took his blood. As expected the blood showed wizard and Rakie blood, they had known that from the day he was found on Ski's doorstep. Ski and the Professor were there and had set up a mini-lab to match Addison's blood to Richard's. They said it would take a while for that. The King had coffee and sandwiches in his room while they waited.

They made themselves comfortable, "Addison, Dillion has set aside apartment for you and Marion, next to Henry's in the outer circle. We thought you two would want to be close, if they are not to your liking after the Coronation, you can move where ever you want." Addison looked astonished. "Don't look so surprised I want you and Marion here as often as possible she is a delight. Eric's Elf Guard have cleaned it out and decorated it for you; you can change that, too, if you like. Those Elf women are wonderful. I have asked the Emperor to let me hire some for the Castle to train our women how to fight. I love a strong woman, nothing like power to give one stamina."

Dillion shook his head. "Father I am sure no one here wants to hear about your stamina. You had fourteen children; we are aware of your stamina."

The Wizard laughed. "I don't know, I might like hearing the King's stories. I agree with him; powerful women make the best lovers; a trait every Wizard looks for. Addison chose well, Marion is the strongest Sprite we have ever come across. He has already found out a little about that this morning. She spoke up to Martin well enough." He laughed, and the King asked how that went.

Addison told them what happened then Dillion said, "So Antioch great Wizard, you have made an enemy of Hex. You are a marked man now; Martin will have his sights on you, be careful. That brings me to this evenings family dinner, and it is formal. We would like just the men to meet in the library for cocktails beforehand where we will confront Richard and my Brothers who are aligned with him. Father will name you a Prince and give you holdings of your apartment and lands.

Richard will not object, but he will to the restitution. Addison, you and Antioch will be eligible for restitution; you can ask for money, properties, loss of title, as they did to Henry, banishment, or his life. You both should take time to deliberate your options. You can decide later; I will ask at the signing of the documentation of Addison's naming as Prince. However, you can take days or months to ask for the punishment."

Henry came in just then. "They took eleven months to decide on mine, it was the worst time of my life. I recommend it, by the time I found I had only lost my title I was grateful. Funny how life turns out. I am so much better off today because I have no title. Casandra could not have married an heir to the throne. She has to be free to rule the Bayonne Temple, and I must be able to support her."

Dillion laughed. "Which is hilarious because now the Brothers who stood against you must stand with you. If she rules the Temple, you will be Emperor of the Continents and the most powerful man in the world. I am sure glad I supported you all these years. I insisted we keep him a Count, just enough nobility to see he was taken care of. Henry, you have surpassed my expectations, and I am happy with it." He raised his coffee cup to him.

The Professor came over to them, "Gentlemen, we have results, there is a 99.9 percent factor that Richard is the Father of Addison, with a .1 percent error. I would say, Addison, we will be calling you Prince before the day is through."

Addison looked like he was going to cry. He stood and walked to Ski, "You will always be my Father Chancellor." He hugged him and said, "What hurts the most is I know the story the Hermit told was true. He murdered my Mother and killed children in the street thinking he was getting rid of me."

Antioch asked them all to sit. "It is time I told you all what I know for sure. I had not wanted to spread rumors without facts. Now that I know you are my cousin and Richard killed my Aunt, you should all understand why she came back here." The Wizard poured more coffee for himself and sat on the hearth of the fireplace. "I was already an apprentice of the Grand Wizard. I told you earlier Addison, an apprentice must train others to master the craft, we even attend to babies. I was your attendee. I was there the night you were born and helped to take care of you until you were two years old. You were born with eyes and hair as black as mine. You were bright and compassionate; even in the playground, you would heal your friends who were hurt. My Aunt Athena could not keep you out of the laboratory as soon as you walked you were mixing and stirring. I ran many tests on you to find your talents, but everything was inconclusive. We found you were just as much a Diamante as Arlequin; maybe even more so. You were taken to a Prophet who told us you must train with the blood; your life should be in Diamante. You would marry on this side of the world and have a Child of Flowers. This young woman would be the champion of the lesser and a hero to all. Now you know why I spelled everyone to name your daughter Zahrah Roselyn. Your Mother had to bring you back to this land."

Addison looked at Henry and then into the fire, "The Hermit told me our child would be a hero as well. I am not certain I like that. It means she will be in great danger, and many heroes end up dead."

The room was silent, and the Wizard said, "We all must die, Addison. Death matters little, our time here guides the world, that matters considerably. She didn't tell me they would change your looks. Athena never shared with me the name of your Father or where they took you. I believe it was because you were my first child to care for, I was distraught about your removal. When my Great-great Grandfather died and gave me all of his powers, he reminded me to keep a lookout for you and your daughter. You know I had this strange feeling when I was around Henry that you were him, my cousin, Aden."

Henry stood, "It seems you are back in the role of taking care of your little cousin again, Wizard. You were our Professor at the University, but you weren't around us."

The Wizard laughed. "Henry, I was in your head the whole time during the Great War. Remember the night you stood on the roof of the Castle at Engelton, and you asked the Night how to stop the King and the bloodshed of your countrymen?" Henry looked amazed and nodded yes. "Well, she sent me to quietly whisper in your ear strategy to take his army to the North Sea. We worked together very well, don't you think? That is good because our principal difficulties are just ahead of us. I suggest we meet tomorrow to start working out how to keep everyone in this room alive. Let's try not to start a war again, too much magic was spilled in the last one."

Dillion put his arm around Antioch and said, "And the one before that." Antioch knew he was referring to his country of Arlequin's demise, and the loss of most of the Wizards. "The King of Hex loves war; the more magic he spills, the stronger he becomes. Henry you and I need to leave, my guards just told me the King of Hex is looking for Elisabeth."

The Tea with the Empress

Queen Rakie, Casandra, and Dillion's wife Audrey met the Queen of Hex and her children at the door of the Castle, then walked them to the private dining room attached to Dillion's apartment in the upper Castle. Audrey asked the Hex guards to wait outside the door to the studios and told them her personal guards were sufficient for a tea.

After all the introductions; the servants brought in the tea, finger sandwiches, and cookies. Then two Elves walked into the room. The girls just stared at them as the Elves went to each of them, then turned to Audrey, and said, "The Queen and her daughters are all wearing listening devices. We have blocked them for now, your Majesty. However, we must remain in the room, or they are required to remove them. What is your pleasure?"

The Queen looked at them and said, "Are you willing to give them up?"

The Queen of Hex said, "I am so sorry your Majesty, I did not know the King had planted one on me. Although I am not surprised. Girls, did you know." They all looked guilty, "Well, do you know what the devices are?" They all reached for their necklaces.

Elisabeth said, "Remove them at once." She was mad and removed her necklace. "I assume it is my necklace too."

An Elf bowed and said, "As well as your Crown your Majesty." The Elves placed them all in a copper dish in the center of the table then set a glass dome over them. The door opened, and the Empress walked into the room. Elisabeth grabbed her chest and broke down into tears. Beatrice went to her and embraced her crying just as hard, neither one could talk. Everyone in the room had tears in their eyes, except the three girls of the King.

Janet finally said, "What is this Mother what is going on?" Elisabeth tried to speak, but she was crying so hard she couldn't get a word out.

Casandra said, "Girls, this woman who came in is Beatrice De Volt, Empress, my Mother, and your Mother's cousin and a good friend. They have not seen one another since the day of her marriage to Kenneth, my Uncle. Until just a few months ago, everyone in our family believed your Mother was dead. We also knew nothing about her children, you or your Brother."

They sat motionless until Audrey said, "I think we should give them some time alone. Let's take our tea into the other room and talk. Casandra, you now have some second cousins to have a reunion with."

Casandra stood up and said, "I do, and I have something right here to start our reunion, invitations to Henry's and my reception next month at the North Castle. I hope your Father allows you to come, it is going to be extravagant. Janet, I understand you are marrying General Martin next year. You must come and get ideas for your wedding. Jessica, there will be plenty of eligible young men for you to choose from."

Joan crossed her arms and stuck her nose in the air, "I don't care about parties, and I hate dressing up why should I come?"

As they walked into the other room, Casandra said, "Because we will have Elves, Sprites, and Fairies. I can also show you the finest hunting Falcons in the world." That got her interest Casandra continued, "Besides Henry loves you and would be hurt terribly if you were not there. What do you say, come to the reception?"

Joan was smiling, "Of course, if Henry wants it, I will be there." Casandra should be jealous she wondered if Henry knew how much this young girl loved him?

The Elves left the dining room but held the two in a secrecy bubble. Elisabeth said, "I hope I can keep our conversation secret. The King knows everything, and he takes so much of my power when he is angry. This meeting will certainly make him angry, it won't be long before the

King knocks on that door to find out why he cannot hear us. He will get our meeting out of the girls. They hold nothing back from him. The poor dears, they trust their Father, they shouldn't! He has given Janet to that brute Martin and has promised my baby to Moondale. Richard is mad he almost killed me several times. Jessica is the only one not promised, and she is just like her Father, greedy and evil. I am not strong Beatrice; I am a coward. My hope is for Devon that he will get free. Will you help him?"

The Empress sighed and told her of the conversation at the healing pool and that an Attachment was partially in his throat. She shared the vision of the Hermit and told her all that had happened as fast as she could. "Henry gave me a drink that will make our conversation private only to you. The Wizard Gadwell has devised it. I will give you a gift before you leave, buried in it is notepaper, the green is for the Hermit, the blue for me. Please keep me informed; not just about the King and your children but you. How you have withstood this for so many years, my heart goes out to you. You are the bravest Sorceress I know. You stand by your children no matter what; that is not cowardice. Please find it in your heart to help Casandra."

Elisabeth said, "I hope she is never in the position that I am her redeemer. I pray to the Night she is spared. We need to get back to the girls I feel the pull of the King." She drank down the syrup, and they took the bowl of jewelry to the girls.

Everyone sat and chatted about Casandra's wedding, the coronation, and Janet's upcoming wedding. Marion had arrived and questioned everyone. The girls knew some of Marion' relatives; that kept them all talking.

Henry walked in and gave each of the King's girls a gift from the islands: perfume which he sprayed on each one. The Empress could tell it was more than aroma it was a spell to have the girls misinform the King.

When he excused himself, Beatrice went to him. "Henry, one moment please." She took him by the shoulders and held him, looked into his eyes and kissed him on both cheeks. "I can never thank you enough for these hours with Elisabeth, not if I thank you every day for the rest of my life. I will never doubt you again. Welcome to our family." She hugged him, and he embraced her. Henry could feel her chest heave she was crying, and tears came to Henry's eyes as well.

Elisabeth was standing there and said, "Henry I have always loved you, I love you even more now." She hugged him and thanked him.

Henry opened the door to the King standing there red in the face. Henry said, "Your Majesty, I was just leaving. I would like to have a word with you if you have the time."

The King took in a breath as if it was all he could do to contain himself. "Not now Henry. I have come for my Queen and children." He walked three paces into the room coming face to face with the Empress. He just stood in astonishment.

The Empress bowed her head and said, "King Hex, I can't thank you enough for saving my Cousin and dear friend from death. She has told me what a hero you were for her and her children. I have found her life remarkable. Without you, we would have never had this reunion. I don't understand why you have kept her a secret from her family, you must explain that to me someday. Today, I just want the joy of our reunion in my heart."

The King could not speak, and Henry backed up into the room just to relish the moment. Casandra moved next to him, watching as well. Then King Hex saw the Emperor walk into the room, and he passed the King and walked straight to Elisabeth. Without a word, Hayden took her into his arms and held her in a long embrace. He whispered in her ear then finally he said, "It has been too long you were my favorite. I am so glad to see you alive, and it looks like you are well. I will see you stay that way." He turned to the King and nodded, "King Hex, at last, we meet face to face. Unlike the Empress, I do not want any explanations from you. I only want her, and her children cared for and kept well." Henry could feel the Emperor press his massive power on the man.

The King had gathered his thoughts and walked to Elisabeth and put his arm around her, "I assure you I take care of them very well. Trust me when I say if anything ill-fated happens to any of them I would surely die myself." He looked to the Empress and said, "I see the strong pull you have Empress. The only reason I kept knowledge of her from her family was my deep love for her. I feared you would come to take my family away from me. I could not stand that. Now, I know my fear was founded."

"Nonsense, we have no desire to rip her from her happy home and Kingdom." The Empress smiled an evil smile. "However, I see no reason she cannot keep family ties strong with us and communications open. I have extended an invitation to Casandra's and Henry's reception Ball to you and all your family. I hope you will come and be our guest at the North Castle."

The King again looked surprised, "Well, I am not sure our schedule will permit this…"

Jessica and Janet ran to him, "Father please, please, don't say no." Jessica said, "This means so much to us, please let us go."

Joan took her Father's hand, "Casandra said she would teach me how to Falcon, and if I am good at it, she will give me one. I have always wanted to learn."

Everyone watched as the King's heart melted, "Casandra said did she, and which one is Casandra?"

As if he did not know, the portraits did not do her justice, she stood firm and beautiful before him. He was beginning to understand Devon's obsession with her.

Henry stepped forward, "King Hex I would like to introduce my Wife, Countess Rakie."

Casandra bowed then stood to look him straight in the eye. "I have looked forward to meeting you King Hex, the pleasure is mine." She flashed him her most charming smile. The King took in a breath and almost fell over.

Henry was enjoying this, "You look surprised King. Casandra and I were married yesterday in Krete."

The King placed a pleasant smile on his face and said, "I had been told the wedding would be weeks away yet. So yes, I am surprised. Congratulations to you both." He took Casandra's hand and pulsed a little energy into her then withdrew it. "I wish years of happiness. May I kiss the bride?"

Henry looked upset he knew the King had probed her, but Casandra only smiled and leaned forward, "Of course." She deliberately shocked him when his lips touched hers. Then she said. "Oh, you are certainly a powerful King, I believe you shocked me." Henry was grateful his Father walked in, and he could turn his head to smile.

"Well, it looks like we all have come together in Dillion's apartments. We planned a very nice reception for all of you downstairs. I suggest we get out of this stuffy room and enjoy some of Henry's good wine." Winsette smiled as though nothing had happened. Henry knew he, Dillion, and Addison had been monitoring the entire scene.

Casandra said, "We are waiting for the King of Hex to accept our invitation to my reception."

The King Winsette threw back his head and laughed, "Your wish is my command, my lovely Countess. I command you and your family to attend her reception King Hex."

The King took in a breath and said, "You cost me Winsette, first the clothes and jewelry for this Coronation, and I know they will not be seen in the same garments twice…" He looked at his daughters and said, "Alright I agree. Now, I really need some wine."

Winsette laughed and said, "You should marry them off as soon as possible it is the only way to save money. Henry, find your own partner; I am taking Casandra." She placed her arm in Winsette's and kissed his cheek. "Henry, I think she likes me more than you." Henry laughed, and they all filed out of the room.

Hezebala's Bed

The reception did not last long, as everyone was worn out from the confrontation in Dillion's apartment and it was awkward standing in the same room with Devon staring at her. Henry and Casandra were the first to leave, saying they were tired from the travel to the Castle. As Henry took Casandra from the reception room all of Henry's men were standing before them with a big box. Sutton walked forward and said, "Count, Countess, we have a wedding gift for you both. This is from all your men. Congratulations and we look forward to serving you both. We vow to protect you and your children with our blood." They all went down on one knee and raised their swords.

Henry and Casandra stepped forward, and Henry said, "Thank you, and we vow to protect all of you with our blood." Henry lifted Casandra's hand and pricked it with the tip of Sutton's sword. Casandra had the strangest sensation, it was as if all her memories rushed out to the men, and all their memories rushed into her, the strength and power overwhelmed her.

They all stood, Perry and Sutton raised the lid of the box and held up two cloaks of black satin, trimmed in a white fur with black spots. Paxton and Bowen stepped forward and retrieved two saddles of black leather trimmed in the same hair. Sutton placed the cloak on Casandra and Perry set one on Henry.

Casandra smiled and touched the fur. "What animal is this fur?"

Sutton said surprised, "It is white Snow Leopard your family's spirit animal, it is in your coat of arms."

She said, "I thought that was the cougar, although I am not sure I ever asked."

Henry remembered the brooch he bought her as a wedding gift, "I thought it was a Leopard, you say a Snow Leopard."

Sutton laughed, "Well, we did our research; it is the Snow Leopard. We asked the Empress, it only makes sense, the snow leopard only lives in Savilla, and Stella, a magical creature and almost as rare as the Unicorn. The fur must be given freely from the pack and can only be worn by a descendant of Savilla or landowner. Henry, you are the landowner now and Casandra you are descendent."

Henry looked at Casandra with awe her black hair, aqua eyes, and creamy white skin matched the coloring of the snow leopard exactly. He should have known she even moved with the grace of the cat and could arouse the power and attraction of the mystical creature. "It becomes you my Countess; thank you, gentlemen. You have given us the perfect wedding present. I see you made the saddle big enough for Shelton. We should ride the Pegasus tomorrow in the parade Casandra, would you want to?"

Casandra squealed, "Yes. Shelton is here?"

Sutton laughed, "We could not keep him away from you, and he is sleeping now it was a long fight for him. When I tell him he will carry you in a parade, he might even let me saddle him. I have never come across a more egotistic animal in my life. He insisted he is on a mission and cannot be separated from you."

Casandra smiled, "He carries the future Empress that is his mission. Tell him the saddle is made of Snow Leopard and of the significance. He will agree."

Henry and Casandra continued through the Castle with half the guard following and half going out to the barracks. Casandra was astounded with the opulence of the Castle; black onyx was everywhere with red jasper and unakite. Every light was gold with crystals of the highest caliber. She had never seen anything like it in all her travels to the most prosperous cities in the world. The historical artwork and sculptures filled the halls beyond what was in many of the museums she had visited. Henry pointed out a portrait here and there, but Casandra knew what she was viewing and told him more than he knew. Servants and guards all stared at them as they moved through the Castle. He knew they made a striking pair with the cloaks on as they walked around but it surprised him she was totally unaware of the stares and whispers.

Henry led her through the courtyard and down the hallway to their apartments. When he opened the door, she was relieved, and he smiled as he thought. Thank the Night, she loved it. The walls were a lovely cream, and although the floor was red jasper, they were covered with stunning decorative rugs. Two tan leather couches faced one another with two blue covered wing chairs at the fireplace. The fireplace was three stories high made of gorgeous white stone. The large room opened to a dining room with windowed doors overlooking the courtyard. To the left of the entryway was a hallway. Henry said, "A restroom and two bedrooms are on the left and a library on the right. The kitchen is at the end of the hallway. Eric is staying in a bedroom downstairs and using the library as his office. There are three bedrooms and bathrooms upstairs one is ours, Grace and Charlie are using the others. They have been keeping the place clean from spies so we can speak freely here. We will also be using the library for our meetings. I have another surprise for you."

Henry knocked on the door. Eric opened the door to the library before she could speak she was bombarded by a large furry dog and a cat was swirling around her legs. Eric laughed. "Meet General, Casandra. I named your dog that because he acts like he runs the place. The Cat is Persnickety, Snicky for short, because she is, blame Grace she is their creator."

She petted and loved both the magical animals and hugged Eric. She noticed the Library for the first time. While it was much smaller, it was almost a duplicate of her Father's. She said, "Henry, it is like Father's, did you do that?"

Henry laughed, "It is your favorite room in the Castle. I thought it would make you feel a little like being home." She smiled, and he led her to the windows and opened the drapes where she saw a small garden of roses and a sitting area by the dining room. "The rose is in our coat of arms, and you will find them everywhere at the Castle. My Mother and Audrey decorated, I think they did a wonderful job. It is just what I asked for."

"Henry, the Castle is beautiful, but I could not live in it. I would feel as if I were in a museum. This feels like a comfortable home." Casandra hugged him.

He pulled her away and said, "I want to show you our room." They went up the stairs to their room. The bed was in the center of one wall with a bed cover of cream, a large red rose was embroidered in the center and pillows the shape of red roses were at the head of the bed. Black onyx floors were covered with rugs in patterns of roses, and the walls held lovely paintings of gardens of roses. The windows were covered in sheer white drapes with white satin drapes covering them. Double doors opened to a bathroom of white marble and gold fixtures, and the other end of the room, double doors opened to a closet with their clothes. The bedroom furniture was striking and beautiful with detailed hand-carved scenes. The bed was remarkable as it depicted leopards and Unicorns running and playing as she looked to the canopy, she saw they were mating.

Casandra looked at Henry and said, "Henry where in the world did you find this bed?"

Henry smiled and said. "At a renown antique store here in our town. The man who sold it to me will be at our table tomorrow that was part of the bargain made. The unicorns were what made me want it for you, I know how special they are to you. The man who sold me this bed said it was the bed of the greatest Sorcerer of all time, Hezebala. It was handed down for generations to the great Queens and Empresses of history. It was held by the Arlequin Queens for years and thought to be lost after the war. It showed up in Roupart's. Brandon Roupart will be at our table at the Ball he is a funny little man but loyal to me."

Casandra sat on the bed and looked up. "Henry do you have any idea what kind of bed this is?" Henry was blocking his memories of the some of the latest histories of the bed. He did not want her to know it was in a harlot house. "Come, lay down, and look at the ceiling of the canopy."

Henry did and was completely taken back by the carvings, "I don't know what to say, other than this is the first time I looked at it from this angle. I am well, embarrassed."

Casandra roared laughing, "I am sure you are." Then she chuckled even harder.

"Should we find another bed?" Henry was unhappy with himself.

Casandra looked at him and said, "Absolutely not! Henry this is a birthing bed look at it closely. If you look at the scenes, it shows conception and birth. Look at the openings to hold while birthing at the end of the bed, the shape and seat for birthing. Henry this is a perfect bed, how fitting to have our daughter right here on the grounds of the Castle of Diamante, Princess Winsette. I will not give up her name Henry. Don't tell your Father but prophets have named her Winsette; she needs that name."

Henry stared into Casandra's eyes he could just look forever at her. "A birthing bed, well if you tell Roupart, he'll charge me more."

Then they laughed, and she said, "I wonder Henry, what did all those men the whore's bed here think they were looking at?" Henry turned white as the coverlet. "We should take this bed for a ride. You have been to whores show me why men go to them. Can I be as seductive as them?"

Henry swallowed, and then smiled and thanked the Night for giving him, Casandra.

After he had bathed and dressed he watched her sleeping in their bed of roses. She was asleep on her stomach, and he pulled the covers down to wake her with a kiss on her shoulder. Then he saw her bruised back, he was hit with the reality of the danger they all faced. She turned and smiled. Henry said, "It is time to wake I have a meeting, and you must get dressed for dinner." He kissed her gently worried that during their lovemaking he had hurt her back. "I will ask Addison to look at your bruises after dinner."

"No, Henry. I am fine; besides, we have another matter to discuss." Casandra sat up in bed. "I believe you owe me for our session this afternoon."

Henry stood up with a grin, "Oh do I, you are not an expert yet. I have much to teach you."

Casandra gave a gloomy look, "I did not please you Count?"

He laughed and said, "I didn't say that at all. Yes, you pleased me, but now I must leave for a meeting. We can talk after dinner."

Casandra stood and threw the covers off, "Count Rakie we have not settled the payment arrangements."

Henry was almost at the door when he turned back and saw his wife stark naked with one hand on the bedpost and the other on her hip. He couldn't help himself he was holding her before he realized. "My darling I must leave, but before I do, I will give you lesson number four in whoring. Always set your price before you render services, or you will be cheated." He kissed her deeply and ran from the room before she could speak. As he closed the door to the apartment, he heard her call, "Count Rakie you cheat!"

The Confrontation

Addison and the Wizard were waiting in the hall for Henry. Addison was laughing, and mentally he said. Henry, what are you teaching your wife?

Henry said, "You were listening again. I don't eavesdrop on you and Marion."

The Wizard was laughing too, "Henry, everyone on this wing can hear you being called a cheat; on your honeymoon, too. How did you cheat on her so soon?"

Henry stopped walking and said, "I didn't, and please there are spies out here."

The Wizard said you're right of course, then he placed his hand on Henry's head and pulled out the information he needed.

Henry stopped. "Don't do that! Why do you do that to me, and not even have the courtesy to ask permission to steal my thoughts? It's a very unpleasant feeling."

The Wizard said, "Stop talking, I can hear your thoughts." Mentally the Wizard said. Henry, you bought a birthing bed for Casandra? You didn't know, Addison, are you hearing this?

Addison was laughing and asked Henry. Share with us the first three lessons you taught her.

Henry stopped and said, "No. Gentlemen get serious and put your head into the game we are about to play." Henry kept walking fast, "We need to end this too many are being hurt."

The Wizard and Addison ran to catch up with Henry the Wizard said, "Sorry Henry, you're right. I will give Casandra healing after dinner."

Two guards stationed on either side of the library doors opened them for the three, and everyone turned in their direction when they entered.

Richard snarled, "As usual, making a grand entrance. What are they doing with you Henry, this is a family meeting. Addison is pretending family, and that Wizard certainly isn't family at all."

The King was seated, and he held up his glass, "Stop, Richard! I will have no fighting. This transition of power is going to be blood free. Wait until you see Henry's bride, you will all understand why he is late. Now, where were we?"

Dillion said, "Help yourselves to wine gentleman. We were discussing the order of the parade tomorrow from the Castle to the Temple, and the returning route. Richard wants to ride in order of assenting beginning with the King of Hex and ending with us. Bernard wants to ride with families and thinks we should parade without personal guards because we have so many dignitaries."

Quintian spoke up. "Why don't we just mount and ride there, I don't understand all the pomp of this. Since we are not deciding traditionally, who cares. It was much more exciting seeing all the Brothers draw swords and fight their way to the Temple. The one left standing was King, fair and square. I don't think anyone really cares about this Coronation." He looked in his glass, found it empty and went for a refill.

The King stood screaming, "That is why I am changing this! And I might add why I didn't choose you for King! You think it was fun and exciting killing eight Brothers on my way to the Temple? Then you're an idiot!"

Samuel said, "Henry would know. Tell us what it is like to kill a Brother."

The King walked to Samuel and slapped him. "I had sixteen sons with three wives I am left with seven! More than half died of sickness, war, and jealousy. I will lose no more. Even though some in this room care little for life, I do. I still love all of you. Days like this I don't know why."

Henry handed his Father a glass of wine. "Father try my new wine. I think we should take a vote. I vote we ride in groups of families. Let the King of Hex lead, then all the visiting nobility and the Rakie's can come last. Who is with me?" Dillion, Bernard, Zakkhar, Henry, and Addison raised their hands.

Samuel said, "Addison can't vote he is not a Rakie."

Dillion said. "He most certainly is. I have his blood work right here." Dillion reached into his pocket pulled it out then slapped it down on the table, "His blood work is a 99.9 percent match to Richard. How many sons does this make Richard twelve or thirteen?"

Everyone in the room was silent.

Richard walked to Addison, who was at least four inches taller than him, but with the same coloring and Rakie family looks. "Impossible, what is your Mother? Some whore I played? Noblemen are one hundred percent noble blood you are surely not that."

Addison calmly said, "You asked why Wizard Gadwell was in the room with us. Well, he is my family, my Cousin, to be exact. My Mother was a Queen of Arlequin, Athena Gadwell and nobler than you Richard." Addison smiled, "I don't believe I will be calling a man who didn't even know that he bedded a Queen, Father. Grandfather was wise not to choose you for King. It is clear you are not the smartest of his Sons."

"This is outrageous where in the world did you come up with this fabrication?" Richard turned to Dillion. "What possessed you to listen to this garbage. Is this the kind of actions we can expect from you as King? You're going to cut us all down with accusations and lies."

Henry stepped in, "Richard, calm down; this is not the first time your infidelity has gotten you in trouble. What is Susanna, your third or fourth wife? How many have come to this Castle begging us to hire your children? Walk the halls, everyone here looks like a Rakie. A prophet read for Addison and told him of you and his Mother. I encouraged him to test his blood find out for certain. Especially since there was murder involved." Henry left that for him and stopped speaking.

"Murder, what murder!" Richard was getting red in the face now.

Addison stepped up to him. "Why the murder of Queen Gadwell. Why did you strangle the Queen and through her body into the river?" Richard stood with horror on his face saying nothing.

Henry said, "Please, Richard, do not tell us you don't remember strangling a Sorceress named Queen Dianna Athena Marquis Gadwell, who came to you asking you to take in your Son. She told you he was extremely talented and mostly Diamentia; he needed training here. You killed her, threw her into the river, and tried to find the boy to kill him too. How many two-year-old boys did you kill in the process? Good thing she was a clever Sorceress, actually Wizard. I bet she knew you would kill her given half a chance. The real reason for this meeting is to call for a Domestic Court Martial."

Dillion said, "Correct, we do not want to diminish the Coronation with ugly gossip and insinuations. It is best to keep this among family. After all, you would not want the same to happen to you as did Henry. It has taken him years to recover."

Richard took in a deep breath, and in a low voice, he said, "Brother I think I would have known if I bedded a Queen or Wizard. The only Dianna I recall was a whore, and if no great importance."

The Wizard had him by the throat before he ended the sentence. He lifted him into the air and dropped him before any of the Warlocks in the room could stop him. Bernard and Quintain grabbed Antioch by the arms and restrained him while Richard laid gapping for air on the floor.

Henry threw back his head and laughed, "Evidently she was no whore, my Idiot Brother. I doubt you know much about Wizards either." Henry pulled him to a standing position and handed him a glass of wine. "Addison's Brother is very much stronger than any of us in this room. It would take all of us to subdue him. I only see two allies willing to help you out. You might as well be truthful." Henry leaned into Richard and softly said, "He has ways of pulling it out of you, very uncomfortable ways." Henry returned to Dillion's side.

Dillion stood confident and said, "Release the Wizard Gadwell Brothers." They did, and he continued, "We do not have time to play petty games. We take a vote or postpone. Which is it?" They went around the room, and the Brothers all voted.

Henry said, "On the matter of Addison's parentage I vote guilty, and to the untimely death of Queen Marquis." All the Brothers voted against Richard, except Samuel and Quintian.

Then Dillion said, "Addison I will instate you as Prince Addison Ski Rakie tomorrow as one of my first dues, and Marion will, of course, become a Duchess. You will have the honor of giving Diamentia a Princess. Congratulations, Nephew. My Brother Richard will see you get lands and holding, come to see me if he reneges, as to the matter of the death of your Mother you are due restitution. You may ask for monies, removal of title, banishment, or death. How say you?"

Addison smiled and said, "I must consider my options, Uncle."

Dillion nodded and kept his expression stoic even though he was enjoying this immensely. "Very well, a postponement. You have one year to name his punishment." Dillion turned to the Wizard, "Since you are Addison's cousin and Queen Marquis was your blood, you are entitled to restitution as well. What say you, Sir?"

The Wizard strutted to Richard with a wicked smile on his face. Henry and Addison almost laughed it was becoming challenging to play this game. Richard was shaking in his boots. "King and Prince Rakie, I am pleased to have this option, I thank you. Yet, what is the proper restitution for death?" He circled Richard and said. "However, the only thing I want from this Warlock is the truth. As Henry knows I can have him speaking in seconds. I ask permission to read his memories, Sir."

Dillion looked at his Father, and the King said, "I would not only like to see that, but I would also like to hear the truth myself. Our land was better off with Wizards and Sprites keeping us honest. However, it is your proceeding Dillion."

Dillion smiled. "Let us give Father his wish. Carry on Wizard."

Just that quick the Wizard had a hand on Richard's right shoulder and the other on the back of his head.

He poured in power and Richard began talking. "The truth is, I did kill a woman named Dianna. I met her in Arlequin on business before the war. I spent a month or more with her, then I didn't see her for at least two years. She came to me with this story of having a son, and I told her I would find work for him in the stables. That was not good enough for her. She began to spell me. I fought her, but it took six of my men and myself to overcome her. We all had our turn with her before killing her, tearing her into pieces and throwing her into the river.

I had no idea she was a royal! I did search for the boy. There were many times I wondered about you, Addison. Sometimes I see her in your face and when your eyes turn dark with anger. But by the time I learned of your existence you were ensconced in Ski's life. I thought it best to let it be."

Everyone in the room stood perfectly still while the Wizard removed power and held on to Richard's head. Henry was beginning to think he was going to kill him right before their eyes. Richard started to fall, but the Wizard caught him, took him to the couch on the side of the library and laid him down. "He will sleep for a few minutes, thank you Prince Rakie and King. I am satisfied, and I know my Cousin will seek justice for our Queen."

He went to the bar and poured a drink. Samuel and Quintian came to him and bowed. Quintian said, "I am sorry for your loss, and I regret voting against you. My Brother has never been a nice man or a nice Brother. I hope Addison chooses death."

Samuel said, "As do I, or at the very least banishment. I know I never want to see him again." A servant knocked on the door and announced dinner.

The men all went to the hallway before the formal dining room. Henry and Addison walked to the Castle entrance to get Casandra and Marion for the introductions before dinner. Addison looked pale and green. Addison mentally said to Henry. That was awful I could see her death as clear as if I were there. I had asked Antioch to teach me how to do that. Now…I am not sure I want to see into other's minds."

Henry thought. I saw it through you, but I believe Richard showed Antioch, and because of our connection, we all three saw it. Richard is lucky. I know my Brother Dillion, had he seen those vivid pictures, he would have done the same to Richard as he did to your Mother. He is a firm believer in equal justice. Did you block your mind from Marion?

Addison turned and looked at Henry and said, "No, and Casandra?" They both quickened their steps to get to their brides. When they caught sight of them, they were both deep into a conversation. They turned to look at them at the same time. They hugged their husbands and Casandra said mentally. Addison, I don't even know what to say. If you wish, I can take the pictures from your mind. No one should remember a loved one like that.

Addison kissed her on her forehead while he held tight to Marion. "Thank you, Casandra, but Antioch has sent me many pictures of her as he saw her. I will remember those. We all need to get to our dinner." He took Marion's arm and led the way for the introductions.

The dining room was stately and enormous with five crystal chandeliers in the center of the room and another twenty dispersed around the perimeter. A large round table was set with a cream tablecloth like the cream and gold marble walls and floors. Deep burgundy drapes hung at the windows with a carpet of the same red and the symbol of the crown under the dark mahogany table. A low arrangement of bright roses filled the center with tall golden candelabras with platers of gold at each place setting.

When Addison introduced Marion to Richard, he asked, "Addison you have blood bonded with your Sprite?"

Addison merely said, "Yes." Then walked on to introduce his stepmother Suzanna. Everyone was dazzled by Casandra and fell instantly in love with Marion's beauty and honesty. The dinner was fabulous, from the table settings to the heavenly seven-course meal. The men sat back and let the Sorcerers take over the conversation, while the deed of Richards glared in their minds. This was the downfall of being blood bonded; little was left to doubt.

The dinner was ended with Henry making a toast with Casandra's wine to Dillion. Henry stood and held his glass up to Dillion and pronounced, "Prince, soon to be King. I pray to the Night you live long in perfect health. May you be embraced in love by all, especially your family, and may you freely return that love to all. May you rule your peoples with justice and fairness and hold our lands in peace and prosperity." Henry smiled genuinely at his Brother showing his authentic soul to everyone there. Casandra was so proud of him she loved him so but had to keep that in her mind and not let Richard see it.

Everyone raised their glass and drank but as Dillion swallowed his wine he was grateful knowing for just that moment Henry had brought them together as a family, maybe for the last time. Who knows where Richard would be a year from then.

When dinner ended, Addison went to Dillion and whispered in his ear. Henry led the four of them and the Wizard in silence to

Henry's apartment. Then he said, "Will you three come in for a night-cap, before bed?"

They went to the library to find Eric, "We need to have a meeting, and we need the Emperor and Empress here but cloak them. No one should know they are here. Can you do that?'

Eric said, "Yes, you don't have to tell me, I already know." Eric walked to Addison and the Wizard. "I do not know how the two of you contained yourself. I would have killed him where he stood."

Eric walked out, and Grace came in, "We are securing the apartment. Eric thought there would be more room for everyone in the living area. He wanted to let the Wizard know we are about to put up a shield."

The Wizard smiled, "Thank you, Grace, I would feel bad if I inadvertently blew someone up. Surprise shields always create havoc with a Wizard's balance."

Addison said, "Well, now that explains a lot. You and I need to talk. Henry thought I was lying about balance and magical spheres."

The Wizard looked at Henry, "Well, look at him, Addison. Have you ever balanced the man out, I have never been around anyone so top heavy."

"I am standing right here…and I am not top heavy." Henry gave them a sour look. "Talking about me is off topic. Would you like a glass of wine or ale?"

Marion said, "Wizard if Henry is off balance, you should fix him. It is important he is at his best until the King holds no threat."

Casandra agreed. Henry objected, but Casandra overruled him. "After this meeting, Henry, you will be put into balance. I know you have asked him to come to heal me if you want that to happen you will be healed too."

Henry squared his shoulders and said, "Being off balance is not an illness or injury. Not at all the same thing. You will let the Wizard heal you."

Casandra said, "You are not ordering me Count Rakie!"

Her Father opened the library door. "I see you two are already fighting like an old married couple. Eric asked that I come to get all of you the Empress is on her way. To answer your question for Henry, Casandra, he is not ordering you to do anything. He is strongly advising you and hopes you consider his point of view. Sweetheart you really should try to keep your voice down; you know how it carries. Henry, bring wine and agree with me." The Emperor walked out of the room.

Henry picked up two bottles of wine and gave Casandra his little boy grin and said, "I agree with your Father." Casandra crossed her arms and growled at him on his way by. Marion and Addison stifled laughter, but the Wizard just outright laughed and said, "I will see he is balanced correctly. Now, let the anger go. I need you with a clear head for this meeting."

Everyone was seated when there was a knock on the wall by the fireplace. Henry pushed against the wall. Dillion, Audrey, the King, and Queen came out. The King said, "Hello everyone, I haven't done that in many years we almost got lost. Henry, there is a cave in halfway across the courtyard before you leave we must fix it." They found a seat, and wine was poured.

Dillion said, "What is so important that a clandestine meeting must take place tonight?"

The Wizard said, "Earlier when I had control of Richard's mind, I took the liberty to do a little searching. I found an assassination plot was lurking in his head so, I probed a little deeper to see more details. Samuel, Quintian, and Richard have hired men to ambush you tomorrow during the parade. The King of Hex is helping them execute the operation with his men. Richard intends to be King, it seems the King of Hex promised it to him."

Henry laughed, "The King of Hex promises that job to everyone, even me."

"What? Well, you must have turned him down Henry, or I would have already been dead. I never could outsmart you. Do you know of the plan Wizard?" Dillion grinned.

The Wizard said. "This is where it gets interesting. Samuel and Quintian think only the King and Dillion will die. However, Richard has other ideas. He wants it to include the Queen and my half Sister, Audrey." He looked at her and felt her anger. "Was I not supposed to tell them we are related Audrey?"

She shook her head, "Well it is a little late now Antioch! I will explain later Dillion. Why does he want me dead? Isn't making me a widow enough!"

The Wizard continued, "Don't take it personally Audrey, he also includes several of your Sisters-in-law and his wife Suzanna, he is tired of her. He believes he can marry up if he is King, which is true. He thinks he can control Bernard, plus, it is Bernard who controls the monies and lands; he is needed at least for a while. But, Zakkhar and his wife will die. He has been sleeping with Zakkhar's wife Harriot for years, I am guessing he doesn't trust her to keep quiet about it. You may want to test the blood of your nephews." The Wizard took a deep drink of wine, while they all stared at one another. "This is not confirmed, but Richard thinks the King will also grab Casandra in confusion. I think it is a golden opportunity to play that hand, I believe he is correct about that. While I was holding his head, I found out Richard was planning to go to King Hex tonight and ask for Henry and Addison's deaths too. By the time he gets there, he will probably add my name he is a greedy little bastard. Forgive me, ladies."

Casandra stood and said, "What a nice little procession of ducks we make marching down to the Temple, King Hex even has the Emperor and Empress in his sites."

Henry asked, "Wizard, do you know at what point in the parade this will happen or who or where the attack will come from?"

"No, he doesn't know for sure. King Hex is the one running the plan. He will signal the attack. That is why he was told to have the King at the front of the procession, and why he wanted the families to ride together making it easier to pick them off. I do know Samuel's wife Samantha and Suzanna will be one of the attackers, their target is the Queen and Audrey."

Henry rubbed his face with his hands and started pacing. "I was so busy planning our game, I didn't look around at others."

The Emperor rose and walked to him. The Emperor said, "Henry, I am insulted. Why does King Hex ride at the front of the parade! I am the one who made the match with you and Casandra, I am the one opening trade with your country, and I am the one who came to honor your Brother. I get sandwiched between the King of Hex and the King of Diamentia. It is outrageous!"

Henry laughed, his eyes lit up. "You are so right Father-in-law!" everyone in the room just looked at the two like they were crazy. "Dillion you must rectify this at once. The Emperor must ride with King Hex at the front, we cannot dishonor my Father-in-law."

Dillion smiled, and the King laughed and said, "Splendid gentlemen, the King of Hex is the biggest coward. I know nothing will happen to the Emperor or Empress while riding with the King."

The Empress rose, walked to Casandra and put her arms around her. "Oh, I will not be riding with you, my Emperor. I will be with Casandra."

Casandra snapped her fingers, "Not quite but close. I will be on Shelton next to you as you ride with Audrey and the Queen, in the Queen's carriage. Between all of us, we can shield out anything."

Eric stood up and said, "My lady squad can surround you. In fact, why we don't place all the women together and all the men together, that way we can fight as one."

The Emperor said, "Eric, take some of my men and put them in the crowd they detect magic at the onset. If we could put military between the three portions, there would be more defense and better separation."

Dillion said, "Yes, it would look like it was planned too, a pretty parade. I have a secret squad for just such an occasion, I have known something like this would take place. I had expected it before now, and they are ready. If we just knew where or had a few seconds notice we could stop them in the act. Here's is what we will do, Emperor and Kings first. Emperor, you must have your personal guard with you, or we will tip our hand. The King will certainly ride with his men. Then navy, women and children, the army, then the heirs to the throne. Ha, this will work."

Addison interrupted, "That's it! Sorry, but the thought occurred to me… Wizard I can speak with you, mentally right?" He waited for him to nod. "Then Eric can speak mentally with Ernst or the Prince. With any luck, they will let Ernst know when or how the attack will be signaled. Ernst will be riding next to the Emperor and Eric. Eric can tell us mentally, and we can relay the message to Casandra and Marion mentally. Oh, this could work. This could work beautifully."

After another hour of planning, everyone left to get to bed. The Wizard sat and poured another glass of wine. Then he waved his hand and gave Casandra a bottle of bath salt. He told her, "Go take a bath with this, and I will be up in a few minutes. I will attend to Henry first. Henry?"

Henry took off his jacket and stood for the Wizard he manipulated the air around Henry. Then he told him to sit, and he gently rubbed his shoulders. "Henry, tomorrow we will all have to be alert and rested. Try to get a good night's sleep. Stop going over the plan in your head you know it will be different when it actually happens."

Henry chuckled, "That is why I go over it again and again until I have worked out every possibility."

The Wizard shook his head, "Your Brother meant it when he said he never outsmarted you, didn't he?" Henry just smiled.

Henry stared at the fire until the Wizard said goodnight. When he entered their bedroom, Casandra was standing against the bed, waiting for him in a red satin nightgown. He walked to her and took her in his arms, and she pushed him away. "Not so fast, we haven't reached an agreement. You will learn, I forget nothing." She crossed her arms in front of her and raised her eyebrow.

Henry stepped back and said, "I see that. My darling wife what is it you want I haven't given you? I have made you the richest women in the world. I have given you my title, my blood. What more do you want?"

The bottom of her gown flamed, and he knew he was in trouble. She stomped from the bedroom to the closet and returned with a purse. She hauled back and threw it at him. He caught it, and she snarled, "All I keep hearing is that I am the richest women in the world, I see no money in my purse. Do you?" Henry knew she was dead serious. "I have expenses, Henry. I have a hairdresser to pay and a magic dresser coming tomorrow to cover my bruised back, and a seamstress to let out my dress for the ball. I need to go shopping for new clothes. In case you haven't noticed, my waist is getting thick. Of course, you haven't noticed you have been planning."

"Stop." Henry looked at her sternly. Henry grabbed her arm and pulled her to a painting on the wall of their room. He handed her the purse and swung the painting out. Henry said an incantation, and a safe appeared. He placed her hand on it and opened the safe. "Here," He reached in and took out a document. "This is a letter of credit. Carry it with you always, but keep it vanquished. Show it at any bank or any mercantile you want to shop at. There is a safe filled with money at Belissa Villa in the house and in the vineyard office. You are welcome to all of it. To enchant a safe, place your handprint on it and it will open to you. Here take as much as you need. I am sorry Casandra I have been a thoughtless husband not to give you any money. Please, don't think I expect sexual favors for money from my wife, and please forgive me." He leaned against the wall and crossed his arms, with a sorrowful face.

She reached into the safe and took out ten bills and a handful of coins and said. "Thank you, Henry."

He took the purse from her and stuffed more bills and coins into it. "You're the richest women in the world; your purse should reflect it."

She smiled at him, and his heart melted. "Casandra please talk to me if you want something from me, or at least think it out loud for me. I am a Warlock; we are not as intuitive as Sorcerers. I thought you were playing games with me. I love you, know there isn't anything I would not give to you. I had one marriage filled with lies, it ended badly. You can ask anything of me."

Casandra put her arms around him. "I am sorry Henry, I will openly let you know what I need. Having liaisons…well, I had no right to ask anything of the Warlocks. I was there for sex only, and to produce a powerful offspring for the family. I suppose I am used to feeling like a whore, I am not so different from one, am I." She turned and walked away.

Twice in one night. How did he not see this? First King Hex's plan to kill them all. Now he totally missed how she felt in all this madness. He tried to imagine a young girl given to a Warlock for propagation. There was no love felt and, in the end, she didn't even have the child she gave birth to. He closed the safe and noticed a jewelry box had fallen on the floor. It was the pin he bought the day he bought her wedding ring. Henry undressed and waited for her to come out of the bathroom. He knew she had been crying. She walked around the room turning out lights and picking up his clothes. He was amused and wondering how long she could avoid looking at him.

"Casandra come here." She walked to his side of the bed. He took her hand and held it open, then he began to make small circles in her palm while talking to her. "Are you afraid?" She pulled away, but he held her tightly. "We all are afraid when we are faced with a fight. What frightens you the most?"

She looked straight into his eyes, "Not seeing you again, not seeing our child live, watching people I love die. Killing the King, you know that is my fate. I must kill the King."

Henry said, "Yes. You have convinced me you will kill the King, but not tonight or tomorrow." He pulled her into bed with him and held her. "Casandra, the Warlocks you have been with were boys, who didn't know how to treat a Sorcerer respectfully or kindly. There was no relationship built with them because you would never be allowed to marry them, they were beneath you. I never understood your custom of the liaison. Until tonight, I had never given it much thought. Now that I have, I understand your reluctance to choose a girl. I pushed that on you; just as everything from your holiday to your wedding has been pushed on you. I will not tolerate our baby girl to grow up as you have. A liaison is not my custom, and I will not allow it. She will not have a liaison." Her head was on his chest, while he could not see her eyes, he felt her warm tears, and her body shake. "You would not make a good whore Cassandra you love too much. I have been lying here thinking you must miss each of your children and that you really did care for each of the boys you bedded. My love if I could promise that tomorrow we would all be safe and free of the King, I would. I will not lie to you, ever." He lifted her head, "King Hex will not die tomorrow. I don't know if anyone will or won't live and I love you."

She fell into his arms and said, "I am the luckiest Sorceress in the world I love you, Henry, with all my heart, and we will not die tomorrow."

The Parade of Kings

The next morning Henry and Casandra woke before dawn by the voice of the Wizard. Wake! It is time to start dressing. Henry snickered, "That Wizard is in my head now. Wake Casandra, I have a present for you."

She lifted her head and smiled, "Am I to get presents every day of my life from you, Henry?"

He handed her the jewelry box and said, "I think not. I don't want to spoil you too much. I found this the day I picked out your wedding ring." She opened the box, and there was a brooch of black and white diamonds fashioned into at Snow Leopard, with aqua blue sapphires for eyes. "The pin had red ruby eyes. The jeweler changed the stones to match your eyes when he removed it from the case. It turned out the man knew you, he fashioned your crown. I was thinking of the meditation you had in the glen at the time."

She sat up in bed and said, "This is a good omen, Henry. We should wear our cloaks."

Henry kissed her. "Yes. Our men will love it. Casandra, I need to take power from you. The King will expect it; no, he will be looking for it on me. I am sorry." Casandra drew him to her neck and pulsed power to Henry's mouth. A surge of energy enveloped Henry, and before he knew it, he had her on her back making love to her.

They barely had time to dress. Casandra and Henry both wore formal black riding pants and boots. Henry wore a burgundy jacket with the coat of arms of Belissa while Casandra wore a burgundy tunic with the emblem Marion designed. The hairdresser weaved her hair with tiny garnets on a thread of gold. Henry pinned the brooch on Casandra cape at her neck.

The effect was striking when Henry and Casandra walked down the stairs. Paxton, Sutton, and the guards were waiting along with the Wizard, Marion, and Addison. Paxton said, "You look exquisite this morning Countess. Shelton is wearing his saddle and will be happy you will match him."

Marion said, "You both look stunning, Diamentia will have a new fashion by tomorrow."

The Wizard said, "You look too powerful and royal you will attract attention."

Addison said, "Yes but it will be easier to spot them if they get into trouble. I like that because Marion will be right next to Casandra." He handed them coffee and said, "This is all you have time for."

The Wizard said, "Wait. I will remind you…this is for Addison and Marion as well. Do not show your affections in front of the King. If he finds you love one another, he will have a card to play, a card that could kill you. Understand me." They all agreed and walked to the courtyard together.

Shelton was elated to see Casandra, she hugged and kissed him before Paxton helped her mount. Paxton took her hand and said, "I should be riding with you to protect you, but Shelton will protect you, trust him."

He kissed her hand, and she tugged on his arm. "Paxton, I want you to protect yourself and take good care of Henry and Addison. We will not die this day."

Paxton smiled and said. "No. we will not die this day." Then he took Marion's hand. "You will ride with the Queen."

Marion stopped. "I will not. I must ride on a Pegasus with Casandra I will need to fly."

Paxton looked shocked, "Addison wants you in the carriage. He told me himself."

Marion pulled her hand from him. "I need a word with Casandra first." Paxton stood back while Marion mentally thought. I want my own Pegasus. I have one, I know Addison showed her to me yesterday. I must ride, and I must be tied on.

Casandra mentally said. Marion, you are pregnant and afraid of Pegasus.

Marion whispered, "Casandra this is important it is the Hermit's orders. She came to me this morning while I was dressing. This is my mission; I must ride today. I must ride. Addison and Henry will try to stop me and if they do… many will die. I am the only Sprite here, I need to change the energy of the spells being thrown to fireworks and harmless confetti. Please, help me. Help…me block my thoughts from Paxton, Addison, and Henry.

Casandra placed them all under a silent spell and called Paxton and said, "I apologize beforehand, but I am putting you under a compulsion spell." She told him to take Marion to the stable, tie her on the Pegasus and hide her until the Parade began. Until it was too late for Addison to stop her. "Shelton, you must shield my thought and Marion's from all the Wizards, Henry, and Addison." He nodded his head up and down. Paxton turned and followed her instructions, and she turned Shelton away from Henry, Addison, and the Wizard to avoid them. She saw her Father and headed Shelton straight to him.

The Emperor saw her and was surprised. He said, "Casandra, what are you doing at the front of the parade?"

Before she could answer a horse turned quickly, and she was face to face with the King of Hex.

The King smiled wickedly and said, "Countess you look quite beautiful and powerful today. I have heard about your mount, he is rather large for a petite young woman like you to handle. Be very careful not to fall from him."

Casandra sat straight in her saddle and Shelton reared his head at the King. "Shelton, behave. I am a competent rider, and Shelton is an exceptional Pegasus. He would never drop me. I have no fear." She raised her eyebrow and stared directly into his eyes. It was hard to do, but she held her gaze.

The Emperor coughed and said, "You do look imposing on him, my Dear. He is impressive, but then you look strikingly beautiful too."

Martin came forward on his horse and said, "Emperor, she should not be riding this beast. Clearly, he is too large for her and why isn't she guarded. Where is your husband, the Count?"

Henry spoke up from behind her, "I am right here, Martin. Casandra, your place is by the Queen. Where is Marion?" He looked upset with her.

She knew he was, but it would a good game to play in front of the King. Mentally she said, Marion is not feeling well she needed to go to the restroom Paxton is with her. This would be an excellent game to play with the King, forgive me, I mean none of this. She turned in her saddle and sharply said, "Marion and I are both grown women, Henry. I am sure she is just powdering her nose. I came to speak with my Father and look who I found." She turned back and looked past the King, and Martin and straight to Devon who cowered. "I need to speak with my Father. Alone."

Henry's eyes widened, and he flushed taking a breath he said, "I will give you a moment alone to speak with him then." The Emperor, Eric, and Casandra rode to the side and spoke a few words. The Emperor looked mad and rode back to the group, and Casandra looked upset too. Eric moved closer to her. Then Casandra's whole demeanor changed as she touched Eric's hand and smiled at him. Henry was shocked she was flirting with Eric in front of him.

The King smiled and broke the silence, "This whole parade is ridiculous if you ask me. Changing everything at the last minute and not guarding the women invites trouble. I don't know how you tolerate it, Henry. What if something terrible occurred to your bride? I would be jealous, as beautiful as Casandra is. Look how she flirts with that Elf." The King looked to Casandra and Eric whispering together. Eric and Casandra rode back to the group, and the King said, "Besides, you two should be honeymooning not attending affairs of State."

A horn blew, and Henry said, "We need to take our places I will escort you back to your place Casandra."

She turned to Shelton and said, "I am perfectly able to find it myself." From a dead stop, Shelton took off and flew above their heads.

Henry looked at the King and Martin grinning at him. "Having trouble with your bride so soon Henry." They turned their mounts and started the parade.

Henry followed her and mentally said. You do not know who you are playing with Casandra. What is this about, and where are Paxton and Marion?

She answered him mentally. They are right here. She landed next to Marion on the Pegasus. Paxton was riding his mount to the rear where the King was. Henry returned to Addison. "Marion is on a Pegasus next to Cassandra." Paxton rode up to them, and Henry said, "What is this Paxton? Marion was to go in a carriage."

Paxton answered, "I know." He looked to the ground and told them, "I can't speak about it."

Addison cradled his head and mentally said. Did they spell you?

Paxton answered, "Yes."

Henry sighed and said, "We can do nothing now…they are walking out the gates."

Addison screamed at Marion mentally. I know you can hear me little Sprite, and you are in so much trouble! Be glad it will be hours before I have you alone I may have time to cool off. Open your mind to us we need to communicate with you. Now!

Eric rode next to the Prince and Ernst. He mentally said. Can you hear me, Father?

The Prince turned and looked at Eric, then to Ernst. The Prince said mentally. Are you my brother?

Eric mentally answered and said. Yes, half-brother, your memory was covered for your protection, ask me about it later at the Ball. We know of the ambush would either of you tell me what the signal is? If you do, we will spare your lives.

Ernst spoke back mentally. It won't save mine if the King dies, I die. I am ready I can no longer live like this. You are my son Eric, and I owe you much for helping Devon and me. There is a woman that will come out of the crowd with two arms full of roses for the Emperor and King. The King will graciously throw a rose to a young girl in the throng, and that will signal to attack.

Eric thanked him and relayed the message back to the Wizard. Eric moved to the Emperor and whispered in his ear. Casandra told the Queens. Marion told Grace and the woman guards. They rode on for at least a mile before Henry told Casandra the King threw out a rose.

Casandra signaled the Empress and Grace. Charlie nodded to their women's unit to surround Suzanna and Samantha's carriage to bottle their powers. The two Duchess felt the containment and shot a burst of energy to the Queen's carriage early, it was a red and orange lightning strike. Marion changed the bolts into confetti before it hit their shield. The crowd roared and cheered, thinking this was part of the planned entertainment.

Marion screamed, "Casandra I must fly, I must be above the parade."

Casandra saw bolts of energy coming at them and returned a stream of light at them. "Grace, Charlie, we fly with Marion," Shelton instructed the Pegasus, and they all shot straight up above the parade.

Marion worked to change the charges of electric into fireworks that shot into the sky, and she turned the spells into confetti that fell on to the parade and spectators. Casandra and the Elves kept Marion shielded while the Warlocks on the ground were fighting off electric charges coming at them.

The Emperor placed irons around the King the moment he threw out the rose. The King began to shout orders to Martin and his Generals to fly. Before he could say more the Emperor silenced him and Eric held Martin, Ernst, and the Prince in irons. The Elf squad flew in to stop the King's Generals and men. General Due Bre was the only one to escape with five of his team.

They heard the boom of spells coming from the women's group first, then magical energy was bursting from the crowds and from the parade riders. The bolts of lightning were turning into fireworks, while the spells flew to the clouds, exploding as confetti. The spectators were roaring with cheers and clapping. Eric said, "They must think this is the entertainment. We need to keep moving quickly to the Temple." They changed the pace of the parade to a trot and moved everyone forward as quickly as possible without putting them in danger. Smoke and confetti covered the sky causing the Emperor and Eric to hardly see anything above or behind them.

As soon as Eric told the Wizard the women had handed bouquets of roses to the Emperor Henry, Addison and the Wizard placed a bubble of protection around the King's carriage. Henry saw bolts of lightning rocketed from the women's group. Spells from the crowd soared toward the Queen, but before he could understand what was happening, they were deluged with lightning bolts. It was all he and Addison could do to deflect and protect the many dignitaries riding with them. The Military of Diamante flanked to the outside of the parade surrounded the nobility and increased the pace as they made the turn onto Blessia Avenue. The smoke, fireworks, and confetti filled the air, it looked as if they were amid a blizzard. Henry tried to reach his men mentally to help Casandra and Marion, but he could not find anyone in the crowd.

Marion was flying low and working hard to contain the energies soaring around them while the others were busy protecting and repelling spells and bolts of lightning. Suddenly six men came from above Casandra, she felt restraints lurching out to her. Shelton immediately flew higher and above the King's men. A large man, who looked to be an officer, flew to meet her. She flung a spell at him, and he repelled it. She maneuvered past him and attached a stream of energy to him, but he raised his hand and burst the stream. Every bolt she sent his way was flung aside. Charlie and Grace were fighting below with the five soldiers he brought with him. Then she saw Paxton and Dillion's squad coming to help, but she couldn't wait for help; the man was after her, and he was relentless. As they fought, he was becoming angrier, and his bolts and streams of energy changed from restraining to harming. Every blow was piercing her and depleting her energies. She knew she had to match his power. She raised both arms to send a blast to push him off his Pegasus. He drew his sword striking her just below her left breast and extending across her midsection to her right side. Casandra screamed with pain and fury, she could only think of her baby. Had this man hurt Winsette? Her anger penetrated the bolt she released, it hit him right in his chest and exploded. His organs flew out and splattered her as his face held a look of disbelief. Then he fell from his mount to ground. Cassandra watched his decent with a sense of pure detachment. Shelton told her to lay against him, and he would heal her wound. As she bent over Shelton's neck, she watched as the five men below fell from their mounts to the ground. Paxton was at her side.

Paxton found Casandra and Marion flying high. He mentally told Addison and Henry, Marion was the one changing the spells and energies to confetti and fireworks. Then Paxton saw Casandra engaged with General Due Brue. He told Henry he would help her and land in the Temple grounds. Dillion heard the conversation and sent his squad to Paxton. Paxton and the men directed the women down to the Temple. Paxton helped Casandra off Shelton and felt the wetness on his hands. "My Countess, you are hurt."

Casandra said, "No, say nothing. Shelton healed me. Look." She opened her cloak and showed him the wound, still red but closed and healing. "Do not tell Henry, I am fine." Paxton could see she was healing but drained, and she was not fine. He pulled a bottle from the air and had her drink a potion. She did and said, "That tasted good, what it is?" She took the bottle back and took another swig.

Paxton laughed and said, "Liquor with healing properties, which you have had enough of. Henry makes everything taste wonderful, even medicine."

General Due Brue fell right in front of the King's carriage. The King stopped the carriage Henry rode forward, and Dillion began catching men falling from the sky. The Wizard asked Dillion, "Where do you want all these up servers King?"

"Wizard would you place everyone in the throne room, even the dead. General Marshall, take your army and guard them. I will be there as soon as the Coronation is complete. Henry, am I to understand Casandra and Marion did this?"

Henry looked at him and said, "It seems so. We need to make you King first, and then we need to get to the bottom of this. I am sure the King of Hex will be fuming at the loss of De Brue and who knows how many attachments have died this day. Casandra has single-handedly humiliated his Kingdom."

Winsette stood up and said, "Welcome to ruling my son. It seems we Diamante cannot crown a new King without someone dying. Too bad."

The Wizard and his sons vanquished Quintian, Samuel, and Richard with the traitors and dead men while the parade rushed through the streets to the Temple. Addison wondered if the crowd had even known what indeed happened.

The King walked into the Temple ahead of his sons. Then walked to the altar, where his wife the Queen stood waiting with the Empress and his Eminence. Dillion and Audrey stood behind the King and Queen while his Brothers moved to sit next to their families.

Henry went to Casandra and noticed blood on her neck; he reached to clean it. She stopped him and wiped it off herself. He leaned in and said mentally. You have been hurt.

She looked at him wearily and answered in her head. No, that was probably a piece of De Brue. Then she faced forward and held her stomach to keep from retching. Henry took her hand and looked forward as his Eminence said the blessing.

Mentally he said. Casandra, you must share with me what happened in the sky. Not just because I want to know, but Dillion and I will need to know to defend you. The King has already called for an inquiry; it will happen following this ceremony. So, show me, or I will compel you. Which will it be?

Casandra was drained and couldn't keep Henry out of her mind much longer. She kept her eyes forward and relaxed. Henry, I do not want to retch in the middle of this ceremony could we wait until it is over? I will share everything, even how I killed a man, and only the Night knows how many other innocents.

Henry agreed and reminded her Due Brue was not innocent.

The Empress removed the crowns of the King and Queen, and they moved to the right-hand side of the altar. Then his Eminence said prayers and blessings, and Dillion and Audrey knelt in front of the Eminence. The Empress raised the crowns they gleamed with the black diamonds of the royal house. Beatrice set one on Dillion's head and one on Audrey's and pronounced them King and Queen of Diamante.

Dillion took the Queen's hand, and they stood and turned to face the congregation they stood like day and night. Dillion had the handsome good looks of the Rakie family with dark brown hair and eyes. Audrey's crown glimmered against her red-blond hair, fair skin, and golden eyes. Henry thought Audrey was as lovely as Casandra.

Together they all said. "Hail, Dillion our King and Audrey our Queen." then they broke out into cheers. The couple kissed and smiled at their people.

Dillion held up his hand for silence. "I have a few announcements to make. First, the King, my Father wants everyone to know they should call him Winsette, and his wife, Margaretta. They have kindly agreed to host a brunch following the service. I regret my Brothers, and I must attend to business immediately after my first official announcements." He looked at Addison and said. "Addison, would you come forward with your wife, Marion." They stepped forward and stood before the King. "It has come to our knowledge that Addison Ski is actually the son of my brother Richard." Everyone one in the Temple started to whisper to one another. "My first proclamation is to instate him as Prince Addison Ski Rakie fourteenth in line to the throne, and his wife, Duchess Marion Donnan Ski Rakie." The King and his wife stepped upon the altar, and she motioned for them to kneel. His Eminence said a small prayer and placed a band of black diamonds on their heads, then everyone cheered. They turned to face the people, and Addison heard clearly Ernst's voice in his head. My nephew Addison, and my daughter Audrey I am so proud of both of you. It is good to know our family will leave something of good in this world. Addison looked at the Queen she was smiling and replied mentally. Thank you, Father. Hello cousin, then she smiled at Addison. Addison smiled back and thanked his Uncle for the kind words.

Henry looked at Casandra and saw she was crying. The King asked them to step to the side and told Henry and Casandra to step forward. Henry mentally said. What is this, Dillion?

Dillion mentally answered. Don't question or argue with your King. I am reinstating you as Prince. It is the only way I can help protect you and Casandra in the judgment with the King Hex! Get up here now and bend your knee to me, fool.

Henry answered. I don't want this.

Dillion said back. You don't always get what you want a baby brother. Come forward now. Winsette, Marietta, Addison, and Marion stifled laughter.

Henry took Casandra's hand and came forward he told her to kneel, and she blindly followed his order, then he tried to reach her mind, but she was far away somewhere.

Dillion and Audrey looked concerned, "My second proclamation is to reinstate Henry Winsette Rakie as rightful Prince of Diamante and third in line for the crown, and his wife, Duchess Casandra Helena

De Volt Rakie." Everyone gasped, and he added, "The false charges of murder have been uncovered, and his name is cleared." Everyone applauded, and black diamond bands were placed on their heads. The King and Queen joined hands and proceeded down the aisle of the Temple with his family following him.

When they were outside Dillion said. "Brothers come to my office, and Henry, bring Casandra," Henry said he needed a moment with her alone, and Dillion told him. "No, she needs to show us all what happened. She is the only one that saw it from the beginning."

Casandra touched Henry's arm and said, "He is right Henry, let's get this over with. Telling it once will take all I have, could you get the Wizard?"

They all started to walk away, and Addison remained. The King turned and said, "Addison come with us you are my Brother. Well... technically a cousin-in-law, but that is too much trouble to get out. When I say Brother, I mean you. Come." They walked across the courtyard up the stairs and turned into the King's office above the throne room. The Wizard and Eric were already waiting.

The Wizard said, "Congratulation King Dillion. I took the liberty to have Eric clean and secure the room. You requested my help?"

The King nodded, "Thank you, Eric would you remain here and accompany us to the throne room?" Eric agreed. "It is the Duchess that has requested you Wizard."

Henry was holding Casandra's arm and brought her to a chair to sit. She said, "Wizard, the King wishes to see the events of today. I am drained of energy if you could help me show everyone what happened, I think I can get through it."

The Wizard came to her and said, "Of course Casandra." He asked the others to take a seat, and he moved her in her chair to the center of the room so they all could see. Then he told Casandra to relax and take a deep breath. He asked her to lay her head back in his hands and told them he would project pictures out into the center of the room.

The day began, as seen through the eyes and ears of Casandra. She started with walking down the stairs of their apartment and the instructions of the Wizard to keep her love for Henry secret. They heard her compel Paxton to help in the girl's plan to hide Marion's mission from the Addison and Henry. They heard Marion say the Hermit ordered her to ride above the parade.

The Wizard let go of Casandra's head and took a step back. "I should have known that Witch was a part of this! She is the bane of my existence! Casandra tell me what you know of the Hermit's visit." Casandra told him what Marion had shared with her, which was not much.

Casandra quickly went on to her riding to the Emperor. She gave them word for word the encounter with the King. She said she rode to the side with the Emperor and Eric telling them she and Marion would be flying in the Parade and said he should not worry. He yelled at her and forbid her to fly then left her with Eric. They heard Eric say to her. "He didn't forbid you, my sweet girl, he only wishes you would not fly today, nor do I."

She looked at Eric with a big smile, "Are you the only one to understand not to order me." Eric laughed, and Henry finally understood. She then said to Eric, "I am trying to make the King think I am in love with you. Do you think it has worked?" She shined Eric a big smile with glamor in it.

Eric shook his head, "It has worked on Henry, look." She turned in the saddle, and the Wizard showed Henry's face infuriated with her. She laughed and rode back to the group. Henry ordered her back with the women, and she took off like a rocket with her words to Shelton.

Then they heard the communications of the women and saw the orange and red bolt of lightning. Her thoughts began to speed up, and the pictures were coming too fast to comprehend. The Wizard stopped her, handed her a glass of something, told her to drink, and he asked her to start again. The red and orange bolts were bursting slowly this time, showing the Pegasus leaping into the air where they could have a bird's eye view of the parade. They saw with every detail the Warlocks who started the attack, their faces and the type of spell and streams of electric thrown. It was fascinating and horrifying at the same time. She unfolded in slow motion the fight on the ground and in the air. Until the six men came to take her, then she started to speed back up.

The Wizard slowed her down again, and the fight between her and the General unfolded. Henry jumped up and ran to her when she showed the blow to her midsection. The Wizard froze him in place, and they all felt the rage she put into the explosion that sent the General's guts flying all over her. Then they saw the look of surprise on the Due Bre's face and him falling off his mount. She bent forward retching out the liquid the Wizard had given her on her boots. The Wizard gently brought her back into the chair and pulled aside her cloak. They all saw the terrific tear in her body, and everyone gasped.

The Wizard said. "Please, no one touch her. I do not know what power she has left to mend together as she has, but we must continue to find out why she is not dead. Arron, I need you."

Arron appeared holding a basin of water and cloth. The Wizard said, "Arron, please clean the wound and be careful not to bring her out of this trance. Once this is started, we must finish."

The Wizard pulled her head back into his hands, and she disclosed how Shelton had healed her. Then they watched as the King's men fell from their mounts. She showed Paxton finding her and taking her to the Temple and giving her a healing potion. They felt the warmth and healing of the medicine, but it made her dizzy. Each time she would think about what happened, she felt her stomach roll. She decided to meditate to keep from thinking about anything. She stared at the ring the Queen had given her throughout the whole Coronation. Her mind went blank until they saw her look up at the Wizard as he asked her to relax.

The Wizard released Henry, and he came to kneel at her side. He was lost for words tears stung his eyes, and he put his head on her shoulder while the Wizard kept her in a trance. Softly the Wizard said, "Henry, with your permission Arron will take her to her room get her cleaned. Henry, would you ask Paxton to bring Shelton to the terrace. Arron that Pegasus has more healing power than I do. Clean her and use ointment on her wound, dress her in loose clothing, use Henry's if you must. Put her on Shelton and let him heal her."

Henry raised her head and gently kissed her cheek. "Eric, would you go with them, and watch over her? I need to see the King suffer."

Eric stepped forward and placed a hand on Henry's shoulder, "Of course Prince." Henry stood back at that and Eric smiled.

The Wizard turned to the King. Dillion, "I have recorded this, and I can replay any portion or all of it for your Court, your Majesty."

The Throne Room

Queen Audrey sat on the throne next to the King as he ordered his Brothers to the island prison along with their wives. Their children would be under house arrest until the Barristers could clear their names. The trial was set in ninety days, and all their assets were frozen. The Mercenaries the King of Hex and his Brothers hired were given to the slave ships.

Dillion called in the King of Hex, his men, his Queen, and the Emperor and Empress. He asked the Emperor to stand for Casandra since she was being healed. The King would stand for Due Bre since he was dead. Dillion told them to take a seat and had the Wizard show the fight between Casandra and the General.

The Queen stood as she watched the General explode. Elisabeth turned and looked with disbelief at her husband. "Tell me you had nothing to do with this Richard!" He went to her and took her in his arms. In his most sincere voice he said, "Of course, I didn't have anything to do with this. Martin, can you shed some light on this?"

Martin stepped forward and said General Due Bre and Richard had devised the plot to take the throne from Dillion. He brought men forward to testify to the collusion between the two that had gone on for years. Of course, this was all without the King of Hex knowledge. Henry was astounded at how quickly they had covered their tracks.

They provided contracts and documentation which would take all three of Henry's brother heads; perhaps their wives too.

Dillion sat on the Throne and squinted at him with one leg extended out and one leg bent. His hands were fingertip to fingertip. He gave the impression he was comfortable and had been King for years. "King Hex, for not knowing anything about this plot you have presented evidence that would take some Banisters months to uncover, and Martin has done this in just over an hour. I am doubly impressed because you are not even a Bannister." King Dillion grinned wickedly. "Martin, to me this presentation does not show your innocence, but your fever to separate yourself from your General."

The King Hex stood to object, but Dillion said. "I have not finished speaking King, sit down. Gentlemen because of our countries long standing relationship, politically and financially, I will take your word of honor you had no prior knowledge of this ambush. I will, of course, expect your cooperation with our Banisters in the upcoming trial of my Brothers. Any information you can give us will be welcomed. Please do not take my actions personally, but after an incident like this, you will understand our right to question your motives in the future. I hope to cement our future together with a new treaty. After today our old treaty is null and void." He smiled and said, "That treaty was Richard's. I can hardly be expected to stand by that after today. You will have to prove your complete innocence before we sign another."

He turned and came down the stairs to the Emperor and Empress. "Everyone can clearly see Casandra was fighting for her life against the General. He sent her a nasty blow first. I find his death self-defense. Casandra will not stand trial or face restitution for any crimes. However, the estate of General Due Brue will pay Casandra one hundred thousand fab fine for pain and suffering. It is the least you could do, King Hex. She has several Wizards attending her now."

Elizabeth stood up and said, "I am sure we will cover all of her healing costs and Beatrice, I hope she will be alright. I would like to see her if possible."

Beatrice went to her and hugged her, "I want to see her myself, we will go right after this is over."

King Dillion turned, "The Queen is petitioning the court to give both her and Duchess Marion a medal for courage. Of course, both my Queen and I cannot thank you, Emperor and Empress, for shielding us during the attack. I understand you also protect the King of Hex, we all owe you our gratitude. This proceeding is over. I am starved, let's get something to eat."

Elisabeth came to Hayden and thanked him for protecting Richard, The King of Hex said, "Yes Emperor, thank you for shielding me." However, the King of Hex glared at the Emperor.

He extended his hand, and they shook hands. The Emperor smiled with superiority, "You are very welcome, King; I am sure you would have done the same for me."

Henry wanted to strangle him, but he wanted to see Casandra more. He slipped past everyone and ran to their apartments. When Henry got to their apartment, the Wizard was standing on the back terrace looking up with a glass of Henry's most expensive wines. He turned and said, "You run very fast I was watching you. If you learned to transport, you would have been here in seconds."

Henry looked up and saw Casandra making loops in the sky with Eric trying to keep up. He could hear her laughing at Eric. "I have tried, I can't but then I would not be in shape for my wife." He laughed and poured himself some wine. "She looks like she is having fun up there. Shelton has her strapped on but what is that, exactly?"

The Wizard said, "I am not sure, I want to examine that when she lands. It looks to be webbing, like a spider. That Pegasus has magic like I have never seen. Do you know where he came from?"

Henry took a drink, "According to Shelton, he was made for her by the Night. He is on a mission, which he refuses to share with me. Casandra has told me if he succeeds he will get his horn."

"You mean they will make him a Unicorn?" The Wizard was impressed.

Henry replied. "Yes and I believe my wife knows what that mission is. I wish she were not pregnant I would convince her to do a full blood bond."

The Wizard said, "She has a strong mind Henry, I tried to find out about that damned Hermit. I want to know what lies and plots she has forced on Marion and her. I think I will try Marion first. Maybe if we work together, we can find a way to open up their minds." He took a drink of wine and said. "Remember your lesson today, never give her an order she is as stubborn as a Pegasus. That is for sure." They both laughed, and there was a knock on the door.

Paxton let in the Emperor, Empress, and the King and Queen of Hex. Henry sighed, "Wizard help me restrain myself. I want him dead." Paxton came out to the terrace and called Shelton down. The Pegasus landed, and Paxton began the laborious untying of Casandra. Henry and the Wizard helped, and while he was where the King could not see, he kissed her cheek. Finally, she was taken down, and Paxton carried her to sit by her Mother and Elisabeth. After a short visit, the Wizard asked them all to leave and let Casandra sleep until the ball. King Hex asked her for a dance, and the Wizard promptly told him she would not be dancing this night. The King of Hex came to Henry and told him he wanted a meeting before he left the country. Henry told him he would speak to him at the Ball.

After they all left the Wizard examined Casandra and put her in bed. Paxton brought her tea and fresh fruit. He said, "Shelton said only tea and fresh foods." She apologized again for spelling him, and he laughed and told her. "You know as I serve you… all you had to do was command me. I must say, that is a bizarre feeling, being compelled. I am glad it only lasted a short while." She smiled and began eating. Henry stood against the wall with his arms crossed watching her. That comment hit home with her she felt deeply about that.

Henry listened to the instructions of the Wizard and turned back in to find Casandra fast asleep. Henry crawled into bed but couldn't help but lifted her shirt to look at the wound. I was just a deep red mark with webbing that Shelton had placed on her. He took her hand and just watched her until he fell asleep.

The Ball at Winsette Castle

Henry, Paxton, and Sutton were in the living area, enjoying a glass of wine while they waited for Casandra. They all turned their heads when she walked down the stairs. Casandra came down from the bedroom in a black shimmering long-sleeved floor-length gown. It was form-fitted with a gathered slit in the front showing her long legs. The neck was high and small crystals reflected the light throughout the material, but Henry's gift, the waterfall necklace was the focal point. Her black hair was tall on her head with her crown of High Sorceress in place. Henry stood, and said she looked lovely. Then he put his hand on her back and realized he was touching skin. He turned her around and was speechless. There was no back to her dress. While the front covered every piece of her skin and hugged every curve, the gown was open from the neck to the below her waist. One-fourth of an inch farther and her butt would have shown, and surprisingly she had no bruises.

Casandra spun around once and examined at all three of the men's faces. "I can't tell if you like it or if you're all just simply shocked. Which is it?"

Henry said, "Well, I must say I am shocked. However, I know you are not going to change your dress nor would I ask you to. It is by far, the most beautiful and sexy I have ever seen. Although I am not so sure it should be seen in public. I hope you are ready to be stared at and talked about. How are you keeping that thing on?"

"I swear you do not listen to me. I told you this morning, magic. They did a wonderful job plastering it to me. I know how you love backless dresses, and I wanted everyone to notice you. You men always wear the same old black and white. Not that you aren't handsome in them, but they will see you now. Sutton, Paxton, you both, look dashing, I hope you find some romance tonight."

Paxton laughed. "We usually do Duchess we had your cloak cleaned, and I am happy we did. It is getting cool outside the walk to the ballroom might be a long one for you in that dress. Not that I don't like it…it is…very fetching."

They all laughed, and Casandra took the cloak Sutton handed her. Henry wrapped it around her, and suddenly she saw Due Bre blowing to pieces. Casandra looked at the fire, hoping no one noticed she was shaking. She reached for Henry's wine perhaps that would ease the pain.

Henry took it from her and said, "No wine, not while the Wizard has you on his tonic." He waved his hand and gave her a glass of juice. "I will bring you home early, so you can get more rest." She started to protest, but he said, "Not tonight Casandra, you have been wounded, and I know you are in pain. I am lucky to have you alive. I will not take any chances with your recovery."

"Henry, I have to stay for the toast; leaving early would insult your Brother. Please." She set down her juice and placed both her hands on his waist and flashed him her most charming smile.

Henry threw back his head and laughed, "And to think I want a daughter just like you." He drew her close and kissed her deeply. Then he said, "I was perfectly willing to stay home with you and watch you sleep. Do not push me we can still do that. I will only promise to take you to the Ball, not how long you will stay…and…no wine and no dancing. You have medicine in fourteen minutes, drink your juice, so you don't have an upset stomach." He handed her the glass of juice.

The reception line was long and seemed to last forever Audrey insisted Casandra sit in a chair, which made her feel helpless. She did meet the owner of Roupart's and his wife, Brandy. They sat at her table, and Casandra found both fascinating. He was a walking historian, and she was a viola player in the symphony. She gave them box tickets to her a performance the next evening as a wedding present. Casandra loved music and begged Henry to go. The Roupart's were so excited to have them for their guest they could hardly stop beaming. She asked if they could bring Addison and Marion and they almost fainted.

Brandy said, "I am sorry about the bed Duchess. Brandon told me about the history, and I almost died of embarrassment. Especially knowing I would be sitting with you this evening."

Casandra laughed, "Why? I love it, you should come to dinner, and I will show it to you. It looks wonderful in our room. I told Henry I want to have my children in that bed. After all, great Sorceresses were birthed in that bed."

Brandy laughed, "You have no idea what life you have brought back to our country, I am so glad you are here. Now I find you love the arts. Dillion, of course, is going to be one of our best Kings. He and Audrey attend almost all our concerts, and Audrey paints. Plus he is just and fair."

Casandra added, "And handsome. Audrey is a powerful Sorceress as well. We had a wonderful visit the other day she has some impressive ideas for women in this country. You will love the changes coming. Girls are going to be schooled in fighting at a young age."

Roupart bent forward and said, "Like what you did in the parade? All the young girls want to learn the old ways and learn to fight again. That is wonderful it gives me hope, we have been too long away from the old ways. I hope you stay a few days in the Castle, so people get a chance to meet you."

Henry laughed, "We are being forced to; she needs to recover. We will see how she feels tomorrow we will do our best to attend the concert. Now I would like to take Casandra around the room and then to bed."

Casandra moaned, "I spent so much time to dress, and you want to leave. I want one dance."

Henry laughed, "The Wizard said not even one dance. I will take you around the room then you are going to bed. I will not be moved on this point." He stood and took her hand.

She turned to Brandy, "This has been the worst Ball I have ever attended, I can't eat, drink wine or dance. You have been the only highlight of my night, I hope to hear you play tomorrow."

Brandy said. "Oh no, my dear. You have made my night I will have wine for you tomorrow."

Henry bent down to Roupart. "My Father wants a word with you; make time for him." Henry winked at him.

Roupart's face beamed, "I certainly will, Prince. Goodnight."

Henry walked her around the floor, and when they came to King Hex, Henry took a deep breath. Casandra said, "Henry don't worry about the King, I will protect you."

Henry laughed and shook his head. "Don't be so sure of yourself, my Dear."

The Queen hugged her, the girls complimented her on her dress and Devon stood nodded to her and left the table. They all inquired about her health. Henry hugged all the girls, Joan begged him for a dance, and Casandra told him to dance with her.

The King said. "Go Henry I will take Casandra for a short walk in the garden. Some fresh air will help her. I want to talk to her about the restitution I feel the offer was too little."

Henry mentally warned her, but Casandra assured him she would be fine. Henry signaled Addison, and he, in turn, told the Wizard. Henry saw the Wizard disappear into the garden. He said, "Very well, be careful with her King; she is not recovered yet." Henry strolled to the dance floor with Joan, and the King led Casandra out the double doors to the garden.

The King offered Casandra a gift of gold and diamonds added to her payment. She insisted she did not need anymore; only the amount to the Wizards for her healing. As they walked, he told her all about his countries of Hex and invited her to visit with Henry anytime they wanted. She listened intently and ever mindful of where they were walking. He was slowly leading her away from the Castle, and she knew she should go no farther. She made a turn into the rose garden. The King said, "Look at the Cereus constellation; it looks as if I could reach out and touch it."

Casandra looked up, "Where? I will wish upon it."

The King laughed. "Don't tell me you believe in wishes, my dear. I have found we don't always get what we wish for."

The King stood behind her and pointed to the sky. "Can you see it right there." He bent his head to her neck and sapped energy. Casandra swooned, and soon she found herself falling back into the King's chest. He caught her in his arms and pulled her in. She remembered the ring Mariette gave her; she concentrated on it and could feel the energy of the stone flow up her body and pull her energy back from him. Then she felt the power of the King, it was sinister energy she quickly pushed it into the ground. The King fell back, and she turned to steady him. They heard Joan calling. Joan ran around the corner and said, "Father, are you alright?"

Casandra moved forward and said. "King, what is it? You seem to be unbalanced." She pushed him down on a nearby bench.

The King glared at her, "I am so tired and dizzy, I don't understand."

Henry and Joan were coming toward them. Casandra said, "Henry help me with the King, perhaps you should have a Wizard look at you."

The King quickly said, "No, Henry I am just tired, really. Just let me sit here a while. I will be fine, really."

Henry sat next to him. He could smell Casandra's scent on him. He turned and stared at Casandra and mentally asked. What did you do to him?

She answered. Henry, I am not sure, I will tell you later. "King it is probably nothing, it has been a long day for all of us I know I am tired. That is all it is, fatigue."

Henry said, "Yes. Let me get Martin and have him take you to your rooms I need to get Casandra home as well."

Joan said, "But Henry, you promised to have Casandra make introductions for us."

Casandra said, "Introductions to who?"

Joan said, "Your second cousin, Thomas."

The King said, "I thought you wanted to marry Henry?"

Joan said, "Oh I love Henry, but he was just a crush, Henry is old."

Casandra started snickering, and Henry grabbed his heart, "Joan, you have ripped out my heart and stepped on it."

Joan rushed to him and place her hand on his arm, "I am sorry, Henry but you had your chance how many times did I propose to you. This is what becomes of not taking someone seriously." She stood with her hands on her hips, and the King was laughing. "Besides, I like Casandra she is perfect for you...and her cousin is so dreamy."

Casandra said, "Well, I will be happy to introduce you. I think you are a very wise and beautiful Sorceress. Thomas is dreamy and a perfect choice. Being the daughter of the King, you will not always be able to choose." Casandra stopped the King was glaring at her, "I am sorry I should not be giving advice. Who do you want to meet Jessica?"

Jessica stood very quietly. "I am not sure I should ask." She looked at Henry, and he said, go on. "The Prince of Talla."

Henry looked at Casandra with a question in his eyes. Casandra said, "My old liaison he is a handsome man, and he knows it. I think he will find you beautiful and exotic."

The King said, "Please don't find them, husbands, Casandra. I can't afford another wedding this year. Girls, we should give them some privacy, and I am feeling fine. I think Henry wants some time with his bride. Into the ballroom." The girls protested, but he shuffled them into the ballroom.

Then the Wizard appeared in front of them and waved his hand, and they heard a bubble pop. Antioch said, "He is not the brightest man, he didn't even know what energy he was slopping up. I am sorry, Casandra, it made you feel so ugly. I thought I could keep that from you, and I didn't mean to push you so hard against him. Your ring is a multiplier; I have never seen any like that."

Casandra said, "I feel better now you had me in a bubble. I am energized."

"Yes, it was filled with energy. I know it felt very confining, but it fed the King. You cannot afford to use any more power this evening, that contest exhausted you. Henry good thing you had me follow her. By the way, you only need call me if you need help. I did mention that did I not?"

Casandra smiled. "Yes. I understand. I was just about to do that when I heard Joan calling. I knew Henry would not be far behind. I can't leave until the toast that would insult King Dillion, and I need to make some introductions."

Henry said, "Thank you, Wizard. We are making those introductions and leaving. If the toast is not made yet, we will miss it. Then I need to make time for the King of Hex."

"I will take her to your apartments and stay with her until you get home. Ah, I hear your Father calling; he is wondering where you are. Excuse me." The Wizard disappeared.

Henry pulled her to him, "As soon as we are finished, you will go with the Wizard. I must stay, I have business to take care of."

Casandra brooded, "I understand why a Ball is really given. It seems business, politics, and commerce are just as important as dancing and flirtation."

Henry chuckled, "You have become a jaded, old married woman. I promise the next Ball will be more fun for you, and I will dance with you all night." He leaned forward and kissed her, then he kept kissing her all the way down to her neck where he pumped energy into her. "Let me know if you need more I love doing that."

Casandra and Henry made the introductions for Joan and Jessica. Henry was not impressed with the Prince of Talla he could see he was still very attracted to his wife. He even made an advance to her, right in front of Henry. A servant came to get Henry just before Henry was going to slug him. It seemed the wine bottles were popping open. Henry didn't tell him that was the way to open them; instead, he used it as an excuse to pull Casandra away. Then they went to the head table, and Henry and Casandra offered their congratulations to Dillion and Audrey.

Henry said, "Casandra is going home right after the toast. I will stay for a while."

Dillion said, "Good, we have some business to get to."

Audrey hugged Casandra. "My Beautiful sister-in-law and my Duchess, you and Marion single-handedly put our women's right to protect herself to the top of this country's list. I am indebted to you. I wish you had not been hurt so badly; you couldn't enjoy this evening, but there will be other Balls."

The Empress was standing right with Audrey. "Your Queen is right, there will be other Balls. I am going to accompany you home. I hope you don't mind, Queen, but I want to spend a little time with Casandra before I leave. I need to be in Bayonne by morning."

Henry said, "Good, I mean, I am sorry to have you leave, but I know Casandra will be resting and not running back here to dance." They all laughed.

Dillion spoke a few words. “I am here tonight as your King because of my Brothers and my loyal men, and the Emperor and Empress and his men. The reason others were not hurt or killed was because of my Sisters-in-law, Marion, and Casandra. They are the reason the treacherous energies turned into the fireworks and confetti, the show the crowds roared and cheered for. Both of you are forever in our gratitude and our hearts. Audrey and I will find a way to honor you and have your courageous story live on in our history.” He bowed to both, and Audrey gave both hugs and the Empress then people came forward to congratulate the King. Bernard made the toast, but all the Brothers had comments to make. The Wizard appeared to transport Casandra home.

Henry asked the Wizard to take Casandra home before she was cornered by well-meaning admirers. He told Casandra he would be home as soon as possible. The Wizard, Casandra, and the Empress disappeared, and Henry walked straight across the ballroom to the King of Hex.

Henry asked the King of Hex for a word alone, and they walked out into the garden. The King sat on a bench and put them in a secrecy bubble. “You owe me, Henry I taught you about the Attachment. You need to turn over Casandra. Tonight!”

Henry sat back and said, “I haven’t gotten an Attachment of my own. What I have learned has been through using Casandra. If anything, I owe her. You, Sir, told me nothing about your plans. Not just for her, but for yourself. Because of that, I am married and sharing my life and wealth with her and her family. Now you want my assets; my power. I don’t see the return for me, enlighten me, King.”

The King smiled, “You are a lucky fellow, Henry. Finding Casandra in the ocean when she slipped out of Devon’s hands. Now, this little plot I planned for months, and you again have taken the advantage and made yourself Prince. If I thought you had any ambition, I would take out your brothers for you and make you King. I don’t believe you want to be King.”

Henry snarled, “Yes… I see how well your promise of the Kingdom of Diamante worked for my brother Richard. No, thank you. I prefer to keep my head.”

The King sighed. "Blame that on yourself whose strategies planned the elaborate security today? Don't try to tell me you didn't have a hand in it. The Emperor was part of it too; he had me in irons, and none of my men could move to help. Due Bre was the only one to get loose he wasn't even the one I had chosen to go after her…that was Martin."

Henry just shook his head in disbelief, "You should have told me. That is the reason this happened. I could have told you Dillion knew Richard was a traitor and believed you were working with him. Yes, I helped Dillion he asked for my help before Martin's engagement party." The King's mouth fell open. "Just like in the war you and your generals didn't trust me. You lost then too."

The King was angry but more depressed on hearing the truth. He needed Casandra now, but he didn't want Henry to feel his desperation. "I understand, Henry I see some truth in what you say, and I can see you don't want to be married. I am not sure you two even like each other." The King sat back and looked at the stars. "If I believed in the Night I would think she is behind saving that girl. I left her for dead at age four. I saw her fight today. Henry, I believe the reason the Warlocks do the fighting, and the Sorcerers hold the balance is a Witch has no mercy. She ripped Due Bre in two. A war of Witches would destroy our world. They don't deserve to have that kind of power." The King closed his eyes and said, "I also know you are not willing to hand her over to me. I ask myself why every hour of every day?"

Henry gave him a wicked smile, "You tasted her, tell me how it felt." The King glared at him. "I watched her fight too. I know what I have in my possession. Tell me, King, did you take her power, or did she take yours?"

Henry stood. "Maybe you shouldn't have poisoned me, or lied to me, or kept secrets from me. Or…not lived up to your bargain. Where is my Attachment and the instructions on making one?"

Henry held out his hand and said, "Not in my hands. I have learned all I need to know about Attachments, and I no longer need your help. King, you have nothing to offer me and your time has run out to impregnate her with your children."

The King stood red in the face. "Where did you hear that? She is for Devon."

Henry laughed, "You and all your little spies. So many it is hard to keep up with them, pay, and reward them all. I warned you in the last war spies are easily turned. You never wanted loyalty only obedience. Well, you have earned neither one of those from me. Perhaps you should change your religion and ask the Night for help. I am not inclined to help you, King." Henry left him in the garden and went to his Brother King Dillion's, meeting.

The Exoneration

Henry returned home exceptionally late, he made a soft nightlight with his hand and laid on the bed and watched Casandra sleep. It wasn't long before his eyes closed. He dreamed Casandra was fighting with him, and she cut him in two pieces. He was at his own funeral, and beautiful violin music was playing. His eyes opened, and Casandra was not in bed, but the music played on. He ran to the bathroom; she was not there. Henry opened the bedroom door, and the lights were on downstairs Henry took a breath. She was probably up early because he smelled coffee. He came down the stairs and found Paxton, Sutton, and the Wizard seated at his dining room table, looking out the terrace doors.

Paxton poured Henry coffee. "I told the Wizard the music would wake you, beautiful, isn't it?"

Henry drank a gulp of coffee and asked, "Where is it coming from?"

The Wizard pointed out the windows, "See for yourself, but do not disturb them Henry this is a sacristy ceremony. It is called the Exoneration. Casandra is cleansing her soul and the souls of those who died yesterday. It is beautiful to watch and hear, sit down and enjoy it."

Henry pulled out a chair and watched. Three spheres of light hung over the terrace to light the ceremony. The sun was not yet up, and darkness filled the courtyard. Casandra was dressed in the white robes and pants of the Monks, and she was doing the War Arts Positions in the fighting stance of the ancients. Many moves were still taught to soldiers, but she was moving to the music. It was more of exotic dance, twirling and repeating the movements as if in a trance. Her grace and poise gave the mortal blow the look of lover's pose. Love and war dancing together, for the first time, he saw the similarity. She stretched from the ground up to the stone railing dividing their terrace from the public courtyard of the Palace. Her leaps were higher than Shelton, he first realized Shelton was standing in front of her. He had been so still, he hadn't noticed him, or Mrs. Roupart sitting on the railing playing the viola.

"Wizard should she be doing that, jumping, she will tear open her stitches. She looks like she is possessed we should stop this." Henry started to stand.

The Wizard froze him in his chair he couldn't move or talk. "Listen to me, Henry. Last night, I was against this at first. I thought the same thing she would hurt herself. The Empress made me understand."

Sutton interrupted, "Look it is getting lighter outside, look at the terraces and balconies. Sorcerers are standing and holding power. I have never seen anything like this, the Queen is standing just across the way."

Paxton said, "More are in the courtyard, and Warlocks are gathering too. Everyone is watching Casandra."

Eric, Grace, and Charlie came out, and Eric said, "What is Casandra doing?"

The Wizard said, "I command you to sit and be quiet. I will explain. As I was telling Henry last night when I examined Casandra after the Ball, I found her split open again. Her Mother helped me to sew her back together and heal her. Beatrice explained to me Casandra would never heal if she didn't release the souls of all those she killed. It seems High Sorceress are made specifically for the release of souls, and the incoming, along with the development of all our souls. That is the simple version, it is much more complicated than that. Holding the balance of the world's magic is only a small part of their abilities; equally important is the gathering and releasing of souls. Beatrice explained the ceremony to me and left me in charge of arranging the necessary components."

He released Henry knowing he would not interfere. "Beatrice spoke to all the Sorceress at the Ball and arranged for Mrs. Roupart to play. The Empress knows her from school, and she knew all the music. It is a piece played for the gathering of souls, which is what Casandra is doing now. The Sorcerers out there are helping too. Evidently every magical person General Due Brue had an Attachment spell on died with him. The music will change, and other musicians in the courtyard will join in. The dance will stop, and Casandra will open a doorway to the Night. The innocent will return to our Mother, returning to the stardust they once were. The evil cannot rise so Casandra will take them to Hell personally."

Casandra's dancing to the music and the Wizard's description of the events had the complete attention of the room.

Sutton said, "They keep the unborn eggs at the Temple…now I know why. It is the best place for them."

Paxton asked, "Does the Empress do this ceremony every day Wizard?"

"I asked, yes, the exoneration ceremony and the encouragements ceremony. It seems we all must be begged to come into this world. Now I understand why so many are reluctant to truly live a good life." The Wizard stood and stretched.

The music changed; the tempo rose, along with the volume as other musicians joined in. Casandra stood with her arms out to each side, and her hands cupped downward as if she was drawing energy from the ground. Everyone went to the window to see more closely. Henry saw Devon and Ernst standing in front of her in the courtyard, watching as intently as he was. Henry began to see white lights coming from the stones on the patio. Hundreds of orbs were coming into Casandra's hands; surely hundreds hadn't died. As they gathered, Casandra rose from the ground, lifting a good ten feet upward. Shelton came to stand underneath her, and she on stepped on his back. The crest moon and morning star shone brightly just over her head. The picture was exactly what had been on the floor of the Temple they were married in. Henry had to remind himself to breathe. Suddenly, the music came to a crescendo, and Casandra brought her hands together in front of her. Then she placed her hands in front of her heart, and the light entered her. She raised her hands above her head and spread them open while leaning back gazing to the heavens. Stars shot out of her mouth like fireworks, brilliant, and hot white.

It was as bright as day and as he looked out the courtyard was filled with people. The King of Hex and Martin stood right behind Devon. Gold threads began to weave around Casandra, Henry knew what that was. Shelton was the one who would make the ride to Hell with her. Casandra spread her legs and slipped onto the Pegasus' back. In her hands she held a blue ball about two feet around in the center of it was a thick black, purple blob, floating and bobbing. Henry had no idea where that came from, it just appeared. The sun was rising, the new day was about to begin. Shelton took off like an arrow and Henry went out on the terrace to watch his wife fly right into the horizon of the rising sun.

The music stopped, and the silence in the courtyard was earsplitting. Experiencing this Henry did not know how anyone could not believe in the Night and the Holy Mother and Holy Father. He wondered if the King had changed his mind about the Night. Now, he wished he had not told the King to ask the Night for help.

The Return from Inferno

Henry refused to leave the terrace for breakfast he would wait for Casandra to come home safely. Paxton and Sutton stayed with him and fixed him breakfast. Eric came out to tell Henry the Elves were going to the Castle to clean the formal dining room for the meeting after lunch. Henry told him if Casandra was not home he wouldn't attend. Then he watched the sky as carriages carried the nobility out of the Castle. The formal activity was at an end, and soon his home would hold no strangers. Finally, he saw Shelton in the distance, as just a small dot. Henry knew it was Casandra he stood and walked to the railing of stone to be closer to her.

When Shelton landed, his mane was white with sweat, and Casandra was worn and sweaty. The three said nothing; Sutton, Paxton, and Henry worked to release Casandra from the golden ties Shelton had strapped around her. Paxton had cold water for Shelton and a blanket to cover him. Henry lifted Casandra from the Pegasus and said, "I will take you to bed now you are exhausted."

She hugged him and said, "Food and water first Henry, a bath, and then I willingly surrender to sleep. She laughed and kissed him. "Set me down, please."

She went straight to Shelton and cradled his head. "You are magnificent. You deserve your horn today my friend. Thank you for carrying me, protecting me, and loving me. I could never have done this without you. Paxton, make sure he has everything he needs."

Paxton jumped the railing and into the courtyard. "Just one little jump, Shelton, and I will walk you slowly to your stall. You'll have the best oats, a long luxurious bath and rub down."

Shelton laughed and said. "All I want is more water, Hell is very dry."

Henry reached out and stroked Shelton's back, "Take him to the healing baths, Paxton. Tell them it is on my order." Henry waved his hand and handed Paxton an official paper. "Shelton, I think I love you. I know I trust you with Casandra and all of my children."

Shelton turned his head and looked Henry in the eye. "You may work out as a good husband to her yet. I am beginning to trust you Prince Rakie." He turned and walked away.

Casandra laughed and said, "Well, you two are making progress."

She turned, and Sutton was standing with a plate of food on a tray with a glass and pitcher of water. "Would you prefer to eat on the terrace or in the dining room?"

She looked around and said, "I think the dining room. People are starting to gather and stare. Thank you, Sutton."

Henry pulled out a chair and watched her as she drank three glasses of water down in record time. Then she took a forkful of food then closed her eyes like she was in a state of bliss. Henry and Sutton both snickered. She swallowed and said, "What? Have you never noticed the taste of food when you are starving? It is like a piece of heaven. Sutton, did you cook this? It is wonderful. I don't know what I am eating, but it is marvelous."

She kept shoveling food in her mouth as Sutton answered, "Yes, I did, my Father was a chef. Living with mostly men who can't even make a decent pot of coffee; I soon became the cook among us. You're eating one of my Father's recipes it is a vegetable stew over rice. I will make you a wonderful dessert if you think you will have room. Henry, can I get you something?"

Casandra gave him a big smile. "Sutton, you never have to ask me if I have room for dessert. The answer will always be yes."

They all laughed, and Henry said. "I will have dessert too, and maybe a cup of tea. Casandra, would you like tea?"

Her mouth was full, but she shook her head yes. Henry reached to her and took her hand. It was red and burnt. He shuddered. "You are the most injured woman I have ever known. Then again, you are the most remarkable women I have ever known. Casandra, watching you today... I can find no words to express the deep appreciation and respect I have for you. I thank the Night she gave me you to love and care for. I am a lucky man."

Casandra squeezed his hand and gave him a loving look. "Henry, my love for you and my reverence for the Night have grown by a hundredfold over the last twelve hours. Today and the evening on the Plains of Pegasus have been life altering for me. I am tired, but after my bath, I will blood bond the experience of those two events for you. I want to share them with you. I want you to know the truth."

Henry smiled as he knew her experiences would be life-altering for him, as well. He said he would be honored as someone knocked on the door.

Sutton walked into the room, "It's Marion and Addison, is it alright to let them in?"

Casandra laughed, "Sure they have both seen me look much worse."

Marion ran to Casandra. "You were spectacular. Casandra, everyone saw; how did you do that? Watching you now, I see what the dancing moves are supposed to look like. I know you are tired, but you must tell me everything. What was hell like? Where is it exactly? How high did you fly?"

Sutton came to the table with dessert for all of them along with cups and a pot of tea, "Miss Marion, give her a chance to answer one question at a time. You are such a magpie but a beautiful one."

Marion gave him a stare, "I am not a magpie. I just have a lot of questions, and they all come out at once. Casandra are you hungry, you ate that whole piece of cake while I was talking?"

Casandra took a drink of tea and sighed, "Not anymore. Sutton has stuffed me to the brim, nice job Sutton."

He smiled lovingly at her and said, "My pleasure, my Father always said never to trust a person without a good appetite. That's why I trust both you ladies you are always ready for food."

Paxton came in and said, "I smell lemon cake, did you beasts leave any for me?"

Casandra said, "How is Shelton?"

"Shelton is wonderful." He sat at the table and cut a big piece of cake. "I had a time getting him in the baths, but then he didn't want to get out. It took four of us to haul him back to the barn. He said Samuel has a softer touch, so he should groom him. Arron is down there, healing his hoofs. They are badly burnt, but the healing waters really helped. King Dillion sent down his horsemen, and he is fussing over him. All the animals in the barn are praising him. I predict by tomorrow he will be unfit to ride or live with. He has a big enough ego he doesn't need this attention." They all laughed.

Casandra sighed, "Marion, would you help me clean up? I love this company, but I am tired. I know you all want to know what really happened. Believe me, I want to share this with you it was extraordinary. I am doing a blood bond with Henry right after my bath, so you will all see firsthand the ecstasy of heaven and the horrors of hell. Much better than my words could describe."

Henry said, "Casandra before you take a bath, give me your hands."

Addison set a bottle on the table, "Henry you rub this into her left hand; I will take her right."

Marion winced as she watched the two Warlocks work to heal her hands. Marion suddenly wasn't sure she wanted to see the sights of Hell. Casandra's hands were enough of a forewarning. Sutton and Paxton brought towels and water to clean them. Between the four of them working on her; Casandra was ready for a bath in a short time.

Marion helped Casandra dress, and she told her there would be a meeting and dinner at the Castle before the concert. Marion was brushing out her wet hair and said, "I can't wait until you can travel Addison said we are going to visit Belissa Villa before going on to the North Castle. He makes it sound so beautiful and peaceful, just think we will live just a half-mile from one another. Our girls will be playmates, it is almost too perfect, like a dream."

Casandra said, "Henry has not said much about Belissa Villa, and I haven't asked. I don't want to think past today. Every time I do something bad happens and the future changes."

Marion was shocked and said, "What? You have never talked like this before. You are the girl that had your life mapped out from start to finish. You are the one telling me to always think the best and it will happen. Now you say don't plan, don't dream?"

Casandra took the brush from her and said. "Pay no attention to me, I am just tired."

"No. This is not like you. Something has changed in you. I feel it in your energy. Was it your experience today?" Marion looked at Casandra in the mirror and saw the darkness there.

"Marion, I can't make plans. If the King lives, it is a waste of time. You're right, today I saw the gates of hell, and they are real. I will waste no more of my time here in this world dreaming and wishing. I will not leave unsaid what is in my heart, or any deed that I want to be done waiting." Casandra turned and hugged her friend. "Ask Henry to come up here before I drop."

Marion turned to find Henry standing in the doorway looking at her with an expression of seriousness. Casandra looked up, she had never seen this look on his face before. He had heard her dark thoughts and words. Marion handed Henry the brush and said, "Her hair is still tangled in back perhaps you can comb it out."

Henry took Casandra by the hand and walked to the bed. "Lie down on your side. I can brush out your hair for you." He began brushing her hair, "You are too tired to do a blood bond, and your fingers are too tender. We will do it another time."

Casandra sat up and took the brush, "Thank you, Henry, but I don't want to wait. I want you and Addison, Marion and all our men to know what we face, now, today. The darkness is powerful and must be understood." She pulled the knife which he always carried from his waist and cut the inside of her arm, then handed him the blade, it was such a sure swift motion that it was done before Henry could stop her. He took the knife cut his arm, pulled off his sash and tied their arms together then laid back on the bed. The first vision was of thoughts and feelings of the dance as the music swirled on their terrace. Then suddenly the sky opened with a blinding light. Henry couldn't see anything, but he could feel profound love and joy; deeper than he had ever experienced. Internally the sensation was of enormous peace, vast knowledge, and bliss. Henry wanted to remain bathed in the cool light. The light suddenly turned hot. He was in burning obscurity, and vague images of dark creatures appeared. While it was just as difficult to see in this place, he knew it was Hell. Hearts were filled with hate, bitterness, hopelessness, and despair. He gasps for air as the heat and stench were overwhelming, along with the terror of screaming. Henry pulled them out of image before it overtook them and waved his hand to heal the wounds in their arms. He pulled her to him, then ran his thumb over her forehead. She was asleep. He held her for a long time before he went to sleep. Henry was well acquainted with the dark, but now his wife had seen the dark magic and the deeds of death, would she never be the same.

Henry awoke knowing someone was in the room with him. The Wizard was standing at the end of the bed. "You have gone too far Antioch, this is our bedroom and private." Henry opened one eye.

The Wizard came around to Casandra's side of the bed and sat down, "If you had answered to my voice I would not have come in here. It's time you are up and dressed. I want to check on her before our dinner meeting, go clean up you smell."

Antioch pulled the covers back. "A sleeping spell, you thought the memories were too dark for her?"

Henry stretched, "Yes I did. I want to see her wound too." Henry lifted her shirt, and Antioch inspected it. "The skin is growing nicely back together; the infection looks gone."

"She still needs to be careful cleaning the wound." The Wizard said, "Yes I guess her Mother was right. She needed to release the dead to heal. I would give her one more day or two of rest before you travel. You could let her ride Shelton; he is healing her better than any of us." The Wizard inspected her hands and said. "You did a nice job on her hands. Addison asked me for lotion. Wake her Henry. I wish to speak to her."

Henry took his thumb and swiped the other way across her forehead, and Casandra woke, "What? Why is the Wizard here?"

The Wizard waved his hand, and a bottle appeared. "Drink this for me, Casandra."

I am finished with all his medicine and healing. I feel fine. My stomach doesn't hurt, and my hands hardly burn."

"Alright, have it your way." Antioch froze her, opened her mouth and poured the medicine in then shut it, and held it closed until she swallowed. "There…that wasn't so bad, was it? Since you have been to Hell, you have gotten a nasty attitude. That medicine will help, and it is the last you will need. I suggest you go out tonight and have a little fun, maybe drink some wine. Your wound is healing nicely, but still no dancing, you did enough of that this morning. A couple of good night's sleep and you will be raring to go. By the way, it looks like you will be having twins. I think it might be wise to keep that a secret for now." He waved his hand, the medicine bottle vanished, and Casandra was unfrozen.

Casandra wiped her mouth with the back of her hand and said. "Henry please, kill him. TWINS!"

Henry was in shock, "Twins." He grinned at her and put his hand on her stomach.

Antioch stood and walked to the door. "He can't kill me I am more powerful; we tested that years ago." He laughed and said, "Besides, you still need me. We haven't gotten that King yet. See you both for dinner." Then he disappeared.

"That man's ego is as big as Shelton's." Casandra sighed, "What did we do to our poor daughter?"

Henry laughed and said, "That is exactly what your Father said when I asked for you before your birth."

Casandra's eyes opened wide. "I was not even going to be High Sorceress then, and you still wanted me?"

Henry kissed her and said. "I have always wanted you. I thought I had lost you when my Brothers died. I loved them both very much, but because of their deaths, I became responsible for Elaine. I had to marry her being the last Rakie not married, although I did grow to love her. I didn't think your Father would allow our marriage after the war. After all, I was on the other side. I am a blessed man; the Night must love me. I think the Wizard is right, we shouldn't let everyone know about having twins. If we have a son I would like to name him after my Brother, he was my favorite, and he spoiled me terribly."

Casandra smiled. "Yes, we can name him Harry."

Henry said, "No, not Harry; he was nothing but trouble, Jack. Speaking of spoiling…" He reached under the bed and handed her a present.

She laughed, "You don't have to do this you know, you already have me." She opened the box to a beautiful, black stole with their initials embroidered on it. "It is beautiful Thank you, Henry."

"Well I will take it back," Henry grabbed it, and Casandra fought him off, "No I like it. Go get dressed and take a bath, you smell." And she laughed.

Magical Music

The Evening began joyously. The ladies all wanted to take Casandra and Marion shopping the next day for the babies. All of them were excited about buying girl's clothes. The men were going hunting, even her Father, and Brother. Casandra thought this was wonderful and how life should be, comfortable and relaxed.

Dessert was served, then Dillion stood and announced a family meeting. The servants left, and Dillion's personal guard entered and locked the doors. "We will make this a brief meeting then we can get to the symphony on time. Emperor, my Brothers and I have asked you and your men to be at this meeting because this family business affects you directly. The interrogation of our Brothers has revealed information we need to share with you." Dillion waved his hand, and all three of the traitor Brothers stood at the head of the table in irons. "Richard, tell these men about the King's plans."

Richard looked at Henry and Casandra and said. "First, let me say to Casandra I am truly sorry. I had no part in the plan to kidnap you; that was Samantha and Suzanna. The truth is they are the ones who created this whole fiasco."

Dillion said, "Richard get on with it."

Richard drew in a breath, "We three have been working with the King for years. I move his illegal products, Samuel laundered his money, and Quintian provides the many spies. There are numerous other deeds he has forced us to carry out. However, the King has made us rich men, and we didn't want to that change. Last year, he came to us with a ludicrous plan. We would kill Father slowly and make it look like old age. You still would have been King Dillion, but you and Audrey would have an Attachment placed on you. He needed to make you more controllable. In return, we would have exclusive rights to the energies of Arlequin. Henry, I am sorry you would be removed to Bezier by the King of Hex, and I would run the winery. However, when the Emperor courted you for Casandra, the plans changed. You could not live, Casandra is to be Devon's Queen."

Casandra was in disbelief; the King had planned this, with or without Henry. He had probably watched her all her life. She was so naïve, stupid, and trusting, nothing was going to stop him.

Richard continued, "When Henry showed up married to Casandra early, I was surprised, and I had a terrible feeling about the whole plan. We knew it would be revised again. I went to the King of Hex the night of our family dinner. That is when the King told me he wanted to kill both you and Addison, along with the Emperor. He even mentioned vague plans kidnapping the Empress and making her ++++++++his prisoner." He looked at Henry, "The King insisted the timeline for everything had been move ahead, he had no time to wait. He wanted to take this opportunity to rid himself of all the vermin. He gave us a list of all the royals he wanted to be killed, and the names of the Arlequin rebels that I was to claim were the attackers. Wizard Gadwell was to be named as the leader of the rebels. He wanted them tied up in a neat little package. I regret this, but what really bothers me is that I was given no choice."

Bernard stood up and said, "Nonsense, you always have choices, Richard. We Brothers have always been competitive, but in the end, we all love one another. We would never do this to you. Ever since the war, and the hatred of Henry, you have been nothing but evil."

"Yes, ever since Suzanna put an Attachment on me, I have not been my own man. My first deed was to get rid of Henry. None of you would let me kill him as the King wanted, and I have suffered ever since." Richard snarled and looked at the floor.

Henry stood and walked to him, "The women, they started this? I can believe it of Suzanna and Samantha, but Gabriella is so..."

Richard said, "Stupid? You didn't think anyone would trust her enough to give details of any plan. Don't worry she knew nothing. She is so stupid even an Attachment would not work on her. Suzanna had all of us try to place an Attachment on that woman, even the King tried, it never took. Suzanna believes she is the reason the King is going to rescue us, of course, we are dead men. We no longer have a use for the King. Now the women, he will keep them for the power he can remove from them. Gabriella was going to that idiot Moondale to be examined."

Casandra coldly said, "Dissected you mean." Richard looked at her with respect.

Henry said, "They have to keep you alive if they want Suzanne alive. Richard who placed the Attachment on Suzanna?"

Richard said, "I know where your head is going, believe me, I tried to unwind the mess she put me in for years. The bond goes back to the fourth, maybe the fifth person who holds the Attachment. If I die, so does she and her bonder, Major Winston, then his bonder Coronel Greystone, and his General Brad. The only one not dead will be Gabriella. What a joke, the stupid one lives. His next planned attack for you is soon, he will not stop."

"When?" Henry was holding his hands in fists.

"I have been tied up Henry. I haven't had many communications with him lately. Mentally Suzanna told me of a plan to escape and said you dared to invite him to your reception Ball at the North Castle. She said the King planned on declining, he would be too busy with Casandra."

Dillion pushed Henry back and told him to go be seated. "Richard if you have anything else to say I compel you to say it now."

"My Brothers and I plead for mercy." King Winsette stood, "Richard no. We need to think about this. Wait for a trial."

"Father, there are too many spies in your dungeon. We will not live until our trial. Have mercy on us, make this quick and take out the Kingsmen. In that, we may gain our restitution."

Samuel said, "We beg you, Father." King Winsette only nodded and sat in his seat. "Also, our children knew nothing of this. I ask you to grant them forgiveness. Richard and I have listed the King's illegal holdings and bank accounts, and Quintian has turn over the spies to the Elves. If you act quickly, you may learn more details about the King's plan. Dillion, I never meant this to happen. We tried many times to elude the King. I am sorry."

Dillion nodded, "I grant you mercy." Henry stood again and opened a full bottle of wine and poured three glasses; the four Brothers waved their hands over it. Dillion said. "Wizard, would you take their minds and souls." Antioch stepped up, one by one he placed his right hand on their head then reached in and pulled out their soul. He placed each soul in a wooden box and waved his hand, and the boxes disappeared. Dillion asked if the Wizard had all the information; Antioch nodded yes. "Brothers I release you from your life with us. May you have a better one the next time." He handed each one a glass of wine.

Richard said. "Thank you, Dillion. You will make a great King, and for what it is worth Henry, I do love you." He drank the wine and fell to the floor.

Samuel said. "I do love all of you, especially Father. I am so sorry. Thank you, Dillion. Henry, I know this wine is going to the best wine of my life." He drank and fell to the floor dead.

Quintian said, "Gabriella is a sweet, naive woman, she does not deserve to be dissected. Thanks for the wine, Henry." He drank and fell.

No one spoke, the Queen came over and waved her hand. The dead men disappeared. "I will take care of Gabriella."

The Wizard said, "Queen Audrey, I beg your pardon, but Gabriella is an unusual phenomenon. Would there be a way I could examine her? I promise not to hurt her, and I would at least appreciate being able to speak with her."

Audrey stood in front of Dillion, everyone knew they were having a private conversation. The Queen finally said, "Please everyone, go on to the concert, I will handle everything here. I will be there as soon as I have completed the task. Brother come with me." She raised her hand they both were gone.

King Dillion turned and cleared his throat, "This has given us much to ponder while we relax to the music this evening. We can speak Gentlemen tomorrow. Casandra, I want you to know you have our full support and protection. There is nothing more we can do this evening." They all left in silence to the concert hall.

Casandra, Henry, Addison, and Marion all shared a carriage. They were the first to leave the gates of the Castle. The carriage slowed Henry pulled back the curtain. The avenue was filled with people silently holding spheres of light. Henry said, "Casandra, Marion, I believe this is for you. I am opening the carriage top they want to see you." Henry magically opened the carriage to reveal hundreds of citizens quietly standing with spheres of light.

Addison said, "Who did this Henry?"

Henry mentally said. We must not speak. Casandra and Marion, this is a citizen's tribute to you both. They are honoring you with their thoughts in silence and holding you in the light of the Night. Usually, this is announced and planned for weeks. I suspect the Roupart's are behind this.

Both women watched the crowd of people who lined both sides of the street. The faces spoke of the appreciation they were held in. There was not a sound on the road only the jangle of the bridals and horse strides on the street. Casandra was feeling very uncomfortable. Marion deserved to be honored, she saved many lives in the parade. Casandra had killed many, there was no honor in that. She held her eyes down, not looking at the crowd.

Henry took her hand and mentally said. They are not honoring death, my dear. They are honoring your devotion to the Night by returning all the soul's home.

Addison said mentally. Casandra before this morning the people of Diamante had never seen the work of the High Sorceress. They thought you were only an antiquated royal with no purpose but to tax their livelihood. One deed and this whole land have a renewed belief in the Night.

Casandra raised her head and looked at Addison and mentally said. You just spoke almost the exact words of my Mother's last night. She had tears in her eyes and said. Mother said Casandra, you must do this action, usually very private, in public to renew the belief in the Night. The Hermit had given her detailed instructions at their last visit.

Henry looked away and blocked his thinking, again the Hermit is deeply rooted in events. Casandra closed her mind to all in the carriage and beheld the crowd. The Hermit had shown her three outcomes. Casandra knew the night of her marriage to Henry in the Temple of Krete, one of those possibilities had fallen away. She didn't like either of the remaining two, but one was the eviler…

"Casandra, come out of the carriage we are at the concert hall." Henry knew she was far away in the Mountain of the Hermit in thoughts imprisoned by the Witch. He would break in that prison, but how?

The concert hall was filled with Witches and Warlocks standing with globes of light. They were led to the royal box seats and stood in silence until King Dillion came in and sat. The lights vanished in a flash, and the orchestra started to tune their instruments. The conductor entered with applause, turned and said, "The musician would like to dedicate tonight's performance to King Dillon and all the royal family, with special gratitude to Duchess Marion Rakie and Duchess Casandra Rakie." Everyone applauded, and the music began. It was almost an hour before Queen Audrey entered and it took that long for the audience to stop staring at Marion and Casandra. After that, the music took everyone away to pleasant thoughts.

The next morning Casandra woke early holding Henry on her breast. He was still sleeping, and she did not want to wake him. She watched him sleep until she could no longer help but brush his dark rich chocolate hair from his face to see him better. He grabbed her hand and gently kissed her palm, each time he kissed her on her palm the heat burned in her veins from her palm to her thighs. She wondered if he was aware of that and if it was deliberate.

Henry opened his eyes and gave her a wicked smile. He said, "Of course it is deliberate. Since the very first kiss at North Castle, I have known how to make you love me. You cannot resist me my wife, and you are stuck with me.

Casandra laughed, "You are full of yourself Henry. You promised no charms and no spells. Here you have been plying me with sexual touches."

Henry laughed and pulled her into his arms, "I cannot help myself. To be near you and not touch you would be torture for me, However, if you wish me to stop…"

Casandra pushed up from him and said, "Absolutely not. I would hate to be the source of anyone's suffering." They both laughed and made love until it was time to wake.

The women were sent off to the town of Winsette to shop, and the men went out to hunt in the woods beyond the Castle. Henry's Sisters-in-law bought everything they could. Never having girls they could not help themselves.

Addison and Henry walked into Henry's apartment with Marion and Casandra sitting in a living space filled with boxes.

They were carrying the pheasants they had shot. Henry said, "Ladies you had a better hunt than we did."

Addison was smiling and said. "We have dinner, but you have emptied the shops. Do I have any money left, Marion?"

The girls both laughed. Marion said, "This is not our doing. Your family went crazy. It came to the point that Casandra and I could not touch or look at anything without it be snatched and taken to the clerk. I do love the Rakie ladies, but they are pushy."

Casandra said, "Marion is right, they overtook the town. It was like watching vultures swooping in on a carcass. I don't even know what is in these boxes. Pushy is a mild description!"

Henry laughed, "Rakie wives all have that quality. Well, I would rather describe it as strong and determined aren't they Addison?" Addison just laughed.

Casandra crossed her arms and said, "So... Marion and I are pushy?"

Addison laughed again and went to Marion, kissed her, and said, "Determined, but as Henry said, in the best possible way. It is why we fell in love with you spirited women. I would not change a thing about you Marion."

Henry kissed Casandra on the cheek and said, "Precisely, I would not change a thing about you either. Now Addison and I are cooking us dinner, and after dinner, we are having a meeting here. We all came up with some great ideas while out hunting. We want the ladies to help us decide."

Casandra took the string of pheasants and said. "Henry, I love you dearly, and you are handsome and manly, a great hunter, a better lover, but..." Sutton was standing right by him. Casandra handed him the pheasants to Sutton and said, "I really need your help going through and organizing all this for the trip to Belissa Villa."

Marion said, "Yes. Addison, we need to get our things separated and into our apartment before the meeting, so there is room for everyone. I am sure you are a good cook, but should a Prince be cooking? I know Sutton is a fabulous chef." She took his pheasants and handed them to Sutton. "Thank you, Sutton."

Sutton said, "My pleasure Duchess." As he walked away, he said. "Rakie women are also very wise. Remember that, Henry and Addison."

He disappeared into the kitchen just as Eric came in and said, "I see the women have been hunting too."

Henry looked at him and put his hands on his hips, "I don't wish to continue this conversation Eric; it leads to a hole I just finished climbing out."

They all laughed, and Addison added, "Come, Henry, we have work to do. Marion where do we start?"

Going Home

After the private burial of the Rakie Princes; the Emperor, Major and all the Rakie royals were standing at the carriages. Marion and Addison were riding with them to Belissa Villa.

The Emperor hugged her with all the love he had in his heart. "That sure feels good to give out all my love, instead of holding on to your crown and torque. Enjoy your days at Belissa Villa. When life calms down, I plan to visit your new home. I love you. Henry, take good care of my baby."

Henry hugged him and all his Brothers and Sisters, with tears in his eyes. It had been many years since he had any contact with them much less touching them. He told them all he loved them and kissed his Mother and Father.

Major took Casandra to the side and handed her a gift, "My gift for you and Henry. I have been instructed to tell you, this is for your children, save it for them. It is a circumpherous and priceless do not let it fall into anyone else's hand. It may be small, but it is a treasure. Your Mother is handling the Rakie souls, do you think I should share that with the King?"

Casandra kissed his cheek and said, "Yes and thank you Major, and thank you for allowing my Mother to be here for me. That was my best wedding present of all. You have always meant the world to our family I think of you as my family. May I tell Henry about you? He will ask."

The Major hugged her and said, "Yes but make sure he knows I like my privacy."

Casandra took him to the King and the Major told them the Empress was holding the souls of their Brothers for atonement."

King Winsette cried, "But they were evil?"

Major said, "No. They were trapped and slaves of the King of Hex. More importantly, they regretted their actions and gave us the truth. Your Sons made their repentance for their mistakes."

Winsette began sobbing, and the Queen took him into her arms as the returned to their carriage. Her Brother Bryan came to her and hugged her. "Be happy little sister. Enjoy your time with Henry. I am going to begin preparations for the King of Hex's demise. We will be ready."

She released her Brother, "I haven't had any time with you at all. Where has Kathryn been?"

Bryan held her tight, "Someone had to stay and take care of the Castle."

He smiled at her, "Bryan you are hiding something from me. Tell me now." She crossed her arms.

"I have avoided you. Kathryn lost the baby, Casandra. I didn't want to ruin your wedding or Ball. She told me she wanted you to be happy, and not to tell you until after the Ball at North Castle."

"I am so sorry, Bryan. Your last child a little girl." She kissed him, "We will be at the Castle soon. Tell her I will spend time with her then. I love you, thank you for being here for me." He smiled and pushed her into the carriage.

The four climbed into the carriage and left the Castle flying over the city of Winsette. She watched her Brother, Father, and Major as the transport lifted. Henry took her hand, and she turned to see tears in his eyes; both Addison and Marion were staring at her. She forgot to block them from her thoughts and Bryan's conversation. She couldn't imagine losing a child, she turned away from them. Looking down over the city the people were cheering; a stark difference to the solemn tribute which had touched Casandra's heart deeply the evening before. The mood of the carriage was solemn they could hardly appreciate the cheers from below.

Henry asked about the small present in her hands. She said it was from Major, "Here, Henry you open it. You haven't opened any presents." Henry took it and unwrapped a small box of wood and inside was a strange object which first appeared like a ball but looking closer Henry could see circular bands of gold were spinning around a single blue diamond. "Casandra is this what I think it is?"

She smiled. "Yes, a circumpherous. Major said it was a treasure."

Addison took it from Henry, "What is it? It is as light as a feather it should have weight with all the gold and huge diamond."

Henry just stared, "It is a legend. I thought it was just a fantasy. Indeed, it is a treasure. I want to find out how this came into the Major's hands. There is sure to be a fascinating story."

Marion said, "Is that the instrument that brought the essence of the souls from Earth to Corenthions?"

Henry smiled and said, "That is the legend, how it worked, no one knows. If this is authenticated, its value is beyond even my vast wealth. Why would Major give this to us?"

Casandra took it from Addison's hand, "He said we should save it for our children. Marion, you hold it. Tell us what you think." She handed it to Marion. "Did you know Major is the thirteenth child of the great Empress Lolita Emerius, and he was a Monk for years. Lolita died just before my Grandmother his Sister became Empress. He lived and worked at Bayonne Temple for thirty. He helped my Mother when she was first made Empress, and he held the world in balance these past days so I could have my Mother with me at the wedding. He knows Henry, the thirteenth child; he holds special powers."

Henry said. "I thought he was with Katheryn, helping at the North Castle. I am terrible I didn't even notice Bryan in the shadows or Katheryn missing from everything. Now, to find they had such a tragedy. Major's Father was Emperor Emerius. Casandra, how old is the Major?"

Marion said, "That is the question no one could ever answer, no one knows." She handed the circumpherous back and said, "Life has been there, this holds much truth, if only we knew how to open it. Everyone discounted his thoughts at the meeting last night. Perhaps we should have given him more consideration. Casandra, you never told me all this about him."

Casandra sat back, rolled her eyes, and said, "Ha, he released me to tell you all with this gift. He trusts us. Although he did ask that we keep his confidence the man is very private. This is a rare treasure indeed."

Addison said, "Major said we should move swiftly and surely. Do you think we should reconsider?"

Casandra said, "No. If he were certain or thought our plans were ill-advised, he would have stood up and said it then and there. Waiting to attack the King at his Castle is still the best plan. Surprise him and take the opportunity to level the Science School at the same time. Kill the snake and burn the venom."

Marion said, "How many will die this time, how many snakes are in his nest?"

Casandra said, "How many more does he create daily?" Casandra did not want to keep going over this all the way to Belissa Villa; besides, Henry had done that last night when he thought she was sleeping.

Henry turned and smiled at her, and mentally he said. You are a trickster wife. She said. "Henry, you have told me nothing of Belissa Villa. Addison has shared with Marion. Why are you so secretive?"

Henry put his arm around her, "I want to know what you think of Belissa Villa. I have my opinions, and they are not likely to change."

It didn't take long, and the carriage was flying over a vast lake, and she saw a settlement of homes and barns. Fields and fields of grapevines, wheat, barley, and hops covered the hills and valleys. It was a vast farm with stone buildings and pathways of stone. The land terraced on hillsides of orchards and woods. Everything was built to fit the landscape; it was natural, rolling, and gorgeous. The colors of oranges and reds, deep purples, and greens crisscrossed the countryside with a massive lake of sapphire blue. Set in the center of the lake like a stone in a crown was a small island. Even from the sky, she could feel the energy of peace, magic, and grace emanating from it. It felt like home. She turned to Henry he was looking at her with a satisfied smiled. She said, "No wonder you did not tell me..." she turned back to look out the window, "There are no words for this. This land is magical."

Marion said, "Addison said Belissa means precious gems of the world in the old languages, I have words. It looks like home to me." Addison kissed her deeply, and Henry and Casandra sighed and watched them smiling.

The carriage landed, and Martin opened the door.

"Here are the newlyweds. I came to offer my congratulations." Martin reached in and took Marion's hand to help her out of the carriage. "And I intend to do a little business." He helped Casandra out of the carriage and bowed to them.

Casandra said, "This is a surprise, here I thought we would have some time alone." She looked at Henry.

Henry mentally said. I mean nothing of what I am about to say out loud, so forgive me in advance. Henry gave her a glare and said, "We will have plenty of time alone. Addison take the women to the house I will be right up."

Casandra stared at Henry in disbelief, "General Martin, will you be staying for dinner or the night?"

Henry said, "Duchess I will take care of our company. Do as you are told." Henry took her by the arm and sipped energy from her neck. "Go with Addison, my love."

Casandra swooned, took Marion's arm nodded and said, "General Martin." Then walked away to the house.

Henry looked at Martin, "Excuse the Duchess she is new at being my wife. What can I do for you, Martin?"

Martin said, "I just arrived; walk with me to the office. I have been sent on this errand for many reasons."

Henry smiled at him, "I didn't think you came all this way to congratulate me. I also didn't think the King's top advisor and General was an errand boy."

Martin chuckled. "That is what I have always been, Henry. A glorified errand boy, and Devon's babysitter. Take no offense Henry, but before we talk honestly, I must ask, have you blood bonded with Casandra? Has Addison bonded with Marion?"

Henry laughed. "What you are really asking is, can either woman hear our conversation. Casandra and I had a small blood bond before our engagement. Doing a full bond during pregnancy is dangerous. Casandra can only hear what I wish her to hear. Addison is another matter he and I are completely bonded. I can block him out, but not forever. Casandra was blocked as soon as I saw you open the door to the carriage."

Martin laughed, "That might have contributed to your spat." Henry glared at him, "Sorry, it is none of my business, but the King mentioned you two were not exactly on happy terms. Addison can listen in, and he may like to know we have not forgotten him. Moondale has captured a few Sprites to experiment on, seems their systems are entirely different."

Henry could feel Marion cringe. "Well, the King's memory of the deal we made is improving. So, you are here with a new offer."

Henry and Martin climbed the stairs to his office in the winery. Martin said, "In a way. The King has had time to think over the conversation you had at Winsette Castle. He has had a change of heart; it seems your arguments hit home with him. He feels the world's eyes are on him and he believes a postponement would be best for now."

Henry sat down and motioned for Martin to take a chair. "He is wise, have you been advising him? I was under the impression there was a timeline for Cassandra's eggs to be used. Would you like a glass of wine?"

Martin said, "Of course, I never turn down wine. Moondale has developed a way to preserve them, don't ask me to explain it. I can't begin to understand half of what that man tells me. The King has also seen the value of keeping you advised of the plan. We believe we have an idea that will not be noticed by anyone."

Henry gave him a glass, "Just an idea, no plan."

Martin grinned, "Yes. The King wants you to develop the plan. After your child is born; the King will invite you and Casandra to visit Hex on a diplomatic trip. He will officially make overturns at your reception, you can plan it at your convenience. We will make sure the countries of Hex, Mento, Machinto, Stella, Antico, and Parragon extend an invitation as well. The trip would take at least months. We could entice her with the exotic Alia Islands. We would impregnate her before leaving Belissa Villa, and by the time she comes home, she will no longer be pregnant. The King will have his children and you your wife and little Winnie."

Henry pushed his chair back, "Something happened to push the King to reason. What has happened?"

Martin heaved a sigh. "Your Brother wasted no time in sentencing and punishment of your Brothers, many died."

Henry wondered who died when Richard died and how close it came to the King. Henry exhaled, "He begged for mercy, we love our family Martin. He was granted his wish. I suspected he had an Attachment at our family dinner. You're telling me that if Casandra dies, I do too? Is that something you know after using an Attachment?"

"You don't know everything about Attachments yet, Henry. Take good care of your wife. I am building a cell for Janet. She needs to be protected while I am gone." Martin sat up and poured more wine. "The Attachments to your Brothers were widespread and extend back six generations. Only one away from the King and Queen. That is when the King realized he should have let you know of our plans. You may have been able to save General Brad and his wife. There are ways to end a life without killing everyone around them. We just needed time to contain it, your family gave us no time. I have to ask, give me an honest answer, could you have given us two weeks?" Martin stared at his wine.

Henry rubbed his face, "I could have demanded a trial. I only had to decent the vote. You could have had months. Brad gave Richard the attachment?"

"No, Suzanna gave him the Attachment. Brad was not like you and I Henry, he didn't find the same sex a suitable partner. The King has been Brads wife's lover for years, he is devastated." Martin sighed, Henry had never seen him so emotional.

Henry stood, "Addison has just told me Casandra has locked herself in our room. I need to get back and unruffle her feathers. However, this is a start to a good plan, one that can work and keep everyone thinking they have won the game. That is always the goal Martin. When everyone is happy, we sell wine. Do you mind if David takes care of you? Give me a few minutes and come up to the house and we will have a drink, and if you would like to stay."

Martin held up his hand, "I do appreciate the offer, but I do have to get this ale to our soldiers. To have loyalty in soldiers, we need to keep them paid and fed. We have been so occupied with other things our business has lacked. Go on, I will stop for a drink before I leave. Try to get your bride out of your bedroom so I can complete my errands."

Henry walked to the door and called David, "Please give Martin what he wants. Tell the King I am happy with our new arrangement. I will consider my compensation."

Martin laughed, "I am freed to tell you he will give you whatever you want Henry. You only need ask, including Joan, even as a mistress."

Henry could not keep his shock from showing, and Martin busted out laughing, "I think this is one of the few times I have surprised you; except for the day we poisoned you."

Henry laughed and said, "Keep Moondale away from her, and I can honestly say you have my interest."

Martin raised his glass, "Done."

Henry almost ran to the house, where he found all three of them waiting for him. Casandra said, "Joan, he would give his own daughters as mistresses? Henry, you should have shared that with me." Henry opened his mind, and she saw the twisted family of the King, she sat down and said. "No, he has Attachments on all of his daughters. Henry, you need to let me see these things I need to know everything. We have to get Joan out of his house!"

"I agree; I have asked the Wizard if there is any way we can help her. He is working on it." Henry went to the bar opened the wine and brought them all glasses.

"When we kill the King, will they all die?" Marion sat down.

Henry said, "I don't know for sure Marion."

"Henry the King invited me to make a visit to his Castle. I think we should stop on the way to North Castle." Casandra took a glass of wine and drank it down.

Henry and Addison both said no at the same time. Addison said, "No more wine for you either. One glass a day, and you just emptied that one. No to King Hex as well. We are not prepared."

Marion said, "All we do is call the Wizard… he brings in all the Warlocks and bam, the King dies, the plan is not that complicated. We are vanquished out and home for dinner."

Everyone looked at Marion, Henry said, "Only a Sprite can be so honest and blunt. That is the plan, Addison your wife has a point. We are not changing the plan, just moving the time."

Casandra said, "I think we should take the Major's advice and be swift."

Addison said, "And sure, are we sure? We need to have everyone informed, and that will take time. Remember the spies, we cannot just send messengers to all the Castles. We need time to get this coordinated. We leave here in five days how can we get everyone in place?"

Casandra said, "This is an opportunity we cannot pass by. I say we make an opening, trust in the Night. If it is right, the way will open."

Henry said, "You are braver than I am my darling to trust the Night. I have found the Night's plans, and mine are not always aligned."

Marion said, "Well, we can always cancel at the last minute. We are two pregnant women there are plenty of excuses between the two of us."

Addison looked at her shocked, "You make things so simple."

Casandra scowled, "Well, she is right. Get the invitation first; if we can't make it work, we will cancel. Martin is coming. Remember, we are not happy couples."

Marion said, "And I am sickly." With that, she turned herself green.

Martin came in with two large packages, he handed one to Marion, the other to Casandra. "Your wedding presents from the King and Queen. Now my errands are complete, I can enjoy a glass of wine while my wagons are loaded."

Casandra handed him a glass of wine and said, "Will you stay for dinner General?"

Martin smiled shrewdly and said, "Not this visit, Duchess. I have urgent business after the wine and beer are delivered. I will take you up for dinner on my next visit. I enjoy Henry's wines and dinners, you have the best cook in the country. Please, do not tell the chief at our Castle as he thinks he is the world's best. You ladies must come to visit sometime."

Casandra said, "I want to. I have always wanted to travel the world." Marion and Casandra had opened their gifts of the finest sheets they had touched. Marion said, "What are these made of? They are so soft and light and what a lovely color of red."

Casandra said, "Ours is white Henry, and look they have the Belissa coat of arms. They are beautiful, three sets, and pillowcases too."

Martin said. "I am glad you are pleased. The Queen ordered them especially made for you both. We grow the finest cotton in our land, and our weavers are world renown. You have been given the very best bedding to be bought. It is fit for a King."

Marion said, "Please tell the King this is a fabulous present, and we love them. Addison, we should visit the King. I really loved the girls, you are marring Janet. Tell us about the wedding plans."

Casandra tried not to stare at the man that grabbed her from Devon at Winter's End. She could still feel the pull of power, and the tentacles burn in her throat. A sudden rush of heat in her groin jolted her back to the conversation. Henry and Addison were taken back as Marion kept up the conversation in Marion style, bombarding him with questions about the land, the Castle, and the wars. All the while Casandra tried not stare at him, but he was handsome and muscular, with green eyes that burnt into her as intensely as the Attachment had. Casandra asked a few questions, but her attention was focused on his uniform buttons. It hit her all at once; the buttons, she remembered them. Henry knew that memory and wished he had the power to block it. Mentally she almost screamed he is the one who carried me to the boat. She couldn't help herself she said. "General, your buttons on your uniform are very unfamiliar. What is on them a bug of some sort?"

Martin laughed, "How observant, Duchess. They are scorpions, a lethal animal from the providence where I grew up as a boy. Hex officers can take the symbol of their lands as insignias on their uniforms. I do wish you would call me Martin that is what everyone calls me."

Casandra looked him in the eyes, "Martin, how deadly is the animal?"

Martin set down his glass then began speaking in a low soft voice. "It is a hideous insect having eight legs and a curved tail with a stinger." He continued speaking in odd rhyme, "Deadly poison is in the tail. It is as light as a feather and likes to hide in a man's boot or crawl up the back of a person. It particularly enjoys cradling in the nap of your neck then places the stinger in your flesh." His words were mesmerizing he was speaking softer and softer pulling them all in. He reached across the coffee table and touched Casandra's neck right on the Attachment. "Right there, that delicate spot. The warm juice spreads down the body, it is said it is like a rapture of heat." His fingers lightly traced the spot where Devon placed the Attachment and Casandra was frozen as heat pulsed down her body. He sat back in his chair and released them all from the spell he had woven with words, "Of course when the poison hits the heart, you are dead." He smiled wickedly. "Rather a nice way to die in a rapture, don't you think."

Casandra swallowed and glared at him, "I could think of better ways."

Martin picked up the wine and filled all the glasses, "Tell me, I am curious. What would be your choice?"

Casandra didn't even think twice, "In a flash, living one second, dead the next. Your choice of death is very sexual. Really, don't you think sex is overrated?"

Martin almost dropped his glass of wine. "No, I do not I have always enjoyed sex."

Casandra said, "You have but have your partners?"

Henry glared at her, "Casandra, this is an inappropriate way to speak to our guest. I think you have had enough wine for the day as well." He took the glass of wine out of her hand. "I apologize for my wife's bluntness Martin."

"Well, Martin, as you see my husband does not approve of much of what I do and say. So, I will change the conversation." Casandra felt more in control, "Do you know if your weavers make bedding for infants?"

Martin answered that he didn't know for sure, but he assumed they did. Casandra turned to Henry and said, "I would like to go to Engelton to order bedding for our baby."

Henry said exasperatedly, "Maybe later, my Dear."

He turned to Martin to speak, and Casandra said, "Now Henry, Martin invited us, and the King did too, the night of the Ball."

Henry looked furiously at her. Casandra ignored him and continued. "Marion would like to go, too, wouldn't you?"

Marion chimed in. "I would love to see the country and the mountains and visit with the girls, why not Addison?"

Addison took the glass of wine from her hand and said sweetly, "Sweetheart you know you don't travel well. I was feeding you medicine all the way here. In fact, you are still a little green. As it is it will take us days to get to North Castle."

Martin said, "The invitation is always open, Duchess. Wait until you have your child before traveling, it is much safer."

Casandra said, "Why can't we just stop on the way to North Castle?"

Henry took in a breath and said. "Because, my Dear, if you remember your geography it is the opposite direction of North Castle."

Casandra stood up and said, "Count Rakie, I do know which direction it is! You enjoy ordering me around a little too much." Henry put his glass down and stood to face her. "You have decided everything I have done over the last few months from where my holiday would be, how long it would be. Wandering out into the ocean for days, while my parents were worried to death, and you changed our wedding day! Even your family is controlling, they have chosen and bought all the needs of our baby. Now you won't even take me to buy some sheets for your child!"

Henry placed his hands on both her shoulders and spelled her to relax. He knew Martin believed this act. However, Henry was wondering how much of it was an act. "Calm down, Casandra. You are working yourself up. This is not good for you, or our baby. I know you have been through a lot over the past weeks, but you really must be more rational. Marion, would you please take Casandra upstairs."

Casandra made her hands into fists and said, "I am not going anywhere until you promise I can order sheets for the baby, bedding that I chose!"

Henry looked at her, astonished, "Very well, I promise you can choose and order the bedding from Engelton; however…" Henry took a deep breath, "I realize this is because you are pregnant, but unless these emotional outbursts stop, you will not be going anywhere. I compel you to go upstairs and lie down, without another word."

Casandra turned and walk to the stairs without speaking, not even a goodbye to Martin as he stood and bowed to her with a big grin on his face. Henry collapsed on the couch and drank down his whole glass of wine then poured another.

Addison joined him and said. "I have some advice for you. Do not get pregnant right away. Enjoy Janet as a regular person for a while. When she gets pregnant, go start a war so you can be gone until the child is out."

Martin was roaring, laughing. "Maybe you should come for a short visit before the reception, it may make your life easier. Henry, what did you tell her about the night on Winter's End? She seems to not remember it at all."

Henry took a swig of wine and opened the conversation to Casandra he could feel the presence of Marion too. "I got there after she dropped from the sky and landed in the ocean. The storm created most of the cover-up, Eric devised the plan to make everyone believe her missing. When she woke, her memories were jumbled, she thought it was a dream. So, I just added to it in her mind with a temporary spell. However, the way she stared at you I thought it might be wearing off. I wonder if her Attachment is not working right, maybe it was damaged by the Doctor, or maybe the Prince didn't get it on correctly."

"You may be right. The King and I thought the energies were different coming from her. It can be overlapped, so we will make another. I was wondering about all the staring she was doing, it was if she could remember me. She is not easy to probe." He turned to Addison and said. "I was telling Henry we are working on an Attachment for your Sprite as well. Send a messenger if you want to come to the Engelton before heading to the North Castle, you are always welcome." Martin gave them a genuine smile and stood to leave.

Addison said, "It might be a good diversion, and then again it might be a trip from hell." Addison took a large swig of wine, and Martin laughed.

Henry said, "I can't wait till you're a married man I hope it goes better with you. I am saying yes, just to get her to shut up about me ordering her around. She is exhausting. We will let you know for sure. Thank you, Martin."

Martin slapped Henry on the back, "You two were not made to handle the temperament of women. Think about that cage Henry."

Henry and Addison stood on the terrace until Martin was out of sight. Addison nudged him and looked to the sky. Henry followed his gaze, crows were flying.

They both went directly to Henry's room, where Marion and Casandra were sitting on the bed. Marion said, "A cage? Henry does Martin plan to keep his wife in a cage?"

Henry ran his hands through his hair. Casandra had learned that jester and the fact he was blocking his thoughts meant he was about to lie. Henry took a deep breath. "I am not going to lie Casandra. I was thinking of how to avoid the answer."

Addison leaned into Henry, "I tried that method too, take my advice, and do not get into a debate with them. It will turn ugly."

Henry raised his eyebrow and said, "Not yet."

Marion said, "So he is planning to put her in a cage?"

Henry said, "Addison, don't you want to show Marion her new home?"

Addison laughed. "I do. However, changing the subject is not going to help you, either." He looked at Casandra her arms were crossed, and her jaw was set with a glare in her eyes.

Henry crossed the room to the windows; crows were coming closer. "Martin is building one for Janet he suggests we consider that to tame our brides, evidently, it was at the King's suggestion. Martin said the King places Elisabeth into it when he is gone for long periods of time for her protection. Also during her pregnancies, she was difficult to live with."

Casandra said. "You mean for the King's protection." She walked toward Henry and looked out the window, "Crows."

Henry shut the drapes, "I have instructed Paxton to release the hawks. I think it is time to show our ladies their new home, and we can come back here and have dinner. Ski is coming he is bringing the dogs. I wanted this weekend to be carefree for you both and want you to have the freedom to roam. I know you are tired of being watched day and night. Fortunately for you, I have the best guard dogs in the countryside. I want you ladies to pick one and have him with you at all times."

Casandra threw her arms around Henry, "I get my own dog. I have always wanted one" Casandra and Marion ran downstairs to meet their dog. The rest of the day was the exploration of Belissa Villa and introductions to Henry's men and staff. They ended with dinner at Henry's house. Casandra loved the home built of solid stone and wood. The furniture was deep hand-carved woods, and the decorations were in the colors of the setting sun and landscapes. Nothing was ornate it was all handmade with care to detail and design. Casandra loved it. Her favorite room was the dining room, it was luxurious. The rug under the table was a beautiful tapestry, paintings of the countryside hung on the wall, the soft lighting of candles glowed as the excellent food filled them. The buffet, table, and chairs were a deep cherry wood. The table was set with white linens, crystal goblets, and hand painted plates rimmed with gold. The conversation was comfortable and relaxed during dinner, and the food was terrific.

Henry asked, "Your thoughts on Belissa Villa, ladies?"

Marion said, "I love it. I have a strange feeling about it. I think I will live here for a long while. All my life I have felt…like I didn't have a home. …we didn't. We lived in the forest and traveled from place to place. My Father, being the magistrate and with so many children we were lucky to have a roof over our head. We would camp or live with a villager while he held court. This, for me, is a dream. A house to have as my own. I can change anything I want." She looked to Addison, "I love it as it is, I don't want to change a thing." She touched his hand.

Henry smiled and looked at Casandra, "I have lived in opulence all my life; for once, I will not be living in a museum. I am home. And…I have a dog." She reached down to pet the dog lying at her feet; a giant black wolf looking male with red eyes stared back at her. Henry's smile broadened.

Bob came in to clear the table and said. "That's a relief, Henry. We will not have to move to the Castle. Henry said if you ladies didn't like it we'd all have to move wherever you wanted. Ruth will be happy too." Casandra tilted her head at Henry.

Ruth came in with the chocolate cake. "Bob, you weren't supposed to say that! Sorry, Henry, I told him we were not to make the girls feel guilty. Really, Bob, you get everything wrong." Everyone started laughing.

Casandra mentally thought. Henry, I really like them they are the cutest couple.

Henry said, "They are blood bonded to me Casandra, they can hear everything you think."

Ruth severed her a big piece of cake, "Sutton told me you like dessert and love chocolate. Good thing you think good thoughts. Now, what time do you want breakfast served Duchess?"

Casandra said, "Ruth and Bob, please do not call me Duchess. Every time someone does, I look around the room for the Duchess. Call me Casandra and I would love to sleep in tomorrow so don't worry about breakfast. I can cook breakfast at least."

Ruth smiled and said, "I understand." She gave her a wink which caused Casandra to blush. Ruth said. "Has Henry showed you the library yet?"

Casandra shook her head no and took a big bite of cake. "Oh, this is the best cake, Ruth. Henry, give her a raise in pay."

Ruth patted her on the back. "Thank you, Casandra, I been telling him that." Then she smiled, "I love to give him trouble. I have been the only woman in his life for some time. He has brought us a winner home this time. I always told him never to trust a woman without an appetite both you girls eat. Means you'll have healthy children too. Oh, and you're the first to buy Henry a present, it is in the Library."

Henry said, "You bought me a present? Hurry and finish dessert, I want to see what I got."

Casandra stood, picked up her plate, and said, "Let's go I am finishing my cake, Henry."

Henry opened the door to mounds of presents, "What is this?"

Bob said, "They have been coming in for days we just stacked them all in here. Marion and Addison's are in here too."

Casandra went in and sorted the presents and found Henry's. "Here this is for you there are three boxes." Henry opened it and found the beautiful tall fluted crystal goblets with their initials on them.

Henry said, "I have never seen any glasses like this. They are beautiful our bubbling wine will look wonderful in them."

They all started opening presents. Addison and Marion got the same glass with their initials on them. Casandra found some of many things she spied on her holiday. Casandra said, "You really did send out the list of my wishes for gifts."

Marion said, "Yes I did. I told the Shopkeepers, and they were delighted to know what you wanted. Your wedding guests were already contacting them wanting advice on what to get you and Henry but who listed my wishes. I wasn't even engaged then?"

Henry started laughing, "Marion your husband can remember everything he sees. No doubt he was watching you like a hawk."

Addison laughed and said, "Yes Henry is right. It is my talent like yours is in changing things. Good thing I could remember because it was the first thing the Queen and your Sisters-in-law wanted from me."

Henry said, "I think we should try out our fluted glasses. Casandra, I just realized, I don't know your special power."

Casandra hesitated and looked uncomfortable. Marion said, "She never likes telling people about it because they always want her to use it on them, very few know. He can read your mind remember he will know at some point."

Casandra snickered, "I can read souls, and I can help them find their way to the Night. That is why it was so easy for me to hear you and Addison. You all know each other's thoughts; I know other's soul."

Henry looked stunned. "When? When was the first time you knew my soul?"

"Let me think." Casandra took a bite of cake.

Marion said, "Knowing her, it was while we were spying on you from the roof of the North Castle."

Casandra laughed, "Marion you are right. I think she can see me do it because she drives me crazy with questions after."

Addison said, "Me, as well?"

Casandra smiled and said, "Yes I knew you were the one for Marion in an instant."

Marion was upset. "You didn't tell me! A friend would have…oh… wait. I am sorry Casandra, you did push me to him."

Casandra laughed again. "It didn't take much pushing if I remember it right."

They laughed together and opened presents until late into the night, as Casandra had promised they slept late the next morning. Eric arrived with Grace and Charlie, and they explored the winery and sailed on the lake. The dogs went everywhere with them. That evening they all had dinner with Ski and his youngest daughter, Rea, and her husband, Derik. Derik was the captain of Richard's personal guard; he was bequeathed to Addison along with Richard's men.

They all separated early to Henry's terrace. It was a chilly evening with stars filling the heavens. As they came down the pathway, they could hear music and see a bonfire through the trees. Henry led them all out into the open patio where all the furniture had been removed, and six of his men were seated with strange instruments in their hands. Henry took Casandra's hand kissed her palm, led her to the center of the patio, and said, "I promised you to dance it's time to pay my debt. This is a Belissa folk dance we usually do at our wedding called the Lavinie; I hope you enjoy this." He nodded to the men and took Casandra in his arms. The music began soft and slow; Casandra had never heard anything like it. It reminded her of the exotic sounds of the Island of Winter's End, but much more seductive. Henry placed her hand around his neck and the other on his hip. He told her to follow his lead, and he pushed and pulled her to rhythms that made her blush and become heated.

Derek and Rae stepped forward, and Derek said, "Watch us, Casandra. My wife is an expert at this dance; she is continually seducing men, aren't you Rea." She glared at him and said, "Oh I would say you are the seducer in our lives." She smiled wickedly and looked at the men playing. They all stopped playing but Paxton. He was beating out a rhythm on the drums, and he was frozen in her gaze.

Henry mentally said to all of them, does anyone else find this a bit sinister?

Addison agreed and broke the spell by saying, "Well, experts show us." Derek pulled his wife to him and pressed her body against him. He turned and nodded to Paxton giving him a seductive smile to start the music. Their bodies fit like a glove as they stepped in the rhythm of the dance. Marion mentally said. Are they going to have sex right in front of us?

Addison mentally said. It is the dance, my love. Addison followed, and before long they were all entranced by the dance and with their partners. They all parted, going directly to their bedrooms.

Casandra woke to find Henry gone the next morning. She knew with just a thought he had gone to do a ritual blood bond with Derek and his new men. Casandra thought Henry, do not share what we did last night! She could feel him laugh. She dressed and went to the kitchen to get breakfast and found Ruth already preparing it.

"Good morning Casandra Henry was up early, and he told me to let you sleep. I heard you stirring, so I made your breakfast. Have a seat. Coffee or tea?" Ruth had several pots on the stove and a basket she was packing with food.

Casandra said, "Coffee, I start my day with coffee. Later in the day, I like tea. What are you cooking, it smells wonderful?"

Ruth put her plate of eggs and coffee on the table with a basket of hot biscuits. "Henry wants a picnic basket for lunch he said you were going on an outing. He wouldn't say where, but I would say you should dress warm and comfortable; a picnic is always outdoors. Have you named that dog yet?"

Casandra laughed, "Well, I should go up and change after breakfast, and no I have not given him a name. I haven't had a dog. What is a good dog name for a boy dog?"

Ruth said, "Well, we have a lot of animals here. Henry has always loved them. We have cats, cows, pigs, and Hennies. Paxton is the animal keeper; you should ask him. I always named them after their personalities. We had a feisty dog named Rascal, then there was the cat that stole all my food out of the pantry…I called him Bandit. What's your dog like, other than big?"

Casandra said, "He is sweet and attentive, he enjoys being petted. He never leaves my side, I almost fell over him getting out of bed. He follows me like my shadow. Shadow, that's what I will name him." She said. "Shadow come." The dog stood, came to her put his massive head in her lap, and she fed him a piece of egg.

Paxton walked in and said, "Casandra don't feed him from the table, or he will come to demand it. You will be sorry." Paxton was leaning against the doorway. "So, his name is Shadow, that's a good name for a guard dog. I can show you how to command him and teach you what to feed him if you like."

Casandra said, "I would love it. Do you have time now?"

Paxton said, "Go get some outdoor clothes on, and we can. Where's Henry?"

Ruth handed Paxton a plate of eggs and coffee, "He is working with his new men. He said he would be back by noon then they are going on an outing."

Paxton just smiled and joined Casandra for breakfast. After they went outside to work with Shadow. As Henry came up to the house running, he watched as Paxton finished up with Casandra. Paxton said, "I will take Shadow to the barn and get Shelton saddled for your outing. Casandra, you did very well. Now command him to stay with me, the last thing you need is for him to follow you out into the lake. Wet dog is not good to sleep with."

Casandra followed Paxton's orders and smiled at Henry. "I am learning, and he actually listens to me, amazing."

"So, his name is Shadow there is much truth that our name becomes our direction in life."

Casandra said, "Well he named himself he follows me everywhere. Where are we going?"

Henry smiled, "You'll see; get a coat and gloves the weather is going to change."

Casandra got the cloaks and met Henry on the path in front of the house. Paxton brought up their Pegasus, and they took off over the lake toward the Island across the way from their home. The Island was almost two miles out into the lake. Henry and Casandra landed on the shore of small pebbles and rocks then walked the Pegasus up the grassy hill toward a knoll. Stands of pine trees banked the knoll with large oaks in the center of the island. As Casandra came to the top of the mound, she could see a stone wall wandering from place to place, through trees and rocks. Henry let the Pegasus walk where they wanted. He walked to a wooden table under a stand of trees with leaves of gold and red. Perched in the tree was a huge black bird with a red chest, staring at them. "Would you like to eat first or walk?"

Casandra said, "I am not hungry, but if you are, we can stop and eat. What is this place? I feel an enormous magical force."

Henry took her gloved hand and walked them to the wall. He pointed out the names on each portion of the wall. These were names she had heard in history class. As they walked Henry pointed out the significance of each individual and the history of the Diamante, "The Diamante was one of the first clansmen to break away from the Monks and shape their own community. They walked to the land filled with vegetation and color and called it the ancient name Diamante meaning vibrate or dimensions of color."

While Henry was telling the history, she knew she was feeling souls embedded in the walls. "Henry, why are souls in the stone wall? Why have they been placed there and not added to the stars in heaven?"

Henry placed a hand on the stone marked Henry Winsette Rakie. "Contrary to the history books, that was the main divide of our tribe from the old religion of the Monks. They took the souls to the Night or to the Day. We believed souls should have a second chance. We are able we keep the souls with us until we are sure they will go to the Night and be placed in the heavens. I was unaware until this week the Empress was doing just that. Many were entombed in these walls. If we are brave enough when we are thirty years of age, we come to the wall and remove a soul and place it in us. We work at the deeds to make atonement for our ancestor. If we are successful, we release the soul. If not, we come back here and return it to the wall. Through my marriage to Elaine, I released Henry's soul."

Casandra and Henry silently kept walking, "I brought you here to explain this custom. The morning you returned the souls to the Night, the Wizard explained what you were doing and why. He told me some souls get lost and remain in this world. He said your people believe those souls get coerced by the evildoers and help them."

Casandra looked at him and said, "This explains so much. Therefore, others believe your clan to be untrustworthy. They believe you are harboring the lost souls who help evildoers."

Casandra placed both her hands on the wall. She sighed, "My Mother's helpers travel the world to plead with lost souls to come to the Temple, it is their life mission." Casandra smiled. "This was the job I was created for. I am my Mother's child, not a High Sorceress. Major was his Mother's child; he did the soul search every day for years." Casandra smiled.

Henry stopped and faced her. "Major, oh…that is why he could be at the Temple for your Mother. Your Mother gave my Brothers a second chance, I am grateful to her. I want to do a small blood bond to show you another one of our customs. Many times, we are given the soul of another for safekeeping at the time of their death. We come here and build a wall for them, or sometimes they ask we take them with us."

Casandra smiled and took his hands. "Is that why you carry Elaine, Harry, and Jack's soul with you?"

Henry's heart stopped, "You have known this all along, do you see them or speak with them?"

Casandra shook her head, "I only sense them. I have asked them to make their own atonement. Jack is ready but not your Brother, or Elaine."

Henry looked back to the house in memory, "I would like to show you the day my Brothers died. It would explain many things, and I want you to see the process of taking a soul, in case…well…we are getting very close to the end of the King. No one knows who will live or who will die."

Casandra was not about to turn down Henry with his request, she would be open and see his world. "Of course, I understand."

Henry lifted her and sat her on the stone of Henry Winsette Rakie the First and drew blood from his finger and hers. As the blood mixed the memory of the fight in the barn unfolded. Jack confronted Harry, accusing him of an affair with Elaine. Jack was holding a cane, and she could feel the pain of the war wounds in his legs. Harry shouted that Jack could no longer satisfy his wife, he should give her up. Jack refused, he loved her still. Elaine tried to stop Harry, but he pushed her aside; he was enraged. Elaine ran to the winery to get Henry, but by the time they reached the barn, Jack had mortally wounded Harry. Henry ran to him, and Harry demanded that Henry kill Jack. As he took his last breath, Harry took Henry's hand and laid it on his chest. Henry pulled his soul from him and sat on the floor of the barn in a jolt. Elaine grabbed the gun from Jack screaming, she pointed it at Jack and shot him dead. Henry screamed and took the weapon from Elaine and ran to save Jack. Jack told Henry he loved him and asked him to help Elaine. Then he took Henry's hand and placed it on his chest. Henry took Jacks, soul.

When Casandra opened her eyes, Henry was sobbing she took him in her arms and held him until he quieted. "There are many ways to reach atonement. You helped one soul that is enough. You know they are with you in every decision you make, even in choosing me for your wife. You can give them to my Mother at any time."

Henry smiled sorrowfully, "I have carried them this long a little longer will not hurt. They are strong, and they have helped me on many occasions. They tell me they have more to do, I will need them."

Casandra knew he was not lying, "Let's eat. The sky is getting darker, we should get back."

The Premonition

Two nights before they would leave for the North Castle. Henry rolled over in bed, and Casandra was gone. He looked around the room and saw the light from the fireplace below in the library flickering. He put on his robe and took the circular iron staircase down to the room below. Casandra was snuggled on the couch with Shadow at her side. Henry smiled and said, "Can't sleep. I see are you worried about our visit to the King of Hex?"

"Worried no. I just can't stop my mind from working. We should place a spell on that iron staircase. The children will certainly be attracted to play on it. I am afraid they will fall. I am also thinking about the colors of the nursery. The Wizard said I will have a girl and a boy it cannot be pink or blue."

Henry sat next to her and watched the fire with her. He had known her long enough, he would allow her to continue until she got to the truth.

She quietly said, "I can't believe we are having twins. I don't want anyone to know until the King is dead. I wonder how many will die when we kill the King. I am having second thoughts about killing him. I don't want to take anyone else to hell, once was enough for me. What about Shadow? He is so big; will he be alright to have around the children? Those sheets and pillowcases the King gave us should be washed before we use them. What will happen to Joan; she is so young? I was wondering should I make a will? I have never thought of that before; funny, isn't it?"

Henry said. "Enough, we can take out the staircase and paint the room yellow; it's a sunny color cheerful and bright, great for girls or boys. The Warlocks will kill the King, and Shadow will be fine with the children he will protect them. We should do more than wash the bedding, there could be spells woven into them. I can't say what will happen to Joan. Perhaps we both should make out a will."

Casandra said, "But I like the staircase. Henry, will I be a good Mother?"

"Casandra, we will be the best parents we can be. That is the real worry here, isn't it? My love, I have found in life if you ask for advice you always get more than you ever wanted. When it comes to children, my family is proficient; I know my Mother will be right here to help us. Sweetheart when your mind starts whirling about, my mind is joined to it. You are keeping me up. I will make you a sleeping draft. If you keep this up, Addison and Marion will be awake in no time." Henry went to the bar he had in the corner and came back with a glass of what looked like water. "Sip some of this."

She did and set it on the table. "I don't like the taste; can you fix it, make it cherry please?"

Henry waved his hand over the glass, and handed it back to her with a chuckle, "Drink. Please." She did, and he took her hand to lead her up the stairs to their bedroom.

When they reached the top of the stairs, Casandra said, "Henry I am still not tired." He turned to find she had shed her clothes on the stairs and was standing naked in front of him. She said, "What did you put in that draft?" then she smiled her most wicked smile, laughed and his heart melted.

Time to Kill the King

The morning of the visit to King Hex, Derek's men and Sutton assembled in front of the barn. It had been decided that Addison, Eric, Sutton, and Grace would go to Engelton Castle. However, Marion would stay at Belissa Villa with Ski, Paxton, and the majority of Henry and Addison's men. They didn't want the King to think any great force was coming on to his lands. Twelve was the size required to move Princes and High Sorceress about the area; they would keep it at twelve. They wanted their party small for easy removal by the Wizards. Secretly Henry and Addison did not want their men to be put in jeopardy. This would also be a test for Derek and his unit. Everyone but Paxton agreed. Paxton thought the trip was fool hearty, and he was insisting on going with them.

In the days before, the Wizard took instructions back and forth to the players. The plan was simple; go to the Castle for dinner. Eric and Addison would call the Wizards when they were secluded in the dining room with the minimum of guards. The Wizard would bring Henry's Brothers, Major, Prince Bryan, and the Emperor. In seconds, the King would be dead. Then they would be transported to the North Castle.

Derek's men all had unique talents to be invisible, and they would leave undetected before returning to Belissa Villa. Henry did not trust Derek or his men. They were told nothing other than to escort them to Engelton Castle. Henry would give them orders after the King was dead.

Henry hated simple plans; they never accounted for the unexpected. The only ones that knew the details were the Sorceress, Warlocks, Wizards, and Elves that would be in the dining room killing the King.

Henry and Casandra hugged Marion goodbye then walked alone to the barn. They wanted Addison to have time alone with Marion.

They all mounted and flew South to Engelton Castle. Once in the air Casandra had butterflies in her stomach. Henry reassured with his thoughts, saying nerves were a part of every battle. The land stretched out as they followed the river through Diamante to the small country of Bezier. The rolling hills faded, and open fields of oats and hay covered the terrain. Henry mentally told her that soon they would cross over to Bezier; one side of the river was Diamante lush with vegetation, and the other; Bezier with rocks, fields of cotton, flowers, and shrubs.

Casandra could see the landscape turn from a lush green to rolling hills without even a tree. Just as they crossed the river, a wind began to blow. It threw her cloak over her head, blinding her, she struggled to pull down. When she did, the sky had grown dark, and lightning was flaring on all sides. Rain and hail poured down on them, and she could feel Devon very close by.

Henry was screaming at her to land Shelton, but there was hardly a place not filled with boulders, and there was nowhere to find cover from this storm. She cried, "This is Devon's storm, he is nearby!"

Henry screamed, "It is a trap expect anything." The rain stopped, but the wind roared, covering them with dirt and small rocks. They couldn't see a thing, only sense where people were. Everyone was scattered among the rocks, unable to gather together for the dust that was flying. Shelton remained with her, but Henry's Pegagus flew off. Casandra could not feel Addison nearby, or Eric. Henry held on to her, covering her with his body.

The wind stopped just as suddenly as it had started and above them were the King's men, firing bolts of lightning down. Henry and his men deflected the first round and began to return fire. Some of the King's soldiers fell from their Pegasus, but she could feel the loss of Derek's men too. They were flying directly into the King's men. Eric and Grace were in the sky also, but she could not see them.

Henry yelled for Casandra to get on Shelton and leave. Then she saw at least fifty more of the King's men coming toward them. Casandra mentally said. Henry, it would do no good, look they keep coming. Where is Addison?

Henry told her he could not feel him, and he wasn't in his head. She was going to ask him what that meant when four men were on Henry. She formed a shield for him, but it was not long before she felt it torn. Shelton reached out and covered both Henry and her in gold threads. Henry had been hurt, but she didn't know how badly. She pushed him aside to fight and throw fireballs at them. More and more came, never aiming at her but always at Henry and Shelton.

One soldier came from behind her and pulled her up by her hair. She was caught off balance dragged twenty feet where she fought him and threw him off his Pegasus. When she looked back, ten men were hammering Henry and Shelton with bolts of energy. She became enraged and pulled the crystal from her neck calling the Snow Leopard out with the multiplier ring. Leopards sprang from every rock leaping into the sky pulling the soldiers from their Pegasus, ripping out their throats. She screamed for the Wizard and blasted the King's men with all the energy she had. It was then she felt Addison dying and calling her name.

The Wizard appeared, and together they defeated the force, killing everyone. Casandra went to Henry; his chest was ripped open and his heart barely beating. Someone let out a scream so deep and primal it shook her to her soul. Henry's eyes opened then she realized the cries had come from her.

Henry's hand came up and pulled her hand to his heart, and he said, "Casandra take it! Take my soul, and my blood it is all I can give you now and my eternal love. Find Addison's soul, my love we will help you. Trust no one there is a traitor among our small group." His heart stopped, and his last breath rushed from his mouth. She bent down to catch it but was too late. She kissed him and sobbed then remembered, Addison.

She ran from corpse to corpse until she found Addison on a group of rocks, dying, with the Wizard trying to heal him. His face was bloody, and his arm was missing, his body had lost almost all his blood. She gasped for breath, and he opened his eyes.

She placed her hand on his chest, and he said, "Receive my soul. Henry, and I will help you endure. At the right time give my soul and blood to Marion." Addison smiled and took his last breath. Casandra was devastated, and then the thought of Eric and Grace came into her head.

The Wizard handed her two bottles and said, "Collect their blood. I will find them."

Casandra worked swiftly and collected both Henry's and Addison blood. She was looking down at Henry's beautiful face and chocolate brown hair when the Wizard came running with Grace's mangled body. Eric was seriously injured holding on to the Wizard for support. Casandra vanquished the bottles of blood and grabbed Eric. In that second of time, she saw the last vision of the Hermits, and she knew how this game would end. It would be the most horrible of all endings. She alone was responsible for all these deaths, and the King was coming, she could feel the coward stalking her.

The Wizard said. "We must go."

Casandra said, "Yes, you must go." She stood up straight and held both hands up and said. "I compel you and Eric to return to Belissa Villa with all of our dead and Pegasus. Give their souls to my Mother, I will keep Henry's and Addison's soul. Keep Henry and Addison's blood for their children. Do not take the King's men or animals. Leave them to rot in the sun. I will stay and kill the King."

Eric screamed. "No don't do this to us, come with us!"

Casandra raised her hands to the sky before Eric, or the Wizard could object and pushed out every ounce of her energy bellowing. "No! This ends now. Go to the Hermit she knows the ending make her tell you the truth, she is evil. Wizard you must rule her. I compel you not to search for me. I rely on you to keep my family from searching. This is my task! Be gone! Now! You are vanquished!" They disappeared.

She looked down to see only blood on the ground where Henry had laid. She sat on the rock beside it and gaped at her hands covered in blood, how much blood had she touched. She saw her rings and took her snow leopard pin and magically buried them with a note, then waited patiently for the King.

She felt the binding around her hands before she saw him land his Pegasus in front of her. Martin arrived second with Devon behind them. Martin dismounted and walked to her. He shrieked at her, "Where are they? What have you done with their bodies? Give them to me now."

Casandra was so weak from sending Eric, the Wizard, the men, and animals away she couldn't even speak. She had never known she was capable of doing that, now she was paying the price. Casandra just looked up and smiled at him. He backhanded her across her face, and she fell from the rock to the ground. Devon jumped from his mount to defend her and Martin threw him to the ground.

He snarled, "I am sick to death of these men defending this pretty face. They are all dead now aren't they, I have shown them who wins the game in the end!"

Devon said, "She is hurt and exhausted, Martin. And…now she is mine. Keep your filthy hands off her!"

Martin took a step toward Devon, and the King screamed. "Stop this at once. Devon, pick her up and give her to me. This will be discussed at the Science school. They will come to look for her. I want this place cleaned up, there will be no trace of her or this fight found. Nothing! And I mean nothing will point to us possessing this witch. Don't come back until it is done!"

Devon picked up Casandra and set her in front of the King on the saddle. The King wrapped his arm around her and took his Pegasus to the sky. He held her tight and said, "You are mine now, little witch. I will tell you this once and make it very simple for you. I will have my way with you for the rest of your life. If you give me children, you will live; if not, you will die."

Casandra leaned back on his chest and turned her head up to look in his face. She gathered a little energy, gave him her most charming smiled and said. "A very wise King once told me we don't always get what we want. I wish you luck."

The King looked down at her and said, "You are astonishing Casandra. I am telling you when I am done, I will have taken everything away from you, and you dare to defy me.

Casandra turned forward and said, "Not everything. Taking my soul is impossible. It can only be offered. I assure you that will never happen."

“Enough! You sit before me dirty and bloody, and still your beauty rivals any Sorceress in the land. This fight has ended.” The King chanted, and memories of the night on the lake so long ago filled her head. And she mentally thought Henry, Henry…but no thoughts came back to her. Henry was dead.

The Conception

Casandra woke in excruciating pain. She felt burning from the inside of her thighs up into her abdomen. Her first thought was her children. She screamed, and a hand came over her mouth along with the face of the King. "Go on, Moondale; I will keep her quiet, insert the eggs. I want her to feel the pain. The least of her punishments for the murder of Due Bre and throwing his soul in hell."

She tried to move but soon realized she was tied down on a table. Moondale said. "Then keep her still. This is a very delicate procedure. We don't want to lose any of these children."

The King said, "Martin and Devon, get over here and hold her still." A bright light was over her head, but soon Martin's face was in hers.

"It will be my pleasure, King. I will love to put my hands all over her." He laughed, and Casandra felt a second probe enter her body, filling her like a hot poker was placed inside her. Martin and the King were grinning, and their eyes began to glisten red. By the time the third probe entered, she merely passed out.

When she woke she was naked and laid out on a bed in the dungeon, the very dungeon of her nightmares. Her first thought was she should have paid attention to that dream instead of only feeling fear. She was no longer afraid; she was long beyond that, she was beyond feeling at all.

A hand came under her head and lifted it. Then a voice said. "Drink." Water flooded her mouth, she tried to swallow, but most of it ran down her chin. A voice said. "She has not stopped bleeding yet. Tell the King not today." The man covered her and waved his hand, and she fell into darkness.

The King's face was over hers, and he said. "Good news Princess. Your eggs are planted firmly. My eggs have already been fertilized, but one egg is for Devon's child. One of your children should look like his Father, or no one will believe you are truly our Princess of Hex."

Casandra looked around. Devon stood with Martin at the sided of the King said. "Take her Devon, you have always craved her this is your moment. Give her your child." Devon looked angry and glared at his Father. "You look like you need a little incentive. Martin."

Martin moved behind him and ripped off his shirt. A scar on his neck pulsed Martin bent and sucked power from him, his body arched, and he groaned. Then the King ripped his pants off and pushed him on top of Casandra. The King and Martin climbed into bed and began to kiss and caress both her and Devon. Devon pulled her head sideways and whispered in her ear, "I am so sorry Casandra, this is not how I wanted to come to you."

Martin took his head in his hands and said. "Drink her power Prince…now." He shoved Devon's head to her neck, and Casandra felt the pull of power and pain in her groin as he entered her body. She could not help from arching her back in agony.

Devon was forced to stay with her in the dungeon. The King and Martin would occasionally come to make sure they were mating to their satisfaction. Moondale was there twice a day to test her for the pregnancy of Devon's child. Casandra tried not to think or feel and held all the energy she could for the protection of the children and their growth. That was hard enough because the King, Martin, Devon, and Moondale would siphon off her power daily. She prayed to the Night that the Wizard and the Hermit were cooperating because she was never left alone. She dared not call the Wizard to plan yet.

Devon was under a spell of the King's, he did not talk, and his sexual appetite was unending. She couldn't wait for the day Moondale would say his child was conceived. There was no clue how many days they had been chained to the bed; the dimly lit room of black stone had no windows. She forced herself not to think of Henry, but her dreams were filled with him. Dreams and visions of his funeral and of standing on the island watching the cremation ceremonies for Henry, Addison, and all his men. She did worry about Grace and Eric and longed for news of Marion.

The Burial of Princes

The Wizard returned from Bezier with little time to do much other than heal Eric and Grace. Although after days, Grace had still not gained consciousness, almost every bone in her body broke when the Pegasus balked, and she slipped from her saddle. Eric had followed her down through the storm, but the attack happened so fast he could not keep the bolts of energy from blasting her brain. The Wizard was confident she would never recover. On the other hand, Eric was mending physically, but the guilt of Grace and the compulsion Casandra had placed them under was weighing on him heavily.

Today was the funeral ceremony, and the Emperor would be there. Questions would come and what could Eric and the Wizard say. Well, he was a wise Wizard and knew he would cross that path when he came to it. The present was all that could be changed, had all the Kings practiced mindfulness this would be so much different. Antioch could no longer sleep. It was because Ruth had given him Henry and Casandra's bedroom. He thought it made no difference, but he could still feel their energy, the aura they left was beautiful and painfully sorrowful. The Wizard had always wanted to feel great love; now, here... he was in the mist of it. He found it oppressive and overwhelming. His mind went to Casandra and Winsette; was his bride even alive. He knew she was in Hex, but she had blocked him entirely. His thoughts were turning darker and darker; he could not function in the depth of the depression. He got up, shaved and bathed then he would check on Grace and Eric.

Eric heard the Wizard motions, now that he was in this heightened state of awareness he could detect the slightest movement around him. He was accustomed to this state of power in war and combat, but since the day on the hills of Bezier he could not turn it off. It was why Eric detected Marion walking into the lake; poor Marion she was utterly devastated. He needed to talk with the Wizard about her. Today was the funerals, and Eric must face the Emperor, Charlie, and his men. He looked at Grace, she was so white and lifeless, he wished he could make love to her just once more. He hoped she could hear him tell her he loved her once more.

"Regrets can take you tumbling down a cliff to your death, or if released they can create the courage to never create another regret." The Wizard walked into the room and began to examine Grace.

Eric waited patiently, "Any change at all?"

The Wizard shook his head and came over to Eric, "Talk to me. You are healing, but your energy is so low. It has nothing to do with Grace."

Eric stood and stretched and went to the window opening the drapes, the sun was just lighting up the sky. "The side of me which is Elf can sense so much. We have the power to turn it on and switch it off. When we are under stress like combat and war, it kicks in. When the danger subsides, it goes off. However, this time it hasn't turned off." He stood watching for the light of day. "I heard you stir this morning and felt your deep sorrow. I can hear Grace's Mother in the guest house crying, she has cried most of the night, and Marion, she is dying of grief. I pulled her out of the lake the other night, Paxton is watching her every move. Ski is strong, but between the loss of Addison, Henry, and his Son-in-law, he is almost crushed. He has endlessly tried to connect with Casandra. I think she has blocked him out like she has me. I cringe thinking about what is happening to her. It is so bad she won't let us see it, my little girl is going to die. I know it just as surely as my love Grace is leaving me too. Can you heal this Wizard, I don't know if I would even let you take this grief from me."

Antioch sighed, "I think today is the day to feel the grief, but tomorrow we have work to do. We must go to the Hermit soon. I fear we must work with that bitter, crazy witch. There will come a day when she dies, and I will happily dance on her bones. She is the reason we are here, she meddles in the tapestry of lives cutting out those that do not fulfill her cause and stitching in the ones who will complete the tasks she is incapable of doing. The heinous part is, she sells her desires as prophecies to young sorcerers. She drew Casandra and Marion in with the allure of great love, romance, and passion. I wonder if she ever showed them the danger and death that would be a bigger part of their lives?"

Eric said, "Well, I know Casandra and Henry had a love that folklores were made. Marion and Addison's love seemed very real. The Hermit showed me Grace's love and convinced me to open my heart to her. If I had to do it over and I thought Grace would live without my love I would not think twice; I would have never allowed her near me. My heart has always belonged to another." Eric turned to look at Grace in bed and held back his feelings. If he let the pressure inside him lose, he wasn't sure he would ever stop crying. He looked out the window, "The Emperor is near."

The Wizard went to the window and said, "Here comes Grace's Mother. She will want to speak to me. I was hoping to have coffee before facing the Emperor."

Eric turned, "I will get you and Mrs. Dryer breakfast. I know she will not stop to eat."

The Wizard said, "Wait, Eric. Before you go, I want you to see something. This might be why you can't turn off your senses. I am not sure what to do about it." He reached down and pulled Grace's shirt to the side. The Attachment was on her neck just at her collarbone. "When was the last time you made love to her Eric?"

Eric said, "Not since we were at Winter's End. She came to Belissa Villa only a day before we left for Bezier. She is our spy?" Eric fell into the chair. "This can't be, she loves Casandra and Marion. The wolf, did you find the wolf pendant?" The Wizard handed it to him. "Her parents will be devastated. The Hermit knew this!"

The Wizard came to him, placed his hands on his shoulders sent him healing then said. "For now I think we should keep this to ourselves."

Eric went down to the kitchen and asked Ruth for a tray. He poured himself a coffee and Ruth plated eggs and toast for Mrs. Dryer and the

Wizard, "You need to eat too you know. You are running on coffee. I thought this was coffee from last night until I touched the pot. Have you even slept?"

Eric gave her a smile and patted her shoulder. "After I face the Emperor's wrath, it is impolite to throw up in front of an Emperor?"

Ruth began to laugh, and then tears were running down her face, "I once asked Henry how he could stand up to Kings and Emperors. He was forever bringing them to dinner. I told him I was scared to death to serve them." She grabbed a handkerchief and sobbed, then just as quickly turned and laughed. "He said he would imagine them naked, and if that didn't work, he would see them drunk and throwing up. If that didn't work he would imagine them shitting on a pot, he was right; it works for me every time." She turned and hugged him. They were both laughing when Eric heard the hoofs of Pegasus and Ruth told him to go on out to greet the Emperor she would take the tray upstairs.

The Emperor dismounted as Casandra's dog bounded up to greet him. Paxton commanded Shadow to sit. Paxton took the leads of his mount and Majors too. "I will see to them, your Majesty. I am sorry about Shadow, he must smell you as part of Casandra's family. Come on Shadow."

The Emperor said, "Casandra has a dog? Henry gave it to her…of course. I have allergies to dogs I would never let her have one." His voice broke, but he recovered and sternly said, "Thank you."

Eric bowed, and the King just stared at him, "Eric, we need to speak."

Eric stood as tall as he could and said, "Yes your Majesty, we have the dining room prepared."

The Emperor and the Major looked to the skies and nodded. The Major covered his eyes and said, "Those crows have flown with us since we left the North Castle. I would have thought they would be tired by now." The Emperor chuckled. They turned and made their way up the path to Henry's home. They met Grace's Father on the trail to the house. He bowed and said, "Emperor."

The Emperor stopped and returned the bow. "Lord Dryer I am so sorry to hear of Grace's injuries. How is she recovering?"

The Lord looked directly at him and said, "It seems she is not recovering." The Emperor was speechless, and Lord continued, "You warned me didn't you, all those years ago, when you invited her Mother and me to the Castle for Casandra's eighth birthday party? You would pay for Grace's education at the Academy and Casandra could have her good friend with her. They wouldn't be lonely or want for anything. It would be such a great opportunity for her. It was…she graduated with honors and was accepted in the elite palace guard. You told me just being around Casandra posed a risk. You were right about everything… and if I could do it again…I would simply say, no thank you, your Majesty." He bowed turned and walked away.

The Emperor sighed and looked at Eric the man was about to burst from grief and guilt. He put his arm around his shoulder. "Eric, I do not blame anyone for this. I just want to know what happened, I just need to know."

They entered the dining room, and the Wizard joined them. Everyone sat and drank coffee then tried to eat breakfast while Eric took them through the events of the day as he saw them. He stopped at the Wizard finding them. The King turned to the Wizard, "Where were you? Why didn't you help them?"

The Wizard stood and poured more coffee, "Your Majesty I regret I cannot speak of it."

"What!" The Emperor stood and ran his hands through his hair, "She did this; was it Casandra?"

Both Eric and the Wizard nodded. "This must be bad to have you under a compulsion spell. Can you not show me anything?'

The Wizard smiled. "Yes, yes I can show you everything. We cannot answer any questions."

The Wizard sat next to the Emperor and Major then held out his hands and pictures of each event unfolded. There was no sound, but the Emperor looked in horror as the Wizard, and Casandra killed man after man. Snow leopards were jumping to the sky as they killed every last one of the King's men. The Emperor saw Casandra screaming over Henry's blasted body. He was amazed the man could speak to her. Then he saw the sight of Addison's body blown away and Sutton's head severed from his body and the Wizard carrying Grace's body with bones twisted in odd ways. He couldn't hear it, but he saw Eric screaming at Casandra, No! Then he watched as she spelled them and vanquished them to Belissa Villa. He clearly saw her say she would stay and kill the King.

The Emperor stood and said. "So she is hell-bent on killing that King all by herself. She was not born for this; she was born her Mother's child. We have all expected too much from her; she is just a girl."

Major looked at his hands and said. "That is exactly what was said of you, your Majesty."

The Emperor turned swiftly and stared at Major, then said. "Power is made, never given. How many times have you had to remind me? Our little girl has become the most powerful and ruthless Sorceress in the world. I almost feel sorry for the King she will decimate him, and he won't even see it coming. She has her Mother's power, my stubbornness, and Henry gave her cunning." The Major smiled.

The Emperor sobbed, then straightened in his chair. "Thank you for showing me the truth. I release you from your mission Wizard. The outcome here must be in the hands of the Night. Now, I can bury her husband and my good friend." Tears were streaming down his face. "I pray to the Night I will not bury her too. Someone informed the King of our mission, who is the spy?"

Major said, "There is only seven left to choose from, only three were not family. That leaves Antioch, Eric, and Grace."

Eric said, "Casandra told us you were your Mother's child, a soul searcher. You know who it was."

Eric and the Wizard felt Graces last breath at the same time and ran from the room. Eric was too late to say the final goodbye. He looked at her Mother and Father grieving over her broken body and leaned against the door frame, praying for tears or screams, but all he felt was emptiness.

Graces body was added to the others laid out on the grassy knoll of the island. Only family and close friends were invited, and King Dillion's army guarded them all. Achille gave the service while Casteglion collected the souls for the Empress. She stood by the Emperor's side with Major on the other. One person came forward to speak for their dead. Eric spoke for Grace, but afterward, he had no idea what he had said. It must have been satisfactory because people told him how comforting his words were.

The bodies were cremated at once by Achille with a spell and Moori, and Casteglion gathered the ashes and poured them in the lake which would spill into the river and out into the sea. After the ceremony, the Monks spoke words of solace to everyone, they spend time with Marion privately. The Wizard led Eric to the lunch and kept an eye on him as King Winsette and the Emperor went into Henry's library to speak secretly. King Dillion and his Brothers left for Winsette Castle, as Arron took the Empress to Bayonne Temple with the souls.

The Wizard walked Eric to the barn. "You need to sleep; I know you won't unless I force you. After taking a walk you are going back to Henry's room, and I am putting you to sleep for the night. Don't even think of arguing with me; we need to leave early by carriage to Crystal Mountain."

Eric said, "I need to know if Paxton or Ski has contacted Casandra before I could sleep."

The Wizard smiled. "That is why we are heading to the barn first, we need the carriage ready early. Then we need to find Ski. What do you want to do about the Emperor?"

Eric stopped and said, "What do you mean?"

The Wizard said, "You are under a compulsion to Casandra just like me. We need to be free to help her. You cannot be the General of the Palace guard and be free to work with me. We also need to decide who we can trust to help us. Who do we tell?" Eric took in a deep breath.

Into the Night

Casandra had lost time and feeling. The King and Martin stopped visiting, but Moondale and his helpers kept draining more and more power. Devon had been locked in with her. The lack of the King's attention pleased her on the one hand and worried her on the other. She wondered what was going on in the outside world and how long she had been in this room.

She couldn't eat the meat they kept serving her. Devon told her if she didn't eat, they would force it down her throat. She swallowed and gagged, threw up and gagged again. She needed fruit and water not wine and turkey. There was only enough water for washing up and never a bath. They both smelled and needed grooming. Devon and Moondale fought, but it did little good; Devon was as much a prisoner as her. Devon was not chained to the wall, but they never let him leave. Moondale was continually doing strange tests on them. Both Devon and Casandra had needle marks up and down their legs and arms. They were both exhausted, drained to the minimum of power by students and guards. Casandra thought she was running a fever. She tried to hold back power to protect the children, but it was getting harder every day. Devon told her it had been weeks since Moondale pronounce that she was pregnant with Devon's child. Casandra told Devon he was a quack, Devon agreed. At night when they were locked in together, Devon told Casandra about his experience with Moondale, his Mother, and Ernst.

Finally, the King came to congratulate Devon on becoming a Father. He walked into the room and just stared at the two of them. Casandra thought she must look worse than she felt, and that was extremely bad.

"Moondale! What have you done to them? We leave for a few weeks, and we come back to this! The Queen was right, you are an idiot!"

Martin threw open the door behind the King and gasped, "Devon, my word, what has been going on here?"

Moondale firmly spoke. "I asked Martin before you went out if I could run some tests. I did, and I let some of my students take their power and use them. You said you wanted her to feel pain. I thought it wouldn't matter to you. Your only concern is the children; they are fine."

Devon was so weak he could hardly move, but he managed to lift his head and said. "He is no scientist; he is a fanatical madman. I hope to live so I may kill him."

The King called the guards. "Escort Professor Moondale to his quarters see that he stays there, and he is to have no visitors but General Martin or myself." They hauled Moondale out as he was shouting at Devon for calling him a madman.

The King came to Casandra and pushed back her tangled hair, "You are burning up. Martin get the keys to the chains we can't leave her here, she will surely die."

Martin had gone to Devon. "The fool almost drained his power out. How did he have enough energy to impregnate her? He has to go, Richard, he has gone too far with his stupid tests."

Martin searched for the keys in Moondale's desk found them and came to Casandra to remove the bands on her wrists. They were bloody and infected she gagged at the sight of them. Martin said, "What will we do with them? We can't take them to a medical. Our plans would be revealed. What am I saying? He brought students in here. Your wife was right, he is an idiot."

The King sat on the bed and shook his head, "I wish I could take them to my wife. She is the only one I know that could heal them. She sees this I will be back at square one with her. It has taken years to have her love me again. You Martin will certainly not be my Son-in-law; she won't let you near Janet. The girls are away at school if we could get them cleaned up."

Devon raised his head and said. "Ernst. Father Ernst could heal us."

Martin said, "He is right, he has brought many to life from the dead. He would at least be able to get them into condition to take to the Castle."

Martin stroked Casandra's breast and said, "I had been looking forward to taking you all week, now…I don't even want your diseased body. You don't look like you have eaten in the months we have had you down here."

The King said, "Get Ernst and guards for the door. Order some hot water and clothing for Casandra. I will stay until you get back."

Casandra would have cried. It had been months, months since Henry had died. Her life would forever be marked by the day Henry died. Ernst came in and laid hands on Casandra he told the King she needed to soak in a warm bath with lavender and ale. Then he went to Devon and politely asked the King to remove the spell, it was no longer needed, and it was draining him out.

After a bath was brought by the guards, Ernst lifted her into the tub. He mentally said to her. I am so sorry girl. This is all my fault. I was the one to take you from your bed that night so long ago. If I could have just let him kill me, you would not be here now. If I die so does Elisabeth, and I love her as much as Henry loved you.

There were tears in his eyes as he began to wash her and clean the many sores and bruises. Mentally he said. If you like, I can have you join Henry. I could make it painless you would just sleep. Two voices in her head screamed No! Ernst almost jumped to the ceiling.

The King turned. He was talking low to Devon. "What is it, Ernst? Is something wrong with her?"

Ernst recovered and said. "She has a serious infection in her female organs; the children need healing. We need the Queen's help with her. I do not know enough about Sorceress bodies."

Casandra smiled at him. She could afford to; her back was to the King. She though mentally. You, Sir, are a liar, and a good one. You must have done that a lot over the years. Did you hear Henry and Addison, didn't you? The King killed them both, but I still hold their souls. He thought yes to her question. I must birth these children Ernst, but if I die so does Devon. He is attached to me now.

Ernst turned his head and moaned in thought. When?

Casandra thought. I don't know. He was that way the day Henry and Addison died.

Ernst thought. This is the first time I have seen him since the hunt they took him on months ago. They had me stay with the Queen to protect her. I heard about Henry and Addison, they had promised to help us free Devon. How do I tell the Queen… it will kill her for sure. She has been so full of hope and love thinking he would be saved.

Casandra took his hand beneath the water. She is stronger than you know, and she will hear, it would be best coming from you. Casandra closed her mind, she was so tired. Ernst said. Sleep little one, I will heal you as my son Antioch did, with perfection. That was when she knew Ernst had taken her to Antioch as a child to be treated.

As he worked on her, he could feel the skin and bone of a Wizard all over her body. However, her female organs were made entirely from Antioch. He wondered how badly Moondale had mutilated her. His son was a master, pride filled him as he worked with even more care. Antioch had constructed her for this purpose he could feel it. He speculated much of these children would be Wizard, and the King's babies were fighting against it even in the womb. Ernst took her from the bath and laid her to sleep on the bed. He saw the bloody chains on the floor and tried not to react to them.

Martin came in, pulled the King aside whispered to him then left.

When he finally got to Devon to heal him, Ernst noticed the Attachment had been healed entirely and covered. The King moved to Casandra and began covering and repairing her Attachment too. It was morning before the King said they were treated well enough to take to the Queen. The King went to the guards and brought in clean clothes. Then he woke Devon and helped him dress. They all dressed Casandra in a gown and robe then he commanded Ernst to wake her.

She woke slowly and for just one second, she had hoped it was only a nightmare, she could smell coffee. Henry had brought her breakfast with eggs and fruit. However, when she opened her eyes, she saw the King sitting on the end of the bed smiling at her.

He softly said, "Good morning Casandra, you look much better today. I compel you and Devon to listen to my words and not speak until I am finished. I also compel you to repeat my story to the Queen; you will never deviate or change it. Nod if you understand." They both nodded.

"We were on a hunting trip when I was called back to Hex on important business. Devon wanted to continue hunting, I agreed and let you go on your own with a few of my army. Devon came across you, Henry, and all his dead men, in the hills of Bezier. Casandra was half dead from the attack, probably thieves, and robbers. You were so injured you can't remember a thing. He told you of Henry's death, and he comforted you then sent for Moondale, he was afraid to move you. Moondale told Devon only one of your eggs had been impregnated by Henry. In Devon's nursing you back to health you fell in love with her son. Now you hold five children in you, four of which are Devon's. You are both distraught and came to me for help and protection. Of course, I will hide you in the tower of our Castle until your children are born, and we can have you married. I will insist on keeping Devon's heirs by naming them Prince and Princess of Hex. Ernst, I compel you to know nothing of this. You have not seen or talked to them." The King came forward with a brush and a comb. "Now come to the table for breakfast, and I will brush your hair, Casandra. I love to brush a women's hair; I can relax you so easily you will see."

His voice was soothing and melodically soft just like the night on the lake. "Devon, you will do this for Casandra every day and be respectful and loving to her. Casandra relax and feel the love Devon has for you. You love him deeply as deeply as you loved Henry. You will do anything for him, you will marry him, have his children and want him sexually every night. Casandra, my darling daughter, eat your breakfast." He turned to Ernst. "Go have the carriage brought around I want them home before dawn."

The King kept giving instructions to both of them sending spells and charms to control them. Casandra just calmly listened she could hardly believe this King didn't know she could not be charmed, but she saw Devon could. The new Attachment was making it harder for her too. However, she needed to act like it was working and not resist.

Henry was in her head telling her this was her opportunity. Listen and take this way to stay close and capture her prey. Addison said if you want to kill this King it is time you learn to play with determination and skill, not emotion. We are here...listen to us, not the King.

The Demise of the Duchess

The Wizard and Eric rose early, and Ruth was up and had their breakfast packed. Marion sat at the kitchen table drinking coffee when they came down the stairs she stood and pronounced, "I am coming with you. Thank you, Ruth." She grabbed the basket and headed for the carriage before either of them could say a word.

Ruth just laughed and said, "Have a nice trip gentleman. I will have a late dinner prepared for you on your return this evening." She grabbed the coffee pot to pour herself some coffee and added, "She is a grieving widow. Don't even think of refusing her this trip. She has something to say to that old witch. Henry's new carriage awaits, it is a long trip, and she will not spend the night there. So be on your way."

The Wizard said indignantly, "Ruth for a servant you speak to us like we were your children. Did you speak to Henry this way?"

Ruth set down her cup and said, "No. As a matter of fact, I did not. Usually, I spoke to him much harsher. Now go."

The Wizard smiled and followed Ruth's instructions.

Eric and the Wizard climbed into the carriage and sat opposite Marion. She handed Eric and the Wizard a mug of coffee then poured a cup for herself. Eric hit the top of the coach signaling Paxton to lift them off the ground.

Marion said. "There are hot sugar rolls for breakfast that Ruth made this morning, and a lunch if we get hungry. I am happy you both didn't argue with me about this trip. I want some words with the Hermit."

The Wizard smiled. "I make it a point never to argue with a pregnant Sprite. However, I will compel you to be very careful with your words. The Hermit is mad, as in insane, you need to keep that in mind when speaking to her or listening to her. Understand Marion?"

Marion said, "Yes, but Wizard both Casandra and I chose paths that led to our husband's deaths. She never showed that to us. If I had known…if Casandra had known…Casandra… I can't image what she is going through." Her voice broke, "I was in Grace's room when she died. I was happy she was released from that torn broken body." She tried to go on, but tears poured down her face. Through sobs, she said, "I wish I could see Casandra…once more. I wish Grace had lived."

Marion's entire body was shaking Eric pulled her into his arms, and he began crying uncontrollably. The Wizard watched as the two of them comforted one another in profound grief and love. He looked away and questioned once more his longing for true love. He could take no more, so he disappeared to sit next to Paxton on top of the carriage. It only took a second, and he was freezing. "It's cold up here how do you stand it?"

Paxton laughed, "Someone has to guide this horseless carriage. I try to dress warmly."

The Wizard waved his hands, and they were covered with a bubble of warmth which also kept out the wind, "Is it alright if I sit with you for a while? There is too much sorrow inside the carriage."

Paxton gave him a half smile and said. "So I heard. You may find too much sorrow out here, as well."

The Wizard waved his hand, and two mugs of hot rum appeared, "A little something to cut the cold and sorrow." He handed Paxton one mug and drank the other, "You're here to protect Marion, aren't you?"

Paxton drank from his mug and said. "Yes for the rest of her life. All the men of Belissa Villa swore an oath to both Marion and Casandra to serve and protect eternally. If you could lead us to Casandra, we would free her. I know the King has her and I believe you know where. We still feel Addison and Henry's souls."

The Wizard didn't want to lie to this honorable man, but he could not allow a rescue now. Casandra had gone through too much pain and torture to quit halfway to killing the King. He looked at Paxton and said, "She is killing the King. This trip to the Hermit is to learn how to help her do that. When the time comes for your help, I will let you know. Addison was my Cousin he was torn from me as a child, and again on the hills of Bezier no one responsible will live, that is my task."

The Wizard peeked in on Marion and Eric they were still in each other's arms but sleeping. He pulled out the bed and laid them down with a comforter over them. He touched Marion's abdomen and sighed. Eric opened his eyes wide with concern. The Wizard shook his head and mentally said. She should have stayed home, her time is near, and I do not want that witch to touch Addison's child. She contaminates everyone she touches. She needs to sleep and so do you, rest my Brother. The Wizard held his hand on their heads to put them to sleep. He returned to sit with Paxton until it was time to wake them for the meeting with the Hermit.

Paxton said, "Wizard could I ask you a question?"

The Wizard said, "Yes go on, but know Casandra has Eric and me under a compulsion spell. I may not be able to answer."

Paxton asked, "Derek and his men; did they fight, or were they traitors?"

The Wizard was taken back by this question. "By the time I got there they were all dead. It was only Casandra, leopards, and me. I believe they were not traitors. Why did you ask that question?"

Paxton looked at him and said, "Well, there were only a few who knew the plan. Derek and his men were not among them, at least I don't think Derek knew...he was Richard's man. Someone told the King they were coming for him. He has never been that bold to attack. I asked because of Rae she was acting strangely."

The Wizard cocked his head, "Rae? Ski's child? Strange? How?"

Paxton sighed, "After the funeral yesterday, some of Derek's Brothers wanted to speak to her. She ran off the island and to her room immediately after the service. Ski asked me to get her and bring to the reception. I went to her room, at the door I heard her laughing." He shook his head and continued, "I swear on the Monks' books, she was laughing hysterically. I peeked through the keyhole and saw her dancing. When I knocked on the door, the laughing stopped. She opened the door, tears were coming down her cheeks. I hardly knew what to say. I told her Derek's Brothers wanted to see her, but she refused. She told me I could instruct them to go to hell. She would never see them again."

The Wizard said, "What did you tell them?"

Paxton said. "Me, I told them nothing, Ski told them she was sick. They were livid, they told Ski she would lose Derek's estate if she didn't speak to them. Let's just say they didn't seem to be gentlemen. There is something not right there, but I just can't put my finger on it. Ski says she is just mourning, and Sorceress handle thing differently, but..."

The Wizard said, "But Ski is all that is left of your family, and you are worried about him and his baby daughter."

Paxton smiled. "I need to tell you Ski, and I did a complete blood bond last night. He is asking me if you would see her soon. She is not eating well."

Wizard looked at him and said, "Of course. There is something else? Are you a Rakie? Did Ski adopt you?"

Paxton said. "No, Jack adopted me. I am a Rakie by name only. Ski has no idea what my parentage is. The Night knows he has taken enough of my blood. Last night Ski told me I am a full partner now in the winery. Addison and Henry named me to run it for Casandra and Marion, and their children. Ski is in no condition to run things now there is too much on his shoulders. I wish I had their talents."

The Wizard said, "Well, I know you are talented with animals. What else do you do well?"

Paxton laughed, "I follow orders well, that is what Henry used to tell me. I don't know why he and Addison put this on me. I am not the man for it."

The Wizard laughed and said, "You are wrong there. They thought long and hard about this, and they came up with one man to take the place of three. Henry wouldn't have put his wife and children in the wrong hands, Paxton. I think I need to find out more about you."

Paxton laughed, "Not much to tell. Wizard I am an open book. Besides, my life is a long boring story."

The Wizard waved his hand, two more hot rums appeared, "You are in luck because we have a long, boring trip to the crystal mountain, start talking."

When they reached the Hermits, Mountain Paxton was taken to the kitchen for warm refreshments while the others were directed into the central living area. The fire was roaring, and the Wizard went to the window to look down at the world below. The Hermit came in and said, "What a nice surprise. Marion, you should not have come your child is too close. Good thing I have a nest made; you are welcome to use it. I insist you stay for dinner." She walked to the Wizard as she passed Eric, "It is good to see you Eric, but then I told you I would see you soon." Eric took in a deep breath and said nothing. "At last we meet Wizard; I have looked forward to this day. You and I working together...well...no one can stop us."

The Wizard looked down on this old shriveled black hair aqua-eyed witch, with a black heart and said.

"No spells can be heard by us.
No lies will penetrate our ears,
I control all the magic on this mountain,
While I am here,
And when I am not...
No evil can be done.

So, it is by order of the Night and the wisdom of the Day. You will only speak the truth Margaretta Selvilla Southerland Duchess of Gregory."

He smiled sweetly and bowed, "We are not hungry, Paxton come out here and drink nothing." He kissed her hand and sent a charm to her soul. Then he sat her on the couch and sat next to her. "Before you tell us what we can do for Casandra, and your plan to kill the King; Marion will speak."

Marion sat up straighter, "I just want to know why. Why didn't you show me or Casandra the truth? Why manipulate us? Why is Addison dead? Why not me? I would have gladly died to save him." She was crying and shaking, Paxton went to her and knelt. He took her hands, and she pulled him to her hugging him.

The Hermit said. "You answer your own questions, my daughter. I needed you alive, and Addison was just a Warlock, just as Henry was, we only needed their seeds. The men were irrelevant." The Hermit looked stunned by her own words. She swallowed and said, "I com… compelled to speak the truth."

She turned to the Wizard who was grinning wickedly. "How does it feel to live under a compulsion? I hope you like it. I am leaving you there for the rest of your miserable life just as you did Eric. Now tell him the truth about his compulsion to love Casandra and Grace."

She tried to hold her mouth shut but her face turned red, and the words broke free. "I forced Beatrice to place a compulsion on you to love Casandra. I wasn't sure she would be the one to kill the King, but I would not take any chances. When Henry married her, I knew it would end at her wedding. The coward Beatrice refused to make it a lifetime compulsion. That is why I brought you here to change the spell to last her lifetime. It was in the potion you drank."

She took a deep breath trying to contain the rest, but she continued, "I needed you to love Grace to keep her near because she was the King's spy." Eric almost fell out of his chair. The Hermit grinned, "I needed him informed of every move Casandra made. He is such a coward he would never take any chances. It was the only way I was could assure he would be in a close position to kill." She looked at their shocked faces, all except the Wizard. "I needed you to bring the Wizard. Don't look so upset, your task is complete. I release…"

She stopped speaking and looked at the Wizard. "You, Wizard, I comp…demand…. I need you to assist Casandra with the King's demise and bring the children to me to raise. I was counting on your agreement with Haden to guarantee me you would finish the game. I have been worried since you ended it. Why Wizard, I did not see that."

He just smiled. "I am asking the questions, Dear. Tell us about the end of the game."

"I will help you find her when the children are born. You will bring the children to me with your air magic. I have a wonderful nest for them here among the crystals. They will have great power from this Mountain. After the children are born, Casandra will advocate for her crown as High Sorceress in the King's presence. You Wizard have already created the King's manner of death." The Wizard gave her a strange look, "Her torque and crown, fool. In her rage of Henry's murder, she will place the crown and torque together then everyone in miles will be dead. It is a plan of beauty my daughter will not feel a thing. She will burst into the Night a pure soul forever."

No one spoke. "None of you understand. I could never get any of my Sorceress close enough to kill him. I thought I had him with Elisabeth. The King was supposed to kill Ernst. Damn him he just used him as a hostage to her heart. I couldn't let that happen again! Henry had to DIE! Casandra's rage will stop him this time! You should thank me; the world should thank me!"

The Wizard calmly said. "I don't like your plan."

She said, "It is a perfectly good plan; nothing is wrong with it."

The Wizard said, "The part that is wrong is you. You're in it. I will fix that." He reached out and took her by the throat.

She croaked. "You cannot find her without me! A man cannot control the magic of this mountain! I build it from a woman's hand your spells will only work here while I am alive. Face it, Wizard, in the end, I still hold all the power."

He lifted her to her feet and said, "Hermit you are a bitter, evil woman, and through the years you have created many powerful people that want to take your job or want you dead. Here is one who wants you dead, and one who wants your job." He waved his hand, and Professor McMillan was standing behind her; Moori was at her side. "What I kept from you is I have bonded with Winsette. I am her future husband. I can find her anytime I want."

The Wizard waved his one hand the windows of the room opened. The Hermit tried to talk, but he cut her throat off from the air. The Professor reached in and tore out her heart and threw it in the fire. Moori took her soul and placed in a black iron box. The Wizard twisted her head off and threw it into the fire. They carried her body to the window and pitched it out. They could hear it crashing against the side of the mountain as it fell miles into the endless ravine below. Marion thought the sound went on forever. Eric just stared at the head in the fire, as if somehow it would jump out to get him. The Wizard closed the windows and walked to the fireplace to watch her face burn black and melt into nothingness.

Paxton stood and said, "Let's go get Casandra Wizard."

He turned to him with a solemn face that showed he heard Paxton. "Casandra commands me just as she commands you." He placed his hand on his shoulder. "She will kill the King, just as the Hermit said, but not in rage. She will kill him with compassion and win with strategies Henry and Addison have planned for her. She carries their souls, just as you have known. You and I, and Eric and Marion are charged with the care of their children. Henry marked her for eternity, in the end, we must give love its wish."

The Wizard went to Moori, "This place is all yours, my Dear. Eric, will you help me clean out the corrupt energy?"

The Professor said, "I am hungry. I will see to a new dinner for us without poison and charms."

Marion said, "I am not hungry. I don't feel well."

Paxton lifted her into his arms and laughed, "Where is that nest? The child is early, Roslyn Rakie is coming."

Marion was crying, "Roslyn Casandra Rakie." She hugged Paxton.

The Wizard said, "Casandra is not going to like that."

The Tower

The King took her to the Castle in the dark, and Martin carried her up the tower stairs where the Queen was working with magic to create a comfortable living space for Devon and Casandra. Martin laid her out on the bed and began to repeat the story they had all been compelled to tell.

The Queen held up her hand and said, "Stop Martin, I don't need to know why or how. I just need to get to work on her. If you would just help me get her undressed and into the healing bath, I made. Guard tell cook we are ready for some food. King would you, and Ernst put Devon on the couch in front of the fire. The King says he needs food and sleep, but he will be fine. My concern is for our grandchildren.

Martin laid her in the tub; it was only when he saw the damage that was done to her he cringed. He had been responsible for some of it himself. More and more often Martin had no control over himself darkness was growing inside him. He stood back while the Queen's healing hands touched Casandra. Martin heard the Queen tell Casandra that Moondale had done the same to her at one time and she recovered. He wondered if the King had done to her what they had done to Casandra. She turned to Martin and asked if he would send in Ernst. He left before she could read his thoughts; he had never been comfortable with the Queen.

The Queen and Ernst spent the following days healing, feeding, and cajoling Casandra to live. Devon was with them, and Ernst worked with him showing him healing techniques and healing potions. They forced her to stand and walk. Each day Devon would carry her down to the garden to walk and talk. Casandra knew the King had spelled Devon to love her, but she felt that had not been necessary. Within weeks she was eating solid food. The Queen announced that Devon could return to her bed. Ernst wanted him next to her all night in case she needed healing with the children. Her internal infection was not going away. Casandra overheard the Queen tell the King to leave her alone if he wanted the children to live. Martin and the King both stay out of her bed.

Several weeks later the Queen told her the King wanted them both for dinner that evening. She had been so sick, no one noticed she was not acting like his spell of loving Devon was on her. Now she would have to gather her energies and begin the game.

Devon helped her down the stairs of the tower; he was telling her the layout of the Castle. She laughed. "Devon, I don't think I need to know this. Your Father has me in the tower. I have a feeling I will be there for life."

Devon turned his head forward, "Casandra I am so sorry, I can never change what happened, but I want to make up for it. I won't ask you to forgive him or Martin or Moondale, but please forgive me."

Casandra stopped walking and placed her finger on his mouth, "Devon, you are not responsible for anything. You and I have both been controlled and manipulated in this game of the Warlocks and Witches. Did you choose to hurt me? Did you want to only love me even before the King spelled you and have you not always wanted to have my kisses?"

Devon turned to her and said, "You fell out of the carriage and into my heart Casandra. I knew you were not a lady of the night, you have been in my head and heart every moment since. And I know you know that. I could not even hide it from Henry." He immediately wanted to take those words back.

Casandra smiled, "I don't wish to talk of Henry or Addison in front of the King or Martin, but I do always want to remember him. Devon, I loved him. I will not hide that from you. You have a pure heart, and true love only a wizard can bring to a woman. It seems we are fated to be together. Your Father will have us married we might as well make the best of it. You are handsome, rich, and a Prince what more could I want."

Henry's voice said. Not enough Casandra, he wants your love, make him believe, make the King believe. She gathered herself and gave the Prince her wicked smile filled with charm and sex. "I believe I could easily fall in love with you. It is hard to think of myself as sexy and beautiful carrying around five babies. I am showing now and getting fatter by the day. You must think the very worse of me." She turned her head, and Devon turned her back to face him.

Devon said, "No, I have known every part of your body over the past weeks and believe me when I tell you, I find none of it anything but gorgeous and beautiful. It is an effort to keep my hands from you or my lips." He smiled and said. "If anything knowing there are children inside you makes you even more desirable." She reached up and put both arms around him and brushed her mouth against his lips. Devon moaned and pulled her in kissing her softly leading into a deep kiss. They heard someone cough and they both turned their heads to find the King and Martin watching them.

The King said, "I so love to watch you two, but dinner is getting cold." Casandra blushed, and wondered how much he had heard?

The King turned walked on with everyone following, "I see the two of you are getting along splendidly. Casandra, you are looking well. We have a lot to discuss."

They crossed the garden into the dining room. The Queen told her to sit next to her. Martin started to pour wine for her, but the Queen stopped him. "I have spent week's healing her, don't ruin my hard work! No wine for her until she gives birth. Now, Casandra do not force anything that does not taste good to you and take your time eating. So many babies are taking up all your room for food." She poured her a glass of milk.

Casandra smiled at her and said, "You are babying me like one of your own children."

The Queen laughed, "Casandra, you are, or I should say you will be soon. The King has told me Devon's plans to marry you as soon as possible. You will be my Daughter, wait till the girls hear! They think the world of you. I can hear them squealing now."

Casandra was not shocked but surprised at how quickly this was unfolding. She looked at the King he was pleased with himself. Then she turned to Devon, and he looked embarrassed. He had wanted to ask you himself, Casandra. This time it was Addison's voice. Play this very sweetly remember you are charmed by the King.

She looked down at her plate then Devon's hand caught hers under the table. "Mother, I had wanted to ask Casandra in private."

Casandra looked at Devon and smiled. "Well, that is not going to work now, is it." She looked to the King. "I wish it were as easy as me saying yes, but this is going to be complicated." She took a drink of milk as the servants were doling out dinner.

The King nodded. "Yes, Casandra is right. This will take a little time."

The Queen said, "Yes, yes, I know she must release herself from High Sorcerers, and there are the paperwork and documentation. But I know you, King, you are working on that right now, aren't you?"

The King smiled, "Yes I am. Our barrister is coming by after dinner to get your signatures on some things and ask you some questions. Is that alright, Casandra, if it is too soon, we can make it another time."

Henry said mentally. My death certificate, my love, and our land. Addison mentally said. Our winery. He is moving fast. If you can handle it, we will be in your head to talk you through it. Better yet open this conversation up to barrister in our family Ski. It is time you stop locking him out.

Casandra set down her glass and said. "Henry's estate? Is that what you are speaking of?"

The King looked at Martin. "Yes, I am sorry if it is too soon..."

Casandra held up her hand. "Oh, I thought you were going to ask me to abdicate from Marais, as well as give the Sorceress position up. Do my parents know where I am or Ski Chancellor? He must be devastated." She looked down at her hands and pushed down the anger. Addison said. No anger; you are in grief and a confused little, brainless witch...act Casandra, and call Ski. She mentally called Ski and put a pained look in her eye as she raised her face to meet the King's gaze. "I am afraid I do not know a thing about how to go about any of this. Putting it off will not make it go away, I know. I just feel so unsure." She pinched her hand hard to bring tears to her eyes.

The King stood, came over to her, and put an arm around her, "Oh sweet girl, you have been through so much, and I am sure the loss of Henry weighs on you as well. In my experience heading straight onto problems is the best way to bring yourself out of them. We are here to help you and give you the best legal advice and counsel. Trust me, we are your family now. I have messaged your Parents; they know where you are Dear. I have even invited them to come to see you. I am sure they will be here soon."

She gave him a smiled filled with tears and said, "Thank you, King. I am indebted to you." She squeezed Devon's hand. While Ski's voice filled her head. Casandra where are you, I have been so worried, what happened? Why did you block me? I am here to help.

Casandra wiped her eyes and said, "Alright let's get the paperwork over with. I will meet the barrister after dinner, but would you mind changing the subject at least for now?"

The Queen said, "Of course my dear, this is not a good subject for digestion. The girls will be home from school soon." They all went on to other subjects, and Casandra filled Ski in mentally with brief details of events in her mind.

After dinner, Devon took her to the library where they had ale and wine, but she was served tea. Martin came in with a tall wizard with black hair and green eyes. He was much older but still very handsome and charming. They introduced him as Barrister Lloyd Webster Camden. He swaggered over bowed and kissed her hand. He spoke insincere offers of sympathy and flowery words of admiration. Casandra smiled and responded politely. She mentally called Ski into her mind. I don't like this guy he has a dirty soul. Ski can you hear him? He is deliberately talking over my head.

Ski answered. Yes, be quiet so I can hear what he is saying. Casandra sat and plastered a look of interest on her face, just as she had done in an ancient poetry class.

Barrister Camden looked at her and said, "Usually in cases like yours Duchess Rakie the Estate is managed by the remaining partner, of course, I will need your permission to go to those holding the estate and request your portion of monies and lands. This could be a long legal battle, but the King has retained me on your behalf. I do need you to sign documents of release to establish me as your legal representative in the matter of your holdings. I also strongly suggest you draw a Will in case you should not live to see your children grown. Do you know if the Count had changed his will to include you and your children?"

Ski said mentally. Tell him Henry has a Will, and you and the children are well provided for. Tell him you would like to have him work up a Will for you. Casandra repeated Ski's suggestion. Read to me the paper he is handing you to sign, just the title.

She silently read. This says release and contract.

Ski said. Skim down and keep reading. Think the words, Casandra.

The King said, "Casandra you don't need to read that; it is just a release form."

Ski said, keep reading, and she said. "My Father told me to read everything I sign entirely."

The Barrister smiled wickedly and said. "Of course, Duchess your Father was correct. I would not want anyone to later accuse me, or this Kingdom, of coercing you into signing any document. Which brings us to the second document, which all of us will sign. It states you signed all these documents of your own free will."

Ski mentally laughed. Antioch is here he knows this man Casandra. She took a breath and looked at him again. Ski said. Don't worry, I have blocked him; he cannot hear us, but he knows something is going on we must be careful. Pick up the other papers, shuffle through them and sigh. Looks like the King is going to use Henry's children for a bid to the Throne of Diamentia.

The Barrister Webster took the papers from her and put them into the envelope, "You can take these with you, take your time reading them. I will be back in a few days for them. This evening we only need these two signed so I can begin the process."

Ski said. Tell him you will be happy to write a letter to me and suggest he make a personal visit to see me here at Belissa Villa. The Wizard wants an introduction. Casandra couldn't help but smile. Also, Eric said, sign with your left hand; remember security, then you will know for sure if he can read thoughts.

Casandra repeated Ski's words and reached with her left hand for the pen. The Barrister said. "Left-handed, Duchess, you drink your tea with your right hand."

Ski said. I am dropping the block, then he will only read your mind. Open to me when you are alone. Careful with your thoughts, and let the game begin. Casandra kept her mind on the documents, signed both, and handed it back. She allowed the pain and tiredness of her body fill her head.

Barrister took both her hands in his. "Your Father is very clever using only the left-hand signature as authentic. I see how tired you are, and you are in pain. Duchess this has been too much for you tonight. You could use a Wizard's healing I would be happy to provide that for you."

She could feel Devon's jealousy he took her hand away from him and said, "I will get Ernst, and take Casandra to our rooms." Casandra turned her thoughts to Devon and filled her mind with as much love as she could. Then she thought the question of abdication just to judge the strength of this man's power along with her thoughts on how attractive Camden was.

Camden drew a breath and said. "To your question Casandra." Then he gave her a very seductive smile. "As far as the legal abdication, I took the liberty of finding that knowledge for you and the King." He bowed to the King and continued. "In this country, the wife of the royal family must give allegiance to the King to be married legally to a royal. Which means Casandra would have to denounce her country before the marriage takes place. I have written for more recent documentation, but so far it states that Casandra must reject her country publicly by placing her Crown or any other station or symbol into the hands of the King of Hex." He paused and looked at her, "The documents are in your hands. A public venue can be provided easy enough. All we need is your crown."

Martin said, "Your crown and torque Casandra you used to wear both all the time. Have you vanquished them? I compel you to tell the truth."

Casandra let the Wizard feel the hatred she held for Martin, and said, "It was removed the night of my marriage. I honestly don't know what happened to it."

Camden smoothly said, "She is telling the truth. Perhaps I could help Casandra, show me the ceremony." Quickly he placed his hand on her forehead, and memories of that night filled her mind.

"Hmm…a Monk picked it up and gave it to the Emperor. Casandra, where would the Emperor place it." She could not help herself she saw the safe in the library of the North Castle. She called Ski back for help saying this Wizard was too strong.

Camden said, "The safe in the library of the North Castle."

Martin laughed, "I will have my spies working on that as soon as possible."

Ski said. Wizard said to faint Addison if you are there help her to faint. Addison pushed on her chest she gasped for air and blacked out.

She woke with the King's face in hers. "You gave us a scare my girl. Camden, thank you."

She looked to the side the wizard Camden was staring into her eyes. She hadn't gotten rid of him, and he smiled and said. "You have simply overdone yourself. I have a healing bath waiting for you, and I suggest you get a good night's sleep. I will be back in a few days to pick up the rest of the papers."

Casandra said, "Thank you. I will read as fast as I can." Then she added in thought to see you sooner. He took her hand and turned in over and kissed her palm. "Take care Duchess." Then he turned and left.

The King said. "Casandra, did you enchant him? He is taken with you; do you not have the attention of enough men?"

Casandra laughed, "You should know, King. A Sorcerers cannot resist a handsome Wizard."

His eyes glinted red, and she noticed that only the King and Martin were alone in the room with her. He softly said, "I think you are too weak. I will help you with your bath."

The Conspiracy of North Castle

The Wizard said, "Well, the torque and crown are gone. Casandra was right they have someone planted there."

Eric said, "Spies at the North Castle. We removed all the animals, and we tested all the servants. That means only the unsuspected could be among the spies. I need to tell the Emperor, but I also need to get back to Marion and the baby. I don't want to leave them too long."

The Wizard smiled, "You have grown fond of them Eric. That is good she needs support right now."

Ski said, "In our culture, a Brother is responsible for his Brother's wife if he dies. Dillion will decide her fate, he will find a man in the family to wed her."

Eric looked stunned, "Why can't she choose for herself? I don't like that rule." Eric loved Marion and always had. He should have gone out into the garden the first night Henry and Addison came and broken up that kiss.

Ski said, "Well, she is Addison's widow and now bound by Diamante law just as Casandra is. I am so relieved I contacted Casandra. Addison and Henry are still with her, but I can feel them getting weaker. We must move this game along. Wizard, will you tell me what this game is, can I help?"

The Wizard stood still with a look of sadness on his face. He said, "You are right. I am bonded to Casandra's child. I can see everything she has gone through, even at this moment and this needs to end. I will take Eric back to Marion and come right back here and tell you everything. Don't try to contact her until I return. We must get her to call me, I must be invited. It is the Wizard's Rule."

The Tower Balcony

Casandra could feel the force of energy around the balcony of the tower preventing her from throwing herself off. She wished she could die, she no longer cared about killing the King. Where were Henry's and Addison's voices, Casandra could barely hear them? She wondered how often they would come and rape her and guzzle her power. They would send Devon on some minimal assignment to have her alone. She was sure Devon would kill them if ever had the chance.

She told Ski they were going after the crown and torque, but it had been weeks, and the King said nothing about it. Every chance she had she would come out to the balcony to dance and pray. Doubts the Night even cared about her filled her mind. When she danced Henry and Addison would wake and speak to her, at least that took her mind off Martin, he was vicious. They loved to bath her, but she hardly felt clean after one of their baths. Perhaps another would help to wash the smell of them off.

She drew another bath, sunk down into it, and relaxed. She looked out the window; a bird was watching her. Spies were everywhere, did they pry earlier? Of course, they watched her every move. She forced her mind to go blank, and immediately Ski was in it. Casandra, it is Ski. I am here with the Wizard, he needs to speak with you in person. You need to call him; it is the only way he can come.

Casandra sighed deeply, "Devon and I have a new attachment. When the King dies, we both die. Besides, the Hermit won't let me change anything, she is evil.

Ski said. We know Casandra. He says he needs to see you now, he will take care of the spies. He asked if you are in the bathtub.

Casandra smiled. Yes. I will call him, funny, I am no longer embarrassed by men seeing me naked. Wizard come to me.

The air vibrated, and the Wizard stood in front of her holding a towel with one finger over his mouth. She said nothing and climbed from the tub as he put the bath towel around her she looked back and saw an image of herself relaxing in the steamy tub of water. He walked her to the full-length mirror stepped in it and pulled her along.

He stood opposite her and said, "It is private in here; no one can see or hear us and as you see you are still relaxing in the tub."

She said, "How did you do that?'

He said, "Parlor magic really, it won't last long an hour maybe. It takes months to create a talking, thinking duplicate. Now we haven't much time I have been to the North Castle. The King has the torque and crown. They must have someone at the Castle, it did not take them long. Eric can't find the spy. The Hermit showed me her plan. I am here to tell you we can change it. Tell me what you want."

She looked at him and said, "I have a new Attachment when the King and Martin die, so will Devon and me." She took in a deep breath, Besides the Hermit won't let me change anything, she is evil."

The Wizard said, "She is dead."

Casandra threw herself into his arms crying. "Thank you, thank you, thank you." She stepped back and said, "I can barely hear Addison or Henry anymore. I can tell you what they wanted. They would keep my mind busy while the King tortured me. They want me to have these children."

The Wizard said. "I know, I was there too."

She said. "The children can never know." He placed a hand over her mouth.

"No, I can protect all the children they will know nothing of the abuse. We must hurry, show me their plans." He placed his hand on her forehead, and everything came rushing out. "Henry and Addison together were geniuses. I hope their children have half the talent they had."

Casandra heard Ski's voice in her head, crying. Casandra said, "Oh, I am sorry, Ski, I should have blocked all that for you."

Ski said I am here for you my Dear please do not block me out from now on. I want every thought, every sigh, this I compel you to do.

She looked away and caught the vision in the tub. "Wizard, you said it takes months to create a duplicate. What about baby duplicates? They don't need to talk or think, they only need to cry, eat, and poop."

The Wizard gave Casandra a huge smile. "It could be done in a shorter amount of time, but they would not last long. We might only have a week before they disintegrate, and we have five to make. However, if the Professor and Ski help we could do it in a month or so."

Cassandra said, "I can't keep Henry's children from coming out much longer. Besides, you only have three to make. The King's children cannot live. I think I can get that Wizard Camden to push along the abdication and marriage. A few weeks…I can stand a few weeks."

The Wizard placed his hands on her stomach and said, "I am not sure you have weeks, there are too many children in you Casandra. I am sure they are expecting an early delivery. I will help develop the King's eggs they will be ready in one month. However, be careful of Camden he is smart. Try to get him to come to Ski as soon as possible. I have had dealings with him before, I need to get my hands on him for only a second." The Wizard smiled and said. "Marion wants to see you, and there are a few others. With your sanction, of course. I would never intrude on your birthing."

Casandra smiled back tears. "Henry and I made the right decision giving you our daughter. Of course, Marion and Eric, and it is not wise to let too many know about the children until they are older."

Ski said. "Me and of course, Paxton." She nodded yes with the first smile the Wizard had seen since he took her from the tub.

The Wizard let his hands heal her and took her back to the bath, where she stepped in. He put his hand in and remove the vision, the water was as warm as she had left it. The Wizard was gone just that fast, and she felt clean.

Crystal Mountain

Eric was forced to tell every detail of Casandra's conversation to Marion, Moori, and the Sprites. Roselyn was sleeping in Eric's arms he could hold her forever, and just stare at her. He was sure there had never been a more beautiful baby.

Moori said, "How soon will we get the other children?"

Eric said, "I don't know. The Wizard said he was coming back here with a crystal ball, he said the green paper was a useless way to communicate. I hope Casandra calls him then we can find out how she is. I know it cannot be good for her." He deliberately closed his mind to that.

Marion said. "I have to see her Eric. Please let me see her."

He smiled his heart opened. "I will. I promise."

The Dance of Schemes

Casandra stood on the large tower balcony the King of Hex had placed her in. The sun poked its head out between the white and black clouds that threatened storms. It had been months since Henry had died and with each day, the voices of Henry and Addison grew dimmer. The children were growing bigger too, soon they would be born. How much longer did she have in their hands. Months of being raped and taken to near death as they drank her energy had taken a toll on her. She couldn't help but worry about how it affected her children. The King and Martin were both fascinated with watching the movement of the children, which scared her wholly.

She returned to the tower room which was one large room. It was a sitting area with a large fireplace to the left from the entrance, three stairs on the right of the door opened to the bedroom and nesting area with windows beyond it. Windows filled all the walls but the wall at the entrance, which was behind the bed and fireplace. A sizeable beautiful bathroom with a sunken tub was the only confined area, but even that had the floor to ceiling windows. A small table sat in front of the double doors leading to the balcony. The place was cold; built with gray granite and floors with occasional rugs of green under the furniture marking out the rooms. Even the couch and chairs in the sitting area were covered in the deep hunter green of the Kingdom. Bouquets of flowers were the only cheerful piece of the décor. There were no drapes on any windows which left her feeling watched, and she was sure she was, she was never left alone. Devon was reading a book on the couch.

"Devon, could you do me a favor? It looks like it will rain. I want to get my dance in early could you move the clouds away for me?" She watched as he looked up. He was a handsome and brilliant wizard his deep emerald eyes were the only thing she found off-putting.

Devon smiled and came out on the balcony, "Of course, but I won't be able to read out here with you dancing." He took her in his arms and kissed deeply. "I love you, I love holding our children so close. This makes me want to keep you pregnant all the time. I can't wait to see them and hold them."

Casandra wanted to cry she truly loved this man. "Devon, how I have grown to love you. I never would have thought I would feel like this." She kissed him and grinned at him, "You know, not all the children are yours." His Father hadn't told him about his children being in her as well.

Devon placed them in a secrecy bubble. "I know, but I will love Henry's as well as mine. Henry was always good to me, he really did try to help me out of this mess. I will love and defend them as much as my own, and I promise I will find a way out of this. First, we have the children and marry; then the King will leave us alone for a while. I will go to my Brother, Antioch will help. You need to be patient it is the only way to handle the King, Ernst and the Queen are helping too. Have faith in me. Sometimes you look so forlorn my heart hurts."

"I am sorry, you're right Devon." She wished she could confide in him and make him understand. Henry screamed in her ear. He has an Attachment! They will know, it is taking all Addison, and I have to keep Martin and Richard from knowing your plan so please be silent.

She sighed, "I love you, remember that Devon, I love you. Maybe it is just that I am scared about birthing all these children. I need to dance to bring up my spirits."

Devon grinned, "I will be here, and Father will always have someone close at hand. I will not let anything happen to you or the children, trust me. Now I am going to move the clouds and raise the temperature, so you are comfortable. And…try to watch you without taking you to the bedroom." He laughed.

"Fifteen minutes, you can't wait fifteen minutes?" She grinned wickedly at him.

She started the dance of the warrior to help strengthen her muscles. She would need all of them to give life to five children. Henry and Addison would bring her ideas as she worked the dance. If her body let her, she would spend all day with them in her head. Henry's soul never stopped working he wore her out with thought. However, as soon as she stopped dancing the voices would leave. She remembered Henry saying running would always help him think, well dancing helped her think. Ski spent a lot of time in her head telling her about the progress they were making with the babies.

Since the night of the Wizard's visited Martin and the King were gone somewhere. Ernst and Devon didn't know where they were. She was happy they were gone but didn't like not knowing where they were. They often traveled to Hex and Parragon she wondered why. Yet, her biggest worry was no one seemed to know where her torque and crown were.

Devon watched as Casandra did her exercises on the balcony. She was always beautiful, but when she danced, it was like watching a swan glide across a still pond. The music she created for her dance was enchanting, and he would just sit and relax. He would envision a life of love with her and their children. Somehow, he would take her and the children to safety.

The King, Barrister Camden, and Martin landed in the courtyard and immediately heard the music. The King's first thought was of the day Casandra threw Due Bre's soul into hell. He stomped through the Castle to the tower. He entered to see Devon entranced with her dance. They all stopped to watch her grace and beauty even as pregnant as she was. He looked to Martin and Camden both were drooling at the sight of her; he hoped he never seemed that lecherous. He would stop this. He walked to the balcony, and yelled, "Cassandra what are you doing? You will harm the children. Stop at once."

Cassandra almost fell over; he had surprised her. Devon jumped up and caught her, "Father you frightened her. Mother said it was a good exercise for her, she needs to build her muscles for childbirth. They will come soon, look how she has grown. There are five children isn't that amazing? Ernst says there are twins."

The King said, "Twins? I can see she is growing larger Devon. Casandra get in here it is cold outside. You should at least be indoors doing that. The whole Castle is watching you." He led her in and said, "I have good news for you."

She went in to find Martin and the Wizard Camden standing in their living area. A Sprite gave her a shawl, and Camden flicked his hand, and a roaring fire started in the hearth. They all took seats, and she asked Ski to help her with her thoughts for the Wizard Camden.

Camden said. "You look much better than the last time I saw you, Duchess."

Martin said. "Stop calling her that."

Camden snapped, "Until the wedding, that is who she is, Martin. Duchess have you had time to read the papers I left for you?"

Casandra gave him a charming smile and said, "I have Barrister. Devon where did you put them? They are all signed and ready. You went to see Ski and have everything in order? King have you heard from my parents?" She tried to look as innocent as possible. Elizabeth had told her she had written her Mother in secret on blue paper.

Camden looked at the King and said, "No, I have not yet visited Belissa Villa. I needed these papers to take to the Chancellor." He reached out and took the papers from Devon. He held them feeling the sexual charm she had made with a hair she had stolen from him. He took in a breath smelling the perfume she sprinkled on the envelope observing her and probing her mind. She showed him her naked body. Why not? Everyone else had seen it. Camden said mentally. My dear, not in front of the King you will get my head chopped off. He smiled and bowed quickly, "I will take care of this as quickly as possible and return them to you personally."

She smiled and looked at the Martin. She mentally thought. Damn, he knows we are talking mentally, block Martin quickly Camden.

Ski said. Excellent Casandra now for the King. You are a great temptress.

Casandra turned her charm on for the King alone and took his hand in hers. "King you said you have good news for me." She was making circles with her finger under his wrist. He looked astonished at her and tilted his head. She gave him a wicked smile and showed him a picture of them in the bathtub. His mouth dropped open.

Martin removed the King's hand from her and placed a wine glass in the King's hand. He sat on the couch between the King and her. "Casandra, we have brought you a present." He opened a wooden box, and there were her black crown and torque. She was shocked and was sure her mouth flew open.

Ski mentally asked. What is it?

Casandra let out a squeal and said, "My torque and crown! You must have wonderful spies. How did you find it? Did you talk to my Father? Does he know I am alright?"

Martin was smiling mischievously. "My spy found it right where you said it was. Your Father sends his best wishes for your happiness with Devon. He regrets he will not be here for your wedding."

Casandra let her heart fall, the bastard was lying, but she had to cover that with sadness. She could feel Martin's pleasure at her heartache. Ski whispered. Casandra, Martin never spoke with your Father. Martin loves pain so much; serve him more.

She reached in the box took out the crown and torque and pitched it across the room. She burst out crying pounding on the box on the top of Martin's lap with her fists. He grabbed her wrists and said. "I am so sorry my Dear, but now you are free to live here with us forever."

She cried even harder and said. "The Emperor has never loved me, he loves Bryan, that is all." Martin pulled her into his shoulders and hugged her, "My poor Casandra." She began crying and sobbing uncontrollably. The damn had opened all the loss and pain of the last few months flooded out, and she dumped it all on Martin. Ski almost felt sorry for him, but he knew Casandra couldn't go on holding all that emotion in. Sorceresses were trained to contain sentiments, Casandra was taught very well.

Martin looked helplessly at the others not knowing what to do with this wailing Witch in his arms. "Someone, please take her from me, she has exhausted me." Devon came to her lifted her into his arms and carried her to their bed. He held her in his arms rocking her and chanting a spell of comfort over her.

Camden sarcastically murmured, "Well, that did not go as planned, Martin."

Martin snarled, "Then why didn't you handle it? I saw your flirtation with her! Remember she is ours. Keep your hands and mind off her."

The King grumbled, "Enough, both of you leave. Between your overzealous sexual drive Camden, and Martin's deep sadistic feelings for her I can barely be in the room with either of you. Both of you will learn to curb your appetite. She is Devon's first." He whispered, "Don't forget she carries my children. No harm can come to her. Go."

The King picked up her crown and torque and went to Devon and Casandra. She was calm now in Devon's arms. He set them on the bed and sat down next to her. He petted her hair as he spoke soft and soothing, "My Dear, Casandra, you will be my daughter to love from today on. The Queen and I will love you. I have plans to make you Queen of Diamante. It will take a little time, but Camden is leaving tomorrow for Belissa Villa to start the process. It is Henry's children who should sit on the throne, with you and Devon as regnant King and Queen. Martin and I have it all mapped out. In a few years, you will be running that opulent Castle, and I will often visit, to love you." She sat straight up and took in a breath.

Ski said mentally. Get more from him, Casandra, you can find out the whole plan right here.

She wiped her face and said, "Really? Henry's child will be King someday? But what of my others?"

The King relaxed and said, "Devon, with Sorceress, it is always the children first. They will do anything for their children." He kissed her forehead and said, "After they are grown I thought Devon's son would be perfect to rebuild Arlequin and it will need a ruler. Your daughter will be a prize for any country she will help us to convince others of our customs and laws. My other Grandchildren will, of course, become Emperor and Empress someday. All your children will be powerful, rich, and great leaders. You may help me map out the destiny of the two that rest at the Temple for your next pregnancy."

Casandra was in a state of wonder; the King had big plans indeed. She looked at Devon and could hear his thoughts we will be miles away from him and Martin, in Diamante Castle. She smiled and kissed Devon's cheek. She sighed and said, "King I have only one request."

He smiled at her and asked, "What is that my Dear?"

She took his hand, "Could I have just one baby at a time? This is painful."

The King roared with laughter. "Of course my girl." He tried to place the crown on her head, and sparks flew.

She grabbed them and said. "Oh, only the Emperor and I can place or remove the crown and torque." She put them on, and the black crown gleamed gold, and the diamond stones sparkled as did the torque. Now her Father and Eric knew exactly where she was. She looked across the bed to the mirror on the dresser and smiled. Only her Father's love turned them to gold. She took a deep breath, sending him love back, and said. "I am starving."

The King laughed. "That is another thing about pregnant Sorceress they are almost always hungry and emotional."

Devon said. "So I have learned. I will take you to the kitchen, and we will steal some food."

King said. "I am going to the Queen we may join you. Depending on her mood." He winked then he laughed.

Devon said. "She will be in a great mood winter break is here. The girls will be home soon." Then Casandra heard Devon's thoughts. Martin and Father will be too busy to visit my bedchamber.

Casandra laughed, and they both looked at her. She said, "Winter break, you call this weather winter?"

The King laughed, "I forget you are from the North, you thought we were still in fall. You will enjoy our winters, my Dear."

Devon laughed and said, "Let's eat and enjoy the peace and quiet while it lasts. When the girls see you, they will not let us alone."

Casandra said. "Well, we better not waste time." Then she leaned in a kissed him hard.

Ski said mentally. Nicely played my Dear. Wizard just got here, he is going to enjoy this story. I am getting some wine. I am here for you just open your mind.

Wizard to Wizard

Camden landed on the path of Belissa Villa to an army of men. Paxton introduced himself and said the Chancellor was waiting for him in the library. He led him up the path to Henry's house. He opened the double doors and entered the library. Paxton said. "Ski, Barrister Camden is here."

Ski looked up and said. "I have been expecting you, Sir. Come in have a seat. So, you are the representative of Duchess Rakie. How did you manage that? Spells, charms?"

Camden smiled, "I have my ways, but she has been very cooperative. She needed no incentive. Easy on the eyes that one."

Ski smiled, "We all love her Camden; we would like to offer you great compensation for help to retrieve her."

Camden held up his hand, "I work for the King of Hex."

The Wizard appeared behind him and held him by the back of the neck. Ski wrapped him in irons from neck to feet. "I am so glad to hear that Webster. I have wanted to kill you for so long, but first, we should have a talk, a reunion so to speak, Ski, some of Henry's wine. Please."

Paxton walked in, "Mind if I listen in. I have never heard a Wizard's argument."

The Wizard laughed, "You don't fool me you're just here for the wine."

Camden said, "Antioch, it has been a while, but I am sorry I can't stay. I am due back to Engelton by dinner. The King doesn't like to be left waiting. Remember he knows I am at Belissa Villa."

The Wizard said. "Do you know where you are sitting? In the library of one of the greatest strategists of all times, just standing here I can think of a hundred reasons you will never make it back to Engelton. I know the King too. He will only care that his paperwork is in order and back on his desk by dinner. Paxton, you know the way to the Castle?"

Paxton said "I sure do. In fact, I am taking delivery of wine and ale to the King today. Soon as Ski signs all the paperwork." He poured the wine for everyone.

Camden's eyes widened, "Antioch just kill me and get it over with. I am sure you have a wonderful plan to explain my disappearance."

The Wizard smiled, "Oh, we will get to that. First, I need to look at what you have been up to over the past hundred or so years. Don't worry I will be as gentle as you were when you massacred all the people of Arlequin." And the Wizard sneered at him.

Ski said. "All signed Paxton. The King will be pleased; he is getting everything he wanted. I just hope he gets to live long enough to know about it." Ski sipped his wine, "This is one of our best wines. I will miss Henry. Paxton tell King Hex Camden fell from his Pegasus when a storm came through. He has broken his leg. I am putting him back together we will bring him back by coach as soon as he can travel." He handed him the packet of legal papers and said. "Don't forget to thank him for the order we are delivering. We wouldn't want to lose a good customer."

Paxton took the envelope and said, "Have fun killing the wizard, Wizard." Then he laughed.

The Wizard placed his hand on Camden's head and began to retrieve his memories. Twenty minutes later he ripped off his head and threw it in the fireplace. He placed his hands on the body, and it lifted in smoke. The Wizard grabbed his soul and put in a glass box. The Wizard sat down and drank down his wine.

Ski watched with curiosity, "I thought one hundred years would take a lot longer. What will you do with his soul?"

The Wizard gave him a wicked smile and said. "It turned out there wasn't much in his head." He laughed and said, "But all knowledge is power. Now as to his soul, I will let the Empress decide on that. Did you know Webster liked to dispose of his wives he lost interest in? He killed his last wife, the beautiful best friend, and roommate of Beatrice? I knew her as well; I was teaching at the Academy when she attended; Casandra Galilahi Greenwald, a High Sorceress."

Ski looked at him. "I assume Casandra was named after her. Does Casandra know she was named for her?"

The Wizard said, "I don't know, but I have a hunch she doesn't. I have never felt it my place to tell Casandra. Casandra Greenwald was Webster's third wife there is suspicion around the death of his first two wives as well. There is a very dark story behind that, and it is Beatrice's to share, not mine."

Ski poured more wine. "Well, Casandra knows now. She asked to be included in this meeting, sorry Antioch."

The Birth of a Wizard, Warlock, and Sorceress

Devon was right, his Sisters were high energy and full of questions. When they heard the wedding would be soon, they took over the preparations. They were picking out dresses and flowers, giggling and squealing. She could hardly keep up with their ideas or words and was happy to go to their tower to rest after dinner.

Devon grinned at her. "You are tired or upset with my Sisters?"

Casandra went to the couch and pulled Devon with her, "Neither, my back hurts. I just wanted to get out of clothes and into my nightgown. I can hardly move without feeling strained. The children are quiet this evening for a change."

Devon waved his hand; her clothes were off and her nightgown on. "Lean against the back of the couch, and I will rub your back." His hands went down her back as the pain was eased, "The children are fine, they are just quiet, stop worrying. I don't think it will be long before you give birth, it is early they will be small. I am glad Father built the crystal nesting, they will need the energy to live."

"I know, and I can't help but worry. That feels so good thank you, Devon." Casandra closed her eyes and relaxed into the wizard's touch. Soon she was drifting to sleep.

"Casandra, we should go to bed." Devon pulled her into his arms.

"No, I want to stay in my dream. A handsome Prince is kissing me and has captured my heart. Let me stay in this dream of love." Casandra pulled him closer and kissed Devon tenderly without opening her eyes.

"Casandra, open your eyes and tell me who is this Prince you are so in love with?" Devon pulled away from her.

She kept her eyes closed, "A handsome wizard, with green eyes. When I gaze into them, I am lost." She opened her eyes and smiled, "Devon, I am not under a charm or spell of your Father's. I do love you. I wish our lives were different, but…"

"Shhh…I know, but I will find a way out of the King's demonic game then we will be happy and free. I love you with all my heart. Knowing you love me is all I could ever want, if I would die tomorrow, I would still be filled with happiness. I have never been this happy."

He bent down and kissed her. Casandra was filled with remorse; how could she kill him? She loved Devon. Her soul would surely go straight to hell. Henry was speaking, but their voices were so faint she couldn't hear a word.

She and Devon had fallen to sleep on the couch in front of the fireplace in one another's arms. At first, she thought she awoke because the fire had gone out, she waved her hand, and new wood and flame came to the hearth. Then a strange pulling of her abdomen muscles created a pain stretching from her back across her stomach to her thighs. She thought. Wizard it is time…help me. He was standing in front of her. He reached down and placed a hand on Devon. Then he helped her up, and an image of her sleeping on the couch remained.

The Wizard waved his hand again, and she was standing in a room of multi-colored crystals, with soft pink spheres of light hung from the ceiling. In the center of the room were cradles made of crystals filled with soft bedding. One held a baby and next to it stood Marion and Eric. Casandra grabbed onto the Wizard before she fell over with joy, he helped over to look at Marion and Addison's little girl.

Marion hugged her as said. "You had to meet Roselyn Casandra Rakie."

Eric said. "Soon to be Princess Rakie. Grandpa is here almost every day to check on her." He looked at her again and said, "You have your torque and crown we have been looking all over for it. The Emperor had it locked in his safe in the library. How?"

Casandra said, "I don't know, there must be a spy close to the Emperor. You will know soon enough."

Casandra hugged and kissed them both, and then a pain ripped through her. The Wizard tried to pull her away, but she said. "No, first I have a gift for Roselyn." She reached into her blouse and pulled a sparkling white sphere out and said. "Addison, do you wish atonement with your Daughter's soul?"

They could all hear Addison's voice say. "Yes I do, release me to her Casandra." She took the sphere and placed it on Roselyn's chest, it was drawn into her heart. Marion was crying.

Eric said, "Thank you, Casandra. Marion has been worried about his soul. The Empress told us she couldn't find it."

Before she could speak, another pain crested across her stomach, and the only words were. "Oh, now Wizard." He picked her up and put her on a table in the room her eyes looked up where Ski and Paxton were standing on either side of her holding her hands. Eric pulled off her boots, and the Wizard vanquished her pants just in time for the first baby's head to pop out from her. After the first one came, they were all running around grabbing babies and cleaning them up. In less than a half hour all five were born, healthy and squalling. Marion put each one on Casandra's chest, so she could know them and give them her milk.

When Henry's boy was placed there, she named him Jack Henry Rakie and put Jack's soul into him and asked if he was ready to make atonement. With each child, she went through the same process. Devon's Son she named Wren Antioch Gadwell and gave him Henry's soul. Henry said he would make atonement and thanked her for making him a Wizard this time and handsome; she could feel a kiss on her cheek as his soul passed in. The King's girl was placed with Elaine's soul, and she put Harry's soul into the Kings Son.

Ski was crying and said, "Thank you, Casandra. The Empress will give them atonement, she never refuses babies a second chance."

When Henry and Casandra's girl was placed on her chest, she began to cry, then swallowed and stopped crying. She said. "I name thee my child, a free soul to be loved. Alexandra Sarah Winsette Rakie

Princess of Diamante and wife of Antioch the Great. She reached into her own chest and removed her soul and placed it on the chest of her baby girl. I, Casandra De Volt Rakie give of my own free will, my soul to my Daughter for atonement to travel through life with her beloved Henry as Brother and Sister.

No one could speak for the tears in their eyes, and Casandra could not look at them, or she would not be able to leave. She stared at the ceiling of crystal and felt her empty body. No children and no soul encumbered her now, Casandra could focus on her task. She handed Marion her girl and sat up with the help of Ski and Paxton. She said, "I compel…no. I will not do that to you, because I love you all so much. I know I only need to ask this of you. I plead with you to care and protect these children and to take care of yourselves and love one another. Make sure they know I love them."

She could hardly speak, she swallowed her tears and continued, "I ask the Night to bless each of you with love and happiness always. I do compel you to say nothing. The weight of separation from all of you and my children is too much pain for me to endure. Wizard take the King's children and me to Engelton so I may end this." She stopped him, "Marion, perhaps you shouldn't name your daughter Casandra. I was named after a dead High Sorceress, nothing good has come of that. Ask my Mother about that. May we please leave Wizard."

He waved his hand, and they were in the bedchamber of the Castle of Englewood with Devon still asleep on the couch. Eric and Paxton were there holding the duplicate babies. She motioned them to the nesting area where they placed the children in their bassinettes. The Wizard set the cords and blooded tissue at each nest on the beds. She went to the wall and positioned her hand on a stone, the wall opened then she reached in and retrieved a wooden box. She handed it to Paxton. "Paxton when you are at Belissa Villa open it and instruct the Wizard in blood bonds. It is for the children and those who wish to know us. I can't decide if you should share it with my Mother, use your discretion. It is my blood and Devon's; please add the blood of Henry, Addison, and Sutton. The Wizard will know how to preserve it until the children are old enough to understand. Keep the darkness from these memories, if you can."

She held onto the Wizard, “Please, make sure Wren knows I did love his Father.” She looked across the room where he still slept, “Wren will be exceptional if he is even half as powerful as his Father and he will love deeper than any of my children take good care of him Wizard. Take good care of all of them. You have my permission to bond with each of them. As a favor to me, I wish you would.”

The Wizard handed her the pants and boots they removed at Crystal Mountain. She dropped them on the floor. “I hope no one saw me traveling through the air half-dressed, oh well, it doesn’t matter to me anymore; I feel like half the people in the world have seen me naked.” She looked at them all sobbing and said. “Please, I can’t bear this.”

Eric grabbed her sobbing put his head to hers and thought. I love you I always will.

Paxton sent her the thought. I will protect and serve your children as will all of Henry’s men, and I love you too.

The Wizard stood crying and thought. I will bond with each child and Roselyn too. I will always call her Winsette, and I will love her as Henry loved you, as I love you. I will love Wren and Jack. You have taught me a great lesson; love hurts. They were gone.

She collapsed on the floor next to the children, and the mirage of her disappeared. Devon fell from the couch and jumped out of his sleep. He looked around the room. The King’s boy began to cry, and she reached for him, tore open her blouse and placed him on her nipple.

The Reign of Justice

Devon ran to her jumping over their bed to the nesting area. "Casandra, my love. When did this happen, why didn't you call me?"

She smiled at him and said, "They all came at once; it was so quick. I could hold them back no longer, but they all live." He looked and saw all the babies were alive and breathing. "I will get help." He jumped over the bed and screamed at the guard to get the King, get them healers, and get his Mother. The babies were here.

He saw Ernst running up the stairs of the tower. Devon grabbed his arm and pulled him to the babies. The very first one Ernst picked up was the false one, his grandson. He held it in his arms, and Casandra saw his mind.

Quickly Casandra mentally spoke to him. Devon's son is safe; he lives. His name is Wren Antioch Gadwell.

He mentally asked her. My true name? How did you know?

She mentally laughed and said. All knowledge is power. Antioch is raising him. He is far away from the King, and so are Henry's children. Please keep my secret Ernst. You owe me that much.

He looked at her and mentally said. Tell me no more; that I will not be able to tell the King. Casandra understood more and more that the King and Devon could read her feelings and thoughts in her energy. She thought it was because of the Attachment.

Ernst said. “This is Devon’s Son, but he has your eyes, Casandra. Devon look.” Devon stood next to Ernst, and he took his son. Tears were in his eyes.

They could hear the shouting in the distance and Ernst ran to the bathroom to get towels to wrap the babies. He carefully started healing and examining each one. By the time she heard the King on the stairs, Ernst was taking the King’s boy away from her and handing her the girl for feeding. He ran back to the bathroom for more towels this time for Casandra to sop up the bleeding from her. “I need to check you, Casandra, come to lay down on the bed.” He helped her up and onto the bed.

The King came into the room and looked at Casandra on the bed feeding a baby, and he stopped dead in his tracks.

The Queen was next, and she almost ran into him. “King move I need to help Casandra. Go get one of those crying children and soothe it, where are the Sprites? I need some water.”

Janet came in through the door with Martin. The Queen yelled at him, “Martin get me a basin of water and some more towels.” Soon everyone was rushing around cleaning babies, dressing them and her. One by one each child was brought to her to feed. She was amazed, the duplicates sucked her milk just as the King’s did, the Wizard and Ski had done a fantastic job. The only difference she could tell in them was Henry’s, and Devon’s children had no soul.

The Queen said. “The wet nurse is on her way. You need food and water there is no way you can care for all these babies.”

Casandra laughed and took the Queen’s head and turned it. “Look, I am going to be lucky to hold even one of them.” Each of the Queen’s Daughters held a child and the King and Devon. “I think there are too many mothers in this room.”

The Queen laughed, “I haven’t held one of them yet.” She went to the King a took a child.

Ernst took his last look at her stomach and pushed once more to get the blood out. “I think you will be fine, but you lost a lot of blood. You need to rest. I will make you a draft and tell Devon to get some of these people out of here to give you quiet.”

Casandra placed her finger on his scar and brought it down the injury, she mentally said. He put that there, didn’t he.

Ernst smiled and mentally answered, yes.

Casandra said mentally. Your Grandson is as handsome as you. I hope he has some of your talents. How was I so afraid of you, you are a loving man Ernst; I am glad I have got to see the authentic you.

He bowed his head and said. "It has been my honor I pray your task is complete."

She smiled and said. "Thank you, Ernst."

The King was right there. "Ernst, thank you for attending to Casandra and the babies."

Ernst waved his hand and handed her a glass, it reminded her of the night Henry made her a draft. Tears came to her eyes. "Sorry, Ernst has helped me with the children and my pain. He should be a healer. He is good at it." She drank down the draft and handed the glass back to Ernst. He had made it taste like cherries.

The King sat on the bed looking out at his family and feeling proud and happy. "You have given us a brood of children my Dear. The Queen hasn't been this happy since we had the four of them running the walls of the Castle. I will send up some Warlocks to expand this wing for you and Devon. I am moving my offices down to the barracks, near to the University. It is closer to where I need to be to do my work, and you and Devon will have more room."

She laughed at him and said. "And you will have a little peace and quiet to do your work. You can't-fool me."

He smiled and said. "Yes, that too." She sighed deeply and thought sadly about Devon.

He asked, "Thinking about Henry?"

She turned and looked him right in the eye, it was time to begin her game. She smiled and serenely said. "No, I wish my Father would be as happy about this as you are. What is that old saying; If wishes were fishes the sea would be full."

He placed his hand in hers and said. "If wishes were horses we would all ride. I never wished for things, Casandra; I make them happen." He said. "I have the paperwork from Ski, you are ready to be married to Devon any time you want."

Martin came over with the King's son. "The Queen says he is hungry."

Casandra laughed and said. "He is a pushy greedy boy. He has been at my breast three or four times already." She opened her clean nightgown, and the babe latched on to her.

Martin said. "I can't blame him." He leered at her.

She said. "I can't wait till you have your own children. Janet says she has seven eggs. I hope she has all of them. Maybe you will be too busy to leer at me." Then she laughed at him.

Martin asked, "Has she been drinking? All I have heard from her is laughter."

The King laughed, "Well, Ernst did give her a draft for pain, maybe it was a little too strong. But…I did just tell her the papers are here and she and Devon can marry anytime."

Martin smiled and said, "The new laws on abdication came. We have accomplished three of the four requirements. All the paperwork is done you just need to sign it. The torque and crown we have." And he nodded to Casandra, "The public place will be at the Science building. It has a large balcony up high where everyone can see the ceremony. We just need the Emperor."

Casandra said, "WHAT! He will never come here." She looked down at her boy and said. "I will never marry, and my poor children will never have a name."

The King put his arm around her and said, "I told you I make wishes come true, trust me." He was watching his son pulling on her breast.

Casandra took the thought of the Hermits and placed it in the King's head.

Ernst came over to the bed and mentally said. What are you doing, Casandra?

She mentally answered. This must be the King's idea Ernst help me. Together they pounded it into his head.

The King looked up at Ernst, and Ernst said, "Casandra do you need another draft for pain?"

She said. "Yes, that was delicious."

Martin said, "Be careful, Ernst she is already happy."

Ernst said. "She doesn't look happy to me." Ernst handed her a glass, and Martin grabbed it and took a swig.

"Make me one of those, Ernst." Martin laughed, "Wait I have a wonderful idea. What if we had a Wizard zap him here. Ernst, if we gave you back your powers, you could bring him here in no time."

Ernst said. "I could, but do you really want him yelling and screaming in front of all the soldiers and people, we need to have him witness it not partake in the ceremony."

Devon came over with one of the babies and said. "Just use a crystal ball he could hear it and see it, but the crowd would never hear him yelling from the balcony."

The King stood up and said, "Devon that is a brilliant idea, nothing is stopping us." He looked at Casandra she smiled and handed him his Grandson. Then she took another baby from Devon and placed her at her breast.

All the while Martin was watching the feeding and smiling at her, "Martin, can I have my drink?"

Martin handed Casandra the cup and stood laughing, "How soon do you want to be married, son?"

Devon sat down next to Casandra put his arm around her and said, "Now." Then he kissed her, and all his Sisters said, "Ahh, they are so sweet."

Joan came over with Devon's son. "Devon, I want to marry him when he grows up, say I can. Janet says I can't."

Casandra laughed and said, "He is your nephew, it is too close to have children with him. What happened to my cousin you were so in love with at the Ball?"

Joan said, "Well he lived too far away, and besides there is this boy at school."

Casandra drank down her cup of medicine and said, "Oh Good Night. I am not ready to have children. Joan, you are fickle, Thank the Night I only have two girls." Everyone was laughing, Casandra turned to Devon and said. "Do you notice how Martin laughs at everything I say. Are you sure you want to marry me, and my crying babies?"

Devon kissed her again, "I would marry you today if I could. Pay no attention to Martin he laughs at everyone, all the time, for no reason. The soldiers call him the laughing General behind his back." Casandra started laughing so hard that she got the hiccups.

Martin bent over and took away her cup. "That is enough medicine for you. I can have the army ready in an hour and people gathered in the square this afternoon."

Janet said. "It would take me a week to decide what to wear. What about the food?"

The Queen said. "I already have Chef making dinner for an open house today."

The King looked at Elisabeth questioning. "What?"

The Queen said, "All your Generals and their wives and Counsel Men will want to see the children. You can't refuse them. Today would work for me we can have a big reception later. Besides we have Sprites here. We can make wedding dresses in a snap. Decorate in an hour."

Casandra said, "Well, I need someone to stand for me." She looked at Devon's three Sisters and started counting her fingers. "I can't decide. I will have all three of you." They all started screaming at once and woke the babies. Then they were rocking and soothing them.

Devon said, "I chose Martin and Ernst they have been by my side all of my life. They should be with me on my wedding day."

The King said, "I need to find a Monk, Ernst bring me a Monk. Sundown, my favorite time of day. I think that is what heaven looks like. It's a good time to marry."

Martin slapped the King on his back and said, "There were times I never thought we would get to this day. Here we are. I believe you, and I can accomplish anything." The King smiled and hugged him. Martin said, "Groom come with me; you have some ring shopping to do, and we need to get the army ready. I think you should wear your dress uniform. Then I can too, easy for us. Ladies excuse us."

The girls handed the Sprites the babies, and they asked Casandra what she wanted them to wear.

Casandra said, "You chose, pick me a dress too. I am too tired to care." She could not keep her eyes open.

The Queen took the baby from her and pulled her gown shut. "Sleep, my child, we will take care of everything. The wet nurses are here. You just sleep."

When she woke, it was already late afternoon, and her breasts were hurting, her stomach was hurting, and her body was sore. The Sprites began bringing her babies to feed, and food to eat. Thank the Night Ernst had left her another draft.

They pushed her into the tub for a bath, fixed her hair and pulled it back from her face, with fresh white flower sprinkled in. Janet came in with a beautiful white gown with gold trim. It was a soft material that clung to her hips and flared out at the bottom with a full train in back. The top was strapless, fitted and covered with gold beads. They added a gold bracelet and earrings, and it looked like they had spent months preparing the dress.

Casandra said, "Girls you have done a remarkable job. I love it." She studied them in their white dresses, each one fit the style and taste of each girl. They were all beaming. "You all look beautiful." Casandra's heart fell, these gentle girls were dressing for their deaths. How horrible had she become? She was just as evil as the King. Then she walked into the bedroom and looked down into the King's baby's eyes and they glinted red. The words of the Hermit rang in her ears, if not you then your Daughter.

Ernst came to stand beside her, and he silently thought. Please release me from this burden. You are not killing us sweet girl. You are freeing us. The Night will give us atonement. He handed her a cup and said. "You look like you need something for the pain." She took it and drank it down, and said, "Thank you, Ernst, I really needed that."

The Queen came in and said. "Casandra you look beautiful. I have one last touch." She placed a gold, sheer veil over her head that covered her from head to toe. They all sighed. The Queen said, "I wore this veil on my wedding day when I married the King. I think we should make it a tradition." All the girls cheered and agreed. Grayson came in with bouquets of pink flowers for everyone and announced the carriages were ready to take them to the University.

The Gazing Pool

Moori called the group into the Seeing Room the second she found Casandra in the pool. Marion and Eric came in first. Marion gazed into the reflection, "They need to put her hair up. She looks the best with her hair in tresses on the top of her head."

Wizard came in and said. "The Warlocks like Sorceress with their hair down." Ski and Paxton were next in the room.

Marion asked, "Eric, is that true?"

Eric smiled and said, "I think that is an individual preference. I am Elf and Wizard. I do not know what the Warlock preference is."

The Warlocks all burst out laughing. Ski said. "Eric, we should make you a politician. You just answered that question without answering it, amazing."

Marion started to object, but the Wizard said, "You can argue with Eric later be quiet and watch the pool now."

They watched as they Sprites dressed and decorated Casandra. They listened as the Warlocks let them hear the thoughtful conversation of Ernst and Casandra. Marion sighed and said how beautiful Casandra was when the Queen placed the golden veil over Casandra.

When Martin and the King took Casandra into the King's office at the Castle to sign the papers of Marriage and Dissolution, the Wizard said. "I still think we should have made fake papers. I sure hope they will get destroyed."

Paxton laughed, "Not to worry, Wizard. Henry had some perfect disappearing ink. Ski has plenty of more if you need some. Casandra's signature starts the process."

The Wizard laughed, but when he looked back to the pool, his heart sank. Martin was holding Casandra's arms behind her while the King sucked power from her neck. Eric took Marion in his arms and turned her head as the King held Casandra for Martin while he pulled down her dress to drink her milk. A guard opened the door and said, "The Queen is coming." They released her and tried to put her dress back.

The Queen came in, took one look at Casandra, and said. "I thought as much. Leave us I will fix this. Both of you try to remember this Sorceress gave birth just this morning. Let her rest!"

They walked out the door like little boys that had been scolded. Elisabeth went to the liquor bottle and poured two shots. She drank one and handed one to Casandra.

"Drink, this it will numb you. I asked Henry years ago to make me something to keep me from feeling. The man was a genius. I have two or more of these a day." Casandra drank it while the Queen worked putting Casandra back together. "I spoke with Ernst." Casandra looked at her, and her mouth opened. "I am not here to discourage you. I welcome an end to this. What you have endured I have done more times than I can count. When I think of my babies being raped and abused by the very people who proclaim to love them. I..." She poured another shot. "It has already happened you know. Those two have taken all of my children, even Devon."

The Queen's hands were shaking so badly that she had done more detriment to Casandra's hair than good. Casandra sat the Queen in the chair and opened the door to the guard. "I need a Sprite's help, quickly please."

He smiled a leering smile and said. "Yes, Princess." He turned to get a Sprite.

Casandra took the bottle and poured the Queen another drink and said. "You know about Devon."

The Queen said. "I am not that dimwitted Casandra. I know what is happening. I just stay in the fog of drunkenness to avoid the pain. I tried to end this so many times, the Hermit even tried to help me. The King had Moondale develop a special cage for me that keeps me from killing him, or myself." She reached out to hold Casandra's hand and said. "My Grandson is safe, that is more than I deserve. Thank you. Any pain of death will not compare to my daily agony." She grabbed the bottle from Casandra a poured a glass full of liquor.

Casandra took the bottle and drank down mouths full. "Henry did have a way with liquor. I once asked him why he didn't make a liquor that would not give hangovers." She tipped the bottle back again and said. "Guess we don't have to worry about a hangover today." She laughed, and the Queen did too.

Eric said. "Oh, this may not turn out well. Casandra is an uncontrollable drunk."

Marion said, "True but she can fight like hell when she is drunk. I know that first hand." They both laughed.

The Wizard said. "We need to go, Eric, time to be with the Emperor."

Eric gave Marion a hug and kissed the baby, "I will be back as soon as I can." He gave her a smile, and he and the Wizard disappeared.

Forsaking the Crown

Devon knocked on the door. "What is keeping you two? The procession is ready."

The Sprite opened the door, "I am sorry Prince, but it is hard to put them right when they don't stop dancing."

Devon walked into the room; the furniture was vanquished, and both were doing the war dance in the middle of his Father's office. "Sprite get Ernst, the King, and Martin."

Devon just leaned against the door jam and watched the show until his Father and Martin showed up. Devon moved into the room and said, "I have a suspicion you two are behind this behavior. They are both drunk."

Ernst pushed them all aside and went to the Queen first. "My Queen let me fix your hair." He placed his hands on her head, and she straightens up and smiled.

"Ernst, is it time for us to leave?"

He answered, "Yes my Queen, you will have a wonderful ride in the carriage. He handed her to the King. "The King and Martin will help you."

Martin grabbed the papers on the desk and said, "This is going to be a fun wedding." They walked the Queen out the door.

Ernst did the same to Casandra and said. "You need your wits about you, young lady but I am grateful you got my Queen drunk."

Casandra stood up straight and said. "I enjoyed getting the Queen drunk, Ernst, but I think it was the other way around. Don't worry, Henry said I was not a drunk to argue with because liquor makes me fearless." She threw one arm over Ernst's shoulder and the other over Devon's and laughed and hiccupped all at once.

The King and Queen rode in the same carriage as Casandra and Devon. They were facing one another, and the drunk ladies were smiling and waving. Occasionally one would say something incomprehensible, and the two would break out into hilarious laughter. Devon leaned to his Father and said, "I just hope this wears off enough that she can say her vows without hiccupping or laughing."

The King took Casandra's hand and said. "Let me try to drain a little liquor before we get there."

Casandra pulled her hand away and shook her finger at him and said. "No, no, no, King. I like this feeling." Then laughed.

When they reached the Science building, Devon and the King took them up the stairs and into a small room.

Casandra said. "Why are we here, I want to get married."

The King said "You will, my Dear. We need everyone in place on the balcony, then we will walk out grandly. You want to make an entrance, don't you?"

There was a knock on the door, and Moondale walked in. "I have it right here, your Majesty." He handed the King two glasses.

The King said. "You both are too drunk to be in public right now. We need a little decorum in this ceremony." Martin came in the room, and the King said. "You will drink this the easy way, or the hard way. You both know Moondale has his ways."

The smiles came off their faces, and Casandra drank the potion then threw the glass on the floor shattering it. All the while staring at Moondale with disdain. The Queen drank hers and pushed them aside to leave, but the King grabbed her arm. "Not just yet. We need to drink a little of that power from the dancing you two did." He bent his head to her neck.

Martin looked at Devon. "I would be happy to help you, Son." Devon turned her to face him and bent down to take her power. She let it happen this would be the last taste of energy from her.

The King had been right for a change. When Casandra walked out on the balcony and up to the Crystal Ball, she was glad she felt more in control. The people roared as they looked out. She didn't realize thousands of people were pushing their way into the square. The King's army was on guard below them and circling around the building. She realized she was still drunk as she leaned in to whisper to Devon. "How many people Devon?"

He placed his arm around her shoulder and smiled. "Three thousand soldiers are here today, about five thousand live in the town. It looks like some farmers and small villages are here too." He couldn't be this close to her without kissing her. So, he turned her and kissed her the crowd roared. Martin stepped up and separated them and turned them to the Crystal Ball. He went to the edge of the railing and held up his hand and yelled, "Silence. The Emperor must hear this ceremony."

Casandra looked down at the crystal and almost fell over; her Father's face was staring up at her. Devon caught her and held her tight. She looked up at Devon and pulled his arms around her waist, "I love you, Devon." His smile melted her heart.

The King began to speak, "Emperor your Daughter is marrying my Son Prince Devon today. I regret you could not make the ceremony." The Emperor started to say something when the King paraded all five children in front of the Crystal Ball, and he said, "Extraordinary, we have five healthy Grandchildren."

She saw her Mother's face and Bryan standing around the Crystal in the library of the North Castle. She blurted out, "I love you all so much."

The King took her hand and squeezed it as hard and he could; she felt a bone crack.

She looked at him in anger, but the Wizard voice came into her head. No, Casandra, you are a child of love; this must be done in love. Do not choose the way of the Hermit; your soul is in Winsette, don't make her suffer. She pulled her hand from the King and removed her crown and torque holding them together down and to the side. She looked happily into the Crystal Ball, then looked in the Kings eyes and said, "Today I am here to abdicate from my country Marais."

Her Brother screamed, "No Casandra we can work this out."

The Emperor was screaming. "I forbid this Casandra." The Empress just stood silent, and Casandra could feel the power of her Mother rushing through her veins. The Empress knew what would happen.

Casandra gazed into the crystal ball and said, "Enough! You are compelled to be silent and listen to me. I am a grown woman; the King has freed me." She looked at the King and sent him a charming smile. She looked down into the Crystal and said, "I release my station of High Sorceress to the North Castle and as future Empress of the Bayonne Temple. I renounce my allegiance to the country of Marais."

She brought her Crown and Torque from her side they were already melting together and sparking.

The Major's face came into view, and he was screaming, "No Casandra."

She looked at Queen Elizbeth's face. Ernst was holding her, and they both were smiling. She looked up and smiled at Devon. Then she gave the King a wicked laugh and handed him the two symbols of power as they bonded together and said. "You are dead King. Henry and Addison have won the game." The King's smile fell from his face, and the world turned white.

The Impact

The Emperor fell into his chair in shock.

Major just stood over the crystal as only white light filled it.

The Prince cover his eyes and mumbled. "What just happened."

Eric stood behind Princess Kathryn as she fell.

The Professor came to the Empress side as she stood stoically looking at the Wizard who was facing the lake hiding the tears running down his face.

The Wizard took his hands down his face, and the tears were gone, he turned and said. "Casandra just killed the King Prince, also his nest of snakes."

Eric stood by the side of the dead Princess and said. "And she has given us the King's spy here in the North Castle."

Bryan looked over and noticed his wife laying on the couch. "Kathryn, what do you mean, she is no spy. Never, she would never." He ran to her and said. "Professor do something save her."

Before the Professor could move, Mags came running in with Bryan's oldest son, with blood running from his neck. Mags was screaming, "He just collapsed in the nursery! I don't know what happened."

The Prince took his son from Mags and took him to the chair in front of the fire. He sat down staring into his innocent face. "I know what happened. It was the only way they could make her spy on us." He looked at Mags and said, "His brothers?"

Mags said. "They are fine, they are fine, Bryan."

The Emperor was sobbing helplessly at his desk. Major turned away and watched as the Empress went to the Princess and took her soul, she silently walked to her Grandson and did the same. Major knew not to stop her or speak to her, she was entranced.

The Emperor came around his desk and began screaming at her. "They are not even cold! Look at you! You do not even shed a tear for your Child, who just blew up most of Engelton if not all of it! The King's spell reaches into my Castle! He is still killing our Children and Grandchildren. You don't even have one ounce of malice or anger! What did I marry…a cold, heartless Witch? How could I ever love you."

The Empress stood looking at him calmly as flames pushed out from her skirts burning the rug beneath her. "YOU MAY NOT SPEAK WITH THOSE WORDS! Your stubborn righteous need for vengeance has taken three of my four children, my beloved Daughter-in-law, and Grandson, and new our new Grandbabies. I must leave to catch the thousands of souls Casandra has freed. You, Emperor, have given life to the Greatest High Sorceress of all times. You and your families name will be imprinted in history. Your ego should finally be satisfied." She turned and flew out of the room leaving flames across the floor.

Mags quickly dashed the flames out but could not save the rug the Empress stood on. Major started to follow her, but the Professor said. "This is my job; you have yours." Major turned to see the King's hands in fists.

The King turned in rage at the Wizard, "You and Eric were only here to protect Casandra and keep her alive. Both of you have failed miserly! You are both released from your duties here. Get out, I can't stand the sight of your face!" They both bowed and walked from the Library.

The Professor was at the door of the carriage and held it open for Eric and the Wizard. They all climbed into a flaming Empress, "Why are they here? The Emperor was right, you have failed me, especially you Eric. I heard Hayden's rant as I left."

The Professor took her hand and with his other hand hit the roof of the carriage, and they lifted off. “My Dear Empress, I feel pain too, but these men did not fail. They were never working for you. I was there when you put the compulsion on both men. You gave their lives to Casandra’s wish; not yours. I always told you to be careful with your enchanted words.”

Eric said. “Today she told you she was a grown woman. Well, she told me that a long time ago. It took me years to let her be a woman.”

The Empress nodded. She opened the curtains looked out and heaved a sigh, “I hear your words, and you are both probably right, but I must hurry to catch her soul. I can be compassionate later.”

The Wizard smiled, “Lucky for you we know exactly where her soul is. We are taking you there now. I can’t wait to show it to you. First I need to use all my energy to speed us to Crystal Mountain.”

Eric placed his hand on her head and said. “Sleep my Empress, you will see her soul soon.” The Empress’s head fell into the Professor’s arms. He began to chant a soothing song over her.

CPSIA information can be obtained
at www.ICGtesting.com
Printed in the USA
LVHW010923170219
607792LV00040B/1457/P

9 781480 976009